I0643200

BAD BILLIONAIRES

ELISE FABER

BAD BILLIONAIRES
BY ELISE FABER
Newsletter sign-up

This is a work of fiction. Names, places, characters, and events are fictitious in every regard. Any similarities to actual events and persons, living or dead, are purely coincidental. Any trademarks, service marks, product names, or named features are assumed to be the property of their respective owners, and are used only for reference. There is no implied endorsement if any of these terms are used. Except for review purposes, the reproduction of this book in whole or part, electronically or mechanically, constitutes a copyright violation.

BAD BILLIONAIRES
Copyright © 2019 Elise Faber
Print ISBN-13: 978-1-946140-32-6
Ebook ISBN-13: 978-1-946140-31-9
Cover Art by Jena Brignola

BILLIONAIRE'S CLUB

Bad Night Stand
Bad Breakup
Bad Husband
Bad Hookup
Bad Divorce
Bad Fiancé
Bad Boyfriend
Bad Blind Date
Bad Wedding
Bad Engagement
Bad Bridesmaid
Bad Swipe
Bad Girlfriend
Bad Best Friend
Bad Billionaire's Quickies

BILLIONAIRE'S CLUB CAST OF CHARACTERS

Heroes and Heroines:

Abigail Roberts (Bad Night Stand) — founding member of the Sextant, hates wine, loves crocheting

Jordan O'Keith (Bad Night Stand) — Heather's brother, former owner of RoboTech

Cecilia (CeCe) Thiele (Bad Breakup) — former nanny to Hunter, talented artist

Colin McGregor (Bad Breakup) — Scottish duke, owner of McGregor Enterprises

Heather O'Keith (Bad Husband) — CEO of RoboTech, Jordan's sister

Clay Steele (Bad Husband) — Heather's business rival, CEO of Steele Technologies

Kay (Bad Date) — romance writer, hates to be stood up

Garret Williams (Bad Date) — former rugby player

Rachel Morris (Bad Hookup) — Heather's assistant, superpowers include being ultra-organized

Sebastian (Bas) Scott (Bad Hookup) — Devon Scott's brother, Clay's assistant

Rebecca (Bec) Darden (Bad Divorce) — kickass lawyer, New York roots

Luke Pearson (Bad Divorce) — Southern gentleman, CEO Pearson Energies

Seraphina Delgado (Bad Fiancé) — romantic to the core, looks like a bombshell, but even prettier on the inside

Tate Connor (Bad Fiancé) — tech genius, scared to be burned by love

Lorelai (Bad Text) — drunk texts don't make her happy

Logan Smith (Bad Text) — former military, sometimes drunk texts are for the best

Kelsey Scott (Bad Boyfriend) — Bas and Devon's sister, engineer at RoboTech, brilliant

Tanner Pearson (Bad Boyfriend) — Bas and Devon's childhood friend, photographer

Trix Donovan (Bad Blind Date) — Heather's sister, Jordan's half-sister, nurse who worked in war zones, poverty-stricken areas, and abroad for almost a decade

Jet Hansen (Bad Blind Date) — a doctor Trix worked with

Molly Miller (Bad Wedding) — owner of Molly's, a kickass bakery in San Francisco

Jackson Davis (Bad Wedding) — Molly's ex-fiancé

Kate McLeod (Bad Engagement) — Kelsey's college friend, advertiser extraordinaire, loves purple and Hermione Granger

Jaime Huntingon (Bad Engagement) — vet, does excellent man-bun

Heidi Greene (Bad Bridesmaid) — science, organization, and *Twilight* nerd

Brad Huntington (Bad Bridesmaid) — travel junkie, dreamy hazel eyes, hidden sweet side

Ben Bradford (Bad Swipe) — quiet, brooding, had a thing for golden retrievers

Stef McKay (Bad Swipe) — lab assistant, dog lover, klutzy to the extreme
Tammy Huntington (Bad Girlfriend) — allergic to relationships
Fletcher King (Bad Girlfriend) — has a thing for smart, sassy women

Additional Characters:

George O'Keith — Jordan's dad
Hunter O'Keith — Jordan's nephew
Bridget McGregor — Colin's mom
Lena McGregor — Colin's sister
Bobby Donovan — Heather's half and Trix's full brother
Frances and Sugar Delgado — Sera's parents
Devon Scott — Kels and Bas's brother
Becca Scott — Kels and Bas's sister in law
Heidi Greene — Kels' friend since college
Cora Hutchins — Kels' friend since childhood
Fred — the bestest golden retriever in the world*Sir Fuzzy McFeatherston aka The Fuzz* — Jaime and Kate's pet rooster

BAD NIGHT STAND

BILLIONAIRE'S CLUB BOOK 1

ONE

Abby

"IF YOU WERE A CHICKEN, you'd be impeccable."

I swirled the sip of rum and Coke in my mouth in an effort to not spit it all over the bar.

Then I swallowed carefully and rotated my head so I could see my friend Seraphina on the next stool over. She was currently holding court over a group of men.

Beautiful, tall, thin, and with a pair of boobs that could knock someone out—quite literally, they had once rendered a man unconscious. Okay, *well*, the sight of her impressive cleavage had caused the man to do a double take and promptly run into a large and extremely hard brick pillar in this very bar, but the point was still there. Seraphina was goddess gorgeous, and she was my very best friend.

"Get it?" the man who'd elbowed his way to the front of the crowd surrounding Seraphina asked. "Im-*peck*-able."

"She gets it," I muttered. "It's just so horribly im-peck-able that only an idiot like you would dare use it."

Seraphina's lips turned up at my caustic complaint.

"Hush, you," she murmured before raising her voice to address the man. "Puns. I do have a certain . . . *fondness* for them." Her reply started him talking, droning on about different languages and double meanings. It might have almost been admirable, the sheer quantity of words orally puking all over our ears, if it wasn't so sad and pathetic.

Whew.

I took another sip of my drink. A bigger one because . . . *bitter much?*

"I'm sorry," Seraphina whispered out of the corner of her mouth. "I don't know why this always happens."

"You're Barbie," I said, bumping her arm with my shoulder. "It's not your fault."

My friend had that elusive *je ne sais quoi*. Unspoken charisma that drew men to her like flies to honey.

And if I was being honest, sometimes that made it hard to be her friend.

I didn't mind being in the background; I preferred it, actually. Given too much attention, I froze and inevitably made a fool out of myself.

But drawing a crowd of slavering men every time we went out made it difficult just to have a drink with my best friend, never mind a full meal.

"I'm sorry," she said again when Bad-Pun was displaced and another man slid forward in an attempt to claim Seraphina's attention. "I honestly thought the jacket would help."

I grimaced. "The jacket is what's doing it, I think."

A bomber made of black leather, it hit just beneath her breasts and managed to emphasize both the bounciness of that particular portion of her anatomy and the slimness of her waist.

"Next time, drinks at my place and takeout."

I saluted her with my glass. "Agree completely."

"Should we go?" she asked, tilting her head toward the door.

"No." I nodded at the Y-chromosomes dotting the space around her like flowers in a planter bed. "Prince Charming may be here."

One blond brow rose. "I doubt it."

"You're the one looking for a happily ever after." I nudged her arm with my own again, knowing my friend was a romantic and, despite her beauty, also very lonely. It was hard for her to find someone who saw her as more than the sum of her parts.

And Seraphina was desperate to be *more* for someone.

"I'm not so sure happily ever after exists," she said.

"Oh, it definitely exists." I held her stare, willing her to believe.

Because happily ever after *had* to exist.

For some people.

Of the goddess variety.

Because if Seraphina couldn't find it, then what chance in hell did I have?

Not that I was looking, thank you very much.

I was just fine with my laptop and my cozy socks and my books.

"Now get on finding that HEA," I said, using the code word from our favorite genre of books—romance, of course. Because what the heck was life without fictional eight-packs and alpha males who actually cared about the women they slept with?

Seraphina bit her lip and I narrowed my eyes at her. "I'll be here to quip nastily about all the bad pickup lines your prince tosses your way."

She laughed, leaned her head against mine. "You're the best."

I smiled, leaned back. "I know."

Seraphina turned back to her admirers and I pulled out my phone, half reading the latest release from one of our favorite authors, and half listening to my friend charm the socks off everyone around her.

"You're a good friend."

The male voice sent a shiver from my head to my toes. It was honey, warm and languid as it slid down my spine and sent my blood pumping.

Which was very, *very* dangerous.

I sighed. This was always the worst tactic, the most under-handed masculine effort to get my friend's attention.

Going through the slightly-rumpled, cute-but-definitely-not-gorgeous, exceptionally-clumsy best friend.

It sent my inner sidekick radar on full alert.

Mostly because I'd been hurt this way before.

So "mmm-hmm" was the only thing I said in response.

"Jordan." A hand appeared directly in front of my face, unfairly positioned between my booze, my book, and my eyes and mouth.

I huffed and finally looked up.

Then promptly felt my lips fall open. Because—*holy fucking shit*—this guy was gorgeous. Way out of my league, of course. But blond and blue-eyed and hard and tall and ripped. He brought every single Thor fantasy to life—the short-haired, shorn, light-ning-bolts-on-the-side-of-his-head version.

Which, face it, was obviously the better variety.

He wore a pair of slacks and a gray button-down that was so sinfully tight around his biceps I half expected it to burst open. I studied those seams for signs of wear. I mean, a girl had to watch out for the rest of humanity, right?

Unfortunately for me, the shirt stayed in place and the signa-ture lightning bolts weren't present in Jordan's hair, but his pants were so tight that his hammer—

I shifted on my stool, thighs unconsciously pressing together as blood pooled *there*.

Which was the exact moment that I remembered he wasn't there for me.

Damn.

He radiated that same allure as my best friend. Wasn't life just perfect sometimes? A gorgeous redhead was perched on the stool behind him, leaning forward in an almost obscene pose in order to compete with Seraphina's cleavage.

She couldn't, of course.

But it wasn't just one woman vying for his attention. No, they were dotted around the room, coquettishly blinking at him, crossing and uncrossing legs, adjusting outfits. Even the bartender—female, brunette, beautiful—had chosen to polish glasses two inches from his right elbow.

He was movie star handsome and he . . . was perfect for Seraphina.

"Abigail," I eventually made myself reply, putting my hand out to shake his.

It wasn't disappointment curling around my stomach. It couldn't be, not when Jordan was so stratospherically far out of my league.

He grinned—nice smile, *of course*—and shook my hand. I suppressed the zing of pleasure that coursed through me at the contact. Instead, I pulled back and hitched a thumb over my shoulder. "Her name is Seraphina. She likes cosmos and hates cheesy pickup lines, despite her kindness in accepting them." I decided to throw him a solid because, really, they were absolutely perfect for each other. "Talk to her about how much you love CSI."

I tucked my phone into my purse, grabbed my drink, and drained it.

"I hate CSI," he said, brows pulling down.

"If you want a chance with her, you might want to discover a newfound love for it."

My legs took a long time to reach the ground—short people

problems—but luckily they'd made contact with the wooden surface before Jordan spoke again; otherwise, they might have kept on slithering until I was ass-down on the sticky floor.

"I don't want a chance with her," he said. "I want a chance with you."

My eyes flew up, and I couldn't help my breath from catching. I wanted that, too. A horizontal, writhing chance. Or hell, vertical. Semi-reclined. I'd take any of it.

My body was very aware of exactly how hot he was.

But then I remembered reality.

"I'm the best friend," I said and lifted my chin, forcing my words to be matter-of-fact. I'd been through this before. "You might be fuckable to the nth degree and perfect for Seraphina, but I refuse to set her up with a liar."

In a movement too quick for my brain to process, my stool was shoved to the side and I was pinned against the bar, heavy hips pressing into me, a hard chest two inches from my mouth.

Seraphina whipped around at the movement and I could just see her over Jordan's shoulder, her blue eyes concerned.

"Hi, Seraphina, I'm Jordan," he said, calm as can be, gaze locked onto my face then my eyes when mine invariably couldn't stay away. "I'm going to borrow your friend for a minute."

"Abs?" she asked, and I knew she'd go to bat for me right then and there if I needed her to.

"Weasel or no?" I managed to gasp out. For some reason, I couldn't catch my breath.

Not that it had anything to do with Jordan.

No, it had *everything* to do with him.

"Weasel?" he asked.

I shook my head, focused on my best friend. Weasel was our code name for the men trying to weasel, quite literally, their way into my pants and then into hers.

I was just about ready to say fuck it—or me, rather—even if

Jordan was a Weasel. He smelled amazing. His body was hard and hot against mine.

And it had been way too long since I'd had sex.

"No chemistry on my part—" Seraphina began.

"Your friend isn't who I'm attracted to," Jordan growled out. "You are, and it's fucking pissing me off that you don't believe that."

TWO

Jordan

THE WOMAN WAS CERTIFIABLE. How could a man even look at her friend when he could have *her?*

Silky brown hair, curves for days, lips that screamed to be kissed.

She was Jordan's every teenage fantasy come to life . . . and somehow she thought that he wanted her friend.

Insanity.

The friend, Sarah-something, nodded at him and he took advantage, tugging Abigail closer as he led them to the dance floor.

He didn't dance as a habit and certainly not after twelve long-ass hours in the office, which had been preceded by several weeks of the same. His workload was crazy at the moment. It had to be because he didn't trust anyone else with the specific details of the buyout.

Oh, he might let them do the work, even knew the company couldn't survive if he micromanaged every detail.

He just waited until they went home to double-check every single contract and calculation.

Jordan hadn't spent the last decade building his technology development firm only to be careless with the details in the home stretch.

And this was definitely the home stretch.

The beach, the surf, and a quiet house where he could get back to invention rather than management was his dream.

He was almost there.

Which meant he could stop and smell the flowers, right?

Or at least a woman who smelled like one.

Abigail fit into his arms perfectly, the top of her head coming just beneath his chin, her face pressing against his chest. He'd have to bend a bit to take those lips, but Jordan had the feeling it would be worth it. Plus, she smelled fucking incredible. Like a tropical island—floral with just the hint of the sea. His fantasy come to life.

She stepped on his foot.

Deliberately.

He smiled, loosening his grip as he glanced down at her. "Problem?"

Her eyes flared in annoyance, and Jordan had to give himself a mental slap to not kiss her right then and there. Those eyes were something special. Streaks of caramel and dark chocolate, gray and green and blue.

He'd never seen a pair of irises so unique.

And they were partially covered by narrowed lids as Abigail glared up at him.

"Why are you doing this?" she snapped.

Jordan grinned. "Why am I holding a beautiful woman in my arms?"

She stomped his foot again. "I'm not beautiful."

He snorted.

"I'm serious!"

"So am I," he whispered, bending so that his lips just brushed the top of her ear.

Her cheeks went pink, her lips parted, and her body wavered, leaning against his before pulling away. She was fighting him, but not because she didn't want him. There was something else underneath, an edge of panic that reminded him of a spooked horse.

"Shh," he said. "Let's just dance."

"But—"

He planted his feet, grasped her shoulders, and pulled her a full foot away from him. Enough to clear his head, enough to give her some distance if she truly did want to get away.

Crouching a bit to meet those gorgeous hazel eyes when hers wouldn't rise to find his, Jordan said, "Just a dance, flower girl, but only if you want it."

He knew he could be pushy sometimes, knew he was a fucking pain in the ass in the business realm, but he wasn't one of those guys who pressured a woman into being with him just because he wanted her. So what if she was gorgeous and her body was off the charts? Having a woman frightened of him wasn't a turn on.

Yeah, not really his style.

Plenty of guys in his universe used their power to get laid, but that had always disgusted him. What was the point in a woman being with him if she didn't want him as much as he wanted her?

Or because she wanted him for his ownership of a multibillion dollar corporation or his fleet of private jets? Or, worse, because she was scared of the repercussions of *not* being with him?

And so he made sure Abigail knew that she could go.

But he also wanted to make certain that she knew *she* was the one he found irresistible—not her friend.

"You can go back over there to your drink and your book,

side-kicking it with your friend, who may be model beautiful, but is also nothing compared to you."

She rolled her eyes.

"I'm serious. Your body is the one a man dreams of—curved and lush, not bony lines and hard angles. A man likes to cuddle with something soft, not a coat hanger."

Abigail glared at him then pointed to her friend and the group around of men surrounding her. "*They* like it. And Seraphina isn't bony, she's got huge—"

His mouth curved. "I'm more of an ass man myself."

"*That* I have plenty of," she said with a rueful smile.

"Dance?" He held out a hand. "I should have asked before I went all caveman on you."

"Not a Weasel." She smiled genuinely for the first time. "Definitely not a Weasel."

Jordan raised his brows, hand out, waiting. "Not sure what that means, but are you going to give a guy a break here?"

She sighed. "I guess I can." Then she started to turn toward a man sitting by himself at a high top table near them. "Do you want—?"

He snagged her arm, pulled her close. "You're impossible."

"Better you know that now, rather than later." Her lips tipped. "You asked me to give a guy a break."

"*I* was the guy needing a break," he said with a mock glare. Amusement swept through him, especially when she looked up at him with mischief in her gaze.

"Noted," she murmured, allowing him to lead her to the dance floor.

"It's hard work tolerating someone who looks like me, I know," he quipped, wanting to see what she'd say.

"Someone who looks like Thor?" She took a step away and pretended to puke. "Yup. I don't know how I'll stand it."

"Come here, trouble," he said, reeling her in.

And then she was in his arms and it was everything.

The music faded, bar noise became a faint buzz, and it was just the two of them in the universe.

His mind felt quiet for the first time in forever.

Quiet until she gave him sass.

Jordan hated sass. Or *normally* he did. But coming from between Abigail's lips and it had a completely different effect. He liked that she gave him shit. No clue why. Well, none except that fire was infinitely more attractive than soggy dishtowels.

"I keep half expecting you to make a quip about Thor's hammer." One of Abigail's brows lifted, a smile curved the edges of those lush lips. "I hear it's mighty."

"I heard it breaks in the last movie," he joked and when that gorgeous mouth dropped open, he had to laugh. "I didn't say *mine* was broken."

"I'm not interested in yours," she grumbled. "I'm interested in Hemsworth's."

The music changed, a faster song that would make it difficult for them to talk and dance. Jordan snagged her hand before she could slip away. "Another drink?"

She shook her head.

"Food then? This place has good appetizers. The crab cakes are fresh and the artichoke dip is perfectly seasoned." *Come on, O'Keith.* Jordan mentally shook his head, knowing that he sounded like an idiotic Yelp review.

When was the last time he'd stumbled over words with a woman?

Hell, when was the last time he'd actually *talked* to a woman who wasn't a coworker? Or his sister?

Or both, since he actually worked with his sister.

He mentally calculated the hours he'd spent in the office— the *months*—and felt horror course through him. How deprived had his life become if he couldn't remember the last time he'd gotten laid?

Abigail's white teeth bit down on her bottom lip and his cock went rock hard.

That right there was the sign it had been way too long.

He was getting random, uncontrolled boners like a teenage boy.

Yes, it had been harder and harder for him to find the time and energy for sex over the last few years. Especially when every woman who was interested in him was the same.

Plastic. Botox. Extensions. Makeup at the Kardashian level.

Sometimes a man just wanted a real woman.

And Abigail in his arms was that in every sense. Her body actually moved beneath his hands, yielded in a way that made him want to strip her naked and stroke her from head to toe. She didn't wear perfume that masked her scent, clothes that were designed to tempt him.

She was herself.

Which was a thousand times more attractive than a woman who tried too hard.

"Not too hungry?" he asked when she opened her mouth. He could see the refusal on her lips. "We could—"

"No," she said, taking a step back. "No dinner."

His heart clenched with something very much like disappointment. *Damn.* He was really starting to like this woman.

He dropped his hand from hers. "Okay."

"I want dessert." She closed the distance between them, breasts pressed against his chest. Her mouth was an inch from his skin, her breath hot and damp on his throat.

"At my place," she added, tongue flicking out to graze his skin.

"Oh," he said, gripping her waist to keep her close. *Oh.*

Articulate? No. But, fuck yeah. He could do dessert.

And seconds too.

THREE

Abby

MY PLACE WAS A BLOCK AWAY, a third-floor walk-up that was perched atop a drug store.

It wasn't much, but it had two bedrooms, a recently remodeled kitchen, and only one shared wall. After my last place, it was practically nirvana.

I'd had the neighbors from hell. On both sides.

In fact, it was as though they'd signed up for a contest to see who could be the most annoying, disrespectful, and downright rude.

Late night parties had been only the start.

Things had progressed to growing their own pot plants and nearly setting the whole building on fire with their heat lamps. Then fighting over said ownership of the plants in the middle of the night. Then throwing the plants out of the window when they couldn't agree.

Onto my car.

And that had just been the neighbor on my left.

The ones on my right were in the Mafia. Or smuggling illegal ivory. Or hiding a hatcheted up dead guy in the freezer.

So moving had been a priority.

It turned out the move was extremely convenient tonight. Especially considering the hot, hard man pressed so closely behind me I could barely walk.

His arm was snaked around my rib cage, brushing the underside of my breasts, teasing me with every breath I took.

"Just up these stairs," I said, raising my chin in the direction of my apartment.

We walked up the private staircase and paused outside my door. I punched in the code above the handle and said to his questioning look, "I can never find my keys." I turned the knob. "This is easier."

"I like easy."

Like what I was about to be. And with that lovely thought, I started to have doubts.

Jordan turned to close the door, locking the dead bolt with an ominous *click*. This was the moment we'd either find out we didn't mesh in bed or he'd really been after Seraphina and had only settled for a late-night fuck from her pudgy friend as consolation. This was the time he'd—

"Maybe we should have a glass of wine?"

Ask if I wanted wine?

I wrinkled my nose. "Can't stand the stuff."

"Really? How about char—"

I put my hand up to stop the how-about-this-wine-that-is-the-most-spectacular-wine-on-the-planet spiel.

People always wanted to tell me I hadn't found the right variety. That I hadn't expanded my horizons enough.

Couldn't a woman just not like wine?

"I've tried them all." My other palm came up when his mouth opened again. "All. Of. Them."

One side of his mouth tipped up. "All?"

I nodded. "As bad as that is. I know we're basically in wine central, but I just don't like it."

"You're allowed to not like wine."

I snorted. "Not according to some people in this area. You'd think it was a capital offense."

Jordan came close, slipped one hand around my waist, and rested the other on the back of my neck. "It practically is."

"Oh God." I sighed and dropped my head back. "You're one of them too."

Lips on my neck, soft, hot words on my skin. "One of who?"

"One of those crazy winos who waxes poetic about hints of sandalwood and notes of rose."

I gasped when his tongue traced up my throat and paused behind my ear where he stopped and inhaled deeply. "Talk about notes of rose. The scent of your hair is driving me insane. What do you put in it?"

"In . . . *it?*" I asked, struggling to hold on to the conversation when the man's tongue was running over that sweet spot just below my ear. I barely held back a moan, which was embarrassing enough when he seemed totally unaffected. "Nothing. Just shampoo and conditioner."

"Mmm." He slid his fingers through my hair, up to the tie holding the unruly locks in place. "And I do like wine, but not as much as I like you in this moment."

Gently, he pulled the elastic free and tossed it to the floor.

I barely had a second to worry about it being lost in the black hole that all hair ties seemed to disappear into before his hands found my scalp and began massaging.

If it hadn't felt so good, been so perfectly erotic—my nerve endings on edge, my skin heated, his hard form pressing so tightly to my spine, his erection like granite against my ass—I might have been a little wigged out.

The dude wasn't taking my clothes off. Instead, he was playing with my hair.

But it felt good.

I relaxed against him, jostling his hands loose. Which was fine because those hands had moved from my hair to my body. And that was really, *really* nice too.

"There you are," he murmured. "In the future, just tell me if you want to stop." He tilted my chin back, our faces mismatched as I looked up and he leaned over me to meet my eyes.

Even upside down, he was beautiful.

"You say stop and I'll stop. Yes?"

I nodded. "Yes."

My eyes closed and my head rested against his chest as his palms slipped under my shirt. Goose bumps broke out on my skin and I realized what he'd done.

Calmed me.

Sensed I was nervous and had taken the time to settle the anxiety instead of pushing.

My lips curved.

"Good?" he asked.

"Good," I said, turning in his arms. Blue eyes bored into mine. "You're so pretty," I crooned, reaching up to stroke his cheeks. Stubble bristled my palms as I cupped his face and brought his lips down to mine.

He groaned, hands on my hips, tugging me close, and my confidence lifted. I felt like the woman in the bar again. The one who'd been secure enough to proposition a god.

I touched my tongue to his bottom lip, and he opened his mouth, transforming what I'd thought was already a hot kiss into an inferno and turning my control of the situation into a flash in the pan.

Jordan took over, hands and mouth working my body like an instrument.

Calloused fingertips slid up my ribs, reached around to unhook my bra, and whipped it and my shirt over my head.

"I—"

He paused, eyes molten, breath fast. "Problem?"

"Only that you're still wearing your shirt."

Buttons popped, cotton tore, and then there was only skin.

Tan, hot skin and hard muscles. That mythical eight-pack? I'd seen the unicorn, apparently, because here was one in the flesh.

"I work out"—he dipped his head, took one of my nipples in his mouth, and I moaned—"a lot."

"Mmm," I said, not caring about the words, only wanting him close, to keep his mouth on me. "Are you a personal trainer?"

"Something like that." He paused and an emotion crossed his face, one that disappeared quickly as he switched breasts. Teeth made me jump, the sting soothed by his tongue as one hand came up to tease my other nipple.

My knees buckled.

"I got you," he said, sweeping me up in his arms and dropping me onto the couch.

The leather was cool against my bare skin, but he was shirtless against me. I had plenty to keep me warm.

My hands came up to his shoulders then into the fine hairs at the base of his skull. I loved that spot, loved how it brought him closer, loved how it made him kiss me harder.

His tongue swept along my bottom lip and slipped inside to tangle with mine, his palms gripped my waist tightly. I was on fire, writhing to get closer.

"Easy," he crooned. "I've got you. I've—"

I released his hair and slipped my hands between us, yanking at the button on his slacks, wrenching the zipper down, brushing the massive erection—excuse me, *hammer*—in the process.

Jordan's head plunked onto my chest and he groaned. "Christ, Abby, slow down." He pulled my hands free of his pants, but my work was done. The slacks were out of my way. "It's been a while since I've done this and I want to—"

"Shh," I said. "*I want to touch.*"

My fingers slipped into his boxer briefs and he hissed out a breath.

"Too hard?" I asked, my mouth finding one of his nipples and returning his earlier favor.

"No—" He groaned again. "It's too good. You need to—"

"No such thing," I said, stroking him with one hand, while I shoved my leggings down with the other.

I was multi-talented like that.

His fingers slipped between my thighs and it was my turn to gasp. That one touch was liquid lightning. I needed him.

"Abby," he whispered and slipped a finger inside. "Fuck, you're wet."

"I want you," I said. "Now."

"I need to—" He broke off when I wriggled my hips free of his hand and brushed the tip of his erection against my center. "Condom," he gasped.

I'd never had sex without one before, but I was safe. From pregnancy, at least. "I've had an IUD for years," I said, rubbing closer to the heat of him, pressing down on the tip and groaning at the size of him.

Barely an inch in and he was stretching me to capacity.

"And I'm clean," I added, shifting to take him a little deeper.

"Me too, but Abby, it's been awhile. I haven't—"

I didn't care about the rest of his words, instead lurching forward so that he was all the way inside.

"Oh *fuck*," he groaned.

"Oh fuck," I moaned. It was so, so good.

Especially when his leash seemed to snap and he picked me up, keeping himself deep while he swept a hand over my coffee table to clear it.

The remotes went one way, my coasters the other. A paperback landed with a smack against the floor.

He knelt, laying me on the wooden surface and dropping to

his knees on one end. My legs wrapped around his hips as he drove into me.

Pleasure rushed through me, rising rapidly. Sweat broke out on my forehead, my muscles locked, and it was right . . . *there*—

"Shit," he said. "*Shit.* I'm sor—" His moan cut off his words, and I barely registered them myself.

What I did register was the thrusts slowing when I needed them to go faster.

I squirmed closer, needing—

"I'm sorry," he said. "It's been a long time."

"I—" My eyes flashed open as he pulled out.

Had he just—?

The throb between my legs was intense. My skin was tight, flushed. My brain was foggy, trying to understand.

"This never happens," he said. "Just give me a second."

"Did you just come?" I blurted, the haze of desire receding as incredulity took over. "*Without me?*"

Fuck if Thor's hammer really wasn't broken.

Jordan scowled. "It's been a long time. I'll take care of you." He hitched his pants up around his hips and reached toward me. "Which way is your bedroom?"

"Down the—"

His phone rang.

I froze. He wasn't going to pick it up. No, he definitely wasn't. Not when I was a twisted pile of need stretched out on a —really uncomfortable, as it turned out—coffee table. Naked while he was half dressed. Orgasm-free when he was not.

So no, he wouldn't pick up the damn phone.

He wouldn't. He . . . would.

His hands reached to the back of his pants and he snatched up the phone, swiping a finger across the screen.

"What?" he barked, eyes on me. I felt the heat of his stare on my breasts, my lips, my puss—

Maybe this night wouldn't be a total implosion after all.

Then I saw his body change.

Whoever was on the other end said something that made him stiffen and rise to his feet.

Then reach for his shirt. And button it . . . or rather attempt to button it since half of the little disks were scattered on my carpet.

"What the fuck?" I whispered, more to myself than Jordan.

Because Jordan was no longer in the room.

His eyes slipped from me as easily as someone ignores a vagrant on the street. One second to analyze, the next to dismiss.

I propped myself up, wincing when the wood bit into my hip.

I watched Jordan as he walked to the door, spouting terse orders, not sparing a single backward glance for the woman he'd left unsatisfied and naked on the table.

Not another look at me.

The door slammed closed.

FOUR

"I'M SEARCHING FOR TREASURE, baby. Can I look around your chest for it?"

My eyes rolled . . . again.

"I need more booze for this," I muttered, bringing my glass of rum and Diet Coke to my lips and taking a sip.

Gross. And I didn't just mean the bad pickup line. My drink tasted horrible. It was probably the absence of the calorie-laden Coke. Sugar helped the alcohol go down easier. But my pants were a little tight and that meant that I needed to cut back on life's extras until my skinny jeans stopped giving me a muffin top.

With a sigh, I took another sip and almost gagged.

Apparently, my taste buds weren't feeling the combination.

Whatever. I was adult enough to not force myself to choke down something that tasted horrible. I plunked the glass on the bar top and pushed it away, pulling my phone out of my purse with my other hand.

"We should go," Seraphina said. "I don't know why we even bothered."

"It was because we got through lunch the other day without interruption," I said, lips curving at her pained expression. "Of course, we were probably naïve not to realize it was because the place was packed with women."

The Tea House was one of our favorite places and not just because they served tea and crumpets—actual crumpets!—but because it was small and cozy and made us feel as though we'd stumbled into a historical novel.

The clientele was also not particularly masculine.

"It's lunchtime now," she whispered. "Don't these jerks have to work?"

"Apparently not," I whispered back as another came up to the bar and leaned close to my friend.

Who leaned away so quickly that she nearly knocked me off my stool.

"You like onions, huh?" Seraphina asked, and I wrinkled my nose.

"Who doesn't?" the man replied back, as much oil coating his words as coated his head. "But what I'm really liking is that shirt."

His eyes drifted down and stuck and I had the overwhelming urge to gag. Not just from his tone and his near orgasm over a flipping T-shirt. But because the rancid onion smell had hit my nostrils.

I stood, clamping a hand over my mouth. "I'm going to the bathroom."

"As soon as you get back, let's go." She glanced at the bartender who all but sprinted over. "I'll settle our tab."

I nodded, leaving my palm where it was, and rushed to the hallway leading to the toilets.

My stomach roiled and I wondered if I was getting sick. The

last time I felt like this—weak, nauseous, sweaty—I'd had the flu. Except then—

"*Oof!*" My hand compressed painfully against my jaw as I collided with a wall.

Or rather, what felt like a wall.

Instead, it was male and very hard and . . . my gut contracted—

Extremely Thor-like.

What. The. Fuck.

My insides heaved and I shoved at Jordan's hands, which had come up to steady me.

"Easy now," he said, and his voice slid over me in the same way as that night eight weeks before.

Jesus Christ, I thought as I shivered in anticipation. *What was wrong with me?*

"Abigail?"

I dropped my hand from my mouth, stomach abruptly settling as I glared at him. "Is that a question?" I asked caustically and yanked myself out of his grip. "Or do you struggle to remember the names of all the girls you screw and leave wanting?"

"I—"

I leaned in and hissed, "I had to get myself off after you used me like a sex toy to get your jollies and then strolled out the door."

"Jollies?" His lips quirked, and I saw red.

"Yes, *jollies.*" My hands found my hips and though I was slightly horrified by what I was saying, I pressed on. He'd had sex with me and left without a goodbye. "You left me naked on my coffee table."

I hadn't heard from him for eight weeks and he was here in the bar saying my name like a question?

Yeah, no.

He knew where I lived, for fuck's sake. Maybe a little pop by with a reciprocal orgasm could have been provided?

Just a thought.

"You ruined what I'd hoped was going to be the best sex of my life and . . . *and* you broke my favorite coffee mug."

He crossed his arms when I paused, chest heaving. "You done?"

I blew out a sigh and started to push past him. "Yeah. I'm beyond done."

Jordan waited until my back was to him before he bent and whispered in my ear, "I didn't want to leave."

"Could have fooled me." I wrinkled my nose when a scent hit me and it wasn't pleasant. Almost sour, it sent my stomach twisting again.

"I had a very important work call I needed to take."

"Now that," I said, "I read loud and clear."

"Abby." He took my arm, spun me to face him.

I would have been irritated by the manhandling if the smell hadn't been so horrible and all-encompassing.

What *was* that?

My brain was processing it as rotting garbage, spoiled milk, and onion breath all wrapped up in one disgusting package.

I gagged, eyes searching the hall for the source of the scent.

I couldn't find anything.

Except for Jordan.

"It's *you*."

My stomach heaved and I shoved away from him, running for the women's bathroom.

"What's me? Abby?" He grabbed my arm again, and I jerked free, pushing into the single stall. I didn't have time to worry about the door closing, let alone locking, barely making it to the toilet as I lost my breakfast.

Tears streamed down my cheeks, my throat burned, and the

nausea didn't abate as my body pitched a proverbial fit for several long minutes.

Finally, when it seemed like I was done, I leaned back on my heels, tilted my head toward the ceiling, and reached blindly for the handle to flush the toilet.

Warm fingers beat me, sending the mess down the drain. My eyes flashed open and, of course, Jordan was there. Unlike me, he'd crouched down, sparing his impeccable suit from the dirty bar tile.

My jeans were probably ruined.

"Here," he said and handed me a damp paper towel.

I took it, turning my head away as I wiped my eyes then the corners of my lips. I pushed to my feet, needing to rinse my mouth out in the sink.

"You okay?"

I spit and took another mouthful from the faucet to swish around. No, I definitely wasn't okay. I'd just puked in front of the hottest man I'd ever seen, the same one who'd seen me naked, who'd been having sex with me, and still decided that his work call was more important than me finishing.

"I'm fine."

Turning, I started for the door, only to have Jordan stop me again.

"I'm sorry about that night."

I snorted. "Me too."

"I didn't want to leave."

With a shrug, I shook his hand loose and headed for the door. "Go away, Jordan."

"I *had* to go."

"Reading that loud and clear." I yanked the handle and entered the hall.

Jordan stepped in front of me and bent down so that his face was near mine again.

That bitter smell curled around my nostrils again, seeping in and making my gut roil.

"Back up," I snapped. "You smell horrible."

His mouth dropped open. "I *what?*"

"You. Smell. Horrible."

He lifted one lapel of his suit jacket, tilting his head down and sniffing. "I smell fine."

I clapped a hand to my nose and took a step back, my words slightly nasally when I said, "If you say so."

He inhaled on the other side. "Nothing. Just my deodorant." He looked up at me. "I wanted to apologize for that night. I was off my game and in the middle of a huge merger. I had no business going home with anyone at that time." His eyes locked with mine. "It wasn't my intention to leave you . . ."

"Wanting?"

A flash of something crossed his expression. Heat? Frustration? Regret?

Since I'd been intimately familiar with those emotions over the last few months, I smirked. Then I turned and walked away.

My exit was almost good enough to make me forget that I'd tossed my cookies in front of him.

Almost.

Because Jordan was still the most gorgeous man I'd ever seen.

FIVE

Jordan

JORDAN WATCHED Abigail's ass as she walked away from him. God, it was a good ass. Two perfectly plump handfuls he'd spent the last eight weeks dreaming about.

And he was finally done with the buyout.

Finally ready to spend the foreseeable future on a private stretch of beach in the Caribbean.

A stretch that he now owned.

His private jet was fueled, the pilot on standby.

So why wasn't he already in the air?

Unfinished business.

With the curvy brunette who was moving further out of reach by the moment.

He trailed her across the bar to the blond model-type, Suzette or Sandy or some S-name. Heads dipped together and twin glares were thrown his way.

That might have made him smile. If he weren't so desperate to improve Abigail's impression of him.

Not just in the bedroom, either. Love them and leave them

wasn't his style. Jordan was more of a serial monogamist. And since he hadn't found a woman in a long time who would tolerate his long work hours, frequently broken dates, not to mention panicked phone calls from his staff at all hours of the day, it had been a long time since he'd had an orgasm that came courtesy of a member of the opposite sex.

Aside from Palm-ela, that was.

Inwardly snorting at his own awful joke, he plastered on a confident smile, and approached the girls.

"Ladies, can I buy you another round? Maybe some food?" The mention of food made Abby's face go pale and he gritted his teeth. Of course she wouldn't want food. She'd just been heaving up breakfast in the bathroom.

"No food," he said quickly.

"Stop mentioning food," Abigail ground out, one hand coming to her stomach, the other to her mouth.

"Abs?" the S-friend asked. "Are you okay?"

"I'm fine," she said. "Just not feeling good."

"Well our tab is paid, so we can go."

Jordan stood like a useless floor lamp shoved into a corner as he watched the girls talk.

He wasn't in the habit of being ignored and though it wasn't something he enjoyed admitting, he didn't like it one bit.

He was important.

Correction, he *used* to be important.

Now he was just an out-of-work inventor. Granted, one with a couple of billion in the bank, but still, he was at loose ends.

Beach ends, he reminded himself.

"I'm just going to head home," Abigail was saying. "Go to bed early and hope that this thing blows over quickly."

"Okay, love. Want me to walk with you?"

Abby opened her mouth but the sound of a cell phone ringing stoppered any words that might have emerged.

Jordan reached for his cell then remembered he didn't have one any longer.

It was relief that coursed through him, not a pang for the job, and certainly not a desire to go back to somewhere he was needed.

His—*the*—company was in good hands. He was going back to his roots. His wallet was just a little thicker.

"Go, Seraphina" Abby whispered, gesturing to the bar's entrance as her friend picked up the call. "I'm fine."

"Talk to you later," Seraphina mouthed before taking off.

"Okay," Abby murmured and tucked her purse over her shoulder. She turned for the door without a glance back at him.

Which was fine.

Because Jordan knew where she lived.

He let Abigail leave, giving her a thirty-second head start before following her.

She was barely a block away and he used his long legs to his advantage, catching up to her in hardly any time at all.

Shortening his stride to match hers, he didn't say anything as he walked next to her.

Her breath caught when she peeked up at him, but the verbal litany he'd expected to greet him didn't come.

Hazel eyes stayed forward, ignoring him.

Ah. They'd progressed to the silent treatment.

He could work with that.

Keeping pace, he stayed at her side as they walked to her apartment.

Patience was his strong suit, and he'd spent every spare moment of the last two months imagining all the ways he was going to make up that night to her.

It hadn't been until hours after the call that he'd realized exactly what he'd done to her. When Abby had said he'd used her like a sex toy, she'd been right.

He'd acted like a premature teenager and then hadn't even

bothered to explain or make it up to her. Yes, that phone call had put his business deal on the razor's edge of falling through the cracks and almost destroyed every single thing he'd been working toward for years.

But he wasn't a user.

That was his father's job.

So now that the deal was tied up in a neat little package and the checks had cleared, he was going to explain and, if she let him, make it up to her.

"I shouldn't have left without a goodbye."

Abigail's feet stuttered, missing a step before her chin came up and her lips pressed into a firm line.

Ruby red and plump, that mouth sent heat right through him.

He wanted to kiss her. He wanted to *talk* to her.

Which should have sent him running.

Instead, he was right there next to her.

"I was in the process of selling my business and the call I received . . . well, it jeopardized everything I'd been working for."

Jordan stopped talking and waited for her to say something.

She didn't.

He sighed. He might need more than patience for another shot with this one.

"I—"

"Will you just shut up?" she snapped.

He paused, rocking back on his heels as she stormed on and for the first time, he wondered if he'd been daydreaming about the wrong woman all these weeks. Yes, she was beautiful, but maybe she wasn't what he remembered.

Fiery yet tempered with vulnerability. Kindness for her friend. Self-deprecating and funny.

Maybe she was just mean.

And he had spent too long with mean to take up with it again.

Jordan hesitated, feet pointed back toward the bar and the lot his car was parked in. Maybe instead of trying to make it up to her, he'd drive to the airport and hit his private stretch of oceanfront.

Then Abby began running.

"Wh—"

They were less than a block from her apartment and she was sprinting for it like the hounds of hell were after her.

He knew he hadn't been that bad in bed. Okay, on the *table*. Right?

But it was her posture that finally snapped him out of his stupor. She was bent at the waist, hand across her stomach, head tilted down, and she was barely watching where she was going.

Thankfully, the sidewalks weren't crowded but she wasn't looking. She could knock over a little old lady, crash into a street sign. Hell, she could miss the edge of the sidewalk and get hit by a car.

Which was the thought that finally propelled him forward.

He ran toward her, catching her arm and tugging her away from a trash can. "Careful, you almost hit—"

"I *need* that," she groaned, ripping free and whipping back to the receptacle.

And for the second time in less than an hour, Jordan watched Abby toss her cookies.

Funny how the sight would typically make him run, but with Abby, he stayed beside her.

Albeit, he still had no idea what he should be doing.

Holding back her hair? Rubbing her shoulders?

She didn't seem to like it when he touched her, so he opted for searching his pockets for a tissue and shifting from foot to foot.

This round didn't last as long as the first. Thankfully. For her. Because he definitely wasn't feeling relief at not having to find something else to keep himself occupied while she was feeling horrible.

"I'm sorry," he said.

She rested her head against the metal rim of the garbage bin. "Me too."

They stood like that for a few moments, awkward and unmoving. He wanted to ask if he could help, but he sensed that she was trying to figure out if she was done.

Finally, she raised her head and winced. "I need to get home."

"I'll help you."

Hazel eyes skewered him. "Help only. Promise," he added when her glare didn't relax.

"Okay, fine." She wrinkled her nose. "I meant, thank you. Yes, I'm still mad at you, but I'm not a total troll and you didn't leave me heaving my guts up on the side of the road, so . . ."

"That counts as something?" He grinned at her.

She huffed out a breath. "A small something."

"Progress. Here." He took her purse from where it had slipped down to her elbow. "Let me carry that for you."

"Thanks," she murmured then squinted up at her building and the three flights of stairs to her apartment. "Why did I like this walk-up so much?"

"Exercise?" he joked as she headed for the building.

"Pish, exercise is overrated. I'd give anything for an elevator right about now."

He touched her arm. "I can carry you."

"I'm fine."

Since she didn't exactly *look* fine, Jordan stayed close. Her skin was waxy and pale. Even her lips weren't as rosy as they'd been minutes before.

He slipped an arm around her waist, shushing her when she started to pull free.

"Just let me help you," he said. "You've still got two flights to go."

She groaned. "I thought I was almost there."

"Forget this," he said and swept a hand under her knees, pulling her up into his arms.

It was a good thing he chose that moment to ignore her wishes because the second she was against his chest, Abigail's eyes rolled back and her entire body went limp.

He cradled her close, spent a half second enjoying the weight of her against him before Jordan realized that he held an unconscious woman in his arms.

He climbed the last two flights of stairs in rapid time then carefully laid Abby against her door as he searched her bag for the keys to her apartment. She'd put in a code on the keypad that night, but he hadn't seen it, and after a few minutes of searching the black hole that was her purse, he dumped the entire contents on the ground next to her.

Nothing.

Or, well, no keys.

There were about a million other articles—junk—in the feminine depths. But no keys.

Shit.

He reached a hand into his pocket and remembered all at once he didn't have a phone.

Which had been a tactical decision at the time. To be unreachable.

To be free.

Jordan realized that had been a really fucking stupid idea.

He'd figured that he could always use someone else's phone if it came down to it. But the only other person around at the moment was unconscious, so that plan was in the crapper.

Except, she *had* a phone.

He'd seen it in the mess on the ground. Shoving tampons and

receipts to the side, he unearthed the smartphone and pressed the home button.

Locked.

He cursed. Of course it was locked, and he knew the PIN to Abby's phone as readily as he knew the code to her apartment.

Abby moaned, and he cupped her cheek.

Maybe she was coming around and could unlock the phone herself. Then he could call someone. But after a long moment of him waiting for signs of consciousness and her not waking up, Jordan recognized that he was well and truly fucked.

He dropped his hands from her face and pressed his fingers to her pulse point at her wrist.

Steady.

So she'd wake up. Right?

But now it had been longer than he was comfortable with. Her hands were like ice, and she was so, so pale.

Damn. He had to do something.

When it occurred to him, he realized he was an idiot.

Jordan picked up her hand, pressed her right thumb to the home button.

It worked. The screen unlocked and he hurriedly keyed in 9-1-1.

"I need an ambulance."

SIX

Abby

I WAS FREEZING. My stomach felt as though it had gone five rounds with the Tilt-A-Whirl.

With a groan, I peeled back my eyelids and winced against the bright lights.

Where the hell was I?

Last I remembered, I'd been puking into another trash can. In front of—and thank you, universe, for that one—Jordan. For the second time.

Awesome. Lovely. The perfect ending to what had amounted to a hellish last two months for me.

"You're awake."

I carefully turned my head to the side and, of course, Jordan was there, looking gorgeous in his suit. It fit his body like a second skin, and *my* body remembered the feel of all that glorious hardness in minute, extremely descriptive detail.

The heat of him. The prickle of stubble against my throat. The way his abs had felt like granite. The press of his hipbones to mine. Hard to soft. Hot to warm. Spicy. Masculine—

Not. Mine.

"I'm awake," I agreed and closed my eyes, shifting my head back to the center of my pillow.

"You passed out," he said.

The lights were uncomfortably bright through my lids, so I tilted my head again. Away from Jordan.

"Yeah," I said. "I'm getting that."

"You scared me."

The words made me jump, not only because they surprised the hell out of me, but also because they came from approximately eight inches away from my face.

I hadn't heard him move, but he was there. Crouched next to the bed and right in my face.

"I'm sorry." And I was. "Thanks for not leaving me."

Jordan's brows pulled down. "Why would I have left you?"

"Um, because I was mean to you and puking uncontrollably."

He snorted. "Fair point. But I don't think you were feeling like yourself."

Now wasn't that the truth? I'd been feeling off for a couple of weeks but had chalked it up to my hypoglycemia. Which basically meant that my body didn't process insulin correctly and my blood sugar dropped unpredictably. But other than small, frequent meals and sometimes getting a little dizzy, it hadn't affected my life all that much.

Trust it to make me pass out for the first time in my life in front of a god.

Now *that* fit in with how things had been going as of late.

"My assistant couldn't find your insurance card."

I blinked, eyes flying to his. There was something in his expression . . . calculating? Careful?

Whatever it was, I didn't like it.

"It's in my apartment." I sighed. "I was using it to apply for new insurance. I was laid off this week."

He grimaced. "I'm sorry."

"Yeah. Me too." My job gone in the span of fifteen minutes. And I couldn't even say it was because I'd screwed up or the owners had been unfair.

Frank and Susan deserved their retirement. Except, I'd all but run their graphic design business for the last few years. It had become my baby, and now it was gone.

"My bosses decided they needed to simplify their life, sold the business, and bought a giant RV." I shrugged. "At least they left me a nice severance package. I'm good for a bit."

Not that I knew what I wanted to do with my life. Did I want to spend the rest of it designing websites and logos?

No, I didn't think so.

But I also didn't have a reasonable source of income.

And a girl needed money to survive.

"That's good," Jordan said.

I pushed all thoughts of my former job out of my head and focused on my immediate surroundings. Which I probably should have done the moment I woke, but there you go. My brain didn't always work in a straightforward, A to B, important to least important way.

Sometimes I got stuck on insignificant details and veered off course.

Sometimes I fussed with the placement of one letter for hours, so focused on that one small point that I forgot about the big picture.

"How'd I get here?"

"An ambulance."

"*What?*" I guess I figured he'd driven me, because damn, being transported to the hospital in an ambulance for my hypo-glycemia was going to be expensive.

Shit.

Jordan's lips pressed together. "You wouldn't wake up, and I couldn't get into your apartment. I was worried."

"I'm sorry. I'm just—" I shook my head. "Nothing like this has ever happened to me before. Aside from a lot of tests when I was younger"—I explained my hypoglycemia and what it meant —"I've never even been in the hospital."

He nodded, looking thoughtful. "The doctor said something about your blood sugar being off."

"Dang," I said. "I—"

A warm hand laced with mine. "Hey, it's okay. The doctors will get you sorted out and you'll be on your way."

My nose wrinkled as the smell of Jordan—was it his deodorant? It almost had a spicy scent, like men's grooming products—hit my nose again. In a second, I went from feeling a little weak but mostly fine, to my stomach tying itself in knots.

"Let go." I pulled my hand free, scooted back on the bed. "Stay there," I said when he leaned in, face concerned.

"What is it?"

I put a palm up. "That smell. You." I tried to breathe through my mouth as saliva pooled around my tongue. "Your . . . deodorant."

Don't puke. No puking allowed—

I gagged.

Jordan backed up.

"I can't with the smell. It's horrible. It's going to make me pu—"

He snagged a trash can from near the door and extended it toward me. "I don't understand why the smell of my deodorant is making you sick—"

The door opened and a doctor filled the threshold, taking in the garbage bin on the bed, my hand over my mouth, and Jordan pressed into the corner.

"Stomach still touchy, huh?" The doctor, a middle-aged man in blue scrubs and a white coat, with gray-blond hair neatly combed, pushed through the door. He used his palm to press some sanitizer from the container mounted on the wall and rubbed it between his hands.

I nodded. "Yes, unfortunately." Though the roiling was subsiding with Jordan out of nose-reach.

"I'm Dr. Williams." He crossed to the computer and typed a few keys before scrolling through several screens. "I think I have the answer to that."

"My hypoglycemia?"

Dr. Williams turned and came close to the bed. "Your hypoglycemia was almost certainly the reason for the fainting. Your stomach upset is for a completely different reason, I suspect."

I frowned.

"When was the date of your last period?"

I pressed back into the bed. "I've had an IUD for years. I hardly ever get periods anymore. It's been months."

Dr. Williams sighed. "Well, here's the thing. We drew your blood"—he nodded at the bandage at my elbow—"and that sample says you're pregnant."

My entire body went numb. That couldn't be right. I hadn't—

I couldn't—

"In fact, your HCG levels say you're about eight weeks pregnant."

I felt Jordan move in the corner, but I couldn't tear my eyes away from the doctor.

"But I have an IUD."

"Unfortunately, no method of birth control is one hundred percent effective." He gave me a sympathetic look. "In fact, my youngest daughter is the byproduct of a failed IUD."

This couldn't actually be happening.

Not now. Not with my job imploding. Not with my dad deciding—

A hand touched mine and I opened my eyes to find Dr. Williams staring down at me, dark eyes kind. "You'll be okay.

The OB will be down in a few minutes to check on you and then you can get out of here. You'll need to make some follow up appointments to ensure you and the baby stay healthy, all right?"

"All right." I gripped the sheets tightly as he logged out of the computer and left the room. The cotton was cool against my clammy hands, but it was more than that. Something concrete to hold on to when the rest of the world was falling apart.

I was ignoring the fact that I was going to have to let go at some point.

Pregnant.

How in the hell was I pregnant?

"Goodbye, Abigail. Take care." And with a small smile, Dr. Williams was gone.

I stared at the ceiling for a few minutes before I frowned and glanced around the room.

Jordan was gone.

How typical.

SEVEN

Abby

"SO YOUR PRESCRIPTIONS should be ready by the time you're out of here, and you'll need to follow up with me in two weeks," Dr. Stephens said.

She was a young blond woman with a perky ponytail and honey-colored eyes. Her gaze was warm and her demeanor straightforward.

I liked her. Despite where her hands were.

"There," she said after a moment and turned the ultrasound machine so that I could see the black and white picture.

My heart stuttered, and I ignored the uncompromising wand between my legs for the first time since it had made its appearance. "Is that—?"

"Your baby?" Dr. Stephens hit a button on the machine, printing out the image. "Yes. Or maybe I should say, there's your raspberry since your little one is just about the size of one of those berries."

"Really?" I asked, my hand coming to my belly.

"Really," the doctor said. "And this here. The fluttering?"

I nodded.

"That's the baby's heartbeat. Which looks nice and strong."

Relief coursed through me. I hadn't even realized I'd been tense, but everything that was happening seemed so fragile. So small.

A raspberry.

I could crush it with barely a thought. An hour ago, I'd thought I was coming down with the flu, and now I had a baby inside me.

Evidence that I could see on the ultrasound, could *hear* on the ultrasound—my baby's heartbeat whooshing away.

And instead of panicking, instead of freaking out, I just felt relief that he or she was okay.

That I hadn't screwed up *this* part of my life.

Not yet anyway.

"So everything looks great," Dr. Stephens said and slid the wand free.

I wrinkled my nose at the feeling of lubricant between my thighs. It was cold and sticky. Gross.

"Because of your health history, I'll want to keep a closer eye on you than my typical patients." Her ponytail bounced as she peeled off her gloves. "That is, if you want to continue your care with me. You can easily see your normal gynecologist for the duration of your pregnancy."

"I don't actually have a gynecologist."

"Good. I'll take you." White teeth flashed before Dr. Stephens frowned. "When was your last pap smear?"

"Uhh." I bit my lip. "Maybe five, six years ago? I'm not sure."

"Well, that won't do. Let me see if I can find anything on your chart. Was it in this hospital?"

"Yes." I gave her my former doctor's name and saw her nose wrinkle. "Yeah," I said, "he wasn't exactly my favorite."

"Honestly?" Honey eyes met mine. "He wasn't my favorite

either. Let's see." She scrolled down several screens on the computer. "Ah. There it is. Seven years ago."

"Oh. Is that—?"

"Don't worry, we'll get you caught up." She smiled. "And it's completely safe to do during pregnancy. That way we'll tick it off the list while I have you here and your results should be in by the next time you're in the office." She pulled out a phone from her pocket. "Let me just find out if there are any kits handy. Hang tight."

The nurse came in barely a minute later, a sealed pack in her hand. Dr. Stephens opened it, arranged it on a tray, and put on a pair of gloves.

"Ready?"

"Joy," I muttered, sliding back down the table to put my feet in the stirrups.

I was in this joyful position, speculum inserted, when the door opened.

At first, I thought it was the nurse and didn't take my eyes from the ceiling.

"Almost done," Dr. Stephens said.

The crash was what made me look.

Jordan had slammed into the tray and was facing the wall.

Jesus Christ.

"I'm sorry," he said to the wallpaper. "I should have knocked. I—"

"Done," the doctor said, covering me as she pulled off her gloves and spun her stool around. "You must be Dad."

"Jordan." He carefully turned, eyes flicking in my direction for a heartbeat before his shoulders visibly relaxed. "I'm Abby's friend."

"Dr. Stephens." She tossed her gloves into the trash and extended a hand before tilting her head in my direction. "Take care of this one, okay?" To me, she said, "Two weeks. I've put the office number on your discharge instructions, so get that appointment on the calendar."

"I will," I said. "Thank you."

With a wave, she left the room.

And cue silence . . . of the awkward variety.

I forced a laugh, crinkling the edges of the paper drape covering my lady business from the rest of the world. "Just when you thought you couldn't see more of me . . ."

I went for a joke because that was all I had.

I mean, really, what could I say? "Here's an even more up-close image of the female parts that couldn't keep you interested. Just what you've always wanted!"

Humor was all I had. Well, that and crying, and I decided that I wasn't quite up to crying in front of Jordan.

Not after our night together.

Tears, panic, and a mental breakdown could come when I was tucked into bed, my softest blanket pulled to my chin, and a worn paperback in one hand.

"What was that doctor doing to you?" Jordan shuddered instead of addressing my lousy joke. "It was like you had a drone up your—"

He broke off, wincing at the same time his cheeks went bright red.

"I'm sorry, I didn't mean it that way." He blew out a breath. "I just mean that it looked uncomfortable, and I wasn't sure if you'd need help and . . ."

"That," I said, deciding to throw him a bone, "was a Pap smear. A lovely procedure where they scrape cells from the surface of a woman's cervix to check for abnormalities. It's uncomfortable, but necessary."

"Was it safe?" he asked. "For the—um . . . for the baby?"

I nodded. "Typical prenatal procedure, I was told." I hesitated for a moment before deciding to press on anyway. "Why are you here?" I put a hand up. "I didn't mean that the way it sounded, just that you heard pregnancy and disappeared. I didn't exactly expect a return trip."

Jordan crossed the room, pausing near my bedside, and I realized that his hair was wet.

"Did you shower?" I asked, incredulous.

He shrugged. "I smelled bad, apparently. I asked Dr. Williams if I could use the physician lounge and he kindly agreed." His smile made my stomach twist, but not in the I'm-going-to-puke way for a change. It looped, knotted itself up in a this-guy-is-the-most-beautiful-specimen-of-manhood-I've-ever-seen, and that bubbly, wiggly feeling actually felt kind of nice.

"Wow," I said and not just because of the wiggly feeling. That he'd showered was perhaps the single most thoughtful thing a member of the opposite sex had ever done for me.

My father included.

"Go on." Jordan lifted an arm, distracting me from the melancholy about my dad and drawing my focus back to him. All things considered, eyeing Jordan's man-meat wasn't exactly a tough job. "Freshly cleaned with unscented soap," he announced. "Your nose should be safe from me."

I gave a cautious sniff and was relieved when my stomach stayed calm.

"Good?"

I inhaled deeper, felt nothing more than a fluttering that had absolutely nothing to do with nausea. "Good."

He smiled and it made my heart skip a beat.

"So," I said, tugging the sheet more fully over my legs, "are we going to talk about this?"

One brow lifted. "About what? The fact that women are way tougher than men could ever hope to be? Or the other thing?"

I bit my lip. "The other thing."

"Want to maybe wait until you're fully clothed for that one?"

Good point.

"I guess. It's just—"

"I know I haven't exactly given you a reason to trust me, but I take care of my responsibilities."

The words might have meant more if I hadn't heard them before, from a man I'd trusted my entire life.

"Okay," I said.

"What is it?" Fingers laced with mine.

I forced a smile. "Let's see, we've danced in a bar, had a one night stand, and a hospital visit, and we haven't even had a first date. Is there anything else on the daytime soap circuit we've missed?"

Jordan laughed. "I don't think so."

"Then let's table all the discussions until I'm no longer bottomless, okay?"

"I can do that." He paused, considering. "So what kind of TV shows do you like?"

"Uh. Are we really doing this?"

"Doing what?"

"The getting to know each other spiel? You've seen my insides."

He fixed me with a look. "I've also seen you naked and know what you sound like when you moan. Though"—his expression went rueful—"not what you sound like when you come. I'd been heading to your apartment, intending to wait around for you. Intending to make that particular part of our evening together up to you, when I saw you go into the bar."

"You saw me?"

"I did." Jordan rubbed a hand against his chin and the sound of his stubble rubbing against his palm raised the hairs on my nape. I remembered the feel of it on my throat, my breasts.

It had all been so good, until it hadn't been. "You wanted to make it up to me?"

"I did," he said again.

"But—" I shook my head.

"That doesn't fit into the image of the asshole who strode out of your apartment without a second glance?"

"Not really, no."

"Well, it doesn't fit into my image of myself either," he said.

Damn.

I'd been so prepared to hate Jordan after our night together, and he was making it really hard to hang onto those feelings.

"So I think it might be best to table all serious discussion and focus on getting to know each other a little better." He squeezed my fingers. "What do you think?"

"I think that's a brilliant idea."

EIGHT

Jordan

JORDAN STOOD NEXT TO ABIGAIL, prepared to catch her if they had a repeat of their last experience on her stairs.

She squinted up at him, rolled her eyes. "I'm fine, you know. Now that I know what's going on with my blood sugar, I'll just be a little more careful about eating."

"Okay," he said, not disagreeing with her, but also not moving from his position behind her. So what if his arms were out and ready to catch?

Abby snorted. "Men are impossible."

"One might make a case—"

"Shh," she said. "I'd stop right there, if I were you."

"Oh?" he asked, all innocence. "So I shouldn't say that women are impossible too?"

"Definitely not," she said, then laughed. "Even if it is very true."

They reached the final few steps and approached her apartment door. Jordan thought she was beautiful in the evening light.

The sun made all the different shades in her hair stand out. He wanted to study it, search out each individual color.

He also had entirely too much time on his hands now that he'd sold the business.

Abby put in the code on the keypad, and he did a very good job of pretending not to watch, all while memorizing the four-digit password.

She opened the door then rotated so she was facing him, blocking the entrance to her apartment. "You don't have to come in."

He tilted his head to the side. "Do you want me to leave?"

"Honestly?" she asked.

He nodded despite knowing that she was about to give him his walking papers.

"No."

The word made him rock back on his heels. "Really?"

She huffed and turned her back on him, tossing over her shoulder as she walked inside, "Don't make me regret being honest. Close the door," she added when he stood frozen. "You can pick which side of it you want to be on."

"Smartass."

"You know it." But she blew out a breath when he'd closed and locked the door. "I'm sorry. You've been nothing but nice and patient today."

"Why do I feel there should be an emphasis on *today*?"

"It's not you—" She shook her head. "Not entirely you, anyway. I've had a shitty couple of weeks and this . . ." Her chin dropped to her chest and she sighed deeply. "What the fuck am I going to do with a baby?"

Jordan felt his heart skip a beat. "So you're going to have it?"

If there were wrong words to say, those were the ones.

"It?" Her eyes closed. She sighed and lifted her gaze to his. "It." Any warmth in her expression had vanished.

"I didn't—"

She walked to the door, opened it. "Out. Don't worry, I won't bother you with *it*."

"Abby." He crossed to her. "That's not what I meant. I didn't want to pressure—"

"*Get out.*"

"I'm not—"

"Get out!" she yelled, tears forming in the corners of her eyes, and just that quickly Jordan snapped.

Crying on cue. Throwing temper tantrums. Manipulating the facts to get something from him.

He'd seen this all before. He'd been through this too many times to count.

He'd just thought that Abby might have been different.

He should have known better.

"Is it even mine?" he hissed, eyeing the worn furniture, the small space. It had seemed cozy and warm all those weeks before. Now he saw it for what it really was.

A play for more.

Abigail gasped. "You—you fucking jerk."

"Now you don't have a job? Oh, and no insurance, too?" He laughed, and if it was bitter, it was because he'd been through this dog and pony show before. He'd seen his father deal with it, had been a victim of the scheme himself.

Lying about being on birth control.

How could he have been so fucking stupid?

His father had fallen for that trick on more than one occasion.

And now, apparently so had he.

Or maybe—

"Are you even pregnant?"

Her jaw dropped open, right on cue. The perfect actress. "You saw—"

"How much did you pay them? God, you had me fooled."

He shook his head, forcing away his blip of regret when hurt slid across her face. This was all an act.

And not even a very good one.

"When did you find out I'd sold InDTech? That my bank account is overflowing?"

That's what she wanted. To pretend to be wholesome as she weaseled her way in.

He pulled out his wallet. Opened the leather case.

"You're unbelievable. I don't want anything from you," she snapped. "Except—" Her breath hitched when he extracted a wad of bills and thrust them into her hands.

She fumbled to take the pile, and his anger was confirmed.

"Except money," he spat.

Abigail carefully stacked the hundreds, putting them into a neat pile that she then lifted up to him. "Nothing," she said softly. "Except for you to get the hell out of my apartment, and never bother me again."

"I should have figured that wasn't enough for you." He shook his head and walked over the threshold. "Consider it a down payment for carrying my baby."

The door slammed closed, barely missing his head.

NINE

Abby

I SANK to the hardwood floor in a daze.

What the hell had just happened?

One second Jordan had been sweet, attentive even, the next he was a raging asshole.

Dr. Jekyll, Mr. Hyde, much?

Or maybe it was more Banner-Hulk, since my insides felt smashed to pieces.

Pregnant. I was pregnant, and the father thought I was trying to trap him.

I'd barely had an hour to come to grips with the fact that *a tiny person was growing inside me* and my baby daddy—who I barely knew—had accused me of being a gold digger.

What level of fucked up was that?

If he only knew who my father was, that notion would be laughable.

"Too bad laughter isn't high on my emotions right about now." I pushed to my feet and when I felt a little dizzy, I forced myself into the kitchen for a snack.

I'd grown up with nannies, a private chef, tutors galore. I'd had a designer wardrobe and any toy I'd ever expressed half an interest in.

But none of that had brought me happiness.

Or parents who wanted to be in my life.

I had a trust fund that ended in a line of zeroes longer than my arm. But I didn't touch the money. I didn't have to.

I made my own way.

And if it was a little—okay, a *hell* of a lot—leaner than my childhood, then that was just fine with me.

I had Seraphina and my other friends. I had my job . . . well, I used to have my job. I had my books, and I had rum and Coke.

Which I couldn't have right now.

I sighed.

"Well, baby," I said, and cupped my stomach, wondering if the little raspberry could hear me, "you've made me puke more times today than I've done in the last decade, you've taken my rum and Coke, and made me expose my lady bits to the world for what I suspect is not the last time. What do you say we take it to the bedroom for an early bedtime?"

I could really use a book, a bath, and cuddly pajamas.

Everything else could hold until the morning.

"He said WHAT to you?" Seraphina all but shrieked into the phone the next morning. I hadn't wanted to ruin my friend's day like Jordan and the pesky hospital visit had ruined mine, so I'd called her as she drove to work the following day.

I winced and held my cell away from my ear. "I know. It was pretty awful."

"Who in their right mind would think *you* would be a gold digger?" she declared. "He's a moron."

"Well, *that's* obvious," I muttered, switching her to speakerphone as I pulled out my laptop. "All of that drama aside, I guess the question really is what I should do now."

"You need a job."

I nodded, though she couldn't see me. "With good health insurance."

"You know." Her voice was careful. "I'm sure your dad's company could use a graphic designer."

"We've been through this before." I sighed. "I don't want to be that person. And if my dad truly wanted me he would ask."

"He *did* ask."

"No, he offered me a fluff position with no real responsibility," I reminded her. "I'm happy to work my way through the ranks, but I refuse to be a puppet that no one respects. Plus, I don't think after our last interactions I'll be ready to work for him in any real capacity for a good long time."

My father wanted me to work for him. *That* I could understand. But he didn't want me to take over the reins.

No, that particular honor would go to my brother.

Me, he just wanted under his thumb.

Which was why he'd bought Frank and Susan's company, effectively putting me out of my job.

It was also why he'd bought the building I was currently living in.

And why he'd had his business manager send me a letter stating he was raising the rent . . . to double my current rate. Oh! But my father happened to have a guest house available on his property and surprise, surprise, it was the monthly amount I was presently paying.

So, yeah no, I didn't exactly feel peachy about working for my dear old dad.

He had a vision of what my life should look like and when that didn't align with mine, he forced it anyway.

"I don't blame you," Seraphina said. "Just with everything

going on—the baby, the job hunt—keep it in your back pocket in case you end up needing something fast."

I sighed. "You're right. Unfortunately."

"They don't call me The Brain for nothing."

"I don't think that's what they call you." I snorted and lay back against the pillows in my bed, tugging the blanket up to expose my feet to the cool air.

She *psshed,* and I could practically hear her rolling her eyes. "I need to get into work."

"Rub it in, why don't you?"

"Shush you and rest up. Apply for some jobs. You'll find something in no time."

"Hope so."

"Know so."

"Love you."

"Love you more," Seraphina said and hung up.

I sniffed, wallowing for one more minute about my circumstances before opening my laptop and pulling up a job search site.

"Anything close," I murmured as I began typing. I couldn't afford to be picky at this point in my life.

I sent my resume off to a minimum of twenty HR departments and five recruiters. I updated my professional profile on social media sites, threw together a quick website, hoping to drum up some freelance design work, and then spent a few hours searching for new apartments.

Two bedrooms.

Now, that was a trip down crazy lane.

With a sigh, I closed my laptop and sat up. I had snack wrappers littered all over my bedspread. It was my attempt at staving off the hypoglycemia as I worked, but the trash combined with bedhead, last night's jammies, and not having bothered with a shower, made me feel like I was one step away from eating bon bons and watching soaps.

I gathered the trash and went into the bathroom, cranking on the shower as I brushed my teeth and wrestled my hair into a ponytail.

I couldn't be bothered with an hour spent blow-drying my mop today.

Especially since I had absolutely zero need to look good for anyone.

When the shower was hot enough, I stepped in and rinsed off, shaving my legs and armpits. I used my expensive body wash, the one that reminded me of my father's rose gardens and the few happy memories from my childhood.

I'd loved to get lost among the flowers, a book in hand, wandering through the maze of planter beds. In the spring, color had exploded around me, a fairy-tale world straight out of a kids' movie. In the winter, the bare vines had looked almost menacing, a villain come to life.

I'd held tight to the escape from reality. In fact, I'd reveled in the chance to get lost in my imagination. Especially when everything else in my life was so cold and artificial.

Calculated.

A battleground.

With me in the middle.

I didn't want that for my baby.

Thankfully, I didn't have to worry about that. Jordan was long gone. My little raspberry and I didn't need the drama he'd no doubt bring to our lives.

It would be easier without him.

Nodding in agreement with myself—*don't judge*—I turned off the faucet and dried off.

Since I had no plans of leaving my apartment, I pulled on a pair of sweats and a "Taco Cat spelled backward is still Taco Cat" T-shirt. I only bothered with a bra because my nipples were so sensitive that I'd probably poke out an eye if I didn't. Fuzzy red and green striped socks completed the ensemble.

I was a mess and that was totally fine because I was all by myself—

I shrieked and stumbled back against the wall, rattling the framed picture of Seraphina and me wine-tasting. I'd, of course, hated all the wine. Which was really not the point at all, I thought as I straightened the photograph and took a deep breath. The important part of the current situation was that my living room was full of suits.

And one of the suits was Jordan.

"Glad you could join us," he said coldly, eyes surveying me from head to toe in one slow glare.

I lifted my chin, the blatant dismissal I found on Jordan's face giving me the strength to ignore my uneasiness with the current situation taking place in my living room. "I wasn't planning on ever seeing you again, so consider yourself lucky to be in my apartment. How'd you get in?"

"You should be more careful about who you let see the code."

Perfect.

"Or maybe you should go fu—"

"Careful," Jordan said.

I sighed and leaned back against the wall. "What happened to you?" I asked softly. "For a moment, I thought we might have some fun together, get to know one another. Since, you know, we apparently made a baby together." I pointed to the room full of suits. Not one of them who'd deemed to take a seat on my couch.

They probably thought the used piece of furniture was beneath them.

I smirked, thinking that Jordan hadn't seemed to mind it during our night together.

"Apparently is the key word," he said.

Sighing, I pushed off the wall, feeling the rough abrasion of plaster against my fingertips before I strode into the kitchen and filled a glass with water. I took the prenatal vitamin the doctor had given me and chased it with a few crackers to prevent any nausea.

Less puking was a good thing.

The sound of a throat clearing didn't draw my gaze.

Or, I didn't *let* it. I was very aware of Jordan standing a few feet away in my kitchen, very aware that the suits were there for a display of strength and to intimidate me.

But I was the daughter of Bernie-freaking-Roberts. I didn't get intimidated. Not by a couple of junior lawyers who were in my apartment for show.

"One partner, one business manager, two lawyers who barely passed the bar, and one egotistical asshole of a baby daddy," I said, placing my glass carefully in the sink and turning to face Jordan.

"Did I forget anyone?"

He just stared at me.

I shrugged. "No? Okay then." I walked out of the kitchen and into my bedroom.

"Where—?"

I closed the door, cutting off the rest of his question and picked up my cell, dialing a number I didn't want to call, but one I knew I needed to.

"Bec? Can you come to my apartment?" I asked. "I've got an issue."

Her voice was crystal clear in my ear, a sharp New England accent with a side of no bullshit allowed. "What is it?"

"Suits. A baby daddy trying to intimidate me."

"Assholes. I'll be there in fifteen." Then, "You're pregnant?"

"Just found out yesterday," I assured her.

I could picture Bec's red lips pursing. "Okay, fine. Was going to give you shit for not telling me, honey. You know I'm prime godmother material."

I laughed, already feeling less on edge just knowing my

friend, who also happened to be a hotshot lawyer, was on her way. "Godmother? Maybe minus the cursing."

"That's an important part of a child's education."

"If you say so."

"I *do* say so." A pause, then beeping followed by the rumble of an engine. "I'm on the road. You just ignore those asswads and let me do my thing."

"I can do that."

"Good."

She hung up and I sat on the edge of the bed, taking a moment to swap my fuzzy socks for a pair that matched my fancy outfit. Or at least a pair that didn't clash so horribly.

Then I went into the bathroom and calmed my mop of hair down, wrestling it into containment.

Also known as a bun.

When I came out of the bathroom, Jordan was standing across the hallway, arms crossed.

"We need to talk."

"Technically, I'd say we didn't *need* to, but I think in this you're right."

"Good." He pushed off the wall. "Come sit in the living room. I'll break it down for you."

There were way too many condescending factors in his statement for me to let any of them slide.

"You'll break it down for me?" I lifted both brows. "Do tell? Oh and maybe if you're going to invite me to sit down on *my* sofa, the least you could do was offer a girl some chocolate and a glass of water."

"Didn't know I was your slave."

I rolled my eyes. "Didn't know being inhospitable was a life goal of yours."

"This isn't my house," he snapped.

"Case in point," I snapped back. "So why. The fuck. Are you. Inside of it?"

"We need to talk."

"That, I think, is overrated," I said. "You're trying to threaten me into agreeing to some shitty contract that lets you off the hook for all responsibility. But"—I gestured at him to lean in—"I don't want anything from you, so you can take your shitty papers, your subpar lawyers, and fuck off."

"Subpar?" one of the suits said. "We're from Lincoln and Associates."

"Like I said. Subpar. My attorney is Rebecca Darden."

One of the suits went pale.

"Yeah," I told him with a smile. "I know."

Rebecca—Bec—was one of the most famous attorneys in the country. And, luckily for me, she also happened to be one of my closest friends.

I wrinkled my nose as I started to push past Jordan. He was wearing that disgusting deodorant again and the smell was enough to make me shudder.

Jerk was probably doing it on purpose.

I shot him a glare when he snagged my arm and halted my progress. "You smell like shit."

He laughed coldly. "You're insane."

"And you're a complete mindfuck! How did you go from nice and caring and sweet to . . . *this*?" I ripped my arm free. "When I say I don't want anything from you—financially or emotionally or otherwise—I mean it. I don't need you or your money or your suits. I am fine on my own."

I plunked down into my cozy armchair, avoiding the couch and the possibility of Jordan sitting next to me.

One of the suits wrinkled his nose as he sat on the worn leather sofa and extended a thick folder toward me. "You'll find our terms very favorable."

I set the contract on the table. "Does this contain a document eliminating Mr . . . .uh . . . " I trailed off, realizing that I literally had screwed a man, practically puked on him, certainly passed out on him, and still I didn't know his last name.

This was why one-night stands never worked out.

"Does this contract eliminate Jordan's paternal rights?" I nudged the folder with my fuzzy covered toe. "If not, it's of no use to me."

The suit looked at me for a moment before flicking his gaze over my head.

"Oh for fuck's sake," Jordan snapped. "We all know that she's using this as a ploy to get more money. Just have her sign the agreement and let's be done with this already."

My vagina was seriously never allowed to pick another man in my entire life.

"She will do no such thing," Bec announced, pushing her way through the front door.

"Is there anyone who doesn't know the code to your apartment?" Jordan drawled.

"I guess not," I snapped. "If you were able to get in."

"Okay, children," Bec said. "What seems to be the problem?"

"Jordan, here," I said, "apparently has a fat wallet and is afraid that I'm trying to take a chunk of it.

Bec froze, eyes wide, then she bent at the waist and started laughing. I crossed my arms, not nearly as amused. The rest of the room was silent, listening to her wind down from roaring laughter to chuckles to the occasional giggle.

When she'd regained control of herself, Jordan pushed off the wall and came to stand between us.

"Care to share what's so funny?" he gritted out.

"I'm sorry," Bec said, wiping a finger under one eye and picking up the folder on the coffee table. "It's just that anyone thinking our Abby is a gold digger is laughable."

Jordan frowned. "And why is that?"

"Because Abby is Abigail Roberts."

His jaw dropped open. His eyes scoured the room as though looking for a billboard that declared in bright flashing lights:

Abigail Roberts—daughter of a billionaire!

Then he focused back on me, something like regret trailing across his face.

"Touché, motherfucka," Bec announced, miming a mic drop.

"Language," I reminded her as she sat on the arm of my chair and started reading.

"You and your language," she murmured. "And the things we do for our godchildren." Bec started reading the document, ignoring the suits. "You're dismissed. I'll contact you with our response."

Her eyes flicked back down as she rapidly devoured what looked to be gibberish to my eyes.

After a moment of the suits not moving, she snapped her fingers. "You're dismissed."

And somehow, that got the men moving. They filed out of the apartment in rapid time.

All except Jordan.

He paused in front of my chair and glared down at me. "This isn't over."

"And you sound like a shitty villain in a B-movie," Bec said before I could reply. "I said we'd be in touch. Your"—her eyes drifted down, then up—"*services* are no longer needed."

Jordan's lips pressed tightly together, but he didn't say anything further. Instead, he followed his team of suits out of the apartment, slamming the door behind him.

I gave the men a few minutes to clear the area then stood.

"Where are you going?" Bec asked.

"To change the freaking code."

TEN

Abby

"OKAY, GIRL," Bec said when I came back inside the apartment. "You need to spill *all* the details."

She'd slid down and taken over my chair, so I plunked onto the couch with a sigh.

"There's not much to tell."

A snort was my only response.

"Look, I'm—"

I was interrupted by a knock on the door. "Oh, come on universe," I muttered, pushing to my feet and moving to answer it.

"It's me." Seraphina's voice was muffled. "The code's not working."

I opened the door. "That's because I changed it."

She breezed into the apartment, bending to kiss my check. "Because of the suits?"

I turned, glared at Bec, who shrugged as if to say, "I called her, so what?" She was still reading the documents and didn't bother to look up at us.

"Because of Jordan," I said. "He memorized the code and decided to let himself in."

Her brows pulled down, but she nodded. "So what's the new one?"

I told her and she smiled. "That was a good date."

"The best," Bec agreed.

It was cheesy, but I'd chosen the night of our senior prom. We'd all gone to the same private school and had blown off our jerks of dates to hang out together instead. We'd busted a few moves—and not very good ones at that—on the dance floor, only giving our aching, heel-wearing feet a break during the slow songs.

It had been goofy and fun and . . . one of the most enjoyable nights of my high school experience.

"Well," I said. "I ran out of good number combos and that one always sticks with me."

"Me too." Seraphina grinned. "Especially since I almost flashed the entire senior class."

"Strapless dresses aren't the best option for you," Bec agreed.

"Neither is dancing to Queen Bey's anthems in said strapless dresses," I added.

"That I learned the hard way," Seraphina said, and we all broke into giggles. She'd caught the dress before she'd fully popped out, but unfortunately, her *girls* wouldn't pop back *in* as easily.

We'd done some sort of crab walk, mad scramble to the bathroom, guarding her assets, and hadn't been able to get everything back into proper alignment until she'd been unzipped, secured, and then rezipped.

I didn't envy her breasts for anything.

"Plus, I can afford better bras nowadays," she said with a laugh. "And I learned that strapless shouldn't be my first choice."

"The boys were disappointed by that." Bec smirked.

Seraphina snorted. "I'm sure they were." Her eyes met mine.

"Nice try to distract us from the real issue, Ms. Abby, but it's time to dish. What's going on?"

I tilted my head to Bec. "Why doesn't the hotshot attorney tell me? I'm guessing it's not great."

"You're right," Bec said, putting the folder down. "He wants a paternity test—"

Well that wasn't a big deal—

"—and if he's proven to be the father, he wants full custody."

"What the fuck?" Seraphina said, but I hardly heard her.

Blood pounded in my ears, and my fingers went numb. "No," I said. "Hell, no."

Bec nodded. "That is definitely a hell no. But you know what this means."

I nodded. "Image is everything."

"Yup."

"I need a job." I sighed. "And a nicer apartment."

"You should call your dad," Seraphina said, then raised her hands in surrender when I glared at her. "I know, I know. And I get it, but if this is about jockeying for position and image, wouldn't it be better to have Bernie Roberts on your side?"

"Except he's never on my side for anything," I grumbled.

"There is that," Bec said, leaning back in the armchair and tucking her feet up underneath her. "I propose this. I'll put together a counter contract, and you'll use your trust fund to find a nicer apartment. Or hell, buy a house. Bernie can't rent control that."

"Oh!" Seraphina clapped her hands together. "I like it."

Bec rolled her eyes. "You're a goof." Then to me, she said, "In the meantime, keep the job hunt up and if you don't find anything in the next two weeks to a month, then you talk to your father."

"Fine," I said, "be perfectly reasonable, why don't you?"

I didn't like the idea of opening up the can of worms that was my trust fund—it was my father's money, after all—but if I was going to use it for anything, I figured that it should be for my child.

"Being perfectly reasonable is my job," Bec said.

Seraphina and I both laughed. Bec waved us off.

"Okay, enough of that. Let's order takeout and watch a Hallmark movie."

"I'll make popcorn," Seraphina said and headed into the kitchen.

"Are you sure you have time for this?" I asked Bec. She was months away from making partner at her law firm and I didn't want to do anything to jeopardize her chances.

She rubbed her hands together. "Are you kidding? You know I live for this sort of thing. Mr. Jordan O'Keith is going to be drowning in paperwork."

"O'Keith?" I repeated, stomach dropping to my feet. "Please tell me that isn't his last name."

She opened the file again and studied it closely. "I can't do that." A pause as she glanced up. "Who is Jordan O'Keith?" Her eyes widened. "Oh. *Oh.* No. Abby, you didn't!"

"I didn't know!" I scrambled to my feet, running for the bedroom and my laptop. "Maybe it's a different one? That's a common name, right?" I pleaded, coming back into the living room, computer in hand.

Seraphina popped her head out of the kitchen. "What is it?"

I opened the browser, typed in "George O'Keith + Son" into the search bar.

"Oh, fuck," Bec said when the page loaded. "Your dad is going to kill you."

"He is so going to kill me," I agreed.

On the screen was a line of photographs of my father's mortal enemy.

In some of them, he was hugging Jordan, and seeing the two men side by side brought out their similar features.

Same eyes. Same hair color. Same build. Same smarmy personality.

Fuck my life.

ELEVEN

Abby

TWO WEEKS PASSED without another word from Jordan or his company of suits. Bec kept me posted on which paperwork she and the other lawyers were exchanging, but because she might as well have been speaking another language, I was unable to say more than, "That sounds great!"

In the meantime, I was house hunting and job searching, the latter of which I'd finally had some success in.

I was heading to a second interview for a tech company that morning. It specialized in research and development of robotics, and they needed someone to oversee their merchandising design.

I was excited. I'd met with the HR representative and the COO the week before to show them my portfolio and we'd clicked. The job seemed to have a lot of moving parts—management of a few junior designers, long-term project planning, and even an opportunity to stick with my roots and undertake some assignments myself.

It was everything I'd been searching for, and I really hoped they liked me as much as I did them.

Why did I suddenly have the image of a little girl standing on the sidelines waving her hands and shouting, "Pick me! Pick me!"

So not a helpful thought going into a very important interview.

"Abigail." The HR representative, Jessica, walked past the reception desk and greeted me with an outstretched hand. "Lovely to see you again. Heather and Rich are ready for you in the conference room."

I stood, shook her hand, and followed her. "How was your week?"

Jessica rolled her eyes to the ceiling. "Craziness! But that seems to be the M.O. these days. We were bought out about three months ago, and while most things have settled, there are still weeks where everything seems to fall apart."

"This was one of them?" I asked.

"Oh, yeah." She stopped at the entrance to the conference room and smiled. "Good luck. I hope to see you around the office in the future."

I smiled back. "Me too."

Jessica pulled open the door and made the introductions. I'd met Rich the previous week, as he was the COO. Heather, the CEO, was new to me, but I immediately understood that she was the most important person in the room.

My father had that air, the one that made people around him sit up straighter and jump through *all* the hoops to impress him.

I considered myself immune to that sort of presence, but even Heather made my heart skip a beat and my stomach— which had been relatively agreeable over the last two weeks —twist.

I hadn't puked since that afternoon, but my queasiness had been intense.

Still, I'd managed with small meals and a package of saltines in my purse.

Today that might not be enough.

No, dammit. I gave my brain a mental slap. *Cut the crap.*

Lifting my chin and swallowing down the nerves and nausea, I shook Heather's and Rich's hands then sat at the table.

I'd brought a few different things with me including some mock-ups I designed of their robotics line for kids. I'd taken some creative license, enjoying the project probably a little too much.

"What's this?" Heather asked, eyeing the small box critically.

"Oh," I said, a bit embarrassed. It wasn't manufacturer's perfect, since I'd printed it at home, but I'd been proud of the packaging I'd created. Now I wondered if it were too juvenile. "Rich showed me a few of the sample products your company has created for kids and I . . . ran with it a bit. I'm sure it doesn't align exactly with what you'd imagined since we haven't spoken, but this is what I came up with. I can totally change anything. This was just geared toward the six- to eight-year-old audience . . ."

I forced myself to shut up.

"Hmm." Heather picked up the box, turned it over, and raised a brow at Rich before setting it back down.

Well, I guessed I'd screwed up this opportunity.

Damn.

I'd really wanted to work here.

After an inner sigh, I forced the negativity down and straightened my shoulders. I would finish the interview with confidence and pride in my work. Who cared what some judgy CEO thought?

"This is the mock website I put together," I said, opening my laptop. "And some graphics for social media ads." I clicked around, showing them the various goodies I'd made. "Some short videos using stock footage and design programs. If we pursued this type of advertising, I'm sure the marketing department could film some original content and we'd make it look a lot prettier."

"I think it looks damn good already," Rich said, and pointed to my favorite graphic. "I like this one the best."

I smiled at him. "Me too."

"Hmm," said Heather.

Holy mother of Batman.

I kept the smile on my lips by pure grit. "So that's what I have. Did you have any further questions for me? Want to see anything else in particular?"

"No," Heather said.

"Okay then." I closed my computer and began stashing my materials in my bag. "Thank you for your time."

I zipped my bag, stood, and slung it over my shoulder.

"I know your father," Heather said.

"Mmm. That's nice." I shook Rich's hand.

"I thought you might be hype."

I extended my palm toward Heather. "Not hype. I like to make my own way, and I love to design. That's the beginning and end of it."

"Hmm," she said, and put her hand in mine.

"Yeah." Super original reply. But I shook her hand and turned to the door. "Thank you again."

Heather waited to speak until I was crossing the threshold. "Jessica will email you the official job description and salary-benefit package. If all meets with your approval, I'll see you in my office eight o'clock tomorrow morning."

My heart skipped a beat before speeding up, pounding heavily in my chest. I turned back to the table where Heather was staring down at her phone. "I'll look it over and let Jessica know."

"Hmm," she said.

I peeked at Rich, who was smiling widely. He gave me a thumbs-up.

I nodded at him, said goodbye, then got the hell out of that conference room before Heather changed her mind.

"YES!" Seraphina fist pumped as she let me into her house. She would be accompanying me that afternoon on my thus far unsuccessful house hunt.

Though the realtor had supposedly found a few more options for me in the competitive market.

Near wine country and in a city with more millionaires than anywhere else on the planet meant that my trust fund only went so far . . .

Okay, that wasn't totally true.

If I splurged, I could probably buy half the town.

But I didn't like using the money in the first place—my father had made it, not me—and if it was just going to be the baby and myself, then I didn't need a gigantic mansion.

Unfortunately, there weren't too many non-gigantic mansions in my town. Not if I wanted to be in the best school district.

And with the baby on the way, I needed to be.

"This job sounds perfect for you!" Seraphina said once I'd showed her the description.

"The salary is kind of low," I said. In fact, it was barely more than what I'd made with Frank and Susan, and RoboTech was a big corporation.

"You could negotiate for higher," Seraphina pointed out.

"Yeah, I could," I said. "But I kind of feel like Heather is waiting for me to pull the 'Bernie Roberts' rich daughter' card."

"You think it's a test?"

I shrugged. "Maybe. Is that crazy?"

"Maybe?" Seraphina smiled. "But by the way you described Heather, I wouldn't put it past her."

"I know."

"Well, only time will tell. And now speaking of things unrelated to both time and craziness, you're a little pale," she said, and led the way into the kitchen. Once there, she handed me a sandwich and pushed me onto a bar stool at the peninsula. "Did you skip a meal again?"

My eyes flicked down at my phone, checking the digital clock on the home screen. "No. But I *am* hungry and tired. I'm sure the interview is what exhausted me. That was a lot of stress for one morning with the prep and then Heather spending the whole meeting *hmm-ing* at me."

"You kicked butt in that meeting, I know it." Seraphina filled a glass with water then sat down next to me. "Now tell me about the houses we're seeing."

"I upped my budget."

Seraphina smiled. "Please say enough so that we can be neighbors?"

"I'm not sure I've upped it *that* much." Her wrinkled nose and pursed lips made me laugh. "Pout much?"

"I want you to buy the house next door and then for you to just randomly pop over for coffee all the time. It'd be like *Desperate Housewives* only less desperate and more fun."

"*Desperate Housewives*? How old are we? That show came out like fifteen years ago."

"Fourteen, thank you very much." Seraphina set the glass down. "I've been bingeing it and it's fabulous."

"You're crazy." I shoved the last bit of sandwich in my mouth, already feeling more energized. I hadn't even known I was exhausted until I'd sat down.

The adrenaline from the interview, I guessed.

"We could binge it together, you know . . ."

"We could . . ." I said, not wanting to commit. Christmas movies I loved. Romcoms, cheesy Hallmark movies. Yes, yes, sign me up.

Dramatic TV shows, not so much.

"Or . . ." Seraphina's expression was way too innocent. "If you moved in *here*, we could watch the whole thing and all the other bad movies we want. We could share books. It'd be great, like being college roommates again."

"Sera—"

"And eat ice cream and stay up late and . . ." I waited for her to wind down, knowing that once she went on a tangent, there was no interrupting her.

"It would be awesome!" she finished on another fist pump.

And since my friend wasn't known for excessive fist pumps, I crossed my arms, raised a brow, and waited. "What's going on?"

"Nothing."

"Mmm hmm," I said. "Spill, girl. You know we tried living together in college and it was nearly the death of our friendship. We are not hospitably compatible."

"We're older now."

"And you're not telling me something."

She slumped, sighing as she rested her head in her palm. "It's really nothing, not compared to what you've got going on."

I reached across the cream-colored marble and put my hand over hers. "My drama doesn't trump everything that is happening in our lives. Your stuff is important too."

"What you're saying is that it's not all about you?" Her lips quirked into a half smile.

"Well, I wouldn't go *that* far . . ." I smirked. "Tell me."

"I was dating someone."

"For how long?" I asked, surprised she hadn't mentioned it. We shared everything.

"I thought he was—" She made a face and shrugged. "I—it's stupid now, but I thought he might be my HEA."

Apparently we didn't share it all.

I squeezed her fingers. "But how? When?"

"Since that day at the bar. When I got called into work. I was running for my car and literally ran into *Him*. Or who I thought was a Him."

Him was our code for that mythical man, the hero from our

novels, the person who we'd run off with into our happily ever after.

A Him was a really big deal.

I gasped. "Why didn't you tell me?"

"You had a lot going on and—" She grimaced. "That's not fair. The truth was, I didn't want to share the fantasy with you. Not because I was worried you'd ruin it or anything," she rushed to say when I sucked in a breath.

Her words stung, but it wasn't about me in that moment. "It's okay."

"No. It's not like you're thinking." Seraphina stood up and began pacing around the kitchen, the glass-tiled backsplash glittering behind her as she walked. "I didn't want to share because I was worried it would all go to shit and then I would be sad, and it did g-go to sh-shit, and I *am* sad and—"

The doorbell rang.

"Damn. That must be the realtor." I stood up, pulled Seraphina into a quick hug. "I'll cancel with her and be right back."

"No." She blew out a breath, swiped a finger under one eye. "I can wallow later. Right now, since you won't live with me, I want to convince you to spend some more money and live next door."

"Are you sure?" I gripped her hands. "We can put on jammies and eat chocolate. I'll even watch an episode of *Desperate Housewives*."

"Tempting." She put an arm around my waist. "But you need a house more than I need chocolate."

I made the sign of the cross and hissed. "How dare you say such sacrilege?"

She snorted. "I love you, dork."

"Love you more."

The doorbell pealed again. "Come on," she said. "Let's go house hunting."

TWELVE

Jordan

JORDAN CLIMBED the stairs to Abigail's apartment and was surprised to find the door was wide open.

He frowned and peered inside, stomach jarring when he saw the living room was empty.

"Can I help you?"

An older man with a beer gut and blue coveralls came out of the hallway. He peered at Jordan suspiciously.

"I'm looking for Abby."

The man's mustache twitched. "She's at the doctor."

"What?" He took a step forward, feeling, for the first time in weeks, the frost seizing him shatter. "The baby. Is she okay?"

The man shrugged. "All I know is that she left in a big hurry." He turned to head back down the hall.

Jordan ran out of the apartment. He'd come . . . to apologize? To make her see reason? To get her to collar her bulldog of an attorney? His lawyer was complaining about an office full of briefs and filings and affidavits.

But Abby was at the doctor and that meant—

He sprinted for his car, stopping at the bar to beg the use of a phone so he could call his assistant.

"I need you to find out what hospital Abigail Roberts is in," he ordered when Brent answered. He pulled out his wallet and opened it to find the business card with the obstetrician who'd seen Abby in the hospital. "Check at Geary Regional first. Dr. Stephens. Call me back."

"For a man who says he doesn't need an assistant any longer," Brent said, "you sure call me a lot."

"Shut up and do it."

"Love you too. Give me five." He hung up the phone.

It only took Brent three.

"Suite 201, Geary. Dr. Stephens," he announced when Jordan answered the return call.

"Thanks."

"A thank you?" Brent asked with mock incredulity. "That might be the first verbal expression of gratitude in the history of all time you've—"

Jordan hung up, thanked the bartender for the use of his cell, and left the bar. He ran to his car, unlocked it, pressed the button to start the ignition, and tore off for the hospital.

The fifteen-minute drive was horrendous, one of the longest of his life. He didn't know why he even cared.

Relief should be coursing through him, not terror.

But . . . he did care.

It took him an agonizing few minutes to find a parking spot, during which time he seriously considered just leaving his car in the middle of the lot.

He didn't do that, one, because he wasn't *usually* an asshole and, two, because the car was brand new.

He'd upgraded to an SUV.

The one with the best safety reviews. He'd even had his assistant order a car seat and a crib.

Okay, so maybe he *had* been putting Brent through the wringer lately.

Jordan guessed it was a good thing his *unneeded* assistant was still on the payroll.

In any event, he parked the car and was hustling for the stairs less than a half hour after walking into Abby's apartment.

He pushed out of the stairwell, ripped open the door and . . . found a waiting room full of women.

All of whom glared up at him with narrowed eyes.

So much suspicion being thrown his way today.

"Can I help you?" the receptionist asked.

He gave her The Smile. The one that had always melted his nanny's heart, even when he was in deep shit for having eaten a gallon of ice cream.

It was the same one that usually got him whatever female attention he required.

Coincidentally, it was also the smile that didn't work on Abby.

But he couldn't think about that now. He had to keep his game face on, find out what was going on, and most importantly, he needed to remember that she was exactly like all of the other women in his life.

Exactly like the women who'd nearly ruined his father's business.

Who'd managed to successfully decimate his family.

"I'm sorry," he said when her look went from guarded to dazed. Yes, he'd mentioned before he wasn't *usually* an asshole, but he knew his effect on women and wouldn't shy away from using it. God knew the female population did it all the time.

Jaded much?

He stifled a sigh, leaned against the counter, and dropped his voice conspiratorially. "I was rushing in because I'm looking for Abigail Roberts. I've never been here before, and she's—"

The receptionist's lips curved up, her bright red lipstick

jarring against the maroon of her scrubs. "Oh, of course. Don't worry, she was running late herself. Go on to the other door, and I'll send the nurse out to get you."

"Thank you," he said, moving to the side. The panic that had been gripping him eased.

The receptionist was calm. Surely if Abigail was in any danger, her demeanor would be more serious, or they would have sent him down to the Emergency department.

Maybe she just wasn't feeling well?

Which probably meant that he should just turn around and leave. It wasn't a crisis. He had no business being there.

Except . . . something inside of him would not let him leave until he'd laid eyes on Abby.

He needed to see for himself that she was okay.

"Here you go, Mr. Roberts," the receptionist said, using Abby's last name like it was his and they were married. He didn't bother to correct her, especially when she ran a hand down his chest and leaned so close that her breasts brushed his arm.

"Oh, I'm sorry," she said when he flicked his eyes down and raised one brow. Hurriedly, she stepped back. "Ms. Roberts will be in the second room on the right."

"Thank you."

"My pleasure."

The way she said those two words was not flattering. It was slightly creepy and very much over the top.

But he supposed that it was his fault for unleashing The Smile.

God, he *was* an asshole.

Instead of letting that stop him, Jordan walked down the hall and opened the second door on the right.

In retrospect, he should have knocked.

"Jesus Christ!" Abby shrieked. "What is it with you and trying to expose my vagina to the world? Get out!"

He stood frozen for a moment, round two of sights he could

never unsee now burned on his retinas, before stepping through the door and closing it behind him. "Dr. Stephens," he said.

"Mr.— oh, you'll have to forgive me. I'm terrible with names."

"Jordan," he said, and released The Smile for the second time. Why not? He was already in deep with the receptionist. He may as well use it to get on the doctor's good side. "You can call me Jordan."

Dr. Stephens raised a brow at Abby. "Got a dangerous one there."

Abby snorted. "Yeah, and his sperm is the most dangerous part." She glared at him. "What are you doing here?"

"I went to your apartment."

She rolled her eyes. "I changed the code."

"The door was wide open," he countered.

The doctor coughed and Abby jumped. "I'm sorry—"

"Carry on," Jordan said. "I'll just sit over here and not bother anyone."

Another snort from Abby, but she didn't protest as he moved to the chair at her side.

"Cold," Dr. Stephens warned and then moved her hand under the paper blanket thing Abigail had draped over her legs.

Abby winced but didn't say anything, just turned her attention to the machine next to her.

Jordan's breath caught. "Is that—?"

Dr. Stephens smiled. "That's your baby. Here's the head and the feet and that little oval there is the heart."

He watched the rapid *flutter-flutter* of his baby's heart, heard the *whoosh-whoosh* as the organ pumped furiously on the black and white screen, and something unlocked inside him.

"Here." Dr. Stephens handed him a printout of the image. "For the scrapbook. Or wallet. Or whatever." She passed a larger stack to Abby. "Everything looks good. I'll see you in two weeks, okay?"

"Okay," Abby said.

"Keep it up with those small meals and call or email me if you experience any dizziness or fainting."

Abby agreed and the doctor left.

Jordan leaned toward Abby to getter a better look at the ultrasound pictures, but she pushed him away.

"Are you serious right now?"

"I just want to see the pictures."

She shoved them into his hands. "Look all you want, but get away from me." She gulped, clapping a hand over her nose. "Haven't puked in two freaking weeks. Five minutes with you and I'm a hairsbreadth away. You're wearing it again, aren't you?"

"Wearing what?" He was barely listening as he flipped through the photos of his baby. *His* baby.

How was this his life?

"Satan's deodorant."

That got his attention and he shifted his gaze to Abby. "What are you talking about?"

"Your deodorant smells like shit." She stood up, careful to keep the drape around herself.

Disappointing, that. He hadn't seen nearly enough of her.

And he was fucking insane to go there. Even if it was just in his head.

"You just turn your back, mister," she ordered, shuffling toward the pile of clothes on the bench. "Last thing you need to see is more of me."

He could argue the point, but Jordan opted not to.

Instead, he did what any normal man would do: acquiesced to Abby's wishes and shifted in the chair—then watched like hell out of the corner of his eye.

THIRTEEN

Abby

WHY THE HELL was Jordan there?

I pulled on my underwear and pants, moving quickly to get decent. The man had horrible timing.

"Okay," I said once I'd slipped on my sweater and boots. "You can turn around now."

Jordan spun in the chair, his long legs cluttering up the small space between the exam table and the wall. The room had been plenty big without him. Then he'd barged in and taken over.

I could smell him. I could feel him, his presence somehow radiating into the space between us and reminding me of the spark that was always there when he was near.

So far, that spark had brought me nothing but frustration and anguish.

I needed to remember that.

Because when he wasn't actively being a jerk, my body seemed to forget the fact that I hardly knew him and that he was batting at a less than ideal average, both in the bedroom activities

—okay, *coffee table* shenanigans—and normal human interactions.

"Why were you at my apartment?"

He sighed. "Should we continue this conversation somewhere that isn't a doctor's office?"

I huffed, slammed my hands on my hips. "Why, Jordan?"

"I want you to call off your lawyer."

I laughed and started for the door. "You're kidding right?"

"No, I'm not."

Turning the knob, I said. "Then you must just be stupid because I'm not calling off Bec—"

The rest of my sentence was cut off as a warm chest pressed me against the door, a slightly calloused palm covered mine on the knob. "I'm not stupid," Jordan said into my ear.

"A-acting like it," I said, forcing my idiot body to stop melting, to stop liking the feel of him against me.

He was bad in bed.

He knocked me up.

He tried to take my baby away.

"Let me go," I hissed and struggled against him.

Jordan released me, backing up a step. His pupils were dilated, the black nearly eclipsing the blue of his irises. He raised his palms when I whipped around.

"What the hell is with you?" I asked, flattening my palms against the wooden panel of the door. "I can barely keep up with your moods. One second you want to fuck me, the next you're gone. Then you're back and I see this glimpse of a nice, caring guy who, oh, by the way, wants to fuck me again." I laughed but it wasn't filled with humor. "Then it's like whiplash because all of a sudden you hate me, accusing me that I'm a gold digger. We hardly know each other. I wouldn't invest this much time into managing some asshole's moods even if I *did* know him."

"Are you done?" he asked when I'd finished, chest heaving, cheeks hot.

Unbelievable.

"Yeah," I said and opened the door. "I'm done here. In the future, communicate through my attorney."

As I walked out of Dr. Stephens' office, I half expected him to stop me, but Jordan let me go, and I was relieved.

Really, I was.

He was insane, his moods yo-yoed faster than I could keep up with, and furthermore, he wanted to take my baby from me.

I forced a smile at the receptionist, making a note to call and speak to the manager about them letting Jordan in without asking me first, before hurrying out of the waiting room and into the hall. I found my way to the stairs leading down to the hospital's lobby and walked out to my car. But when I pulled the door handle, it didn't unlock. Frowning, I pulled again. I had one of those cars with the locks that automatically disengaged when the key fob was near, because, well, history told me repeatedly that keys and I didn't mix.

But the theory of automatic locks only worked when I had my purse. Or rather, my keys *in* my purse.

Which was likely sitting on the counter in Dr. Stephens' exam room.

Dropping my head back, I stared up at the clouds. November wasn't the coldest time in California, but the sky was gray and there was a definite chill in the air. None of which would help me get my purse back.

I was exhausted. I didn't want to walk back into the hospital. I didn't want to do a damn thing except cozy up on my couch with a blanket and a book. But I needed to go back to my apartment, make sure everything was moved out and locked up, and then drive across town to my new house.

Which was on Seraphina's street—actually directly *across* the street from her home. We were both excited.

Separate but close by worked for us.

Of course, none of this changed the fact that I still didn't have my keys.

I made a face, wanting to be in the jammies-on-the-couch portion of the day already without the rest of my adult responsibilities.

Unfortunately, life didn't work that way and with a sigh, I pushed away from my car.

"Looking for this?"

Jordan.

I made a sound, a whiny little cry that would indicate to any of my friends that I was nearing the end of my rope.

He didn't pick up on the signal. Instead, he stood there, my black purse gripped in his hand like it was a clutch rather than a good-sized handbag.

I'd forgotten how big he was.

Big.

I giggled at the absurdity of it all, especially when my thighs clenched and I felt moisture pool between my legs.

He was horrible in bed, you little hussy, I thought.

Well, not horrible so much as premature. With a little practice . . .

Oh, my God. I was going insane. It was the hormones. Had to be. All the books said that my sex drive might increase. *That* was the only reasonable explanation for why I could possibly still be attracted to him.

Jordan rattled the bag, like he was shaking a toy for a dog. Annoyance flared. Really? Should I trot over and rub myself on him in thanks?

My body liked *that* idea. Especially when the movement lifted the hem of his T-shirt, exposing a couple of inches of hard, flat abs. It liked the rubbing-all-over-him option a lot.

I tilted my head to the sky again and tried to find my freaking brain.

I was losing it, switching personalities faster than the man in front of me.

But what could I possibly say?

"Come closer. Let me smell that Satan's deodorant of yours and remember all the reasons why I can't fuck you."

His brows drew down. "What was that?"

Oh come on, Abby, I yelled internally. *Filters. Stop allowing your thoughts to vomit all over the sidewalk.*

"Nothing," I said. Thank God I hadn't spoken loudly. "Just thanks for grabbing that."

"Did you say—?"

"Uh-uh. I didn't say anything. I most definitely did *not* say that my body is a confused asshole that still wants to have sex with you, even though you are maybe the worst lay of my life and—"

Oh. Good. God. I clamped my lips closed.

"You want to have sex with me?" Jordan closed the distance between us and I backed up until my spine was pressed against the cold metal of my car.

"I didn't say that."

One hand came up, caging me in. "I think you did."

"Nope." I lifted my chin. "What I *said* was that my body wants to fuck you. My brain, on the other hand, is very logical and understands that while you may be pretty to look at and have a rather large . . . *hammer,* you're not equipped with the knowledge to use your apparatus properly."

I smiled when his jaw dropped open.

"And let it also be noted that you're a jerk."

After snagging my purse from his limp fingers, I slipped under his arm—gagged, because his deodorant was seriously the worst—and pulled the door handle.

Thankfully, the locks disengaged and I slipped inside, locking them behind me before Jordan got any ideas. I pushed the button to start the car, put the engine in gear and began reversing, forcing him to move back or get run over.

Unfortunately for me, he chose option A.

I glanced out my window just before driving away and saw that his expression was stormy. I could have sworn that his lips had formed the words, "I'm not done with you," but I pretended not to notice.

I was done with Jordan O'Keith. Once and for all.

FOURTEEN

Abby

MY BLACK PENCIL skirt was a little tight and I was struggling to suppress the urge to adjust it as I walked across the lobby toward the bank of elevators leading up to my new job.

Usually, I'd take the stairs, but RoboTech was on the fifth floor which was about four floors too many in the heels I was wearing.

"Ms. Roberts?"

I turned and smiled at the security guard. "Oh," I said. "Was I supposed to check in with you? I didn't realize—"

The younger man smiled, eyeing my too-tight skirt in a way that made me feel instantly uncomfortable.

"I've got your badge," he said, gaze most definitely not on my face. I knew I was a little extra boobalicious because of the pregnancy. My ass and breasts were the only parts of my body to increase in size thus far. "Mr. Sutter"—Rich, the COO—"said to give it to you. You'll need it to access the elevators."

I took it from him, feeling gross. This is why I'd begun to hate corporate jobs, why I'd worked at the graphic design firm with

Frank and Susan. They'd had a family business, full of under-standing and teamwork. With big corporations, the attitude and, often, the whole Mad Men-type climate that still existed in some circles, was deplorable.

One word to my father and this troll would *literally* be bank-rupt, but I didn't equate being sleazy on the same level as ruining someone's life.

Unfortunately.

"Thanks," I said and reached for the pass. "If you'll just hand it over, I'll be on my way."

"You know," the guard said as he pulled the rectangle of plastic back and held it out of reach. "I have a lot of power here, and if you go out with me, I can show you how that power works."

Gross.

"I'm confused," I said, tilting my head to the side and blinking doe-eyed up at him. "How would you *show* me your power?"

A wink. "That's for me to know and you to find out." Barf. "But I do have keys to every office in the building. I have access to some . . . interesting projects."

And great, the guard had escalated from sleazy pickup lines to corporate espionage. Now I'd definitely have to report him.

I sighed, and his expression went from supremely confident to more than a little desperate.

Idiotic man-child.

Didn't he understand what he was saying?

Hadn't he signed an iron-clad NDA like I had? That paper-work alone should give any reasonable person pause. And he was just offering this up like candy to get a *date*? With me?

I stood by my idiot statement.

"I'll show you," he said when I didn't reply. "In fact, just the other day I went into one of the offices and saw—"

"You're fired."

My head whipped around. Heather stood there, furious.

"I—" His arms flapped at his sides, the desperation from the previous moment turning into pure panic.

Heather picked up her cell phone and dialed a number. "Stan. Get your ass up here. Now."

I bit my lip in nervousness when she hung up and stared at the guard. "Uh"—I hitched a thumb toward the elevators—"should I go on up?"

Heather shook her head fiercely and not one strand of her hair dared to disobey. It was pulled tightly into a bun that stayed perfectly in place. My ponytail—that I'd spent a good forty-five minutes attempting to wrangle into some semblance of control—looked positively messy in comparison.

"You'll stay." Her eyes flew up, pinning the guard in place with laser focus. "And you as well." A sniff. "For the moment."

Our trio stood there for an awkward ninety-six seconds—yes, I counted. Several people walked through the lobby, a few even pausing as though to offer help, but one shake of Heather's head sent them on the way.

I couldn't help but be mesmerized by the bun, or more realistically, how the bun didn't move a millimeter.

"What?" she asked, catching me staring.

My cheeks heated. "Sorry," I muttered. "I have hair envy." I pointed to my mess of brown hair, which I could already feel sliding loose. "Mine is hopeless."

She raised a brow.

"Totally inappropriate, I know." My nose wrinkled, knowing this was my boss, but not able to stop the verbal diarrhea, I continued talking. "But in stressful situations, I tend to focus on the minute details."

"Sharing flaws on your first day?" she asked, her mouth almost curving into a smile. "Most wouldn't risk that."

"I'm assuming you like me more for my work than my

personality at this point," I said. "Might as well give you reasonable expectations to start."

Heather shook her head, but I definitely saw a smile. It lasted a whole four and a half seconds—yes, I counted again—before it disappeared.

A door behind the security desk flew open and a man with gorgeous olive skin came out. He was sporting a trimmed salt-and-pepper beard and had a network of lines around his eyes that made him appear more friendly than harsh.

"What's up?" he asked.

"Stan," Heather said, "meet Abigail."

He shook my hand. "Nice to meet you, Abigail. I'm Stan. I'm in charge of security here at RoboTech."

I nodded. "Nice to meet you too."

"Introductions made, let's get down to business," Heather said. She nodded at the nervous looking guard. "We've got another one and this one is extra stupid."

"Fuck," Stan said then winced. "Sorry. Not so much as for the language as for this asshole." He turned, gestured for another man to come from the back. "Go with Francis," he ordered. "Now."

"I didn't—"

"Diego," Stan said. "That wasn't an invitation for you to speak. Do yourself a favor, shut the fuck up, and go in the back."

The guard hung his head and I felt a moment's pang of guilt before I shoved it away.

This mess was his fault. Not mine.

"How many more are left?" Heather asked when he'd gone.

"Of the old staff? Two. But I actually like those two." He sighed. "Then again, I liked Diego, *or* I thought he had the potential to change."

"Mmm," Heather said. "If they step one toe out of line—"

"Gone," Stan agreed. "What specifically did Diego do?"

"Offered to exchange corporate secrets for a date with this

one." She pointed at me. "Admitted to going into RoboTech offices to look at projects. Not to mention sexually harassing my new employee on her first day."

"Fucking moron."

"I mean for a minute there I actually felt bad for him," I said. "Then I realized he was a giant idiot."

Stan snorted, and I winced.

"Sorry, I probably shouldn't have said that."

"It's the truth," he said. "I'm sorry you had to deal with that. My company recently took over security and cleared house." He sighed. "Or I thought we had. That's not how I expect my employees to act. He'll be gone before you come down for lunch." His eyes tracked to Heather. "I'll talk to him, see what he knows."

"Make it clear to him what he'll lose if he chooses to blab again," she said. "Lucky it was here and now. All of these leaks need to be plugged."

Stan nodded and left them.

"Let's get to work," Heather said and led the way to the elevators.

FIFTEEN

Abby

"WELL, that was one way to make an impression," Seraphina said. It was just before lunchtime, and I'd spent the morning learning the lay of the land from Rich and meeting the staff who would be working for me.

Two senior designers. Five junior designers. Seven people for whom I was now responsible.

The notion was daunting—the most employees I'd managed with Frank and Susan's company was three and two of those had been college students on an internship. These employees were serious workers and enthusiastic about the projects they were designing.

"After lunch, Heather wants to meet with me to discuss timelines."

"Did she mention anything else about the guard?"

"No," I said, slipping my feet back into my heels and standing up. "But I also didn't ask. I got the feeling she didn't want me to, and since I'd been with the company for all of a half hour at that point, I didn't think it was appropriate."

"Getting someone fired in your first hour." Seraphina grinned. "Why do I think your father would approve?"

I snorted.

"Speaking of the elder Mr. Roberts, have you told him yet?"

"He knows I moved," I hedged.

Seraphina sighed. "It's going to be worse if he finds out from someone other than you."

"It's going to be terrible if he finds out from me."

"Abs."

"Sera."

Silence.

"I'm going to tell him."

"When?"

I turned to the window and sat on the edge of my desk. If I looked into the distance, ignored the streets and highways and houses and buildings in between, I could pretend the rolling hills covered in grape vines was my only view.

Somewhere up there, my father owned several wineries. His house was in those hills. As a kid, I'd spent more time running through the vines and the gardens than inside. It had been simpler. Quieter. Less imposing.

Less scary than dealing with my dad. No, less scary than *disappointing* my dad.

Of course, that was before I'd realized that everything I did would disappoint my father.

This was no different.

"I'll tell him."

Seraphina caught the change in my tone as any good friend would. "Abs, it's going to be—"

"I'm fine," I said, and forced my voice to be chipper. "I've got to go. Don't want to overshoot my lunch hour on day one."

"Are you sure you're—?"

"See you tonight?"

She blew out a breath. "See you tonight."

I hung up and blinked away the tears, knowing that it was the hormones making my eyes a little watery, not because I was torn up about my father and my childhood.

I was twenty-seven, for God's sake. A grown woman with her own life.

I could *not* have daddy issues.

I suspected I did anyway.

"Gross," I grumbled and picked up my purse. There was a soup and sandwich place just down the block. I'd fill up on some carbs and maybe splurge on a cookie.

I walked into the hallway, passing Heather's office, and nearly plugged my nose at the hint of sour in the air. It reminded me of—

Nope, not thinking about Mr. Thor Wannabe.

I breathed through my mouth until I'd gotten far enough from the scent that I didn't feel like puking. Hopefully, one of the staff didn't wear the same deodorant as Jordan.

After popping into Rich's office and asking if he wanted me to pick up something for him—no, since he'd brought his lunch— I took the elevators down to the lobby and walked out into the fresh air.

Today the sky was clear, but it was cold and I immediately regretted not bringing my jacket.

Still, it wasn't bad enough for me to go back upstairs. I toughed it out to the deli and ordered a salad and soup, sitting at a little table in the back while scarfing the two down and reading a book on my phone.

And I did splurge on a cookie. Double chocolate chip.

Belly pleasantly full and my body warmed from the soup, I headed back to the office.

This time no security guards accosted me on my way to the elevator. The extent of my excitement was when Francis—the guard who'd escorted Diego off to what I now imagined as a scary interrogation room, complete with two-way glass and intimidating lighting—smiled and waved at me.

I smiled back and got on the elevator. On the way up, I began regretting the double chocolate chip cookie. In the span of five minutes, I'd gone from pleasantly satiated to overly full. A good walk would have probably cured the feeling, I thought, and made a mental note to ask Rich where the stairs were.

The elevator opened with a ding and I stepped out onto RoboTech's floor.

My office was down the hall to the right, in between Heather's and Rich's. It had a glass door and a large window in the front. Both had blinds that could be closed, but I hadn't bothered.

Unless someone actually knocked—and even sometimes not then if I was really engrossed in a project—my focus was completely devoted to whatever I was working on.

There was still a trace of the smell in the air, so I hurried into my office and closed the door.

I plunked my purse on the table near the window pointing out to the vineyards and sank into my office chair. Immediately, I toed off my heels and stretched my aching feet. The black pumps might look amazing, but they were absolute torture to wear. And though they definitely appeared professional, I wouldn't be wearing them again.

Flats all the way, baby.

After the shoes, I was tempted to release the zipper on my skirt but figured that probably wouldn't send the right message on my first day.

With a snort, I logged into my computer and pulled up my calendar. There was a request for a meeting with Heather in a half hour to discuss the projects she wanted to move on and their timelines. It was to be held in the conference room directly across the hall from my office.

I glanced up, noted the blinds to that room were closed, and shrugged as I got back to work. My email account had been set up and waiting for me that morning and it was already filling with messages. I had the feeling that just managing my inbox was going to be a challenge.

I set an alarm on my phone for twenty-five minutes later and got to work weeding through the messages. There was the typical new hire paperwork, most of which I'd already completed. There were project descriptions and proofs, an employee handbook, and several requests from the designers for meetings the following week.

After putting all the requests in my calendar and seeing the lack of available space, I decided that it was a good thing I'd started on a Friday. I might need all of Saturday and Sunday to recover from the scheduling nightmare.

Hopefully things would calm down after I'd settled in and had a chance to meet with everyone. Still, I couldn't help but feel that this job was going to be trial by fire.

My phone buzzed and I jerked up from the computer, silencing the alarm. I slipped on my heels, gathered a notebook, pen, and my cell and crossed the hall. Unfortunately, I also got another sniff of the scent along the way. Jesus, was someone rubbing it on the walls? Why was it so strong?

Shoving down the nausea, I pushed through the door. The blinds were still closed, so I wasn't ready for what I saw.

For *who* I saw.

"What are you doing here?" Jordan and I said at the same time.

He jumped to his feet and closed the distance between us.

"No." I took a step back as his smell inundated me. My stomach churned. I felt saliva pool in the back of my mouth. "Stay there."

"Why are you here?" He didn't exactly look happy to see me, but he also didn't appear angry.

"I work here," I said, swallowing hard and pressing myself

against the door. The wooden blinds rattled and screeched as they moved against the glass. I turned, straightening them before I did real damage.

In. Out. Don't breathe through the nose. Do. Not. Puke.

"Why are you here?"

"I own this company."

"Owned," Heather said as I whipped around, noticing her for the first time. I hadn't been able to see anything more than Jordan from the moment I walked in. "You *used* to own it," she said.

Jordan's jaw clenched. "I still hold the majority of shares, Heather."

"Come sit down, Abigail."

I blinked at Rich's voice, feeling extremely overwhelmed, but nodded and crossed to the conference table.

"Mr. O'Keith, I'd like you to meet Abigail Roberts, our new Vice President of Design and Marketing." Rich's gaze shifted between Jordan and me. "But I suspect you two already know each other."

Away from Jordan, I found I could breathe a little easier. The nausea was still there, but it wasn't like I was going to poltergeist vomit in the next few seconds.

I might actually make it to the trash can if needed.

"No," I said. "I'm not all that familiar with Mr. O'Keith."

"Yes," Jordan said at the same time. "I know Abigail."

I glared at him. "You do not *know* me."

He raised a brow. "Are we going to do this here?"

"No." I sniffed, pulling out my notebook and taking the cap off my pen before looking around the room.

Well, I looked at Rich and Heather. Jordan I deliberately ignored.

Both of Heather's brows were up. Rich's eyes were darting between his phone and the rest of us.

"Let's get started, shall we?" he asked after a moment.

"Yes," I agreed, and if it sounded a little desperate then it was because I *was* a little desperate.

To forget that Jordan was sitting in the room with me.

To forget that Jordan's baby was currently cooking in my womb.

Jordan sat down next to me. Even though there was an empty chair between Heather and Rich, he just plopped down and invaded my space.

His slack-covered leg brushed my thigh, making me shiver, but his eyes were on Heather as she began talking. I couldn't concentrate on her words, not when he was sitting next to me, his heat seeping into the space around me, all Thor-like and handsome.

". . . don't you think, Abigail?"

I started, my eyes jumping from Jordan to Heather.

I had no idea what she'd been saying.

Fuck me.

"I'm not sure that six months is a reasonable timeline to bring something like the kids' robot to market," Rich said. "The engineers haven't finished the programming. We have to test it with our focus groups. Send out early versions to bloggers—"

"The coding is almost done," Jordan said, drawing my gaze back to him. "I'll finish it by Monday. Then the engineers need two months tops. That gives four months for focus groups and bloggers. That's plenty."

"Okay wait," I said. "So you'll want market-level packaging ready to go in *two* months? We have nothing but a mock-up I made. Two months is not nearly enough time."

"Hmm," Heather said, making a few notes on her laptop.

"That mock-up you made is nearly perfect," Rich replied, leaning back in his chair. "I've been consulting with our manufacturers. We have the supplies to replicate it already available in our warehouses. It can be used with very few manipulations."

"All right," I said, nodding. "Just to be clear, do you want my focus to be this before all else? Because if there are indeed no major changes and we're using the design I laid out, I could probably get what we need in eight weeks. All the other projects will need to be back-burnered though."

"Heather?" Rich asked.

Another few taps on her keyboard, another "Hmm."

"Jordan?"

He inclined his head. "This needs to get to market as quickly as possible."

"Why?" I asked. "A kids' robot isn't exactly a new concept. What's the rush? Why not take our time and line up the toy for next year's Christmas season?"

Heather nodded.

Rich nodded.

Jordan frowned. "It needs to be out as soon as possible."

"If that's the case and we're being realistic here," I said, "I'm going to need to pull all the designers from their other projects and put them on this with me. Is that going to impact other deadlines?"

"No," Jordan said. "Our Christmas push has come and gone. We have nothing due until the spring."

It was my turn to say, "Hmm."

I couldn't figure out why this was so important to Jordan. Why was he pushing the project forward in such a rush? Wouldn't it make more sense to hit the market during a major shopping season? Why did he want to release in May?

Something was off, but I couldn't pinpoint what it was.

"Use whatever resources you need," he said.

"You're overstepping your bounds," Heather interjected. "This isn't your company anymore."

"It was my company for a decade, Heather," he snapped. "And my R&D is what keeps it alive during lean times."

"We're not in lean times," she countered. "I'm signing the contract with the Army."

"Which is idiotic at best."

"You sold the company to me. You trusted me to make the best decision for its future when you took your payday and checked out," she said, her chin lifting. "All was well and good until you decided that you couldn't hack it doing nothing on a beach."

"Now who's overstepping?" He leaned forward in his chair. "You know damn well why the military is a horrible idea."

"No," she said. "I know why *you* think it's a horrible idea. What *I* see as a businesswoman is an opportunity for sustainable and stable income for the next twenty years."

"Fuck," Jordan muttered and shot to his feet. The action was so abrupt that I jumped, knocking my phone, notebook, and pen to the floor.

He and Heather froze, turned to examine Rich—who looked as uncomfortable as I felt—and me.

"We'll continue this later," Jordan said.

Heather closed her laptop and stood, much more calmly than Jordan had. If her spine was as rigid as granite, then that was the only outward sign of her being upset. "There's nothing further to discuss. You wanted out of the business side. You're out."

"I'm still the majority shareholder."

She strode toward him, laptop under one arm. "I will bring Dad into this, if I need to, bro." Heather walked past him.

"You wouldn't."

"Hmm."

Jordan rolled his eyes but didn't say anything further.

"And you know exactly what he'll say," she chirped. "Rich, a word in my office?"

Rich gathered his things and was out of the room in less than thirty seconds, leaving me alone with Jordan and his dark storm cloud of anger.

Yeah, that I didn't want directed at me.

Carefully and *quietly,* since Heather's words seemed to have triggered some sort of contemplative coma, I slid my chair back and knelt to pick up my notebook.

My pen had rolled under the table and I had to crawl underneath to retrieve it. I was on hands and knees, arm outstretched, fingers just grazing the cap when I realized I should have just left it.

I had a box of twenty-three identical others in my office.

"You're killing me in that skirt," Jordan said softly.

I gasped and tried to stand, which basically meant that I tried to give myself a concussion by cracking my head against the underside of the heavy oak table.

"Shit," he said and crawled under next to me. "Are you okay?"

"No," I groaned, collapsing on my side, one hand covering the aching spot on the back of my head. "Why would you do that?"

He touched my arm cautiously. "I didn't mean to startle you."

"Well, congrats." I glared over at him. "You did anyway, plus you messed up my hair."

He grinned. "I like your hair messy."

My stomach fluttered before I reminded myself of who exactly Jordan was. No flutters. Nope. No freaking way.

"Here we go again," I said. "Am I going to get Dr. Jekell or Mr. Hyde?"

"Neither." He crawled closer. "You're going to get Jordan. Just me, none of the other bullshit that's colored my past or our interactions. You're going to get the real me."

The words might have been considered sweet if I could have actually processed them.

But I couldn't.

Because Jordan coming closer meant that he'd exposed his armpit.

"Satan's deodorant," I gasped, clamping my hand over my mouth as the smell hit me.

Nausea roared and that too-full feeling from a half hour before exploded.

Literally exploded.

Everywhere.

SIXTEEN

Jordan

JORDAN DESERVED IT. Really, he did.

"Oh, God," Abby said, heaving again.

He shoved the trash can under her nose just in time, holding back her hair with his other hand.

Yes, he might have researched what to do if a pregnant woman was puking on the Internet. Yes, it should have been obvious before the search what to do.

But he was a guy. He didn't have a lot of experience with vomiting or pregnant women. And he definitely wasn't used to dealing with long hair.

He had congratulated himself on the wet towel thing when that came up in the search. *That* had been genius.

Well, technically it was his mom's genius since she'd done that for him when he was sick. His heart clenched at the memory. He didn't think of her often, not when it always hurt so much.

"Get. Away." Abby shoved him hard enough that he toppled

backward onto his ass. He barely had the presence of mind to let go of her hair.

"I'm trying to help," he said.

"You've helped enough," she gritted out. "Now stay out of nose-reach. Please. For the love of all that's holy."

He finally clued in. "Is it the deodorant again?"

Hazel eyes flashed up to his. "You think?"

Jordan pushed himself back until he was on the outside wall. From the waist up, he was covered in puke. It soaked into his shirt and he unbuttoned it, peeling it free. His undershirt had survived a little better, so he walked over to the sink, shoved the shirt into the garbage bin there, then washed his hands.

Luckily, his sense of smell sucked, otherwise he might have been joining Abby at the trash can.

"What can I do?" he asked.

She moaned and pushed the bin away, lying curled up on her side on the floor.

Jordan was a total dick for noticing her skirt had ridden up and that her panties were just a sexy as those four-inch pumps.

Which—he frowned—she shouldn't be wearing. Not in her condition.

What if she fell?

"Abby?"

"Shh," she said.

He fell silent, waited for her to say something. When she didn't, he cautiously moved across the room and glanced down.

Her face was flushed, her eyes were closed. At first, he thought she'd passed out again and his heart skipped a beat. Then her lips pursed, forming a little "o" as her breath puffed through.

She'd fallen asleep.

In a conference room. In the middle of the day. On her first day of work.

She was going to kill him.

He debated whether to wake her or not and after a moment decided not to. How could he? She was carrying his baby, and if she needed rest, then he'd damn sure make certain she got it.

But his conscience pinged as he slipped through the door, closing it behind him. He knew that the kids' robot project was going to put her under more strain and he knew he should extend the timeline or maybe table it all together.

Except . . . he couldn't do that.

"What are you doing?" Heather hissed.

When her eyes locked onto his shirt, blatantly eyeing his state of undress and the closed door behind him, he put his hands up. "Come on," he said. "Like I would ever have a relationship with someone in the workplace."

She raised a brow, pointed at his shirt. "Hmm."

"You and your fucking *hmms*. You think you sound smart by just uttering a syllable? Use words like a normal person."

"You want words?" she asked. "Why in the hell are you partially dressed after spending an extra half hour with an employee you obviously have a past with? Why does she hate your guts?"

He crossed his arms. "She doesn't hate my guts."

Heather laughed. "You're more delusional than I thought."

"It's not like that," he said. "We—" Jordan sighed, thought *fuck it*, and laid all the cards on the table. "She's pregnant. It's mine."

"Uh . . ."

For once, Heather using only one syllable didn't annoy the shit out of him.

"You—" She shook her head, dropped her voice. "You fucking idiot. You're kidding me, right? Don't you know who she is? Who her father is?"

"I know," he said. "Well, I didn't know that night. But I, uh, learned a couple of weeks ago."

"And this project. *This* project we have her on. Don't you

realize how that's going to look—" She put up her hand, eyes widening. "Wait. Did you say you *just* learned who she was?"

"No, I found out weeks ago."

"Before or after?"

He rolled his eyes. "Before or after what?"

"Before or after you found out she was pregnant?"

Jordan hesitated, and Heather groaned, pacing away a few steps before turning back toward him. "Oh, my God, you're a bigger idiot than I've ever given you credit for. You did it, didn't you? Acted just like Dad."

"I— It wasn't like that—"

His sister pretended to hit her head on the wall. "It was. You did exactly what Dad would have done. Tried to pay her off." She started laughing. "You tried to buy off Abigail fucking Roberts."

"Shh," he said. "You'll wake her up."

Heather's laughter abruptly halted. "My new VP is asleep in there?"

"My mere smell makes her puke."

His sister started giggling, albeit quieter this time. "Oh, this is too good."

"She's exhausted," he said, and if his tone was accusatory, it was because he felt no little amount of guilt about the stress he must have caused her over the last few months. Leaving her that night. Serving her with papers. Being a total asshole at every opportunity.

"I'm not going to fire her," Heather said. "She's the best designer I've ever met, *and* she seems to be good at managing people."

"I don't want you to fire her," he retorted, crossing his arms and leaning back against the wall of windows next to the door. "Just cut her a little slack."

"Don't fuck this up for us. If you want your pet project to go, we need to keep her happy."

Jordan sighed. "Noted."

"So why isn't she on Roberts' payroll?" Heather asked.

"Unlike Dad, good old Bernie doesn't like women on staff."

The lights above them turned on automatically, telling them both that it was getting late. The office generally closed early on Fridays since many employees worked longer days during the rest of the week, so the space was quiet.

"Dad liked women on staff a little too much."

Jordan smiled ruefully. "That he did."

"Bernie's missing out."

Jordan nodded. "I know. Today was the first time I'd seen her work. It's genius."

Heather didn't say anything for a long moment, just studied him closely before shaking her head. "Careful, brother, or you'll end up like Dad, a brood of half-bloods gathered under his wing."

"Just because you have a different mother doesn't mean that you're not my sister." He paused, made sure his words were calm when the anger in him was a real thing. His past—his *father's* past—did not define him any longer. "And I'm not Dad. When I'm with a woman, I'm only with that woman.

"I know." She patted his arm, eyes warming for a brief second before her normal devil-may-care, taking-asses-not-prisoners demeanor returned. Another shake of her head. "You knocked up Abigail Roberts. What a fucking idiot."

And with that sisterly idiom, she walked away.

Jordan listened to her pack up her stuff in her office, watched as she walked by. "I sent Rich and the others home," she tossed over her shoulder. "Lock up when you leave."

He nodded his thanks and sat down to wait.

SEVENTEEN

Abby

MY NECK ACHED, and there was a very persistent, very annoying buzz coming about six inches from my left ear.

I groaned and rolled over, wondering when my bed had gotten so uncomfortable.

Groping for the phone, said source of annoying, persistent buzzing, I blindly swiped my finger across the screen. "Hello?"

"Are you okay?" Seraphina's voice was concerned.

"Yeah, I'm fine," I said. "I was just tired so . . ." My words trailed off as my eyes adjusted to the dark room.

This could not be happening.

"I'm sorry!" Sera said. "It's just that I got home and saw your lights were off. I didn't realize you were sleeping. Go back to bed and call me later."

She hung up before I could say anything in reply.

Which was a good thing, because the fact that I'd fallen asleep after puking my guts out in the company conference room on my first day of work was a fact that was not going to be spoken about until I died.

I banged the back of my head against the floor then whimpered when the sore spot connected with the hard surface.

"This literally cannot be happening," I moaned, pushing to my feet. My shoes were lined up like a pair of perfect soldiers next to the trash can, both of which had been moved closer to the door.

I started for them and almost ate shit as a jacket I hadn't felt draped around me, slipped to my feet.

It was a man's jacket. Jordan's. I knew that because it smelled like him. Not like that terrible deodorant, but like Jordan the man. Slightly spicy and with a hint of salt. There was nothing sour about it when I brought it to my nose and sniffed.

And now I was randomly sniffing objects that belonged to my baby daddy.

Psycho, much?

I gathered up my notebook, cell, and pen, all of which were piled nicely by where I'd been laying.

I felt a wave of embarrassment flow through me. Not only because Jordan had seen me puke again, but also because everything my father said was proving to be true.

The weaker sex. Unable to hack it in a corporate world. Pathetic.

If he could only see me now, I thought sarcastically.

There was no way I still had a job after this.

Bending over, I grabbed Jordan's jacket and then walked to the door to snag my shoes.

I'd write my letter of resignation and email it to Heather.

I sighed. Not even one full day on the job before I'd screwed up. Classic.

Jacket draped over my arm, notebook, pen, cell, and shoes gathered in my hands, I struggled to open the door.

After a moment, it pushed inward a couple of inches.

My stomach dropped, all hope of slinking out unnoticed vanishing.

"Hey," Jordan said.

I hooked an elbow in the door and opened it all the way. "Hey." I couldn't even meet his eyes, I was so embarrassed.

I slipped out into the hall and hurried to my office, flicking on the light as I did so.

Quickly, I dropped my things onto my desk, shoved my feet into my shoes, and picked up my jacket. I was just thrusting my arms into it when I heard Jordan's voice.

"Are you okay?"

I dropped my head back. Why couldn't the man let me wallow in peace? I was beyond embarrassed. I wanted the floor to open up and swallow me whole. I wanted—

To be left alone.

Instead of saying any of those things, I forced a smile, finished buttoning my coat, and grabbed my purse. "I'm just peachy."

"Abby . . ."

So what if my throat felt tight? So what if my eyes burned? I was just fine, dammit.

I sniffed, closed my eyes hard, and lost the battle with tears.

They poured down my cheeks in hot tracks and I quickly turned around, not wanting Jordan to see. Everything else was awful enough. This was just that extra cherry on the sundae he didn't need to see.

Chin to my chest, my foot tapping on the floor in pretend irritation—because it was actually tapping in my-feet-really-fuck-ing-hurt-and-it's-still-not-as-painful-as-the-ache-in-my-heart—I said, "I'm totally fine. You just go ahead."

Okay, that sounded watery. But, hell if it was all I had in me.

"Dammit!"

I jumped, whirling around.

Jordan was five feet away from me, his hands at his sides and clenched into fists. "I want to hold you but I can't because I make you puke!"

I laughed.

Because of the absurdity of the situation. Because it was better than crying. Because I couldn't do anything else.

I laughed until my stomach hurt and I slid to the ground. I laughed until Jordan started laughing too. And finally, I laughed until he sank to the floor across from me, safe-smelling distance away.

"If you just changed deodorants—"

His smile took my breath away.

Suddenly, I couldn't look at him. My eyes drifted from the window to my desk, to my feet . . . back to Jordan.

"Hi," he said softly.

"H-hi." Oh, my God, I was such a dork. My voice was shaking and my fingers were trembling. I felt like we were on the precipice of something huge and I couldn't decide if it was good or bad.

"Can we maybe try to start over?"

My thumbnail had a chip in the red polish adorning it. Actually, my pinky did too. I needed to redo all of them. Maybe in blue? No. That wasn't really office-y. I could do silver sparkles. That would be pretty and just in time for Christmas. I—

"Abby?"

I straightened my shoulders, forced my gaze to his. "I'm not sure how to do this," I admitted. "We haven't exactly had the best start."

"I know," Jordan said, "and it's my fault."

"Not going to disagree with you there," I muttered.

He laughed but then went sober. "Can I tell you something? I think it might help make sense of everything. Not that it's an excuse, but just . . ."

I studied him as he trailed off. "Give some clarification?"

"Yeah."

"Okay."

"I—" He stopped. "It's just that—" A shake of his head. "Damn, this was easier in my mind."

My heart started beating faster. I wasn't sure if it was because he was uncomfortable or because what he was about to share was something big. I just knew that he looked nervous and I felt for him. "I know the feeling." He glanced up. "Of things making more sense in my mind than in real life."

He tilted his head to the side, eyes piercing as they locked on mine. "I don't know how I ever thought that you could be like them."

I picked at the hem of my skirt. "Like who?"

He grimaced. "Like the women I grew up with. No," he said when I frowned. "Like the girls my father slept with after my mother died."

"I'm sorry," I said. "I didn't realize you'd lost—"

"It was a long time ago and it's not important."

"Well, it's clearly important." I crossed my arms. "Otherwise you wouldn't have brought it up."

Jordan smiled again, this time not the take-my-breath-away version, but a sadder, smaller one. I didn't like it.

"You're right," he said. "It *is* important. My mom was the glue that held my family together."

"How many of you are there?"

"There were four of us. Now there are two."

My brows drew down. I knew Jordan's dad was still alive and Heather had called him brother. Maybe that was a nickname?

"I see you're mentally calculating," he said. "There were four of us before she died. My mom and dad, Zach—who was two years older—and me. After my mom . . ." His eyes dimmed, blue becoming icy cold with sadness. "Well, my dad's drug of choice to forget was women. It got worse when Zach died five years ago."

"How old were you when your mom . . . ?"

"Eleven." He rolled his eyes. "Zach was sixteen. Both of us

saw the never-ending parade of women—of *girls*, really, they were barely legal—coming through the house."

My stomach twisted itself in knots, my heart absolutely ached for the little boys who'd lost their mother and then, for all intents and purposes, their father as well.

"I'm so sorry."

Jordan shrugged. "It was what it was. I stopped blaming my father for it a long time ago. And I got some pretty cool half-siblings out of it."

"How many?"

"Six. Well, seven, including Heather." A pause. "You're doing that mental calculating thing again."

I froze. "What?"

"When you think really hard, these pull together." He scooted a little closer, near enough to reach up and brush the skin between my eyebrows before dropping his arm and sliding back. "Okay?"

I sighed, still able to feel the brush of his fingers on my forehead. The skin was warm, marked by his touch. "Yes," I said, breathless, and felt my cheeks heat.

"I like touching you."

I ignored that, wanting to lighten the mood instead. I liked it when *he* was on the spot, not when his focus was on me. "Lovely," I said, rolling my eyes. "Just thinking is going to give me wrinkles."

"I can smell the smoke," he said.

I snorted.

"Not to mention, it's cute. *You're* cute. Well, you're beyond beautiful, but then you make a joke about yourself or start talking about marketing and design and my breath catches. You're so much more than the outside."

That was the dream, right?

For someone to see me as more than just the sum of my parts.

For someone to see inside my heart and decide that I was worthy of being loved.

God, I was so fucked up.

Not a shocker, given my past. But instead of focusing on the uncomfortable feelings blooming inside my brain and body, I concentrated on Jordan.

Why was he doing this?

Did he really want to start over?

Realistically, I wasn't sure I could. I'd seen so many versions of Jordan at this point that I wasn't certain which was the real one. How could I reconcile the kind, thoughtful man in front of me with the jerk surrounded by suits in my apartment?

How could I trust that he wouldn't change right back?

"You're doing it again."

I reached up, felt my wrinkled brows, and relaxed my forehead. "I don't know if I can start over."

He grimaced. "I understand. I'll leave you alone."

But despite our words, neither of us moved.

I stayed still, watching him watch me and decided that while I couldn't be certain he wouldn't revert back to asshole Jordan 2.0, I was also quite certain that I was willing to take the chance.

"Heather doesn't look younger than you," I said, and it was a question even if it wasn't phrased as such.

"She isn't."

"Then—"

"She's six years older."

I frowned and felt it that time. Dammit, I *did* do that a lot.

"My father was with her mother before mine. We didn't find out about each other until her mother died when she was eighteen."

I whistled. "I bet that was dramatic."

Jordan's lips twitched. "Considering she crashed a dinner my father was throwing for his shareholders, yes. It was quite the moment. Though"—he shrugged—"she was the third half-sibling that I had found out about, so not much surprised me at that point."

"Still must have been hard."

"Everyone has their own challenges. My father's is, apparently, wrapping his tool."

"Gross," I said, laughing.

"Yeah, tell me about it. My father's youngest is four years old. The man is sixty." He shuddered.

"I bet he gets a lot of grandpa comments."

A smile. "Like you wouldn't believe. But I think it's well deserved. His last mistress—he doesn't even bother getting married anymore—was younger than me."

"Yikes."

"I know."

"Okay." He sighed and pushed to his feet. "Well, that's enough about me. It was a dick move to assume that you'd be like them. I've seen the custody, alimony, child support thing pan out a half dozen times now." He raised one palm. "Not an excuse. There was no excuse for my behavior. Just an explanation."

I nodded.

"I'll wait for you in the hall. Walk you to your car, if that's okay? I'd feel better knowing you were—"

"My parents are still married," I blurted.

He stopped, hands at his sides, and stared at me.

"I haven't seen my father since last Christmas." I swallowed. "As for my mother, I haven't seen her in fifteen years."

EIGHTEEN

Abby

I TOOK A DEEP BREATH. Aside from Bec and Seraphina, no one knew this part of the story.

Not my brother. Not my father. Neither of them could understand why my mother had run.

But I did. Intimately.

"You ready for the big guns?" I asked.

"Big guns?"

I swallowed, already feeling a little shaky at the prospect of admitting this. But Jordan had laid his past out for me. He deserved to know why I tended to keep people at a distance.

"You ready to hear why I'm so fucked up?" I asked. "Because it's a doozy."

"You don't have to—"

"I do," I said. "I tend to hide in my own world because of it, and if we're going to have a baby together, you need to understand why I sometimes engage the hard retreat." My lips trembled and I pressed them together tightly.

Jordan froze, face serious. He nodded tightly and sat down a couple of feet away from me, back against my desk.

I shifted so my shoulders were resting on the wall below the window.

"Okay?" he asked.

"What?"

"The smell." He pointed at his armpit.

The tension in my gut uncoiled slightly. "Don't worry, you're out of smell-shot."

He snorted. "I'm throwing away this deodorant as soon as I get home."

"That would be much appreciated," I said.

And then there was no avoiding it. I just had to say it. To get it out there.

"I was eleven when it happened." Jordan's eyes shot to mine, and I forced my lips into a rueful smile. "Eventful year for both of us, I guess, huh?"

My legs were flat on the ground, still in the heels.

Jordan rested his palm on my ankle, glancing down at me.

I nodded. He waited for me to find the words.

"I was really into gymnastics and I was really good. I'd just moved up a level and had a new coach. I was practicing my splits —it was the one thing he said I was behind on." I stared down at my hands. "And me being me, I just had to work on it until I had it. I—" My voice broke.

Jordan squeezed my ankle lightly and the touch brought me back to the present. Away from that night. Away from that room.

"The coach took me from the main floor to this room that was walled off from the rest of the gym. No parents went back there. Not that mine would have come anyway. They were too busy with their own lives. They didn't have time to waste on something as insignificant as their daughter's gymnastics class."

"Abby."

I was shaking, but made my eyes meet his.

"You don't have to do this."

I nodded. "I do. I haven't—I should have done something. I found out about five years ago that he'd gone to prison for molesting girls. But the dates were ten years after he'd done it to me." A tear streaked down my cheek. "He touched little girls for ten years because I didn't do anything. Because I believed when my mother told me it was my fault. Because I was too ashamed."

"It's not your fault."

"I should have told someone else. I should have pursued it."

"You were eleven."

My head dropped to the wall. "I know."

"Did he hurt you?" Jordan's words were soft, but there was a deadly edge.

"No. Well, not physically. He had me get into the splits and I remember him kneeling behind me, resting his hands on my shoulders—the coaches did that sometimes, put a little pressure on you to help the stretch—but then he took it further. He slid his hands up and down my arms, down my chest. I hardly had boobs at that point, but I remember him probing, rubbing at what little I had there." My voice cracked. "I remember freezing. I remember feeling that it was wrong. But most of all I remember feeling ashamed."

I carefully met Jordan's gaze, wondering if I'd find the same expression of disgust I'd seen on my mother's face.

There was nothing there. He was staring forward, unseeing, and not one emotion was discernable in his expression. Not anger or revulsion. Not pity or fury.

Just nothing.

Then he blinked and saw me looking. "What did you do?"

"I told my mother. She said I was making the whole thing up." I clenched my fingers together. "I found out later that she was sleeping with him."

Jordan's chest rose and fell in a long, slow breath.

"She never did anything. In fact, she forbade me from telling anyone. Said I was a slut who'd asked for it." I swallowed. "I know better now, but it took me a long time to confide in anyone."

"What'd your father do when he found out?"

"He doesn't know," I said. "You, Bec, and Seraphina are the only ones who— It's stupid, but every time I tried, I just pictured my mother's face. The disgust. I couldn't disappoint him that way." I laughed, bitter. "No, I found plenty of other ways to make him unhappy with me."

"That can't be true."

"It's true. But that's a story for another day. I switched studios and ended up quitting gymnastics altogether when he came into the new gym one day as a guest coach. I panicked, lied to my father about losing interest, and shoved the events deep, deep down." I sniffed. "If only they'd stayed there."

"Pain has a way of resurfacing."

I nodded. "That it does."

We were silent for a long moment before Jordan spoke again. "I'm admitting defeat on the whole starting over thing."

I laughed. "I didn't realize you were still stuck on that."

"Like a dog on a bone." He squeezed my ankle again. "How about instead of starting over, we move forward?"

"Throw out that deodorant, and we've got a deal."

JORDAN WAS quiet as he walked me to my car. The air was cold and our breath blew white clouds as we crossed the parking lot.

I would have been just fine on my own getting to my car, but honestly, I was glad he was there. It was dark and I felt raw on the inside after sharing so much.

Given the tentative way he held himself, I suspected he felt the same way.

"Thanks," I murmured when we got to my car. I pulled the handle and the car unlocked with a beep.

"No problem. So . . ."

"Give me your phone," I said, reaching into my purse and snagging mine. "I'll get your number and text you with the information about my next appointment with Dr. Stephens."

It was a peace offering. And perhaps a way to move forward like he'd suggested.

Jordan rocked back on his heels. "See, here's the thing—"

I flushed, shook my head, shoving my cell back into my purse. "Oh. It's okay. You don't have to go. I just thought—"

"I don't have a cell phone," he said. "I threw mine away after I sold the company."

"You *threw* away your phone?"

"Not you too," he said, rolling his eyes. "Everyone is so glued to those damn things these days—and believe me, I used to be one of those people—but when I sold the company, I promised myself that I would take a break from all that. That I'd look up from my screen every once in awhile."

"I get that," I said. "But what about an emergency or if you really need to get a hold of someone?"

He smirked. "Don't know if you know this, but nearly everyone on the planet has a cell phone."

I laughed. "Okay, so you can't give me your number. How are we going to communicate to do this *moving forward* thing?"

"Landlines?"

"I haven't had a landline in years."

"Reasonable point," he said. "Email?"

"Which you could access better from a phone," I teased.

He leaned against my car, close enough to make my stomach flutter, but far enough to not trigger my bloodhound of a nose. "What's with the phone obsession?"

"Cell phones are great," I said, espousing on the merits of phones rather than investigating the underlying attraction that never seemed to go away when Jordan was near. "They play movies and hold thousands of books. You can text. And maybe even call someone on it."

He laughed. "All of that is true. So tell me," he asked, "what's your favorite book?"

"Which is like the world's hardest question!" I said, turning to match him, my shoulder resting against the driver's side window. "But if I had to pick one"—I reached into my purse and pulled out a worn paperback—"it would have to be *Pride and Prejudice.*"

"What do you like about it?"

I ignored the fact that we were having this conversation in the parking lot. That both of us should get into our cars and go home. I focused on nothing aside from the fact that he seemed genuinely interested in my answer.

"I guess I love that deep down Darcy and Elizabeth are perfect for each other, no matter that their circumstances and personalities attempt to keep them apart."

"Hmm."

"Now you sound like Heather."

He laughed. "Can't have that." His fingers laced with mine. "So tell me, how is it that you can't find your keys, but you can find your phone and book in that black hole of yours on the first try."

"Priorities, I suppose."

His thumb brushed against my palm. "I wish I could kiss you right now."

My heart leapt. Did I want him to? Did I dare risk pursuing something with him? Our situation was already complicated enough with the baby and now work. Not to mention the fact that our fathers hated one another. "O-oh. I—"

"I'm not going to because"—his lips twitched—"Satan's deodorant, and I don't want to get puked on again."

"That was *not* my fault."

He brought our laced hands up, pressed a kiss to the back of my hand. "I'm not saying it is. In fact, I think if we're going with pop culture references, wouldn't all of this be my fault?"

"Yes," I grumbled. "It *is* your fault. Well yours, and also the manufacturer of my IUD since they promised baby-free sex and then didn't deliver."

A gust of cold air blew around my legs, up my skirt. I shivered.

"I should let you go," he said. "You're cold."

"Yeah," I said.

But I didn't want to go. I wanted to stay. I wanted to talk to Jordan all night.

"See you Monday?" he asked.

I nodded then winced. "Though I should probably turn in my resignation. With our relationship and your sister working here, not to mention the puking and the whole falling-asleep-in-the-conference-room thing, I didn't exactly make a good impression on my first day." I wrapped my coat a little tighter around myself. "That's not even considering the interaction with Diego."

His face went thunderous. "What happened with Diego?" Then he waved a hand. "Never mind. I'll find out from Stan." He squeezed my hand. "Who, by the way, can arrange an escort to your car if you're ever here late and I'm not and you're uncomfortable. Not that you would be uncomfortable working here, or want me to walk you to your car regularly. Or, well, that you couldn't take care of yourself. I just meant if—"

"Jordan." He stopped talking. "I understand." A beat. "Thank you."

"And Heather already told me she wouldn't accept your resignation."

"What?"

He nodded, pushed up to standing. "So there's that. You're working here and that's final."

I gave him the look. "Are you pushing it? Or just trying to be funny?"

"Maybe both?"

I huffed good-naturedly. "Men."

"We're exasperating, I know." He released my hand and I ignored the fact that I missed the warmth of his touch. "So Monday?"

A nod. "Monday."

He opened my door. "Good night, beautiful."

He waited until I was buckled in with the engine started before he closed the door then turned and walked back into the building.

I couldn't help but feel as though a piece of my heart went with him.

NINETEEN

Jordan

JORDAN STRODE BACK into the office and used his badge to enter the security office. Walls of television screens showed cameras from all angles. Every elevator. Every hallway. Every entrance and exit.

Stan glanced up from his desk, unsurprised since he'd been able to watch Jordan's approach the entire way. The light from the computer monitor made RoboTech's security chief's skin appear pale and ghostly. "Hey, boss. What's up?"

"Don't let Heather hear you say that," Jordan said with a smirk. He skipped the pleasantries. "What happened with Diego?"

Stan sat back in his chair. "He took the bait."

"Damn. I liked that kid." Jordan sighed and leaned against Stan's desk. "Any word on where he's trying to share it?"

Stan shot him a look. "Shouldn't I be discussing this with Heather?"

"Probably." He crossed his arms. "But discuss it with me too."

"Same buyer as three months ago. Wants specifications for the drone."

"And did Diego get them?"

"The ones we planted?" Jordan nodded. "Yup. I've got my guys trying to track the buyer. They're slippery as always, but the transaction has got to be clumsy if the hormone-riddled moron was using it as fodder for picking up girls."

"Girls?"

Stan shook his head. "Girl. Not plural. Abigail Roberts."

"He hit on Abigail?" Jordan's voice was a growl. Pathetic, but there it was.

"Who wouldn't?" Stan asked. "Not only is she gorgeous but that body—"

"Shut the fuck up."

Stan froze, eyes narrowed as he studied Jordan. "Something we need to discuss?"

"Nope."

"Abigail is a nice girl," Stan said.

"And how would you know?" Jordan said. So what if it sounded like an accusation? Who the hell was Stan to say such a thing?

A flash of humor crossed the other man's face before it went blank. "I worked security for her father about five years ago. Doubt she remembers me since she wasn't around much. But it's kind of hard to forget her . . ."

"I'd be careful with your next words."

"You've got a big ego, O'Keith, if you think you could take me," Stan said, amused. "But that's not what I mean. There's something vulnerable about her. I didn't like seeing the hurt in her eyes."

Neither did Jordan. Especially when he was the cause of it. "Yeah."

"Her dad is kind of a dick."

Jordan snorted. "I know the feeling."

"That you do." A pause. "So the specs?"

He released a frustrated breath. This whole thing was a fucking mess.

"They won't do the buyer any good. They're flawed and incomplete."

"You know that," Stan said. "*I* know that. But the rest of the staff doesn't. And they're getting pretty ballsy if they're entering Heather's office to steal information."

Jordan rose to his feet and thrust a hand through his hair. "Keep the last two around for a bit, see if they get pinged and are stupid. It might give us the information we need."

"Might not," Stan countered. "It's a risk."

"We've got to plug the leak."

"Thought you were supposed to be on a beach right now. That this all was Heather's problem."

"Things change."

One brow went up. "Not *that* much."

"It's complicated."

A smirk. "It's a girl."

"Abby is not a girl—" Jordan grimaced at the admission.

"So, Abby, is it?" Stan's smirk grew into a grin. "You know what your father would say about that."

"Something disgusting, no doubt." He sighed. "I knew the interest from the Army was a bad thing."

"It's a profitable thing, from what I understand."

"But at what cost?" He shook Stan's hand, headed for the door. "They never bring anything except frustration and heartbreak."

"How's Hunter?" Stan asked just as Jordan reached the threshold.

"How do you think?"

The last thing Jordan saw before heading up to his office was Stan's face creased with sadness.

He knew his own face was a mirror image.

"Done," Jordan announced, pushing into Heather's office. He was bleary-eyed, hadn't left his desk except to grab food and pee since Friday evening.

He hadn't had a weekend like that in a long time, and though he was exhausted, it came with exhilaration. He'd figured out the issue with the code, and he'd finally finished the program. It was running flawlessly.

His previous position as CEO hadn't allowed him the joy of finding a problem and then a solution and following both to their fruition in a long, long time.

And the action brought with it a sense of completion he hadn't realized he'd been missing.

Okay, that wasn't quite right.

He knew he'd missed the grunt work. He knew he'd wanted to get back into the ranks.

He just expected to want that after a nice long break.

A few months ago, he'd been near burnout. No creative juices flowing, no new ideas. He'd been ready to throw the whole company into the fucking ocean.

Then Hunter.

Then Abigail.

Then Heather offering to buy into the company and taking over the business side.

Meetings and schmoozing and finding investors had been the worst part of his job, but he'd always figured he was good at it. The buyout offer falling through the night he'd been with Abby had proven otherwise.

The investor he'd planned to sell to had managed to turn key members of his staff against him, and they were stealing projects that were RoboTech's—then InDTech's—bread and butter.

They'd successfully taken a piece of programming that had been the company's future.

Not that he could prove it.

But Stan would, Jordan had no doubt of that.

In the meantime, Heather had bought him out. She'd taken over the company, renamed it, and cleaned house. All typical behavior of a buyout, except she'd kept those loyal to them and weeded out the rest.

Or so they'd thought.

Now three months down the line, Jordan wondered how many snakes in the grass were still out there.

"Done with what?" Heather squinted up from her computer screen and blinked. "Holy shit, you look terrible. What'd you do? Not sleep for the last forty-eight hours?"

"Yup," he said, his voice almost giddy from lack of sleep. "I'm done with the program."

Her jaw dropped open. "You're done? That's it? Two days when the rest of the crew has been working for weeks to figure out the glitch?"

He sank into a chair and propped his feet on her desk. "Yup. That's because I'm the best."

She shoved his feet off. "You're also delusional from lack of sleep."

"Maybe. But the program is airtight." He stood. "Have the crew test what's on the secure server."

Heather took his meaning right away. The program was there, or part of it, but the key was in his possession and his alone.

"Will do."

"You good with that?" he asked.

She gave him a look. "I trust you, Jordan."

The words made his heart give a little squeeze. "Yeah?"

"Plus"—her smile was evil—"I know *you* know that I'll cut you in your sleep if you screw the company over."

"So violent."

"You know it." Heather stood, kissed his cheek. "Get some sleep." Her nose wrinkled. "And take a shower. You smell."

"Noted. See you tomorrow."

She said goodbye and turned her focus back to her computer, dismissing him before he was even out of the room.

Jordan didn't mind. In fact, he respected the fact that his sister was such a good CEO. It reminded him that not all women were like those his father managed to get tangled up with.

He closed the door behind him and strode out into the hallway. It was early still, the workplace just waking up as staff trickled in. This had always been one of his favorite times of the day. The hum of a few computers, the quiet of only a couple of voices. Later the space would be awash with activity, punctuated with laughter and ringing phones, but this was the time that reminded him of the early days. Of scraping by, refusing to use his father's money to start the business, hoping on a dream that he'd make enough to pay the rent, let alone make millions of dollars.

Back then he'd slept in the office, kept his clothes in the one and only closet, bathed in the sink, hauled his laundry down the street to a Laundromat.

That had been before he'd owned an entire building, before he'd employed hundreds of people.

Before he'd flamed out.

Jordan shook his head and walked toward the elevator. The lights were off in Abby's office, but he tried to convince himself that he wasn't disappointed at not seeing her.

It was probably better anyway. He hadn't been home to shower and smelled horrible. God knew what that would do to Abby's stomach.

He pressed the elevator button, head shooting up when it dinged straight away.

The doors open and Abigail started to walk off, only to stop and stare at him. "Jordan? Are you okay? You look terrible—"

"I'm fine. Just worked all weekend." He smiled and took a step back, aware of his smell all over again. There was no way he was making Abby puke again.

She came closer and frowned. "You're wearing the same clothes. No, is your shirt is different? But your pants—you haven't gone home?"

"Got caught up with a project." She reached for him and he put his hands up to shield her. "Stay back. I haven't showered in two days either. I keep a spare shirt in my office, but that's it. I smell and don't want to make you—"

Her head tilted to the side, glancing down his body and back up. The slow perusal set his blood on fire and he suddenly wasn't tired any longer.

"You"—she sniffed—"smell *incredible*."

"What?"

Abby came close, her nose brushing against his throat as she inhaled. "Mmm," she moaned. "If you smelled like this all the time I'd rub myself—"

Jordan coughed, put his hands on her arms, and gently set her away from him. He was rock hard and aching. "I—uh. As much as I like it when you do that, this probably isn't the place."

She put a hand to her forehead. "I'm sorry. Whew. Is it hot in here?"

"No," he said, concerned now. "Are you okay?"

Her hand dropped. "Besides feeling like an alien took over my body? Hot. Cold. Aroused. Puking. This ride isn't for the faint of heart, let me tell you." She gave an awkward laugh and turned for her office.

He snagged her hand, slipping the briefcase she carried free of her fingers and taking her purse from her shoulder. "I'll walk you."

"Don't get too close," she said. "You might regret it."

"That, I doubt."

They strode in silence down the hall to her office. She opened the door and flicked on the lights. "Thank you."

"You're welcome." He handed over her bags, hesitated when she turned her back on him and went to the window.

"I used to play out there, you know?"

He frowned, crossing the room to look out the window. Busy streets bookmarked by multistory buildings for as far as the eye could see. "Were your parents insane?"

She smiled. "Sorry, no. I meant there." She pointed way out in the distance, to the vineyard-covered hills. "My father has an estate there."

"Mine too," he said. "Did you play in the vineyard?"

"All the time. And the rose gardens." Her face turned toward him. "Hide and seek was the best. Though"—her expression dimmed slightly—"now that I think about it, no one ever found me. I always thought it was because I was the best hider, now I'm thinking that they probably didn't want me underfoot."

"Abby—"

"No," she said, "it's okay. I'm not going to get all maudlin about it. I'm well aware that my childhood was firmly in the realm of fucked up. But damn, how much of a dick move is it to send your daughter out for a game and then not follow her?"

"A big one." He paused. "But, I have to admit, I'm guilty of sending my siblings off to play a game without intending to join in."

"I think *siblings* is the keyword here." She grinned. "How many of them lived at home?"

"All six of them still do. It was quite a rude awakening to come home from college and be assaulted by a gaggle of three to five-year-olds." He grimaced, thinking of those brutally early mornings and being barely twenty-one. Going out, drinking too much, hungover, and. So. Much. Screeching.

"Does your dad share custody?"

"This probably isn't the best conversation for us to be

having"—he gestured to her stomach—"in our current situation."

"No," she said. "But I want to know anyway."

"Of course you do." He sighed. "Get ready for *The Jerry Springer Show* but in real life."

She straightened her shoulders, turned fully to face him. "Okay, I'm ready."

"I'm not sure if I am," he muttered. "But here goes. Six baby mamas, six kids. Of those, two became wives, then ex-wives. Those two still live at the house, albeit in separate wings." He rolled his eyes. "According to my father, they've bonded over what a jerk he is."

Abby snorted.

"I interpret that snort as agreement." Her lips curved into a full-blown smile and, *damn*. When she smiled at him like that, it took his breath away. "God, you're beautiful," he said.

Another snort. "No distractions, mister. You've started the family drama, you can't stop in the middle of the story."

"I could talk all day about family drama, just so you know."

"Oh, *I know*," she said. "Believe me. I know. What's with rich people and so many skeletons in their closets anyway?"

"Too much money, not enough common sense?"

She laughed. "I think it comes along with the trust funds." Her face went serious and she gripped his arm. "Promise me we won't screw up our baby. Promise me that we'll raise a well-adjusted, normal kid."

"God, I hope so."

He couldn't help himself, not with her so close. Not with roses swirling through the air and images through his exhausted mind.

Abby's stomach swollen with his baby. Abby holding a little girl with brown curls and hazel eyes. Abby in his bed. Abby smiling up at him like she was doing now. But she was in a wedding dress. She was *his*.

Jordan was spinning out of control. It was too much, these

feelings that were developing. He should be running the other direction.

But he found he couldn't.

And when Abby's tongue slipped out, wetting her bottom lip, he couldn't resist.

He *had* to lower his head.

That first touch of his mouth to hers was explosive. Desire flamed low in his gut, his mind demanded that he move quickly, that he strip her clothes off and kiss every inch of her. He wanted to set her on the edge of her desk and lick her until she came. He wanted his fingers, his *cock* inside. He wanted—

She whimpered and all of that heat tempered.

Because he also wanted to love and stroke. To trail his fingers across her belly, to press his mouth to the place their child grew. He wanted to cup her breasts, kiss her throat and the spot behind her ear he'd discovered that first night.

He wanted to make her come so many times that she was limp and satiated and their first horrible evening together was forgotten.

Horrible for her, that was.

His orgasm had been life-changing.

Hers had come from batteries.

She deserved more.

He gentled the kiss, soft brushes of his tongue, gentle nibbles of his lips. He teased and coaxed until she was soft and limp, resting against his chest.

And when he pulled back and she looked up at him, those hazel eyes warm, he felt a piece of his heart go off into the abyss.

This was a woman a man fell in love with.

Her lids slid closed, her arms slipped around his waist, and she inhaled deeply.

It was the perfect moment . . . until she stiffened and stepped back, hand coming up to cover her nose.

"Satan's deodorant," they said at the same time, and smiled.

Hers was rueful. "I'll just sit over here," she said, and plunked down in her office chair, rolling it a few feet away.

"I should let you get settled."

"Nope."

His gaze flicked to hers, took in her amused expression. "What?"

"Don't think you're getting off the hook that easy, mister. I need the rest of the baby mama drama if I'm going to have a hope of focusing for the rest of the day."

He laughed. "You're ridiculous."

"Nope," she said again. "I just love *Real Housewives* and this is definitely on par with that. So the two ex-wives live at the house?"

Jordan shook his head but acquiesced. "Plus, one ex-mistress. Along with Parker, Steven, Mitch, Gabrielle, Victoria, Theo, and Hunter—my nephew."

"I didn't realize Heather had any kids."

"Hunter isn't Heather's. He's Zach's. Or was Zach's." Jordan forced his voice to stay neutral. It had been years. He should be used to it. "My brother was killed in Afghanistan five years ago."

Abby winced and stood up, crossing to him. She took his hand. "Oh Jordan, I'm so sorry. I didn't realize that he'd . . ."

She trailed off and Jordan squeezed her fingers. "It was a tough time for all of us. We didn't find out about Hunter until a year ago."

"How old is he?"

"Seven and a half."

"Damn." She sighed. "I'm sorry. That seems so inadequate but . . ."

He squeezed her fingers. "Thank you."

"What branch of the service was Zach in?"

Jordan stared out the window. "He wasn't. Zach was a contractor with the Army. My father sent him over to keep an eye on their company's prospects."

Her inhale was rapid and pained. "Oh, Jordan."

"I know."

"So the argument with Heather about the contract—"

He rubbed his free hand on the back of his head. "I shouldn't have gotten into that with you and Rich in the room. It wasn't—"

She hugged him. Tight. For a long time.

Long enough for the strain in his shoulders to relax minutely, for his arms to come around hers. Long enough for the ice around his heart to begin to melt, for the dark, heavy hurt about his brother to recede slightly.

"I'm breathing through my mouth, I'll have you know," she said, startling him into a laugh. "I promise I won't puke on you again."

"I think I deserved it," he said.

"Oh, I *know* you did. But a girl's got to have some pride, you know?" She loosened her grip slightly and leaned back. "Thank you," she said, softly. "For sharing that with me."

He brushed a strand of hair off her face. "I hope you're adding that to my positive points column," he joked.

"You've been adding to that for a little while now."

"I really should let you get to work."

"One more thing." Abby bit her lip. "Never mind. I've already been way too nosy."

"What is it?"

Her cheeks flushed, she opened her mouth, closed it. "I was wondering about the other kids' moms, is all. Wanted to complete my real-life reality show binge."

"The other three weren't interested in being parents. They took a payoff and signed over all parental rights." He smoothed his thumb over the streak of red on her cheek. "But that wasn't the question you wanted to ask and we both know it."

"I—"

He cupped her jaw. "It's okay, sweetheart. If we're going to make a go of this, then we need to be open."

"That's just it," she said and dropped her arms, stepping back from his hold. "I don't even know what *this*"—she pointed between the two of them—"is. Are we dating? Are we trying to get along for the baby's sake? Are we nothing more than strangers who got to know each other a little by pure accident?"

"We're more than strangers," he said, "and you know it."

Her chin dipped forward. "I'm not really sure what I know anymore. A week ago, I hated your guts. Today I want—"

She broke off, shook her head.

"Abby." He waited until she looked at him. "Today you want what?" Another shake of her head, but he moved close, refused to let her avoid answering the question. "What do you want, sweetheart?"

"Dammit." She blew out a breath. "I want you. *Okay?* And not just your body—which I want to lick like a freaking Popsicle —but the rest of you. Or the part that I've gotten to know over the last couple of days. The sweet and thoughtful man who carried my briefcase into my office without asking and shared his past with me even though it was painful." Her breath came in rapid exhales. "I want the man who kisses me like I'm precious and who looks at me like he wants to tear my clothes from my body. And"—her shoulders slumped—"I find that I can't even dislike the man who was a jerk in my apartment. Not when I understand the context."

She fell silent as he was struggling to digest all that she'd said.

"You like my body?" he asked.

"That?" she nearly shrieked. "I admit all of that, and you're focused on that fact that I love your abs?"

He nodded, a smile tugging at his lips.

"You're unbelievable." She turned away, grumbling, "You don't even know how to use your hammer—"

He growled and pulled her close. "I know how to use it. I just need a chance to prove it."

"Been there, done that." She crossed her arms with difficulty since he'd snaked his hand around her waist and was holding her against his chest. "If I puke on you, it's your fault," she warned.

"Noted." He brushed his mouth against hers. "Abby?" Her stare met his. "I feel all of that too. And more. I want you. I picture you in my bed, in my shower, in my kitchen. I want you against the wall and spread out on your desk. But I also want the woman inside." He touched a finger to the spot above her left breast. "The one who I'm still getting to know. The one who has a huge heart. The one whose eyes get sad when she thinks about her past and the one who isn't afraid to sass me."

"I—"

He touched a finger to her lips. "Let me finish?"

She nodded.

"I like you so much that it's scary and I know that the stakes are high because of the baby, but I want to spend time with you. I want to know what irritates you, what makes you smile. I want you to show me the books that have made you cry, and I want to pummel every ex-boyfriend you've ever had." He held her gaze. "I want that coach to burn in hell, and I want to see you cradling our baby. It's crazy. I know it's too soon, but I can't stop myself from wanting to take the chance."

Jordan dropped his finger.

"I can't—"

His heart sank.

He should have known. These types of feelings didn't exist in real life. Not in *his* life.

"—stay away from you."

Her words hit his gut with the force of a blow.

"What?"

"Can we try?" She lifted a shoulder, her face earnest, her eyes laced with fear. "I think we owe it to ourselves to at least try?"

"Yes." He hugged her tight. "We need to at least try."

TWENTY

Abby

JORDAN PAUSED as he headed to the door of my office. "What question did you really want to ask me earlier?"

My heart was both raw and hopeful, and though I knew it was probably a nosy question, I asked it anyway. "Where is Hunter's mom?"

His blue eyes frosted over. "Left. Couldn't handle it."

"Handle what?"

"Hunter is sick."

My hand came up to my throat. "How sick?"

Jordan shook his head and I knew. *I knew.*

"I'm sorry."

I dropped my gaze to my hands. Such inadequate words. So useless. So *stupid*. Why had I pushed?

"Abby?" I glanced up.

"Thank you for caring."

I nodded. "Go get some rest."

He started to leave, paused again. "Dinner later?"

"I don't know what time I'll get off," I said, feeling behind already. I'd come in an hour early and that time was now gone.

Not that I'd take any of it back, I just knew that this project was important to Jordan and didn't want to screw it up.

"Email me when you're done."

"And you'll, what, be waiting around for my message?" I rolled my eyes and sank down into my office chair, rolling it with my feet close enough to my desk to reach my keyboard.

"Something like that," he said with a smirk.

I sighed. "You know there are advantages to having a cell phone."

He crossed his arms, leaned against the doorframe. "Name one."

"Sexting."

His jaw dropped open before he turned to leave.

"Where are you going?" I called.

"To get a new phone," he called back.

Laughing, I shook my head and got to work.

I SHUT down my computer and stretched my arms behind my head.

"All right?" Rich asked, knocking on the doorframe.

"I'm great," I told him honestly. "I'm loving this job."

"Two days in and you've still got the rose-colored glasses on?"

I laughed. "So far, so good."

"You out of here?"

I nodded.

"Cool. Me too. I'll walk you to your car, if you don't mind. I wanted to pick your brain about the placement of the new logo on the website."

"Sure," I said. "I noticed the parking lot was pretty dark on Friday."

He nodded. "I just approved a work order for new lights. They're due to start the end of the week. In the meantime, have someone walk with you."

I slipped my feet into my flats and picked up my purse and briefcase. "Is there a reason that everyone keeps mentioning that?"

"We had a few robberies around the time of the buyout. I think that's why Heather brought in the new security." He lifted a shoulder. "I haven't heard of any issues lately, but I don't think it hurts to be cautious."

"Of course." I flicked off my light, smiling. "And thank you."

He smiled back. "It benefits me, you know. I get a little more time with that graphic design genius brain of yours."

I scoffed. "I'm far from a genius."

"How about a natural? If you won't give me genius, then at least give me that."

"You're a charmer, aren't you?"

He grinned. "Twenty years ago and minus one wife. Yes. Nowadays, I stick to honest."

My cheeks felt hot, but I ignored them . . . along with the compliment. We walked down the hall, and Rich pressed the button to call the elevator. While we waited, I asked, "Doesn't this building have any stairs? I feel like I'm always waiting for these metal death boxes."

He snorted but nodded to a door I hadn't noticed before. It was tucked into the corner near the bank of elevators. "Right there. But this old man has bad knees, five flights and I wouldn't be walking for the rest of the week."

"Oh no," I said. "What happened?"

"Football. And too much of it."

The doors dinged open and we got on. "I hear that can be a brutal sport."

"It sure can," he said, then grimaced. "Without risking monopolizing your after-work hours, can I get your opinion on the logo placement?"

I pictured the mock-up of the website the junior designers had emailed just before the end of the day. There was a lot of good in it: fun colors, clear tabs and font, but the logo wasn't right.

"I don't think it's the placement so much as the proportions. It's too big."

Rich pulled out his phone, accessed the link, and held it up so I could see the screen. "Damn, if you're not right."

"Words a woman lives to hear."

"Don't I know it?" We shared an amused gaze as he put his phone away.

"So tell me about this wife of yours."

"Well, she . . ."

I listened as we rode down, laughing at Rich's description of his wife and kids and their latest vacation, then at the misadventures of a new puppy at home that the three kids "just had to have."

"So then the dog took off through the house, one stiletto in his mouth, a pair of my daughter's underwear around his neck, just as she and her new boyfriend walked through the front door."

We were both chuckling as we walked off the elevator and into the lobby.

"Oh." Rich paused then patted my arm. "I don't think my escort services are needed. See you tomorrow." He turned for the exit.

I hardly saw him go.

Because my eyes were on Jordan.

Whose smile took my breath away. I found that I couldn't make my feet move, not toward him, not away. I just stood still and waited for him to approach, my heart thudding. *Thump-thump. Thump-thump.*

"Hi," I whispered when he was close.

"Hi." He put out his arms as though to hug me. "No deodorant. I promise."

I laughed, the spell that had surrounded me shattering. "Thank God for that."

"I got something for you," he said, taking my briefcase and my purse, slinging the former over his shoulder and holding the latter in his fist. I marveled again at how he made it seem so small.

Then again, what was the saying? Large hands, large . . . hammer?

I huffed out a laugh and Jordan gaze skimmed over me.

"You'll have to share what's so funny with me later," he said.

"Not happening." I grinned when he frowned. "What are you doing here? I thought you were waiting for my email."

"With bated breath." He tangled my fingers with his. "Don't you want to know what I got you?"

"Sure. But I like surprises too."

"Noted." He released my hand and reached into his pocket.

What he pulled out made me laugh.

"Isn't that more for you than me?" I asked of the shiny new cell phone.

"It is if you hold up your end of the sexting bargain."

My cheeks went red-hot. "Now wait a minute. I never said —" I broke off when I caught his mischievous expression and smacked his chest. "You're terrible."

"You like it," he teased and held the door for me as we left the lobby.

"Nope." But I did. I liked this version of Jordan a whole lot.

I could only hope he stuck around for a long, long time.

Or maybe even indefinitely.

TWENTY-ONE

Abby

"THIS ISN'T EXACTLY what I had in mind," I said an hour later.

Jordan had conned not only my cell number but my new address out of me before we'd left the parking lot.

"You said you were craving Chinese."

"That's not what I'm taking issue with," I said, pulling takeout containers from the brown bag Jordan had brought in.

"Then what is it?" he asked before starting to go through the cupboards. "Plates?" he asked.

"They're not unpacked yet," I admitted. "I couldn't lift the box. I've been using paper ones."

"Hmm." He pulled out his phone and pressed a button. "Hey, it's me. Yeah, yeah. Can you arrange the movers to come out and unpack the boxes Abigail has left?" He glanced up at me, brows raised. "What time?"

"I'm fine," I said, plunking my hands on my hips. "I'll get to it—"

"Why should you have to?"

"Because I—"

He turned his back on me, probably because he knew his next statement would piss me off. "Six tomorrow night. She'll tell them where she wants everything. They do all the heavy lifting." A pause. "Good."

Jordan tucked his phone away in his pocket and gave me a look that should have belonged to a little boy. It was guilty, full to the brim with remorse. The only thing missing was a toe making a hole as it dug into the ground.

I sighed, all the annoyance I'd felt in the previous moment slipping away. "You're lucky you're cute, you know that?"

His expression turned obstinate. "Well you shouldn't have to—"

"I'm perfectly capable—"

"I didn't say you weren't. But, sweetheart, I have the money and you're carrying our baby." He took a step closer. "Now can't you let me just take care of you? Just a little bit?"

Taking care of me was fine. It was the becoming used to it—relying on it—that I was afraid of.

But I'd decided to try this thing with Jordan and that meant pushing old fears away.

Even when it really, really scared me to do so.

I forced a smile. "You can." A pause. "Just a little bit."

He studied my expression, and I had the feeling that he understood exactly how much that acquiescence had cost me.

"Thank you." A brush of his lips against mine. "So tell me, where are the paper plates?"

"Second cupboard on the left. Forks are in the drawer next to the dishwasher."

He followed my directions and pulled out the plates and silverware, bringing both to the kitchen island, where I'd set up shop and was plucking fried wontons from a container I'd already opened.

"Oh, my God," I moaned. "This is the best thing I've ever had in my mouth."

"Setting yourself up there," he said.

"I'm surprised you resisted the innuendo," I teased.

"Me too."

I broke out into giggles, filling my plate with fried rice, chow mein, sweet and sour pork, and lots of wontons. "I almost commented on their salty deliciousness."

He smirked. "Now I wouldn't have been able to resist that one."

"Me neither."

We both laughed and sat down at the barstools, eating our fill.

"Dare I ask what you were taking issue with earlier?" Jordan ate a mouthful of rice. "Or should I let that sleeping dog lie?"

"You're brave," I said, having almost completely forgotten about the bags that were cluttering my counters. "But I'm fed now. I was protesting the fact that my kitchen looks like a drug store exploded inside of it."

"I need deodorant."

"Yes." I popped a wanton in my mouth. "That's a certainty."

"Smartass." He dropped his hand on my thigh.

"You know it."

A squeeze. "I do. But I'd like to not smell like a caveman while still being able to interact closely with you."

"You want me not to puke every time you're nearby."

"Well, yes, there's that."

"So"—I waved a hand at the bags littering my beautiful white marble—"drug store explosion?"

"No. Sniff test."

I groaned, dropping my forehead to the cold stone, before sitting up and glaring at him. "We should have conducted the *sniff test* before I had a full stomach."

Jordan set his fork down next to his plate and wiped his

mouth with a napkin. I didn't have any of those unpacked either and figured it must have come alongside the food. "Damn. You're right. Sniff test will have to wait till tomorrow."

"Well, it'll have to at least wait until later," I told him. "Don't ruin Chinese food for me, okay?"

"I'll do my best."

"That's all I ask." I sat back in my barstool and patted my belly. "How did we eat so much food? I swear, I always have left-overs when I order in."

Jordan lifted one leg, placing it between both of mine. The action made my breath hitch and desire sweep through me, so much and so rapidly that I nearly missed the horrible joke that went along with the action. "Hollow leg."

"Oh my God," I said when I could speak without sounding like a breathless buffoon. "The dad jokes start already."

He huffed. "It wasn't *that* bad."

"Oh, but it was." I started giggling and Jordan joined in, his rumbling laughter making the leg between mine vibrate.

Now wasn't *that* nice?

"So no sniff test for the present," he said once I'd managed to pull myself together. "What should we do to pass the time?"

He waggled his brows mockingly, but the heat in his eyes belied the joking exterior. Jordan wanted me and I knew it.

"I've got a few ideas," I said, sliding from the stool then taking his hand in mine.

"This isn't what I had in mind," Jordan grumbled, sitting cross-legged next to me at my coffee table.

The coffee table.

Which looked ridiculously tiny with him sitting next to me. Solid little thing. I couldn't believe we hadn't broken it that night.

And I wasn't supposed to be thinking about sex. Nope, that was the road that led to ruin and failing IUDs.

You can't get any more pregnant at the moment. The thought popped into my mind and I pushed it away.

Not the point.

This was our chance to take things slow.

"No complaining," I told him, picking up my crochet hook. "Crocheting helps my brain relax."

"If anyone ever saw me doing this—"

"You going to invite Heather over for a crochet party?" I asked.

"Fuck no."

"So, shh," I said. "And concentrate. Loop." I looped, showing him, trying not to laugh as he fumbled with the yarn. After a moment, he got it. "Pull the outside loop under the inside." I demonstrated. "And repeat."

He started to do it then mishandled the hook and the yarn slid off. A curse slipped from his lips.

"We can do something else," I offered. "Or you can just relax while—"

Blue eyes met mine and they were determined. "Show me again."

I did.

He followed my actions, tongue pressed into the corner of his lips as he concentrated fiercely. The yarn slipped off again. Another curse.

"Really—" I began.

A growl. "Again." His mouth softened. "Please."

I put down my hook and slipped between him and the table, forcing him to slide backward as I settled myself into his lap.

"This," he murmured, snaking his hands around my waist, "I like."

I shook my head, leaned back against his chest. "You need to relax," I told him, even as my actions made me do the opposite of my words.

Jordan's scent wrapped around me and that spicy maleness made me want to cuddle closer. That coupled with the heat of his body and the solidity of his muscles, and I was aroused beyond belief. I wanted to rub all over him, like he was catnip, curl up close and forget about the crocheting.

I wanted him. Maybe more than he wanted me.

But if I was doing this—making a go of the dating thing with Jordan—then I wasn't going to jump into bed with him again. That had been the crux of our problems, and I was determined to avoid that stumbling block this go around.

And dammit, the man was going to learn to crochet. It wasn't that hard.

I put the hook in his hand and placed mine over his. Then I did the same with the yarn.

"Loop. Tuck. Pull," I said and guided his hands through the actions. "Loop. Tuck. Pull."

He got it. Of course, the man got it. Two times through and perfect stitches, perfect tension. He repeated the action one more time. Two. Then he dropped the hook and yarn.

"That's good enough," he said, mouth coming close to my ear, his husky words making me shiver.

"There are other stitches—"

"I don't give a damn about the other stitches."

"Then what—?"

I didn't finish the sentence as Jordan spun me in his lap.

His mouth slammed down on mine.

And suddenly I didn't give a damn about the other stitches either.

TWENTY-TWO

Abby

I WAS ON FIRE. Oh God, I was on fire.

Jordan's hands were holding me tight against him, his lips plundering mine. It was too much and not enough. Our clothes were in the way. I wanted skin-to-skin. I wanted him on top of me.

And then with a shift of his mouth, everything changed.

The touch softened, his hands came up to gently cup my cheeks. His tongue was gentle and probing.

I sighed and he caught my breath.

"Hi," he said, pausing to stare down at me.

"H-hi." My heart was still pounding, that gnawing desire bubbling just under the surface.

His forehead dropped against mine. "You undo me."

I snorted. "Except you're not the one with wet panties right now."

He laughed, the sound puffing against my skin, filling my heart with a lightness that only seemed to appear when Jordan was nearby.

"True," he said. "Wet isn't really my problem at the moment."

My eyes drifted down and I smirked.

"No hammer jokes," he grumbled.

I couldn't help it. Apparently, I couldn't resist an innuendo.

"But there are so many good ones," I said, laughter punctuating the words. "It's—"

He kissed me again and it wasn't the hot, searing-me-to-the-soul kind. Nor was it gentle and coaxing. This one was demanding. He knew what he wanted from my mouth and he took it.

We broke apart, both breathing heavily.

I glared at him with heavy eyes. "Did you just kiss me to shut me up?"

"Did it work?" I opened my mouth indignantly, only to close it when he shot me a teasing look. "I kissed you because I can't seem to help myself." His lips twitched. "The shutting up part was just bonus."

I poked his chest. "Incorrigible."

"Your big words must come from all the books you read."

I fanned myself, fluttered my eyes. "Oh darling, you say the sweetest things."

"You *taste* sweet."

My breath caught. Jordan's hand stroked my waist, inching lower, slipping under the waistband of my slacks. "It's the fortune cookie."

"It's you." A dip of those fingers, calloused skin brushing the top of my underwear. "I bet you taste sweet here too."

"Jord—"

"Would you like it if I kissed you there?"

Now that was an image. Who wouldn't like Thor between her thighs? But . . . I'd been at work all day and wasn't sure how *fresh* I was.

"I—"

He tilted his head, fingers running back and forth, back and forth. I wanted them to dip a little deeper, to slide home. "You what?"

One lock of hair had slipped over his forehead and I brushed it back, feeling both extremely self-conscious and turned on. *He* smelled great. I, on the other hand, probably had B.O. and needed to douse myself in Purell.

"Sweetheart." He kissed my throat. "What is it? Do you want to go back to crocheting?"

The angst dissipated as I laughed. "God, no."

"Then what's the matter?"

"Just having a girl moment." I waved a hand. "Ignore me. I'll be fine in a minute."

His eyes narrowed and I sighed, knowing him well enough by now to understand he wouldn't let the point go without further explanation.

"I want you to go down on me, but I'm not sure how"—I waved a hand in the direction of my vagina—"good things are down there at the moment."

"Because of the baby?"

I shook my head. "It's been a long day. I haven't showered—"

Clarity finally dawned on his face. "You want me to eat you out but are worried about how you smell?"

I'm sure my cheeks were bright red. "Yup. That's pretty much the crux of it."

"Women."

"Hey! I'm trying to be considerate—"

"Shush, you." He picked me up, tossed me on the couch. "I'm trying to lick my girlfriend's pussy."

"Jord—" But my protest and embarrassment faded the moment he unzipped my pants and yanked them down my thighs. He dipped a finger beneath my underwear, eyes hot when he found me dripping.

All the air left my lungs when he put that finger in his mouth and sucked.

"Sweet," he said, voice gruff. "Like I said."

"Okay," I whispered in awe. "That might have been the hottest thing I've ever seen."

"No, that would be you writhing beneath me."

"But I—"

He didn't let me finish, instead yanked my pants past my ankles and started on my shirt. Something ripped. Buttons flew. My underwear disappeared like magic.

And in less time than I could have imagined, I was naked.

Jordan didn't give me a second to catch my breath. He spread my thighs, tossed one leg over his shoulder, and dove in.

"Oh my God," I moaned, and then hissed when he chuckled and the sound reverberated through me. He hadn't shaved for a few days, so his jaw was covered with stubble that added just the right amount of friction. If I'd been wet before, two seconds of his mouth on me and I was absolutely drenched.

His tongue circled my clit, flicking lightly for a few strokes before settling into the perfect rhythm. One warm palm slid up, cupped my breast.

"Oh," I moaned. "Just like that." My fingers tangled in his hair when he squeezed my nipple, teasing the hard nub as he licked me.

He switched breasts, sped the movement of his mouth until I was writhing against him. Both hands slid to my waist and he pulled me firmly against his lips, teasing, tormenting, winding me tighter and tighter and *tighter* until—

Explosion.

White stars flashed behind my closed lids. Pleasure spilled out from my center, radiating into my limbs and leaving me lax.

"Sweetheart?" Jordan's voice was gentle though laced with just a bit of stiffness. It brought me to my senses.

Slightly.

"Mmm," I said softly, words not having returned yet.

"Can you?" He shifted between my legs.

I sighed. "Hmm?"

"Can you let go?"

I blinked, trying to understand what he was talking about. "Killing my buzz, O'Keith."

Warm hands grasped mine, wrapping around my fingers and unlocking my fists. My eyes shot open to see my hands still wrapped in Jordan's hair.

And not gently.

I winced. "Sorry."

"I'm not." He grinned. "Hang tight." He rose and went into the kitchen.

A moment later he returned with a towel, wiped my thighs and in between.

"Beautiful," he murmured, kissing my cheeks. I knew they were red, but I ignored them.

"Not hardly," I said. "But thank you all the same."

"No arguments." He wiped his chin then sank down onto the couch and pulled me to his chest. "We've been through this all before, remember?"

"I remember," I said lazily, playing with a button on his shirt. "I also know what I look like. I'm fine. I like myself. But I'm not a supermodel."

"You're the most beautiful woman I've ever seen."

"And I'm going to accept that compliment, difficult though it may be." I yawned. "It's hard to undo years of Weasels with only one prince."

There was a moment of silence before I processed what I'd said.

"Not that *you're* a prince or—" I began.

Jordan laughed. "You think I'm a prince. No take-backsies."

"Oh lord," I groaned.

"Tell me more about these Weasels."

His hand was stroking my hair, petting me, making my eyes

drift closed. The gentle caresses—and perhaps the best orgasm I'd ever had—loosened my lips.

"Oh," I said. "They're just jerks who sleep with me so they can get close to Seraphina." Another yawn. "We've gotten really good at picking them out."

"Hey." Warm fingers under my chin, tilting it back. I blinked my eyes open. "How many?"

"Many what?"

"Weasels." He clenched his jaw. "How many men have slept with you to get to her?"

I tugged my head free. "Does it matter?"

He dropped his hand to my arm. "Yes."

Well, he knew everything else about me. Might as well give him the last of it. "Three? Wait. No, *four*."

"Assholes."

I didn't deny the fact. "Good news is that we've gotten really good at detecting them." I lifted one shoulder. "Especially when you lose your virginity to one."

Jordan's nostrils flared. "And you thought I might be one?"

"I don't think you see yourself clearly," I said. "You're Thor reimagined. Tall and blond and all muscle-y. Put that with me—curvy, short, dark—and it doesn't make sense. Physically, anyway." My lips twisted. "*Physically* you're Seraphina's perfect match."

"I've never wanted her."

I smiled gently, running my hand down his chest. He was angry and tense, his words sharp. But not at me.

And I felt another part of my heart become enchanted with the man next to me. Pieces were falling for him left and right and I knew that sooner or later I would be fully gone for him.

I might already be.

"You're in the minority," I said softly. "And that's okay," I added when he started to protest. "I'm comfortable in my own skin." A press of my lips to his cheek. "It helps that I've ensnared a god."

"What's with your obsession with Thor?"

"Have you *seen* Chris Hemsworth?"

"Of course."

"Abs. Chest. Arms. Hair." I tugged his lightly. "Grow yours out, and you'd give him a run for your money."

"Hilarious," he muttered.

"Regardless," I said, cuddling up against him. "You do it for me. And not just your body. I like the Jordan from the last few days very much."

"I like him too," he said, laughter in his voice.

"And modest too."

His chest rumbled and I let my eyes slide closed, enjoying the warmth of him, the feel of his fingers running through my hair. I sighed deeply.

He shifted, pulling free of my hold. I moaned in protest. At least until he picked me up from the couch and held me close. "Where's your bedroom?"

I wasn't sure I had the energy for a romp but decided I'd give it my best effort. After all, he'd graced me with the orgasm of all orgasms. "Upstairs. Last door on the right."

He carried me up, depositing me carefully beneath the comforter. I expected him to drop down on top of me. Instead, he asked, "Pajamas?"

I frowned. Was this some sort of kinky fantasy? Pajama fetish?

"You don't want to keep me naked?"

A masculine chuckle. "Believe me, you could stay naked for the rest of your life if you wanted." His lips touched mine. "But what do you normally sleep in?"

"A tank top and granny panties."

He smiled. "And where are said granny panties located?"

I was concentrating on the conversation, but between the

post-orgasm glow and the fatigue seeping in, it was difficult. "In the closet. Top drawer on the far right. Tank tops are the drawer below. But what—?"

Without preamble, he spun and walked into my closet. My room was still in shambles, boxes piled against the walls. I'd gotten my clothes put away and the bed made, which was something. But just thinking about what was left to be unpacked made me break out into a cold sweat. The task seemed overwhelming.

Not that I was about to mention that to Jordan and encourage his highhandedness about the movers.

I might be relieved they were coming, but I wouldn't admit it. Nope, a girl had to have *some* pride.

A minute later, the man in question emerged with my jammies in his hand. He pulled the comforter back, slipped the tank top over my head, and tugged my underwear up and over my hips.

His eyes were scorching the whole time, his gaze scouring me from the inside out.

But he merely kissed my belly, tucked the blanket up under my chin, and then pressed his mouth to mine.

My head dropped to the side when he leaned back. His hammer was directly in view and he was packing a mega-sized version, not a compact. "Shouldn't we"—I indicated with my chin, since my arms were cozy warm under the comforter—"take care of that?"

He adjusted the waistband of his jeans and gave me a grin that held a tinge of discomfort. "I think it's due a pass, don't you?"

I frowned. "Just because I didn't get off that night doesn't mean that I want to punish you now."

"I know," he said, but smiled to soften the words. "I want to take things slow with you, honey. And you're tired. Feeling you come against my mouth was enough."

I shifted to my side, glancing up at him and stifling a yawn. "When you say things like that I don't feel quite so tired."

Jordan kissed my cheek. "Go to sleep."

"Why not go for a quickie?" I asked. "There isn't any way I could come again this soon, but I'll enjoy it and that way, you'll get off too."

"I'm filing that statement away for future use," he said, cupping my cheek for a second before stepping back. "Plus, I don't want *anything* quick with you."

My eyes were drifting closed, but the words made me smile. "Jordan?"

"Hmm?" His voice sounded far away.

"What statement?"

"What?" he asked.

"What statement are you filing away?"

"Nothing, sweetheart. Sleep well." His footsteps were quiet on the carpet.

"Jordan?"

"What, baby?"

"Key on the counter in the kitchen." I yawned. "Take it. I don't need it."

"Okay, honey." He flicked off the lights. I heard the door start to close.

"Jordan?"

"Yes?" Even falling headlong into sleep, I could sense his amusement.

"Not quick sounds good to me, too."

TWENTY-THREE

Jordan

JORDAN STRETCHED and pushed back from his desk. His eyes were burning, but he and the team had finally managed a successful test run of the robot project.

"Have a name yet?"

He looked over his shoulder, a smile already on his face. It didn't matter what time of day it was, how long he'd been working, or who'd pissed him off. Abigail made him happy.

"No name yet," he said, crossing to where she stood leaning against the doorframe of his office.

Her chin tilted up and he kissed her, a soft touch that nonetheless had him going rock hard. He was a man starved . . . or maybe living on the edge. But he wasn't a man satisfied.

It had been two weeks since that night at Abby's house, and he could still taste her on his tongue.

But they'd both been swamped with work, and though he'd followed her home every night with dinner, he hadn't managed to carve out more time than that.

Hunter had been in the hospital and Jordan had tried to spend every spare minute with his nephew. It was tough to see the vibrant little boy laid low, to see his body covered in wires and tubes. He was an innocent seven-year-old who had no one except Jordan, a mother who skipped town, and a nanny, who had spent more time with him than both of his parents combined.

Jordan honestly didn't know what he or Hunter would do without Cecilia. Luckily, though she was technically an employee, Cecilia seemed to love Hunter as her own.

As for George O'Keith, well, he might be paying the hospital bills, but he wasn't anything more than a checkbook.

Which had bugged Jordan at first. What was the point of opening his wallet if he wasn't going to spend time with Hunter? Jordan himself could afford the bills without strain, but his father had insisted to the point that he'd given in.

Then he'd understood.

It was too much like Mom.

His mother's illness and death hadn't been sudden. Cancer was a real asshole and it had chipped away at her body and soul, piece by piece. She'd wasted away, taking a part of all of them with her.

Hunter didn't have cancer.

Unfortunately, what he did have was congenital heart failure. He was weak, immunocompromised, and in desperate need of a transplant.

And neither Jordan nor George O'Keith could buy that for him.

Abby squeezed his arm, making him realize that he'd blanked out on her. "Are you okay?"

"I'm fine." He tugged her over to his desk chair and tapped her shoulder, guiding her down into it. "I was just trying to finish up everything because Hunter comes home today."

Her face brightened. She knew what was going on with Hunter's illness and about the extended hospital stay. "Oh, that's great!"

"Yeah," he said, leaning against his desk in front of her. "So I'm going to have to cancel tonight."

"Of course," she said and though there was disappointment in her tone, her words were genuine. "Of course you have to. Hunter is way more important than a date night."

That was the moment it finally happened. The last piece was placed on the scale, finally tipping the balance and making him feel something he'd never thought possible—love.

Abigail hadn't met Hunter. The little boy wasn't anything more than a vague personality supported by pictures Jordan had shown her. And yet she was putting his nephew ahead of herself.

"You're important too," he said.

Her hand rested on his thigh. "He's an innocent little boy who's already been through too much. He needs you."

Jordan shoved a hand through his hair. "I hate that he has to deal with this bullshit. It's not fair."

Arms slid around his middle, held tight. "It is definitely not fair."

"I'm sorry to cancel," he murmured, slipping his arms around her in return and squeezing gently. "Though probably not as sorry as the rest of the team."

"What do you mean?" She leaned back, stared up at him.

"Sniff test being delayed again means that stinky Jordan is here to stay."

She laughed. "Is it better to be stinky or to be puke-causing?"

"I'm not sure."

Abby rose on tiptoe, pressing her nose to his neck and inhaling. "For what it's worth, I think you smell fabulous."

"Stinky turns you on?"

She grinned. "Apparently."

His cell phone buzzed and his eyes flicked down to where it sat screen up on his desk. The message was from Cecilia.

Heading home.

Abby touched his hand. "You'd better go."

"Yeah." Keeping one arm around her, he lifted the phone, sent back a response, then slipped it in his pocket. "But first I need to do this."

He kissed her, pouring all the desire he'd been banking for the last few weeks into it. All the frustration from finding his satisfaction with his hand, from waking up hard and aching. He poured *everything* into that kiss.

Including the love.

Eventually, they had to break apart and gasp for air. Abby dropped her head against his chest, breaths coming rapidly.

"You may . . . not . . . be able"—she sucked in a deep breath, steadying her words—"You may not be able to use that hammer, but your tongue is damn good."

He cupped her chin, pressed one more kiss to her mouth. "If I never hear another hammer innuendo, it will be too soon."

Another laugh, another shot of joy directly to his soul.

Damn, he loved this woman.

And somehow, that love grew even more when she paused in the doorway and said, "I think you should name the robot, Hunter."

A moment later, she was gone.

But she was the first one to give voice to the truth. He was pushing this project because of Hunter. Because his tech-savvy nephew not only wanted a robot he could play with from a hospital bed, but one that could also be taken apart and put back together again and again and again.

It was a simple request, but not an easy one. There wasn't

anything on the market like that, so Jordan had decided to delay his beach plans to create one. Hunter had needed him.

But Hunter also needed it soon.

Because without a transplant, the doctors gave him six months.

TWENTY-FOUR

Abby

I SHOULD HAVE BEEN CONTENT, all curled up on the couch in a pair of cozy pajamas, a book in my lap, a cup of tea steaming on the coffee table.

My boxes were unpacked. My belly was full. My house wasn't half bad.

Okay, my house was awesome. I hadn't realized how much space I'd been lacking in my apartment until I'd upgraded and gotten over my guilt of using some of the trust fund money as a down payment.

My new, slightly better salary meant I could actually afford the mortgage, so I was considering the down payment my father's first gift to the baby.

Which he didn't know about yet.

I made a face and tried to focus on reading, a prospect that would typically suck me right in, especially since it was a good book from one of my favorite authors.

But I was restless for some reason.

Okay, not *some* reason. I was restless because I missed Jordan.

I peered out my front windows, saw that Seraphina's house was still dark. She'd invited me to a late dinner with her and Bec —who'd finally managed a few hours out of the office—but I hadn't felt like going.

Now I wished I had.

Because I was lonely.

How gross was that?

"Super gross," I muttered.

I placed my book across my knees and took a sip of tea, feeling it warm my body as I drank. After setting it down, I tried to pick up where I'd left off but only managed to reread the same paragraph three times.

My mind was wired, too pumped to focus, and I decided to save the book for a time when I could actually enjoy it.

"No sense in wasting a perfectly good alpha." I stuck in the old receipt I was using as a bookmark and set it on the arm of the couch before standing and walking into the kitchen.

I pulled my laptop from my case, settled into one of the barstools at the kitchen counter, and logged into the secure work server, deciding to get a bit ahead for Monday. I was just pulling up the folder I'd labeled *Project Hunter* when the doorbell rang.

"Hmm," I said, wondering who might be coming to the door at—I squinted at the clock—nine o'clock at night.

The bell rang again and I sighed, closing the laptop screen before sliding off the stool.

"Coming," I called as it chimed a third time. It cut off mid-ring.

I could feel the other person's impatience through the wooden panel as I approached and I knew that should have made me hurry. But I had this sinking sensation of who it might be.

He might be.

I'd been studiously avoiding his phone calls for the last couple of weeks and should have known better.

My father tilted his head to the side, face coming into view in one of the glass panels that bookended my front door. His hazel eyes were familiar—they matched my own—as was the fire shooting out of him.

I sighed. He must really be angry if he'd come himself.

"Here we go again," I said, glancing down at my stomach. I was in what I'd like to term the fat stage of the pregnancy. My butt and boobs seemed to have grown disproportionally, but my belly was still relatively flat, the little curve well-hidden beneath my loose pajama pants.

I unlocked the door and reached to open it, but my father beat me to it, pushing it open so quickly that I had to jump back to avoid being smacked in the face.

His bodyguard, Mac, trailed him closely, gaze searching my house for would-be assailants. Not finding any in the immediate vicinity, he smiled and winked at me.

I finger-waved. I'd always liked Mac.

"Hi, Dad," I said.

"Abigail." He strode right past me with barely a glance.

And the flash of eye contact I received was wholly dismissive.

I wished that dismissal still didn't cause a pang of hurt. I bit my lip. Unfortunately, it still did.

Ten seconds in my father's presence and I was a hurt little girl again.

I reached for the door to close it, but Mac beat me there. "Go ahead," he murmured, tone gentle. "I'll lock up."

"*Abigail*," my father said, impatience lacing each letter of my name.

And, shame on me, I hurried to him anyway.

I told myself it was because the sooner this was over with

then the sooner he'd leave. I'd get back to my book or the project and—

But it wasn't about getting him to leave.

I wanted his approval. His pride.

My feet carried me to the kitchen, where my father stood stiffly, arms crossed fiercely over his chest, and I knew I wouldn't be getting either of those.

Nope. Fatherly appreciation wasn't in my future. Instead, a fight was heading my way.

I filled the kettle with water to stall the inevitable, setting it on the stove and turning on the gas.

"Tea?" I asked. "Or maybe coffee?" I opened a cupboard. "I think I have some somewhere."

"No."

"Okay." I reached for a fresh glass, not bothering with the one on the coffee table. I'd deal with that after The Reckoning. One tea bag in, then the hot water once it began steaming. While it steeped, I snagged the carton of milk from the fridge.

I didn't bother speaking to my father. His silence was typical. He used it with business associates—waiting them out, pushing them to crack.

I was accustomed to the tactic, so I kept myself busy making the perfect cup of tea.

It was either that or start blurting out all the reasons he might be mad at me.

And—peeking up at him as I poured milk into my tea—given the expression on his face, he didn't need any more ammunition for his fury.

He didn't speak as I put the cup on the island near my laptop. Nor as I returned the milk to the fridge. He didn't say a word as I walked by him and climbed back up into my stool.

Fine.

I opened my laptop, typed the information to log into the

secure server again, and pulled up the design for the back of the packaging. It wasn't quite right yet.

I'd just started to adjust the shading when my father finally deemed it time to talk.

"Nice house."

Now *that* was a loaded two words, considering the last time I'd spoken to my father I had expressly told him to take his trust fund and shove it up his—

"Hmm," I replied, taking a page out of Heather's game plan.

I tried one filter before discarding it, not accomplishing much except to partially ignore my father.

Bernie Roberts wasn't a man easily ignored, and I was no different than the rest of America. Except that when it came to my father, I always had this pulsing hurt. Like a scraped knee exposed to the air. Stinging. Throbbing. Aching . . . for something different.

My eyes burned and I blinked rapidly to diffuse the waterworks. I was lucky. I was healthy, had a home and food. Mine was a life of privilege, and I wouldn't complain.

But sometimes a girl just wanted a hug from her dad.

The laptop screen closed, and I jerked my hands back to avoid my fingers being smashed.

I forced my eyes to my father's.

"What did you need, Dad?" I asked. "As you can see, I'm trying to get caught up on some work."

Fury darkened his gaze. "You're working for O'Keith."

My phone buzzed. I examined the screen, saw it was Jordan. Impeccable timing, that one. If my father saw his name—

Fireworks.

"I'm working for Heather O'Keith," I said, picking up my cell and placing it in my lap. "Her tech company needed someone to oversee design and marketing."

"Why would they want *you*?"

Ouch. That one struck home and hard.

I forced my voice to remain calm. "Because, Dad, that's what my degree is in. That's what I spent the last six years doing with Robert and Susan before you bought up their business."

He leaned against the counter, position stiff and arrogant. His hair was still brown, not a hint of gray despite the fact that he was in his sixties. Wrinkles radiated out from the corners of his eyes and around his mouth.

Some might call them laugh lines.

I called them something different.

Asshole etching.

"I bought them out so you'd come to work for me."

Snorting, I took a sip of my tea and felt my phone buzz again. "Tell me, Dad," I said, placing the cup back down, "would the position at Roberts Enterprises involve real work?"

He scoffed. "Of course it would. Your brother needs help, someone to run his calendar. Make sure he doesn't miss lunch—"

"Doesn't he have an assistant for that?"

"I would have paid you better than an assistant," he said.

I allowed my eyes to travel around my kitchen, taking in the gray cabinets, marble countertops, top-of-the-line appliances. The rest of the house was the same. Wide moldings. Tall ceilings. Expensive flooring.

Yes, I was paying for it.

But only because my trust fund had given me enough of a head start to do so. And the fact that what I'd borrowed from it hadn't even made a dent should tell the world something. Should tell *my father* something.

Why would I need *more* money?

When had money ever given me something that wasn't strictly material?

I got it. I had privilege, had been born into it, never had to struggle, always had something to fall back on if I'd needed it.

But I also preferred to make my own way, on my own dime. And since I'd graduated from college, I had lived by that motto.

That I'd finally decided to cave and take a shortcut should have told my father something had changed.

He was just too wrapped up in himself to notice.

I sighed, slid from the stool, and gave my father a hug that he didn't return. "I love you," I said, pulling back. "But you would have never given me the opportunities I've found at RoboTech. I'm good at what I do. And, I'm sorry, but you missed out on that when you tried to shelf my abilities."

"Abigail, how dare—"

I closed my eyes. Breathed out deeply. Then I opened them and strode to the front door. "I'll see you in a few weeks at Christmas."

He sputtered as he followed me. "That's not the end of this conversation. You can't work for an O'Keith."

My brows came up. "I think I already am." I put one hand up, seeing the storm raging on his face. "And before you get into the trust fund talk—which by the way, you've pressured me to spend on a house for *years* now—I have something I need to tell you."

His jaw fell open, probably because I'd never taken that tone with him before. I'd never had a backbone when it came to my father.

Today, that changed.

"I'm pregnant." A pause as I sucked in a breath and decided to just say it and worry about the fireworks later.

His teeth clicked closed.

I lifted my chin. "By an O'Keith."

TWENTY-FIVE

Abby

ANY RESPONSE my father might have made was cut off by the sound of the doorbell ringing.

Good lord, my house was the revolving door tonight.

Mac slipped past us into the hall and started for it, only to step back and place his hand inside his jacket when the lock turned.

Oh shit.

Jordan.

My newfound courage slipped as he pushed open the door.

The only sign of his surprise at finding my father, me, and a bodyguard in the hall was a brief halt in motion. It was a millisecond, really, one I might have missed had I not been watching him so closely.

But I *was* watching, so I saw him take in the situation in an instant.

My father red-faced, skin mottled, smoke all but pouring out of his ears. Me, chewing on my lip, nerves starting to swell.

Mac, ready to reach for his gun.

I frowned at that. My father had kept a bodyguard with him for as long as I could remember, but I'd never really processed the fact that he might actually be in danger. Further that, I knew Mac had been with him for the last four or five years and I'd never seen him reach for a gun.

Well, I hadn't been around all that much, had I?

And now guilt was trickling in. Because how well did I really know my father? Was he truly in danger? Was I viewing him, perhaps unfairly, through the lens of my childhood?

Could he have changed?

Then I remembered our interaction in the kitchen and put the thought out of my head.

My father might have changed, but it wasn't a drastic difference, and it certainly hadn't changed the way he viewed me.

Bodyguard or not.

Jordan closed and locked the door behind him before striding casually toward us, stopping to shake Mac's hand as he walked by. "Haley," he said. "Good to see you."

Mac nodded then moved to stand in the corner, trying to give privacy to a situation that was impossible to ignore. Kind of hard when his charge was in the middle of it.

"Hey, sweetheart," Jordan said, stepping between my father and me, snaking a hand around my waist, and bending down to kiss me.

My father made a choking sound.

"Did you get my text?" he asked.

I shook my head, hands gripping his button-down tightly. He was still in his clothes from work, and I guessed he hadn't had the time to go home yet.

"No." I took in a breath, let his warmth and scent wash over me, steady me. I stepped back, tilted my head toward my father. "Jordan, this is my dad, Bernie."

"Good to see you again." Jordan put out his hand.

My father's remained at his side. "O'Keith."

Jordan raised his brows, turned toward me. "I finished early. Thought we might have our date after all."

"She's not dressed for it," my father burst out. "Obviously. So go."

Jordan's jaw tightened. "I'll have you know—"

"Jordan," I interrupted softly.

He looked down at me. I mouthed, "I got this."

His eyes searched mine for a long moment before he nodded. "Want a cup of tea?"

I smiled, not having realized that he'd noticed my addiction. I *should* have because he was thoughtful and considerate and always seemed to notice all the little details.

"Sure. Thanks."

He bent to kiss my cheek. "Holler if you need me," he whispered and headed into the kitchen.

"Him?" my father snapped. "You cannot be serious."

"Good to see you, Dad," I said, and walked to the front door. "I'll be over for Christmas as usual. Otherwise, if you want to discuss anything further, have your assistant call me and we'll coordinate calendars."

"That's it? You tell me you spread your legs for an O'Keith and you want me to coordinate calendars?"

"I'm twenty-seven years old," I said. "I don't need your permission for who I'm friends with, let alone who I sleep with."

"This is some convoluted revenge, isn't it? You think your childhood was so tough and now you're trying to deliberately—" Spittle flew as he ranted and I found the angrier he got, the calmer I felt.

"I didn't deliberately do anything. I'm just trying to live my life the only way I know how."

"This—" He shook his head. "I can't believe you—"

I let my head fall back to rest against the wall. I had hung two framed pictures of Bec, Sera, and me, centered above a console table that held a bowl for keys—my attempt at mending my losing ways.

"This is why I can't be around you," I said softly. "Everything is about you." I tipped my chin back down, met his eyes square on. "But *this* isn't and I suggest that if you want anything to do with your future grandbaby, then you stop judging me and let me live my own life."

"As if I'd want anything to do with a child that has O'Keith blood in it." He laughed, harsh and cold. "God knows if you are associating with *that* family, then you're as much of a whore as the rest of them."

The verbal blow took my breath away.

"Nice, Dad."

"You need to go." Jordan had come back into the hall and was standing very close to my father. Mac straightened from his position in the corner, but Jordan didn't do anything except say, "It's time for you to leave."

"Fuck you, asshole." Then my father punched him square in the jaw.

Jordan's head snapped back, his hands clenched into fists at his side. But he didn't even bother to address my father. Instead, he looked at Mac. "You need to get him out of here otherwise—"

"Coward."

The word drew Jordan's eyes down.

"I'll give you one freebie because she's your daughter and you're an old man." His voice went deadly. "But talk to her like that again and we're going to have a serious problem."

I stepped between them, leaned back against Jordan.

"Just go," I told my father.

Jordan was rock hard behind me and the fury radiating from him was almost a tangible thing. But when his arm wrapped around my waist, it was gentle.

Mac walked over and leaned down to whisper in my father's

ear. My dad listened for a minute before turning disdainful eyes in my direction.

"I can't deal with this"—he sniffed at Jordan and me—"I have more important business to attend to."

Mac glanced at me and shook his head. I knew he'd made up whatever he'd told my father to diffuse the situation.

I nodded my thanks and locked the door behind them, collapsing back against it with a huge sigh. Tears were threatening but I didn't want to let them fall.

My dad was a jerk. No sense crying about it.

"Come here," Jordan said gruffly.

My eyes flashed open. He had his arms held wide and I didn't hesitate, just walked into that embrace.

"It's going to be okay," he whispered.

And even as I held the words close, I couldn't help but mentally shake my head at the irony.

I may not have gotten this comfort as a child, but I found that receiving it as a grown woman was just as good.

Actually, it may have been better.

"WHY AM I SO NERVOUS?" I asked Jordan the next morning as we drove to his father's house. He'd stayed for a little while the night before, long enough for me to heat up some leftovers for him and crochet a couple of rows on the baby blanket I'd decided to make for the nugget cooking in my belly.

He'd passed on the crocheting, opting to sit next to me watching the sports highlights as I'd worked.

The scene had been domestic and, scarily, I'd liked it.

He wanted to hang around longer, but I'd made him go home. The dark circles under his eyes spoke volumes. He needed more sleep, and that meant I couldn't monopolize all of his free time.

Even though I wanted to.

Even though I was quickly realizing that I wanted to spend every spare moment with him.

Even though I was as horny as a teenager.

"There's no reason to be nervous," he said, resting a hand on my thigh as he drove.

I mentally reset the conversation in my head and focused on the current task at hand. We were going to see Hunter, and I was freaking out.

I didn't do small children well. I was the youngest, had never been around little kids. And this one was sick. And special to Jordan. What if I said the wrong thing? What if—God forbid—I made Hunter cry? What if—?

"Why are you emotionally spiraling over there?" Jordan asked.

The question made me blink and squint over at him. Blue eyes flicked from the road to mine before returning forward.

"How—?"

"Sweetheart," he said, "I notice a lot of things about you."

"Scary," I muttered.

He squeezed my leg. "No hiding now," he said. "Not when I'm finally cluing in."

"That's what I'm afraid of," I said. But I felt the smile tugging at the corners of my lips.

"Spill."

"I'm scared Hunter won't like me."

"Sweetheart." His voice was gentle. "Just be yourself, and I guarantee he'll like you."

Aw.

"You think so?"

He winked. "I know so."

I blew out a breath and nodded. "Okay. I've got this."

"Yes, you do." His eyes met mine for a moment and there

might have been a dash of nerves in the blue depths. "So," he said, tone far from confident, "I wanted to ask you something."

The thread of nervousness in his voice made me study him closely. "Go ahead," I said carefully.

"Do you want to go on a date?"

I cocked my head to the side, relief pouring through me. "Isn't that what we've been doing for the last few weeks now?"

"Well." He winced. "Sort of."

"We've spent almost every night together," I pointed out. "And had lunch. And"—I smiled—"you've brought me breakfast nearly every day. Now that I think about it, just about the only thing you do with me is try to shove food down my throat."

His cheeks went a little rosy. "It's important you eat. No more passing out."

"I agree." I put my hand over his. "And thank you," I said, joking aside. "I haven't felt dizzy since you started making me fat."

"It's nothing." His shoulders came up and I put my hand on the one I could reach, stopping the shrug in progress.

I didn't want him to dismiss what'd he'd done for me.

"It's not nothing to me," I said. "Thank you."

A moment of quiet then, "You're welcome."

"Okay, since we've established the whole spending-loads-of-time-together thing. Which I think is dating, isn't?" I asked. "What's this about taking me out?"

"You deserve a nice dinner at a restaurant. Maybe a movie or a play. Flowers. Whatever." I didn't stop his shrug this time. "You deserve to be courted, Abs. We did this thing all ass-backward, I know. But I'd like to change that. Start from the beginning and have a do-over."

I laced my fingers with his. "I don't want a do-over," I told him. "I like where we are now. It's . . . easy? I'm not sure if that's the right word and maybe this is completely too soon and ridiculous or I'm addled with pregnancy hormones, but I feel like I know you better than any other person on the planet." I hesitated, biting my lip before I just decided to say it. "Maybe even better than Bec and Seraphina and I . . . I guess I kind of like it." I made a face. "No. That's a lie. I *really* like it."

Jordan was quiet for long enough to make me want to take what I'd said back. Then he turned his hand palm up and gripped mine tightly. "I really like it too."

I released a breath, feeling like we'd made a big promise that I didn't yet know the words to.

"Still, I wouldn't mind a nice dinner."

His laughter filled my heart. "Good," he said. "Tonight, I'm taking you on a date."

TWENTY-SIX

Abby

"JORDAN!" A tiny pair of arms wrapped tightly around Jordan's neck and I felt my eyes burn, my hand coming to rest protectively on my stomach.

"Sorry I missed you last night," Jordan said. "You were asleep by the time I got here."

"I'm always tired." Hunter's little freckled nose wrinkled. "It's annoying."

"Yeah," Jordan said, ruffling his hair and leaning back. "I bet it is. Hey, buddy. This is my friend, Abigail."

"Is she your girlfriend?" The wrinkle stayed in place.

Jordan looked solemn when he nodded.

"Ew. Girls are gross."

We both laughed as Cecilia, Hunter's nanny, came back into the room. "Hey," she said, putting her hands on her hips, her voice laced with mock-outrage. "*I'm* a girl."

"Well, that's okay because I love you, CeCe," Hunter said, and *I* promptly fell in love with *him*. "What's in your hand?"

It took me a minute to realize that Hunter was talking to me and then I examined the little bear I'd crocheted and felt embarrassment course through me. His room was jam-packed with stuffed animals and books, all of which looked a hell of a lot nicer than the lopsided bear with unevenly placed eyes I held.

"Oh," I said, turning it over in my hands. "It's silly, but when Jordan told me you were in the hospital, I-I made this for you."

Hunter tilted his head to the side. "Why?"

I nibbled on my lip. There was something about the fierce way his eyes focused on me that made me feel like a bug under a microscope. "I just thought you might be a little lonely and want something to cuddle." I resisted the urge to slide it behind my back. "It's not much, really."

"Can I have it?" he asked.

I nodded. "Of course."

I walked a little closer to the bed he was lying in. It was hospital grade, cleverly disguised with blankets and pillows to hide the institutional materials. But it was still a hospital bed, and that drove the seriousness of his situation home. I'd give this little kid anything he wanted.

He took the little green bear with the goofy eyes and studied it closely. "It's lumpy," he said.

"It's the first one I've made." I laughed. "I could use a little practice."

"First ones are special," he said solemnly, and hugged the bear. "It *is* cuddly."

"Good. At least I got *that* right."

Jordan was still sitting on the side of Hunter's bed and he tugged me down into his lap. "So tell me all about it, bud. What have you been doing this morning?"

"Causing trouble," Cecilia chimed in. She was sitting on the floor folding laundry.

Jordan raised his brows and Hunter stubbornly put out his bottom lip. "I wanted to play with my aunts and uncles."

It took me a minute to comprehend that Hunter meant

Jordan's half-siblings, who currently lived in the house. From what I knew, they were all around Hunter's age and would have been perfect built-in friends.

"He wanted to play *football* with his uncles and aunts."

Jordan hissed out a breath.

"I miss running," Hunter said, and crossed his arms. "It's not fair."

"I know, buddy." The anguish in Jordan's tone killed me. "I wish that I could make this go away for you. But—"

"You can't." A sigh. "I know."

"I've got an idea," I said, turning to Cecilia. "Can Hunter go outside?"

"He can *sit* outside."

"No running. No jumping. No playing. No fun," Hunter grumbled.

I stood and tugged Jordan's arm. "Give us twenty minutes," I said, "and I'll see what I can do about the fun part."

"READY, HUNTER?" I asked, adjusting Jordan's shoulders so that he was standing straight.

He giggled. "This is going to go really bad."

"Yes, it is," grumbled Jordan.

Which only made Hunter laugh harder.

Cecilia tucked the blanket tighter around his shoulders then sat down in the empty chair next to his.

Chairs weren't the only things we'd brought out onto the patio, but I had used a lot of them in my plan. And rope. And potted plants. And . . . a blindfold.

That was currently wrapped around Jordan's eyes.

"Okay, remember what to do? You tell Uncle Jordan what direction to walk and when to stop and try to get him through the whole obstacle course without running into anything."

Hunter nodded, his smile huge.

"Try not to make me fall off a cliff," Jordan said.

Hunter broke out into peals of laughter.

"The pool's not too far," I stage-whispered and Jordan growled, making Cecilia and me join in with Hunter's amusement.

"I fall in," Jordan said, "and I'm taking you with me."

"You'd have to catch me first."

His arm snaked out and caught my wrist. He tugged me into his arms and pressed a kiss to my mouth, aim true despite the blindfold. "I always know where you are, sweetheart."

"Abby-dar?" I said, my heart pounding in my chest.

He released me, fingers brushing the sides of my breasts as he set me away from him.

"Jordan," I hissed, "Hunter is right there."

"They're not paying attention."

I glanced over my shoulder to where Hunter and Cecilia sat. Jordan was right, they were in heated debate, the words "pool," "uncle," and "no" featured loudly.

"How would you know that they're not—" I gasped, spotted one blue eye peeking beneath the blindfold. "You're such a cheater."

He grinned. "A man's got to do what a man's got to do." He swatted my butt, pretended to stretch and then said louder, "Okay, bud, time to stop plotting. Should we do this?"

"Yes!" Hunter yelled, eyes mischievous.

"Wait!" I grabbed Jordan's arm and fixed the blindfold. "No cheating."

"Woman—"

"Walk forward," Hunter commanded.

I bit back my smile as Jordan took a step forward and promptly walked into a rope, knocking several chairs out of alignment.

"Sorry," Hunter said, maybe a little too cheerfully.

"Hang on," I told Jordan, and righted the chairs, then took his shoulders and aimed him in the proper direction of the course's start.

"You're doing this next," I called. "So you'd better be nice to your uncle."

Hunter's mouth made a little "o" and just that quickly, he got serious about helping Jordan through the course.

"Walk forward. Stop." He turned to Cecilia and held up a palm. "What hand is this?"

She whispered the answer.

"Go right!" he yelled.

"*His* right," I said to Jordan, who turned left and managed to avoid the potted plant blocking the other path.

"Now crawl," Hunter ordered.

Jordan dropped and attempted to squeeze through the cardboard box we'd found in the garage.

The sight of Thor on his hands and knees getting stuck in the tiny hole I'd cut out of the side of the box was too much for me. I started chuckling and couldn't stop. Not when he managed to struggle through, not when Hunter told him to go left and he knocked over a plant, not even when he managed to get wrapped in the duct tape I'd strung between two chairs.

"Which left?" he called, covered in silver stripes like a metal mummy. He was bent over, trying to remove the pieces from his ankles and his voice was desperate. "Mine or his? *Mine or his?*"

"His," Cecilia and I managed to get out while still chuckling.

Two more turns, one more crawl, and Jordan was free of the maze. He took his blindfold off and glared at me then Cecilia.

"This is not that funny!"

I held my stomach as I giggled. "My abs. Oh my God, laughing through that was the hardest workout I've had in months."

Cecilia rubbed her cheeks. "Even my face hurts."

"You're in so much trouble," he said and though he was looking at Hunter, I knew the words were directed at me.

"You can make it up to me later," I joked.

He turned to me, eyes sharp. "You'd better count on it."

"SNIFF IT," Jordan ordered.

"Uh-uh," I said, shaking my head and turning my face away. "The last one was bad enough."

My stomach was *still* queasy. I'd smelled twenty-something deodorants at this point and they were all bad.

All of them.

"This is the last one," he said, offering it up to me like it was a piece of broccoli and I was a finicky toddler. "Smell it, and I promise this is the end."

"Promise?" I raised my eyes to his and when he nodded, I sighed in resignation. "Fine." I carefully took the deodorant from his hand and removed the lid. I brought it about a foot from my nose and took a cautious sniff.

Blegh.

I capped it and shook my head, dropping it to the counter and backing away.

"Damn," he said. "That was supposed to be the unscented stuff."

"Well, it's not unscented to me."

He dropped it into the trash can then removed the bag and walked through the garage to throw the offending deodorants into the outside garbage bin. A minute later, he was back. "What type do you use?"

I was wiping my nose on a tissue, trying to somehow remove the scent from my nostrils. "Of deodorant?" I asked, slightly nasally.

"Yeah."

I told him.

"Do you mind if we try it?"

"You want to put on my deodorant?" I asked.

"Want is the wrong word. I'd like to be able to not stink my office up and also not make you sick. What you're wearing doesn't make you puke, right?" He shrugged. "Seems worth a try."

I stood up and inclined my head in the direction of my bedroom. "Seems like we should have given it a try before you made me smell all of those other gross ones."

"At least we did it before dinner?"

I groaned, stomach feeling a bit raw. "Don't mention food right now."

"Sorry." He pressed close to my spine. "I'm trying to help."

"I know." I turned in his arms and hugged him. "Thank you."

Hands slid down my back, cupped my hips. I wanted them to slide lower, to keep going and cup something else.

Unfortunately, Jordan released me, taking my hand and tugging me up the stairs.

"Jordan?" I asked as we walked through my bedroom door and headed for my bathroom. "Is there a reason you haven't fucked me again?"

His fingers spasmed on mine. "What?" He turned to face me.

"I-I just—you haven't seemed interested." I shrugged, dropped my eyes. "You've held me and we kissed a few times. But it's mostly—" I broke off.

"Mostly what?"

I grimaced. "Well, friendly."

"You think I feel *friendly* about you?"

"I mean, I guess not. I just— We haven't— Not since that night you—" I pointed south. "It's okay. I just . . ."

Was making a royal mess of this.

"I've jerked off to the image of you coming against my mouth every night for the last three weeks." His stare bored into me. "I've imagined the taste and heat of you. I've pictured myself inside of you." He grabbed my hand, placed it on his . . . hammer, which was hard enough to pound nails.

Or maybe pound something—*someone*—else.

"I want you, Abigail. Don't you ever doubt that."

"Then why haven't you—?"

"I was trying to give us time to get to know each other. We both have a lot of outside pressure right now. I didn't want to add to it."

"I don't think giving me mind-blowing orgasms is a bad type of pressure."

One brow rose. "Mind-blowing?"

"Oh yeah," I said. "I thought you were well on your way to redeeming you and your *hammer* skills. Then you backed off."

I waited to see if he'd deny it.

He didn't.

Instead, his expression went thoughtful. He nodded. "I did back off. I think . . . I think that things have been so intense between us that I gave distance when I should have closed it. You're not like any other woman I've ever met, Abby. You've got me so twisted up that I don't know how to move forward."

"I—"

"It's not a bad thing. Just unfamiliar ground to navigate." He cupped my cheek. "Like how you were with Hunter today—that killed me. You were so perfect, so sweet. Then I think about you with our baby, and I just get lost in this fantasy." A sigh. "And then I remember we went from step A to step Z skipping everything in between and I keep thinking I owe it to you to give you B through Y. It's almost paralyzing."

"I don't need B through Y," I said. "I just want to be with you. I want to know everything about you. I want to watch bad movies and crochet with you and not put any expectations on anything."

"I'm not used to having no expectations."

I couldn't have expectations, not when every person in my life aside from Seraphina and Bec had completely obliterated the ones I'd had for them. I couldn't expect perfection and happy endings, not when what I was developing with Jordan already meant so much.

If I started dreaming of the other end of the rainbow, of picket fences and family holidays, I thought I might be thoroughly decimated when we were through.

"I know," I said. "But can we try? Can we keep moving forward without all the pressure of worrying about whether or not we're doing it right?"

He nodded.

"Thank you." I rose on tiptoe to touch my lips to his.

Jordan's expression altered, turning a little hotter, slightly playful. "So no planning, right?"

"Right. We just live in the moment and—*oof!*"

He jerked me to his chest. "Shh. For now, we're going to live."

And then he lowered his head to mine.

TWENTY-SEVEN

Jordan

ABIGAIL in his arms was the best thing in the world. She was soft and warm and smelled like roses, and when she moaned against his lips, pressing harder against his chest, Jordan's arousal went from hanging on by a thread to roaring out of control.

He put his hands on her shoulders, tugging her back.

"But—"

One move and she was in his arms. He carried her to the bed, ripped back the comforter, then set her on the sheets.

Pink cheeks, swollen lips, mussed hair. She would have said it was crazy, that her locks were out of control, but he thought the way they were spread out across her pillow was the sexiest thing he'd ever seen.

"Hi," he whispered, coming down beside her on the mattress.

Her mouth quirked up. "Hi."

"You're so beautiful." A roll of her eyes—another dismissal that was so typically Abby. He gripped her chin, forced her to look at him. "I gave you no expectations, so you need to give me this. You are the most beautiful woman inside"—he pressed his palm to her heart, felt the rapid *thump-thump* of her pulse—"and out."

"Jordan." She sighed, covering his hand with her own. "What am I supposed to do with that?"

"Accept it."

A snort.

"Now shh." He kissed her before she could protest further, slipping his tongue into her mouth and coaxing hers to join in. The heat, the *spark* he felt at just the press of their mouths was insane. His entire body felt on the edge of implosion, just from one kiss.

Her hands threaded through his hair, gripping tightly, and the slight bit of discomfort propelled him headlong over the edge.

He found the waistband of her pajama pants, shoved them down, then tore his mouth free from hers to pull off her shirt.

In less than ten seconds, she was naked except for a tiny pair of blue panties. Pale skin flushed pink, breasts stiff-peaked and waiting for his mouth, the slightest hint of her arousal soaking through her cotton underwear.

His mouth watered.

Slowly, wanting to savor the moment, to make it better for her than their first encounter, Jordan traced his hands up her waist.

Gooseflesh erupted on her skin, and she hissed out a breath. "That tickles."

"Mmm," he said, bending so that his mouth could follow the same path. Her waist, her stomach, and then up . . . up until he reached her breasts. He rubbed his nose against the underside of one, before leaning back slightly to blow on her nipple. "I read they can be extra sensitive. Is this okay?"

"Uh-huh." She arched back, pressing her breast closer. "I want—"

He licked the hardened nub, relished her moan. "What do you want, sweetheart?"

"I—" Hands came up to his head again and tugged him back down. "They're—" Another swipe of his tongue. "Not . . . *ah* . . . sensitive. I want—" She pulled his head toward her breast and groaned when he held steady, staring into those gorgeous, lust-filled hazel eyes. "You. Jordan. I need your mouth."

He'd wanted the words, *needed* them, but they nearly shattered what remained of his tattered control. He wanted to make this perfect.

And it meant more to him than his own pleasure.

It meant more to him than anything else did in that moment. More than the company, the robot project, the beach.

The only thing that mattered was pleasuring Abby.

He closed his mouth around her nipple and gave her everything he had, every skill he'd honed, every tactic he knew. Jordan paid more attention to her responses than any other woman from his past, noting every moan, every hitch of breath. He exploited the information, using it to discover what set her on fire.

From her breasts, he moved up to her mouth, feasted on her throat, and then kissed his way down her body.

There was a soft curve just below her belly button and his heart squeezed, his desire banking for a moment as he glanced up and met Abby's eyes. He saw in them what he felt in his heart. Hope, fear, and love.

He felt love for the baby and . . . for Abigail.

Carefully, he pressed his lips to the little bump. He was in love with Abby.

Holy shit, he was *in love*.

Shaking fingers touched his cheek. "Jordan?"

"I know, sweetheart," he said. "I know."

It was like one of those moments in a movie, where the main characters stare at each other and a montage of their past interactions start playing. Except this was real life and the moments were a blur, the huge feelings he felt for this woman so much more.

"I need you." One shift of her hips and the time for emotion was over.

He slid lower, spread her legs, and began feasting.

Fuck, she tasted amazing. Sweet with just a hint of tart, it was the best meal of his life.

"Oh, God," Abby moaned, hips writhing. "That's"—he slid one finger home—"oh, fuck. *Jordan.*"

Another finger and he moaned at the tight fit, remembering what she'd feel like, imagining himself sliding home. His slacks were uncomfortably tight and he was slowly dying from the need to be inside her.

"I—" She gasped. "That's—" Her head rolled from side to side on the pillow, her hips bucked against his mouth. "Oh . . . *fuuuck.*"

She pulsed against his finger, squeezing him tightly as her orgasm pulled her over the edge.

Her chest rose and fell, breasts jiggling, a sheen of sweat coating her skin. Her pussy was pink and glistening, and he had to force his eyes to the ceiling and count backward from one hundred to not blow his load.

"Jordan?" she asked after a minute.

"Yeah?" He was still counting.

"Why aren't you inside me?"

His head jerked. "What?"

She sat up, hands finding the buttons on his shirt and sliding one free. Then the next and the next and the next. He shoved it off when they were all loose. The buttons on the cuffs caught on his wrists and he yanked them through, not giving a damn when he heard the fabric rip.

Because Abby's hands hadn't stopped.

They'd continued to unbutton his slacks and then had progressed to zipper sliding.

Hot palms on his chest, his stomach, beneath his boxer briefs and—

"Oh fuck," he groaned when she gripped him tightly.

"There you are," she whispered, but she wasn't talking to him. No, the words were for his *hammer*—fuck, now *he* was the one making hammer references—and the way she licked her lips nearly made him come right then and there.

Which made alarm bells blare in his head.

"Next time," he said, extracting himself from her hands and bending to kiss her. He thrust his tongue past her lips and slipped his fingers back between her thighs. She jumped then moaned when he gentled the strokes, knowing that she was still sensitive.

Abby was so responsive that he wanted to spend the night making her come over and over again.

He wanted to claim her, body and soul. To mark her from the inside out. To tattoo her heart with his name.

To tie her to him for an eternity.

But most of all, in that moment, he couldn't wait another second to be *in* her.

He kicked out of his slacks and knelt between her thighs.

I love you, he thought, and thrust home.

TWENTY-EIGHT

Abby

I REALLY LOVED *this man's hammer,* I thought, gasping as Jordan slid inside me with one firm stroke. It was too much yet not enough. Well, not the hammer part—*that* was great—but the rest of it.

What we were sharing wasn't just physical. It was more.

And that scared me.

I wanted to keep emotions out of it, but I couldn't.

Every time we were together, whether it was sexual or not—and more often it had been *not*—I felt another thread connect us.

Or, rather, I felt another string attach *me* to *him.*

And I worried about what might happen when he inevitably severed the ties.

Because it would have to come from him. I was too addicted to his particular brand of perfect to distance myself now. I'd jumped in with both feet and prayed that he wouldn't find me lacking—

Which was seriously fucked up, I realized.

My worth shouldn't come from another person. But it had

somehow become interlaced with his . . . what? Acceptance? Thoughtfulness? Approval?

Oh, my God. I was *so* fucked up. How was I going to raise this baby without screwing him or her up? How—?

"Abigail."

Jordan was on top of me, *inside me,* and I was having a panic attack. "It's not you," I said. "It's—oh, God"—my hands came up, covered my face—"*oh, God.* I'm ruining this. I'm sorry. I'm so sorry."

I was hiccupping now, sobs escaping my chest, tears leaking, and I didn't completely understand why except that when he'd slid inside me it had felt so perfect and I knew perfect couldn't last. I just knew I'd do something to fuck it up.

And now I was. I was screwing it all up.

"Sweetheart." He tugged at my hands, but I shook my head. I was embarrassed enough, he didn't need to see my snot-covered, splotchy face.

Because I wasn't crying pretty.

This wasn't one perfect tear sliding down my cheek, like a romance novel. These weren't tears symbolizing the fruition of a relationship and hope for the future.

These were frightened sobs from a woman who felt too much.

This was me being unable to take that final leap and just put it all on the line.

This was—

"I love you."

I froze, sobs sticking in my chest. My arms went lax and Jordan gently peeled them from my face. He leaned close, close enough that I could see the specks of gray-green lining the deep blue of his irises.

Beautiful.

"Abigail Roberts," he said, one palm cupping my cheek. "I. Love. You."

It scared me, those words. But it scared me more to do this without them.

Because . . .

"I love you too."

He shuddered, reminding me that he was still hard, still deep inside.

"I like hearing you say that," he murmured, resting his forehead on mine.

Serenity swept through me in that moment, erasing the fear, eradicating those persistent doubts.

There were just the two of us in this bed. The rest of the world could wait.

Calmness reigned . . . but just for a minute.

"Okay?" he asked.

I nodded. "Sorry I freaked out."

"If you're feeling what I'm feeling then I say we're due a freak out every once in a while."

"When are you going to freak out?" I asked, pushing back a strand of hair.

"Probably not when I'm inside your heat and dying to move." He gave me a pained look. "You feel incredible."

"I know." I smiled, before tugging his mouth down to mine. "Now move."

He didn't need to be told twice.

THE PHONE CALL came eleven days before Christmas, while Jordan sat next to me in Dr. Stephens' exam room. She measured the baby's growth and it was crazy to see the difference that just a month had made.

Fourteen weeks since that bad night stand.

Fourteen times seven—it was too early in the morning to do the math—days since my life had taken a sharp left.

Jordan had all but moved into my house, even going so far as to sneakily claim a drawer and buy an extra tube of my deodorant to leave on my bathroom counter. And though we worked long hours and we spent a lot of time with Hunter, we were managing to carve out time for just the two of us.

Time that I relished.

Time that I loved—even if it was just streaming a bad TV show and eating takeout, even if it was just working opposite one another on my kitchen island, laptops dueling.

Even if it was crocheting together and making fun of the garish and mismatched colors he'd chosen for the scarf/blanket/lumpy-square-handkerchief.

I didn't want to share him with the world.

But I wasn't the only one who needed him.

So when Jordan's cell rang and he turned it to silent instead of answering it, I touched his hand. "That's Hunter's ringtone."

"It's—"

I shook my head. "Answer it. What if he's—?"

Sick. Hurt. In the hospital. Lonely and all by himself.

He studied me for a second before pulling out his cell and excusing himself to the corner of the room.

"His nephew," I told Dr. Stephens. "He's in need of a heart transplant."

Her eyes dimmed. "How old?"

"Seven," I said softly. "Mom bailed. Dad passed away."

"Damn," she said, peeling off her gloves and patting my knee. I slid up, tucked the drape back over myself. "It's always so much worse when it's kids."

I nodded. "I agree completely. He's the best kid, too. Smart and precocious—"

"He got it," Jordan said, his face blank. "I—*he got it.*"

"Got what?" Dr. Stephens asked.

"A heart." Jordan's voice was stunned. "Hunter is on the way here with Cecilia. They have a heart for him."

"Oh, my God." I started to stand, remembered I was bottomless and froze.

Dr. Stephens squeezed my hand. "You're all set here. I hope everything goes okay. Call me if you need anything."

"Thank you," I said.

She left, closing the door behind her.

"Jordan," I said. "He'll be okay. It's—"

"I want to get custody of him," he said. "Once this is all said and done. I don't want him alone. I want him with me." His eyes met mine. "With us."

My breath caught. "I—I—"

I breathed in then out, very slowly. I wanted that too. So much. I already loved Hunter like my own.

"We'll get him through this," I said, knowing that he had a fight ahead of him. "Then we'll figure out what Hunter wants." I wouldn't take him from Cecilia, the one other solid in his life. If—no, *when*—Hunter was healthy and strong, we'd figure it out.

And it would involve Jordan and me.

I couldn't let that little boy grow up without us.

We met Cecilia and Hunter in the waiting room of the transplant center.

"Did you grab the papers?" Jordan asked.

"I did." Cecilia handed a folder over and Jordan flipped through it, sighing when he reached a page.

"Good," he said, pulling two legal documents out, glancing quickly at both, then sticking them back inside. "Everything is here."

"Want me to hold that?" I asked, leaning up to whisper in his ear. "Hunter looks like he could use a little Uncle Jordan time."

We both glanced over at the little boy, whose typically pale skin was even paler than normal. Jordan handed me the folder then bent to pick up Hunter. "All ready, buddy?"

Hunter's bottom lip trembled. "Uh-uh."

One big palm wrapped around the back of Hunter's neck and pulled him against Jordan's chest. He bent his head, speaking softly into Hunter's ear. I couldn't hear the words he whispered, but I saw the effect: a gradual relaxing, a growing confidence, and finally two little arms being thrown around his uncle's neck.

Cecilia sniffed and I wiped a finger under each eye.

"Sometimes I wish that Jordan was Hunter's dad," the younger woman said.

"I think he wishes that too," I told her.

"Do you think—?" she broke off. "Never mind. We need to think about the surgery right now."

"Would you mind if he—if *we* . . . someday?"

It was barely a coherent sentence, but Cecilia understood me anyway.

Her lips pressed tightly together. "I would love it if Hunter found his own family." She stared at me, fury in her eyes. "She signed away her rights, you know?" A nod in the direction of the folder.

"What?" I opened the cardstock cover and my heart sank. "How could . . .?"

"I know." Cecilia touched my arm. "And I know that you have a lot happening." Her eyes drifted down to my stomach even though neither Jordan nor I had mentioned the baby to her or Hunter. Hell, as far as I knew, he hadn't even told his father.

Heather knew, of course, because of the whole sleeping-on-day-one-of-my-new-job situation. Yet she hadn't mentioned it to me.

But Cecilia, a women who barely knew me, had picked up on it.

She smiled. "I'd love it if you two could take Hunter. He

worships Jordan and he adores you. He deserves more—" She shook her head. "He deserves more than just a nanny."

"Hey." I turned to face her fully and though I wasn't the most touchy-feely person, especially with people I didn't know all that well, I hugged Cecilia tightly. We hadn't spent years together, but I felt like I knew her heart.

And that heart was pure.

"Hunter is lucky to have you."

She sniffed and pulled back, glancing up at the ceiling and blinking rapidly. "I'm scared," she said softly. "I shouldn't be. I need to be strong for him. But I'm petrified."

"Me too," I admitted. "But we're going to pretend otherwise. Deal?"

Cecilia nodded, blew out a long, slow breath. "Deal."

"And," I said, as a few nurses pushed through the double doors and began walking toward our little group, "when Hunter becomes an official part of our family, I hope you will too."

Her jaw dropped open and she looked at me, dumbstruck. But she didn't get a chance to respond because Hunter ran over, grabbed both of our hands, and began tugging us forward.

"Come on, CeCe and Abby. Today I get to become a superhero!"

TWENTY-NINE

Abby

"I CHECKED OVER THE ORGAN MYSELF," the lead doctor said. "Everything looks perfect so we'll begin prepping Hunter for the surgery and get him feeling better."

Hunter was in bed, his little body dwarfed by a white hospital gown covered with pouncing tigers.

The image fit him.

Launching himself forward for a chance at the future.

"Do you think my new heart will be working by tomorrow?" Hunter asked. "Because I'd like to have it in time for me to turn eight."

"Is it your birthday tomorrow?" the nurse asked, placing a blood pressure cuff on his upper arm.

"Uh-huh," he said around the thermometer.

"Well, if the doctor okays it tomorrow, I'll save you a celebratory Jell-O." She noted a few items on the chart.

"I love Jell-O!"

"Great!" She fist bumped him. "What's your favorite flavor?"

"Cherry!"

"Done," she said. "I'm going to mark one in the fridge with your name on it right now."

"Yay!" Hunter bounced on the bed. "That's awesome."

"What do you say?" Cecilia prompted.

"Thank you!" Hunter called as the nurse moved toward the door.

She smiled, waving her goodbye.

The doctor walked over to Hunter and began talking to him, explaining what was going to happen in vague, kid-friendly terms. Ten minutes later, and after answering about a hundred questions from Hunter, he left with a promise that the anesthesiologist would be in soon.

I watched from the corner as Jordan and Cecilia sat and joked with Hunter, not wanting to intrude.

I probably should have gone to the waiting room, but I didn't want to take my eyes off Hunter until the last possible moment.

And when he asked me to come over and hold his hand so the nurse could start his IV, I knew that little boy owned me, whether he was aware of it or not. His whimpers of pain, the tears in his eyes, all of them slayed me.

Thankfully, the procedure was quick and within minutes, the anesthesiologist was in the room, giving Hunter a medication that made him drowsy.

A few moments later he was being wheeled away, a piece of my heart rolling alongside him.

"How is he?" Heather asked from the doorway of my office the next afternoon.

I winced. "In some pain," I said, honestly. Watching him hurt was probably the worst thing I'd experienced in my life to date. "But the doctors said that everything went perfectly."

She came in and closed the door. "Did you want to take some time off to be with him?"

My eyes flew up, surprised.

"You've been a mess today. Unfocused. Out of sorts."

My stomach clenched. "I'm sorry. I'll make sure I don't—"

"That's not what I meant," she said. "I get it. I'm worried too, and the kid isn't mine."

I shook my head. "It's not like that. Hunter's not my—I mean it's just . . . you don't have to—"

"Abby." She smiled. "Hunter is Jordan's, and Jordan is yours. So Hunter is yours."

"Is this some sort of if X equals Y and Y equals Z then X equals Z nonsense?"

She groaned, dropping into a chair in front of my desk. "Stop. You're bringing back horrible memories of algebra class."

"You're incredible with numbers," I reminded her.

"Yes. With real numbers. It's the alphanumeric ones that get me every time."

I laughed then sobered. "I want to be with Hunter, but I also want to make sure I do this project right. It means so much to Jordan. I don't want to be the one who—"

"Screws it up?" Heather asked, rather unhelpfully if you asked me.

"Yes. That," I said, grimacing.

"So keep working," she said. "Just do it remotely."

"What?"

Heather rolled her eyes. "You're already doing it anyway." Her brows went up at my expression. "Don't think I've haven't seen how frequently you log in to the server from home. Plus, that's going to be how you work when the baby gets here, isn't it? Think of it as a trial run."

"Wait, what?" I asked.

"You are going to keep working here after the baby, aren't you?"

"Y-yes," I stumbled out. "I mean I'd planned to, I just hadn't thought that far ahead and—"

"Good. I'll plan it for you." Heather grinned. "I kind of like doing that, if you hadn't noticed."

I snorted. "Yeah. I think I managed to pick up on that."

"Okay, great. It's settled then. Pack up and get out of here." She stood. "I don't want to see you until Hunter is home from the hospital."

"Heather?" I asked as she turned to the door.

She stopped, rotating back to face me.

"Thanks."

Her lips twitched and she shrugged. "Don't know if you know this, kid, but I kind of like you."

"Somehow I like you too." She laughed and started out again.

I stopped her. Again.

Because something she'd said had triggered alarm bells in my mind.

"Before you go, can you tell me how often, exactly, I've been logging into the secure server?"

THIRTY

Jordan

JORDAN READ the press release with a mixture of growing horror and extreme fury.

This is why he'd gotten rid of his cell phone in the first place.

What he'd thought was going to be an innocent—or very naughty, he liked both options—text message from the woman he loved had turned into something far more sinister.

He glanced over at the hospital bed where Hunter slept. It had been a week since the surgery, a week of seeing Hunter for small slices of time, of trading places with Cecilia and Abby so that one of them was always in the waiting room in case Hunter might need them. In fact, Abby had spent so much time in the waiting room that she had her own desk. Or rather, the nurses had encouraged her to rearrange a table and chair next to a plug so she could work remotely.

And now he wondered what exactly she'd been working on.

Fuck. Jordan sucked in a breath, blew it out slowly, and focused on Hunter. This wasn't about work or betrayals. This was about a little boy who had spent most of the past week sedated or sleeping. He'd been moved from the cardiac intensive care unit to a room in the general cardiac ward the night before. Though it was an improvement, his nephew still had a long journey ahead of him.

A soft knock on the door drew his attention from Hunter. He tore his gaze away and saw the nurse who was on shift, Rebecca, standing in the door. "I'm sorry," she murmured. "Visiting hours are over."

"Okay." He crossed to Hunter, pressed a kiss to his forehead. "'Night, buddy."

His nephew stirred slightly but didn't wake.

"He's doing well," Rebecca said, shutting the door behind her.

"Yeah, he is," Jordan agreed. He slipped his phone into his pocket, but the device might as well have been burning a hole in the fabric after what he'd read on it.

"Your girlfriend is in the waiting room," Rebecca said with a smile. "Sally tucked a blanket around her because she'd fallen asleep. She's tuckered out."

His heart pulsed as he thanked the nurse and asked him to pass on the gesture to the charge nurse, Sally. He'd seen the hours Abby had been pulling, knew that she was working hard for Hunter and wanting to be there for him. He also knew that she was the most golden-hearted person he'd ever met.

It didn't make sense.

Why would she sell out RoboTech?

Why, after all of the hours she'd spent on design, would she give the information to RoboTech's number one enemy?

To Roberts Enterprises.

She wouldn't.

Abby didn't have any love lost for her father, and she'd been damn loyal to Jordan, to Heather, to Rich.

She wouldn't betray him.

He pushed through the double doors that led out into in the waiting room, holding on to the notion.

Please let that thought be the correct one.

Abby was curled up in a chair, laptop perched on her knees. The screen was black, but she shifted, her fingers brushing the mouse pad. A document came to life, a spreadsheet with rows and rows of information.

Jordan frowned, snagging the laptop before it hit the floor when she moved again, unconsciously seeking a more comfortable position in the rigid wooden chair.

Several lines were highlighted in yellow, and a column on the far right was titled "Me" and filled with periodic "Xs."

Other lines were highlighted in red. And still more in blue, with question marks corresponding in the "Me" column.

He studied the rest of the sheet, trying to make sense of the information. It was mostly numbers: time stamps, length of time, IP addresses.

"Jordan?" Abby asked, her voice hesitant.

He lowered the laptop and stared at her. "What's this?"

Her face went pale and his gut clenched. Dammit, had he been wrong?

"Jordan—" she began. "It's not like you're thinking. I—uh—well. It's complicated . . ."

His stomach sank further and further with each stumbling word.

"—my father, he said—"

Jordan shut his eyes. Breathed. Then opened them.

Of course.

"I need to go." He dropped the laptop onto the chair next to her and walked away.

"Jordan!"

Footsteps echoed down the tile floor.

"Wait."

He yanked open the door to the stairs and rushed down. His

feelings were a tangled knot. He didn't know how to coax them free. Abby couldn't have—

His feet stopped at the bottom of the first flight.

But she hadn't denied anything. She hadn't—

No. He shook his head. This wasn't the time to draw out motivations. He needed to sleep. He needed to think.

But he couldn't walk away. *Dammit.* It wasn't that easy.

Jordan couldn't walk away from Abby.

The door at the top of the stairs flew open, and Abby ran through. Her eyes were wild and there were tears on her cheeks. She'd left the computer, her purse, *everything* behind.

And that was the moment he knew for sure.

She'd left it all behind.

For him.

"I didn't!" She gasped out, sliding to a stop at the top of the stairs. "That was what I was trying to say. Someone was logging in under my name, accessing Hunter's project. Heather and I have been tracking it since last week." Abby sank to the top step, sighing as she put her head in her hands. "But I didn't expect that my own father would try to betray me."

Jordan walked up the steps and sat next to her. "Your father hates my family."

"Why?" Abby asked, glancing up at him. "I don't understand how hate could turn him against his own daughter. I didn't want to believe it. Then I saw the press release and knew . . ." One tear slid down her cheek. "What could make him do that to me?"

Jordan brushed a hair back from her face and told her, "My father seduced your mother."

She rolled her eyes and he blinked, surprised.

"It's true."

"I don't doubt it. Just know that my mother had more affairs than a tabloid queen. If my father tried to ruin all the other men in her life, he wouldn't have time to actually run a business."

Jordan put his hands up. "I don't pretend to understand it, all I know is that after my mom died, they were . . . close."

"Ick."

He winced. "Yeah."

Abby sucked in a breath then released it. "I didn't betray you," she whispered.

"I know."

Her eyes went to his. "You do?"

He nodded. "I admit, I freaked for a second, but"—he reached for her hand—"I know you, sweetheart. I was coming back when you barreled through that door like a charging bull."

She glared, but her lips were twitching. "I'm going to let the bovine joke slip for now, but know that in a few more months that'll get you throat punched."

He laughed, wrapped his arms around her. "I love you, Abigail Roberts."

She dropped her forehead to his shoulder and hugged him back. "I love you too, Thor, God of Thunder." A pause. "And your hammer."

Right there in the hospital stairwell, four days before Christmas, he tugged Abby into his lap and kissed her.

And when she told him about the trap she and Heather had laid to trip up the corporate spies, he kissed her again.

Then once more, just for good measure.

THIRTY-ONE

Abby

JORDAN WAS ASLEEP BESIDE ME, sprawled amongst the pillows and comforter, but I was wide awake, my laptop open and at the ready. I just needed to click the button that would upload the final layer to the trap.

I could only hope they would take the bait.

That *my father* would take the bait.

Christmas Eve and I was trying to screw over dear old Dad. Now *that* was the spirit of the season.

Not that he hadn't tried to screw me over first.

Which was the part I didn't understand. Why bother with such a small project when Roberts Enterprises had so much already? It was a nothing product for RoboTech as it was, quite literally Jordan's pet project for Hunter.

So why would my father bother taking it on?

The only reason I could comprehend was revenge.

Ruining a company's reputation for little more than vengeance. It wasn't like I could say it was the first time I'd heard that particular notion.

It's just that . . . I'd thought my father was better than that.

Sighing, I closed the laptop and picked up my phone, texting Heather to let her know the final trap was planted.

I was giving the family of my father's greatest enemy enough material to blackmail him for years. And I was doing it without a second thought.

Because I trusted Heather and Jordan.

Because this all needed to stop.

Because, dammit, I had to believe my father might have a slice of good in him. Despite my childhood, despite the bullying attitude, despite the neglect and distance and disapproval.

My dad had to love me.

Right?

I went into the bathroom and closed the door, leaning back against it for a moment before I turned on the taps to fill the big tub. We were staying at the nicest hotel in town, which happened to be located just a few blocks from the hospital. It was a convenient location and though I'd argued with Jordan about the unnecessary expense of reserving the Presidential Suite, considering we were hardly in it, I was definitely feeling the tub right in that moment.

There were perks to dating a billionaire.

I filled the bath with warm—*not hot*—water and stripped down. I was just about to step in when my phone rang.

Thinking it was Heather, I answered without looking at the caller ID.

Big mistake.

"Abigail."

My father.

"Hi, Dad." I was proud of myself. My voice was steady.

"What have you done?" he hissed.

"I don't know what you're talking about," I said, wondering if he'd come clean and admit to screwing with his daughter's career for ego or revenge or whatever. I wondered if he'd finally tell me why I meant less to him than my brother.

"I should have known," he said, completely obliterating the last bit of hope I'd held for him, "that *you* would do something like this."

I grabbed a towel, wrapped it around myself. "Something like what, Dad?"

"Don't call me that," he spat. "As if I'd want someone like you to—"

My fingers clenched on the towel. "Call you what?" I whispered, but it was apparently enough to cut through his tirade.

"I'm not your father, Abigail," he said, voice icy cold. "I may have given you my name, but I've never acted like a father to you. God knows you should have gotten a fucking clue."

I swallowed. "What are you saying?"

"Little idiot," he snapped. "I'm telling you that I am *not* your father."

A frigid calm swept down my spine. "Who is?"

"A fucking yoga instructor your whore of a mother slept with in Maui. Can you believe it? She tried to come to me, to get me to fuck her. Probably thought she could hide the truth, but I knew. I knew! She—"

I breathed out slowly, trying, one, to come to terms with my Star-Wars-Luke-I-am-your-father-moment and, two, to thank my lucky stars that Jordan wasn't my brother.

That would have been the flipping twist to end all twists in the sordid tale that was my childhood.

"So why didn't you divorce her?"

He scoffed. "Robertses do not divorce. I wasn't about to pay her half of everything just because she couldn't keep her legs closed."

"Wow," I said. "I would have thought that a Roberts wouldn't get married without a prenup."

"Prenups are a requirement *now*. Believe me."

I sat down, leaned back against the tub. "I don't know if I can believe anything you say," I said.

"I think that's my line."

I ignored the quip and instead asked, "Why didn't you send me away? If you hate me so much, why keep me in your life?"

"I don't hate you," he said, then his voice went hard. "Or I didn't until you pulled your little stunt today."

I shrugged even though he couldn't see it. "Hopefully that will teach you not to take things that aren't yours."

"I've got some of the best coders in the industry."

"*Some*, I think, is the key word," I shot back. "RoboTech has the absolute best working on this and"—I pulled my phone from my ear to check the time—"I'd open my email in about five minutes. I think you'll be canceling that release."

"What did you do?"

"Let's just say, if you're pissed now, I expect a monumental explosion when you open that email." I pressed on when he tried to interrupt, saying, "I don't understand anything about what happened between my mother and you. Why the elaborate gifts and birthday parties?" I laughed though it wasn't humor-filled. "I guess I understand why you were so forceful when it came to sending me away to boarding school after she left. But everything beyond that, I don't get. Why the job offer? Why the trust fund? Why pay for college?"

He was quiet for so long that I thought he'd hung up.

"Money is the easy part," he said. "Emotions are too complicated."

"That's it?" I asked when he didn't say anything else.

"That's it."

Wow. Somehow, that didn't make me feel any better. No wonder my mother . . . *no*. That wasn't an excuse, no matter how cold and difficult my father—*Bernie*—was. There wasn't a justifiable reason for parading through lives and men and marriages, wreaking havoc as she pranced.

There was no reason to leave me behind.

"I guess I won't be over for Christmas tomorrow," I said.

"No. I don't think you should come."

A slice of pain pulsed through my heart.

"For the record," he said. "That trap you and Heather pulled off today was pretty good."

"I almost think that was a compliment," I said, forcing my feelings down and trying to keep my tone light. I could cry later, after I'd digested everything he said. Now, I wouldn't let him hear me crumble. "From the discerning Bernie Roberts. Someone knock me over with a feather." A fake laugh. "Good chat. Can't wait for the next one."

Just before I hung up, he spoke. "You were a beautiful baby, Abs."

Then he was gone.

God, my family was seriously fucked up.

SPENDING CHRISTMAS DAY at the hospital just a little more than a week after spending a birthday unconscious in the *same* hospital wasn't on any kid's wish list, but Hunter was a trooper nonetheless.

He was more alert than the days previous and super excited about the package Jordan brought in.

Which contained a prototype of RoboTech's robot. Complete in shiny, brightly colored packaging that I had designed.

Which looked amazing—but that was just my opinion—so I was extra nervous as he tore off the Santa print wrapping paper and studied the box.

"A robot!" he said, immediately ignoring all of the painstakingly designed details and tearing straight into the cardboard. "Can I make it move?"

Jordan nodded and helped him retrieve the little robot. "You sure can."

"And jump?"

Another nod.

"And talk?"

"Yes," Jordan said. "At least a few words."

I could have waxed poetic to him about the balance and composition, how I'd spent hours looking for the perfect shadow-free image that didn't have the models—a pair of six-year-old twins, one boy and one girl—looking like they were insane, crazed, or trying to murder each other.

But I didn't.

Because his enthusiasm to get inside the packaging was exactly why I'd spent so long creating it.

I didn't want kids to study the box in confusion—to try to figure out what was inside.

I wanted them to know the contents immediately . . . and then be unable to wait another second before tearing it open and playing with that toy.

Hunter doing just that pleased me beyond belief.

However, there was one detail he'd missed in his enthusiasm that I wanted to make sure he noticed.

That the little girl inside me, who'd felt so lonely and discarded, *needed* to make sure he understood. Because he was special and good and sweet and even though his father was gone and his mother had left, he still deserved to know that he was loved.

That Jordan loved him.

And that I loved him too, but that portion of the story could wait until another day.

Jordan was installing the batteries as I rounded the bed and started scooping up the paper and cardboard.

"Hey," I said, holding a piece up to Hunter. "Whose name is that?"

He frowned, little blond brows coming together for a half second before his eyes went wide. "That's *my* name!"

Jordan nodded. "Yeah, bud, it is."

"Cool!"

And then Hunter's attention went right back to the robot.

Which was exactly how it should have been.

I tossed the trash into the bin and then went to sit by Cecilia.

"This," I said, reaching into my purse and pulling out a card, "is for you."

"What?" Her eyes widened. "I-I didn't get you anything."

"You didn't have to," I said, closing her fingers around the envelope. "But a little birdie gave me hints about something you might like. And this is open-ended so you can use it when you're ready."

Cecilia's expression was careful. "Uh, okay?"

I smiled. "Okay is good. Just open it. I promise it will make more sense if you do."

She carefully tore open the envelope and pulled out what was inside. It was a round-trip plane ticket to Finland and behind that a voucher for a very special hotel.

Cecilia gasped. "For—"

I nodded. "For the Northern Lights. I heard that you really want to see them."

Her eyes filled with tears, her chin bobbed jerkily. "I-I do. I've always wanted to go, but I can't accept . . ."

Carefully, I closed her fingers around the papers. "You can." I narrowed my eyes at her. "Or rather, you *will*."

"Abby—"

"Shh," I said. "Just hug me and accept. And"—I touched her arm—"promise me that when we're out of the woods here, you'll go."

"I—" She sighed. "I don't know what to say."

"Don't say anything," I told her. "Hugs." I extended my arms, gesturing with my fingers at her to come on and do it already. "Then tuck that envelope into your purse and plan a trip."

"You're stubborn," she said, but hugged me all the same.

"Thank you for being there for Hunter," I whispered. "I don't know what he would have done without you."

"I love him," she said simply.

"And he loves you."

We both sniffed, holding tight until the sound of Hunter's unmistakable giggles reached us. Then we pulled back and gazed over at the boys. They were huddled on the bed, Jordan's arm around Hunter as he showed him how to program the robot.

"He loves him too," Cecilia said. "And you."

"I know." I smiled. "And the feeling is completely mutual."

THIRTY-TWO

Abby

"YOU!" Bec pointed a finger at Jordan, who'd answered the door. It was just after the New Year and we'd been planning a take out and movie night. "You need to shoo. And you"—she turned that finger to me—"need to be sitting on the couch, getting ready to be pampered."

Seraphina stood behind her, arms laden with bags. "Move it, princess," she said, nudging Bec to the side. "You were so worried about your manicure that you couldn't carry the bags, the least you could do is move that big ole butt of yours out of the way."

Bec made to smack her then stopped, flashing me her freshly painted nails. "Gel manicure," she stage-whispered. "I just didn't want to carry the bags."

Seraphina gasped in outrage. "You—"

"Ladies," Jordan interrupted firmly. "What's going on?" His gaze flicked to the doorway again. "Cecilia? Is everything okay?"

She nodded, glancing around uncomfortably. "Hunter's fine. Umm. Bec wouldn't take no for an answer."

"Heather's with Hunter for a few hours," Seraphina said. "Auntie time." She shooed him toward the hall. "Which means that you are going to go see a movie or go to the mall or something."

"What am I going to do at the mall?"

Seraphina rolled her eyes. "I don't know. I don't care. What I *do* care about is sneaking in a few hours of Abby time without you tagging along."

"Hey, that's—"

"We like you, God of Thunder," Bec said, "but you're cramping our style."

"I-uh—" Jordan turned to me and I tried not to smile. I knew my friends, knew they could railroad just about anyone, let alone someone with a soft heart like Jordan. All things considered, I was rather enjoying the show.

"Don't look at me," I said. "I love spending time with you."

Bec made a barfing sound. "Gross."

Jordan shook his head, crossed to the couch—Bec had pushed me down onto the cushions and covered my lap with a blanket. He kissed me, long and slow and deep, leaving me a breathless lump before he pulled away. "I'm coming back in two hours."

I nodded, maybe dumbly, definitely dazed as he climbed the stairs to our bedroom.

"Damn," Seraphina said, setting the stacks of bags on the coffee table. "I think I came just watching that. What happened to Hair-Trigger Hammer?"

I snorted. "Apparently he was just out of practice."

"I'd take some of that *out of practice*."

We all froze and stared at Cecilia, whose cheeks were bright pink.

"I—uh—" she stammered.

"Told you you'd love her," Bec said to Seraphina, nudging her with her elbow.

"Shh," Seraphina said. "You're being rude."

"*Both* of you are being ridiculous," I said and patted the couch. "Sit over here, Cecilia. I think I smell chocolate."

"We have dark chocolate," Bec said, dropping to her knees to begin unpacking bags. "It's good for the baby."

"And for us," Seraphina said, pulling out a pair of pajamas from a bag and tossing them at Cecilia. "These are for you."

Cecilia's eyes bugged out when she saw the tag. "These—I can't! They're too expensive."

"Girl," Bec said. "Your innuendo now means that we're forever friends and as such, you will accept all gifts of chocolate and ridiculously expensive pajamas forevermore."

I snorted.

"You must have really low standards for friendship," Cecilia muttered.

Then promptly clamped a hand over her mouth.

Seraphina and Bec glanced at each other then at me, bursting into laughter. "Well, that much is obvious," Bec said.

"Hey!" I laughed.

"Oh, my God." Cecilia closed her eyes. "I did not just say that."

"You did." Bec grinned. "Which just proves our friendship standards. We live by three rules: be snarky, make every conversation dirty, and wear extremely pricey but excessively cozy pajamas."

"Now go," Seraphina said. "Bathroom is the third door on the left."

I rolled my eyes at the idea of my best friend giving directions in my house—Cecilia had been over enough times by now to know every nook and cranny—and caught the pair that Seraphina tossed me.

"Maternity edition," she said, brushing her hand over the little bump that was my baby. "Go change."

"I'll help," Jordan quipped, waggling his eyebrows at me as

he came back into the room. He'd changed into jeans and put on a jacket.

"I bet you would," Bec cackled. "But we don't have seconds to spare."

Jordan's gaze met mine and he shook his head. Still, his eyes were amused. "Your friends are something else."

I grinned. "I know."

Bec took Jordan's arm and led him to the door to the garage. There she patted his cheeks—the upper then the lower—and shoved him out. "You'll do, Thor. You'll just do," she said as it slammed closed.

Clicking the lock, she turned back toward us. "Okay. I need chocolate and a movie that will make me cry. STAT."

Two Weeks Later

"Can we go? Can we go?" Hunter asked, little butt wiggling in his bed. "I'm ready to go home."

Hunter was being discharged today. Finally.

Well, the finally was all him. I personally thought that the stay was too short, that he should be monitored and under watch just to make sure everything was going okay. He had a new heart and so many things could go wrong and—

"Abby!"

I blinked. "Sorry, what?"

"Is it time to go?"

"We just need to wait for the doctor to put in the discharge instructions and we're out of here, bud," Jordan said, gathering up the last of Hunter's things and putting them into a clear plastic bag. "I'll run these to the car. You two good?"

Hunter sighed. "I want to go home."

"I know, honey," I said, signaling to Jordan that we were fine. "Unfortunately, these things sometimes just take time."

He scowled. "Where's CeCe?"

"At home, getting everything all ready for you."

Another sigh, but he turned back to the robot, tinkering again, adding more details, tweaking the programing—not that he would call it that. The Hunter robot was just learning a new trick. But I could see why it was the perfect toy for real life Hunter.

Something that would keep him semi-stationary.

It was hard to tell he'd had a transplant not even two months before. I'd never really realized how sick he was, how pale-gray and weak, until compared to this version of Hunter.

Healthy and pink-skinned.

"I want to come with you and Jordan," he said.

"Soon," I told him.

We needed to be within a half hour of the hospital and its transplant center for a few more months. Then Hunter would move into my—to *our*—house.

"But we'll visit every day," I said. "And Jordan will be there and—"

"Yeah."

I frowned. "What's going on, honey?"

"I—" Pale blue eyes filled with tears. "Are you going to leave, too?"

My heart clenched, but I forced my voice to stay calm. "No, honey. I'm afraid you're stuck with me."

"Okay," he said, but the word wasn't confident.

I wished there was something I could say that would make him believe that I was going to be around for the long haul, that I loved him too much already to possibly think about leaving and never coming back.

But I knew from personal experience it wasn't that easy.

Once a child's trust was truly broken . . . well, some things couldn't be repaired.

There were always cracks, valleys that never quite healed.

"Did you know my mom left too?" I asked, brushing back his hair.

His eyes flew up to mine, surprised.

"I was sad for a long time," I said. "But eventually I realized she hadn't left because of me."

Hunter's gaze fell to the bed. "If I hadn't gotten sick . . ."

I wrapped my arms tightly around him and said the only thing I could. "It's not your fault."

He shuddered, sniffed, and I held on.

"Sometimes things in life really suck. Sometimes things aren't fair. Sometimes people are mean." I pressed a kiss to his head. "But that's the time to hold on to people who are nice, who love you, and who see you for the awesome, wonderful eight-year-old you are."

Hunter's little arms wrapped around my waist. "I do have a robot named after me."

I smiled, feeling tears well in my eyes. "That you do."

My stomach fluttered and I gasped, pressing my hand to it.

"What?" Hunter asked, pulling back.

"It's nothing," I said, trying to memorize the feeling. It was the baby moving. I knew it. I felt that in the depths of my soul. And the tears that had been welling escaped from the corners of my eyes.

"Abby?"

"I'm fine," I said, dashing them away. I cried at cleaning commercials lately, so it wasn't a surprise that feeling my baby for the first time made me teary. But I didn't want to make Hunter worry.

"Is it the baby?"

My jaw dropped open. We hadn't mentioned one word about

the pregnancy, not wanting to add another layer of stress to the already stressful situation for Hunter. He'd been through so much that I didn't want him to think Jordan would drop him for a new baby.

But apparently, we hadn't been so good at hiding the fact that I was pregnant.

"The baby is fine," I quickly assured him when I saw the worried look on his face. "I just felt him or her move for the first time."

"Maybe it was my voice," Hunter said with a grin. "I bet he likes me already."

"That's a guarantee," I said, head spinning a bit with the speed of Hunter's conversational U-turns. "What makes you think the baby will be a boy?"

He lifted his chin. "I know."

"Okay," I said and stood. "Should I go see if we can hurry this process up a bit?"

"Yes!"

"Oh. Hunter?" I paused in the doorway. "How did you know about the baby?"

He gave me a look that was way too mature for someone his age. "I'm eight, Abby. I know things." A pause. "I hope Uncle Jordan marries you."

My breath caught as Hunter began tinkering with the robot again and I left the room thinking the child was right.

He knew things . . . *way* too many things.

I made a vow right then and there that he would know less of the adult—less hospitals, less family drama, less pain, and fear. I made a vow to let him get dirty, to help him make friends his age, to play football with him in the backyard, to break windows with foul balls, and stink up the laundry room with his shoes.

I made a vow to love that little boy like my own.

EPILOGUE

PART ONE

Jordan, Four Months Later

JORDAN SLID CAREFULLY from the bed and tucked the covers up under Abby's chin. Her brow puckered and he pressed a kiss there, loving the way the lines relaxed at his touch.

He loved everything about her, in fact.

Which was what today was about.

It was Abby's first Mother's Day, and he and Hunter had a hell of a day planned.

Well, it technically revolved around pajamas, cuddling on the couch, and watching cheesy movies.

Carter whimpered again, and Jordan turned to their week-old son, feeling his heart expand to the size of a watermelon. It was amazing how so much love could grow in a second, with a single glance, with only one touch.

People who didn't believe in love at first sight must not have had kids.

"Shh," he said softly, scooping him up and slipping from the room before the noise could wake Abby. She'd been up feeding him every two hours the night before and deserved a break.

As much as he wanted to help her, he didn't have the right parts. So aside from changing diapers and walking the halls with Carter to get him to settle, he couldn't do much to relieve the exhaustion that Abby must be feeling.

Hell, he felt half dead and he had hardly done anything.

Jordan walked down the hall and into the kitchen, putting a pot of coffee on to brew as he smiled down at his son.

Rosy cheeks, blue eyes that matched his own—he thought they would stay blue, though Abby thought they'd turn hazel— and wispy brown hair.

He was a squishy faced, chunky, little lump.

And Jordan loved him more than life itself.

"You're pretty special," he said. "Did you know that?" Wide eyes stared up at him, and he kept talking. Carter was probably hungry, but he wanted to give Abby as much sleep as possible.

He'd avoid waking her until he had to.

"You're so lucky. Your Mommy and I both love you very much, and you have a brother who's crazy about you." Jordan touched Carter's nose, smiling when his son rooted around. His delay tactics may not last long. "Because that's what Hunter is to you," he said, blabbering on against the losing battle anyway. "You're more than just cousins. You're brothers."

"Uncle Jordan?"

He looked up at the sound of Hunter's voice. It was as sleepy as his rumpled appearance—jammies wrinkled, hair askew.

"Yeah, bud?"

"Is that true?"

Jordan bounced Carter. "Is what true?"

"Is he really my brother?"

"Come here," he said, patting the barstool. "Family is a tricky thing. People get hung up on moms and dads and who is technically related to whom. But I don't think any of that matters." He held up Carter, who locked eyes on Hunter, the same way he did every time Hunter was in the room. "All I know is that Carter is going to need a big brother. That he's going to need lots of people in his life to love him." He wrapped one arm around Hunter's shoulders. "Just the same as you."

"I think I'd make a good big brother," Hunter said.

Jordan grinned. "I know you will. Window-breaker."

"It was an accident!" Hunter hung his head. "I didn't realize that it would . . ."

Jordan raised a brow. "Break? If you hit a ball really hard?" He nudged him. "I thought Abby would lose a gasket."

Hunter nodded emphatically. "Me too."

Instead, all she'd done was smile, shake her head, and tell Jordan to call someone to fix it.

Carter let out another squawk, this one more determined and louder.

"I think Mommy's time is up," Jordan said. "While Abby is feeding Carter, let's get everything ready, okay?"

"Okay!" Hunter nodded and ran off in the direction of the living room. "I'll get the pajamas!"

He stared down at Carter, his first biological son but the second son of his heart. "I love that kid."

Carter cooed.

Jordan crossed the kitchen, opened the cabinet above the fridge—the one Abby deemed as unusable because she was so short—and pulled out the little box he'd stashed within.

Pajamas. Chocolate. Bad movies. Check. Check. Check.

He stashed the ring in her basket of yarn and set it on the coffee table as Hunter ran like a tornado gathering the pajamas and a cozy blanket and turning on the T.V.

"Good?" he asked.

Hunter gave him a thumbs-up and Jordan turned down the hall, cuddling Carter close as he walked. Carefully, he turned the knob and crept into the bedroom, wanting to wake Abby gently.

But she was already up, eyes heavy, hair crazy, and more beautiful than anyone else on the planet.

"Hey," he said.

She smiled. "Hey, honey."

"Someone is hungry," he said. "I tried to delay him, but I wasn't successful."

"Tell that to my boobs." She pointed to the part of her body that had grown to rival Seraphina's set and grimaced. "They apparently know that Carter is hungry."

He set Carter in her arms. "I'm going to take a quick shower while you feed him."

In reality, he was taking a quick shower for two reasons: one, boobs—as in, hers were on display and giant and he wanted to touch them, but he couldn't—and two, he was nervous about proposing.

Which was ridiculous. They'd discussed marriage. They were planning on adopting Hunter, had just had a kid together.

It was a sure thing.

And he didn't want to screw it up.

"Okay," she said, her focus on Carter.

Probably a good thing, otherwise she would have seen that he was a mess.

Ten minutes later, he was clean and ready. Hunter knocked on the bedroom door as Jordan emerged from the bathroom in fresh clothes . . . or fresh pajamas. He glanced at Abby, who nodded. Carter had finished eating. He reached for the knob—

"Happy Mother's Day!" Hunter announced, launching himself on the bed.

Jordan shook his head. The boy never walked when sprinting would do.

"Thanks, sweetie," Abby said, hugging him with her free arm. "Did you sleep okay?"

"Yup. Here." He dropped the package on the bed. "These

are for you. Jordan and I planned a day with your favorite things."

Her eyes rose to meet Jordan's. He nodded. "Chocolate. Hallmark movies. The works." One side of his mouth quirked. "We'll even let you have a shower first."

"My heroes," she quipped and slid from the bed. "Or maybe you're saying that I *need* a shower?"

"Definitely."

She snorted, rose on tiptoe to press a kiss to his lips. "Thanks for that." A glint in mischievous hazel eyes. "Do I need to bust out the hammer jokes?"

"God, no." He took Carter from her. "Enjoy your uninterrupted shower," he told her. "I've got the boys."

"I love you," she whispered.

"Right back at you."

Shaking her head, she went into the bathroom. Hunter helped him change Carter—or rather picked out fresh clothes while Jordan dealt with the *nasty* diaper business, as Hunter liked to call it.

By the time they'd gotten Carter settled and Hunter a bowl of cereal for breakfast, Abby was done with her shower.

Hunter dropped his bowl in the sink when she came into the kitchen. "Come this way!" He took her hand, dragging her into the family room.

Jordan's heart skipped a beat and he wiped sweaty palms on his shirt. "This is it, bud," he whispered to Carter. "I hope she says yes."

Carter blinked up at him.

"I know." Jordan laughed. "I'll be lucky if she does."

He walked into the next room, smiling when he saw Hunter fussing over Abby—arranging the pillows behind her back, positioning the remote at just the right distance. He met Jordan's eyes and nodded at the basket, a nonverbal cue to get moving.

"Can I hold Carter?" he asked, moving to the armchair and sitting down, arms extended.

"Sure, bud," Jordan said, helping him to settle back and support Carter's head.

Abby's eyes were soft. "They're so sweet together," she said, watching Hunter hold Carter.

"Yes, they are." He reached for the basket, opened his mouth—

"And *this* is sweet," she said. "You guys are going to spoil me. How did you get these chocolates? I've never seen them anywhere except in Switzerland."

He shrugged. "I flew them in. Abby—"

"You *flew* them in?" She gasped. "That must have been ridiculously expensive."

"I wanted to make today special."

"It would have been special without chocolate." Jordan lifted a brow and she grinned. "Okay maybe not."

"Abby"—he went down on one knee next to the coffee table —"I wanted to ask if you would—"

"Oh, my God. Is that new yarn?" She clapped her hands together before reaching for the basket. "It's gorgeous."

"*Abby.*" He caught her hands before she could grab it. "Shush for a second, okay?"

She blinked.

"I'm trying to ask you something."

Her eyes drifted from the basket in his hands to his position on one knee.

"A-are you—?"

"Yup." He held up the basket. "I wanted to ask if you would crochet with me."

There was one beat of silence before she smacked him in the chest. "Jordan O'Keith, so help me . . ."

He pulled out the box and set the basket down. "Abigail

Roberts. We've done this all sorts of backward, but I can't imagine spending my life without you. Will you marry me?"

The box made a little creak as he opened it, showing off what was an obscenely-sized princess cut diamond ring inside. But he'd never had any restraint when it came to Abby, and he'd definitely not had any when it came to the ring she was going to wear for the rest of her life.

"No."

Or maybe not.

"What?" He set the box down, took her hand. "It's okay if it's too soon. I just—"

She laughed, yanking him close. "I'm sorry, I couldn't resist." She kissed him. "I would be honored to be your wife."

He kissed her long enough to warrant a "gross" from Hunter and pulled back to slip the ring on her finger. "I'm going to pay you back for that one," he said.

Her hand came up to cup his cheek. "I hope so," she murmured. "For the rest of our lives."

And he kissed her again, ignoring the retching sound Hunter made.

He had his happily ever after, dammit, and he was going to enjoy it.

BAD BREAKUP

BILLIONAIRE'S CLUB BOOK 2

ONE

Cecilia

CECILIA SAT ON THE PLANE, her first-class seat luxurious and insanely comfortable. It might have been the first time in her limited travel experience that she didn't feel like cattle shoved into the back of a truck, and instead, like an actual person with wants and needs.

"Your champagne, Ms. Thiele."

"Thank you," she said and took a sip, leaning back into the butter-soft leather with a sigh.

She'd just closed her eyes when someone sat down in the empty seat next to her.

Rustling accompanied the movement as the person got settled.

"Can I get you anything?" the flight attendant asked.

"A whiskey."

Every hair stood up on Cecilia's neck. Oh, *God* no. It couldn't possibly be—

She clenched her lids tightly, refusing, absolutely refusing to open them. No. She was imagining things. It had been years since she'd heard that voice.

Too many years.

"Here you go, Mr. McGregor."

Oh, fuck.

Her eyes flew open, but she didn't move her head. She couldn't chance it. But she did risk a peek out of the corner of her eye, and that was enough to have dread twisting her stomach into knots.

No. It couldn't be.

She'd booked this flight last minute, deciding to use the voucher gifted to her by Abby—her friend and employer—after she and her husband, Jordan, had returned from their honeymoon.

Cecilia's life had felt stagnant.

She'd needed to get away, and she'd had the free flight and hotel.

It made sense to use it, however last minute.

Plus, everything had worked out. There had been one first-class seat open. Only one cabin at her dream resort.

And now she was sitting next to Colin McGregor.

"Flight attendants, arm the doors," the pilot's voice chimed through the plane's speakers.

A *thud* signaled the disappearance of her last avenue of escape.

She was trapped on a nonstop flight for twelve hours.

With the man who'd left her at the altar.

How was this possibly her life?

"Cecilia?" that masculine voice asked. "Is it really you?"

And just like all the times before, her eyes were drawn to him. She'd never been able to ignore him. Not Colin. Not even when he'd—

But this time was different.

She wasn't weak. She wasn't a vulnerable girl in a rough place.

She'd been through Hell and back.

Colin had no power over her.

Not anymore.

Cecilia put in her earbuds and turned her back on the man who'd devastated her world six years before.

TWO

Cecilia

SHE WAS GOING TO YELL "BOMB!" on an airplane.

She *had* to.

It was the only way to get the plane to turn around, for CeCe to find an escape route from the awful man sitting next to her. He'd been staring at her for three hours twenty-two minutes and forty-six seconds. Forty-seven. Forty-eight—

Okay. The precise timing wasn't important.

But the heavy weight of his gaze was smothering her, a stifling cloud that threatened to drive her insane. And it was exacerbated by his smell, all spicy and male. It floated around her, making her toes curl.

He was the same as before.

As in, he had *exactly* the same effect on her body—an accelerated pulse, sweaty palms, a tense quivering abdomen, and heat between her thighs.

She wanted him.

Despite it having been six years since she'd seen him. Despite what he had done.

Cecilia's body still wanted Colin's with a longing that was so intense it was almost scary.

Her lady bits wanted her to tug him up from his seat by the tie—a new addition, as she'd never seen the man in a suit—drag him up the aisle, and lock him in the ridiculously small bathroom to have her merry way with him.

Hence, the bomb threat.

Which, obviously, she couldn't make.

It might be torture sitting next to Colin, but there were three hundred other people on this airplane, all with places to be, people to visit, sights to see. She couldn't ruin that for them.

Not that Colin McGregor would care he was ruining it for *her*. He crushed dreams, smashed hearts, tore tender emotions to shreds.

He was her Godzilla, and she was the decimated city.

Had been the decimated city.

But now she was rebuilt. She was stronger, her heart reinforced with rebar and steel, and she didn't give one damn for Colin McGregor.

If only she could convince her body of that fact.

Damns to give or not, she still didn't want him within arm's reach and so, shortly after takeoff, she'd risen and discreetly asked the flight attendant if there was any way she could switch seats, only to receive a regretful glance and an apology as the flight was completely full and all the first-class seats were occupied by couples or families traveling together.

She'd even started to ask about moving back to economy, thinking to make someone's day by offering them a seat by the gorgeous Scot, but the flight attendant had looked so harried that Cecilia had relented.

She knew they had a job to do and that she was getting in the way of it, and while she didn't want to be a pain in the ass, her current situation was truly untenable.

"You're even more beautiful than I remember," he said, and

the rough edges of his accent hacked at the words, making them more of a growl rather than a soft sentiment.

Her breath caught, and she found her eyes drawn to the stormy blue of Colin's.

And she stared again, utterly entranced before she remembered how it had all ended.

Her in a white dress.

Alone, except for the priest, who'd given her a pitying look and invited her to stay as long as she needed.

But it had always been like this, Colin's gruff words winning her over. They were unexpected from him—he was typically so reserved and taciturn. And that compliment, freely given as it was, chipped away at any defenses she had managed to erect.

The problem was that his words weren't always followed up by action. In fact, they were typically trailed by pain for her and fury for him.

The hurt of those memories—of Colin so angry, her so broken—helped shore up her resolve.

"Don't say things like that," she snapped and started to pop her earbuds back in. Her friends at home had filled her phone with a slew of romantic audiobooks, and she decided that she much preferred fictional heroes at the moment.

At least if they broke their heroine's heart, it was only once.

Colin had already broken hers twice.

She wasn't looking for a round three.

But before she had the chance to insert the earbud, his fingers gripped her wrist. "Don't ignore me," Colin said, all high-and-mighty, all arrogant, rich Scottish duke.

Well, she wasn't a little girl anymore, wasn't a fresh-faced recent high school graduate taking a summer trip, wasn't even a slightly disillusioned college dropout. *No.* She was more experienced, and at twenty-six, she knew she'd had enough of wealthy, powerful men.

"You don't belong here."

"If you were worth anything at all, your parents wouldn't have disowned you."

The memory of Colin's words were bullets, stealing her breath as they shot forward in her mind to strike home.

She'd been so naïve, so stupid, so . . . completely in love.

And he'd destroyed her.

Twice.

What was the saying? Fool her once and shame on him, but fool her twice and shame on her?

Yeah. *That.*

Shame on her. For being a fucking idiot. For putting herself out there. For being a glutton for punishment.

"Let me go, Colin," she said, yanking at her wrist until he was either forced to release her or make a scene. He chose to let go. Of course, he did. Because McGregors didn't make scenes. They functioned in the background, skulking, stalking, waiting for the moment their prey faltered and they could pounce.

And to show her that he was still in control, that he was stronger than her and was only loosening his grip because *he* wanted to, Colin did it slowly, sliding fingertip by fingertip free, dragging them across her skin and raising goose bumps in their wake.

"I already did that once," he said, putting his arm back onto his armrest. A lock of jet-black hair fell across his forehead as he leaned in to meet her eyes. "And it was the biggest mistake of my life."

"Twice," she whispered, her throat tight, her heart pounding. There was an invitation in his gaze. He would accept her. She could crawl into his arms, get lost in an embrace that once upon a time had protected her from anything bad in the universe.

Except with Colin, that peaceful, sheltered feeling never *actually* lasted.

His expression clouded and she might have said he looked

confused. But Colin was never anything less than one hundred percent completely sure of himself.

That was why he'd broken her so completely the second time.

So, she ignored the invitation in his eyes, turned her back on him again, and tried to pretend that she didn't feel like crying.

Her once-in-a-lifetime adventure was off to a brilliant start.

THREE

Colin

SHE STILL SMELLED of vanilla and jasmine. Her head still fit perfectly under his chin.

Colin inhaled deeply, knowing that if someone caught him, he'd end up looking like a bloody idiot. It was worth it anyway. Cecilia's scent hit him right in the gut, unfurling in his stomach and spreading through his limbs.

It smelled like home and also like his biggest regret.

She sighed in her sleep, turning over and nuzzling close, and her hair tickled his nose, just like it used to. God damn, did that make his heart ache.

And now, she was in his arms again.

What was the American expression? A summer fling? They'd had two of them. Except, it hadn't just been a fling for him. Not *either* time.

He'd given her a ring.

Had actually been heading to the altar when he'd discovered she'd run off with his best friend.

He'd been hurt and too angry for answers at the time. Then

later, when that fury had finally calmed enough that he'd wanted those answers, his family had imploded, and he hadn't been able to spare a moment for his idiotic emotional needs.

A month after CeCe had left him, his father had dropped dead, apoplectically screaming at a tenant for some perceived slight. And while Colin wasn't terribly sad to see the old bastard go, he *had* been nearly sunk by the responsibilities of inheriting the multitude of McGregor estates and businesses. He'd needed to dive in, to streamline because the family was bleeding money and would have been out on their asses if he hadn't taken the time to learn every detail of each of the companies before deciding which to sell and which to keep. It had taken years before he'd been able to breathe freely, but he was there.

And the deal with RoboTech further ensured that.

The McGregor coffers were secure. His family was safe. And . . . now what?

Or at least, that was what he'd *been* thinking before he'd sat down next to Cecilia on the plane.

Now, his focus was clear and revolved around a certain waifish redhead with piercing green eyes.

Though he supposed waifish wasn't the right term for her, not any longer. Six years ago, she'd still been a girl. Today, Colin found himself holding a woman, still slender and petite, but full of curves that his hands itched to cup.

She sighed and shifted in the circle of his arms, and he knew that it wouldn't be much longer before she woke. She'd slipped off about forty-five minutes after deliberately trying to ignore him again, but though her mind might be in favor of rejecting any interaction with him, her body seemed to have a different tack. As sleep had swept through her, she'd slumped against him, first her back then her shoulders and head, and then nearly all of her when he'd slid an arm around her to shift her into a more comfortable position.

Her head was tucked just beneath his chin, one arm

wrapped around his waist, the other dangling between them and resting on the outside of his thigh.

Thank God it was on the *outside*, otherwise he might have embarrassed himself.

She shifted again, and Colin took one more inhale, knowing that she would hate both him and herself when she woke and found them tangled together.

The cabin lights flicked on, and CeCe breathed out slowly. She inhaled, and he felt her breath catch through the cotton of his shirt. Her back went stiff, her hand at his waist curled into a fist.

It was obvious the moment she was fully awake. Mainly because the second she was, Cecilia did her best impression of a cat being wrangled for a visit with the vet. She clawed at his chest, trying to shove herself back into her own seat, and in the process managed to both nearly unman him and catch a chunk of her hair on the buttons of his shirt.

"Jesus, woman," he ground out, grabbing her hips to steady her flailing movements. She struggled, her elbow connecting with his midsection and then *lower*. Okay, that was enough. He pinned her against him, trapping those dangerous limbs between them. "I'd like to keep that part. Just hold still."

"Let me go," she snapped.

"Certainly," he replied. "Or at least I will, once you've released yourself from my shirt."

Finally, she stopped fighting him. "What?"

"Your hair is stuck . . ."

Fingers came up to feel her scalp, and she winced when she found the tangle. "Oh."

"If you'll allow me"—she snorted, and he ignored it—"I'll release you." But despite the tension in her frame, CeCe didn't move as he gently worked the locks free. "There," he eventually said, smoothing a hand down her head and tucking an errant strand behind her ear.

She lurched off him and back into her own seat. "Thanks," she muttered and swept her hair up into some sort of intricate twist that exposed the back of her neck—

His heart stopped.

He reached across the armrest and gripped both of her arms, fury suddenly filling every cell in his body. "What have you done?"

Where once there had been soft red tendrils, curls he'd loved twisting around his finger as he'd trailed kisses down her nape, now there was nothing but shorn locks, so short that he could see—

CeCe frowned. "It's been six years. I cut my hair. Big deal."

"Not the haircut," he gritted out. "*That* I like. It suits you." And it did. The bigger question was, "Why the fuck do you have another man's name tattooed on your neck?"

FOUR

Cecilia

SHE FROZE at Colin's question, struggling to comprehend, her brain still foggy from sleep.

No. Her brain was a mess because she'd woken up in Colin's arms.

"*Cecilia*," he said, and her fingers drifted up to the name tattooed just beneath her hairline.

She was unused to people noticing it, since she usually wore her hair down or in a low ponytail, but she'd just gotten her hair cut and liked the feel of the air hitting her scalp where the stylist had used clippers to trim it short. There was something about the way it felt . . .

Free.

She rolled her eyes.

Or so she'd thought.

Cue her sitting next to the man who'd broken her heart.

"Who's Hunter?" Colin snapped, dropping his hands from her arms, preferring, apparently, to glare down at her.

CeCe stiffened. Hunter was . . . well, he was special. The special-est—was that even a word?—boy she'd ever met. And she—

"I love him," she said softly, not thinking what the words would mean to Colin, who couldn't begin to understand her relationship with Hunter.

He was hers, but not.

Kind of like the man sitting next to her had been.

Colin made a noise very much like a growl and scowled at her. "You *love* him?"

It was truly a pleasure to make a man like Colin McGregor squirm. One might be frightened because he was huge, with arms like tree trunks, shoulders nearly twice the breadth of hers, brows dark black and yanked together, but Colin had never hurt her.

Not physically anyway.

And besides that, he couldn't possibly begin to understand what her relationship with Hunter was.

She'd been part nanny, part mother, part sister, and *all* friend to the sick little boy before he'd gotten a heart transplant the previous year. Now, he was still a friend and a little brother and a son and . . . not hers. He belonged with Abby and Jordan. He had a family. He was happy and adjusted and finally, *finally* healthy.

But he would always hold a chunk of her heart.

"He's eight," she murmured. "Or rather, he's nearly nine now."

Colin stiffened. His eyes were wide, almost panicked, and it only took her a heartbeat to understand why.

"Your math's off," she said lightly. Because she understood with crystal clarity why he was so concerned. "If you'd knocked me up, we'd have a *seven*-year-old."

They'd slept together eight years ago. For the first time. She internally sighed since it had also been the last time. But the crazed look in Colin's eyes wasn't so much because of Hunter or her tattoo or even whether or not she'd been pleased by the events (and yes, she had been, despite fumbling on both their parts). Instead, the terror was because he was worried she might have kept a child from him.

Rage filled her. Did he honestly think she wouldn't have told him when they'd nearly gotten *married?* What would she have done after the wedding? Surprise! Here's the two-year-old you helped create!

Fucking moron.

"Hunter isn't mine," she snapped. "Or yours, either." One earbud in. "He was just a boy I nannied for." She shoved in the other. "And while your family may lie about information that could make or break another person, I would never do such a thing. You didn't get me pregnant, Colin, and I thank God every day for that fact."

"What?" His brows rose. "That's not—"

But she didn't hear the rest of his words because she cranked up her audiobook.

And heard all of one sentence before Colin plucked the buds from her ears and snatched her phone from her grip. He glanced down at the screen. "This rubbish comes in audiobooks now?"

Once the brogue would have sent warmth down her spine. Today, that warmth was still present, though it was in the form of embarrassment.

Because the audiobook was about a Scot and an English-woman, the former stealing the latter away and teaching her all there was to know about pleasure and life in the Highlands. It was filled with kilts and beards, with sporrans and fabulous dresses and it was . . . so fucking embarrassing.

Once, he'd been *her* Highlander.

She'd drooled over his kilt, admired his legs as he'd straddled his mount.

He'd shown her pleasure. A single night of glorious, soul-shattering pleasure before disappearing from her life for years.

"Give that back," she hissed, but he merely ignored her and put one of the earbuds in and—horror of all freaking horrors—began to listen in.

A strand of black hair curled across his forehead as he turned his stare to hers.

His innocent stare. Except it wasn't innocent. The man next to her was about as far from that sentiment as one could humanly be.

"Stop," she snapped, extending her hand. "You're not cute, and the guileless little boy eyes won't work on me. Give. Me. My. Phone."

"I don't sound like that," he muttered, but took out the earbud and returned her cell. "That is the most inaccurate genre of books I've ever come across. I can't believe you still read—"

"I don't care if it's accurate or not"—she glowered—"but these authors do a ton of research, so I have faith in them. And plus, it's *fiction*. I'm allowed to get lost in the story, just for the pleasure of it. Just because I enjoy it." She stopped, chest heaving, cheeks hot. She hated when people judged her because of the books she read. So, what if she read romance? The stories and writing were good, and didn't everyone deserve a happily-ever-after?

Even if those HEAs didn't always materialize in real life.

"If you want to really learn about Scotland, you should read a history book," he said. "Or maybe a biography. Or *visit*."

Her heart squeezed tight at the old argument they'd had on a regular basis. "I've read loads of history books," she whispered. "And I did visit. Or don't you remember?"

Blue eyes held hers. "I remember." A pause. "All too well."

Ouch.

She blinked before glancing down at her hands. "Yeah, well. I wasn't exactly planning on this."

"On what?" He turned to face her more fully, his elbow encroaching on her armrest, his scent teasing her nose, that damned lock of hair still falling across his forehead and making her ache to smooth it back into place. "On being trapped next to me for twelve hours?"

She shook her head. "On ever seeing you again."

FIVE

Colin

THE WORDS WERE a physical blow to Colin's gut. He knew CeCe was hurt. That *he'd* hurt her. But frankly, they'd hurt each other, and to actually hear her speak words like that aloud was brutal.

On what?

On ever seeing you again.

Like an idiot, he'd pressed her, and like a moron, he'd expected to hear something different. Some explanation for why she'd left him for his best friend. Why the woman he'd imagined spending the rest of his life with had betrayed him so deeply and abandoned him.

"Well, you nearly accomplished it," he said. "Do you live in San Francisco now? Or was that just a stopover?"

She sighed. "Are we really doing this?"

"Doing what?"

"Small talk." Her words were like ice, little frosty bullets that threatened to wound. "Pretending to be old friends."

His hold on his temper was getting decidedly more tenuous.

He bent so his nose was nearly pressed to hers. "You left, sweetheart. *You left me.* So, if anyone has a right to be pissed, it's me. I needed you, and you fucking *left.*"

Her shoulders had risen with each of his snapped statements until they were practically covering her ears. He'd hated when she used to do that, curling into herself, protecting rather than fighting.

She'd done that, he remembered, far too often with his family during their engagement, after he'd won her back the first time. When his family had lobbed their quote, unquote *friendly* rejoinders her way.

And she'd done it that day on the cliffside eight years before when she'd declared her love for him and he'd panicked, before walking away from her.

But now CeCe dropped her shoulders, and *her* temper joined the party. "I left? *I. Left. You—*" Her eyes closed for a heartbeat, and he watched a deep breath slide through her lungs. "You know what? It doesn't matter."

It mattered to him. A whole hell of a lot.

But she was still talking, and he soaked up all the information he could.

"I live north of the city. I've"—she shook her head—"I was at loose ends for a while, but then I got the job as a nanny. Hunter is the sweetest boy."

Her lips curved, teasing him, reminding him of how it had been to kiss that smile, to twine his hand through her hair, tug her close, and feel those lips against his.

"He got sick pretty young and needed a heart transplant. But he got one last year and—"

Colin touched her hand when she faltered, and those green eyes went shiny with tears.

"He's just so much better now. Healthy and running and . . . I just love him so much." She sniffed. "But he doesn't need me anymore, and so I'm"—she laughed darkly—"God, I don't even know why I'm telling you any of this."

"Except that maybe I understand what it's like to be at a crossroads."

CeCe froze and glanced up at him. After a moment, she murmured, "Yeah. I suppose you would."

"How are your parents?"

It was the wrong question. Her face closed down, and she slipped her hand out from beneath his, clutching it to her chest as though he'd burned her.

And maybe he had.

"They're fine."

"Cecilia." He reached for her again, cursing under his breath when she cringed away from him. "What happened?"

"You know what happened," she said, her words soft and yet somehow more piercing than her harsh tone from earlier. "They said if I went, they were done." A shrug. "And I went."

"*What?*" He'd expected them to have come to their senses, to have put aside the grudge they'd harbored when she'd chosen not to go to their preferred college.

How could they have shut her out?

An unpleasant feeling unfurled in his stomach. Same way he had, he supposed.

She laughed, but it sounded off. "Oh, Colin." The pity was palpable. "I know you're used to breaking your promises, but there are plenty of people who hold firm to theirs." Another laugh, this one filled with so much fatigue that it physically made his heart ache. "And my parents have always been nothing but firm."

His tongue was glued to the roof of his mouth. She implied that he'd broken *his* promises? She was the one who'd betrayed him and then left. But more than that, how could her parents have abandoned her? How could they have just left her to make her own way because she hadn't done exactly as they wished?

What the fuck was wrong with them?

He hadn't realized that he'd spoken the last aloud until CeCe touched his hand. "I knew what I was getting into. And I was a grown woman. It was time that I found my own way."

"You were *twenty*."

She pulled her hand back, twisting in her seat so that she faced him, but also so she was physically as far as possible from him. "An adult."

He scoffed. "A foolish one." Everyone was an idiot at twenty.

Hurt flashed across her emerald eyes, but she nodded before saying softly, "Yes. Yes, I was."

The foolish for trusting *him* was only implied, but it still weighted the air between them.

"Why did you leave me? Why did you run off with Ewan?" He finally asked it outright, needing to hear it from her lips. Maybe then—

Maybe *what*?

"You really don't remember?" she asked.

He shook his head. "I remember the whiskey. I remember seeing the papers, the journal, the *pictures*. But the rest of it is black." He thrust a hand through his hair. "When I woke up, you were gone. And I couldn't find you."

"Colin." She sighed. "I can't do this. Not again."

Another clench of his gut. "But—"

She waved a hand through the air in a slicing motion. "I *had* to go. Can't we just leave it at that?"

No. They damn well couldn't. Not when he'd pictured her in his arms for eternity. Not when he'd imagined their children. Not when he'd fantasized about waking every morning next to her. Not when—

"And it was for the best anyway. We were too young, too immature. It would have never worked out."

"*It would have worked out*." He pressed his thumb to her lips when she opened her mouth to protest. "I would have bloody well fought tooth and nail to make it work."

Her eyes filled with tears again, making those green irises shine with a force that hit him exactly where it hurt.

"Except you didn't fight for me, Colin." She yanked her head back. *"You didn't."*

SIX

Colin

HE STARED into CeCe's eyes, hating that they were filled with unshed tears. That *he* had been the cause of her hurt.

"Except you didn't fight for me, Colin," she'd said.

He hadn't gotten a chance to respond because Cecilia jumped out of her seat and bolted for the bathroom. By the time she came out, ten minutes later, the flight attendants were serving breakfast and she had plenty of time to erect her walls of privacy against him.

Namely those earbuds.

But also, by striking up a conversation with the woman in front of them, who'd dropped a book that CeCe had returned.

By the time the women had finished chatting and the breakfast plates were cleared, the plane was descending.

And Colin was trapped beside her, unable to break the silence.

Well, *unable* wasn't the correct word.

He *could* just start talking. The trouble was he didn't even know where to begin. The past was a series of landmines between them, and he'd always thought that he was the one most wronged, that CeCe had returned to Scotland the second time to punish him for his idiotic immaturity of their first summer together, that she'd seduced him and purposely broken his heart because he'd hurt her in the past. Now, he was wondering if it were possible that he'd gotten it all wrong.

His mother, *hell*, even his sister had confirmed that Cecilia had run off with his best friend—*former* best friend, that was.

But she'd said he hadn't fought for her.

Was it possible . . . could he have it all wrong?

Especially because Colin was beginning to understand that his family could sometimes manipulate him.

It was both fortunate and not, that he'd witnessed the manipulation firsthand when they had sabotaged his buyout of Jordan O'Keith's technology firm the previous year. They'd cost him millions of dollars and hundreds of hours of his and his employees' time because they *"couldn't stomach being associated with an American."*

It was only by pure dumb luck that he'd run into Heather O'Keith, Jordan's half-sister and the woman who'd ended up buying out InDTech, now named RoboTech, at a conference a few months ago and had been able to explain himself.

He'd apologized, knowing there was no going back and that the millions were lost for eternity.

But Heather had surprised him by offering to hear his ideas for a mutually beneficial working relationship . . . if he had any. Which he hadn't, of course. Not at that time, anyway. He'd been stuck on the missed opportunity and disappointed he wasn't working with technology that would truly make the world a better place.

So, he'd told her he would put something together and contact her with an agreement she couldn't refuse.

What a fanciful thought. She'd rebuffed his first three offers, until finally he'd struck the right cord, and they'd begun brainstorming on unmanned aircraft technology and how it could be implemented in the third world.

War zones. Natural disasters. How could they get food, water, and medical supplies in when the conditions were too dangerous for personnel?

They didn't have all the answers yet, but now his biomedical robotic company was going to be working closely with RoboTech for the next five years on developing such technology.

He was finally getting close to something that wasn't just money, that wasn't solely based on shareholders and profit-and-loss statements.

Colin was finally doing something worthwhile.

It had taken him long enough.

Still, Heather's initial refusals on his projects had changed him in a way he hadn't expected. Typically, if someone didn't want to work with him, he said fuck off and went and completed the project on his own. And when it was complete, he then made it his life's duty to make them regret the rejection.

So, there were not many people who didn't work with him.

Until Heather.

"You going to go cry to mama?" she'd interrupted as they'd spoken over the phone, scorn in her every syllable when he'd begun to threaten along his usual tack. *"Not used to being subpar? Going to run off and pout like a little boy who doesn't want to try harder to make it better?"*

He'd been so infuriated that his words had stoppered up in his throat.

"RoboTech is the best," she'd gone on. *"And we never stop trying to get better. Until you're ready to be all in with that, I'm sorry, but both you and your projects are useless to me."*

And then she'd hung up.

He'd sat there, stunned, surprised, infuriated. But she'd been right.

He *had* been a spoiled brat in his business dealings, throwing his temper around when he didn't get his way.

He'd been a twenty-eight-year-old man throwing a bloody tantrum.

Pathetic.

Colin was more thankful for Heather than she would ever know. She'd propelled him into a change for the better, and he was finally, *finally* a man who could hold his head high.

Pride was a fickle beast, and he'd always gripped his tightly—whether he'd been right or wrong or somewhere in between. But Heather had helped him see differently, and so he was truly on a healthier path now.

His businesses functioned better, he wasn't chained to a desk all day, every day, and he was finally finding a way out of the dark tunnel that had been his life after his father's death.

And what was the first thing he'd seen after emerging from the opposite end?

Cecilia.

More beautiful than ever, but with shadows in her eyes and hurt coloring every word.

What had he done to her?

What had his family done?

They'd witnessed her running off with Ewan Campbell. He'd *seen* the proof in pictures.

But what if he'd been wrong?

What if he'd stopped searching for Cecilia too soon? What if—?

Fuck.

He was filled to the brim with "what ifs" and not any of them made a difference. Because she was here. Now. And this time, he wasn't going to let her go.

SEVEN

Cecilia

CECILIA WAS thankful to be staying in London for a night. She wouldn't really get to see anything, but she planned on a longer stopover on her way back to the States.

For now, she was happy for a hotel, some non-airplane food, along with a hot shower and soft bed.

Not that she'd been uncomfortable in Colin's arms.

"Shut up," she muttered, reaching for her phone and stuffing it into her tote bag, along with her pillow, her lip balm, and the seventy-three other things she'd managed to strew around during the twelve-hour flight.

"Pardon?" Colin's voice was slightly rasped, almost sounding unused, and not at all indicative of the fact that they'd just been arguing an hour before.

"Sorry," she said. "I was talking to myself."

His lips twitched, his beard glinting slightly in the airplane's overhead lights. And why hadn't she noticed it earlier?

The beard was very Chris Evans as Captain America—the second Avengers version where he looked all yummy and scruffy and beyond sexy. Except Colin was a Scot and his accent added a whole other layer of deliciousness that was truly unfair to the female populace.

"So. Not. Fair."

One black brow sprang up.

She sighed, mentally slapping herself. "Sorry. I'm doing it again."

He grinned and her panties melted, just slipped right down off her thighs. Okay fine, so the underwear magic act was a complete and utter fantasy, but his effect on her lady parts was not.

She still wanted him.

Once had definitely not been enough, and their single attempt at learning one another certainly highlighted that fact.

He'd given her an orgasm . . . before penetration, that was, but he'd promised her more, better, *longer* later.

Only later had never come. Not even during their short-term engagement—his family had made sure of that.

It had taken years of self-exploration and several diligent partners for her to understand her own body. For sex to finally be spectacular. Or, if maybe not spectacular, then at least pretty damned good.

"I always liked it when you did that."

For a moment, she panicked, thinking she'd been expounding upon her sexual delights aloud before she realized that Colin was referring to her proclivity for talking to herself.

"Well." She shrugged. "Apparently, it's a habit I won't ever be able to shake."

Blue eyes locked with hers. "I hope you don't ever change."

She gave him a sad smile. "Everyone changes, Colin. It's a fact of life."

"I was hoping you'd say that because—"

"Ladies and gentlemen, please ensure your tray tables and seatbacks . . ." came the flight attendant's voice through the loudspeakers, declaring them ready for landing before discussing connections and the weather in London.

Cecilia deliberately focused on the woman's words as she opened her window shade and stared out at the landscape.

But she wasn't really taking in the view of the gorgeous green countryside or the massive sprawl that was London. Instead, she was trying to forget Colin's words.

"I was hoping you'd say that because—"

Because what?

No. It didn't matter. The rest of that sentence was *not* important.

Except it was.

She closed her eyes.

Dammit.

The rest of that sentence was really, *really* important.

Her bags were lost.

She was planning a trip to Finland with no end date, followed by backpacking around Europe, also with no deadline, and her bags were nowhere in sight.

"All right?"

Colin. Of course.

He held his carry-on in one hand and looked dashing and unruffled despite the long flight.

She'd expected him to be long gone after the hellish line she'd had to wait in to get through the passport check while he'd breezed through the other shorter queue.

Stupid sexy Scot.

She turned back to the conveyor belt, but her bag had not miraculously appeared.

And so, her trip was continuing its fabulous start.

"I'm good." CeCe straightened her shoulders and pasted on

a smile. "Lovely to chat with you." She turned away but didn't get far. Colin slipped his fingers through the strap on her bag and halted her escape.

"Is this all you brought with you?"

"I'm fine." She lifted her chin in the direction of the airline's well-lit office. "I've had airlines lose my bags before. It's not a huge deal. It'll turn up, so if you'll excuse me . . ."

He released her and she left, not looking back, not daring to make eye contact with him again, lest he see the longing in her eyes.

This was her trip to find herself again, to prove that she was as strong and capable as she hoped to be.

So off she went to file a lost luggage claim.

Like a calm, responsible adult. Not like a mid-twenty-something who wanted to throw a temper tantrum or lie down and cry . . . or better yet, to lie down and *sleep*.

Instead, she adulted.

And hated every minute of it.

EIGHT

Cecilia

CECE FOLDED the printout from the luggage report and smiled at the woman's assurances that her bag would be found and delivered to her hotel by the morning. With an inner sigh, she turned and walked through customs with only her carry-on.

Thank God she'd brought a toothbrush and a change of clothes in her tote.

She checked the signs and started walking in the direction of the taxi stand, the mental image of her forthcoming soft and fluffy mattress almost too much to bear.

"Cecilia." A hand grasped her arm.

"Shit!" She jumped, lost her grip on her bag, and watched as the contents of her long-ass-plane-ride survival kit rolled in all directions.

Her Chapstick skidded end over end until it slid under a fully occupied row of chairs, her phone skittered beneath a massive rolling suitcase guided haphazardly by a small child and narrowly missed being crushed by its menacing metal wheels. Her pencils and sketchpad scattered in all directions and her clothes . . . no, her underwear, *that* went floating across the floor, wafting to a gentle stop on Colin's foot.

He bent and picked up the flimsy scrap of deep green lace—it matched her eyes, okay? And plus, a girl needed to feel sexy every once in a while.

Or at least that was what Bec had said when she'd gifted Cecilia a trunkful of expensive lingerie before her trip.

"*For those sexy European guys,*" she'd mock-whispered before her face had gone deadly serious in that fierce lawyer mask of hers. "*And for you. Because you're amazing and beautiful and deserve to feel that way.*"

Colin coughed, cheeks going faintly pink. "I-uh . . . sorry about that. I didn't mean to startle you." He held the ridiculously small thong clenched in his fist, and the sight made her stomach tighten.

Well, not just her *stomach*. She got that squidgy feeling just beneath her belly button, traveling lower, throbbing, aching, until her thighs squeezed together in a vain attempt at soothing that empty feeling within her.

She blinked before regaining her senses.

Her heart was empty, and she was going to Finland to fill it with beautiful green-tinted lights and the wide-open night sky. There would be snow and animals and a glass-roofed cabin of her own. She was going to sort out the loneliness inside her, finally find her place in the world.

And that place didn't include Colin or his yummy hands *or* her panties scrunched up all sexily in his palms.

Enough.

In a quick movement, she snatched her underwear from Colin's hand and stuffed it into her bag. Then she began crouch-walking as she hurried to gather up all her other items.

Which didn't take long because he helped.

Colin McGregor just could not take a hint.

"Cecilia—" he began but coughed again, probably because she'd just stuffed an entire string of condoms back into her tote.

Protection wasn't just a woman's responsibility, but damned if she was going to rely on a man to keep her safe.

That's what led to accidental pregnancies, and *that* wasn't a romance novel trope she was interested in living . . . not in real life anyway. Between the pages of a book was another thing entirely.

"Goodbye, Colin," she murmured, slinging her bag onto her shoulder.

"Wait." He hesitated before touching her arm again. "Let me see you safely to your hotel." When she started to shake her head, he gave her puppy dog eyes. And the infuriating man gave damned good puppy dog eyes. "Please, CeCe. I know I don't deserve your consideration, but will you at least let me know that you're safe and sound?"

She sighed. Was she seriously considering spending more time in a confined space with the man who'd broken her heart twice?

Ugh. She totally was.

"Fine," she said, giving in because she was too tired to fight, too tired to resist stealing just a little bit more of Colin.

He smiled, and the brilliance of it sucked the air from her lungs. *God*, he had the best freaking smile, wide and slightly crooked on one end, his teeth straight and white but not perfectly aligned. That little bit of imperfection mixed into all of the flawlessness that was Colin McGregor just added a whole other layer.

It was too much, and it wasn't enough.

She wanted him. She was scared.

She was hurt but remembered the great times they'd had together. The brilliant moments when they were alone, when she was with someone who saw her as her true self.

When she'd belonged.

Sadness swept through her, and she dropped her eyes to the floor, hurting, absolutely *aching* for the loss of that time in her life, no matter how brief it had been.

"Cecilia?"

She forced her gaze up, made her lips tip into a smile. "Should we go?"

"Sweetheart?" A brush of his thumb across her cheek. "What is it?"

Her heart turned over in her chest, that long old scar throbbing. But she couldn't tell Colin that. Not now, not here, not after all this time. "I'm tired," she said. "Can we go?"

Blue eyes searched hers for a long moment before he nodded. "Of course."

He grabbed her bag, slinging it over his arm, and pointed in the direction of the automatic doors.

Cecilia frowned. "Where's *your* bag?"

"The driver has it." He nodded at the man wearing a black suit and tie with a pristine white button down, standing next to a black sedan. "Thanks for waiting, Danny."

Danny nodded, opening the door without a word, but the look he gave her was assessing.

And immediately made her spine go stiff.

She'd seen that look before. Too many times over. From his family. From his friends. She was the calculating American trying to take advantage.

"You know—" She hesitated, ready to say, 'fuck it all' and take a cab like her original plan, but Colin had anticipated her actions. He snagged her wrist and tugged her into the car in a move so quick the rest of her sentence was swallowed up in a gasp and the sound of the door closing.

"Hotel." He gripped her chin between his thumb and forefinger. "Then I'll leave you to your life."

Her breath caught. In relief? In disappointment?

Who knew?

Except . . . she *knew*.

And what she knew but didn't want to admit, even to herself, was that those words left her with a trace of displeasure—no, *more* than a trace. What she felt was a torrent of regret that was nearly impossible to ignore. She should have fought, should have done something.

But she'd been young and vulnerable and . . . *so damned hurt*.

So, she ignored the blip of sorrow at the thought of never seeing Colin again.

She tucked that hurt down, shoved it all away, and did what she did best.

Pretended to be completely fine despite the fact that she was totally shattered inside.

LONDON WAS BEAUTIFUL. The buildings were like nothing she'd seen before. Tall, huge walls of gorgeous architecture full to the brim with arches and curls and wooden doors. Brick houses transformed into gothic churches before pivoting again into another style and then another as traffic weaved and bobbed and turned through narrow and twisted streets.

Every building was multistoried and towered over the car. Which should have made her feel closed in.

But instead she felt safe and cozy, like she was tucked snugly under a soft comforter.

London was nothing like her little town north of San Francisco.

There were multistory buildings at home, of course, but not like this. Not packed in, crowded together, taking up every millimeter of available space.

Good thing she wasn't claustrophobic.

"Different from Scotland, isn't it?"

Cecilia stiffened, somehow having forgotten that she was trapped in a car with Colin. She removed her hand from where it was pressed against the window, purposefully wiped what was almost certainly a sappy smile from her face, and turned to face him.

They were nearing the clogged streets close to Buckingham Palace, and she knew her hotel wouldn't be far off.

Though . . . traffic.

They could be trapped for days.

Le. Sigh.

It was easier to be closed off from Colin when he was more of a painful memory rather than a living, breathing human.

Who was nice and waited for her and gave her rides and—

Broke your heart, girlfriend, she imagined Seraphina saying. Her beautiful blonde bombshell of a friend would tell her to woman up and harden her heart. *Forget him. Move on and hook up with a hot Finnish guy. They make man buns look sexy.*

She just wished it were that easy.

Because amongst the painful memories were good ones. More than the bad, more than the ones that shattered her teenage fantasies.

She sighed. This trip was supposed to be about relaxing, enjoying herself after spending so long wrapped up in Hunter's appointments and treatments and medications. This was supposed to be about her having an adventure where she wasn't trying to think of ways to get Carter—Abby and Jordan's baby— to eat peas when the little toddler hated all foods that were green.

This—

She sighed again, wanting to slap herself. She shouldn't be missing them. It hadn't even been a day.

Fingers on her cheek startled her.

"You okay?" Colin asked.

She leaned into his touch, inhaling the spicy scent that was solely Colin—leather and sandalwood and pine.

"I—"

Then she realized who she was leaning closer toward, whose hand was cradling her face, and who apparently had as big a hold on her body and mind as ever.

P.A.T.H.E.T.I.C.

That was her.

"London is different than Scotland," she said, finally getting a grip and circling back to safer topics than her idiotic brain and heart. "I mean, all I'd seen of it before was Heathrow, and that wasn't exciting. And I know it doesn't make sense for my travel plans, with me leaving for Finland tomorrow, but I couldn't miss a chance to be here without at least seeing Buckingham Palace and Hyde Park—"

"You're leaving *tomorrow*?"

The car slowed, pulling to a stop at the curb. And *seriously*, she was tipping this driver big time.

CeCe took one glance at Colin's stormy expression—the one that used to make her crazy. Crazy to kiss him and smooth it out. Crazy to piss him off further so he'd yank her close and kiss *her* with all that pent-up frustration. Crazy to—

Run.

"Oh look, we're here," she said, popping the door handle and climbing out onto the sidewalk, thankful that they were on the "wrong" side of the road, so she didn't have to clamber over Colin's legs.

Because it wouldn't be clambering over so much as clambering *onto,* and that would be very dangerous indeed.

She grabbed her tote bag, tucking it over her shoulder while slamming the door shut, and thrust a fifty-pound note at the surprised driver, who was just sliding out of the car.

She needed to get to her room, slam the deadbolt, and hide.

The smiling attendant waved her forward, and CeCe

handed over her passport all while trying not to glance behind her like she was a fugitive on the run.

This just in . . . she felt like one.

"Here you go," the woman said. "You've got a lovely room on the fifth floor. You'll find the elevator right down that hall."

Cecilia thanked her, hurrying away from the desk and ignoring the fact that the space between her shoulder blades was prickling.

Risking a quick glance back gained her nothing. Colin was nowhere in sight. He'd left after she'd so unceremoniously slammed the car door in his face.

Obviously.

So, what if she felt the tiniest bit disappointed and, well, guilty for slamming said door in said handsome, dark, and brooding face?

She pressed the button for the elevator, stood back when the doors dinged open, and then started to select the fifth floor.

The hairs on her nape rose before he even spoke.

As though she had a built-in Colin-detector.

And frankly, she needed to face facts. She did have a built-in Colin-detector.

It was called her vagina.

As in, it got wet every time he was nearby.

"You actually need to press six," he murmured from too close behind her, reaching over her shoulder to push the button with that number. "Floors are counted differently in England than the United States. Here, they have a ground floor and *then* the numbers start counting up from one."

CeCe glanced down at the envelope housing her room key and sure enough, she was in room six-twenty-two.

Fifth floor. Lies.

Shaking her head as the doors slid closed, she stuck her room key in her pocket and then sighed, dropping her chin to her chest, warring with herself—

"Fuck it," she muttered, sliding her tote bag from her shoulder and letting it fall with a *thump* to the floor. She whipped around, launched herself at Colin.

He jumped and fumbled, and she thought for sure they were both going down, but then he regrouped, regaining his balance and holding her tight against his chest.

And—*God*—it felt fantastic, being in his arms, being this close.

"Cecilia?" he asked, blue eyes wide but filling rapidly with heat.

He felt it, too. He understood the attraction, the never-ending pull that seemed to yank them together time and time again.

That attraction was the only reason—the *only* reason, take that her damned smug conscience—that she kissed him.

And promptly lost her head.

NINE

Colin

COLIN SPENT APPROXIMATELY six seconds in heaven before it was torn from his arms.

Or rather, before CeCe ripped *herself* from his hold.

He'd had just a tease of soft curves and floral scents, felt the press of her lips, her breasts, her tongue against him.

Then the bloody elevator had dinged, its doors had slid open, and she'd run.

Again.

This pattern was getting frustrating.

He slammed his fist against the metal panel as it tried to slide closed and bent to pick up the paper envelope that had fallen from Cecilia's pocket when she'd thrown herself into his arms. She'd grabbed her tote bag, so there was that, but she wouldn't be getting far without a room key.

Sighing, he tucked his messenger bag over one shoulder and left the elevator, bracing himself for her presence, for the punch to the gut that stole his breath every time he saw her.

She was beautiful, inside and out, there was no doubt about that. But she was also . . . scared. Hurting.

And he wanted the full story, for fuck's sake.

Not a piece of information here and there. Not a slice of the past and vague words. He wanted to know what had happened six years ago.

Because by all rights, *he* should be the wounded one.

But Colin had the feeling that he wasn't.

He glanced at the key holder in his palm, searched out the sign on the wall, and headed in the direction of Cecilia's room.

She wasn't far, around one corner, head in her hands, bag still over one arm but resting on the floor, as she squatted against a door.

He ignored the jump of his pulse and stretched an arm over her head, swiping the key against the lock. It disengaged with a *click*. When he shoved it open, bright green eyes flew up to his, and her mouth opened, no doubt to put him off again.

A shake of his head, a swift movement to scoop her up off the floor.

"Col—"

"Hush." He growled when she flailed her arms, that damned annoying tote bag whacking him in the head. He slid it free from her arm, then set it carefully on the luggage stand before carrying CeCe further into the room, flipping switches all the way.

"*Colin.*"

He didn't bother to reply. Instead, he ripped the comforter free of the mattress with one hand.

"Hey! You can't—*oof!*"

He took a breath, shaking off the tempting sight of the woman he'd obsessed over for years, hair mussed, looking up from a bed at him in invitation.

No. Confusion. With a little irritation mixed in.

Colin bent and removed her shoes, lining them up next to the nightstand, before turning back and staring at CeCe.

Yes, it was probably creepy.

No, he couldn't stop himself.

Especially when her lips parted and there *was* a hint of invitation in her expression. He leaned down, felt the hot whoosh of her breath on his mouth, and kissed her . . . on the cheek.

"Good night, sweetheart," he murmured, pulling up the blanket and tucking it around her. Gritting his teeth, he set the keycard on the nightstand and rose to his feet.

And then he did the opposite of what every cell in his body was demanding—namely stripping CeCe naked, leaving her limp with orgasms, holding her close afterward, whispering all the words he'd felt, *still* felt, into her ear, and watching her fall asleep.

Did she still snore in soft little puffs of air?

Would she still whisper his name and snuggle closer?

Could they possibly forget the past and find a way to build something new?

He wanted to find out the answers to all those questions. He wanted her body, her heart, her soul.

He wanted *her*.

That was why he had to leave.

Colin tried to ignore the fact that she didn't stop him as he went.

It didn't work.

HOTEL BARS WERE THE WORST. The scourge of the earth, the cesspool of all humanity, the bottom of the proverbial barrel.

Either that or he was being dramatic.

Okay, he *was* being dramatic.

And that wasn't like him.

But he'd sent his driver away, intending to walk the city until his nerves settled. The trouble was he had only made it as far as the hotel bar.

He had always felt like this . . . not about the bar and not acting like a gross creeper stalking a woman who wanted nothing to do with him. Rather, he meant that it had always felt as though there were a piece of string attaching him to Cecilia. It had been stretched taut, threatening to snap for many years, and now that he'd found her, he didn't have the strength to risk that tenuous position once more.

What if he couldn't find her again?

Dramatic meet maudlin meet terrible Shakespeare-esque drama.

He should have just talked to her when he'd been in her room.

Better that than brooding over a bottle of whiskey like a pathetic idiot.

"Another?" the bartender asked when Colin drained the last drops from his glass.

"No, thanks." He shook his head and tossed enough bills on the bar top to cover his tab plus a healthy tip. The man had been quick, efficient, and didn't ask nosy questions.

But Colin was bleary-eyed, exhausted after the flight, and the days had been packed with meetings before then, and he really needed to sleep.

He was also slightly drunk.

Which was probably why he headed to the elevators rather than pulling out his cell and calling his driver. He pressed the button for the fifth floor and waited calmly—albeit with a slightly faltering stance . . . the floor's fault for not being level, thank him very much—as the elevator rose.

Then he pulled out the spare key to CeCe's room, the one he'd put in his pocket earlier for *safekeeping*, and unlocked the door.

It was mostly dark, with only the bedside lamp on, and she'd fallen asleep with a book on her chest.

One of those bloody historical romances.

For fuck's sake.

He carefully picked it up, lest it stab her in the eye or something as she slept, and started to close it. Only a word caught his eye. Then a sentence.

Then a *scene*.

And hot damn, *what* a scene.

He sank to the floor next to the bed and turned the page.

And another. And another. And . . . he read the whole damned thing. The sex, the horses, the kilts, the conflict that drove the hero and heroine apart—conflict driven by the hero's intervening family that left a nasty aftertaste in his mouth. He even read the happy ending and the epilogue where their castle was full of children and the couple lived in a state of unending bliss.

The book made him sigh like a sappy sod, and it made him ache. To *long* for the fictional happily ever after.

It also made him sleepy, and Colin found himself listing to the side, curling up next to the bed, and closing his eyes.

TEN

Cecilia

CECILIA WOKE with her mouth feeling as though she'd swallowed an entire desert worth of sand. Her breath certainly could have made any desert-dwelling creature drop dead on the spot.

She never went to bed without brushing her teeth, without religiously using mouthwash and flossing, and now she'd done so twice in the last day.

Gross.

But she'd been so exhausted—emotionally and physically—after everything that had happened with Colin, that she hadn't moved from the bed, except to grab a book, toss her leggings to the floor, and slip off her bra.

She'd waited for him to come back, to knock at the door and demand answers.

He hadn't.

And she wasn't disappointed.

Because she was a strong independent woman and was fine

on her own. Cue her wagging finger and her podium-worthy rant. She didn't need a man, dammit. She was traveling through Europe. She had plans. She—

Had been frozen in place by his kiss. On her cheek.

Ugh.

Running her tongue over her teeth and wincing at the furry feeling, CeCe tossed the covers back and stood.

Who knew what hour it was, but she'd slept enough of her time away in London already. She wanted to go see Buckingham Palace and the Crown Jewels. And if she had time, she wanted to walk through Hyde Park with a coffee.

Dropping her chin to her chest, she took a moment to stretch out her stiff neck. No matter how expensive the room, hotel pillows still sucked.

A sigh. One more quick stretch, and she headed for the bathroom. Or attempted to, anyway, because she had only taken one step in that direction before she tripped over something.

No. Some*one.*

A huge, male someone.

Her scream caught in her throat, and she sucked in more air, trying to clear it, before she realized the male someone was actually a Scottish male someone named Colin.

"Shit," she hissed, heart pounding, hand coming to her throat.

Colin was sleeping on the floor between the bed and the hotel wall, on the gross, hard industrial carpet. And he had . . . her *book?* It was resting open on his chest, rising and falling with each of his breaths.

He had read it?

Oh, God.

Heat scorched her cheeks. The book was a steamy one, and *of course* the hero was Scottish and had broken the heroine's heart in the past.

Which was too damned close to home, but she hadn't been able to stop herself from finishing it, from crying at their trials, and then sighing in contentment when they'd finally found their happily-ever-after.

CeCe reached for the book, wanting to get it far away from Colin. Frankly, she wanted to chuck it out the window, but since that was probably sealed shut, she'd settle for it to be shoved deep down into her tote bag, never to be seen by steely blue eyes again.

The book's cover was smooth beneath her fingers, that soft, almost velvet-like feel that some paperbacks had.

The spine was in good shape, hardly creased, but then again, she was very careful with her books in general.

Not the point at the moment, yet a nice distraction, none-theless.

But the distraction wasn't to last because the moment she caught a whiff of his scent, sandalwood with a hint of whiskey, she was ensnared.

Enraptured.

Entranced.

Her hand slid from the book to Colin's chest, resting lightly as she shifted her position, so her knees were next to his shoulder. And she studied the man, truly looked at him for the first time in years.

Not quick glances before avoiding his gaze, dodging old memories and pain. Not a flick of her eyes then away because he was so beautiful and hot and sexy and . . . overwhelming.

She *really* looked at him.

And noticed the changes in his face, the faint wrinkles around his eyes, the beard covering his cheeks and chin. It was a deep black, but there were a few gray hairs here and there. Enough of the silvery strands that for the first time she stopped to wonder about all that Colin had been through.

She'd been so wrapped up in what happened to *her* that she hadn't stopped to consider him.

Wow. So, that was what guilt felt like.

Snorting at herself, she turned her eyes back to Colin. A curl of hair had slipped over his forehead, and she smoothed it back before starting to stand.

"You're in dangerous territory, sweetheart," came his rumbling, sleep-laden voice, hand snaking out to wrap around her wrist.

"C-Colin," she stammered. "I j-just—"

"You're the most beautiful thing I've ever seen," he said.

Or rather *whiskey-ed*.

Holy entire bottle of the amber concoction, Batman.

"You're drunk," she said.

He shook his head, goofy smile on his face.

"You smell like you took a bath in a distillery," she told him, slipping her wrist free of his grasp.

He tilted his head in the direction of his armpit and wrinkled his nose. His face fell.

That puppy dog expression had always been too much for her. The need to comfort him was compulsory and impossible to resist. "Yours is still my favorite smell in the world," she blurted.

Then wished she'd kept her damned mouth shut because it revealed *way* too much.

The last bit of sleep slipped from Colin's eyes. They sharpened, and she quickly stood.

"I should ask why you're in my room, but I'm not going—" Her breath hitched when his hand went to her ankle, rough fingers tracing gently on the bare skin there. She cleared her throat. "I'm going to take a shower."

"Want company?"

Her heart clenched and her . . . well. Suffice to say that she had a lady boner.

He was fully clothed, touching one of the most innocuous parts of her body, and she had a serious moisture problem.

Which he could probably see, since she was standing almost directly over him.

His fingers slipped higher, tracing little circles along the back of her calf, her knee, teasing at her thigh.

"I-I—"

He leaned up onto one elbow and those fingers slipped higher, until one tip slipped under the elastic of her underwear.

Just the tip.

She giggled.

She couldn't help it. Bec, Abby, and Seraphina had corrupted her.

They were bad influences, especially because they would have encouraged her to . . . well, *encourage* Colin.

And she wanted to. Really, she did. Forget the past in that moment. She had a sexy Scot with his finger in her panties, and she was wound so tight that it wouldn't take more than a brush of said finger to send her toppling.

But he was drunk.

"You're going to say no," he murmured, slipping more of his hand under the elastic and cupping her ass with one rough palm. "I know you are."

She nodded. "I'm going to say no." Then added in a mutter meant for her ears only, "Not that I want to."

Except apparently not quiet enough because Colin's lips curved and his free hand came up, cupping her other cheek. "I can make you feel good," he said, and she knew he could. He *had*.

But. He. Was. Drunk.

"Climb into the bed," she said, pushing his hands down and out of her underwear.

He scrambled up to his feet in a movement way too fast for someone who was inebriated. His arm slid around her waist and his mouth was on hers before she had a chance to realize what she'd said.

She'd meant for *him* to climb into bed. By himself.

Except she was there. With him. Surrounded by his scent, pressed into the mattress by his bulk. His lips were teasing hers open. His tongue was tangling with hers.

And *fuck* did it feel amazing.

ELEVEN

Colin

CECILIA WAS WRAPPED TIGHTLY against him, pressed firmly against his chest, her legs intertwined with his. Colin moaned and pulled her closer, leaning down to press a kiss to the valley of her breasts.

Then frowned.

Her skin wasn't as soft as he remembered, her curves not as lush. It was almost as though she weren't—

His eyes shot open when something tightened around his neck.

He blinked, searching the space around him, abruptly aware of the cold bed. The linens were soft for a hotel but rough when compared to his woman's skin. And they might have been wound around him, but they were decidedly *unlike* CeCe's curves.

The room was also dark.

Colin cursed and sat up, tearing away the cotton sheet that had somehow become wrapped around his throat.

He saw the clock and cursed, seeing that he'd slept the day away.

And Cecilia was gone.

He knew that in his bones.

"Fuck," he muttered, trying to sift through his sleepy mind, trying to understand how he'd come to wake alone when last he'd remembered, Cecilia had been beneath him on that very bed.

His eyes lit on a note faintly illuminated by the clock and propped onto the bedside table. A little bottle of water and some aspirin were positioned next to it.

Thanks for the lift. Drink the water and take the aspirin. I imagine you'll wake with quite a headache.
Have a nice life,
CeCe
P.S. Don't worry, I paid up the room for another day. Take care.

COLIN GRUNTED, starting to crumple the note before stopping and instead carefully folding it and putting it into his pocket. "Have a nice life," he muttered, getting out of bed and ignoring the pills. He wasn't a child any longer, and he didn't have a hangover. Yes, he might have drunk a little more than normal the previous night, but he'd been in full possession of his abilities.

Except somehow you fell asleep with the most beautiful woman in the world in your arms, you arsewipe, his brain conveniently reminded him.

Because yes, there was that. He'd had Cecilia in his arms, pliable and warm and delicious and . . .

That was the last thing he remembered.

So, maybe he was slightly out of practice in the whiskey-bingeing department.

Sighing, Colin reached into his satchel and pulled out his

phone, checking his emails and sending a text to his assistant to clear his schedule for the foreseeable future.

This was why he'd trained his COO and CFO. So he could have a life.

And he intended to finally have one.

Which was why he called his *other* assistant—the one who specialized in remembering birthdays and selecting the perfect arrangement of flowers for his mother. Joanne had been around the McGregors for decades and had been managing his life since his father died.

She'd also loved Cecilia.

"Joanie," he said. "I have a problem that doesn't involve an artistic arrangement of lilies. Or well, it might involve them. *If* she likes those, which I can't remember—"

"She?" Joanne asked.

He shoved his feet into his shoes, pinning the phone between his ear and shoulder. "I'm getting Cecilia back."

"Finally," Joanne said, and he could almost hear her smile through the airwaves. "But, Colin dear, it's yellow daffodils that she adores. Though, I don't think flowers are going to mend—"

"I don't need flowers," he said. "Though I'm sure I will at some point," he added, filing CeCe's preference in flowers away. "For now, I need you to ready my plane for a flight to Finland."

"Ohhh." Joanne's breath slid out on a sigh. "The northern lights. *Colin*, that was always her dream. It's so romantic."

"Except she left without me."

He heard Joanne's teeth click closed. "Okay, that's less so."

Colin snorted. "I agree." He rattled off the name of the resort he'd seen on the brochure that had fallen out of her bag at the airport. "I need a flight as close as possible to there."

"And a room?"

"No," he said. "I'm hoping she'll take a poor sod in out of the cold."

Joanne huffed. "I wouldn't be so sure, my dear. After what you and your family did to that poor girl—"

Colin's gut tightened. "What Joanie? What did we do?"

A pause. "You don't know?"

His blood iced over. "What?" he asked, barely able to force the word out.

"Colin," she whispered. "Honey, it's—" A sigh. "You were too drunk to remember?"

"I was drunk for weeks," he reminded her.

She sighed again, and the silence stretched between them. "The plane will be ready in two hours."

"Joanie, I need you to tell—"

"No. You and CeCe need to talk this out." A pause. "But, Colin, if you don't want your arse to be frozen solid in Finland, I would be prepared to get on your knees and beg."

Fuck.

"It's that bad?" he asked.

"My boy," she began before clearing her throat. "It's not good."

He opened his mouth to press for details before clamping it closed. The person he needed to discuss this with was Cecilia.

The person he apparently needed to beg for forgiveness was Cecilia.

Colin grabbed his bag and hoped there wouldn't be any snow on the ground because his damn slacks weren't the least bit waterproof.

TWELVE

Cecilia

SHE WAS SITTING on a bench in Hyde Park.

She'd left Colin sleeping in her hotel room much earlier that day, stored her suitcase at the drop-off facility near the hotel, and was now counting the time until she had to leave for the airport.

Buckingham Palace hadn't materialized, but she had gotten a glimpse of the Crown Jewels, and now she was drinking her coffee in the late afternoon sunshine. CeCe had done plenty of traveling on her own, was quite comfortable with silences and navigating cities by herself.

She was happy with that.

Except . . . she wasn't.

Sitting there with a hot carafe of coffee in her hands, the steaming liquid not yet cool enough to drink, CeCe felt very much alone.

"You're over this," she murmured, deliberately turning her focus to a narrow, winding path that veered off to the side. "You've always been alone. You *have* to be over this."

But . . . she wasn't.

She'd always been able to feel self-contained, to be satisfied in that, because she'd spent so much of her time alone. But she hadn't been alone these last few years. She'd had Hunter and Jordan, and now she had Heather and Sera and Abby and Carter along with them.

She had more of a family now than she'd had growing up.

But there was still something empty inside her. Longing. She wanted someone who could be hers, first and foremost. She wanted to be the most important person in someone's life.

Maybe that was selfish, to want to be someone's top priority.

Maybe she needed to understand that love wasn't finite, that just because she wasn't in a relationship, didn't have romantic love that she meant as much to Abby and Jordan and—

No.

That wasn't right either.

Love wasn't finite, but romantic love and friendship weren't the same.

Jordan and Abby had something more.

A more that she was desperate to have, and maybe that made her weak, but also . . . fuck that. For as much as she had been hurt over the years, her ability to care for, to love those around her hadn't been broken. She cared and loved deeply.

So, she fucking deserved to have someone love her in that same way.

Devotedly. Passionately.

She deserved to have a man look at her with the same warmth and affection she saw in Jordan's eyes when he looked at Abby.

"I deserve someone to love every part of me."

Because she knew that she'd loved every part of Colin when they'd been together, the good and bad, the annoying and sweet. She'd made the mistake of thinking he'd felt the same, and . . . maybe he hadn't.

But also—she thought of the confused expression on the plane, how good his family had been at gaslighting her.

Should she have stayed?

Back then? Should she have ignored the hurtful words, volleyed back some of her own? Should she have fought to understand why he hadn't come to the church?

Now, she would have.

Now, she wouldn't have just stopped at a phone call, or let someone whisk her away to safety.

Now, she'd built a life for herself. Now, she'd taken care of a really sick kid who had gotten through to the other side, who had made her understand that even when things are really fucking hard, they were still worth fighting for.

She pulled her phone out of her pocket and checked the time.

Hours yet.

She stood, her fingers slipping into her other pocket, the one with the keycard in it. The keycard to the room where she'd left Colin sleeping. Maybe seeing him on the plane was a sign that unless she figured out where they went wrong, she would never be able to fully move forward.

But could she go back? What if she was wrong and his family hadn't orchestrated their breakup? What if it was . . . just her?

Sighing, she pocketed her phone, sat back down on the bench, and drank her coffee.

It had cooled too much, didn't taste as good as she had imagined.

Or maybe—she shot to her feet.

Fuck it. She didn't take this trip to be a coward. She was done running from her life, from experiences she wanted to have. She wanted to confront Colin, to tell him what a fucking asshole he'd been, and if that was the only resolution she garnered from the conversation then great, moving on.

But if she got more . . .

Because maybe she'd find something more.

Maybe she'd find a way to fill in that great yawning hole in her heart. By herself. Because *she'd* taken action and decided her future.

To take a risk. Or maybe to play it safe.

But CeCe decided.

Heart thudding, she dumped her coffee in the trash can and made her way through the streets to the Underground, took a train back to the stop for the hotel, and slipped into the elevator.

She almost lost her courage at the door.

But then she lifted her chin, whispered, "You deserve answers." And that gave her the courage to unlock the room, to step inside.

The air was hot and damp, as though someone had just been in the shower.

But the room itself was empty.

Sandalwood and leather and spice . . . and empty.

Disappointment slid through her at being denied her opportunity for resolution, but there was also some pride mixed in. Because she'd been brave enough to not run. Because she'd begun to understand the tangle of feelings inside her. Because she was no longer hiding like a weak ninny.

CeCe had found her strength.

And she wasn't giving it up.

Bump.

With a sharp gasp, her cell slipped from her fingers and hit the floor of the shuttle van. CeCe winced and watched it slide under the seat in front of her. She'd been trying to return a text from Hunter, had been craning her neck and holding the phone out in a vain attempt to not lose the signal and—

Bump.

The roads weren't ideal.

Bump-bump.

Her cell slid farther forward and very much out of reach.

"Fuck," she muttered and then immediately winced and smiled apologetically when a mom with her two young sons slid her a look.

One of them was about Hunter's age and whispered, or rather attempted to whisper because somehow when kids that age tried to whisper, their voices ended up carrying. And the shuttle they were in wasn't large.

Which meant she heard the little boy's excited statement with crystal clarity. "Mom, she said the *f*-word!"

The younger of the two boys said, "I thought the f-word was fart. She said fu—"

"Oh look," CeCe said, leaning over him to point out the window. "That tree is huge!"

It wasn't really, but it got the boys' attention off one another and their focus out the window rather than on her unfortunate use of the non-fart f-word.

The mom gave her squinty eyes for a second before grinning. "Definitely not the first time they've heard it, nor will it be the last." She shrugged and retrieved CeCe's cell, handing it back to her. "Just trying to keep that one"—she tilted her head in the direction of the littler brother—"out of the loop for as long as possible. He always saves that kind of stuff for the most inopportune moments."

The dad chuckled and slung an arm around his wife's shoulders. "Like the grocery store checkout line."

"And the dentist." The mom grimaced. "*And* the school play."

"I'm sorry," CeCe said again. "I should know better. I'm a nanny."

"*Oh*," the mom said, a faintly calculating note in her voice. "Well then, maybe in payment for your *huge* transgression, we can hit you up for a kid-free night while we're here. How long are you staying?"

"Lizzie," the husband warned. "You're laying it on really thick. You're the one who taught Tate his first bad word, after all."

She wrinkled her nose. "Well, at least he used it correctly."

"At the dentist. 'Get the goddammed thing out of my mouth,' were his exact words if, I remember correctly."

CeCe giggled as the woman popped him on the arm. "Shh! I just got him to stop saying it." She glanced up and smiled. "I'm just kidding about the babysitting," she said as the shuttle slowed to turn into the resort. "But if you're ever lonely and want a little company, here's my cell." She passed over a card. "We'll be here for ten days."

Cecilia glanced down at the paper and noted the California address for a company she didn't recognize. She'd known they were from the States, given their accent, but they both had a hint of twang that didn't scream the Golden Coast.

"Oh, how funny," she said, noting the location was near the firm where Abby and Jordan worked, RoboTech. "I live just outside of Marin."

Lizzie clapped her hands. "So, we've traveled halfway around the world to meet someone who only lives thirty minutes away?"

"Small world," the husband said and extended a hand. "I'm Sam. It's nice to meet you . . ."

"Cecilia," she supplied. "Nice to meet you, too. And it's lovely scenery all the same," she said to Lizzie. "I hope you and your boys have a fabulous trip. I'm sure we'll see each other around."

"Text me!" Lizzie whispered as they departed the shuttle. "We can do a spa day! I need some girl time."

CeCe couldn't help smiling at Lizzie's energy. There was something incredibly infectious about her, like a little old granny whom nobody could deny anything. "I will," she whispered back.

Then she gathered her suitcase, which had been delivered to the London hotel overnight, and pulled it in the direction of registration. Thirty minutes later, she was on her way to her very own glass-roofed cabin.

And it was *ah*-mazing.

The first thing CeCe did was drop her bag on the floor and hurry over to the window-encased dome at the end of the cabin. A bed sat beneath the glass, and she jumped on top of it to stare up at the sky. Though it was still daytime, it was already getting dark.

Would this be the night that she saw the aurora borealis?

Hopefully. But maybe not. She at least had time. *Lots* of time, and she would see them, dammit.

For once in her life, one of her dreams was going to come true.

Sighing at the oh-so-lovely thought, she pushed off the bed and set about hanging up her jacket and tucking away her clothes. Then she cranked up the sauna—her cabin had a private one—because that seemed like a very Finnish thing to do.

Later she would walk over to the restaurant for dinner before double-checking the forecast.

Solar activity was predicted to be low for the next few days, but CeCe didn't plan on letting that stop her.

She'd tape her eyelids open if necessary.

Her clothes ended up in a pile near the bed, but she didn't bother picking them up. She could be messy for once and not worry that she would potentially be setting a bad example for her charges.

Naked, she strode toward the sauna and had just sat on the wooden bench, ladle of water in her hand, ready to dump over the hot rocks, when there was a knock on the door.

"Dammit," she muttered and spooned the water onto the

rocks before standing and reaching for a towel that was hanging outside the door. It was probably a staff member, having forgotten to tell her something important.

The steam hit her skin and beads of moisture slid down her chest, between her breasts and lower, between her thighs.

She was hot and wet all over, but that had been a common problem of hers of late.

"Seriously," she muttered and headed for the door, throwing it open without glancing through the peephole.

Which was *seriously* an idiotic thing to do.

Because standing on the other side of the door wasn't a staff member with a forgotten bit of advice or a slightly pesky query.

Nope.

Standing on the opposite side of the pane of wood was none other than Colin McGregor.

And she, Cecilia Thiele, idiot of all idiots, lost her grip on her towel.

THIRTEEN

Colin

COLIN'S EYES bugged out of his head for a second, his gaze traveling every inch of CeCe's lush body— gently swaying breasts, narrow hips, flat stomach . . . flaming red curls.

Holy fucking shit.

Then he blinked and realized that any person walking by Cecilia's cabin would be able to see that gorgeous body.

The body that should be for *his* eyes only.

Yes, he was an arrogant asshole. Yes, he knew that Cecilia was a woman and it was technically *her* body first and foremost.

But fuck if Colin wanted another lecherous prick to lay eyes on her.

"Can I come in?" he asked, his voice sounding as though he'd swallowed a bloody flamethrower. He'd called in a favor to an acquaintance that specialized in hacking to find out CeCe's cabin number, had been all the more thankful for that small victory when he'd driven onto the huge property belonging to the resort.

In the meantime, Cecilia was still frozen in shock, her mouth gaping in a way that made him want to kiss her senseless, so he picked up the towel, wrapped it around her and pushed her gently backward.

Her feet moved without protest, allowing him to step forward into the room. She didn't do *anything* without protest, so Colin knew she was thrown completely for a loop. She didn't speak a word when he closed the door behind him, didn't say anything when he brushed by her to set his bag near the closet. Hell, she didn't even comment when he set the bag of takeaway he'd grabbed from the restaurant on the counter of the little kitchenette tucked away in one corner of the cabin.

In fact, the only thing that seemed to startle her out of her stupor was him dropping his pants to the floor.

"Col—" she began but gasped when his underwear joined the pile.

His socks were next, stuffed into the boots Joanne had sent along with a suitcase of warm clothes, followed by his jacket and shirt.

And then he walked toward Cecilia, wanting nothing more than to strip the towel from her hands before tossing her onto the bed and making love to her under the darkening sky.

But she'd been in the middle of something when he'd knocked.

Colin intended that she finish it *and* was fully committed to naked reciprocity.

He'd seen hers. It was only fair she saw his.

Okay, that wasn't the *only* reason.

He worked out a lot and knew his body was in shape. If seeing him parade around naked somehow convinced CeCe to transform into one of those crazed women at a *Magic Mike* show, then he was all for it.

Yes, he was well aware he was a fool, but a man had to be cognizant of his shortcomings.

A narrow hall opened into a bathroom, but the water wasn't running, and the telltale humidity of an interrupted shower was absent. He closed the door behind him and opened the next, feeling the gust of heat spread over his skin on a rush.

A sauna. Of course.

When in Finland.

"What are—?" Cecilia began from behind his left shoulder, but she didn't get to finish the question because he merely wrapped his fingers around her wrist and tugged her toward the open door.

"Let's finish your sauna," he said, sitting on the bench. "It was rude of me to interrupt."

"As if you give a damn about interrupt—"

He ladled a spoonful of water onto the heated rocks, cutting off what would no doubt have been a scathing remark about his insensitivity.

"Colin!" she exclaimed over the hissing stones and steam filling the air.

"What?" he asked innocently.

"Oh, my God," she said, exasperated. "You're still the same."

"No." He placed his hand over hers, leaning close to stare into her eyes. He needed her to see, needed her to understand that this was their chance at a fresh start, and that he wasn't the same moronic asshole from their past. "I'm not, sweetheart. I've changed. For the better. My family doesn't control me, not any longer." Her fingers pulsed beneath his, startled. "I don't know what happened with them, what they did to you. But I should have known better than to believe them when they said you ran off with Ewan. You're kind, CeCe. Honest, compassionate. You wouldn't do that to me."

Colin's chest was heaving, and his palms were damp . . . and not from the heat of the sauna.

He had to make her understand. He—

"No," she said. "I didn't run off with Ewan." She slipped her hand free of his, pressed it firmly to her chest, just above the towel she still wore. "But I *did* leave with him. It's only . . ." She hesitated, and then sighed deeply. "Ewan gave me an escape route after you shattered my heart into a million pieces."

FOURTEEN

Cecilia

NOW THAT THE time to confront Colin was here, she found it hard to focus.

Maybe that was from shock—how was he here?

Maybe it was because she'd watched him strip naked and just let it happen, enjoying the show.

Stupid.

As in, she was. Yes, the view was great. But attraction to Colin wasn't the problem.

It was all the rest of it. His family. Their breakups. The person she'd become with him. Bending and bending and bending until she'd no longer resembled the woman she wanted to be.

But . . . she was different now.

And she wanted answers, naked or not.

"Why are you here now? After all this time?" Cecilia asked into the silence that descended in the wake of her admission. Her apparent heartbreak had come as a shock, based on Colin's expression of pure horror. Which just further confirmed what she knew in her heart.

This was a tangled mess, one they'd both tangled more by not sitting down and talking.

If she could only go back and kick her twenty-year-old self into action.

She'd corner Lana and Bridget, demanded they admit they were trying to break up her and Colin, and then she'd confront Colin himself, tell him what he'd said was absolutely horrendous and unacceptable.

And *then* she would float off into the sunset, her answers found, her pride restored.

No. More. Weaklings.

"I—" He stood, closed the door to the sauna, and sat back down next to her, naked except for a small hand towel tossed haphazardly over his . . .

Penis, Cecilia Thiele, her mind shouted. *It's his penis, and it's giant and glorious and you want to lick it like a lollipop!*

She forced her eyes up and focused on his face, but then got sidetracked by the little scar above his lip and then by his lips themselves. They were yummy and lush and just so flipping kiss-able. What kind of universe gave a man a mouth like that?

And then he had to go and talk.

To be sweet and make his words both simple and heart-wrenching.

"Because, sweetheart, I couldn't stay away."

"Dammit," she muttered, glancing up at the ceiling, studying the single bulb hanging from the paneled wood. Condensation had gathered on the glass, and the drops sparkled as the light shone through. The effect was beautiful, even though it was slightly blurry through the lens of her tears.

Except, she was trying to channel Heather or Bec, here. To be strong and kickass.

No. She was channeling *herself.*

Maybe her inner strength wasn't so loud or overt, maybe his words called to that hole inside of her, tempting her to just put the past behind her and jump the man and his glorious, naked penis.

But that wouldn't solve her problems.

Her mind was getting clearer. Her confidence was growing.

But . . . she still had work to do.

Case in point was not avoiding the conversation with Colin by thinking about anything and everything except what they needed to discuss.

It was just that he sounded so genuine, and she wanted nothing more than to believe that he wanted her. But, how could she?

And yet . . . maybe he did?

No. Part of her couldn't help but think that people didn't change, not truly, not deep down, and though he might want her now, that would inevitably change, and then he would push her away, and she would end up broken all over again.

She *couldn't* end up broken again.

"But why, Col? What do you want?" she asked.

His blue eyes were pained. "I . . . I know what I'm going to give you are just words, and that they're not nearly enough. I know I must have hurt you badly, but I can't remember anything from those days."

Her throat went tight, and she tried to speak, but he covered her hand with his.

"I'm so sorry I hurt you. It was . . . inexcusable to do that to the woman I loved, and I'm so fucking sorry it took me years to grow up and understand that being a man didn't mean taking what I wanted or threatening or proving my dick was big." His fingers convulsed. "I thought I was all grown up, but, in truth, I didn't know a damned thing."

She dropped her chin to her chest. "But what's changed Colin? We're still the same people inside. Yes, we're attracted to each other, but I'm not convinced that we're good in a relationship. I've taken very few leaps in my life, and they've ended up blowing up in my face every time." A sharp shake of her head. "I can't regret them, can't regret the good times I had with you. But I *do* regret the person I was *with* you."

Hurt flickered across his face, but to his credit, his voice was calm when he asked, "Why?"

CeCe sighed. "Because I was weak. Because you loved me, and I loved you so desperately, and I wanted this fairytale to work out." She blinked up at the ceiling again. "But that's not real life. One person can't give and give and *give* while the other takes. *I* can't be that person again."

"I'm not asking you to," he said. "I just want another chance to make things work. For me to be able to prove to you—"

She pulled her hand back.

"I *can't*," she said, shaking her head when he went to reach for her. "I can't do this, Colin. I can't hurt this much and have all this regret and pain and angst. My life is supposed to finally be about me. I need to find out who I am without my job and the remains of our relationship hanging over me. Without my parents' disappointment weighing me down. I need to—"

"I understand." He scooted closer, took her hand in his again. "I get not knowing who you are and your whole world imploding. The fallout from my father's death aside, I've spent the last few months in the same perpetual cycle—thinking I understand how my life revolved, but then recognizing that maybe I didn't know anything at all." He touched her cheek. "I'm different now. I've grown. I know I still have work to do, but I'm not the same stubborn asshole who thinks his shit is made of gold."

His words tempted. His earnestness made that hole in her heart seem a little smaller.

Then he kept talking.

And some of the anger she'd banked over the years flew to the front of her emotions.

"I understand that you were hurt, and I'm sorry that—"

Sweat trickled down between her breasts when she shot to her feet. "No, you *don't* understand," she snapped, "because you weren't the one left shattered. You weren't the one who was devastated when all you'd hoped for a future was fucking *gone*."

He was quiet for a long moment, eyes on hers, the blue unfathomable.

Then he stood and cracked the door, reaching for a robe and handing it to her then repeating the process for himself.

When they were both covered, he brushed his knuckles over her cheek. "You weren't the only one devastated, CeCe. I thought you'd left me for my best friend and then just a month later, my father was dead, the business was one wrong decision away from collapse. I was in over my head. I was scared and . . . you were gone." His voice tightened. "You can't say I was unaffected because I *was*. My life was fucking broken, too."

Her breath caught as the truth of his words hit home. Her anger faded. "I-I'm sorry. I know I should have handled things differently. I should have demanded an explanation, not run off because I was hurt."

"We both shared in the immaturity and stupidity."

She wrinkled her nose, knowing it was true, but still hating it all the same. "Yeah."

Maybe she could convince Heather to invest in time machines and go back six years to give herself and Colin a sharp smack on the forehead.

Silence stretched between them as they stared at each other. She didn't know exactly what to say. Part of her felt better, part of her felt worse, and looking into Colin's blue eyes, seemingly filled longing, made an answering yearning rise within her.

As stupid as they'd both been, she wanted to go back to those easy times. Back to the hikes on the cliffs, to sketching until the sun went down, to the picnic lunches packed by Joanne and the rides on his horse, the kissing, and . . . more.

If only they could go back.

If only they could forget the past.

But life wasn't that easy. Or at least *hers* wasn't. And as much as she wanted to, she couldn't just put the pain aside and pretend everything between them hadn't happened. She ached and burned and *hurt*. But maybe . . .

Maybe they could move forward.

Maybe she could find a way to give them both a chance to figure out if they could have something healthy . . . together.

"Col?" she asked, when all he did was continue to stare at her. "What are you doing?"

"I'm memorizing every detail of your face so that when you kick me out into the bloody cold Finnish weather, I'll remember that you have a freckle just beneath your left eye and another on the top corner of your lip. I'll remember exactly the way your eyes curve near their corners and how your top lashes are thicker than the bottoms. I'll remember the hint of pink"—he swiped a finger over both of her cheekbones—"just here and here. I'll remember every part of you for the rest of my life. I let the details get blurred in the past, and while I couldn't ever hope to forget you, at least now I'll be able to remember you as perfect as you are in this moment."

Her pulse had picked up its pace during his speech, and her skin had gone taut, heating with desire, with embarrassment, with *awe*. "I think that's the most words I've ever heard you say at one time."

One half of his mouth curved. "Probably."

Silence fell between them again. "Do you really notice all of that?"

A nod. "Aye."

She groaned. "No fair busting out the full Scottish accent."

"All's fair in love and war, lass."

CeCe groaned again, but it was to hide the way her heart

had skipped a beat at the word *love*. Though truth be told, it skipped another when Colin called her *lass*.

Ugh.

But also, aw.

And also, shit, *shit*, she was really going to do this. "Col—" she began.

"Aye?"

Or something like *it*.

"You're laying it on real thick. But"—she reached up and placed a finger across his lips when he opened his mouth, presumably to protest—"that wasn't what I was going to say." He nipped at her finger, and she jumped back. "Hey! *Behave*." And yet, Cecilia was grinning and felt light for the first time in years. "I was going to say that maybe we could bring the food over to the bed beneath the glass roof, lie down, and—*Colin*! Stop grinning. I was going to say lie down and watch for the aurora borealis."

"Well, that's disappointing." But he grinned and pushed her in the direction of the bed. "Get comfortable, and I'll grab the food."

She curled up and watched the sky grow fully dark, popping grapes and cheese and crackers into her mouth almost as fast as Colin handed them over. They talked, not about the past, but about the places she wanted to visit next.

Paris because the Eiffel Tower and the Louvre were a must.

Copenhagen because her grandfather had lived there, and she wanted to visit the palaces and see the colorful buildings next to the harbor.

The Alps. Barcelona. The Colosseum. Maybe Fiji and Malta and Indonesia, somewhere warm and tropical when the weather got cold.

And then back to London.

Because Buckingham Palace and old English manors and

changeable weather and small twisting streets surrounded by tall buildings.

And also, she thought, her heart catching when the sky lit up with a magical green hue, back to London because it was closer to a confusing, sweet Scottish man who'd stolen a piece of her heart and had never given it back.

FIFTEEN

Colin

CECILIA MADE the most adorable sounds when she slept—soft mewls as she cuddled closer, gentle sighs that tickled the side of his throat.

She was as beautiful up close as from a distance, and though they'd stayed up late into the night, waiting on the aurora borealis and then finally seeing that distinct glimmer of green light up the dark sky, Colin hadn't allowed himself to sleep.

He was waiting for the other shoe to fall.

He was waiting for Cecilia to see sense.

He needed for her to be more attached to him before it happened. He needed her to love him.

As he'd never stopped loving her.

She yawned and turned in the circle of his arms, stretching and pressing her ass back against his crotch. He tried to shift slightly, so she didn't rub against the giant problem threatening to burst free of the underwear he'd slipped on before they'd settled into bed, but he didn't move quickly enough.

Lights flashed behind his lids, and he hissed out a breath as those luscious curves slid against his cock.

"Fuck," he muttered, placing a hand on CeCe's hip to stay her motions.

"Mmm," she murmured, slipping free and sliding closer.

And, he might as well be honest, it felt so fucking good that he didn't try very hard to keep her away.

"CeCe, baby," he began, but groaned when the soft cushion of her ass tucked right against his erection. Fuck, but she felt good against him.

"Mmm," she murmured again and then went ramrod stiff.

Shit. Colin tensed, preparing to haul his ass out into the cold.

She rolled over and opened her eyes, those green irises startlingly clear. One hand reached up to cup his cheek. "I thought it was a dream," she said softly.

"Not a dream." He turned his head and pressed a kiss to her palm. "Did you know your eyes are the same color as the northern lights?"

One half of her mouth curved. "Really?"

He kissed that curve. "Aye."

She shuddered and he smirked. "Still not playing fair, are you?"

"When it comes to you?" he asked, not giving her a chance to reply. "Never." Another kiss. "I'll never play fair when it comes to winning you back, sweetheart. Letting you go was the biggest mistake—*mistakes*—of my life."

She smiled and it lit up the room. Or maybe that was his heart. "I like it when you don't play fair."

Then that smile faltered and the brightness faded. He tried to figure out the underlying meaning of her words, why they'd hurt her so much.

"You—" he began.

But he didn't get the chance to finish the sentence because

then Cecilia's mouth was on his and her hand was on his cock and . . . his head was spinning.

He pulled back. "Wait, baby. What—"

She sat up, tearing off the robe she'd fallen asleep in, and fuck but she was more gorgeous than ever. "Do you want me, Colin? Because I *need* you to make me feel good. I need you to make me forget that we were only together the once. I need you to help me forget what came after."

"I don't think that—" He shook his head. "We need to talk. We shouldn't just bury—"

"Then just get the *fuck* out!" she screamed. "Because you're going to leave anyway, and then I'll be broken again, and I can't. I wanted to and I thought I could, but *I can't.*" She shoved off the bed, snatching the robe and trying to wrestle it on as she ran.

Which didn't go well.

Colin saw her start to go down before she realized what was happening, saw the tie of the robe tangled around her ankles as she started to sprint down the hall.

He moved, not thinking, not trying to process the words nor the frustration he felt for not knowing what the fuck was going on.

"Ah!" CeCe stumbled and went down in a jumble of limbs.

But he was there.

He caught her.

As he should have done all those years ago.

He righted her, tugged the robe over her shoulders, and tied it snugly around her waist. She wouldn't look at him, but he didn't need to see her eyes to know they were shimmering with tears.

"Right, then," he said, as he should have in the past. "We're not leaving here until we have both said all there is to say."

Her chin came up, and her eyes went cold. "I can leave here whenever I want."

Fuck. She could. And he had no fucking right to demand

anything from this woman. "You can," he said. "*Of course,* you can."

She scoffed, didn't look at him.

"But, sweetheart, I don't want you to go," he said. "I've spent years feeling empty, years being a fucking idiot, years knowing I'd lost you, that I lost the absolute best thing in my life."

Her lips parted. Her eyes squeezed closed. "I can't do this again, Colin. I fell for you after high school and then you broke my heart. I fell again after I got hurt, was barely picking up the pieces of my life when you barreled in and won my trust, despite my best efforts to keep you away." She shoved back her hair with a shaking hand. "And then you left me at the altar, and when I called you on the phone to find out why you weren't there, you said horrible things th-that shattered me into even smaller pieces. I—" Her exhale was shaky. "I can't do that again."

Joanie's words paired with CeCe's, and his throat went tight as the truth settled on his heart, heavier than ever. Fuck, he'd known he'd done something wrong. But he didn't realize it was this *horribly* wrong.

And he couldn't fucking remember.

For a second, that old darkness, the immaturity and ego, threatened to well up. To demand she give him the explanation he deserved. To convince her she would be stupid to not just immediately forgive him.

Then, just as quickly, it passed.

He'd grown and changed and become a better person. If he wanted a shot with this wonderful woman, he needed to show her that the change was real and permanent.

"I don't want there to be any more secrets or pain," he said. "I want to move on."

"I don't know," she whispered. "It's not that easy to just close the chapter and move forward."

He knew that. But he also knew that he needed this woman in his life. "I want to understand exactly what happened, and I want you to understand what *I* thought happened. At a minimum, I think we both need that." He placed both hands on her shoulders. "We've run long enough. We've let circumstances and our families manipulate us. But we're not young or naïve or gullible anymore. We can have the truth. The *full* truth."

He sucked in a breath when she finally looked at him, and the force of her pain socked him in the gut. Her words were equally as impactful. "I'm not sure I want it."

No. She had to. Otherwise—

Inhaling, he forced himself to calm, to speak from the heart. "From the moment I met you on that hillside, red hair flowing behind you as you corralled that horse"—a beast of a horse that had belonged to his sister—"I knew we had a connection." Colin clenched his jaw, regret pouring through him all over again. "I didn't trust in it like I should have. I wasn't strong enough to treat you as you deserved. I understand that. Just as I understand and will abide by your wishes if you want me to go."

He'd go if she asked.

But he wouldn't stay away. He'd find a way to make things right. No matter what.

She swallowed. "He was scared."

He touched her jaw. "Me or Ab?"

Ab being the horse that had belonged to his sister. The horse that brought a smile to CeCe's lips for a brief moment before it was gone like so much smoke, before quiet descended, a long, stretched-out silence that scoured his skin.

When she finally spoke, her voice was gentle. "For a long time, I assumed it was just Ab." Green eyes on his, holding his gaze, prompting him to speak.

"I did, too," he said, cupping her cheek. "But the truth is that I was terrified. I was trying so hard to be the man my father wanted, the one my family demanded. I locked all my extra emotions away and pushed them down after we were over until I wasn't sure I would ever be able to feel anything again." He sighed. "Maybe you're right, maybe we wouldn't have worked out because I didn't have the strength to be the husband you deserved." He let his hand fall from her face. "But I loved you, and I searched for you, sweetheart, and seeing you again, now, after all this time, I know that I want to try to make things right between us." Unable to stop touching her for long, not when she was in front of him, not when the giant cavern in his chest was finally beginning to be filled in, he brushed a lock of hair off her forehead. "So, I guess the question is, do you want me to try and make things right? Do you want something—a relationship, *more*, that might be *us* again?"

She sucked in a breath, her eyes closing for so long that his gut twisted into knots, and then those knots twisted into more knots.

"It wouldn't have to be an us," he said when it seemed she wouldn't speak, or worse, when the answer might be no. "Or at least not the *us* from before. We could build something stronger. We could have more." He braced himself for her refusal, even as the words kept coming. "I'm stronger now. I know my family isn't the perfect entity I'd made them out to be. I've seen their manipulation—"

Her eyes flashed with hurt, and his heart sank like a stone.

"That's it, isn't it?" he asked gently. "They did something to you."

"Col—" She broke off, shook her head.

He squeezed her fingers. "I know they were good at manipulating me to get what they wanted, but that's changed. I don't let them do that anymore, and I haven't for some time," he added. "If you give me this chance, I won't let anyone or anything come between us."

More silence. Longer this time. And the longer it went on, the more clearly he felt the pain of her rejection lick up his spine.

She was going to say no.

And he'd deserve it.

Because even without all the details, he could see the hurt, knew that whatever had made her leave with Ewan was grievous.

"I've grown up, CeCe," he said. "I won't hurt you. Not ever again."

She was still and quiet, so damned quiet. But as he studied her closely, Colin watched the pain in her eyes fade, saw the thread of hope faintly creep in on their edges.

And for a heartbeat, he dared to hope.

"Technically," she whispered, "that was two questions."

"Pardon?" His brows drew together, hope displaced by confusion.

"Before," she whispered. "You asked two questions—do I want you to make things right? Yes, I *do* want you to make things right. But . . . I also want to make *my* part in this right. Because I made mistakes, too. I'm not perfect. I should have—" A shake of her head, a sigh. Then she smiled, small and tentative, but it was there, as was the fire in her expression, the determination. His pulse slowed. Those knots untangled. "As for the other question —do I maybe want to be an *us* again?—the answer to that is—" Her teeth pressed into her bottom lip, released after a moment. "Yes. And I know it's probably stupid, that I should turn in my feminist card. But . . . I missed you. I miss what we had. I want to see what we might be, now that we've grown up."

"I'll make it up to you," he promised. "I'll make things right." He didn't miss the flicker of uncertainty in her eyes, knew that it would take time for her to trust him again. "Now," he said, trying to sound casual but no doubt failing horribly at it, "is this a tea or a whiskey conversation?"

Silence. Another bout of the tense quiet.

Then she grinned, laughing when they both answered at the same time, "Whiskey. Definitely whiskey."

SIXTEEN

Cecilia

"I DON'T REALLY KNOW where to begin," CeCe said, whiskey in hand. She took a sip of the fiery liquid, relishing the burn as it went down, soaking up the notes of oak and honey and—

She was delaying.

But she really didn't know where to start.

The image of him walking away on the cliff side eight years before, the wind mussing his hair, the moonlight transforming his solid form into shadows in mere seconds had broken a piece of her CeCe knew would never be the same.

Her innocence.

No, *that* part had been freely given. But even though they'd gotten back together two years later, their first breakup had stripped her of her emotional innocence, had dismantled her ability to . . . dream.

Happy endings were no longer guaranteed. She wouldn't ever be rescued by a man on a white—or in his case, a *black* —stallion.

It had taken her a long time before she'd begun to appreciate that having her heart broken had ultimately been a good thing. She couldn't have continued in this world with those naïve, rose-colored glasses on. She certainly wouldn't have survived college if not for Colin's cold treatment.

And she probably never would have spoken to him again at all if he hadn't messaged at one of her lowest times.

A torn rotator cuff.

A hugely significant tear that had required surgery.

She remembered being helped into a sling by the sports therapist, Sally, pain scorching her left arm with each tiny adjustment, but that hurt had been eclipsed by the conversation echoing through the closed door to her coach's office when he'd phoned her parents to tell them of her injury.

The voice that had been alternately stunned then shocked into silence then furious when her coach told her parents she'd been injured.

"What do you mean, it serves her right?" he'd shouted, making her wince and Sally apologize for hurting her.

CeCe hadn't the heart to tell Sally that her shoulder was nothing when compared to knowing that her parents were cold-hearted assholes, who just couldn't put their own egos aside to love their daughter as she was.

It had been stupid to hope, to dream that her parents might one day see reason and find a way to care for her.

But that wasn't possible.

Then Colin had messaged while she was hurt, and hadn't stopped messaging, even when she ignored him. He'd pestered her until she finally knew she would either have to block him or respond . . . and she'd been so lonely and so distraught by the agonizing recovery process, by her parent's estrangement that she'd finally sent something back. Of course, it had taken approximately two point six million emails and DMs from Colin before she'd even begun to forgive him.

But he'd been there. And he'd been her only constant.

They'd first rebuilt their friendship over long online chats about anything but her shoulder, her family—she'd wanted to forget her injury, what her parents had done. So instead, they'd spent most of their time discussing TV and movies, their likes and dislikes, the things they'd wanted to do together in her free time. They'd stolen moments in between all her couch surfing, around her hectic schedule as she'd worked any job she could muster in order to pay her medical bills—everything from fast food to contract drawing work.

But she'd never reached out to her parents again. Not after the surgery, not after the physical therapy, not after all the blood, sweat, and tears had left her with a shoulder that would never be good enough to swim competitively again.

God, how her shoulder had hurt, and, *God*, how the bills had piled up.

She'd lost her scholarship with the college, along with her health insurance.

But eventually she'd been able to get caught up enough to rent a room, and then later when their friendship had once again turned into something more, when because of his support, CeCe had been able to move past the hurtful relationship with her parents, to tuck it away and push forward and work harder, she had accepted his offer to stay with him in Scotland.

What more had she to lose?

Of course, if she'd known how much more she *could* lose, she would have never gone back.

Yay for hindsight.

But also yay for growing up, for no longer running from her problems.

Warm fingers brushed her cheek. "I don't care where you start, sweetheart. Just tell me *anything*."

She sighed and glanced down at the glass in her hand, running one finger over the curved edge. "I think, if you hadn't messaged me again right at the moment you did six years ago, I wouldn't have come back to Scotland, wouldn't have wanted to start over with you. No matter what."

"I wouldn't have stopped." A pause, blue eyes locked on hers. "*No matter what.*"

Her lips twisted. "You say that so confidently."

"I almost flew over when I found out you'd been hurt."

"What?" She glanced up and saw the truth in his eyes. "Why didn't you?"

He took a sip of whiskey. "I didn't think I'd be welcomed by your parents, and I didn't think it would be good for your recovery to have me there, mucking things up."

The sky outside was already beginning to darken, the hours of daylight being swallowed up as easily as krill into a blue whale's mouth.

CeCe thought of all the times she'd skirted his questions about her parents, where she was living, why she was working so much after recovering from a major surgery, and she wished again that she'd had it within her all those years ago to communicate effectively.

She'd held all the wrong things in. She'd made so many childish mistakes.

Then again . . . she'd been a *child.*

But she was grown now, and she sure as hell wasn't going to do the same damned thing. She was going to be better, to demand more of herself, of Colin. "I wish you would have come."

He held her gaze. "Me, too."

Tilting her head back to stare up at the ceiling, she took a few moments to gather her thoughts.

"So, you know I got hurt. I'd had a great season after"—she straightened and gestured between the two of them—"after *us.*"

"You told me you had a real shot at Nationals," he said.

"Yes," she agreed, "I thought the possibilities were endless from there. International competitions, maybe the Olympics, who knew, but things were looking really good. I was swimming faster, had never been in better shape." She took another sip. "And that continued over the summer. I swam every day and worked two jobs, since my scholarship didn't cover me for the non-school months. But that meant I didn't get out of shape and had an okay amount of money saved by the time school started."

"But then you got hurt," he said. "You never wanted to talk about exactly how it happened."

The memory still stung, one of those perpetual *if onlys*, but she went through it again, needed him to understand that it had framed so much of her thinking at the time. "It was in the first competition of the season. I felt something tear but kept swimming because it was in the final stretch of the race. I won." CeCe shook her head. "Turns out, if I hadn't pushed through the pain, I might still have a racing career."

Colin took the empty glass from her hand and set it on the table. "You couldn't have known that."

She shrugged. "A fact I understand *now*, but one that also haunted me for a good long while."

He brushed his knuckles across her cheek. "How long did it haunt you, sweetheart?"

"Frankly?"

A nod.

"It *still* bothers me," she said with a huff. "But you can't go back and change the past. The worst part was my parents never came, never called. Hell, they never even sent a card. Their only daughter's life and she had needed a pretty serious surgery followed by physical therapy, but they never once came to check on me."

"You never told me that."

"It was easier to forget," she said. "And avoid." Her eyes met his. "I'm really good at both of those, in case you haven't noticed."

He stroked a hand down her arm. "And *I'm* good at not seeing what's in front of me, at ignoring problems because I don't want to create conflict." Blue eyes flashed. "It's fucked up. If only—"

"We'd done things differently," she said softly.

"Yes." He swallowed hard. "That."

CeCe's eyes burned, but she felt the edges of those jagged wounds close slightly, their ache easing enough that she could breathe a little easier.

Colin touched her cheek. "I'm sorry about your parents."

She shrugged, her voice resigned. "That's the way they are. It just took until after my injury for me to truly understand they would never change. And, truthfully, I'd broken something in them, too. I wasn't their perfect daughter. I didn't stay close to home and go to the college they'd decided on for me. I didn't marry the man they'd chosen and start popping out kids. I wanted to travel and draw and swim fast." She laced her fingers together, pressing them to her heart. "I wanted to live my own life, and that would never *ever* be compatible with their expectations."

"It's their loss," Colin said fiercely, brushing back a strand of her ponytail that was lying around her throat. "I know I'm far from innocent in this, that I fucked up royally, but I don't know how a parent could do that to a child."

"I know." She laughed, and it sounded broken. "We both really got screwed in the parental department. I mean, I got disowned because I wanted to take a trip I was paying for myself and then swim competitively a few states away from home, and your mother—"

Colin straightened, eyes going flinty and cold. "What did my mother do to you?"

"Well, it was more to you." CeCe opened and closed her mouth. Damn, she hadn't wanted to go about it this way. She didn't want to hurt him, and her next words would *definitely* hurt him. "Though I guess you could say it was to *us*—"

The trill of her phone cut through her words.

She reached for it.

He stopped her. "Don't."

"I have to." She slipped her fingers from beneath his. "It's Hunter's ringtone, and I haven't talked to him yet."

Colin sighed, chin dropping to his chest. "Then, of course, you have to answer it." His tone was sincere, absent of sarcasm, and that settled some of the raging storm inside her.

Cecilia swiped across the screen, a smile breaking out on her lips when Hunter's little face appeared on her phone.

Saved by FaceTime.

That was a new one.

"Bye, CeCe!" Hunter shouted and then disappeared from the screen. A heartbeat later, Abby's face appeared in his place.

"Not you!" CeCe joked. "Where's my little squishy's face?"

Abby laughed but turned the camera around so she could see Carter toddling around the floor, a large plastic truck clutched in one hand. "And I'll have you know he told me just this morning *Carter no squish-squish.*"

"No!" CeCe said, collapsing back onto the bed and watching the darkening sky through the windows. "He's growing up too fast."

"I know." Abby sighed. "But that's not the only thing that's going to be growing." She pointed at her belly.

"What?" CeCe's jaw dropped open. "Are you saying what I think you're saying?"

Abby nodded. "Yup. Jordan is once again banned from wearing deodorant."

CeCe burst into laughter. "Don't tell me the smell of it is

making you sick again!"

Her friend rolled her eyes. "Every freaking type." But then she laughed. "My nose told me I was pregnant before the pregnancy test could."

"Oh, my God."

"I know."

"You're having another baby."

"*I know.*" Abby widened her eyes. "What the hell were we thinking?"

CeCe smiled. "That you're good parents?" A beat. "Plus, you have a hell of a nanny."

Abby blew out a breath. "About that . . ."

Cecilia's gut dropped.

"I was wondering if you would consider working for me."

Pregnancy brain was already striking her poor friend. "I *do* work for you, Abs."

She waved a hand. "I'm screwing this up. I meant, I want you to put your art skills to work in my department." Both palms came up. "No pressure, but your drawings are so amazing that I was hoping to hire you as a freelance artist. You could work from here or on your travels. I just . . . you're family, CeCe, and my kids and I are so lucky to have you. But I don't want to be the one to hold you back, not when you're so talented, honey. You deserve to have all your dreams come true."

Cecilia's eyes filled with tears. "Dammit, Abs. You had to go and do it."

Her friend sniffed and wiped a hand across her cheek. "I'm sorry. I mean, *I'm not sorry*. But I'm also a hormonal mess and have been emotionally puking all over everyone." Jordan appeared briefly on the screen, a box of tissues in his hand. He put them in Abby's lap and looked into the phone. "She asked you yet? You're going to say yes, right?"

"Ugh." Abby slapped his arm. "Stop being so pushy, dammit."

"Language." He smacked a kiss to her lips and glanced back at the camera, winking at CeCe. "Yup, she's definitely going to say yes."

"Jordan!"

"*Abigail*." He kissed her again, a little longer than before. "I love you to pieces."

"Congrats," CeCe murmured when he broke away to look into the camera.

He studied her through the screen, eyes concerned. The man was an emotional ninja, somehow always knowing when she'd needed a hug or a break from the stress of Hunter's care. Today was no different. One look and he knew something was up. "You doing okay?"

She nodded. "I'm fine. I just . . . I had some stuff come up."

His brows pulled together. "Do you need me to—?"

"*I'm all right*." CeCe put enough emphasis on the words that Jordan stopped talking and studied her. "If you say so," he said after a moment.

Her lids narrowed. "I *do* say so."

One half of his mouth turned up into a smile. "Okay then. Enjoy your travels, and I'll try to make sure Abby doesn't bug you too much—"

"Hey!" Abby protested.

"Be safe and don't hesitate to call. What?" He glanced off screen and CeCe could hear a female voice shouting something in the background. Rolling his eyes as he turned back, he said, "Apparently, Heather will be in Germany next week and wants me to plan her social calendar for her. She asked me to ask you about possibly getting together if the dates work out."

Jordan's sister, Heather, was another part of their raucous, romance-reading, ridiculously-expensive-pajama-loving quintet. She was also a true ball-buster and really fun to hang out with.

"That would be great. I'll text her."

"Awesome. Enjoy yourself, CeCe." He shifted slightly to the

right so Cecilia could see Abby on the screen again. "Say good-bye, sweetheart."

"Wait!" Abby said. "I didn't get to ask if you finished reading the book. Chapter Sixteen has that scene with the—"

Jordan sighed and waved to CeCe. "Bye." Then he bent to kiss Abby again, pressing the button to disconnect the call.

All the noise cut off in a split second, and she sighed into the silence, surprised at how much she missed her friends, Hunter's sweet face, and even Carter's little squishy toddler legs.

They were her family, and she was homesick for them.

Funny how she'd never felt homesick before, but her little motley crew of kids and adults had become more of a real family to her than her own blood.

They were her anchor in the way she'd once hoped Colin would be.

Her breath caught because *Colin*.

As in, she'd forgotten he was in the room with her.

CeCe sat up from the bed and whirled around. He was on the couch, a book in his hand. Her heart was pounding for some reason. No, not for *some* reason. She felt like she'd accidentally shown the table her hand in poker. Okay, that was a terrible analogy, but him overhearing the conversation was almost as though she'd stripped off too many layers of skin and was now a throbbing and vulnerable *and* homesick mess.

Colin looked up from the book. "Your friends seem nice."

The breath she'd been holding slid free. "They're the absolute best."

"*You're* the best." His lips tipped up.

She crossed over to the sitting space and picked up a glass of whiskey—his, hers, she didn't know at this point—and had just lifted it to her lips for a sip when she recognized what he was reading.

What. He. Was. Reading.

"What are you doing?" she gasped.

He turned the page. "She said chapter sixteen, right?" A tilt of his head. "Oh. *Oh.*"

"Colin!" She tried to grab the book from his hands.

"He puts his . . . *what?*"—Colin's eyes went wide—"*where?*"

"Oh. My. God," she muttered. "This is not happening."

"And his tongue? Holy . . ." He trailed off and looked up at her. "You read this?"

Cecilia's cheeks were burning. "Seriously, just stop. Oh, my God." She groaned again when he kept the book out of her reach and still managed to turn another page.

This book was dirtier than the last. A contemporary romance about a boss and his best friend's sister. He was a sex god and really, *really* adventurous in bed. Which was hot when reading it by herself or reflecting on it with her little Energizer Bunny of a vibrator.

It was also critically embarrassing when it was Colin reading about the sex god's . . . *godliness* and then giving her incredulous looks.

"And then he—" Colin dropped the book low enough for her to rip it out of his grip and launch it across the room. She barely heard the *plunk* as it smacked against the floor. Instead, she was suddenly aware of his body beneath hers, of his hard *Scottish broadsword*—to steal a surprisingly fitting term from her historical novels—pressed against her thigh. She was draped over him like a blanket and when he looked at her with heat in his gaze, she couldn't possibly be held responsible for her reaction. "You read that?"

"I'm not innocent any longer."

His eyes heated further. His hands slipped to her waist.

She lost the battle with herself.

Her hands went from his chest to his head. She dropped her mouth down to his.

And she kissed him with all the pent-up heat and emotion and yearning from the last eight years.

SEVENTEEN

Colin

THE WOMAN COULD *KISS*.

Her mouth was urgent yet soft, hurried but somehow giving him the sense that she was still savoring every second.

Colin didn't realize he'd been sitting there frozen, lost in the sensation of CeCe being his arms but not actively participating in her kiss, until his woman pulled back and glared at him. "Kiss me, dammit."

He didn't need to be told twice.

He wrapped his arms around CeCe's waist, and leaned back against the couch cushions.

Curves beneath his fingertips, breasts pressed against his chest, and then skin . . . And *fuck*, yes. Her skin was like velvet, silky smooth, and flushed pink from the blood rushing beneath the surface.

Not that his blood was calm and hanging out below his skin . . . or at least not *all* his skin. It had shifted so it was in a very specific, very hard and aching location.

CeCe shoved at the T-shirt he'd shrugged on when her phone had rung, not wanting to be half-naked and scarring a child if he happened to get caught on the screen.

But instead of being caught *in flagrante delicto*, he'd been captivated by the voices coming from her phone. Jealous of the easy familiarity between her and her former employer. Touched by how good she'd been with Hunter. She loved those people.

He was glad.

But it also made him ache.

Because he wanted her more.

He wanted this kiss to be about the future more than the past.

He wanted this moment to be the beginning of some magical happily ever after, like in one of her books.

"Colin," she said, tearing her mouth away, her breath coming in short gasps, her hands on his chest, his abs . . . teasing lower. "Your head is working too hard." She grinned. "And not this one," she added with a punctuating pat on his cock.

His hips shot up at the touch, and he groaned. "God, sweetheart. I love your hands on me. But—*ah*—I feel like we should finish the conversation—"

Her hand reached into his boxer briefs and squeezed. Hard. "Fuck now. Talk later."

Considering that Colin's eyes were rolling into the back of his skull, he couldn't argue.

Except, he *had* to argue.

Because somehow, he was lucky enough to have a third chance with the woman he loved, and he could not afford to fuck it up.

"CeCe." He gathered his wits, pulled her hand from his pants, and yanked her so she was flush against him. Which almost shredded his already tenuous control, because she was soft to his hard, smelled so damned amazing, and when she undulated against him—

Fuck, he wanted her.

Except . . . Cecilia might be determined to live in the moment, to pretend the past didn't still have its claws in him, but he knew they couldn't do this, not yet anyway.

Not without them both understanding *exactly* what had happened six years before.

"Stop," he said. "Sweetheart, *just stop*."

CeCe finally froze, though her chest heaved, and her green eyes gleamed with pain. "I just want to forget," she said, tears leaking out of the corners of her eyes. "I just want to move on."

He wiped away that glistening moisture, pressed a soft kiss to her lips.

Then he waited.

Her first instinct was always to run, but he couldn't let her. Not this time. Not when it meant their future.

Luckily, his patience paid off.

Glassy emerald eyes met his, and her exhale was shaky. "I don't want to hurt you."

God, she undid him.

"Haven't we hurt each other enough?" he asked softly. "We've let the past come between us, the secrets chip away at everything that's held us together. We both need to know *everything*."

A nod before her chin dropped to her chest. "You're right."

"So, tell me, sweetheart. Please."

Another shuddering breath. "Okay." One more shaking inhale and exhale. "Okay." Her gaze met his. "What do you remember from that day?"

He closed his eyes, tugging at the swirling twisted memories. He'd gotten up and dressed in his kilt, knowing that CeCe would love it, and then his mother and sister had come in with . . . "My mom showed me your journal. You'd written"—he swallowed against the hurt those words, in her own hand, had wrought. "You said you coming to Scotland, taking me back—" A shake of his head. "You'd written that your forgiveness after our first breakup was all a ruse, a way to pay me back for hurting you. You said I was just a pawn and you were going to wring every pound out of me then break my heart in revenge—" He broke off, opened his eyes.

"I didn't," she said and shifted so she was sitting beside him instead of on his lap. "Lana"—his sister—"had borrowed a journal. Ewan told me that one of her friends, Olivia, used to forge notes for you in school. He thought she'd done it, especially"—one half of her mouth curved into a bittersweet smile—"because I've never referred to a vacation as a holiday or a trunk of a car as a bonnet or even a shopping cart as a trolley . . ." She trailed off with a shrug. "A lot of things were off about the journal. But perhaps, you had to be me or at least an American, anyway, to see the word choice was completely wrong."

His throat had tightened the more CeCe talked. Because, of course, she was right. His family hadn't wanted him to marry Cecilia—both because she was American and also because she wasn't the woman they'd chosen for him . . . Olivia.

Olivia had been a neighbor, Lana's closest friend, and she'd also had a crush on him since they were children.

And Olly *was* beautiful, but she was also weak and went along with everything Lana said. There was also the fact that his mother and sister had thrown them together more times than he could count after the botched wedding.

Not that he'd been having any of that. He'd been too heart-broken and devastated—

Fuck.

If only he'd taken a moment—

He should have taken a *fucking* moment.

"But it wasn't just the journal, Col," she asked, resting one hand on his shoulder. "Was it?"

He shook his head.

Her expression softened. "See? And this is part of *my* regret, of wishing I did something, *anything* different. Instead, I got hurt and I ran. I hate that I did that"—a sigh—"that I *still* do that. I want to be kick ass, like my friends. To be tough and strong. To push back and demand. But all I ever seem to do is run to avoid conflict." Haunted green eyes drifted to his, made his heart convulse.

"No," he said. "This is all *my* fault. I'm such a fucking idiot. I believed them. How could I have believed them?" He shoved a hand through his hair, yanking at the strands. He'd known letting her go was the worst mistake of his life, but knowing why—that'd he'd thrown it all out over a few forged words, made it infinitely worse.

"Col—"

He locked his eyes with hers. "Will you give me another chance, sweetheart?" he asked. "I know I don't deserve it, but I'm asking—no, I'm begging you to let me prove to you that I've changed."

"Col—"

He touched her cheek. "And, if you give me this chance and we fight or something goes wrong and you run, know I'll find you," he said. "Know I won't stop looking, that I won't give up. And if someday you're done with me, if you want to break my heart, it'll be on a silver platter for you. Always. Forever."

"I don't want to hurt you, baby," she whispered.

"I know." He touched her chest, just above her heart. "Because even though the world, even though *I've* done my best to scar this"—he tapped the spot lightly—"it's pure. It's filled with love and joy and sweetness, and that's part of what makes you so fucking impressive."

Colin knew the words weren't exactly the most elegant or romantic. But they had to be said. And he'd say them to her over and over and *over* again until she began to believe him. She had to believe that she was special. That she was important and valuable—

Six years of damage. *No.* Longer than that. He'd broken her heart when she was eighteen, when he'd fallen for her but had been too scared of disappointing his parents to fight for her. The irony was that CeCe thought she was weak, but she was the strongest woman he knew. She'd fought for her independence, had gained it at great cost. And she'd never looked back.

That was strength.

What Colin had done in turn—catering to the demands of his parents—was the personification of pathetic.

"And you're not weak," he said, knowing she needed the words, better words, and wanting to give them to her, wanting her to see herself as *he* saw her. "You didn't become your parents' puppet. You fought through a serious injury. You survived a broken heart—twice." He cupped her cheek. "And built a life for yourself. With wonderful people who see your value. Who love you." He brushed his thumb lightly over her skin. "You did good."

Her breath shuddered out. "I just did my best," she murmured. "Put my head down and pretended I was fine."

That was such a CeCe thing to say.

To discount and minimize. But she needed to know she'd done something wonderful by not letting the hard, the heart-breaking events stop her from living her life.

"Sweetheart," he said. "I don't *want* you to pretend you're fine. I want to know everything that's in your heart, your mind. I know that we had—we *have*—a connection. I know we had an intense relationship, but I also know we couldn't really talk about the important things. Maybe it was maturity. Maybe I just wasn't able to be the partner you needed." He sucked in a breath, released it slowly. "But I do know I don't want that for you, for us."

Her eyes drifted away. "I don't know if I have the strength to be real." A beat as Colin opened his mouth, a rebuttal on the tip of his tongue, but Cecilia beat him to the punch. She shook her head in one abrupt movement. "No," she said. "Fuck *that*. I'm done being that. I'm done running or being a weakling." She stepped away from him, started to pace. As she moved, she shoved her hands into her hair, shifting the heavy locks, giving him a glimpse of that tattoo on her nape. He now had a crystal-clear understanding of exactly why Hunter was so important to her.

He was so damned proud of what she'd become.

And he was so damned ashamed of how weak he'd been.

She reached the hall, paused, and Colin watched her shoulders rise and fall on a breath.

Then she spun to face him.

"So, if I'm done running, if I'm taking this trip so that I can find myself, so that I can prove I can be strong and mature and valuable then I need to put my money where my mouth is and *stop* running, *stop* being weak, *stop* thinking that just because my parents, because *you* didn't love me the way I deserved, that I don't have value."

God, that hurt.

But she was right. He hadn't valued her or her love. He'd jumped to conclusions and hadn't believed in her.

She'd run. He'd let her go.

Her chin lifted. "Okay, so talk to me. What else went down, because if it had just been the journal, I think we . . ."

"Might have been able to work it out?" he asked, and she nodded. "Yeah. I think you might be right. But it wasn't just the journal. My mother had receipts for expensive clothes and the wedding dress—"

"I didn't ask for—"

He laced his fingers through hers. "I know. *Now*." He cursed, anger once again eating at him. Why hadn't he realized? "But that's no bloody excuse. I should have known then."

"There are a lot of things we both should have done," she said, squeezing his hand before exhaling deeply. "Then the bank account added even more fuel to the fire."

Surprised she knew that piece, Colin's eyes shot to hers.

She nodded. "Ewan told me when he came to confront me at the church. After he realized what was happening, he gave me his phone, had me call you. Do you remember?"

Colin frowned, searching through those memories. "I think so? I started drinking right after they showed me the journal and kept drinking through the receipts, the account, the boxes of wedding china you supposedly *had* to have."

Which was fucking pathetic. He thrust a hand in his hair, spun away, unable to believe that he hadn't just talked to her.

Whiskey. Anger. Not listening. Just like his father.

What a fucking lineage he came from.

But the past wasn't as important as this woman, as understanding and taking ownership. So, he turned back, crossed to her. "What did I say to make you leave?"

A shadow crossed her face. "It doesn't matter."

Every cell in his body filled with ice. Because *this*, this was the truth of what had torn them apart. "It matters, sweetheart," he whispered. "Don't run. Don't pretend it's okay. Just tell me, so we can move on." God, he hoped he could find a way for them to push through because otherwise, it would just hang over them forever.

Tears filled her eyes, but CeCe blinked them away and lifted her chin. "It wasn't a big deal—or, well . . . it isn't *now*. I've moved past it. I'm okay," she said, affecting a casual tone despite him knowing that the memories had to be shredding her inside.

"Sweetheart."

Her gaze went to his, steady and even and . . . filled with old pain. "You insinuated that the events . . ." A sigh. "You said they'd made you understand exactly why my parents had disowned me."

Fuck.

He paced away. "*Fuck!*"

How could he have said such a thing?

What special kind of bastard was he?

"God." He thrust a hand through his hair. "I'm such a fucking—"

Arms wrapped around his waist, a shaky chuckle punctuating the action. "Feel better?"

Shocked laughter burst out of him. "No," he said, turning around so he could take her in his arms. But she'd managed to slightly temper the anger he felt for his own idiotic actions. *Slightly* was the key word there because he knew it would take him a long time for him to forgive himself. What he'd said was unforgiveable. It had taken her softest, most vulnerable spot— that her parents hadn't loved her enough to appreciate her independence, to be there for her even though they didn't want the same things for her life—and exploited it.

He'd purposely chosen the way to hurt her the most.

After he'd won her trust again.

"Damn." She rose on tiptoe, pressed a kiss to his cheek. "Way to kill the mood, McGregor."

He smiled at her joke, but his words were serious. "I will spend every single day for the rest of my life making it up to you."

"No." She shoved at his chest, any trace of amusement fading away. "*No.* You don't get to do that, Colin. You don't get to shoulder everything like it was all your fault. *I* was there, too. I could have done things differently, pushed harder, refused to leave until you knew the truth." She raised her hands then dropped them back at her sides. "I ran. And I shouldn't have."

God, this woman. She was it for him.

Always had been, always would be.

So, when she ended her rant with a firm, "Got it, mister?" he nodded. And when she asked if he wanted to take a walk, he nodded again, got dressed alongside her then grabbed both their coats and helped her into hers.

Colin knew he wouldn't ever be able to deny her anything.

Cecilia Thiele absolutely owned him.

EIGHTEEN

Cecilia

CECE SHRIEKED with joy as they went over a huge dune of snow. Dune? Was that even the correct word? She knew there were sand dunes, but were there *snow* dunes?

Clearly, she'd been out of the Midwest and in California for too long if she couldn't remember the correct term.

Pile?

Drift? Ah, yes! That was it.

They'd gone up and over, their sled bumping to the ground with a jolt that threatened to steal her breath, but then Colin had his arm around her waist, tucking her safely against his side and all the hard muscles there. He was taking his job of keeping her safely in the basket very seriously, so her breathlessness was purely sexy Scot related.

Also, it was fun.

The dogs were barking as they towed the sled forward, little doggy smiles on their mouths, tails bouncing as they ran.

Adorable. If they weren't so noisy, she'd almost want a team for herself.

Yup, that would be *super* practical in California.

Hold on Hunter and Carter, let's jump on the sled and take the dogs down for a Happy Meal at McDonald's.

Totally doable, right?

Colin leaned down, the stubble on his chin teasing the skin behind her left ear. "What are you smiling about?"

She turned her head and spoke directly into his ear, so he could hear her over the barking, knowing she had a giant grin on her face. "How much the kids would love this."

His face softened but his eyes heated, and that space between her thighs, went tight.

And wet.

Which Colin apparently knew because *his* lips curved up and his tongue flicked against that spot behind her ear that she really, *really* loved when he teased. "Later," he said. "Later, I'll . . ."

And her jaw dropped open as he detailed every dirty thing he planned to do to her when they got back to their cabin.

Her pulse was pounding when he'd finished. Because, damn, his words were better than Abby's chapter sixteen.

"But first," he continued, "you're going to enjoy your sledding and gold panning, and then we're going to have a nice dinner."

"And a sauna?" she asked breathless.

"As long as you're naked and in my arms," he said, hand tightening on her waist.

Her lips tipped up even as her hand drifted down for a squeeze. "I think that can be arranged."

"I've decided that I don't like gold panning," CeCe declared, falling back onto the bed.

Her arms ached, absolutely ached after an hour of shaking

the pan from side to side and not finding anything more than silt, rocks, and mud.

"Not convinced you'll find your fortune in the river?"

"Even if I'd been dreaming of finding a huge nugget, *a la* Sutter's Mill, I think that this afternoon would prove I'd be crazy to continue with that fantasy."

Colin smiled as he plunked down next to her and gathered her in his arms. "What's Sutter's Mill?"

"Oh," Cecilia said, realizing that he probably wouldn't know much about U.S. history or what had sparked the California Gold Rush. "I got on a Netflix documentary kick awhile back and watched a ton of historical ones. This dude named James Marshall found gold in the 1800s and people came flocking West."

Colin kissed her forehead. "I like it when you say *dude*."

She chuckled. "I'm apparently a true Californian now. I say it to mean man or woman, senior or child, and as a curse, a plea, or an exclamation."

He nodded sagely. "You're a master of all things dude-related."

She smirked. "It's funny to hear you say *dude*."

"It's not that common of a word in Scotland."

CeCe rolled over in his embrace, settling atop of him with her chin resting on her folded arms. "But it has *so* many uses."

"Apparently." He stroked a finger down her cheek. "But the marvelous uses of dude aside, are you okay?"

"I think so." She paused, raising a finger when he started to open his mouth. "No. That's not entirely true. I *am* okay, but I feel almost . . . flayed open? I don't know how to describe it. Like I'm too vulnerable, and I keep waiting—" She bit off the rest of her sentence, knowing the words weren't entirely fair.

But even though they remained unsaid, Colin heard them anyway.

His eyes darkened. "You're waiting for me to hurt you again."

She hesitated.

He sighed and cupped the back of her neck, forcing her gaze to his. "No running. No pretending. I'm glad you're talking to me." He brushed a kiss over her forehead. "I'm so sorry you were hurt, sweetheart, and *I* won't hurt you."

Her heart squeezed. "But you can't promise that, Col. You can't predict the future. You can't wrap me in cotton to protect me from the world, and you can't realistically promise to not hurt me again. That's not real life." She stared into his blue eyes, seeing the truth dawn there. It was obviously something he didn't care to admit, but no one knew the future.

How could he promise to never hurt her?

It was unrealistic. Impossible.

People hurt each other all the time.

It's just that . . . she *really* wanted that promise from Colin, wanted for it to be the truth. That he would magically transform into that mythical hero, sweep her off her feet, and they would ride off into the sunset.

But myths were myths for a reason.

They were stories. Fantasies.

Fantasies that are grounded in reality, her heart argued. *That's where fairy tales come from. There's always a kernel of truth and reality within them.*

And great, now she was bickering with herself over the future of a relationship that would probably never be.

"I want to be the man you deserve," he whispered, and the torment in his expression made her heart ache.

"I want that, too," she whispered back. "So, so much."

Except she didn't believe in fairy tales.

She couldn't allow herself to.

Not any longer.

THE SUN WAS ALREADY low in the sky, but it did beautiful things to the silhouettes of the trees, made the snow glimmer with sparks of gold from the remaining rays of light.

Beautiful. Stark.

Alone.

Kind of like CeCe herself.

Except, she wasn't quite that any longer, was she?

Colin was there. They'd talked and she hadn't run and there were no more secrets and . . . he'd stayed.

Part of her brain couldn't believe it. Part of her heart was still in its protective casing.

She considered herself a generous person by nature, not one to hold grudges, someone who gave affection freely. After having the parents she'd had, she knew exactly how important compassion and understanding was.

But she was cautious.

Because she had given freely. Twice.

Her pencil began moving faster on the paper, remembering the whirlwind romance the first time—and the second—the big feelings, the way she'd loved Colin to the detriment of all else.

Trees flew onto the page, their shadows looking like disturbing skeletons sprawled onto the snow. The sun became an ominous orb. The sky a swirling fury.

Then she relaxed.

Because she wasn't that person anymore.

Yes, she was drawn to Colin.

But, no, she wasn't going to lose herself again.

She'd crawled, pulled herself through proverbial broken glass to get where she was. Maybe she didn't have it all figured out. Maybe she wasn't ever going to be as kickass as Heather or Bec or as self-assured as Abby or even with a hidden steel rod of a spine like outwardly sweet Sera. But she didn't *have* to be any of those things.

CeCe just needed to be herself.

Or the self she'd figured out so far.

She knew she could survive a broken heart. She knew she could work and support herself. She knew that she was loveable —despite her parents' best efforts to prove the alternative.

That was enough.

Which meant she got to decide what her life would look like.

So . . . did she want Colin in her life?

Maybe it was stupid, but yes. Plus, she was allowed to be stupid because it was. Her. Freaking. Life.

And she wanted *this* Colin.

She wanted the man who'd spread out a waterproof blanket on the snow, along with snacks, her drawing supplies, and a pile of extra blankets, before waking her with slow, hot kisses that had threatened to melt her from the inside out. She wanted the sweet man who'd brought her to the blanket and who'd left her to her sketchbook that morning when she'd mentioned in passing the night before that she was itching to draw.

She wanted the man who was giving her space to do what made her happy, somehow knowing that she wouldn't be able to concentrate on drawing if he *was* there because she would feel guilty ignoring him while she drew. Instead, he'd stepped back and had gone to do something she had absolutely no interest in.

Ice fishing.

But it was more than that. Because she also wanted the adventurous man who suggested she continue ticking off all of her bucket list items for this resort, starting with horseback riding that afternoon. The one who'd apologized and owned up for his behavior, his mistakes, accepted her apology for her own.

She'd grown up.

And so had he.

"Which is why you haven't kicked his ass out of your cabin,

Cecilia," she muttered, setting her pencil down and staring up at the sky. "Because no matter how much part of me wants to hate him for what he did, I know I'd have to hate myself, too. And I'm not that person anymore. I'm *not*."

Colin wasn't either.

Trust in that. But . . . don't *only* trust in that.

CeCe was going to trust in herself, too. In her ability to be strong and know her value, to stand up for herself and to leave if she wasn't being treated right. No more manipulations or punching bags.

Her life.

Her life.

Yes, she could do that.

Crunching footsteps drew her attention to the path that led to her cabin. Colin was making his way toward her, bundled up like crazy, but still giving major popsicle vibes.

She might have been outside for the morning, but the man had gone fishing.

On ice.

She shivered just thinking about it.

He stopped next to her, crouching down to brush a finger over her cheek, no doubt rosy from the cold. "Hey, sweetheart."

She shivered again, though she was uncertain if it was because he was touching her or because the finger that was on her skin was frosty.

"Hey, yourself." She cupped his cheek.

He winced. "Christ, woman," he said, hands coming up to cup both of hers. "Your hands are like ice. Did you even use the blankets I gave you?"

Meanwhile, he'd been out on literal ice.

She grinned. "I'm wearing snow gear and was wrapped in a dozen blankets. I'm fine."

He shifted, wrapping a blanket around her shoulders, one she'd just shrugged off as she'd readied herself to move back inside because she was, in fact, cold. "You're a bloody icicle," he muttered, setting another heavy weight of blanket on top of her, hands rubbing briskly up and down her back.

She didn't move or complain for three reasons.

One, she was cold, and this was warming her up.

Two, *Colin* was cold, and this was warming *him* up.

Three—which was the most important reason—she liked being in his arms.

"I have a thought about how to warm me up," she said, interrupting his grumbling.

He froze.

She leaned back enough to shift in his embrace, enough to bring her hands to the back of his neck and tug him down on top of her. This time, he didn't complain about the temperature of her fingers, probably because she was determined to warm her . . . mouth.

On his.

Ha.

And with laughter on her lips, with hope in her heart, she leaned back onto the blanket and kissed Colin until she was warmed straight through.

"My thighs are so freaking sore," CeCe said on a groan. She flopped back onto the bed, phone pressed to her ear, as silence greeted her through the airwaves.

"Hmm," Heather said.

"Shut up," CeCe told her. "My legs are sore from riding."

"*Hmm.*"

One syllable from her friend. One syllable that spoke volumes.

CeCe rolled her eyes. "From *horseback* riding."

"Is that what the young kids call it nowadays?"

"Ha," CeCe said. "You're only a couple of years older than me. I don't think you can consider me young."

"Young at heart."

That made Cecilia burst out laughing. "Oh, Heather," she said, once she'd regained a semblance of control. "I know we don't talk about heavy stuff all too often, but I stopped being young the moment my parents disowned me."

A pause.

"I know about your parents, CeCe."

Any amusement faded. "What do you mean?"

"I—" A sigh. "You know we ran a background check when Jordan hired you to watch Hunter," she said quietly.

"Oh." CeCe sat up, feeling a little sick to her stomach. Heather had known? Jordan had known? That her parents didn't want her. That Colin had—

Heather's voice was gentle. "You don't own the monopoly on bad parents."

"Yeah—"

"You share it with Jordan and me, with Abby, with Sera, with Bec. Hell, it's practically the glue that binds our quintet." Heather's voice went earnest now. "We all have baggage. We've all spent a long time being a mess or dealing with the mess that is our family."

"I—"

"And further that, you proving that you could make a life for yourself, even after what happened to you, shows that you're fucking incredible, Cec. You can slay proverbial dragons. You can persist and keep going, and"—she heard the smile in Heather's tone—"you're somehow still nice."

"Heather—"

"No arguing," she said. "Accept the compliment and—"

"Will you just be quiet and let me get a word in edgewise?" CeCe snapped.

Silence.

She immediately felt guilty for snapping at her friend. Heather was just trying to be kind and was being a good friend, and CeCe had unleashed on her. "I'm sorry," she said. "I didn't mean—"

Then Heather began laughing.

"See?" she asked when she pulled herself together. "Nice." A beat. "But steel underneath."

CeCe was quiet for a moment. "I've never thought I had steel before." Heather sucked in a breath, probably to argue with her about the presence or absence of steel. Cecilia beat her to the punch. "But then I came on this trip. Then I realized I'm not weak. Then I realized that even though my strength is different than yours or Bec's, it's still there and rock-solid and important."

"Hmm."

CeCe snorted. "I see why Abby wants to punch you when you say that."

Heather laughed. "It's my superpower."

"Well, superpower or not," CeCe said, "it's annoying."

"My work here is done." She heard Heather clapping her hands together, as though she were dusting them off. "I should probably get off the line anyway. I'm getting on a plane in a few hours." A beat. "But CeCe?"

"Yeah?"

"I'm glad you went on the trip, glad you're using the time to recognize that steel inside."

She smiled, at ease. No, *loving* that one of her kickass friends thought she was tough.

Nice, but strong.

Yeah, CeCe would take that.

But she also had a little sliver of mischief, a piece of her personality that tempered all that nice, that made her just the tiniest bit wicked.

See? Her friends were rubbing off on her.

Which was why she said, "As for the riding . . . I *was* talking about horses earlier." She bit back a smile. "But I don't think it'll be *just* a horse for much longer."

Quiet, then, "You'd better not have picked up an interspecies kink."

"A man," CeCe said. "I'm seeing one." This time she couldn't hold back her grin and spoke through her smile. "And for the record, I'm planning on doing a lot of riding with him. *A lot.*"

Heather began sputtering.

CeCe laughed. "Bye, Heath."

She hung up, giggling, at the same moment Colin pushed through the door to the cabin, takeout bags in hand. He took one look at her face and dropped them on the counter, then closed the distance between them and kissed her until her pulse thundered in her veins, until her breath came in rapid gusts.

"Do I get to know what had you laughing?" he asked, pulling back, his breath hot on her lips, his fingers in her hair.

She shook her head. "Nope."

A wicked smile. "Should I keep trying to convince you to tell me?"

She lifted a brow. "Is that what you were doing?"

He nodded.

She wrapped her arms around his shoulders, tugged him closer. "Then yes," she murmured against his lips. "Keep convincing me."

Colin took her at her word.

And just for the record, the man could fucking kiss.

"I DON'T NEED you to do that," she muttered, wondering how she could have gone from having so much fun with Colin over the last couple of days to wanting to throttle him within an inch of his life.

"I'm trying to help you," he said. "I can set up an account for you, enough funds to cover your travel expenses."

This man.

This infuriating man.

They'd been arguing for the last ten minutes because she'd discovered that he had put his credit card on the room to replace hers.

A fact she wouldn't have found out at all if she hadn't gone to pick up their dinner and realized the last four digits of the card slip she was signing didn't match those from her card.

Probably why he'd said he would pick up the food after his shower.

Instead, she'd gone down, wanting to save him a trip, especially since he'd been practically waiting on her hand and foot.

Then the receipt.

Then the stubborn man in front of her when she'd come back to confront him.

Of course, he was just wearing a towel, and the white cotton hitched around his hips made it hard to hold on to her anger. But she was strong. She was steel. She would not get distracted by tiny beads of water dripping down a luscious chest she wanted to capture on her tongue.

Get it together, CeCe!

Blinking and forcing her gaze from his chest, she lifted her chin. "I changed it back to my card."

A cavalier shrug. "I'll change it back."

CeCe glanced up further, tilting her head back to study the ceiling as she struggled to keep a hold on her temper. "Colin," she gritted out, "it is very important for me to pay my own way. I worked hard to afford this trip, and while I was very touched that Abby and Jordan paid for my flight and gave me the voucher for this hotel, my intention is for the rest of the time and for all of my incidentals, to travel on the funds that I have worked hard for." She dropped her gaze, met the piercing blue of his. "I need to do this myself. *For* myself. Otherwise"—her voice gentled—"it won't mean as much."

He was a statue across from her, hands clenched into fists at his sides.

But by the time she got to the last sentence, his hands had relaxed, his jaw unclenched. His palm came up, cupped her cheek, and he sighed.

She braced herself, some small part of her expecting fury to accompany their argument.

Instead, she got, "I understand, sweetheart."

One half of his mouth curved. "I'm a stubborn bastard, I know that, and I want to take care of you. I have the means. But —" He ran his thumb over her bottom lip when she began to protest. "But," he said again, "I understand what it means to need to be strong enough to take care of yourself and to work hard for something and want to put it to good use."

Her breath shuddered out, and she nodded. "You'll leave the card then?"

A nod. "Aye."

She shivered, and he grinned, knowing it did something to her when he talked to her like he was her rugged highlander rather than a suave businessman. Which is probably why he pressed his advantage and said, "You'll let me pay half when I'm here?"

CeCe considered that. "That seems fair."

"And take care of you in other ways?"

This man. Stubborn as hell, and yet she really, really liked the perseverance, liked that he wanted to look out for her. "So long as you let me take care of you right back."

He grinned, brushed his lips over hers. "I'm getting the better deal."

"Who says?" she asked, raising on tiptoe and shifting closer. "Plus, I wouldn't turn down a private plane trip," she joked. "I know Heather raves about hers."

"Good thing I have one."

She shook her head. "Of course, you do."

He opened his mouth, probably to explain about the plane, but she found she didn't care about the plane, couldn't summon up any worry about making sure things were exactly equal. She'd brought up her concerns, and he'd listened. He'd backed up. Stopped and they'd worked together to find a compromise.

And that made her relax, made her able to enjoy this time with him, this process of building something new that wouldn't break either of them.

Also, her newfound wicked streak had made an appearance.

"Oops," she said, nudging his towel loose.

It hit the floor with a soft *floof*.

Colin made a strangled sound, but by then she was on her knees, was sucking him deep into his mouth.

He groaned, fingers weaving into her hair. "Cecilia—"

She put her tongue to good use, paired it with her hand. Maybe she'd taken a while to come into her own, maybe she'd been shy and a late bloomer. But she knew Colin, she knew how to touch him in ways that drove him crazy, and she knew that it turned her on beyond belief to have his cock in her mouth.

To give him pleasure gave her pleasure.

She pumped and sucked and licked and—

Found herself dropped onto the bed, her jeans torn off her legs, her boots hitting the floor, and her panties . . . well, they disappeared like so much smoke.

And then his mouth was on her.

CeCe forgot about giving him pleasure. She forgot about everything except the pleasure he was giving her.

His tongue on her clit, fingers circling her entrance, pumping inside. One warm hand slipping under her shirt to pinch her nipple between thumb and forefinger. "I—*oh*—like that, Colin. Just right—"

He pressed the flat of his tongue against her, curled his fingers, and—

She exploded, sparks bursting behind her eyes, moans pouring out of her lips.

It took a minute for her to be able to peel back her lids, another for her to push herself up on her elbows. She wrapped her fingers around the still hard length of him and began pumping.

"Sweet—"

"Not fair," she said lazily, although she tightened her grip when he tried to pull her hand off. "You interrupted me and my evil plans. I wanted to make you come."

His breath caught as she stroked him. "That's not—"

"I like you in my mouth," she murmured.

"You don't have—"

"And"—she leaned forward, traced her tongue over the head of his cock—"the best part of fighting is the mutual makeup orgasms."

"Mutual make—"

She took him deep, put her hands to good use, and—

He exploded.

"See?" she asked when they both could breathe again.

Colin cuddled her close, pressed a kiss to the top of her head. "I bow to your all-knowing greatness."

"Got it in one." CeCe snuggled in, yawned, and fell asleep with a smile still on her lips.

NINETEEN

Colin

HE STARED down at the woman who'd stolen his heart when he'd barely been a man and had never given it back. She was sleeping, making those soft noises in the back of her throat that he thought were the most adorable things he'd ever heard.

But the fact of the matter was that CeCe was it for him.

He'd almost ruined that, twice, but he had another chance, and there was no way he was going to waste that.

Her mouth had made him see actual stars, his orgasm burning a hot trail down his spine that he was almost surprised hadn't left him with third-degree burns. He'd been planning on just treating her to an orgasm. Instead, she'd surprised him, and then surprised him again after he'd had his mouth on her by taking him again, by sucking and stroking and—

Colin closed his eyes and breathed.

Patience. Slow, steady.

Not waking the woman he'd never stopped loving because his cock was in a constant stage of hardness around her.

He tugged her a little closer, rested his chin on the top of her head, and held on to this moment.

The rest would come.

Colin wasn't going to fuck things up for a third time.

———

SUCH A BLOOD-CURLING scream would usually send Colin running in, his proverbial sword at the ready.

Instead, he just glanced over and smiled.

CeCe was running around with two little boys, along with their mother, as they had a Boys vs Girls snowball contest.

Spoiler alert: the boys were winning.

Snow clung to the red strands of her hair, stuck to the back of her winter parka, clung to the waterproof pants she wore. Her cheeks were tinged with pink, the tip of her nose was red, and . . . she was happy.

The sight was a vice on his heart.

He'd nearly lost that forever.

"I think your CeCe is going to need a hot shower after this."

Colin blinked and turned to the man standing next to him. Sam, the father of the shrieking hooligans, who'd doused CeCe and their mom with snow, huge grins on their faces, laughter peppering the air.

The younger boy slipped and went down face first, accidentally knocking his mom down into the soft, fluffy stuff.

Colin chuckled. "After this, I think everyone is going to need a shower *and* a nap."

The mom, Lizzie, who CeCe had apparently befriended on the shuttle ride to the resort, grabbed the leg of the other boy, tugging him down and smushing a handful of snow into his chest.

Who then grabbed a handful himself and pelted CeCe right in the face, leaving her sputtering, green eyes wide.

Sam laughed. "Right. I think I need to get in there and referee."

"I'll come help—" His phone rang. "Sorry, I've got to take this. I'll be there in just a minute," he said after glancing at the screen and seeing it was the office. Since they were under strict instructions not to call, Colin knew this must be the equivalent of the building being on fire.

He stepped away, swiped a finger across the screen, and brought it up to his ear. "Hello?"

"Colin, we have a situation."

It was hard to hear Francine over the voices shouting in the background.

"What's the matter?" he asked. "What's all the yelling?"

"Your mother is here."

"What?"

His exclamation had CeCe looking up in concern, but he quickly slapped a smile on his face and shook his head. He'd deal with his mother. He'd just wanted a little more time, wanted to have a plan in place to make it clear to her that he would no longer tolerate her interference.

Apparently, there wasn't time for that.

He needed to diffuse this situation, make sure the business wasn't impacted, that his employees weren't dealing with the manipulation that was his mother. Okay then, he'd lay the groundwork of his boundaries.

And then he was calling his solicitor.

Because he'd wasted too much time. Because he'd let them hurt CeCe.

That wasn't happening again.

"Give her the phone," he said.

"You sure?" Francine muttered. "This is a lot. Even from her."

Heaven help him. "I'm sure," he said.

"Okay."

Colin listened to the rustling, to the loud, shrieking voice getting even louder. Then his mother's voice came on the line.

"Colin," she declared. "These . . . *people* will not tell me where you are."

As though his executive staff were peons of no value. Meanwhile, they ran the corporation that made it possible for him to step away, that paid for so many of the things his mother *had* to have.

Fuck.

He'd always known she was spoiled and selfish.

He'd . . . always been a bit of both, too.

But he wasn't that person anymore. He'd changed, and though what he'd done to CeCe, how he'd treated others still made him cringe, Colin knew he needed to be done with regrets and looking back. He wouldn't stop trying to make things right with the people he'd hurt, wouldn't stop showing CeCe how precious she was to him, but he also couldn't keep living life with the engine in reverse.

Push forward.

Devise tactics to handle his family.

Execute them properly.

He was planning on doing the same thing with his mother, his sister, and he was damned sure going to confront them, to make them own up to their piece in all of this.

He just needed the plan in place first.

"Well, you have me now," he said.

"I—" Her voice dropped to a hiss. "I'm part of this company, as well. I've made sacrifices and—"

"Have you?" he couldn't stop himself from interrupting.

"I—well. Yes, of course, I have."

"What sacrifices?" While Colin had been burying his father, while he was taking up the reins and ensuring that McGregor Enterprises didn't collapse in on itself, his mother had continued on as usual—burning through money, buying anything she wanted.

And Lana, his sister, was right in line behind her.

"What?" his mother asked.

"Exactly what sacrifices did you make, Mother?"

"I—well—*I*—" He could almost picture her chin lifting, her shoulders straightening as the imperiousness reentered her tone. "I don't owe anyone an explanation of my actions."

Colin wanted to snap back, to demand that explanation.

But . . . patience. Plans. Calm.

Slightly more centered, he tempered his voice and asked, "What did you need, Mother?"

She went off on a tangent about needing access to additional funds beyond what was in her account because there was a fashion designer in Edinburgh designing the "most exhilarating boots."

How footwear could be exhilarating was beyond him.

"How much?" he asked, interrupting the soliloquy. His gaze was on CeCe, his mind already shifted to the woman in front of him. The group was all doused with snow, their expressions filled with warmth and laughter.

Colin didn't want the ice on the phone.

He wanted CeCe. He wanted *that*. The joy, the fun, the laughter.

She was the sun, and he'd been cold for years.

His mother named a figure. A ridiculous figure for boots— unless they were made out of solid gold. "Fine," he said. "I'll reach out to my accountant." CeCe shrieked when one of the boys shoved a handful of snow down her jacket, and Colin had the distinct out of body experience of wondering why in the fuck he was standing there on the phone when all he wanted to do was be next to the woman he loved. "I have to go—"

"Where are you—?"

"Goodbye, Mother." He hung up, and cognizant that his

mother would be persistent, especially when money was involved, he sent a text to his accountant.

Then he shut off his cell and shoved it into his pocket.

Scooping up some snow, he made his way over to the group, lifted his arm, readying to loft the ball—

"3, 2, 1. Now!"

CeCe jumped to her feet and launched a snowball at him. A snowball that was accompanied by four others, courtesy of Sam, Lizzie, and the boys.

Colin sputtered, dropping his own snow, and ran a hand over his face.

When he could see again, CeCe blew him a kiss.

He grinned . . . and tackled her to the ground.

And then, just because he could, he kissed her.

Then when she was breathing hard, when her eyes were glazed with pleasure, when there were plenty of '*ew!*'s from the boys . . .

He got her with a snowball of his own.

A LITTLE WHILE later they returned to the cabin, the tension from the conversation with his mother having dissipated along with the fading sunlight.

"Sauna?" he asked, closing the door behind them and rubbing his hands together. CeCe's nose and cheeks had turned pink in the cold and though she'd assured him repeatedly that she was fine, she was shivering.

"No," she said. "No sauna."

Then she unzipped her coat and dropped it to the floor.

"Wait," he said, rushing over to where she'd left her robe. "Put this on. You're freezing."

Her shirt followed her coat. Then her pants. She stood in

front of him in a bra, panties, and socks. It might have been the sexiest thing he'd ever seen.

"I'm not cold," she said, walking toward him and yanking down the zipper on his own coat.

"You're trembling."

"Because I want you," she said. "So damned much."

"Sweet—"

CeCe shoved his coat off his shoulders, started tugging at his shirt. "Col. I *need* you."

"I—"

"Please," she said. "Please, don't deny me this."

Colin swept her up into his arms. "I was just going to say, I can take off my own clothes."

"Oh."

"Yes," he said. "*Oh.*" He set her on the bed and stared down at her for one long moment. That was all his ragged control could take. Then he reached behind her, unhooked her bra and exposed those gorgeous breasts. Her nipples were hard points, demanding his mouth.

He obliged, sucking one deeply while teasing the other with his free hand.

"Col—" She broke off as he switched sides.

"You're so fucking beautiful," he murmured, releasing her and kissing a path down her body. He stopped to tug off her panties, to nibble at one hip, to trace the path of freckles along her waist with his tongue. But those were mere distractions, side trips from what he really wanted.

Which was Cecilia's wet pussy pressed firmly against his mouth.

And it was *wet*. He could see it glistening, smell that musky scent even though he was still six inches from the motherland.

Her hips shifted, tilting slightly, legs spreading as he came closer.

"Mmm," he said. "You want my mouth, sweetheart?"

"Get your tongue inside me, Colin," she demanded, head dropping back to the pillow and her legs spreading further. "I need you."

He traced a finger through the damp heat, cock throbbing when she moaned.

Then he stopped delaying and put them both out of their misery.

One lick sent his arousal sky-high. It threatened to burn him to ash, to snap his last semblance of control. He was finally going to be able to make love to the woman who held his heart, and the only thing that was stopping him from thrusting deep and rutting like an animal was how strongly he wanted this to be about Cecilia. He needed to make it perfect for her. He needed her to see how perfect *they* could be together.

The next touch of his tongue shattered something within her.

She gripped his head, pressing it more firmly against her center and ground herself against his mouth.

"More tongue," she ordered, and who was he to deny her anything? "Oh fuck. *Yes.* God, Colin. Like that."

"Mmm," he murmured, loving the way the sound made her buck and grip his hair tighter. He firmed his tongue, found her clit and unleashed every trick he'd learned over the years.

"No," she said when he circled instead of flicking his tongue. "The other was be—*better*. Mmmm," she moaned.

Goddamn, but there was something unbelievably sexy about a woman knowing what she wanted in bed.

"Like that." Her breath caught. Her hips jerked and every muscle in her body went granite hard. "Oh, God. Yes. I'm so—mmm—I'm so close, Colin. Please—"

He slid a finger deep, curling it up and forward.

And she shattered.

Feeling her clench around his finger, her hands in his hair, her legs over his shoulders was fucking incredible.

But what was even better was her tugging his head up and kissing him before staring deep into his eyes. "Thank you." A whisper, but accompanied by a confident smirk that made him want to drop right back down between her thighs and repeat the process from the beginning.

She must have read the intent in his gaze because she grabbed his shoulders then reached behind her into that tote bag of hers.

Out came the string of condoms.

"Any interest in helping me use these?"

TWENTY

Cecilia

COLIN'S LIPS curving into a grin was just about the sexiest thing CeCe had ever witnessed.

Okay, fine. *That* was a lie. Even sexier was what happened next.

Namely, Colin making his clothes disappear with all the aplomb of a magician. There wasn't any room for embarrassment or insecurity. Hell, he'd had his mouth between her thighs mere minutes ago.

But this did feel a little different.

More intimate.

Especially when he hesitated by the side of the bed and just stared at her.

She propped herself up on one elbow, lifting her other hand up to rest on his stomach. "I like the way you look at me," she said quietly.

There was that grin again.

"I definitely like the look of you, lass."

"Not that again," she said, all drama as she flopped back onto the mattress. "You'll transform me into a puddle of goo at this rate, I swear, McGregor."

"So long as you let me watch your diddies jiggle like that," he said, his use of Scottish slang for boobs making her crack up.

"Oh, my God." She slapped a hand over her mouth to contain her laughter. "You're terrible."

"And you have the most incredible breasts I've ever seen."

The intensity in his eyes made her breath catch, but she just tore a condom from the strip and waved it at him. "Enough pretty words. If you truly believe that, then prove it to me."

She didn't need to ask twice.

In a heartbeat, he was on top of her and kissing her with all the pent-up passion of a man on the edge. But, CeCe wasn't a passive participant.

Nope. She got in on the action.

She stroked and squeezed. She petted. She kissed and licked and nipped.

Until she could barely see straight from all the longing.

"Please, Col. I need you inside me now."

He didn't argue, just grabbed the little plastic square from near her head, tore it open, and rolled on the condom. He paused, knees between her open legs, cock two inches from where Cecilia needed it. But when she tried to cage him with her thighs and tug him down, he resisted. Instead of sliding home— where they both desperately wanted him to be—he stopped. Waited for her eyes to find his. Colin's warm palm cupped her face, the pad of his thumb stroking across her cheekbone. "You're sure? We don't have to do this now. We can take longer—" A shake of his head. "Keep doing other things." His eyes widened. "Or not do *anything*—"

Her heart swelled and she placed her fingers over his lips. "I'm sure."

Despite everything—the heat of him so close, her desire

raging low and hot and desperate, the past, the present—she *was* sure.

They'd been moving toward this for eight years now.

"I've dreamed about having you in an actual bed," he said, almost reverent as he nudged at her entrance. "About making up for . . . before. I thought often about making it better. Making it everything you wished it had been."

CeCe wrapped her arms around his shoulders and tugged him down so he was pressed tightly against her chest. "You're all I ever wished for, Col. You're all I've ever wanted."

He filled her in one stroke, gentle but insistent as he buried himself deep.

Tears blurred her vision.

Because it felt so damned right.

Because this was the piece she'd been missing. This wasn't a release, a mutual sprint toward orgasms.

This was . . . *Colin*.

His hips flexed, drawing back and out before pressing in, deeper and a little harder.

She moaned, and he repeated the movement. Then repeated it again. And again. Until the tears dried in her eyes and she was more focused on sensation than feelings.

Until she was groaning and screaming, demanding "More" and "Faster" and "Harder."

Until she was flying over the precipice and Colin was trailing her, growling her name as he tumbled, too.

Until her heartbeat slowed and reality returned.

He cradled her close for long moments, brushing back her bedraggled hair, pressing a kiss to her temple. Then, eventually, as though he were supremely reluctant to let her go for even a second, he slipped from the bed with a murmured, "Be right back."

His footsteps echoed down the hall to the bathroom. She listened to the sounds of the taps turning on and then off before he returned with a washcloth. He cleaned her, returned the towel to the bathroom, and came back to bed.

There weren't any words exchanged as he pulled her into his embrace and tucked the covers over them.

CeCe didn't say anything as the sky lit up with green in a breath-stealing display, though the air caught in Colin's lungs as frequently as it did in hers.

She didn't speak until Colin's breath evened out and came in slow inhalations and exhalations.

Only when he was deeply asleep did she dare to murmur the thought that was circling her brain.

"What have I done?"

She had tumbled headlong into love with Colin McGregor.

For a third time.

Only time would tell if that would be the third biggest mistake of her life.

TWENTY-ONE

Colin

HE WATCHED CECILIA SLEEP, her chest rising and falling in slow, even breaths. The green in the sky had been short and breathtaking, though that hadn't stopped her from staying up too late, waiting and hoping for the northern lights to make an another appearance.

Of course, the hotel had installed an "aurora alarm" in the cabin, one that would be activated if the aurora borealis made an appearance.

Not that CeCe trusted that.

She'd said the first night as they'd lain bundled up in their robes, lying under the glass roof, "I've waited my whole life to see this. I'm not trusting it to technology."

Colin smiled at the memory.

She'd been like a kid on Christmas morning the first time the sky had lit that otherworldly green and it had made his heart catch, that little slice of the Cecilia of the past, the one who appreciated the beauty of the world. The one who'd stared endlessly over the cliffs near his home, studying the ocean and trying to commit the sounds of the waves breaking against the rocks to memory. It had reminded him of the girl who'd been captivated by the small details in a stained-glass window, the one who'd so appreciated the curls and different shades of color in his horse, Bowen's, mane that she'd spent long hours sketching every minute detail.

That had been the woman he'd fallen for.

The one with a zest for life, who'd been so freely giving with her love and affections. She hadn't been like the other women in his life, always calculating which power play would gain the most or throwing a temper tantrum when they didn't get their way.

Cecilia had been different.

And it had been their downfall.

"Fuck," he muttered under his breath, carefully sliding free of the mattress while being sure to keep CeCe covered with the blankets.

He had to make a call.

A long overdue call that would probably involve an apology.

Och. He hated apologies. Giving them, that was.

Quietly, he stuffed his feet into his boots and shrugged into his parka. He grabbed his phone from the side table before slipping through the front door.

Then he dialed a number he knew by heart. One he'd blocked six years before.

One he unblocked now.

The sun was just coming over the horizon, but it was already close to eight in the morning. Of course, Finland didn't get much sun this time of year, and it would already be setting by one in the afternoon, so there wouldn't be much of a chance to soak up its rays.

But none of this had anything to do with the call he needed to make.

Except to delay the inevitable.

"Fuck," he muttered again and pressed the green button on the screen.

Colin had a moment's regret when he realized it was two hours earlier in Scotland, but by then the phone was already ringing.

And ringing.

And ringing.

Then going to Ewan Campbell's voicemail.

"Well, fuck." He started to shove the phone back into his pocket, but it started vibrating, and one glance at the screen had his gut churning.

The arsehole was calling him back.

He glanced heavenward for one long moment before swiping his finger across the screen. This was what he wanted. Right?

Right.

He put the phone to his ear. "Aye?"

"You're a stubborn fuck, aren't ye?" Ewan said.

God that voice was his childhood, and the longing it set off in his heart was almost shocking. It wasn't a surprise that he'd missed the friend he'd grown up with, the one he'd gone off to Oxford with, but what *was* shocking was the depth of that emotion.

They'd shared so much, and Colin didn't realize until he'd heard Ewan's voice how empty he'd been the last few years.

"Aye," he agreed. "I think I might have misunderstood a few things."

"*A few—*" Ewan broke off then continued with a lowered voice. "A few things?" he whispered. "You misunderstood a whole hell of a lot, Colin."

"I'm sorry."

A pause, probably surprised, because he hadn't been the type of person to apologize outright for anything.

"Right." Another pause, longer this time. "You wouldn't let

me or CeCe explain. Do you even remember what you did to her? What you said?"

Colin sighed. "She told me—"

"*You've seen her?*" he exploded. "After everything, she's let you near her?" There was a female voice in the background, a muffled protest. "Sorry, baby," Ewan said, and the sound of rustling filled the airwaves.

"Is this a bad time?" Colin asked.

"It's barely six in the morning," Ewan retorted. "That's never a good time. Especially when a couple is dealing with all the demands of a newborn."

Ewan had a kid?

"You're married?"

Ewan sighed. "Two years now. And my son is six weeks old."

"Fuck," Colin murmured.

"I know," Ewan agreed. "We're getting old. Growing up."

"I don't know if that idiom can be applied to me," he said. "Or not until recently, that is."

A pause, then, "You've seen Cecilia?"

"We're on holiday together." He kept the explanation as simple as possible.

"So, she trusts you?" Ewan bustled around in the background, turning on and off water as he filled a container. Probably for coffee. His friend had never been able to live without the caffeinated beverage.

"I don't know that she trusts me." Colin sighed and sank down onto the snowbank a few feet away from the cabin. "She's waiting for me to hurt her again."

"And you don't want to hurt her?"

His spine went ramrod stiff. "What the fuck?"

Ewan spoke over the sounds of coffee percolating in the background. "Hurting Cecilia seems to be a pattern for you. She's been happy and has a stable job. She's made friends."

"You've kept in touch with her." His voice sounded dead, even to his own ears.

"Yes, Col. She needed someone to look after her."

When you couldn't, was the portion of his sentence that he left unsaid.

Colin heard it anyway.

"I was in a fucked-up place. Not an excuse," he hurried to say when Ewan started to speak. "I made my first fuck up right, but I don't know how to fix the second one."

Silence.

Dammit. He dropped his head to his knees, a long tense quiet the only response to his words. At this point, he was ready to beg.

"Please, Ewan. I need you to tell me how to fix it."

A long breath hissed through the speakers of his phone. "There is no easy fix, you bloody idiot." A pause. "What you said to her was beyond cruel, and the only way you might have half a hope of truly repairing things is to give her time."

Time. *Fuck.* Why did it always come down to time?

TWENTY-TWO

Cecilia

COLIN WAS QUIET. *Too* quiet.

He'd come in a half hour before, his arms full of yummy-smelling baked goods from the restaurant near the lobby. He'd woken her with a gentle kiss and by waving a chocolate croissant under her nose.

But he'd been too quiet as he'd drunk his cup of coffee. All notes of teasing had disappeared, and it was making her uneasy.

"I'm going to take a shower," he announced, pushing back his chair in an abrupt motion that made her jump.

"Okay," she said, her heart picking up its pace.

Perhaps this was the moment he'd decide to get on with his life.

Without her.

Well then, so what? She wasn't that girl anymore. Her chin lifted, and she straightened her shoulders. If he wanted to go, then he could just let the door hit him on the ass—

He kissed her.

"I love you, Cecilia Thiele," he said softly, when they'd

broken for air. One brush of his thumb between her brows. She was probably frowning again. Then he strode down the hall, closing the bathroom door with a *click*.

But . . . had he just said *that?*

Why? How?

Blowing out a breath, she shook her head then ate some more of her chocolate croissant. Not in confusion exactly, but definitely in bewilderment.

"I love you," she murmured, touching her lips. "*He* loves me."

And he'd walked away again.

Well, that wasn't going to stop her. Not this time.

She put down the chocolate croissant—

Why did that make her giggle? But she could imagine a voice through a megaphone blaring, *"Put down the chocolate croissant and go attack your boyfriend*—was he her boyfriend at this point? Maybe? Did she want that? Also, maybe. But also, yes, she thought she did.

Anywho, she digressed.

Because Colin was in the shower, and her mind was still shouting, *He needs a blow job, STAT!"*

Cecilia didn't know what was wrong with him, what had happened overnight or earlier that morning, but he was off and unlike in the past, where she'd tiptoed around, afraid to rock the boat, she had already decided she wasn't going to be in a relationship like that again. So, she was taking a page out of her friends' books. She was going to bend less. She was going to clearly state what she needed in this relationship (yes, she'd decided that she wanted to explore what a relationship with Colin would look like), and she'd demand they talk things out.

No more secrets. No more sweeping things under the rug.

Because if they'd come together six years ago instead of drifting about, caught up in their own traumas, things might have been different.

They might have still been together.

She stood and pushed back her chair.

Or maybe they wouldn't be together, maybe their marriage would have imploded in the end. But what CeCe was realizing with a growing certainty was that the past was the past and if she really did want to move forward with Colin in her life, then things between them were going to have to change.

Old patterns needed to break.

She stripped off her tank top, dropped her pajama pants to the floor, her underwear.

Naked, she pushed through the door to the bathroom.

Then froze.

Colin was fully dressed, sitting on the closed lid of the toilet, his head in his hands, the shower on full blast with steam filling the space in little gray, damp curls.

He glanced up at her intrusion, his jaw dropping open even as his eyes went scorching hot. His gaze dipped to her breasts, lower.

And while her stomach clenched in return—this man made absolutely every cell in her body stand up and take notice—her mind was more concerned.

She sank to her knees, feeling the damp air curling around her skin, placing her palms on his knees, the fabric of his jeans almost rough against her bare skin.

"What is it, baby?" she asked, slipping closer when he didn't touch her in return.

Nothing. Except his eyes closing and a deep breath expanding then collapsing his lungs.

CeCe reached up and put a hand on his cheek. "Colin? Has something happened?"

His eyes flashed open. "I spoke to Ewan."

Oh, fuck.

"Uh—"

"Why didn't you tell me?" he asked, agony in every line of his expression.

"That I still talk to him?" she asked when he nodded, keeping her tone gentle, considering that he'd thought she'd run off with Ewan six years before. "I didn't even think about it. Ewan has been good to me. He got me out of a bad situation, helped me get back to the States. But he's never been more than a big brother figure, checking in on me now and then." She sighed. "I wouldn't have let him be anything more, anyway. I wasn't capable of letting anyone in for a long time. But none of this makes any difference to what we're building now. Not with us looking forward instead of back. We should leave the past where it belongs."

Blue eyes full to the brim with pain. "I'm worried that I broke something we won't ever get back."

"You did," she said then hurried to add when he winced, "*We* did, Col. But we also don't want to go back, right? Isn't the whole point of this, of us being here, to build something better?"

Silence, then, "*I* should have been the one who was there for you."

Oh.

She understood now. He wasn't jealous of Ewan, rather her relationship with him was just one more reminder, one more regret, one more should-have-could-have-would-have. But before she could tell Colin that, his hands came up to grip her shoulders and though his tone was fierce, his touch was gentle. "Also, your logic is flawed. We are both holding on to anger and fear that is doing neither of us any favors, and if we can't let that go, we can't begin to build something better."

She paused and considered that. "What I feel for you isn't anger."

He stilled. "Then what is it that you feel?"

Love. But she was too scared to admit it.

"This," she said, stretching up to kiss him rather than confessing her feelings.

Colin allowed her lips to briefly collide with his before he pushed her back. "*That's* a distraction. We need—"

"No," she said. "What I need is for you to press your body to mine and hold me close. I need your kisses to show me what I mean to you, I need your touches to ground me in the here and now. Words are so easy, don't you see?" She dropped her head to his shoulder. "But actions are everything. Please, Col. Please . . . just give me everything."

He stood, helping her step into the shower before stripping off his clothes. "You already have it all," he said and kissed her.

Water sluiced over their skin, warm enough in actuality but almost freezing cold in comparison to the heat of his body. Nothing felt as good as him pressed flush against her, hard where she was soft, spicy where she smelled sweet. He didn't have the body of the gym rats she saw in Northern California, but his abs were hard and defined, and his pecs were squeezable to the nth degree.

So, she indulged, palming them, loving the way he groaned as she ran her nails over his nipples.

"I love you, sweetheart," he murmured, his breath hot near her temple, his lips kissing the delicate skin there. "I don't know how you can ever forgive me for what they did to you, for what I did and thought, for what I said."

"Don't—"

"I know. Actions." Colin's arms tightened around her. "But I *have* to say this. Yes, I was manipulated. Yes, they did a bang-up job of doing it. But, fuck, *you were mine.* I should—" He swallowed hard.

"I *am* yours, Colin McGregor." Her lips curved. "Always. Even when I was fighting very hard against it, I could never deny this . . . this *thing* that ties us together. I knew it from the first time

I saw your muddy boots on that hillside, stalking toward me, all brooding-hero-style"—she grinned up at him, relieved to see him smiling back—"and I know it in the man you are today. The one with agony in his eyes and regret in his voice. We both screwed up, but keeping hold of those old hurts will get us nowhere."

"I could just throttle them—"

"Baby." She rose on tiptoe, stared him in the eyes. "You know everything now. Can you let it go?"

He dropped his forehead to hers. "I'm so angry. We lost years because—"

"Because we couldn't find the strength in our relationship to talk it out." She brushed back a lock of his hair. "If we couldn't even talk through our second major hurdle—and I don't disagree it was a damned big one. But we didn't let it bring us closer. Instead, the deception imploded everything we had, and I think that means we were too young, and it wouldn't have worked out anyway."

"It damn well would have," he snapped.

She sighed, wrapping her arms around his neck. "I know I'm just riding this wave of crystal clarity that has come six years too late, but no, I don't think it would have. Sooner or later your family would have found a way to drive us apart."

Colin didn't say anything for a long moment, just held her tightly. But finally, he slowly exhaled and said, "You're right. I hate that you're right in this case, but . . . yes, I think they would have found a way."

"Words a woman dreams to hear," she deadpanned.

He released one hand from her back and used it to tip her chin up then brushed a kiss against her lips. "You didn't deserve any of the bad things that happened to you, and I will do my best to ensure every day from this one forward has something good in it."

"As long as that something good involves you," she said,

closing her eyes and inhaling the clean, warm scent of him, "then I'm sold."

"And this *thing* between us?" he teased. "As long as it involves that?"

"Shut it, mister." She kissed his pec, flicked her tongue over one nipple, grinning when he moaned. "We can't all be Lotharios spouting perfect romantic sentiments." He opened his mouth, but she rose up to slant her mouth across his. "Now show me exactly how *romantic* you can be right here in this shower."

So, he did.

Twice.

And when they fell into bed later that afternoon, the sky already dark, the stars blinking cheerfully down on them, Cecilia fell asleep with a smile on her lips.

TWENTY-THREE

Cecilia

"I'M GOING to meet my friend Heather in Berlin next week," Cecilia said over dinner.

She and Colin had finally emerged from the cabin after doing little more than sleeping, having sex, and waiting for the night sky to light up with that otherworldly green of the aurora borealis for almost three days. But today she'd spent the morning sketching then several hours in the afternoon with Lizzie, enjoying the spa and getting in a little girl time while their various boys had whittled away the hours doing who knew what.

They'd also made plans to get together when they both returned to California, and CeCe was excited over the prospect of a new friend.

And then there were the magical auroras.

It still made her breath catch, the way those waves of emerald seemed to streak across the sky. She'd managed to see it twice more, bringing her total up to four incredible views.

And each time they appeared, the air still froze in her lungs and awe welled up in her heart.

But she was also going a little stir-crazy.

They'd panned for gold, done the dog sled thing, gone horse-back riding, eaten at the restaurants, had food delivered. They'd read and talked. They'd fucked like rabbits.

Items were being checked off her bucket list left and right, but she missed the sun.

By the time they got up in the morning, the sun was already on its downward trek and when early afternoon rolled around, it was pitch black. The short days were messing with her mind, as was the isolation.

The staff at the resort were great at being unobtrusive, but she needed some people around. Needed to be able to walk down to the corner coffee shop and grab a pumpkin spice latte. She wanted to wear cozy sweaters and black leggings and infinity scarves, not parkas and snow boots.

She missed being home.

She missed Hunter and Carter and Jordan and Abby and Bec and Seraphina.

She missed her family.

But she had Colin, her heart reminded her, swelling like a balloon when he replied to her statement about meeting Heather with, "Do you want me to go with you? I know a great restaurant near . . ."

She squeezed his hand. "Don't you need to get back to work?"

He grinned. "I haven't taken a personal day in almost six years. Not since—" His smile faltered, but he pushed on. "Not since I buried my father."

"But—"

"It was the perfect way of hiding," he murmured, snagging a piece of meat off her plate. "But I'm done with throwing myself into work at the expense of a life that doesn't involve conference calls and emergency client meetings."

"Yeah?" she asked.

He captured her hand and kissed her fingers. "Plus, I think I can spare a few more days for the woman I love." Her heart skipped at the words. "My business partner, who also happens to be named Heather, will be in Berlin for a conference at the end of next week. It would be good to touch base with her before this project takes off."

"So, work even outside of work?" she teased.

His expression went guilty. "I—"

She stood up from her chair, crossed around the table, and plunked herself into his lap. "I'm teasing." A kiss to his cheek. "And you don't have to stealthily check your emails. I'm going to start doing some freelance design work for my friend Abby's company, so I might be chained to my laptop more than you."

"Why work on holiday?" he asked.

"So I can pay for my travels," she said. "And maybe visit a certain Scottish hunk on my way back to the States."

"Mmm, I like that idea," he murmured. "Though that would mean I'd let you out of my sight, and I'm not sure I can do that yet."

"Col." She touched his cheek, heart starting to pick up its pace. How could she have not considered the fact that they lived an ocean and a continent apart? How would they manage the distance? She couldn't drop everything and move to Scotland. Not again. "We're going to be okay, right? I mean, we'll manage the distance? I—I mean, I live in California—"

One hand rested on her hip and squeezed. "I'm rich, remember? I have a private jet that is always at the ready."

"But—"

"Plus, my new venture is based in California. It's why I was flying out of San Francisco in the first place."

"Yeah, about that," she said. "If this private jet is such a great perk, why were you on a normal flight with the rest of us cattle?"

"I'd loaned it to a friend." A shrug. "Next time, they're on their own." He grinned. "Especially since I'll be in California more than Scotland for the foreseeable future. This project is why I've been working so hard to consolidate the McGregor businesses, to make sure they're strong and healthy." He tilted his head down so his eyes met hers. "It was stifling, and I wanted to live my own life."

"But the dukedom? Don't you have to run it? You can't just leave it to flounder—"

"Being a duke isn't like one of your books. I might have the title, but it's all in a trust, and I have very good managers to make sure it's secure," he said, giving her a soft kiss before gently pushing her off his lap. "Now, eat your dinner. I've been planning to step back for a good long while from the non-technology ventures and turn it over to people I trust, people I've trained, who are long overdue to take up the reins."

There was something he wasn't saying, CeCe realized as she sat back in her seat and studied him. "It's not just that you were overwhelmed." She tapped a finger against her chin. "There's something else you're not saying."

He speared a piece of fish on his fork and announced like it was no big deal, "I was coming to find you."

"What?"

"I was going to start with your former coach and keep going with friends and family, talking to anyone and everyone until I found you." He smiled self-consciously. "Hell, I even considered trying to go viral. An I-messed-up-and-broke-the-woman-I-love's-heart post on Facebook or Instagram. I even set up an account on YouTube."

"You didn't!"

He pulled out his phone and showed her. "I did."

"Oh, my God." She dropped her head to the table. "I'm so glad you found me on that plane."

"Me, too," he murmured. "So, so much." And he took her hand, lacing his fingers through hers.

They finished their dinner in contented silence, their eyes passageways to all the overwhelming feelings in their hearts.

TWENTY-FOUR

Colin

"ARE you going to argue with me about this, too?" he grumbled.

Cecilia glanced around, taking in the tall stone buildings that lined either side of the street. They'd driven by an open-air market and several roadside cafes before arriving at the flat Joanne had reserved for them in the Bergmannkiez neighborhood of Berlin. Just down the street, treetops were visible, signaling a park.

"No," she murmured, and her face went soft. "It's perfect. Thank you."

"Good," he said. "Next time you see Joanne, you can thank her. She picked it out."

Cecilia huffed out a laugh. "You know, most men would take credit for making their woman happy."

Fuck if he didn't love the way she'd declared herself to be his woman.

Not that it wasn't true, but the sound of it coming off her lips was something special.

"So, a flat is okay but not a plane ride?"

"A *private* jet ride is fine *if* it's convenient for your business, but you redirected your plane so we could jaunt over to Berlin. That's a little different from a few days in a flat." Cecilia rolled her eyes then snagged the keys from his hand to let them into the building. "We could have just hopped on a plane."

"We *did* hop on a plane."

"*Your* plane." When she reached for her suitcase, he shooed her hand away, grabbing it and his bag. The rest of their luggage —their heavy snow gear—had been stored on the plane.

He tipped the driver, thanked him, and followed Cecilia inside the building. "What's the point of owning a plane if it's not at my beck and call?"

"What if the business needed it?" She shook her head and started climbing the stairs. "What if my little jaunt to Berlin did something to jeopardize your livelihood?"

Colin dropped the suitcases to the floor and ascended the few stairs between him and Cecilia. He snagged her hand, turning her to face him. "Is that what you're worried about? Each of the major divisions has their own plane, sweetheart. The one we flew on is *my* personal jet."

"I—" Her mouth opened and closed a few times, tempting him until he gave in to the urge to kiss it.

"Everything will be fine." He bent a little to meet her gaze. "Always the truth, remember? I promise, I won't hold anything back, but you have to as well." A kiss to her nose. "No brooding or throwing a fit when I want to give you a little treat."

"Brooding is a male characteristic," she said, testily. "And I'm not agreeing to being spoiled. If this"—she waved a hand around her—"is a *little* treat, then I'll eat my hat."

"*That* is a sexist comment." He grinned. "And I'll keep the spoiling in check if you promise to accept it graciously."

"Fine," she said, crossing her arms. "But that also goes in reverse. If I want to buy you something, you'll accept it without grumbling."

"Deal." He snagged their suitcases and they climbed the rest of the stairs to the flat's door. Once inside, he set the bags inside the hall, shoved the keys on top of them, and scooped Cecilia up into his arms. She squealed as he kissed her, swallowing the happy sound, before using his foot to make sure the door was shut. Then he carried her down the hall, checking each of the rooms before finally finding one with a bed.

He tossed her on the mattress and followed her down. "Now, how about you accept something else without complaint?"

TWENTY-FIVE

Cecilia

SHE SMIRKED, staring up at the beautiful specimen of man above her for a moment, before wriggling to reach into her back pocket and retrieve a condom with all the flourish of a magician pulling a rabbit from his top hat.

"I think I can accept *something* without complaint," she said, pushing him to his back and tugging down the zipper of his jeans. "But first, it's my turn to give you a *little treat*."

Colin folded his arms behind his head, raised a brow. "Little?"

She snorted and tugged at the hem of his T-shirt, silently telling him to take it off. "Nice try," she told him, yanking off her own tee when he obliged. A shimmy later and her leggings were off.

He got a glimpse of what had been revealed and grinned.

"You like?" she asked, sliding her hands down over her breasts and teasing her fingertips under the band of her panties. The set was pale pink silk and very, *very* sheer. "My friends gave me a few parting gifts before I left California." She smirked.

"Told me to use them on a hot European man." A tap of her finger to her chin. "Hmm. Where am I going to find one of those?"

"Behave." Colin reached up and tweaked one nipple through her bra, making her jump even as pleasure arrowed straight between her thighs.

She brushed her mouth over *his* nipple, flicked her tongue out. "I don't think you want me to behave." She bit down.

He hissed, fingers coming up to hold her head to him.

"Do you have more?" he asked hoarsely, when she slipped free and started tracing her tongue down.

She paused at the waistband of his boxer briefs. "Yes." CeCe pushed both his jeans and his underwear down, freeing his cock so she could suck it into her mouth.

"I'm going to kiss your friends," he groaned.

Releasing him with a soft *pop*, she glared up at him. "You'll save all your kisses for me."

"Of course." Colin nodded rapidly, arching his hips up, encouraging her back to her *little* treat.

"Good," she said with narrowed eyes before gliding his cock back between her lips, stroking her hand up and down its length until she found a rhythm that had him moaning and thrusting up, fingers clenching and unclenching in her hair, breaths coming in rapid gasps.

"Enough."

Suddenly, she found herself on her back, Colin pressing her down into the mattress. His eyes were wild, his hair askew, and his cock was hard and glistening against her stomach.

He didn't give her a second to process the gorgeousness of that image before his mouth was moving on her breasts, his fingers slipping between her thighs.

"Col—"

She broke off with a scream when he thrust his fingers inside of her.

He froze. "Too much?"

"No," she said, quickly. "Just give a woman a moment to catch her breath."

"No, I don't think I will." He was a flurry of action—sucking on her nipples, kissing his way down her stomach, flicking his tongue against her clit, stroking his fingers in and out, in and out.

Pleasure rose inside her with all the subtly of a tsunami approaching shore. One second, she was merely turned on. The next, she was catapulting up the mountainside, hurtling for the peak, screaming again as she plummeted down the other side.

There was a crinkle and then Colin was pushing inside, not giving her a second for her body to adjust to the rigid intrusion of him before he was pounding into her in a way that intensified the waves of pleasure still radiating through her, fanning the embers of her desire into flames that threatened to engulf her all over again.

"Col—" She broke off and groaned when he hit just the right spot. "Yes. *God.* Mmm."

"Look at me."

Her eyes flashed open and she met his, saw the need in their depths, the razor thin control he was grasping at, but what captivated her most was the love.

The last bit of fear, the piece she'd been holding back to keep safe. They both slipped away.

She was Colin's.

Forever.

"Give me everything," she whispered, her hands coming to his shoulders. "I'm not scared anymore, Col. Just . . . give me *everything.*"

He didn't hesitate, just leaned down to kiss her, his tongue thrusting in synchrony with his hips, taking them both over the cliff, driving them headfirst into pleasure on the other side.

And when he held her close afterward, their exhalations still jagged, both of their hearts beating a rapid tattoo, Colin murmured, "Everything is already yours, sweetheart."

———————————

She was drunk in a bar in Germany.

With a sexy Scot at her side.

Giggling, she leaned against his shoulder, loving when his arm wrapped around her.

They'd ordered schnitzel.

Actual schnitzel.

Another giggle had him gathering her closer. "You're well and truly gone, aren't ye?"

Heat bubbling in her stomach, pleasure coiling between her legs. "Mmm," she moaned softly, winding her arms around his waist and snuggling closer. "Talk to me some more in that sexy accent."

"You mean *my* voice?" he teased.

"Yeah," she said. "That, too."

Grinning at her silliness, he bent his head and began whispering all sorts of sexy Scottish sayings in her ear. And the man must have taken notes from her books because the things he said to her had her waving down the waiter and paying their bill.

Her turn, despite his glowering.

But the fact that he let her pay, paired with the gentle way he held her, and all the soft murmurings had ratcheted her desire to a fever pitch.

They pushed out the front door, headed down the stairs to street level, and began making their way to the rented apartment.

She'd just given into her urge to push him back against one of the brick walls and kiss Colin senseless when her phone rang.

She ignored it.

It rang again.

CeCe was just drunk enough to continue ignoring it.

Colin wasn't.

He pulled back and reached into her purse, grabbing her cell. "Answer it," he said. "Otherwise, you'll worry."

She would, too. And that he knew her well enough to understand that not answering the call would have kept her up when she finally sobered up enough to realize she'd ignored someone who was reaching out to her, unlocked another piece of her heart.

Time.

He was giving her all the time she needed.

Smiling, she cupped his cheek lightly and took the phone from him, sliding her finger across the screen and lifting it to her ear.

"Hello?"

"Cecilia?"

"Mom?" she whispered. Her fingers went limp. All hint of drunkenness left her system. The cell clattered to the ground, and she wavered.

Colin caught her around the waist with an arm and bent to grab the phone. He went to put it up to his ear, lips parting, but CeCe took a breath, finally centered herself enough to say, "No!"

Blue eyes on hers.

"I need to do this," she whispered.

A long look filled with pride, but also a battle. He was warring with himself. He wanted to take this over for her, and maybe she once would have wanted that, too.

She'd changed.

So had he.

Sucking in then releasing another breath, she took the cell phone from him. "Mom?" she asked, "are you still there?"

The voice was familiar and yet critically different.

"Yes, Cecilia," she said. "I'm here."

She sounded old. Frail. Stiff.

"How did you get my number?"

A pause then, "It's the same as before."

Oh. Yeah. That was true. She'd kept her number after she'd begun paying all her own bills. She just figured her parents had "lost it" since they'd never bothered to call.

The memories of that time had the final tendrils of the cocktails she'd been drinking drift away, had her focusing on what was important. "Why are you calling?" she asked, forcing down the sharp ice pick of pain that thinking of her parents brought. Colin slid an arm around her waist and held her close as he propelled her forward on the sidewalk.

Taking care of her, but not taking over.

More defenses fell.

"Your father is ill."

CeCe waited, part of her expecting to be gripped by terror. Instead, she felt sympathy, *empathy* from the piece of her that didn't want anyone to be sick, anyone to suffer, but she also didn't want to drop her life and run home and play nurse by her father's bedside.

Maybe that made her a bad person.

Or maybe that made her someone who'd created her own family after her flesh and blood had cut her off, had abandoned her.

Abandoned a child. Because, for all intents and purposes, she'd been just a child.

All because she hadn't wanted to be molded into their form.

But her family—her *true* family—wouldn't abandon her. The one she'd created over the last few years. The one who'd brought her Jordan and Hunter, Heather and Abby, Sera and Bec. They would be there for her. They'd stuck by her side, and she knew they would continue to do so, even if she didn't do exactly what they wanted.

That was family.

Having each other's backs. Calling them on their bullshit, if necessary, but loving them even if they ignored advice or made a decision that wasn't the smartest.

Love. Loyalty. Support.

It was as simple as that, and the disparity between what she currently had, and what she had growing up, what was on the other end of the line was vast enough that Cecilia wasn't distraught.

Instead, she was resolute.

"I'm sorry he's ill," she said.

"Right." A clipped response. "So, when will you be home?"

"I *am* home," she said, and glanced up at Colin, felt warm when his pale blue eyes held hers, even despite the cool air.

"*What?*" her mother exclaimed. "Your father wants to see you. You will be on the next plane—"

Old patterns. More mortar for her foundation. For the decisions she'd made.

And maybe she should have unloaded, should have listed all the indiscretions that had hurt her over the years—cutting her off financially, not coming to her side when she was injured and recovering from surgery, slamming the door on her face when she'd returned home searching for some semblance of love and understanding.

But . . . the moment they'd slammed that door in her face, a door inside her heart had closed.

They were biologically related to her.

And that was the end of it.

"I'm sorry he's sick," she said, interrupting the tirade, "and I hope he'll be okay. You as well," she added when her mother began sputtering again. "But I've moved on with my life."

"You can't *move on*—we're family—"

"Funny story," she said, interrupting again, not caring it

wasn't the least bit polite. "Once, I would have agreed with you." She closed her eyes, took one more breath. "Be well."

She hung up

Colin stopped their forward march, turned her in his arms, held her tight. "Do we need to fly back to the States?"

CeCe shook her head, another barrier falling at his use of *we*.

More proof they were building something together. More proof that the family she had created was stronger, more understanding, more supportive than the one she'd grown up with.

"No," she murmured. "We're flying forward, not flying backward." A pause, CeCe tilting her head, before starting to walk again. She wanted to be back in the apartment, alone with Colin —preferably with a *naked* Colin. "I'm not sure that makes sense, and now I'm sober, so I can't even blame it on that."

He snorted.

"But that part of my life is gone. It doesn't have any power over me now."

He stopped, tugged her tightly against his chest for one brief moment. "God, sweetheart," he said, cupping her cheeks. "You are so bloody amazing."

She started to shake her head, but then Colin kissed her.

Long enough that her pulse pounded. Long enough that her lungs burned for air.

He pulled back. "So *bloody* amazing," he said again.

Then he took her hand and they walked back to the apartment, the cool winter air a kiss on her cheeks, but the man next to her warm and solid and everything she had ever hoped for.

THEY WALKED up the stairs to the apartment the following afternoon, CeCe having slept late as she recovered from her overindulgence the night before. Colin had woken her at noon then had coaxed her into the shower and fresh clothes before plying her tentative stomach with several hangover cures—fried food and plenty of fresh air as they'd walked to a shopping area and hit several stores.

But it turned out that his cures were effective because she was feeling much better when they reached the top of the stairs and Colin opened the door for her.

"What do you want to do for din—" She glanced up and nearly jumped out of her skin, her shriek lodged in her throat.

There were people in the apartment.

Strangers.

And flowers. And a massage table.

And a rack of dresses.

Gaping, she glanced from the group of people, to the dresses and table, to Colin.

"Just a little treat," he murmured, nudging her forward before slipping back out into the hall, the door closing with a soft click.

"A *little* treat?" she asked, aghast.

"If this is a little treat," one of the women—a slender brunette with a hint of a German accent—said, "then I'm almost scared to see what a big one is."

"You know what it is," the other woman—also a brunette, but as curvy as her companion was thin—said, waggling her eyebrows. Her English was a little more accented, but perfect.

As was the innuendo.

"Ladies," the male of the group said, coming over and taking CeCe's arm. He sounded American and tugged her toward the massage table. "Give Cecilia a break. She's been thrown a curve-ball by the sexy Scot who hired us"—his pale brown eyes dropped to CeCe's—"to spoil you."

"He's *been* spoiling me," she argued, though Colin wasn't there to hear it.

But he had—taking her to several art galleries that day then shopping, during which he'd bought her a set of pencils that should be gold-plated for how expensive they were. She'd taken one look at the price after admiring them then had nearly skittered back in her haste to avoid accidentally breaking and buying.

And Colin had bought them anyway.

Stubborn man.

She smiled despite herself. Stubborn man that she loved.

Yeah, that was a *pitter-patter* in her heart, but it was also the truth. The man held a piece of her heart, had always had it, and the fact that he was so carefully cherishing it now undid her.

"Well, let us spoil you some more," the man said. "I'm Fredrick. This is Martine, and that lovely lady is Helene. She's your masseuse. I'm on hair. Martine is on makeup, and we're all opinionated as hell and will give you our thoughts on your dress."

He nudged her onto the edge of the table.

"Dress?" she asked.

"Yup." He glanced at his watch. "We've got two and a half hours to get you ready for dinner. Massage. Shower. Makeup. Hair. Dress." He clapped his hands. "We're your fairy godpeople."

Helene rolled her eyes and handed CeCe a headband to keep her hair off her forehead. "Come on fairy godperson. Let's let Cecilia change." Her gaze met CeCe's. "Clothes off. Face down under the sheet."

"Okay."

They disappeared down the hall and she looked around the room, stunned and touched and heart full. Then she stripped down.

Because she loved massages.

Because she'd never had one like this.

Because Colin had arranged it for her.

Smiling, she slipped off her clothes, pushed back her hair

with the headband then slid between the sheets and got comfortable.

A few minutes later, Helene called out to her.

"I'm good," CeCe called back.

The other woman came in, and they spent a few minutes discussing what CeCe liked in massages and what she didn't and problem spots before Helene dimmed the lights.

Then gave Cecilia the best massage of her life.

An hour later, she blinked open deliriously relaxed eyes and slipped into the robe Helene left her. Frederick appeared, leading her down the hall and to the bathroom where he'd filled the tub.

"I thought you might like a soak better," he said, setting a couple of towels on the counter then fixing CeCe's headband so her hair would be safely above the water. "I'll knock on the door in a half hour when it's time to get out."

She nodded. "Thank you."

The door closed, and she hung up her robe. Then she was in the tub, warm water up to her neck. Someone had put a few roses in the water, rolled a towel into a pillow for her to rest her head on. She started to do just that, but then she noticed the book on the soap shelf.

Her heart thudded, and she dried her hands before reaching for it.

A note was tucked between the cover and first page, and she knew even before she began reading that Colin had left it for her.

Her eyes hit the words, their meaning processed in her brain. She giggled.

Chapter Twelve is good in this one, too.
—C

Fuck, he was good.

Smiling, she leaned back and started reading, and though it

went against her normal rules of book engagement, CeCe began with Chapter Twelve.

She barely made it through, heart pounding, heat curling between her thighs when Frederick knocked on the door. She dried off and slipped back into the robe, carefully leaving the book on the counter. And then she let herself get swept up in the moment, in the pampering.

She'd never had her hair and makeup done.

Not even on her aborted wedding day.

She hadn't wanted to spend the money, so had done it herself. But that Colin had thought enough about what she might need to do to get ready for a nice dinner tonight, to have arranged Martine and Frederick and Helene, touched her beyond belief.

But even as her hair was curled and her eyes were lined, her cheeks contoured, and her body encased in silk and lace, she felt the streak of wicked make an appearance.

Which was why by the time the trio of her fairy godpeople had left, disappearing like smoke the moment Colin knocked on the door, that streak of wicked was in the forefront of her mind.

She pressed a kissed to his mouth, glad she'd forgone lipstick when he deepened it with a growl, tugging her tightly against him.

"You look beautiful," he said, voice husky when he released her.

"Thank you," she whispered. "For everything."

He brushed his knuckles over her cheek. "I love you."

Her lips parted, but before she could say anything, and she damned well was ready to say it in that moment, he kissed her again.

And she got back to wicked.

To chapter twelve.

When he pulled away to let her breathe, she slipped her hand into his pocket, leaving a little present behind.

Okay, a tiny scrap of lace.

Because the hero in the book had taken a souvenir home from the heroine after they'd gotten busy.

Because her wicked meant that she wanted Colin to have a souvenir to think of her all night.

"Wh—"

He reached into his pocket as she was slipping on her coat, as she moved casually to the door, and his growled out *"Cecilia"* made her desire bloom between her thighs.

"Chapter twelve," she said, smirking over her shoulder as she turned the knob.

Before she could open it, she found herself pinned against the wood, back against the door, front against all the hard, muscled, gloriousness of Colin. "Col—"

She didn't get any more out.

He simply . . . kissed her absolutely senseless.

And when he released her, holding her close as they made their way down to the car waiting below, CeCe knew that being a little wicked was absolutely worth it.

TWENTY-SIX

Colin

MUCH LATER THAT NIGHT, his phone buzzed, and he reached over to retrieve it from the nightstand.

Then grinned when he saw it was Ewan.

His friend had sent him a picture of his baby, a cute little bundle of unidentifiable gender, but held by a woman with love in her eyes.

The impact of that easy affection took Colin's breath away.

The reason I stopped drinking coffee for nine months.

Colin found out he was good at typing one-handed.

They're both beautiful. But . . . you gave up coffee?

Another buzz.

Yes, they are. And yes, I did. Without a second thought.

A beat before another message came through, before Colin had a chance to reply to the insanity of his friend having given up the beverage he'd all but built a shrine to in their younger days.

You know how you asked me how to make things right?

Yeah.

You make CeCe know she's yours. It's not just about giving up coffee because the woman you love can't stomach the smell. But rather that you will clear any hurdle for her, that you'll find ways to take care of each other and won't disappear at the first sign of trouble. It'll take time, especially given the past. But, you're a good man, and I know you can give that to her.

Colin sighed.

I'm not sure about the good man part, but I'm going to do my best to be one from now on.

The ". . ." of a message being typed, appeared and disappeared. Then Ewan's message came through.

Just love her.

That, Colin knew, was something he would spend the rest of his days doing.

———

"What time are we meeting your friend?" Colin asked the next day, running a towel over his hair as Cecilia shaved her legs in the shower.

They'd slipped into a comfortable pattern of living together, sharing space and even a bathroom without a moment of awkwardness. Though . . . he grinned, thinking of CeCe's fantastic body covered in suds his hands had helped create in an effort to make sure she was *clean*. Co-ed showers certainly helped that along.

"At six-thirty for a pre-dinner drink and then maybe a meal if she can stay away from work that long," she said. "Heather's as much of a workaholic as you."

"Reformed," he said. "Your man is a *reformed* workaholic."

She peeked her head out of the shower curtain. "Who was up at three a.m. checking his emails."

"Fine. *Mostly* reformed." He kissed her, slipping a hand around the curtain to cup all his favorite curves.

"Mmm," she said, leaning into him before jumping back with a screech. "The plastic on the shower curtain is cold! Plus, as much as I like your mouth and hands and"—her eyes flicked down and she licked her lips, which pretty much turned his hard-on into blue balls—"*certain* other parts of your anatomy, I don't want to be late to meet Heather."

He rubbed his thumb across her nipple. "I can be quick."

"No, you can't," she said with a smile. "Which is why I love you."

Colin was grinning when she suddenly stiffened, and her face went serious. "What is it?"

She dropped the curtain. "Nothing. I just—I had better finish shaving."

Mentally repeating what she'd said gave him the insight he needed. He dropped his towel and slipped back inside the shower, carefully retrieving the razor from CeCe's hand before gathering her into his arms. "I love you, sweetheart. I've told you, nothing you say will change that."

She released a shuddering breath. "I know. It's silly, it's just last time I said that—"

He'd told her to go.

"You don't have to say it." He wiped a thumb below her eye, swiping away the moisture there. "I know how you feel. But things are different now, and if it accidentally slips out, I'm not going to run for the hills or be too drunk and angry and stupid to not recognize your words for the wonderful gift they are."

"*Colin.*" She thunked her head against his chest.

He wove his fingers into her hair, lightly tugged her back up. "What?" he asked, brushing back the water dripping down her forehead.

"You absolutely slay me with your words."

He waggled his eyebrows. "That's because I'm amazing."

She mock-scowled. "And modest, too." He grinned as he kissed her, feeling her answering smile against his lips. But then she gave him a little shove and tilted her head in the direction of the door. "Now, get out of here, I've got to finish showering so we can meet Heather."

"Okay," he said, giving her a sad puppy dog look.

"None of that," she declared, but her face was filled with amusement . . . that turned to heat when he trailed his hand down her front and slipped his fingers between her thighs.

"I'll leave," he said, giving her clit a teasing stroke before pulling away.

Her hand snaked out and caught his wrist, returning it to her heat. "Heather's always late anyway," she murmured. "She'll get caught up in emails and *ah . . .*"

The rest of her words were lost on a moan.

They were late getting to the bar, and even though he wanted to make a good impression on her friend, Colin found he didn't care.

Not when he was with CeCe.

Not when his heart was finally full.

TWENTY-SEVEN

Cecilia

"I DON'T HAVE to come with you," Colin said as they walked hand in hand down the street. "I can leave you to your friend and keep myself busy for a couple of hours."

She stopped and rose on tiptoe, giving him a heated kiss. The man was on fire, he'd made her come with his fingers then his mouth in the shower, all before he'd bent her over the vanity and given them each a release that had made them see stars.

"You don't *have* to hang out," she said, pulling back. "But I definitely want you there."

One side of his mouth tipped up. "Okay."

With just that, he took her hand again and they strode forward to the restaurant.

A simple request, a simple acquiescence.

Effortless.

He was just so easy to be with.

A happy sigh had him glancing down with a raised brow, and she just blurted it out, no fear this time. "I love you."

His hand twitched in hers. "I love *you*," he said and pressed a kiss to the spot behind her ear. "You're the other half of my heart," he murmured.

Her own heart twitched, and she bit her lip. "Romantic," she teased.

"Apparently." He tucked her against his side.

She tilted her head to glance up at him. "Besides me wanting to monopolize all your time, I'm sure Heather is dying for gossip to send to the ravenous crew at home after I told her I was seeing someone."

"Yeah?" He glanced up at a street sign and pointed ahead. "The restaurant should be just ahead." Then, though his tone stayed casual, she knew he was fishing. "What did you tell her about me?"

She smirked. "That you were trouble."

He huffed. "Women."

"Men." But she snuggled closer as she said it, loving the feel of his arm around her. "Thank you for chasing me down, Colin. I didn't think it was possible to feel this happy again."

The arm that was around her shoulders twitched, and he whispered, "I want to take you back to the flat and strip you naked all over again for saying that."

Cecilia turned her head to press a kiss to his biceps. "I want that, too. But first, food." They'd reached the restaurant and Colin held the door open for her. "Oh, look! There's Heather. I can't believe she beat us here."

CeCe waved, lacing her hand through his, and waded her way through the crowded space, feeling Colin falter for a moment before his steps picked up behind her. "Hi," she said when she'd reached the table and hugged Heather, who returned the gesture almost woodenly. CeCe pulled back. "You okay?"

But Heather wasn't looking at her. She was looking over Cecilia's shoulder. "McGregor?" she asked. "I thought we weren't meeting until later in the week."

Cecilia glanced up at Colin. His face was as surprised as Heather's. "That was the plan," he said.

They both looked at her.

She glanced between them, smart enough to have put the pieces together, and lifted her hands, palms up. "Um. I guess our Heathers are the same?"

"Hmm," Heather said, shaking her head. "Well, sit down. How did this happen? Do I need a drink?"

"I've known Colin since I graduated from high school," Cecilia said, picking up a menu as Colin settled in next to her.

"What is it with all my employees fraternizing?" Heather grumbled.

Cecilia shook her head at the same time that Colin raised a brow. "Employee?" he asked incredulously.

"Fine," Heather said, holding up a hand. "Don't go all alpha male on me. *Business partner*. But first, there were Abby and Jordan, and now you"—she pointed at CeCe—"and McGregor. Abby just told me you accepted her offer, and you"—she continued her pointing streak, this time singling out Colin—"the ink on our contract is barely dry. How did this happen?"

"I love her," Colin said with a shrug. "Always have. Always will."

CeCe's heart gave a little *aw*, and Heather's mouth clamped shut at the words. "Damn," she said, glancing at CeCe. "You've got a live one."

"I know," Cecilia said, grinning.

"You also know the girls are going to want every *single* detail."

A sigh, but CeCe was secretly thrilled that Heather seemed to approve. "I know. I'm expecting it'll take several FaceTimes to satisfy everyone's curiosity."

"More than that." Heather chuckled and nodded her head at Colin. "Just *look* at him."

Col frowned, glancing down at himself in a confused way

that made CeCe smile. "You're gorgeous," she murmured in his ear. "And perfect for me in every way."

He squeezed her thigh, murmured back, "What was that about *me* being a romantic?"

They stared at each other, eyes saying all the things their mouths couldn't in a crowded restaurant . . . at least until a *click* startled them out of their reverie.

"Sorry," Heather said. "I had to. You guys are just—" She shook her head, and Cecilia felt her phone ping on the group text she and the girls shared.

"Really?" She sighed. "There will be no end to it now."

Heather laughed. "Not for me." A grin. "I have to get off to a business meeting in a few anyway." She waved at the waitress. "This asshole from Savant Technologies is trying to undercut one of my deals. He thinks he's so flipping"—she rolled her eyes —"amazing and manly, and that just because he possesses a Y-chromosome, he knows how to run a company better than me. Idiot."

She asked the waitress for a drink then paused her diatribe as Colin and Cecilia ordered after quick glances at the menu. "I swear if he thinks that he can get the best of me, he's got another thing coming. *Ugh*. Sorry." She waved a hand and pivoted subjects so quickly that CeCe felt her head spin for a moment. But that was always the way with Heather. "I want to hear all about Finland. Was it amazing?"

"*So* amazing," Cecilia said, placing her palm over Colin's where it still rested on her thigh and then proceeding to chat away with Heather.

Aside from a few words here or there, Colin let them have their fun, and Cecilia did manage to shut up long enough about the aurora borealis to let him and Heather touch base on a few business details that had come up since he'd left San Francisco.

But then Heather was checking her phone and cursing, yanking her wallet from her purse.

They both waved her off, promising another get together in the near future and watching with wide eyes as she bustled out the door, fury in every line of her body. The crowd parted before her like the Red Sea, and a man scrambled to open the door, looking blindsided when Heather unleashed a smile in his direction.

"The man who's trying to undercut her is a bloody idiot," Colin said.

"Agreed." The door closed and CeCe turned back to *her* man, the one that was lifting her up instead of cutting her down. "So, your Heather is my Heather?" she asked.

His thumb came up, touching the corner of her mouth. "Apparently."

"Small world," she said.

"Very small." He smoothed back a lock of her hair, tucking it behind her ear. "But mine is so much bigger with you in it."

TWENTY-EIGHT

Colin

"I DON'T HAVE TO GO," he told Cecilia a few days later as they packed up the Berlin flat.

"No," she said. "It's important that you go and check in. I'll head to Paris for a couple of days and then if things work out, we can meet up there."

Paris. The City of Love.

He should be seeing it with CeCe.

"Promise you won't visit the Eiffel Tower without me?"

"Ah, Colin McGregor," she said, traipsing over to him and throwing her arms around his neck. "I keep forgetting that you're such a romantic."

He gently tugged her arms free and set her away from him. "*Woman.*"

"*Man.*"

"A promise, please."

She mock-glared, but her eyes were bright. "I'll wait on the Eiffel Tower, but I'm damned sure not waiting for you for croissants."

"I can deal with that."

Cecilia grumbled as she kissed him. "That's because you don't *like* croissants."

"Maybe," he said, deepening the kiss, sliding his tongue between her lips, loving the way she tasted so sweet, reveling in the heat of her mouth and the soft little sigh of pleasure that emerged when he was doing it exactly right.

They were both breathing hard by the time he broke away.

"I'm going to miss you," she said.

"I'll only be a plane ride away."

She laughed. "And you've got a private one at your disposal."

"True." He snagged her hand. "Come on. Let's get to that plane so we can drop you in Paris."

"I could have taken the train, you know."

Colin stroked a hand down her spine then gave her ass a smack. "I know. But—"

"You have a private plane. Blah, blah. I know." She stopped, abruptly turning around.

He froze. "You okay—"

Her arms wrapped around his waist and he struggled with the bags for a second before letting them fall to the floor. Who gave a damn about luggage when his woman had her arms around him?

After a few moments, she released him, heading for the door, explaining her actions with a casual, "I hadn't hugged you yet today. Oh." She paused; beautiful green eyes locked onto his. "I love you. Somehow more than yesterday, which should be impossible."

This woman was going to be the death of him.

But he was smiling as he followed her out of the flat and to the car parked below.

Damned if he didn't love her more every day, too.

COLIN DROPPED CeCe off in Paris with a driver to take her to the flat Joanne had reserved in the 6th Arrondissement then boarded his plane again and headed for Edinburgh.

He smiled at the memory of her pursed lips when he'd told her on the flight over to close the travel search site on her laptop because he had her accommodations covered. Those lush lips had puckered, her brows had pulled together, a fire starting in those green eyes, before she'd sighed, smiled, and given him a kiss.

"Thank you," she'd murmured.

"Have an extra croissant for me."

"I won't fit into my jeans if I keep that up."

He'd nuzzled her throat. "Then we'll buy you bigger ones."

She'd broken into giggles at that, and they'd spent the rest of the short flight chatting about all the things she wanted to see.

And now he'd left her in Paris, along with his heart.

"Damn," he muttered, knowing that he was turning into a sap. He needed to get his head in the game, to focus on business so he could get back to Cecilia.

He also needed to decide how to deal with the other thing.

The *thing* being . . . how he was going to ensure his mother and sister would never *ever* come between him and Cecilia again.

TWENTY-NINE

Cecilia

SHE WOKE WITH A GASP, hating that the old memories had arisen again now that Colin had flown home to Scotland.

During the day, it was easy to pretend everything was different and better, but without him, without the other half of her heart, old doubts began to creep in and make her uncertain. Was it inevitable that things would eventually go bad between them again? Would he misjudge her?

Would she end up all alone again?

Sighing, she glanced at the clock and saw that it was just before four in the morning. Too early.

But her friends should be available, Heather depending on which time zone she was in, of course.

CeCe opened the text chain and scrolled back up, past the Outlander gifs teasing her for finding her very own Jaime, past the pictures she'd sent of the croissant she'd devoured that morning and the very long line she'd waited in for admission to the Louvre. She kept going back until she tracked down Heather's travel plans.

And upon seeing that her friend had returned to San Francisco after brief stops in Rome and Madrid, Cecilia sent the S.O.S.

I need girl talk. I'm freaking out.

Immediately, texts began pouring through.

What's the matter? Abby.

How can I help? Seraphina.

Who do I have to kill? Bec.

Hang on, I'll videoconference us all in. Heather.

The screen of her laptop lit up and within a couple of seconds, each of her friends' faces was staring back at her from a different corner.

"It's the middle of the night in Paris," Abby said. "Why are you awake?"

Cecilia rubbed the aching space between her eyebrows. "I had a bad dream." Bec smirked, but CeCe waved her off. "Not like that. I dreamed about the day Colin and I . . . well"—she sighed, knowing that she was going to have to dish all. Their relationship status took *It's Complicated* to a whole new level—"We were supposed to get married."

"You're getting married?" Seraphina shrieked and clapped her hands together, her beautiful face shining brightly with joy. Sera *loved* happy endings. "That's amazing! That's—"

"Not what's happening," CeCe interrupted. "Colin and I were *supposed* to get married six years ago."

Sera clamped her mouth shut. Heather said, "Hmm." Abby's eyes widened. But Bec said in typical rough and ready East

Coast Bec fashion, "Well, fuck, the newest to our corrupted quintet of dirty old women has been holding out on us."

Already, Cecilia felt better. "I didn't expect to see him again. We . . . obviously, we didn't part on good terms. His family kind of conspired to break us up, and he believed them over me. I was hurt, so *damned* hurt, that I left and never looked back."

"And then what happened?" Abby was perched on the edge of her chair, clearly riveted.

All the girls were as she detailed the plane ride, the hotel in London, and Colin following her to Finland. Her life had all the drama required for their very own CeCe-centered romance novel.

"How's the sex?" Bec asked with a cackle.

Cecilia's cheeks went red-hot. But she answered anyway. "Incredible," she said, unable to hold back her sigh.

Seraphina giggled. "I'll take what she's having."

Heather spoke for the first time. "So, it seems like everything is going good and that you worked out a lot of your issues. Plus, he couldn't keep his eyes—or hands—off you at dinner the other day. What's going on now that has you doubting him?"

"I'm not doubting necessarily . . ." she prevaricated.

"Try that line on a different group of horny old women," Bec said.

"I resent the term *old*," Abby said.

Bec waggled her brows. "But not horny?"

"Clearly not." Abby pointed at her slightly rounded belly.

"Ladies," Heather interjected. "I know you think you're amusing, but CeCe needs to answer the question."

She flopped back onto the bed, staring up at the gorgeous antique ceiling. It was coffered and the swirling white woodwork was so gorgeous that she physically ached for her sketchbook. "I'm not doubting his intentions." She groaned. "I'm just doubting our . . . *I don't know*, our staying power, I guess. I mean, he's been sweet before, and now he's not here, and what if it all goes to shit again? I can't—I don't know how—"

"You miss him," Sera said.

"Yes," she wailed. "And now he's back in Scotland, and what if his family gets their claws into him again?"

"Then he's a fucking idiot," Heather said bluntly.

"And we cut off his balls with rusty scissors," Bec added.

CeCe sat up, nose wrinkling. "Why rusty?" she asked.

A shrug. "Because that's worse."

"Okay," she said, not able to disagree with that logic.

"Why not just fly to Scotland?" Abby asked. "If you're not going to enjoy your solo time in Paris, you might as well visit him and spend some more time together."

"And hot sex," Bec said. "She needs more of that."

Seraphina nodded. "I agree. This will give you both a chance to flush away those bad memories and move forward. It's not like he can avoid his family forever."

"I bet he wishes he could," Heather grumbled. "Family is a giant pain in the ass—"

"Hey!" Abby said with a glare.

"Present company excluded," Heather said, smirking. "But his business is also based in Scotland, so he'll need to go back regularly. If you can't get over that . . ."

Heather didn't finish the rest of the sentence, but Cecilia heard it anyway. If she didn't get over her discomfort with Scotland—going there, him returning home, his family—they would be stuck in this same painful cycle forever.

It was better to rip off the Band-Aid.

"I guess I'm going to Scotland."

"You pack, and I'll get Jordan's assistant to book you on a flight," Abby said. "I'll text you the details."

"What's it with billionaires and assistants?" CeCe muttered.

Abby just grinned. "You know you love it."

She rolled her eyes. "Fine. I do." A glance at her friends. "You guys are amazing. Thank you."

"Pish," Bec said.

"Love you!" Seraphina called.

Carter ran onto the screen and waved at CeCe. "We love you, too," Abby called over his chattering.

"Remember," Heather said. "Our demons only drag us down if we give them the power to do so."

Cecilia's breath caught; she opened her mouth to—

Bec beat her to it. "Fuck, that was deep."

"Language!" Abby chided.

Sera just smiled as Heather shook her head, hand reaching forward in her little corner of the screen. "Talk soon." CeCe's laptop screen went black.

"I guess I'm doing this," she said and headed for the bathroom to shower.

Scotland, here I come.

THIRTY

Colin

HIS PHONE RANG, and a grin broke out on his face. "Sorry, gentlemen," he told the group of investors sitting at the table with him. "I've got to take this, but Francine has the matter well in hand. You can direct any further concerns to her."

Hopefully, him saying the actual words would prevent Colin from having to make this type of trip again.

Tetchy investors not wanting to work with his female CFO.

Bloody idiots.

But if this impromptu meeting didn't work, if they continued to circumvent Francine, then they could take their money elsewhere. McGregor Enterprises wasn't desperate for investment, and Francine was the best person for the job—male, female, or otherwise.

"Sweetheart," he said after he'd swiped a finger across the screen and made sure the conference room door was closed behind him.

"I-is this a bad time?"

Colin frowned as he strode into his office. "No." He wanted

to find the words to put her completely at ease but knew there wasn't one perfect thing he could say. That, unfortunately, rebuilding the trust she had in him would take time. "Cecilia, I'm here for you," he said. "Whenever you need."

Her breath rattled through the speakers. "Well, I'm glad you said that because I . . . uh . . .I—"

"Sweetheart, what is it?"

"I kind of flew to Scotland to surprise you," she blurted. "But I didn't think about where you would be. I don't know where your office is, and I'm at the airport and—"

He cut her off. "Cecilia."

"Yes?" she asked, her voice small.

"I'm sending a car to pick you up. Neil was already dropping off someone for a flight to Dubai, so he can get to you sooner than I could. What terminal are you in?"

She told him, and he put her on speaker to fire off a text.

"Okay. He'll be there in ten minutes. Can you go wait on the curb for him?"

He sensed her nodding, heard the sounds change as she began to move. "I'm here."

"Good," he said then hesitated before asking anyway. "What's the matter?"

"I—uh . . . I'm sorry. It was stupid to come here."

Colin started packing up his briefcase. "Did I somehow give you the impression that I don't want you here? I just wish I could have had someone waiting. I don't like you standing out in the cold."

"I should have told you."

"Cecilia," he said again. "I'd already called to have the jet readied for takeoff to Paris in a couple of hours."

"Oh," she said softly.

Colin decided to lay all his cards on the table. It was the only way they'd be able to keep building something healthy between them. "The truth is, I was missing you desperately. I hate being here when you're not." He smiled at his receptionist as he left. "I'm so, *so* glad you're here."

She released a shuddering breath. "Really?"

"Really," he said and too impatient to wait for the elevator, he pounded down the stairs to where his driver waited. "Now, Neil is going to take you to my flat. I'll be there and waiting by the time you arrive from the airport."

"Okay." Her next word was light. "Naked?"

He laughed, a full bark that made his driver, Mick, send a shocked glance in his direction. Colin didn't think he'd ever smiled at the other man, let alone laughed. He wasn't an asshole, but he hadn't had much to laugh about over the last few years.

"Your flat?" Mick asked, opening the back door.

Colin nodded. "Thanks." To CeCe he said, "Stay on the line with me until Neil gets there."

"Okay," she said then, "Did you really miss me?"

"Sweetheart." He smirked. "Don't ask stupid questions."

"Hey!"

"Is for horses," he said, stealing one of her lines.

"Oh, my God," she muttered. "I can't believe you remember that."

"A certain redhead might have taught me a few American idioms."

She snorted.

"And, yes, I really did miss you," he said. "Did you have enough croissants?"

CeCe huffed out a laugh. "Never! Oh, I think he's here. Dark hair, green eyes, and glasses. A Mark Wahlberg lookalike?"

"Not sure who *that* is," he replied. "But Neil is supposed to show you his identification."

"*Hi, ma'am*," Colin heard. "*Can I take your bag?*"

"He flashed a fancy badge," Cecilia whispered, and Colin relaxed.

"Good. See you in thirty minutes, sweetheart."

"Can't wait," she murmured before clicking off.

And Colin knew he had the biggest, dopiest smile ever on his face, but he found he didn't give a damn.

Then his phone rang again.

"Sweetheart," he began. "It's only—"

His mother's voice was shrill as it screamed through the speaker. "Colin Douglas McGregor, what *have* you done?"

Fury filled his every cell.

After everything, every-*bloody*-thing, his mother and sister had done, *this* was her first reaction to his request?

Fucking hell.

There would be no more playing nice.

His lips twisted into a smile that must have been more feral than kind. "Mother," he said. "So good to hear from you. Cecilia and I will be over for brunch tomorrow." A pause. "That should give you plenty of time to pack."

"You—"

"Great," he interrupted. "I'll see you then."

Colin hung up the phone, silencing it when she called back, and then several more times when she continued trying to get through. Finally, when it seemed as though she'd taken the hint, he shoved his cell into his pocket, pushed her from his mind, and asked Mick to stop the car for a moment. He cleaned out a bakery of their croissants—not French, but they did look damned good—and then picked up a bouquet of yellow daffodils.

See? He'd listened *and* learned.

Now was his chance to prove that to the woman he loved.

THIRTY-ONE

Cecilia

SHE SMILED and stroked a finger down one of the yellow petals of the daffodils Colin had surprised her with. "Thank you for the flowers."

He pressed a kiss to her bare shoulder. "I didn't think you'd even noticed them, given the way you launched yourself at me when I opened the door."

"*You* grabbed *me*."

A chuckle against her spine then a sharp nip at her cheek . . . the lower one.

"Colin!"

"Mmm." His tongue darted out to soothe the sting. "I really liked *your* surprise."

She played innocent. "Me flying in?"

"Not that one."

"The bottle of wine?"

He kissed over the rounded curve of her butt, drifting slowly down and inward. "Nope."

"The cheese—"

He licked, and she broke off on a gasp.

"Uh-uh." Another lick. Calloused fingers spreading her legs a little wider.

"My lingerie?"

"Mmm-hmm." He pressed an open-mouth kiss to her clit and she jumped, then sighed as his fingers joined the party, showing just how much he'd enjoyed the sheer lacy garter belt and bra set.

It had been another gift from the girls, and it matched her eyes perfectly. It also enhanced certain other parts of her anatomy.

She'd sent them a mental thank you when Colin's eyes had nearly popped out of his head.

Colin licked her again and any thoughts of lingerie faded from her mind. No, *all* thoughts faded. Her brain was hazed with the desire for more. For faster. For *again, right there.*

"Oh God, please do that again," she moaned when his tongue executed some twisting movement that nearly toppled her over the edge.

And he did, but thank everything that was holy, he did it again. And again. And then once more. Until she was hurtled into space, and pleasure coursed through every cell of her body.

"You're really fucking good at that," she said, once she'd managed to regain one half of a wit.

He grinned, like a cat that had gotten into the cream.

And he had *gotten the cream*, she thought with an inner cackle that would have made Bec proud.

"Give me five minutes," she said, "and I'll be smiling that way at you."

Colin crawled up the bed, hauling her into his arms. "I didn't do it because I wanted something in return."

"I know." She sighed and cuddled closer, still limp and satiated but knowing that she needed to broach this subject sooner rather than later. Cecilia really wanted the black cloud that was hanging over them gone forever. "But I like doing it and"—she prepped herself for the rapid left turn in conversation she was about to throw at him—"Colin, I think we need to go see your family."

He shuddered. "Those two topics should never be spoken about in the same sentence."

"I—" She shook her head, smacked him across the chest. "You know that's not what I meant."

A brush of his fingers across her cheek. "I know. And funny that you should bring it up, but I told my mother we were coming for brunch tomorrow."

"*What?*"

"Right after I sent her an official letter from my solicitor demanding that she and Lana vacate the estate within thirty days."

"But—"

"They're not going to be destitute. I've bought them a house." A shrug. "It's on the other side of the country, but it's opulent, and they'll still receive their portions of the company's profits." He stopped and stared down at her. "I can't look at them. I can't pretend to love them after all they've done to you. It wasn't right."

"They're your family though."

"Real family doesn't act that way."

Cecilia thought about her own parents, about all they'd done —and *hadn't* done—and knew he was right. Jordan and Hunter, Abby, Heather, and the girls were more family than her own blood.

"You're right."

"Of course, I am." He smirked but cupped her cheek with gentle fingers. "You don't have to go if you don't want to."

"Oh no. I definitely want to clear the air. Now, about that cocky smile you were sending my way a few minutes ago," she said, her hand snaking down his stomach.

Colin's groan was enough to rid her of any doubt.

This was right.

He'd talked to her. He was going to have her back with his family.

He loved her.

CeCe sighed contentedly. This time they were going to make it.

COLIN OPENED her car door then laced his fingers through hers as they walked up the drive. The McGregor Estate, informally called Rock Hill, loomed large and gloomily overhead.

She used to love those spires and the way the windows curved at their top corners.

Today it looked as bleak as she felt inside.

The last time she'd seen this place—

So. Not. Going. There.

Colin released her hand but snaked an arm around her waist, tugging her flush against his side. "I'm here."

CeCe melted. This man . . . he was it.

The front door opened before they could knock, and CeCe was surprised to see Joanne.

"Oh, look at you!" she said, running toward them to grab Cecilia's shoulders. "You're as pretty as ever." Then she hugged her tight, whispering in her ear, "Did my Col make things right between you?"

"Yes." Her lips twitched as Joanie pulled back. "Now I know how he heard about the daffodils."

Joanne winked before turning to hug Colin.

"Your mother and sister are in the study and . . . Olivia is there, too."

Cecilia's heart clenched, she'd only met Olivia a handful of times, and most of those had only been in passing because Lana,

Colin's sister, and Olivia were friends. Olivia Stewart was beautiful and had seemed sweet, at least until Ewan had implicated her in her and Colin's breakup.

Colin just nodded grimly at Joanne's words, pulled CeCe close again, and led them inside. "Can you send a tray into the study?" he asked. "We haven't eaten yet."

They'd been too busy christening his shower.

And then his kitchen counter.

And the front door.

Those memories shored up her spine. She could totally do this.

But that was before they actually walked into the study, because the trifecta of beautiful and cold women standing before her was beyond intimidating.

No one spoke as Colin settled her in a chair and then sat on the arm of it.

He placed a hand on her shoulder when she opened her mouth to break the awkward silence. *Wait*, he seemed to be telling her.

She gave him a small nod.

Bridget, his mother, was the one to cave. "How could you do this to us?" she wailed. "This stupid American bitch has you on tenterhooks again, and you'll just throw over your family for *her?*"

Olivia winced, but Lana inclined her head, encouraging her mother along.

"First. Don't ever talk about Cecilia like that again." Colin's tone was frigid, and she shivered from the force of it. "Second, is that *really* all you have to say for yourself?"

"All *I* have to say?" Bridget pointed a bony finger at CeCe. "She—"

"Actually," Olivia interrupted, looking extremely frightened but determined all the same. "I *do* have something to say." She stood and crossed over to where Cecilia sat. "I'm so sorry. I was"

—her eyes were glassy—"well, it doesn't matter what I was. It was horrible and wrong, and you need to know that I forged—"

"Shut up!" Lana snapped. "You're supposed to be helping, not—"

Colin leveled a glare at his sister that had her paling and clamping her mouth shut. "Go on," he said, his tone so soft it was almost deadly.

Olivia took a deep breath, releasing it before the words poured out. "I took Cecilia's journal and helped Lana set up an account to make it look like she was stealing. Then I sent Ewan to the church, following him with my camera so I could take pictures, making it look like she'd run off with him." She bit her lip. "This is all my fault."

"Why?" CeCe asked. "Why would you do that?"

Olivia's eyes dropped to the carpet. "I wanted to marry him."

"Oh," CeCe said dumbly. It was an obvious reason, she supposed, just not one that she'd ever considered. Her eyes lifted first to Bridget then to Lana. "You wanted that, too."

Not a question.

Lana still answered it as though it were one. "Obviously."

"I—" CeCe shook her head. "Wow."

"I'm so sorry," Olivia said. "I know it was wrong and—" She reached out a hand, as though to touch Colin's arm, but the look he gave her had that palm freezing midair and returning to her side. "I was a jealous coward," she told them. "No. *Worse* because I didn't confess my part in it until now." A tear slipped from the corner of her eye. "I robbed you of y-years. I'm so sorry."

What could CeCe say? *It's okay*? But it wasn't.

Instead, she settled on, "Thank you for telling us."

Olivia dropped to her knees in front of them. "Colin. I'm so sorry. Please, forgive me."

His gaze flicked in her direction then away, fury in the clenched line of his jaw. "No."

Olivia wilted, and CeCe found she didn't have it in her to

make the other woman feel worse. Not when she was already so torn up. "We've all made a lot of mistakes." She patted Olivia's hand. "Should we try to move forward now?"

A tearful nod. "I'd like that."

"Good."

Colin shot a dismissive glance in Olivia's direction. "Anything else?"

She shook her head.

"Good. Leave."

Bridget and Lana gasped. "You can't talk to her like that," Lana said, but Olivia just sent them one more apologetic look before leaving the room.

"What have you got to say for yourselves?" he lobbed the question to the room.

"You can't honestly believe her," Bridget attempted. "They must be working together—"

Colin stood, hands fisted at his sides. "Shut. Up."

"You know what I don't get," Cecilia said, touching Colin's back in an effort to calm him. Then pushed past her discomfort to ask the next question. She needed to know the answer. "Why go through the effort? Why befriend me? Why make me feel like part of the family?"

Lana rolled her eyes, but Bridget's were as cold as those nights in Finland. "You took him from me," she hissed. "You were never supposed to come back."

Cecilia snagged Colin's hand when he would have strode over to them.

"I guess fate had different plans because I never did expect to be back here again." She tangled her fingers with his. "But I'm so glad I am, because everything you did to tear us apart has actually made us stronger in the end."

"You can't have him!" Bridget shrieked. "He's mine. The money is mine—" She broke off, panic on her face for one brief second before her tone took such a dramatic turn—bitchy to sweet—that CeCe could see how easily they'd been manipulated. She'd seen the sharp side of Bridget many times during their engagement, but it had been so quickly covered up by softness, by supposed caring, that it had been far simpler for her brain to chalk it up to *her* misunderstanding, rather than because Colin's mom was a complete and utter asshole.

"Colin, dear, I love you," Bridget began, so sickly sugary now that CeCe understood the truth beneath those words that it made her teeth ache. "I need you, especially with your father gone. I'm so lonely—"

"Enough," Colin said, sitting back down on the arm of the chair. "Let me make this easy on you. Your *money* is safe, but the only way you'll see another pound is if you get the hell out of this house and *never* come back."

"You can't cut us out of the business's profits," Lana said, chiming in at precisely the wrong time. Especially when she wasn't tempering her tone with any of the falseness her mother had adopted. Her expression was predatory and calculating.

Colin's smile in response was wolfish. "Oh, but I can."

"You wouldn't."

He shrugged as if to say, *Wouldn't I?* and the smug expression on Lana's face slipped.

"Now, you can enjoy your fat inheritance far, far away from here in the home I bought for you or buy one in another bloody country for all I care, but neither of you will ever be welcome in this house again."

"But—"

Joanne bustled in, a tray heaped with food held aloft. "Hungry, dears?"

"No," Lana and Bridget snapped.

"Great," Colin said, tilting his head toward the open door. "Then you can finish packing your things."

THIRTY-TWO

Colin

A FEW WEEKS LATER, Colin rode out from the stables atop his black gelding, Bowen, heading in the direction of the outer edge of his property. He knew that CeCe had probably ended up there, even though his groom had told him she'd started that morning in the opposite direction.

His woman was a creature of habit, enjoying a morning walk or ride before spending her afternoon hours sketching—via paper or electronic tablet, depending on if she was working for Abby at RoboTech or creating something for her own enjoyment.

The little grassy knoll was her favorite spot, a place where the rolling green hills gave way to a jagged outcropping of rock. The ocean beat against the shore far below, salt-tinged air wafting up the cliffside to tangle her hair and muss the pages of her sketchbook.

God. He couldn't wait to see her.

He'd been in Edinburgh for the past few days, tying up a few projects before they headed off to winter in the Southern Hemisphere.

Bali, Fiji, New Zealand, and Australia were all on CeCe's travel list.

But before then, he had plans.

And those plans involved Paris and croissants and the Eiffel Tower.

Grinning at the fit she'd throw about not fitting into her jeans because of all the baked goods they would be consuming, Colin headed toward the stables. The wind sliced right through his clothes as he rounded the building, and he decided that spending the coldest part of the year somewhere warm sounded damn good at that moment.

Joanne waved him down as he rode past the front door.

He stopped, bent to take the basket she held up to him. She tsked. "Cecilia didn't take lunch with her."

Colin shook his head, knowing the woman he loved had gotten carried away with sketching again. "I'll make sure she eats."

"Every bite."

A serious nod. "Of course."

Joanne smiled. "You're a good boy, Colin."

He secured the basket then took off at a gallop. Almost a week apart was way too much time.

Her spot appeared in less than twenty minutes, and his breath caught. He shook his head, trying to clear it when all he could concentrate on was CeCe in front of him with long, *long* legs encased in tight denim. Her back was toward him, red curls flying in the breeze, and when she turned to face him, the warmth in her gaze set his heart pounding.

"Hey," she said, once he'd jumped from Bo's back and tied his reins on a nearby log.

She stood, calmly stroking Abharsair's—Devil in English, Ab for short—neck. Ab had technically been his sister's horse, but he was so ill-tempered—part because of his personality and part because Lana hadn't taken the time to train him properly—that he wouldn't let anyone but CeCe ride him.

Six years ago, she'd tamed the horse with sweet words and a few sugar cubes, and now he was still devoted to Cecilia.

Colin's lips twitched. She managed to inspire that feeling a lot. Joanne, Ab, her friends. Him.

"Hi, sweetheart," he said, coming over and slipping an arm around her waist. Ab tolerated a pat on his forehead before turning away with an expression that bordered on disgust when Colin kissed her.

"I missed you," she said, turning in his arms and hugging him tight.

"Hardly," he teased. "Joanne told me that you've been so busy working and sketching that you haven't eaten."

A guilty expression crossed her face.

"I—"

He tugged her toward Bowen and unstrapped the basket. "I'm to make sure you eat every bite."

She laughed before leading him back over to her blanket and shoving her drawing materials to the side. "With Joanne's cooking, I'm sure that won't be difficult."

He held up a croissant with a smile. "Especially when she packs your favorites?"

She snatched it from his fingers, flopping back onto the blanket and taking a huge bite. Her words were slightly muffled. "I'm going to get fat"—she chewed and swallowed—"And I can't even find the energy to care, not when Joanne makes me homemade croissants every day."

"Careful, you don't choke," he said, lips twitching. "I kind of want to keep you around."

"Meh," she joked. "You'll just find another redhead."

Colin snorted and grabbed an apple from the basket, shifting when CeCe moved to rest her head on his thighs. They stayed like that, eating as they stared out at the cliffs and ocean. Well, *she* was staring at the cliffs and ocean. He was staring at her.

"For the record, I like your spot."

She'd finished the croissant and had closed her eyes. "Hmm?" she asked. Apparently, she'd been doing more dozing than staring.

He bent to press a kiss to her lips.

"Nothing, sweetheart. Go back to sleep." Colin brushed his fingers through her hair, watching as the woman he loved fell asleep on his lap, knowing that they were lucky to have more time together, knowing that he'd cherish every single second— heartfelt or teasing or otherwise.

Knowing that he had the other half of his soul in his arms.

And he wasn't letting her go.

EPILOGUE

PART ONE

Colin, six months later

HE WAS SITTING in the waiting room of a hospital when Cecilia burst through the doors, a huge smile on her face. "It's a girl!"

She launched herself into his arms, kissing him soundly on the mouth. "Abby had a perfect little girl."

Colin stole her lips for another kiss. "How are they?"

"Tired. But healthy and resting." She pushed herself up from his lap. "We should go relieve Bec. She might not *do delivery rooms*, but I'm sure Hunter and Carter are running her ragged."

He smiled, having just spoken with Bec only a half hour before. CeCe's friend *was* being run ragged, but she'd also been in on his plan and enthusiastically *for* it. "I was thinking," he said and held out a gold ring. On it was an obscenely large diamond surrounded by emeralds that matched Cecilia's eyes. "We haven't exactly had the best of luck with planning weddings, so maybe we should go to Vegas instead?"

Her jaw dropped open. "Are you serious?"

A nod.

"I—oh, my God. *Col!*" Tears streaked down her cheeks, but she eventually managed a "yes" and let him slip the ring on her finger.

"How mad do you think your friends will be to miss it?" He nodded in the direction of the door that lead back to where Abby, Jordan, and Seraphina were sequestered.

"Furious." Cecilia grinned. "But I don't care." She threw her arms around his neck and stole another kiss. "We've waited long enough for this, baby. Let's do it."

THE JET WAS ready and waiting, so he just grabbed her hand and led her out to the waiting car.

"Should we stop by the house and pack some clothes?" she asked when they'd buckled in.

Colin pointed to the trunk. "All taken care of."

Cecilia's brows pulled together. "Really? Did you pack me underwear?"

"You doubt me?"

A huff. "How many pairs?"

"Bec packed it for me."

Her face relaxed. "Oh. So, at the hospital, why did you ask—?"

"I didn't want you to miss out on anything you might want." He cupped her cheek and rested his forehead against hers. "After all we've been through, you deserve *everything* you could ever dream of."

"We deserve," she said. "*We* deserve a happily ever after." A beat. "And the only thing I dream of is a future with you. *That's* what's important. Not some silly fantasy, but the fact that I love you with every part of my being."

Her chest was rising and falling in rapid breaths, teasing his lips, and Colin gave in to the urge to kiss her.

He never had any hope of resisting anyway.

Cecilia tasted as sweet as ever, as intoxicating as a bottle of whiskey, and *fuck* did he love kissing this woman.

But eventually, and as much as it pained him, he had to take his hands off her.

"We're here, sir," the driver said with a cough.

CeCe jumped in his arms and pulled back, the tops of her cheeks stained pink.

"You see our need for Vegas," he told the driver then chuckled when CeCe smacked him across the chest. "Come on." He snagged her wrist and tugged her up the stairs to the plane. "Let's get married."

It turned out that though Bec had helped him keep his plan from Cecilia, she hadn't kept it a secret from the rest of their friends.

Case in point, Heather.

Who was standing outside the chapel he'd reserved, phone in hand, and three tiny female faces crammed into the screen on the other side.

"Don't mind me," his business partner said, pointing the phone at them while the interfering hens cackled through the airwaves.

He narrowed his eyes at Bec. "You promised."

An unrepentant shrug. "We'll hang up if you guys really want us to, but we love her and need to see her happy."

"You're nosy," he said.

"That's true." Another shrug. "But also, the other. We want CeCe to be happy."

Sighing, he turned to the woman who would soon be his wife. She was radiantly happy.

"Do you mind?" she asked. "It's kind of perfect that they're here this way."

As if he could ever deny her anything.

He pointed his thumb in the direction of the door. "I guess you ladies are witnessing a wedding."

They squealed as he held open the door for Cecilia and Heather.

"But you'll be witnessing it with the volume on mute."

Heather smirked, adjusting her phone so the noise coming through the speakers wasn't ear-piercing, then twisted her thumb and forefinger in front of her mouth. "My lips are sealed."

He shook his head as his fingers found Cecilia's. "I love you," he whispered, "and can't wait for you to be my wife."

"Awww!" the peanut gallery's sighs were audible despite the low volume on Heather's phone.

Colin rolled his eyes. "Really?"

"Shh, guys," Heather said. "Or you'll get us kicked out."

CeCe gave him a smile that hit him right in the gut. "Let's go grab our happy ending, shall we?"

BAD HUSBAND

BILLIONAIRE'S CLUB BOOK 3

ONE

Heather

HEATHER SNIFFED and swiped a finger under each eye as Colin and CeCe drove off in their car.

"So, the master businesswoman known as Heather O'Keith has real human emotions?"

She stiffened, whipping around to glare at Clay Steele, successful businessman, rival entrepreneur, and sexy as fuck male . . . despite the awful porn star name.

"I have plenty of feelings," she snapped. "Just because I don't make a practice of showing them in my fucking boardroom doesn't make me less of a woman."

Clay's stare drifted down and then back up. "Anyone who says you're not a woman has lost their fucking mind."

Heather froze.

Had he—?

Had the man who'd done nothing but dog her steps in the business world, who made it a point of tormenting her by stealing clients and undercutting bids, had *he* just complimented her?

How in the . . .?

Then she saw the glassy look in his eyes.

Ah. Drunk.

"You've had a few too many," she said, waving a hand to signal the town car parked at the corner. Of all the things that came along with busting her ass to have a flush bank account, having enough money to afford a personal driver was a perk that she really enjoyed.

"So?" he asked, not quite belligerent but close.

Idiot man. But she'd seen way too many of them in this situation to be the least bit cowed. "I hope you're not an angry drunk."

"No." Both brows came up, waggled. "I'm a horny one."

Despite herself, she chuckled. "With a porn star name like yours, I'm not surprised."

"Hey!" he said and followed her when she strode toward her car, the back door now conveniently open. "I'll have you know, my name is a family one, passed down generation by glorious generation."

A roll of her eyes as she pushed through the open door, plunking down on the plush leather seat. "Maybe so. But you're still drunk."

His expression sobered enough that she stopped short of slamming the metal panel on his head.

Didn't stop her from wanting to do it, though.

His next words made her regret the thought. "Rough day for me today."

Dammit. Why did he have to go and show that he had a human side? Heather wanted to loathe him, not have sympathy for the man.

Clay seemed to realize he'd said too much and so he stepped back, shoving his hands in his pockets. He tilted his chin in the direction Colin and CeCe's car had disappeared. "Who were they?"

"Friends." *No. At this point they were family.*

"Ah." One of his hands exited his pocket and shoved through his hair, leaving the thick brown locks mussed. Not that it detracted from the image. Rather, it made Clay Steele appear slightly more human instead of his typical.

Which was godlike.

Tall, broad in the shoulders, lean in the hips, with chocolate-colored hair and unusually vibrant mocha irises.

He'd been in her mental spank bank for months.

"I'd give a lot to have one of those again."

His words made her frown in confusion before she realized she'd spoken aloud, though thankfully about CeCe and Colin being more than friends, and not about her tendency to mastur-bate to the image of Clay bending her over the bed, pinning her against a wall, grabbing her by the ankles and—

"A family?" she asked, blinking the images away.

"Yeah." A sigh as he turned for the sidewalk. "See you at the next convention, O'Keith."

"Wait!" Acting on an instinct she didn't want to examine too closely, Heather put one foot out of the car, reached to snag his wrist, and hauled him to a stop. "Let me at least take you back to your hotel."

"I'm getting drunk," he said but allowed her to pull him inside the sedan so her driver could shut the door behind them.

"You're already drunk," she said.

He stiffened. "*More* drunk."

"Fine," she said, half-worried he was going to launch himself from the car. She'd never seen Clay like this. Usually he was so cold and uncompromising, impenetrable, even under the toughest of negotiations. He was . . . well, he was typically as *Steele*-like as his last name decreed.

She wrapped her arm through his to prevent any unplanned exits from the vehicle and gave the driver the name of her favorite bar. "If you really want to drink, let's do it right."

And *then* she'd drop him at his hotel.

Except it didn't happen that way.

Yes, they hit the bar.

Yes, they drank.

Yes, they got plastered.

But then they woke up . . . or at least, *Heather* woke up.

Naked.

With a softly snoring Clay Steele passed out next to her in bed.

That wasn't the worst part.

Because Heather woke up naked with a softly snoring Clay Steele in her bed *and* she was wearing a giant diamond ring on her left hand.

Still not the worst part.

That came in the form of a slightly crumpled marriage certificate tucked under her right cheek.

And not the one on her face.

She pulled it from beneath her, a cold sweat breaking out over her body, dread in every nerve and cell.

She *still* wasn't prepared for the horror she found.

The marriage license had been signed by . . . Heather O'Keith and Clay Steele.

Holy fuck, what had she done?

TWO

Clay

HE WOKE WITH A SPLITTING HEADACHE, a mouth as dry as the Sahara, and . . . completely naked.

"Fuck," he muttered, rolling over on the mattress and testing the severity of his hangover by slitting his lids the tiniest bit.

Pain blared through his skull.

"Fuck," he said again and slammed them closed.

Noted. His hangover was at DEFCON 1.

Not a surprise, considering what day it was.

Clay kept his eyes closed and pushed up in bed. His muscles ached like he'd run a marathon. Or . . . he supposed he'd fucked one.

That was his typical M.O. on this particular anniversary.

His closed eyes were probably why he didn't notice that he wasn't alone, that he wasn't even in his own hotel room. But between the pounding in his head and the increasingly pressing urge to take a piss, he didn't notice either one of those critical facts.

Another "Fuck," to emphasize the fact that his body felt—

and not that he would *ever* admit such a thing to any other living soul, but his heart felt the same—like it had been run over by a train.

"Is that the only word in your repertoire?"

Clay went ramrod stiff, his eyes flying open to send lightning strikes of agony through his brain. He knew that voice.

It had made him rock-hard from the first moment he'd heard it.

Confident, cool, and with just the hint of rasp. Heather O'Keith was sex incarnate, not that anyone who dealt with her in the business world would dare to say such a thing.

Not when she was so buttoned up and controlled in those suits she wore. Fuck if Clay hadn't jerked off to the image of tearing her shirt open, pearl buttons flying every direction, and then bending her over and pulling those slacks past her thighs. He'd drop to his knees and eat like it was his last meal. He'd—

"I'm taking your silence as a yes," she said, smirking before staring down at her perfectly painted nails as though considering whether she needed a manicure. Her right hand drifted over her left, and his eyes caught on her ring finger, remembering something.

He winced and rubbed a temple. How much had he drunk last night?

The last time he'd had a hangover this bad he'd been newly twenty-one.

"Fuck," he said and dropped his chin to his chest.

Heather snorted and he glanced up, one half of his mouth curving.

His voice was rough. "Apparently, I can only use the F-bomb directly upon waking."

"Or upon hangover," she quipped, her left hand coming up to brush an errant strand of hair off her forehead.

There was something about that movement, about the color of her polish—red with silver sparkles—that was familiar.

But then again, how did he know there were silver sparkles on her nails?

They just looked red from here.

And he was losing it. Completely and utterly losing his mind.

"What's the matter, big guy?" Heather asked. "I can practically smell the smoke from here."

God, he liked this woman.

She was spine and fire and spunk, confident enough to sledgehammer a man's balls when he was fucking up or trying to take advantage. More than that, Clay had way too much respect for Heather as a businesswoman to minimize her skills by qualifying her solely as a ballbuster. Her mind for business was unparalleled, and she had outmaneuvered him more times than his ego cared to admit.

His eyes finally processed the wall color behind her chair. The rug beneath her feet. He stood, whipped around, and realized all at once that this wasn't his hotel room. Not his bed, not his room, and judging by the décor as he snatched a throw pillow off the floor and used it to cover himself *way* too late, he wasn't even in his hotel.

"Why am I here?"

A huff of laughter had him turning to face her in time to witness another brush of those sparkly red nails against her shirt.

A shirt that . . . he tilted his head, studying her closely, because it wasn't buttoned correctly. No. That wasn't it. Her shirt was *missing* buttons.

Pearls flying. A freckle on her left ring finger that he'd kissed. One on her right hip that he'd nibbled.

"Did we have sex?"

"Ding. Ding. Ding," she said, her eyes clouding with some emotion as she tapped her nose. "I knew you could get there in the end."

Clay's eyes were locked on her face, trying to recall if she'd unfrozen at all in the sack or if she'd stayed so utterly in control.

Aside from flashes of naked skin, his brain wasn't much help. But he did know that if he hadn't been able to shatter that famous control of Heather O'Keith's, then he clearly hadn't done his job correctly.

He sank onto the edge of the bed. "Damn. I wish I could remember it."

His words made her flinch, a flinch he would have missed if he hadn't been studying her so carefully. Somehow, he'd said the wrong thing without trying.

That was his specialty when it came to Heather O'Keith.

He should have just stuck with fucks.

"Hey," he said, rising from the bed and walking over to her. "I'm sorry, I didn't—"

She put up her hand. "Stop your alpha I-need-to-fix-every-thing brain for a hot second. I'm fine. And frankly, we've got bigger problems."

And then she held up a piece of paper that made him halt in his tracks.

THREE

Heather

HEATHER WATCHED as Clay's stride faltered before he continued forward.

The man turned heads as he walked down a sidewalk, but coming toward her, only that stupid pillow tucked across his hips, all rippling muscles and sun-kissed skin . . . *fuck her*, it took her breath away.

She wasn't lucky like Clay. *She* remembered every moment of their night together.

Calloused fingertips across her skin, hot lips pressed to hers, to her neck, to the space behind her ear that made her head spin. Hard against her soft, him sliding home, filling her to capacity before he'd proceeded to hit *all* the right spots. He'd known exactly how to please her, almost better than she knew how to please herself.

So, yeah, her Clay Steele fantasies hadn't done the real man any justice.

She shifted in her seat, pressing her thighs together as the memory of him kneeling before her the previous night sent all her nerve endings on high alert.

His eyes flicked down, and moisture flowed south.

Ugh. He was so not helping her little issue.

That issue being her lack of control and her drunken idiocy. She'd been fuzzy on the details upon waking, but a long, hot shower and her attempts at locating her missing pearl buttons and then fumbling to reattach them to her shirt with the ridiculous sewing kit from the tray in the bathroom had ensured she was fully sober and in possession of every single one of those memories.

She'd only utilized her pathetic sewing skills in the first place because she hadn't expected to spend another night in Vegas and had sent all of her luggage ahead to RoboTech's private plane.

Which had been fueled and waiting for her—she flicked a glance down at her watch—for the last eight hours.

To take a page out of Clay's book, *fuck.*

She should have called for the butler to buy her a new shirt and ran, taking the ring and marriage license with her. She could have gotten her lawyer friend Bec to arrange a quiet annulment as quickly as possible and then send Clay the details when it was taken care of.

But she hadn't been able to leave.

Not when Clay had been . . . what?

Vulnerable. Fragile. Different from the man she knew and understood.

Yet as he strode forward and took the paper from her fingers, Heather didn't know what she'd been thinking. He wasn't the least bit vulnerable. He was strong and, not that she would admit it, intimidating.

Clay Steele was far too smart for his own good, and he made her want too many things.

Things she couldn't have.

Commitment wasn't in her DNA.

"What the fuck is this?" he asked, eyes boring into her.

"*That* is a marriage license," she said. Rather helpfully, she thought, despite the glare he shot her way. "With our signatures, if you haven't gotten that far down yet," she added with a wave of her hand, trying to keep hold of her cavalier this-is-just-a-little-hiccup attitude she used frequently with the flightier members of RoboTech's board.

His brows pulled together, twin slashes of dark chocolate that made her want to sidle close and kiss his frown away.

Kiss his—?

What the fuck, Heather O'Keith?!

She cleared her throat and stood. "I'll get my lawyer working on an annulment as quickly as possible." She moved close to Clay, close enough to snag the paper from his fingers while forcing herself to ignore her body's reaction to him.

Heather was a strong, independent woman, dammit. Just because a man was sexy as shit and could find her G-spot without a four-hour tutorial and diagrams, didn't mean she could afford to lose control.

Look where that had gotten her mother. And for that matter, her father.

Even the one time her half-brother Jordan had lost control, he'd created a mess so huge that he'd nearly obliterated his business *and* his personal life.

Colin and CeCe were no different. Running free and loose had nearly killed any chance of their future together. It was only by a fortuitous trapping on a twelve-hour plane ride that they'd managed to work out their differences.

So no, she wouldn't be repeating her friends' mistakes. *If* she decided to take the non-drunken plunge into matrimony, it would be a carefully considered choice. She definitely would *not* wake up with a crinkling paper under her ass and find herself married to the man who was her adversary in the business world.

But as often happened with Clay Steele, all of her best-laid plans went to hell.

His lips—the soft, skilled set she'd feasted on the night before —quirked and he moved, faster than she could blink, plucking the marriage certificate out of her grip and turning away.

The sight of his delicious ass rotted her brain.

That was the only conceivable reason for her just standing there like an imbecile as Clay strode to the bathroom and paused, a mischievous light in his mocha eyes.

"Oh no, Heather," he said, carefully folding the paper into thirds. "You're not getting off that easily."

Then he closed the bathroom door.

It locked with a *click*.

FOUR

Clay

CLAY BRACED his hands on the marble counter and dropped his chin to his chest.

This was a mess and a half, and he had the marriage certificate to prove it.

An annulment was the right call, the easiest solution to resolve the shitty consequences of his idiotic tour of All Things *Not* to Do in Vegas, but then Heather had gone and declared it all but done in that imperious tone of hers. With his brain throbbing and his body aching—because though the memories weren't there in his mind, his body clearly remembered how much fun they'd had together—and he'd just . . . he'd wanted to make her mad.

The paper that was as dangerous as a nuke crinkled in his grip, and Clay blew out a sigh.

An annulment it was.

It *had* to be.

So why then was something inside him revolting at the thought?

"Fuck," he muttered, leaving the license on the counter and turning to crank on the shower. The first thing he needed to do was scrub away the remnants of his drunken night from his skin.

Well, the *first* thing he needed to do was to brush his teeth, because hello, dragon breath.

Anyway. The point was he'd accomplish the simple things—e.g. general human cleanliness—and *then* deal with the giant mess he'd made of his life.

He groaned and picked up a toothbrush and tube of toothpaste on the counter. Both were open and clearly used, but considering he'd probably spent half the night with his tongue on or *in* Heather, he figured he'd risk the germs in favor of clean, minty-flavored breath.

After, he set the shower to scorching and by the time he stepped out and toweled off, felt well on his way to his normal self.

Of course, that was before he realized he had no idea where his clothes were.

Or his cell.

Or his wallet.

Clay sighed and tilted his head back, staring up at the fluorescent lights.

Naked walk of shame down the Strip. Yeah, that would be just about perfect on this day.

He shivered despite the scalding shower he'd just taken, the memories doing what they always did. Freezing him from the inside out, the cold seeping into his extremities, raising goose bumps on his skin. No matter how many layers he put on, he was still always cold.

Frost on the windows.

His breath coming in rapid clouds of white.

Fingers going numb.

And blood. So much blood.

Clay wrenched open the door and stumbled into the room.

The *empty* room. His clothes had been folded and sat neatly on the end of the bed, alongside his wallet and phone.

Why did that feel like it was less an act of kindness and more of a parting shot?

Not that it mattered.

He needed to get dressed and get to the airport. He had meetings in London and Berlin then a sit-down with a prospective client in Amsterdam. *Then* he needed to fly to San Francisco and finalize some contracts before heading back out to New York to check in with his CFO.

So no, his life didn't need any hiccups, and it definitely didn't need one Heather O'Keith throwing another wrench into it.

The hesitation he'd felt before his shower was gone, chalked up to his blurred, fuzzy, hungover mind. He'd taken the license from her because that was his way. He liked to be in charge, and he didn't trust anyone, least of all the woman who'd been so adversarial over the last months. Clay would give the contract to *his* lawyer and demand an annulment as quickly as possible.

Heather was just going to have to deal.

He was handling this *his* way, and that was the end of it.

"Exactly," he grumbled, agreeing with his internal dialogue as he tugged up his slacks. "She's not always in charge."

He shrugged into his shirt and as he did up the buttons, a memory sparked. Heather had undone them the night before, kissing along the path of skin she'd revealed, smirking up at him as her fingers had drifted toward the waistband of his pants.

He'd been rock-hard and aching, and that smirk had snapped something in him. Clay had reached for her, grabbing her around the waist and tossing her onto the bed. Buttons had flown, her blouse torn open. Except . . . his fingers went to the pocket of his shirt and he found the little white sphere he'd tucked there for safekeeping.

It was a tiny thing, a fussy piece of femininity designed to frustrate clunky masculine fingers.

He should have tossed it in the trash or maybe made a mental note to save it to return to Heather, but Clay found himself tucking it safely into the pocket of his slacks, shoving it deep down, so it wouldn't fall out. Then he walked to the bedside phone and located the name of the hotel he was in.

Ten seconds later he'd texted his driver and received an ETA.

Since it was only a few minutes away—*his* hotel was only two resorts over—he decided to head down to the lobby.

He was nearly out of the room when he remembered the marriage license.

"You're an idiot, Clay," he said and turned back for the bathroom.

The used toothbrush was there, next to the open tube of toothpaste. But where thirty minutes earlier, the certificate had been neatly folded, placed carefully out of the splash zone of the sink, now the counter was empty.

He knew.

He *fucking* knew, but he checked the floor to make sure it hadn't fallen off anyway.

"Heather," he growled, his blood boiling in a way that only she ever managed to create. With everyone else, he was calm and collected. With *her,* he lost his goddamned mind.

The note he found perched atop the trash can confirmed that.

Later, porn star.
P.S. Look forward to hearing from my lawyer.

He'd locked the door. Clay had locked the fucking door.

So why was some part of him not surprised that Heather O'Keith could pick a lock?

"Okay, baby," he said, shoving the note into his pocket. "Now, it's on."

FIVE

Heather

"WHY. Do. I. Do. These. Things. To. Myself?" Heather asked, punctuating each word with a thunk of her head on her pillow.

She was somewhere over the Atlantic and was supposed to be sleeping in order to be bright-eyed and bushy-tailed for her meeting with the board of Colin's company in Scotland. She was taking over communications of the robotic arm of their partnership while he and CeCe were on their honeymoon. After that, Heather had brief stops in London and Berlin before meeting with a prospective client in Amsterdam.

It was going to be seventy-two straight hours of meetings, frantically reviewing client notes and finalizing PowerPoint slides, paired with clothing changes on the go, snatching bits of sleep on the plane, and eating whatever crap food she managed to cram into her mouth in her free minutes . . . no free *seconds*.

So she should be sleeping, not holding a crinkled piece of paper that had the potential to ruin her.

"Get it together, Heather," she said, tossing the license onto the nightstand and forcing her eyes closed. A couple of deep breaths would settle her, would help her sleep. They always did.

Except where normally she could drift off in the blink of an eye, her blinks only brought her images of Clay.

Of Clay over her.

Of Clay *inside* her.

Of Clay's mouth and hands and *fuck,* his mouth.

She'd never lost control like that before. Not with her own hands—or devices, rather—and certainly not with a partner.

And yes, she did say partner in a non-gender specific way. She had always intimidated men, and so she'd experimented with women during her college years. Not just in a fling sense or a stolen kiss here or there, but in a full-fledged exploration of that part of her sexuality. She'd had real relationships with real feelings.

There just had been a piece missing inside of her that those relationships had never been able to fill.

That missing piece came in the form of a penis.

She snorted, rolling her eyes at her idiocy. It wasn't just a penis—it was the hard to her soft, that spicy smell, the arms, the abs, the bristles of hair on a chest. Hell, she might have been still fighting it, trying to prove to herself and the world that she didn't conform to quote-unquote normal heterosexual rules, if not for the combined power of Bec and her college on-again, off-again, Lexy.

"I'm not saying you're not attracted to women, Heather," Bec had said. *"Obviously there's a piece of you who is. But I also do think that some part of you wants to stick it to your mom's image of the perfect daughter who gets married to the man she chooses and has two point two kids and a picket fence."*

Lexy had chimed in. *"And then there's the fact that you're not really into me."*

Heather had frowned. *"You're beautiful, Lexy. You—"*

"You don't want me." Pale blue eyes had locked onto hers. *"Not really. Trust me, I can tell."*

Heather hadn't liked that. She didn't like being wrong about anything, but most especially about herself. But she couldn't deny what Bec had said, nor Lexy, if she was being entirely honest with herself.

So, she'd stopped trying to turn her mother's hair gray and had focused on her father. He thought men were better at business? Well, fuck him, she'd prove him wrong. He thought only men could have one-night stands and relationships where they don't let emotion get involved? Double fuck him, she'd sleep with so many men that . . . she'd started to hate that part of herself.

And so . . . therapy.

Her dirtiest, darkest secret was that she'd started therapy about five years before.

No more empty sex. No more trying to be something she wasn't. No more trying to stick it to her parents.

She was her own person. She worked because she enjoyed her job and the challenges it created.

She was sane and stable and the person people went to for advice. She wasn't crazy Heather who slept with anything with a pulse or even sad, torn up Heather trying to find her own place in the world.

She was content.

And so what if content meant a little bit lonely . . . or that her lady bits felt shriveled with disuse.

At least she had her friends and her work.

But now, Clay *fucking* Steele.

Goddamn it.

What the hell had she been thinking?

She hadn't been. That was the problem. He'd touched her, and five years of celibacy had gone up in flames. She'd wanted so, *so* badly.

And he'd given. So, *so* good-ly.

Heather snorted again and flopped an arm over her eyes. *God*, had he given it "good-ly." Probably the best ever, if she was being completely honest, and since she was alone and didn't need to hide anything from anyone, she could freely admit that Clay had skills. Even drunk, he'd used every single one to play her body like she was his personal instrument, celibacy be damned.

But marriage? Commitment?

Down that path led ruination.

Yes, she was well aware that she was sounding like a bad gothic novel, but Heather wasn't like CeCe or Abby. She wasn't built for commitment. She was her parents' daughter and didn't have the capacity to care for another person in that way.

She was broken deep inside, and no amount of therapy could fix *that* part of her.

Friends she could do.

Love? Breaking down every single barrier between herself and another person? Being open and sharing all the intimacies that came with building a solid relationship?

No.

That ability was just not in her.

And so she grabbed her phone, sent an email to Bec asking her to schedule her some time when she got back to San Francisco to discuss a few "legal matters"—ha!—then set her cell onto the nightstand and closed her eyes.

One breath. Another.

Sleep stole her under.

SIX

Clay

THE PLANE TOUCHED down with a jolt, and Clay attempted to shove Heather from his mind.

Not that it was easy.

The woman had wormed her way deep inside his psyche from the moment he'd met her, six months before.

Blonde hair the color of sunshine peeking through clouds, blue eyes that mimicked the indigo of the early morning sky. A body that should have sonnets written in its honor—curvy and soft and with an ass that he wanted to . . .

"Mr. Steele? Is everything all right?" Julian, the flight attendant, asked.

Clay blinked, shooting out of his seat and tucking his briefcase under one arm. His cheeks felt hot—from embarrassment or desire, he didn't know. Okay, so maybe he didn't want to examine too closely that he'd been caught daydreaming like a horny teenager.

"Yes," he said, after clearing his throat. "Thank you."

He nodded to Julian and disembarked the plane, heading

toward the car that was waiting at the bottom of the jet's staircase.

"The office, Mr. Steele?" his driver asked.

"Yes, thank you, Frank," he said as he sank into the plush leather and turned on his cell.

It began to vibrate almost immediately, texts and emails pouring through. WiFi on the plane made it so he hadn't gone a solid twelve hours without communication, but he'd turned even that off for the final two hours of the flight and had forced himself to sleep.

A snort. So much for that.

He'd spent the entire one hundred and twenty minutes picking through his fractured memories of the previous night, trying to remember every detail.

Except that hadn't really helped his scrambled brain, his memories still in bits and pieces.

Smooth porcelain skin. Those sparkly red nails. Dusky pink lips. Breasts that had pillowed against his chest.

"Dammit," he muttered as his cock hardened for what felt like the hundredth time in the last few hours.

It somehow remembered, but his fucking mind was useless.

"Everything okay, sir?" Frank asked as he drove them out of the airport, reminding Clay that he needed to lock this shit up tight and focus on the deals ahead. There was a reason no one ever asked him how he was.

And that reason was because he was always fine.

Or at least he was good at projecting "fine" and faking it until he was actually fine in truth.

But now two people in the last ten minutes had shown concern.

Clearly, he was losing his touch.

"Fine, Frank. Thanks," he clipped, annoyed at himself for the lack of discipline. If his father could see him now . . . he'd be extremely disappointed.

Steeles are steel, son. Emotionless. Strong under pressure. We don't break. We don't bend. We endure.

Except they *hadn't* endured.

"Fuck," he said under his breath. This trip was happening at the wrong time, too close to the anniversary of—

"I can get you to the office in just under an hour."

Work. He needed to focus on work. On the deal, on making Steele Technologies more successful than his dad had ever dreamed.

And his dad could *dream*.

"An hour's fine," Clay said after a beat. *Endure,* he reminded himself. *Strength under pressure.* "Thanks, Frank. In the meantime, I need to make a phone call."

"Absolutely, sir." The divider between them rose almost before Frank had finished the sentence.

The call was a lie—well, at least having to make a pressing one. Yes, there were always people he needed to touch base with, but at that moment there wasn't anything that couldn't wait. Except sitting in the silence created by the divider *snicking* closed was a mistake. The quiet, the isolation made his devil come out.

His mother had always said he could be a holy terror when he put his mind to it and, well, Clay always put his mind to it.

Always.

Smirking, he sent a text to his assistant and got a response in less than two minutes.

Which was why Sebastian got paid the big bucks.

His lips tugging up, he keyed in the number.

It rang once. Again. A third time. And just when Clay was composing the message he was going to leave, a breathless female answered.

"O'Keith," Heather panted into the phone.

There was noise in the background, a rapid *pat-pat-pat* that reminded him of something he couldn't quite place, but Clay forced that out of his brain and focused on the way Heather's voice had softened on answering.

It would harden as soon as he spoke, he knew that, and he wanted to hold on to that softness, before his voice raised her hackles, turned her tone into an icy blade.

He wanted to hear her as she'd been that night. And his instincts told him that she'd been sweet, almost gentle.

A concept he would have laughed at months ago, but one he knew today was—

"Hell-o?" she said, less breathless, more sharp, and already those rounded off edges were being honed into precise points.

"My dear Heather O'Keith, are you taking a shower?" he asked, finally cluing into what the *pat-pat-pat* in the background was.

There was a long pause.

"Clay." Another beat. Then a sigh and, "How did you get my number?"

"Husbands should know where their wives are, don't you think?"

He could hear her teeth grinding. It made him grin.

"Clay, I'm naked and dripping, what the *hell* do you want?"

His lips curved. "Words a man lives to hear."

She muttered something under her breath that sounded suspiciously as though she were counting to ten. "What can I do for you, Steele?" And though it was posed as a question, Clay knew it was more curse than concern.

He really irritated Heather, and for some reason that gave him great joy.

"Clay!" she exclaimed, impatient now.

Okay, fine, so he was acting like a second-grade boy with his first crush.

But he didn't care, couldn't find the strength to care. Not when his lack of reply made her sigh again. Her eyes would be flicking up toward the ceiling, her lips pursing as she breathed in and out on a long, slow exhalation.

"I don't have all day, Steele. Give it to me now or so help me—"

"More words a man lives to hear." He chuckled at the feral sound that came through the airwaves. "Ah, Heather, baby, you're so sweet to me."

Now her shoulders would drop as she attempted to rein in her temper, her chin joining her eyes in tipping up at the ceiling, the slender column of her neck exposed and delicate. That angle was a tease, he'd press his mouth, his tongue—

Fuck.

Many dreams—none of them of the PG variety—had been made envisioning all the things he'd do to Heather's throat, sucking and licking and marking the smooth skin there.

And he *had* marked it. Just last night.

He'd nipped behind her ear, nibbled down to her shoulder, sucked a hickey on the gentle curve where her throat met her collarbone. He'd kissed, he'd caressed, he'd *necked* like he was a teenaged boy in the back seat with his first girlfriend.

"I'm hanging up now," she said, the background noise growing as she apparently moved closer to the shower.

"You have something that belongs to me," he said before she could disconnect.

A huff. "I'm taking the license to *my* lawyer."

The *click* cutting off his words was probably a good thing.

Because something stupid had been about to come out of his mouth.

Like, "Not the license, *you*, you infuriating woman."

And Heather O'Keith didn't belong to any man . . . least of all him.

SEVEN

Heather

HEATHER DROPPED the phone onto the granite countertop. It clattered, skidding to a stop near the complimentary shampoo/shower gel/old-fashioned bar of soap/lotion tray.

No matter how much her room cost, the hotels never seemed to provide conditioner.

Didn't they understand women at all?

Shampoo just didn't do it.

Not that it mattered.

Her assistant had already unpacked her toiletries and clothes before Heather had even left Colin's office.

The meeting had gone well, the woman who was overseeing the European portion of his business, competent and confident.

Heather slipped back into the water, sighing with relief as the hot water hit her cooled limbs.

She was also smiling.

Not because of the disturbance of the phone call—though she had the feeling Clay would probably like being referred to as a disturbance. No, she was smiling because the woman Colin had left in charge of his business operations reminded her of herself.

Francine was smart as hell and tough as nails, but she was also young in a way that Heather hadn't been in ages.

Or maybe not ever.

Still, it made Heather like Colin even more for having chosen to put his faith in a woman like Francine.

Her business partner liked strong women. He respected them. He—

Clay liked strong women, too.

"And that, my stupid, sex-melted brain," she said as she smoothed conditioner down the length of her hair, "is not a helpful sentiment at all."

Because it didn't matter what Clay liked.

It didn't matter how she felt when Clay was around.

He was dangerous to her on a fundamental level.

She had seen it too many times. The risks were too close to home.

"A man is *never* going to change me," she promised and let the hot water stream down her back, rinsing the conditioner away, leaving her hair soft, the rough edges smoothed over, temporarily or perhaps, permanently mended.

Which was fine for her split ends.

But men weren't as effective as beauty products. They didn't fix *anything*.

They were chaos and hurt and bending, and *bending* until he was happy at the expense of all else.

Of *everyone* else.

So no. Heather was perfectly happy with her rough edges.

They kept her safe, made her strong and tough and invulnerable.

You weren't invulnerable with Clay, her brain reminded her, rather unhelpfully, she thought.

"And look where it got me," she said, cranking off the water.

"Married to a man I don't know and everything I've worked for at risk."

Her brain, conveniently, didn't have a reply.

"Typical," she huffed and reached for a towel.

AFTER A FEW HOURS of restless sleep, Heather was aboard her plane and heading for Berlin.

It was such a beautiful city, one of her absolute favorites, but she doubted she'd see anything this trip except the insides of hotels, conference rooms, and cars.

Upon arriving, she went straight to the hotel to drop her bags and order room service then poured over the files for her first meeting. The hotel would be her temporary home base for the two days she was in Berlin, one that would allow her to sleep in a bed that wasn't thirty thousand feet in the air while conveniently providing her decent meals at all hours.

Her business life wasn't so easily managed.

At the moment, several new products were being proposed for development and while she'd already made a soft decision on each of them based on market projections and the scientific reports the research heads had sent her way, she always liked to meet directly with the development teams. Sometimes there was something in a person, an unquantifiable "something" that didn't come through on reports and cost/expense ratios.

Passion or intensity or the ability to do good in the world.

And while Heather may be a businesswoman at heart and may seriously enjoy making deals and exceeding expectations when it came to the bottom line, she also truly wanted to make the world a better place.

Sometimes it was via a little robot that had made one child—and then about six million others—happy. Other times it was the project she and Colin were undertaking, trying to find a way to muster supplies in the wake of natural or man-made disasters and deliver them quickly to those people most affected. Occasionally it was partnering with the government to get better equipment to the military.

She'd never cop to it, of course, but those "side projects" were what fed her soul, what kept her going when she met another man who thought he could bully or manipulate or coerce her into doing something just because she was a woman.

Of course, she couldn't deny that she derived great pleasure from turning the tables on those men who underestimated her.

Clay doesn't underestimate you.

"Shut it," she gritted and picked up her briefcase. Her phone buzzed at almost the same instant, informing her that her car was downstairs and her assistant would be up to unpack momentarily.

Her assistant was freakishly efficient.

When Heather didn't give Rachel time off, that was.

Her assistant had just about shit a brick when she'd seen the state of Heather's clothes as she'd boarded the plane for London, and had promised she would never take another day off again.

Meanwhile, Heather had thought she'd done a fairly decent job of seamstress-ing, considering her limited resources.

Not good enough, apparently.

Rachel was a little dramatic, but Heather liked her anyway.

Young, sweet, and slightly naïve, her assistant always managed to know what Heather required—often before Heather even realized she needed it.

And that's why Rachel was getting a raise after this trip *and* a week of vacation.

No burnout on Heather's watch, not when she wanted to keep her assistant around.

There was a knock before the lock disengaged and Rachel pushed the door open, thrusting a stack of files in Heather's direction.

"Don't bother reading them now," she said. "These are for the next set of meetings. You'll have a half-hour lunch break to review them."

"Perfect," Heather said, taking the folders and stashing them in her briefcase. "And the Pierce file?"

Rachel wrinkled her nose. "Still waiting on their firm to provide details."

Heather frowned as she considered their planned stop in Amsterdam the following evening. "If they don't have them to me by five tonight, the meeting's off."

"Good," Rachel said, and at Heather's raised eyebrow explained, "I told them they had to have them to me by four-thirty."

"And that is why you're getting a raise," Heather said with a grin, adding at Rachel's shocked expression, "I was going to wait until we were home, but how often has that been lately?"

A nod, though Rachel was still wearing a surprised expression that made Heather's stomach sink. "What is it?"

She better not be planning on quitting.

Rachel's chin wobbled before she waved a hand in the air. "Ignore me, I'm being ridiculous."

Heather raised her eyebrow again, staring until Rachel caved.

"Fine." An irritated huff, but despite that, the rest of Rachel's words were genuine and maybe . . . a little embarrassed. "I'm surprised, I guess," she said, smoothing a nonexistent wrinkle in her skirt. "I've . . . I just have never actually been good at anything before, at least not at anything that mattered."

Damn, but Heather liked this girl's honesty—though it broke a piece of her heart to hear the sadness lacing Rachel's words.

"Well, that may be," Heather said, bumping Rachel's shoulder with her own, "But I also know I couldn't have pulled this trip off without you. I would have been a hell of a lot more stressed and less prepared *and* less rested if it weren't for you taking care of the million little details that come along with a trip like this." A pause as she waited for Rachel's eyes to connect with hers. "So, thank you for doing your job with such scary competence."

Rachel laughed, the uncertainty finally melting from her features. "No problem."

"And we'll discuss the specifics of your raise when we're flying home. Deal?"

"Deal." A pause as Rachel checked her watch. "Now get out of here. If your butt's not in that car in the next five minutes, you'll be late for the first meeting and put the entire schedule out of whack."

Heather saluted, leaving Rachel to finish the unpacking, and headed down to the car. Her mind was so full, so busy with reviewing key details for her first meeting as she walked through the lobby and out to the street that she missed Clay Steele standing at the reception desk.

But he didn't miss her.

EIGHT

Clay

CLAY TOOK one step in Heather's direction before he forced himself to stay at the counter.

Careful. Watch. Wait.

The woman helping him paused briefly in her frenetic keyboard pounding. "It'll be just a minute."

He nodded and thanked her, but his gaze was trained on Heather.

God, those pearl buttons just killed him.

Heather's lips were moving as though she were reciting facts to herself, and knowing her, she probably was. He had never been in a situation where she didn't seem to have all of the pertinent information on a topic.

Part of that was probably because, like him, she picked projects and investments that were in her wheelhouse. The other part was that she was just really damned smart and even if she didn't know the particulars about a topic, she was able to listen openly and then provide valuable insights from her own experiences.

It frustrated a lot of the men in their world, but then again, a lot of men in their world also liked to feel superior.

Clay didn't appreciate feeling like an idiot, of course, but he also didn't need to feel like the smartest one in the room in order to be important to the conversation. And he enjoyed learning and conquering new challenges.

Life was pretty boring otherwise.

But Heather's big juicy brain wasn't the only thing that attracted Clay.

Her body was amazing and her heart . . .

He would have said it was icy before Vegas.

It wasn't.

He remembered the way she'd looked after her friends had gotten in the car, straightening the "Just Married" sign before they pulled away, snapping a picture and then wiping tears from her eyes as they'd driven off.

There was emotion there.

Buried under some heavy armor, but it was still there. It—

Why is today hard for you?

She'd asked the question as she'd traced nonsensical patterns with one finger on his naked chest.

Clay grabbed on to the memory, pulling it to the forefront of his mind. Had he told her? His gut clenched hard. Fuck, what had he told her—?

It took a long moment, but the images finally teased themselves free. Then he breathed a sigh of relief as he remembered catching her little finger and bringing it to his mouth. He'd trailed his *own* finger down, traversing over her silky curves until he'd reached the damp space between her thighs.

And then she'd been moaning instead of asking questions.

It had been safer that way.

Heather disappeared from view, the revolving door swallowing her up, and he turned back to the woman at the desk. She was placing the plastic key card into an envelope. "Here you are, Mr. Steele," she said and directed him to the bank of elevators.

He lifted his messenger bag onto his shoulder and tucked his garment bag under the other arm. Berlin was only a quick stopover for him, so aside from a lunch meeting with his client that afternoon and a chat over dinner with his CEO of European operations, Clay planned on spending most of the day catching up on a few overdue projects before his flight out to Amsterdam the following morning.

Though, he frowned, pressing the elevator button before pulling out his cell phone, he wouldn't be stopping in Amsterdam at all if he didn't get some useful information from the folks at Pierce.

There was something about the company that wasn't sitting right with him.

So far, everything they'd sent had looked perfect, but almost too perfect. Pierce was growing fast and making money hand over fist, without a single mistake in sight, but if that were truly the case, then why were they shopping so aggressively for a buyer?

He knew for sure they were talking to RoboTech via Heather as well as several others from their circle. They'd also approached him about Steele Technologies buying them out.

It could be they were simply hoping for a bidding war, and while Clay didn't necessarily doubt that, he was also hesitant, especially based on the speed they wanted the buyout to occur and the lack of additional information he'd asked for.

His gut told him they were hiding something.

He just wasn't sure what.

The elevator dinged and he stepped off, checking the sign for the direction of his room. He was almost there when a door to his right flew open and a girl stormed out, almost colliding with him.

"Sorry," she mouthed, cell glued to her ear.

"It's okay—"

"*No.* That isn't going to work," she snapped, moving around him toward the elevators.

He stopped at his room and extracted one of the keycards from the envelope. He was just swiping it over the panel when he heard the woman say, "Heather O'Keith doesn't operate this way. Either provide the information to us today by four-thirty or we're done. I don't care that . . ."

Clay glanced down the hall and watched as she turned the corner.

Could Heather's room actually be next door?

He turned the handle, shoving his luggage inside before stepping back into the hall and . . . glancing toward the room in question.

What were the odds that fate would throw them together again?

He snorted.

Pretty damned high based on the last six months. He was just about to turn back to his own room when he noticed the door to hers hadn't quite latched. He reached forward to pull it all the way closed. If Heather saw him, she'd probably make some quip about him stalking her, or bust his balls over his attempt at breaking and entering.

Not that it mattered, because Heather wasn't there.

Heather. *Wasn't.* There.

And the devil inside him pushed to the surface.

Instead of tugging the door so it closed and locked, he found himself nudging the panel inward.

As the door opened, it caught on a garment bag hanging near the entrance—the same bag that must have slowed it enough so that it hadn't latched—and so he shifted the luggage slightly, wanting to prevent the same thing from happening in the future, wanting to keep Heather and, presumably, her assistant safe from . . . well, strange men barging into their hotel room.

"I'm not barging," he muttered. "I'm just making sure they're safe."

His conscience mocked him and he knew if his words were true, then he would have fixed the door and headed directly out of the room.

But he didn't leave.

And he also didn't bother kidding himself.

He wanted to scope out Heather's space, however tempo-rary. He wanted to see all of the little idiosyncrasies and he—

Voices echoed in the hall and he froze, six inches from her bed.

He was going to get arrested.

"Shit." Clay was losing his fucking mind. He needed to get the hell out of this room and back into his own. He needed to concentrate on *his* businesses and interests.

He needed to get his shit together.

In one swift movement, he turned away from the bed and back toward the door. Of course, though the motion was fast, it wasn't in the least bit graceful and he managed to knock over both a suitcase and a small tote bag, dumping its contents across the carpet in multiple directions.

Cursing, he reaching for a tube of lipstick that was rolling its way under the bed. He snagged it and shoved it back inside the tote, along with a pair of fuzzy socks, a package of tissues, a clear zippered bag with hand sanitizer, a mini deodorant, and wet wipes, and three paperback romances.

This is why women were way more successful than men. They traveled prepared.

He was just shoving the last book back into the bag when a paper slipped from between its pages.

Clay picked it up, a huge grin breaking out on his face.

NINE

Heather

HEATHER WAS EXHAUSTED by the time she made her way off the elevator and began walking down the hall toward her room.

Her brain throbbed and her feet ached, despite the expensive-supposedly-meant-they-were-comfortable heels. Because no matter how pricey and how well designed, stilettos were just not comfortable after ten hours on her feet.

She was dying to toe them off and then chuck them across her suite.

Or maybe not, since they cost enough to feed a small village, but the notion was there.

So bare feet—with a tiny shoe toss instead of a launch—followed by a bath and room service.

That was her plan.

Her plan seemed obtainable for all of two minutes.

Because when she reached her door, she realized her key wasn't working.

"Why?" she groaned, dropping her head to the smooth panel of wood. "Why. Won't. You. Work?" She punctuated each word with a thunk of her forehead against the door before trying the key again.

Nothing.

She tilted her chin up toward the ceiling. "Universe, help me out here."

The door opened.

Heather's lips parted in surprise and any hope of words was lost the moment she saw the pair of surprised mocha eyes staring down at her.

A pause before Clay's shock turned into amusement. "Well, who do we have here, knocking on my door?"

She frowned. "This is *my* door. What the hell are you doing in my room?"

He *tsked* and pointed up at the plastic placard on the wall. "Sweetheart, you need to look again."

Which was the moment that Heather finally studied the numbers outside the door, finally *read* the numbers closely.

And, *fuck her*, but Clay was right.

Her room was . . . not this one.

Groaning, she took a step toward the proper keypad and swiped the little plastic card.

It didn't work.

Oh God, was she on the wrong floor? Had she—

Clay plucked the key out of her hand and took a step . . . but not toward her. Nope, he went to the room on the other side of his and pressed the card above the knob. The little light on the door flashed green and the lock *clicked* open.

Heather sighed. Perfect. Now she not only owed him an apology but also a thank you.

He pushed the door open, flicking the dead bolt forward, probably so she wouldn't have to battle with the keycard again, because apparently her brain was incapable of both reading and operating simple technology. Then he rotated to face her, an expectant look on his face.

Ugh.

"Thanks," she grumbled and started for her room.

Clay didn't move as she brushed by him, and she couldn't hold back her shiver, not when her body remembered every moment of their night together.

She cleared her throat, shoving those memories down deep.

Her body, the treacherous beast, was reminding her how good it had been.

They were already married, so what would it hurt if she slid a little closer instead of away?

The amount of heat in Clay's eyes told her that was all it would take.

"Sweetheart—"

She snapped out of it. "I'm not your *sweetheart.*"

"Heather, then," he said, stepping closer, forcing her to either back up or let his chest brush against hers. It was second nature to stay in place, to feel the hard planes of him press close to her softer ones.

"Heather," he murmured again. Gently. One hand came up, cupped her cheek.

And that was enough for her to unstick her feet, to remember the trouble it caused last time.

The trouble *Clay* caused.

For her work. For her future. For her . . . heart.

"I'm sorry for disturbing you," she said and retreated to the threshold of her room, pushing the door open.

Clay didn't follow.

She tried to convince herself the little slice of disappointment cutting across her heart didn't actually exist.

"You're not a disturbance, sweetheart."

Her brow rose, her eyes narrowed, but Clay's only response was a lopsided grin.

"So, what do you think of the Pierce deal?" he asked, propping one shoulder against the doorframe.

Instantly, she relaxed. Business, she could do, even with a tired brain.

"I'm only telling you this because I owe you for the"—she waved a hand between their rooms—"*thing*, but something's off about Pierce."

He nodded. "I agree. The reports are almost too perfect."

Heather tilted her head to the side. "Do you think they're doctored?"

"Could be." A shrug that drew her eyes to his clothes for the first time that evening. He was dressed more casually than she'd ever seen him. Well, aside from their naked time together.

She bit her lip, her eyes glued to the sliver of exposed skin at his throat, the way his sleeves were rolled back to reveal strong forearms.

"What just went through your mind?" he asked, jarring her from her reverie. He'd moved closer, close enough to touch.

The thought made her shiver.

"Nothing," she said quickly, trying to remember why she shouldn't invite him into her room to continue what they had started in Vegas.

"Mmm." One of his hands rose and cupped her cheek. "You should sleep, baby."

Her lips pressed into a flat line before she stepped back. "Not your baby. Not your sweetheart."

"Noted." He nudged her back, pushing the dead bolt to the side and tugging the door closed as he said, "Sweet dreams, honey."

"*Clay—*"

It shut completely.

His chuckle echoed through the wooden panel.

"Lock up," he said, and she did so, only then hearing his footsteps move over to his room, his door opening and closing.

"Not your honey, either," she muttered, toeing off her shoes and grabbing the Pierce file for one final review in the bath.

Then she hesitated, her hand resting on their shared wall.

"Goodnight, Clay," she whispered.

TEN

Clay

CLAY SECURED the dead bolt to his suite, a grin tugging at his lips.

Heather.

Knocking on his door.

God, that was just perfect.

He chuckled and headed back for the bed where his laptop sat open, files strewn over the comforter. Maybe two more hours until he could wrap up for the night?

His eyes traced the stacks of papers.

Okay, probably three.

"Focus, Steele," he muttered as he sat down with his back against the headboard. "And not on the woman in the next room over." But it was virtually impossible to ignore the fact that she was probably already naked and taking either a shower or a bath, based on the noise the loud ass pipes in the shared wall of their bathrooms was pumping out.

So what. Big deal. Heather may be all naked and wet just a few feet away. She was just another woman he'd slept with.

Except she wasn't.

His stomach clenched at the thought, twisting and clawing in a way he hadn't felt in a long time.

It wasn't fear.

No, it was abject terror. He couldn't care about another person. Not like—

And in what was probably the most perfect timing in the history of all time, his lawyer took that moment to return his earlier text. They spent a few minutes exchanging messages until Clay had scheduled an appointment for some necessary "discreet services" when he returned to the States.

She probably thought he had a mistress that needed paying off or an illegitimate baby that needed a trust fund.

Which was just as it should be. He was a billionaire . . . or nearly so. Give him another year, and his father's dream of that milestone would be accomplished. But the point was that he was obscenely rich, so he was certain to have his eccentricities and dalliances. Not that he'd ever needed her to take care of something along those lines before, but there was a first time for everything, and she was the best out there. He'd take care of his little issue before it became something bigger.

Done.

Finished.

He and Heather would go back to being business associates —*cough*—adversaries, and that was it.

It was for the best.

"Yup," he agreed, carefully folding and sliding the marriage license in his briefcase. It was simpler that way. Safer.

And so what if his brain was accusing him of being a coward.

Many people had laughed at him for refusing to buy a private jet until the company was stable enough to afford one, for not spending thousands of dollars on each of the suits in his closet, for not renting out the penthouse in every hotel he stayed in.

Small expenditures. Controlled actions. *That* was how he'd made his money . . . and how he kept it.

By being conservative with his assets and not risking more than he was willing to lose.

So, now his wardrobe *was* filled with suits that *were* expensive, and he owned a jet, but he still didn't waste money on the penthouse or caviar or red-soled shoes. This suite with its single bed, room service available twenty-four hours, and location near the airport was perfect for his lifestyle.

Work hard. Eat hard. Sleep hard.

He snorted and picked up the file.

No wonder he got all the ladies.

No one could resist a burger at three A.M.

"Which is going to be the time you finish this if you keep going at the rate you're going, Steele."

So he pushed away all thoughts of Heather and the marriage license . . . and the tenterhooks of his past that always crept close to the surface this time of year and got the fuck to work.

His fingers clicked across his keyboard as he began going over the reports one more time, inputting figures himself, testing and manipulating the data. The puzzle of the Pierce deal had triggered something in his brain and he knew, *knew* that he wouldn't get a good night's sleep until it was completely unraveled.

Papers were sorted into different piles as he worked, spreadsheets were created and reports were made, over and over with different variables at work.

This was his strong suit. Data, reading between the lines, understanding the pieces that were left out.

And it was nearly three hours later that he understood.

"Holy fuck," he whispered as he stared at the screen of his laptop. "They can't be serious."

He stood, stretching his back, his neck, shaking the numbness out of his legs.

Because this was—

Buying into Pierce was going to be a huge mistake.

Clay was moving before conscious thought caught up to him, grabbing his key, the files, his laptop, unlocking his door and moving a few feet down the hall to knock on Heather's.

He didn't look at the time, didn't consider that it was nearly one in the morning, that she'd had a long day and probably didn't know what time zone she was in. He didn't consider how exhausted she'd looked when he'd seen her three hours earlier and that he was probably waking her up.

He didn't consider any of that.

And yes, deep down, he knew he was a Grade A Asshole for not doing so, but this was more important than sleep.

This was business.

She answered his knock in a pair of silky blue pajama pants and a cream-colored tank top with no bra.

Yes, despite the information rattling around in his brain, he noticed.

Grade A Asshole, remember?

The material was thin and did more to enhance than contain. His fingers actually ached with the need to touch. His mouth watered.

Heather snapped her fingers in his face. "Eyes up here, Steele."

He blinked, physically shook himself and forced his gaze up to meet hers. "I need to show you something."

If he hadn't been staring at Heather's face at that exact moment, he would have missed her eyes flick down toward his waist.

His lips tugged up, and he snapped *his* fingers.

"Not *that*." A beat. "Though I could be convinced if you're extra nice to me."

"Shut up, Steele," she retorted. "I was staring at your laptop."

"That's what all the girls say." He waggled his brows.

She huffed and turned away. "Come in or don't. I'm tired."

Clay followed her, closing and locking the door, and found himself wondering when in the hell blue pajama pants had become his favorite type of lingerie.

Because Heather's ass was just—

Not the point.

He trailed her down the hall and into the bedroom, ignoring the twinge in his gut when he saw her bed was a mirror of his, down to the stacks of papers, the files, the laptop. She'd been working, too.

Of course she had.

She scooped up some of the files, stacking them carefully before perching on the edge of the mattress. "So, what are you doing here?"

Clay snagged the desk chair and plunked it in front of her, not daring to sit on the bed next to her. Not when—

Focus.

"I was going over the Pierce files—"

"Me, too," she said, gesturing to the piles next to her. "I'm guessing the reason I'm graced with the presence of Clay Steele, porn-star-in-training, is because you've found something?"

He pretended to wince. "You're mean at one A.M."

"I'm mean all the time."

"Maybe," he said, turning the laptop so she could see the screen. "But sometimes, I think you're more bark than actual bite."

Her lips twitched. "You'll ruin my image."

"Don't worry. You're still the smartest woman I've ever met." He was glancing down at the spreadsheet as he said it but looked back up when her anticipated comeback didn't materialize. "What is it?" he asked. Her face was unreadable, but there was something in her eyes . . . vulnerability? Fear?

But Heather O'Keith wasn't vulnerable, and she definitely wasn't scared of anything.

Case in point, she erased that trace of emotion between one heartbeat and the next. "Never mind," she said, her tone brisk. "What did you find?"

Clay hesitated but decided there was nothing gained in pushing her. "This."

Anyone who tried to force Heather over to their side, who tried to out-stubborn or outmaneuver her, rather than dealing with the facts, with information that was black or white, found themselves looking at her backside as she strode away into future successful endeavors.

But all things considered, Clay supposed her backside wasn't a bad view.

Of course, he'd rather view her from the front.

Which wasn't the point, so he pulled up the spreadsheet and began showing her the information he'd found.

"Oh," she said, snatching up her laptop and pulling up the file she'd been working on. "And if you compare it with this . . ."

"I know," he said, opening the profit loss statement they'd been supplied. "It means this couldn't possibly be accurate."

"They're operating at a loss," she murmured, "but don't want us to know it. Why? Plenty of start-ups looking for investors aren't profitable in the first year but are still good investments."

"Right." He nodded. "I think that's what pinged my mind first. Numbers that are too good to be true are usually too good to be true."

"Exactly." Her pointer finger touched the screen, all red and sparkly.

Clay blinked away the memory of those nails tracing down his chest, the feel of them digging into his back. They had leaned closer to one another as they'd talked, and he could smell the mint of her toothpaste, the floral scent of her shampoo.

She tilted her head to get a better view of his screen, reached over and highlighted a square on the open spreadsheet. "*This* is the biggest issue. Because Pierce *should* be profitable, but this number showing as it is means that someone is skimming off the top."

Her left hand had landed between his legs and somehow she didn't seem to notice.

She. Didn't. Seem. To. Notice.

How could she not *fucking* notice that her hand was half an inch from his cock?

His dick had sprung to hopeful attention and was getting harder by the second, but Heather was completely oblivious as she selected another cell on the spreadsheet and then another, filling them with alternate colors.

"What do you think?" she asked, eyes glued on the computer.

Clay managed a nod . . . and nothing else.

"And then"—she leaned closer, almost sprawling herself across his lap—"because the numbers—"

She froze.

Probably because he hadn't been able to control himself, and he'd shifted just the tiniest bit closer to her fingers.

He was a pig.

But fuck if he didn't want her hands on him.

"I—" Her breath hitched, her eyes finally left the computer's screen, connecting with his.

But she didn't move her hand.

Slowly, *carefully*, he lifted his palm and rested it on her hip, waiting for her to back up, waiting for her to tell him to get the fuck away.

Instead, she surprised him by taking the laptop and tossing it onto the mattress.

"Well, I guess we don't need to take that trip to Amsterdam after all."

"What—"

She kissed him.

And Clay suddenly started feeling pretty damned optimistic about life.

ELEVEN

Heather

HEATHER WAS BEING AN IDIOT—SHE knew that, she understood it.

She just didn't give a damn.

Not this close to Clay, not with his hands on her, his mouth against hers.

So she kissed him for all she was worth, wrapping her arms around his neck and pulling herself forward so that she straddled his hips. His arms banded around her waist, bringing her flush against him and reminding her all over again that she wasn't wearing a bra.

He was still in the button-down and slacks, and the stiff material teased the bare skin of her arms and chest.

"Mmm," she moaned when he broke the kiss to nibble along her jaw, down her throat. When he nipped the space just above her collarbone, her grip shifted to his hair, holding him in place.

"You like that," he murmured against her skin, and it wasn't a question.

"Yes," she answered anyway.

She had liked it when he'd done it before. She loved it when he did it now.

Fingertips that were surprisingly calloused for a man with a white-collar job traced the scooped neck of her tank top. Her nipples pebbled, aching for his touch to drift lower, for his mouth and teeth and tongue to follow suit.

Instead, his hands slid up, cupping the back of her head and stealing her mouth in a kiss that made her head spin.

"Sweetheart," he eventually said, pulling back, both of them gasping for air.

For once, she didn't rebuke the endearment.

In this room, in this moment, it seemed perfect.

Alarm bells blared in her head, but then Clay continued speaking, and she couldn't focus on the internal warning. Hell, she could barely comprehend his words with his fingers massaging gentle circles against her scalp.

"We should stop," he said, and the statement took a long time for her desire-addled brain to process. "You don't want this, not really."

"I *really* do," she said with a wicked grin. "Because I *really* like orgasms, and I know you're the man who can give them to me."

"Still—" He groaned when Heather's hand snaked down to grip the hard length of him.

"You don't want me?" she asked, using her free hand to urge one of his out of her hair and down to her chest, pausing to rest it over her breast. Her nipples were hard and aching, standing out sharply against the cotton. And while the action made both of them groan, she didn't let Clay focus his attention there, instead, she coaxed his hand lower . . . under the waistband of her pajamas and directly between her bare thighs. "Because I want you."

He hissed when she shifted so that his fingers caressed the hot, damp center of her. "*Fuck.* I want you, baby." He let out a pained breath. "I know you can fucking feel how much, but I'm trying to be good here. You're tired, and I'm an asshole, and you need to rest."

She undulated her hips, teasing herself and him as the movement made his fingers inch nearer her entrance.

Her teeth found her lip, bit down. "I'd rest a lot better after an orgasm."

His head dropped back. "Fuck, Heather—"

"Yes," she said, pulling her hand away to strip off her shirt. "*Fuck* Heather." She tossed the tank aside just in time to see his head pop up, Whack-a-Mole style, those mocha eyes darkening to espresso.

And it was like she'd snapped the leash on his control.

One second she was on top, teasing, urging, the next she was just along for the ride.

He tossed her onto the mattress, decimating her organized stack of files, snagging both laptops just before they joined a stack of papers in tumbling to the floor. The papers he left, the laptops he plunked into the chair, and then there were no more distractions.

It was just her and a very aroused Clay Steele.

Except this time, he wasn't drunk.

He was sober. And very, *very* focused.

On her.

His hands found the waistband of her pajamas, yanking them down her legs and tossing them onto the floor. In between the space of a heartbeat, she found herself naked with Clay fully dressed, random papers and file folders biting into her skin.

It was pretty much the hottest thing ever.

To find a man who was as driven as her, as smart, as focused was fucking rare and this man—this hot, gorgeous, sexy, surprisingly sweet man—was one in a million.

Especially when he paused to stare down at her.

One corner of his mouth turned up. "Never thought this particular fantasy would come true."

She blinked, smiled. "You've had fantasies about me?"

He scoffed. "Fuck yes, I've had."

"Really?"

Both hands dropped onto the mattress next to her head, his legs coming over her to straddle her thighs. "Too many nights over the last six months, sweetheart."

She wove her fingers into his hair, tugging his head down so that she could whisper in his ear. "I've thought about you, too. Mostly as I've stroked myself to sleep."

His curse almost blistered her ears. "You can't say things like that."

Heather let her head drop back to the bed. "Why not?"

"Because." He bent and kissed her throat, the tops of each breast. "I'm trying to make it good for you." Another kiss, this time to each nipple.

"Then"—she gripped his head, pulled it flush to her skin— "no more talking."

Clay took her words to heart.

His mouth latched onto her nipple, sucking deeply and making her back bow off the mattress. He rolled the aching nub of her neglected breast between his fingers. They weren't his tongue and teeth, but it was close enough for the moment.

Especially when he switched sides and alternated tasks.

Stars spun behind her eyelids, heat arrowed from her breasts directly south, and if she'd thought that she was wet before, now she was absolutely drenched.

Clay released her nipple with a soft *pop* and kissed her rib cage, her navel, one hip then the other.

Then in between.

And good God did he kiss her in between.

In one of those swift movements he seemed to be so good at, Clay was between her hips, one of her legs over each of his shoulders. He didn't give her a second to think, to protest that she'd been teased enough and just wanted him inside her. Nope. He just dove between her thighs, used his fingers to spread her wide, and drove his tongue deep inside her.

"Clay!"

"Mmm," he said against her, the vibrations driving her crazy. He hadn't shaved, and the stubble on his chin was providing just . . . the . . . right . . . amount . . . of . . . friction.

Whoever said that friction was a bad thing during sex had never had Clay Steele between her legs.

His thumb stroked up, gently circling her clit, and the sensation was almost calming—wholly pleasurable, but it was like he was stroking her down from the edge, bringing her back from the precipice.

But then he pressed firmly the same time his tongue drove deep, and any notion of calm was gone.

He'd lulled her down only to ramp her back up again.

And then he did it again. And again. And the bastard would have driven her to that fucking edge for a fourth time if Heather hadn't reached down to grip his hair, holding him in place as she ground her hips against his mouth.

She came. Loudly.

Fingers traced softly along her thighs, her stomach, her waist, but this time she didn't mind the gentling touch because aftershocks of pleasure were still coursing through her limbs.

She took a minute to let her brain reset, for feeling to return to her arms and legs.

Then she pushed Clay onto his back. "Stay."

A darting trip to the bathroom for a string of condoms, but she probably hadn't needed to rush, because he'd remained on his back.

Albeit he was still clothed, but that was an easy problem to fix.

She shoved a few more papers to the floor as she climbed back onto the bed and tossed the condoms within arm's reach.

"You could have asked if I had any," he said.

"I like to be prepared," she replied, busying herself by beginning to unbutton his shirt. Unbutton. Kiss. Unbutton. Kiss. Unbutton— "Plus, don't tell me that you're one of those guys who always has a condom in your pocket."

He sucked in a breath when she finished with the last button and spread his shirt wide. "In my wallet, maybe."

A nip to his hip. "And do you have your wallet?" She flicked open the top button of his slacks, darted her tongue underneath.

"No."

"So." Another lick. "Case in point. Women are more prepared than men."

For some reason that made him laugh and lean up to strip off his shirt the rest of the way. Since that was what Heather wanted, too, she didn't object. Instead, she enjoyed the view of all that yummy muscled goodness.

His pecs were defined, perfect handfuls she wanted to spend some time with, his waist was trim—no desk job pudge in sight—and while he wasn't sporting a six pack, his abs were flat and defined enough that her mouth watered with the urge to lick.

In fact, she wanted to lick it all.

Trouble was, she didn't know where to start.

"What are you thinking?" he asked.

Her lips twisted. "That you're a dessert bar loaded with my favorites, and I don't know where to begin."

He laughed, and she joined in. "So sugar is your weakness?"

One of her brows lifted. "I wouldn't dare state such a thing." A beat as her mouth curved. "But bring me cinnamon rolls, and I would lick your feet."

"I'd rather you lick me somewhere else."

Heat shot down Heather's spine, making her insides clench

in anticipation. She would rather lick him somewhere else, too. Many somewhere elses. But—

"How do you get away with it?"

He froze. "With what?"

"With using those sort of lines and somehow not sounding like the worst sort of creeper?" She smacked his chest. "That was a terrible line, and my vagina was still like: Woohoo! Let me join the party, 'kay?"

Clay stilled, his lips pressing together in a straight line before he lost it.

Absolutely lost it as laughter burst out of him.

But she was laughing, too, somehow *laughing* in bed with a man who she'd always thought was gorgeous but icy cold.

How?

Heather didn't know. She also wasn't going to examine anything too closely.

This was one of those chances that came too few and far between, demanding that she grasp life by the horns and *live it* into submission.

"You're amazing," he said once they'd quieted.

She undid his zipper. "And *I'm* going to lick you like you're my favorite lollipop."

Clay's breath came out in a whoosh, and his eyes darkened to espresso again, but he didn't tell her that he was the one in charge, didn't flip her over and do licking of his own—and frankly, while she really wanted to get her mouth on the man, she wouldn't have tried too hard to stop him if he'd gone that route.

But instead of snagging the reins back, he merely crossed his arms behind his head and smiled.

"Do your worst, Heather O'Keith."

TWELVE

Clay

CLAY WAS A FUCKING MORON.

He was going to blow his load like an eighteen-year-old boy.

When he'd told Heather to do her worst, he hadn't been thinking. Well, he *had* been thinking, but the thoughts going through his mind were that he was going to be on the receiving end of a blow job from the most beautiful woman he'd ever seen.

So no, he hadn't been thinking . . . or at least not straight.

Because Heather had taken him at his word and was doing her damnedest to drive him insane.

If he'd thought it was a good idea earlier to tease her to the edge of her orgasm, this was her payback.

With interest.

But dammit, he knew the teasing had made it better for her. It had been for her own good. It had—

Pot. Meet kettle.

"*Fuck*," he groaned when her tongue traced the underside of his cock. He wanted in her mouth. Or better yet he wanted to flip her over and—

"Uh-uh," she said, her mouth hovering just above the tip of him. "Behave."

He hadn't even realized that he'd moved.

"Lay down," she said, that mouth so close, yet so far.

"Heather," he said, dropping back onto the mattress. He was almost begging and didn't give a damn. She'd licked his fucking cock like a lollipop, as promised, but she hadn't put her mouth *on* him and he was running out of patience. "Please, baby, give me your mouth. Or better yet, let me inside you." A flick of her tongue had every muscle in his body tensing. "Fuck, baby. I promise I'll make you feel good."

"Okay."

His eyes flicked down to hers. "Okay?"

"Blow job later." A shrug. "Fucking now."

Thank God.

He tore off a packet from the strand of condoms, ripped it open, and rolled it on. Then he lifted Heather up, positioned himself, and plunged deep.

She screamed.

Shit. *Shit.* His hands tightened on her waist, ready to lift her free. Had he hurt her?

But then she was moaning and rocking on top of him and he relaxed. She'd screamed earlier when she'd come. Maybe that was just her thing.

Still, he had to be certain.

He stayed her hips and nearly lost his breath at the look she shot him. Her teeth were pressed hard into her bottom lip, her eyes hazy, her cheeks tinged pink. She groaned, the one almost begging now. "Please, Clay."

"Did I hurt you?"

"No." A shift of her hips slid him deeper, and they both hissed out a breath. "Now, please, let me move."

He released her waist.

Instantly, she began riding him, taking him way too high,

way too fast. He leaned up, sucking a nipple into his mouth at the same time as he slipped a hand between her legs and pressed down hard on her clit.

Another scream as the liquid heat of her gripped him tightly. He exploded right alongside her, thrusting deep, holding her tightly to him until they both collapsed back onto the bed.

Hearts thudding, breathing rapid, they stared into each other's eyes.

Clay didn't regret the moment. Fuck, how could he?

But lying there with Heather, hugging her close . . . well, that created a whole other set of consequences he wasn't prepared for.

She shifted in the circle of his arms, wincing before pulling a file folder from beneath her ass. She huffed out a laugh. "Why am I always finding papers here when you're around?"

He chuckled, and her face went serious.

Probably because his laugh hadn't sounded remotely natural.

"You okay, big guy?" she asked, glancing down at him. "You know you don't have to stay, right? That this isn't anything more than two people scratching a mutual itch."

Her words pissed him off. They were absolutely *infuriating—*

For reasons he wasn't going to examine too closely.

Still, he didn't tell Heather that. Instead, he reached behind his back and dumped a stack of papers to the floor. Then he pulled back the blankets and tugged her until she was settled against the sheets.

A quick trip to the bathroom took care of the condom.

When he came out, Heather was looking through a file that had somehow survived their horizontal mattress antics.

Clay snagged it from her hands and tossed it to the floor.

"What—"

"I'm not leaving," he said, hauling her into his arms.

"It's—"

He kissed her, long and deep and slow.

Then Clay scratched their proverbial itches one more time for good measure.

CLAY WOKE UP NAKED, in a strange bed again, but this time instead of being alone and hung over, he held a beautiful woman in his arms.

He liked this version of events, as compared to those in Vegas, so much better. Sighing, he closed his eyes and settled back into the pillows. He really needed to grab another hour or two of sleep.

They'd stayed up for hours, enjoying each other as they took deliberate care to work their way through that string of condoms. But now, Clay needed to make up for some of the sleep he'd lost, especially considering the potential confrontation with Pierce later that evening.

But sleep wasn't on the agenda.

Because the moment his lids closed, there was a quiet knock at the door.

He flicked his gaze to the clock, saw it was just after six. Too early for housekeeping.

Another knock, this one a little louder than the previous. Heather sighed, shifting in her sleep, rolling onto her back as a frown pulled her brows together. Clay carefully extracted himself from her body and the tangle of blankets to answer the door.

He'd set exactly one foot into the hallway when he heard the *click* of the lock disengaging, the metal against metal scrape of the knob moving, turning, and felt the shift in air pressure as the door opened.

The *crash* as it collided with the dead bolt he'd engaged hours before.

He whipped around, yanking Heather to her feet in a motion that had her instantly awake, a startled yelp emerging from her lips.

"Run," he ordered, mind spinning, the memories vivid and all too intense.

She needed to get out of there. He needed to get her safe.

"Clay?" she asked, hand coming to rest on his chest. "What is it?"

The door crashed again, the dead bolt bringing it to a shuddering halt, but he knew it couldn't hold forever. He *knew* it wouldn't.

Both of their heads turned to the hallway, to the door he could see was open a scant inch or two. A sliver of light illuminated the space as pale fingers worked their way up to the latch.

"Go! Get out of here," he snapped.

"It's probably just—" She took a step toward the door, but Clay gripped her wrist, tugging her back.

The dead bolt wavered and memories exploded in his brain. In a second, he was transported back to another time, another door. He hauled Heather behind him and squared off against the intruder.

He'd been too weak to save them before.

Too small. Too pathetic.

But he wasn't weak now.

And he was going to tear them limb from limb.

THIRTEEN

Heather

HEATHER KNEW SOMETHING WAS VERY, very wrong.

You don't say, genius? her inner asshole sneered, but she didn't have time to worry about her internal monologue, not when every muscle in Clay's body was taut with tension, not when he'd thrust her behind him like the worst sort of threat was about to barrel down the hallway.

This wasn't about her.

Not really.

This was something else entirely.

Clay took a step forward, jerking her thoughts to crystal clear focus. She grabbed his elbow, would have been shaken off if not for the fact that she'd shoved herself in front of him at the same moment.

The movement gave her a fraction of a second to confirm that, yes, the intruder was her assistant, Rachel, before she found herself shoved back behind Clay again.

Rachel froze in the now open doorway, a to-go cup of coffee in her hand.

"Uhh, Heather?" she asked.

Clay's shoulders relaxed for a heartbeat before an entirely different kind of tension solidified his spine.

Embarrassment.

Fuck.

Heather cleared her throat. "Can you go down to the lobby and get another cup of coffee? We were just . . . *discussing* the Pierce deal and could use some caffeine."

To her credit, Rachel didn't smirk at the obvious lie.

Instead, she nodded and turned for the hall. "I'll text you when it's ready," she said, closing the door behind her.

And cue silence.

Heather coughed. "My assistant."

Clay kept his back to her, his words frosted over. "So I surmised." A hesitation then, "How did she get in?"

Turning, Heather searched the room for her clothes. She bent and picked up her pants, stepping into them.

"Here."

She froze then took the tank top he held out. "Rachel's dad was a locksmith. The first thing she did when I hired her was to tell me how easy hotel locks were to bypass if someone knew what they were doing. See that?"—she pointed to a tiny wedge on the nightstand—"I'm supposed to use that, too."

Clay found his pants, pulled them on. "I see."

"It's pretty cool," Heather said, rambling on about the idiot gadget because it was obvious that something was very, very wrong with Clay. "It's got an alarm you can set and if you put it in right, the door can't open enough for anyone to get at the dead bolt. It's great, especially with all of the traveling I do."

His chin dropped to his chest. "You're prepared."

She nodded. "I am."

"Good."

More silence.

Then, "I've got to go."

"Are you okay?" she asked, taking a hesitant step in his direction. He was wound almost frightfully tight, as if one wrong word would shatter the crumbling façade he was struggling to hold on to.

"I'm fine," he said. "Just lots to do today. Thanks . . . for the—"

"Let's leave it at that," she interjected before he said something that would bruise the tender feelings that were developing for this man, despite her best intentions in keeping him at arm's length.

He nodded, grabbing his shirt from the floor and shrugging into it as he hightailed it down the hall and out the door.

She let him leave without an argument.

Because sometimes a person needed some time to figure out what the fuck was going on in their head without pressure and questions and inquisitions.

This was clearly one of those times for Clay.

Had he been assaulted in a hotel room?

She'd noticed he'd been extra careful with the locks earlier. Making sure she'd locked up when he'd left her the night before, flipping the bolt closed and double-checking it was secure when he'd come to show her the files.

Heather had assumed he was just aware and cautious. Neither of which was a bad thing, not when they were wealthy and important people—*now don't I sound fancy?* she thought with an inner eye roll—but seriously, sometimes it paid to be a little suspicious.

Except Clay had been more than a little suspicious.

He'd been ready to kill whoever had come through that door. She had no doubt about that.

But why?

Sighing and knowing that the answers she wanted wouldn't be forthcoming, she turned for the bathroom, wanting to shower and officially start her day.

Unfortunately, that start was going to be a lot different than she'd hoped.

Namely, with Clay inside her, using the moves she'd enjoyed from the hours before to give her multiple orgasms.

Rolling her eyes at herself, she took a step and nearly ended up on her ass as a file full of papers slid on the carpet, taking her for a ride . . . and not the one she wanted, dammit. She cursed, scrabbling at the wall as she tried to catch herself.

It worked. Sort of.

One nail broke, and she landed hard on both knees, but it was a slow sort of tumble rather than breaking her fall with her face.

She wrinkled her nose, staring down at her now ragged pointer fingernail. That color had been one of her favorites, and now she'd have to find a spare hour to have them redone.

Le sigh. Her life was *so* difficult. Multiple orgasms marred by broken nails.

Her phone buzzed, and Heather picked her way through the files to where it rested on the nightstand. Though she wasn't sure why she bothered to avoid the mess of wrinkled papers. They were in absolute irreparable disarray. Hers, Clay's, a mix of each. They'd never get them just right again.

Their laptops were perched haphazardly on the chair, so she straightened them. When they were both safely stowed, she grabbed her cell.

A text from Rachel was waiting on the lock screen, just as she'd expected.

She opened it, hit the little circle at the top and called her assistant. As it rang, she began scooping up the papers and jamming them into a single, but wrinkly and generally untidy pile.

"Hey," Rachel answered without preamble. "Is it safe to come up?"

"Yup," Heather said and dropped the stack onto the bed. "He's run as though the hounds of hell were after him."

"I'd say you were being dramatic if not for the look in his eyes." A pause. "So, sleeping with the mystery man next door? That's a new one for you."

Heather sighed and walked into the bathroom to turn on the shower. "More like sleeping with the enemy."

"En—*excuse me*—enemy?" Rachel said, and Heather heard the din of street noise decrease. "Sorry, it's nuts out there."

"Big shopping days before Christmas," Heather said, stripping off her pajamas. "Sorry to send you on a useless errand, but I'm going to pass on the coffee . . . and on the trip to Amsterdam."

"What?"

Heather explained about the numbers not adding up and her —and Clay's—suspicions.

"Holy shit, I can't believe they tried that."

A shrug, though Rachel couldn't see it. "They're desperate. But I'm not."

"True."

The conversation lulled for a moment before Rachel said, "Hey, so before I go change our travel plans . . . oh, never mind. It's not my business."

Heather picked up her toothbrush. "Nonsense, what is it?"

"I shouldn't. You're my boss."

"Well, I'd hoped that we were working our way toward friends." Heather's lips twitched. "And that means you can ask me questions that you wouldn't normally ask your employer."

"This feels like a trap."

Heather huffed. "It isn't."

"Well, then, obviously you're way too nice."

"Don't ruin my dragon lady image by uttering those words aloud. Now spill."

Rachel laughed. "Okay, fine. You mentioned something earlier about sleeping with the enemy?"

"Well, yes, there is that," she said, swiping a line of mint toothpaste onto her toothbrush. "The man who was all naked and yummy—"

"And built."

Heather grinned. "*And built.* That man was no other than Clay Steele."

"Holy fucking shit, *that* was Clay Steele?"

"In the flesh."

Rachel cackled. "Literally."

"Oh my God," Heather said, unable to hold back her laughter. "Now I'm for sure keeping you around. You'll be a perfect addition to our quintet of horny old ladies."

"I resent the term old." A pause. "But sign me up for the horny quintet, anyway. It sounds like fun."

Heather grinned. "That'll make us a group of six, so I guess we'll be a . . . sextant?"

"Why do I think that's perfect?" Rachel asked.

"Because it is."

Heather hung up as they both erupted into laughter.

"Sextant," she murmured and shook her head.

Yes, that was the perfect term for her and her friends.

FOURTEEN

Clay

CLAY PACKED up his things and was on his plane on the tarmac of the Berlin-Tegel Airport within an hour.

He didn't see Heather before he left, and that was a good thing because he had a snowball's chance in hell of explaining the fucking catastrophe that had occurred in her hotel room.

I was responsible for my family's death. Super smooth.

I've been obsessed with making sure doors are locked since I left ours open when I was eight. Ridiculous, actions, woe-is-me attitude.

My sister, my brother, my mother, my father died because of me.

The truth.

The horrible, gut-churning truth.

It had been *his* fault.

"We're cleared for departure, Mr. Steele," the flight attendant said. "Can I get you another drink before we strap in?"

"No. Thanks, Julian," he said, despite the fact that his glass of whiskey was empty. He allowed himself one day a year to numb the memories. One day to pretend his life wasn't—

This.

"Fuck," he said between gritted teeth as he leaned back in his seat, ready to force himself to catch a few hours of sleep before he pulled out his laptop and got to work. Now that the Pierce deal was off the table, he needed to figure out his next step.

He *could* spend some time reconsidering the contract with the military, but he didn't necessarily want to be tied up with NDAs and non-compete clauses.

Even if the money was good.

The plane began to move, speeding along the tarmac and lifting into the air.

Maybe he would take a second look at the start-up based out of Sacramento. It was close to his headquarters in San Francisco and had shown a lot of promise.

Clay let his eyes slide closed and kept running through his list of potential projects as the plane leveled out and his mind, now focused on reports and data and numbers, drifted off into peaceful blackness.

THE PEACE DIDN'T LAST AS LONG as he would have hoped.

Mainly because Clay's laptop was back in Heather's hotel room, so he couldn't use work to distract himself once he'd woken.

He turned on his phone, wanting to text her.

Except, he didn't have a clue what he should say. *Hey, let's just ignore my meltdown and oh, by the way, can you snag my laptop for me? Maybe overnight it? Or bring it back to the States for me?*

Fuck that. He'd just buy a new one. He was nearly a billion-aire, could afford to burn through some of that capital.

Yup. That was his plan.

Plus, his work was constantly backed up onto a secure server, so that wouldn't be an issue. He'd get back to San Francisco, have Sebastian pick him up a new computer, and he'd forget everything about Vegas and Berlin.

Done.

Even better, he'd have Sebastian buy him one now, so it was ready and waiting when he got home.

He opened his messages, began typing one out to his assistant.

Two words in, his phone buzzed. The little banner at the top showing the message was from Heather.

A photo.

Clay's mood brightened a little, his imagination running wild with the potential picture she might have sent.

Of course, he realized he was an idiot three seconds later when he actually opened the message and saw the photograph.

Not naked. Not sexy.

A picture of their files—neatly stacked, though still very wrinkled—along with a promise to return his share to him when she finished her trip.

He should have known better, because putting herself at risk was definitely *not* Heather's M.O. And parading that type of picture of herself across the beast that was the Internet and cell service was a risky thing to do.

Heather *wasn't* a risk taker.

Except, his mind rebelled, she *had* married him at some point during a drunken one-night stand. But then again, he'd taken that same plunge, and he was pretty much the biggest stick-in-the-mud around.

His phone buzzed again, drawing his focus back to the important things at hand.

Literally. In his hand.

His mouth twitched, thinking Heather would have appreciated the pun.

It would have been accompanied by a roll of her eyes, of course, but the pale blue would have been laced with amusement, her lips would have quirked into a smile, lush and kissable.

He actually laughed out loud when he studied Heather's next picture, drawing Julian's focus.

Clay raised a hand, letting the attendant know he could keep reading his book then returned his gaze to the photo. His laptop was "restrained" with a pair of . . . panty hose? Eyes had been drawn on two Post-It notes that were now stuck to the cover and a curling iron was aimed threateningly at the charging port. A ransom note had been propped up in one corner of the frame, *Return the license or else. MY LAWYER.*

He snorted, couldn't have stopped himself if he'd tried.

It was just so ridiculous.

It was just perfect.

He sent a gif, a child shaking his head firmly in the negative. Then added, *No. MY lawyer.*

Three dots appeared mere seconds after his text went through, and another picture popped up only moments after that.

More laughter bubbled up in his chest.

One manicured hand held his trussed laptop over a trashcan.

You drive a hard bargain, he wrote. *But no.*

A picture of a broken fingernail. *Your files ruined my manicure. You owe me. MY LAWYER*

I believe they were our files, he replied. *And no, MY lawyer.*

A buzz. *You're not funny.*

But you are, he typed.

If you add 'funny looking' to that statement, I might just stab you.

He sent another gif, this time of a creepy-looking serial killer. *Now, you've gone and tempted me.*

She shot back a gif of a woman peering between two bushes. *I'm watching you.*

Clay chuckled as another text came through.

But seriously, I can ship your laptop home. Or I can just bring it when I return in two days.

Will you personally deliver it? he texted, adding a gif of waggling eyebrows.

A gif back, this time a comedian mouthing the word "Nope."

He countered that with puppy dog eyes.

Doesn't work on the woman with the heart of steel.

Heart of Steele, he thought before shaking his head at the romantic, idiotic pun. Then he typed, *Your heart isn't hard, Heather.*

And . . . nothing. She didn't reply. Not for a full two minutes. Two minutes that somehow became the longest two minutes of his life, but then he saw the dot-dot-dot flicker to life below his last text, settling the unease in his gut.

This thing between them wasn't over.

Just so you know, I'm not going to ask any questions about this morning. Another pause, another buzz. *Except—*

His breath caught.

Except ask if are you're okay.

He stared at those six words, and for the first time since his family had been taken from him, answered truthfully.

I'm working on it.

Her words appeared a heartbeat later and somehow, they managed to make things a little better, to ease the weight of the baggage he carried on his soul just slightly, just enough that he could breathe a bit easier.

Fair enough.

She'd made it easy, even without knowing the demons he was battling, giving him permission to grieve, telling him it was okay that he was flawed and imperfect.

Telling him that someday everything might just be perfectly fine.

Also, she wrote, *I sent you something, so check your email. For now, I'm off to a meeting. See you in San Francisco.*

That sounds like it should be a Sinatra song.

True. A beat. *Bye, Clay.*

Bye, sweetheart.

Not. Your. Sweetheart.

Clay drifted along at thirty thousand feet, wearing a smile he'd thought impossible just hours before, his heart lighter for the first time in ages.

He thought he just might keep Heather O'Keith.

Especially when he opened his email and saw what she'd sent him.

FIFTEEN

Heather

HEATHER GRINNED at the thought of Clay opening his email to find the steamy romance novel she'd gifted him.

The book was one of her favorites—both hysterical and hot as hell—and she hoped he'd actually read it. The man could use an excuse to laugh.

She knew that because she'd spent the hour after her shower researching.

And not the Pierce files, which Rachel was organizing, but finding out every bit of information she could about Clay, Steele Technologies, and his life growing up. She probably should have begun the search months ago, when he'd come blazing into the picture, all sex appeal and disruption to her normal business ventures. But she'd been swamped since she'd taken over Robo-Tech from her brother Jordan.

Excuses, she knew.

Because really, she'd been running.

Avoiding.

Losing herself in work because it was a hell of a lot easier than risking her heart.

And her heart had liked Clay from the moment she'd first seen him all broody and self-assured at a conference. His words and demeanor had been like ice upon introduction, but somehow, he'd managed to drum up enough charm to steal her client from her.

Her body had liked the way he looked. Her brain had been alternately furious and intrigued.

No one bested her.

But Clay had.

And that made it easier for her to compartmentalize him. To shove him far, far away from her tender insides.

Tender insides?

Holy balls of Batman, she was losing it. Ab-so-lute-ly losing her mind.

The bottom line was Clay made her feel vulnerable. It was as simple as that.

And if there was one thing Heather O'Keith couldn't stand, it was feeling vulnerable.

Dammit. She almost wished she could say the reason she avoided men and sex was because she'd been burned badly. It would be so much easier to lament a broken heart or trash a shitty boyfriend who'd dumped her via a Post-It, a la *Sex in the City*.

But she didn't have a Post-It breakup or a broken heart sob story.

She was just really, *really* good at keeping people at a distance.

Plus, parents, man, they seriously fucked people up.

Still, feelings aside, the Internet was a vast place, and there was plenty of information about Clay and Steele Technologies exploding into the market as they'd made one good business decision after another. Then there were the typical top ten hottest bachelor lists from Page Six and similar, and shots of Clay with a parade of gorgeous women on his arm at various events.

Everything was exactly as expected.

Until she stumbled upon an old newspaper article from more than twenty years before and everything, suddenly, became crystal clear.

Heather knew she should close the page. Not only was it a horrible invasion of Clay's privacy—one that he hadn't wanted to share—she'd just been texting him an hour before promising to not ask any questions. Now she was reading a graphic article describing how his entire family had been murdered before his eight-year-old eyes.

A home invasion.

Failed security measures—someone had left the front door unlocked, and the perpetrators had walked right in.

Clay was the only survivor.

Her heart broke for him, for the scared little boy. She sniffed and dashed away a tear, knowing that crying on Clay's behalf was a useless gesture at this point. The horrific deed was done, the pain already caused.

There was no going back.

But she still hurt for him.

And that was Heather's deepest darkest secret, the soft spot she hid from the world.

She cared.

About *all* the things.

Sometimes it was just easier to pretend she didn't.

Her phone buzzed, and she answered, assuming it was Rachel calling to say the car was ready. "Yo, what up?"

"Hey, sis." Jordan's voice was amused. "Is that how you answer all those important business calls?"

She rolled her eyes. "So says the man who escapes to the beach anytime he wants."

Jordan scoffed. "Not since you commandeered my plane."

The familiar argument had Heather grinning. "It's the company's plane, remember?"

"Details. Details," he said, and she could picture him waving his hand through the air.

"So, what's on fire?" she asked.

Confusion filled Jordan's tone. "Huh?"

"You usually call me with a crisis." She closed her laptop then pressed the phone between her shoulder and ear so she could stow it in her tote bag.

"Lies," Jordan replied. "Plus, I can handle my own crises. And anyway, can't I just call my sister to say hi?"

Heather plunked onto the edge of the bed. "Well, I guess you *can*."

"Fuck." All teasing drained out of Jordan's voice. "I've been a really shitty brother, haven't I?"

"What?" she asked. "That's not what I meant at all, Jordan. It's just that—"

"I only call you when I have a problem? Shit, I'm sorry. I know I suck."

"Jor, *bud*. It's not that." She gripped the phone tightly, hating that she'd let her mouth run and now he was feeling guilty. "You've had a hell of a couple of years. I shouldn't have assumed that—"

"I'd have my head up my ass?"

And the tension broke.

Heather felt her lips tug up. "Maybe. Or maybe not?" They both laughed. "Head-ass position aside, how's Abby?"

"Working too hard. Loving being a mom of three."

Heather lay back, crossing her ankles so they hung off the end of the bed. "That sounds like her."

"She misses you, and Hunter is requesting an Auntie day when you're back in town."

"Done."

"So." The two letters were serious.

She closed her eyes, so tired from the previous night that she could have fallen asleep right then and there. "So what?"

"Are you okay?"

Her lids flew open. "I'm fine. Why?"

He coughed, and she pictured him running his hand through his hair, mussing the blond locks. He did that when he was stressed or uncomfortable, and she always had to resist straightening the mess he'd made of his 'do. But it was one of those quintessentially Jordan things that made him so damned endearing.

A giant teddy bear had nothing on him.

"Well," he said, "it's probably stupid, but I just had the feeling that I *needed* to call you because you . . . never mind. It definitely *is* stupid."

"No." She sat up. "What is it?"

"Well—" He sighed. "It's just . . . Abby was up all night with Carter yesterday. He was running a fever and was a total snot monster, and she's already exhausted just being this far along in her pregnancy. But she was trying to do it all anyway, even slept in his room so he wouldn't wake me up. And I just thought, Abby's my wife. She knows I'm here, that I would walk through fire for her, and she is still trying to shoulder it all herself."

Tenderness for the big lug swept through her. "Well, knowing you, I'm sure you took a lot of that burden back."

"Hunter and I tucked her into bed with new pajamas and free reign over the Netflix account."

Heather laughed.

Jordan did too before growing solemn again. "So anyway, it just occurred to me"—a squawk pierced through her cell's speaker—"dang, give me a second to grab Carter. I don't want Abby to get up again." Rustling filled the airwaves, alternating with Carter's babbling and Jordan's soft, "Hi, buddy."

A minute later, Jordan came back onto the line. "Okay, he's good for a bit. Hunter is entertaining him."

Heather grinned. "Well, we all know that Hunter is Carter's favorite person."

"True," her brother agreed. "And so anyway, my meandering point is that Abby has me and Hunter and Carter, but who do you have? Dad is useless. Your mom is—well, *your mom*. But more than that, you're my sister, Heather, and I worry that I've been so wrapped up with my own life that you might be feeling—"

Her pulse thudded in response to the words.

"I just . . . had this feeling that you might need me, okay?" He blew out a breath. "So now you can tell me I'm crazy."

Her heart melted. "Oh, Jor."

His laugh was forced. "Stupid, see? You don't need anyone, Heather. You're the strongest, most self-sufficient person I've ever met."

If he only knew her weakness when it came to Clay, when it came to him, to Hunter and Abby and all her friends.

Strong wasn't the right word for it.

Fragile and self-conscious was more like it.

Had she said the right thing? Or more likely, had she put her foot in her mouth again? Was she a good friend? Was she too cold? Too distant? Of course, she was, she'd spent her whole life perfecting that distance.

But the worst, the most nagging, dastardly question of all . . .

Could anyone really, *truly* love her?

"Yeah, well, appearances aren't always what they seem."

"Heath," Jordan said. "What can I do—?"

"Dad!" Hunter yelled in the background. "Carter *pooped!*"

"And that's my cue," she said, forced lightness in her tone. "But if you really want to do something for me, you can take me to see the new Captain Marvel movie when it comes out. Abby's hopeless with superheroes."

"Just a second, bud." Jordan's voice was muffled before he

came back on, talking over a babbling Carter. "Not *all* super-heroes. She really, *really* likes Thor."

Heather made a fake vomiting sound.

"Regardless," he said over her, "you're on for the movie. But Heather?"

"Yeah?"

"Can you do something for me in return?"

Her shoulders straightened, her chin lifted, and calm settled over her soul. She was good at that, good at accomplishing tasks, at doing something for someone else. "Of course, I can."

"Will you just . . . will you pick up the phone when I call?"

And her heart melted all over again.

"Yeah, Jor. I can do that."

"Great." He blew a raspberry, presumably on Carter's tummy since her nephew giggled loud and shrill. "Unfortunately, for now, dad duties will prevail."

Her smile was wide. "Enjoy that diaper change."

"You're evil."

She cackled and hung up the phone, thinking she was damned lucky to have Jordan in her life.

SIXTEEN

Clay

TWO DAYS LATER, Clay hung up the phone and stood up from his desk. It was Friday evening and late enough that it had already been pitch black outside his office windows for several hours.

Considering he'd entered the building before the sun had risen that morning, he figured it was time to pack it in.

Plus, he was supposed to be meeting his lawyer at a bar outside the city in a little over an hour.

A lawyer in a bar . . . now that was the starting line of a crappy joke.

Still, he'd already canceled on her yesterday—for business reasons, not because he was trying to draw out his marriage to Heather. They had both agreed an annulment was the best option.

No. There was no other option.

They were two exceptionally busy people with businesses that took up every waking moment.

Neither of them should be considering a relationship at this stage in their lives.

But the memory of their night together wouldn't stay relegated to the back of his mind.

And not just the part where she'd given him three of the best orgasms of his life. What burned just as brightly was the laughter they'd shared, how Heather had teased him, the way they'd worked together—discussing data, arguing its various meanings, teasing conclusions out of each other until they'd functioned as a perfect unit of two.

A portion of Clay liked the idea of being part of a unit, a team, a . . . family.

The rest of him was terrified.

Which was why he was keeping his appointment with Rebecca.

He grabbed his satchel and slung it over his shoulder. Time to stop delaying.

Obviously, marriage was out of the question, but Clay had been thinking hard over the last twenty-four hours and had come up with a way he could still get his fix of Heather.

Business partners.

It was the perfect way to utilize their joint brainpower, to harness their chemistry and put it to use in a mutually beneficial way.

Now he only had to convince Heather—and his cock—of the matter.

He exited the elevator, waved at the security guard in the lobby of his building, then took the stairs down to the basement level, where his car was parked on site.

There were perks to being the boss, and one of those meant he never had to troll through San Francisco's streets looking for parking.

A few steps later and he was inside the car, the powerful engine purring to life.

Yes, it was cliché to have a nice, sporty car that cost a ridiculous amount of money, but this particular car had been a dream of his father's, and frankly, it wasn't like Clay had been forced to buy it. Thirty seconds in the driver's seat and he'd been sold. His Maserati was sleek, fast, and hugged the curved roads of the North Bay like it was spandex wrapped around a certain celebrity's ass.

The late hour meant light traffic and a quick drive, so he arrived at the bar Rebecca had chosen almost a half hour early. He circled the block, found a parking spot, and was just about to get out of his car when his phone chimed.

He glanced down at the screen.

Sorry, Steele. I'm going to have to reschedule. One of my junior partners made a major mistake.

"Damn," he muttered, thinking he could have spared himself the drive. Still, he was already there and parked so figured he might as well go inside.

No problem. How about Sunday?

A buzz.

I'll make it work.

He tapped his fingers across the screen.

So, since I just got here, any recommendations for food?

Another buzz.

Shit, I'm sorry. I'm an asshole.

He replied.

Who was canceled on yesterday because her 'asshole' of a client had his own crisis to deal with? I understand. Don't sweat it.

Dots appeared beneath his text.

We'll be assholes together. Have the wings. Sunday 11 am.

Clay grinned.

Done.

He pocketed his phone, snagged his satchel—because confidential files—and double-checked his wallet was in his back pocket.

It took approximately two point two seconds for him to regret his decision.

Music blared, and the bar was *packed*. Which was fine; he could deal with people if he really had to. But the real issue was the bar and dance floor were packed with a completely different crowd—read, college-aged kids— than he was used to.

He had to be older than ninety percent of the people in this bar.

Frowning, because he hadn't expected a place like this to be Bec's type, he turned to leave.

Forget this noise, he'd hit the drive-thru on the way home.

But just as he was about to leave, his phone buzzed again. He pulled it out and shook his head at the message.

Don't panic, pretty boy. Go to the room down the hall. That's where the old folks hang out.

A chuckle as he decided to go with Bec's instructions and squeezed down the narrow hallway into the room beyond.

It only took one glance for him to understand why she had recommended *this* place—wood furniture that was the perfect amount of worn in, a smaller bar, quieter music, and a few round-topped tables. People his age were gathered in little clumps and talking rather than trying to feel each other up on the dance floor. Though, there *were* a few couples wrapped around one other, swaying in one corner to the melody of a song that the front group would no doubt consider an "oldie."

The other space was fine, a typical club with kids who were just growing into themselves and their adulthood.

And there was nothing wrong with that, nothing except that it made him feel about a hundred and ten years old.

He hadn't been that carefree for twenty-two years.

Shaking off those painful memories, he took a step toward the bar, only to halt in his tracks.

Blonde hair that shone like honey in the soft light. A delicately curved jaw he knew each minute detail of. Slim shoulders, narrow hips, and an ass a man wanted to drop to his knees and pay tribute to.

Heather.

Straight out of his dreams.

Or not.

But she was dressed more casually than he'd ever seen her —blue pajamas and silky tank aside. She was propped against the bar, one hand holding her phone up to her ear as she spoke on her cell. She wore dark jeans, heeled boots, and a close-fitting flannel shirt with a tempting line of buttons down the front.

What was it with this woman and buttons?

He needed her to invest in clothing with snaps or better yet, T-shirts. Those were less dangerous for his psyche.

His eyes trailed down to her hips and that gorgeous ass when she turned to signal the bartender, then back up to her face when she rotated to lean one hip on the bar. She'd wrinkled her nose, but her lips were curved up into a smile, and he watched them form the words, "It's okay."

A second later, she hung up and tilted forward to pass the bartender some cash, but when it was clear she was going to leave, Clay found himself pushing through the crowd.

He slipped an arm around her waist, bent to whisper in her ear, "I hear the wings are good."

Then he internally groaned. She was right. He had really horrible lines.

But Heather didn't comment on the line. Instead, she was already spinning around, extracting herself from his grip in a move that left his wrist in a vulnerable position. "Back the fuck off—*Clay?*" she asked, incredulous. "What the hell are you doing here?"

He would have laughed at the shock on her face, except for

the fact that his wrist was currently being bent in a direction that he definitely did not enjoy.

"Can you—?" He glanced down.

"Oh!" Her fingers opened. "Sorry." A shrug. "Force of habit."

Clay wanted to ask her why that particular move was a force of habit and also the names, addresses, and social security numbers of every man she'd used it on, but figured he would try and play it cool.

Frankly, just being this close to her already made it difficult to play it *cool*, but add in the fact that he hadn't seen her in two days, and he was barely able to do more than stand there and stare like a thirst-stricken man dying of dehydration in the desert. Just being within a foot of her, and he felt like he'd stumbled onto an oasis.

"Hey," he said.

Her lips twitched. "Hey."

And . . . silence.

Heather broke it by slipping her arm through his and tugging him over to a booth. "We're scintillating conversationalists, aren't we?"

"The best," he agreed with a smirk.

She slid onto the bench seat, tugging him down next to her. "So, are you dogging my steps now in my personal life, too?"

"For the record," he said. "I had a meeting, but she canceled."

An emotion crossed Heather's face, here and gone so fast that it was indiscernible. "Well, that's convenient."

"A business meeting," he clarified, maybe not able to see through the many layers of defense she possessed, but also not a complete idiot. "With my lawyer."

"Oh." She visibly relaxed. "Not my business."

"So, wings?" he added, suddenly happier than he'd been all day. "They come highly recommended apparently."

Heather turned so her back was against the far wall, bending one leg and rotating it sideways so that it lay across the bench seat. "Is this the moment I tell you that you don't know your wife at all?"

He frowned, though scarily, not because she'd referred to herself as his wife. "What do you mean?"

"I'm a vegetarian."

"Oh damn, sorry," he said. "Then not wings. How about—"

She had him going for a second, her expression so perfectly controlled that he nearly missed the twinkle in her blue eyes.

But then her lips curved at the same moment a server set a giant basket of wings down in front of her. "Here you go, Heath. All flats, just the way you like them."

Clay's brows drew down. "You—"

She dissolved into laughter. "Your face. Oh my God, your face!"

"Words a man lives to hear?"

Her giggles cut off as she looked at him, one brow raised. "*Really?*"

Now his mouth was twitching. "You asked for it."

"You would think that I had said that I was a serial killer for how crestfallen you looked." She snagged a wing then shoved the basket in his direction. "Plenty of people are vegetarians."

Which wasn't the reason he'd been upset.

Her admission had shaken him because he hadn't wanted to believe he could have missed that big of a detail about her. Not when they'd already eaten more than one meal with each other, not when they'd spent a good amount of time together.

He hadn't liked thinking that he might not know her at all.

She shoved the basket his way again, and he picked up a wing, grinning as she took a bite and managed to get a smear of sauce on her cheek. "I think I might actually be able to be a vegetarian"—a bite—"well, except for bacon. Bacon is just"—another bite—"too good."

"And wings," he added.

Nodding, she finished her piece then dropped the bone into the basket. "Eat up, Steele. You snooze, and I'll take more than my share."

"Why do I feel like that was your motto in kindergarten?" He took a bite and nearly moaned because, goddamn, was it a good wing. "Did you used to take all the crayons? Refuse to share your juice box?"

"First," she said, gesturing with a half-eaten piece of chicken. "That would mean sharing straws, so gross. And second, so what if I didn't share my Oreos? They were *mine*, dammit."

His breath caught. "You're amazing, Heather O'Keith."

She froze for a beat before snagging another wing. "You're just trying to distract me."

"No," he said and kissed her, sauce and all.

He barely felt the wing in her hand plunk onto his lap.

But he certainly didn't give two shits about the stain it left behind.

SEVENTEEN

Heather

"AHEM."

Heather didn't hear the voice, not at first, not when Clay's lips were on hers and she had all but crawled into his lap as he'd kissed her. His lips, *good God*, she could write some really dirty poetry about his lips and the way they were somehow both soft yet demanding, hot yet soothing, lush and sexy as sin.

She especially loved when he slid his tongue slowly across hers then nipped at the corner of her mouth.

It gave her goose bumps, every single time.

"*Ahem.*"

Luckily, Clay wasn't as lost to his surroundings as she was because while the throat clearing managed to penetrate her plea-sure-addled ears, it still wasn't jarring enough for her to pull her mouth away from his. But Clay, thankfully, had some sense left. He stiffened, gently setting her away from him, and turned to face the interrupter.

"Yes?" he asked coldly and the tone was so different than the one he'd been using with her that it brought Heather back to their initial introduction.

He'd been so standoffish months before, so frosty that the reemergence of that same quality made her realize how long it had truly been since he'd used that imperious voice with her.

"Mind not sticking your tongue down her throat in my bar?"

"That's none of—"

Heather poked her head out. "It's my fault, Bobby. But it won't happen again."

"See that it doesn't. I can't have my sis making all of my customers vomit." Bobby grinned. "Another basket of wings?"

She nodded. "Yes, please. And two of whatever's on draft tonight."

Bobby left, and Heather didn't waste any time in answering the question she knew was coming. "He's my half-brother, but on my mom's side." She rolled her eyes, wondering why her parents were incapable of using any form of birth control. "I'm sure you know that Jordan is my brother, but he's technically only a half-sibling as well. We only have the same dad. Our parents banged before his mom married his dad. *My* mom had me then went on to have a gaggle of other children."

"I—uh—" He rubbed his forehead. "So that's a lot."

"That's not even the tip of the iceberg. And it's not just my mom, my dad gets around *a lot,* too. I've got a pack of half-siblings on his side as well, they're all just much younger than Jordan and I."

"That must make for some really interesting family reunions."

She cleared her throat. "It's some serious *Jerry Springer* bull-shit up in here. Or it would be, if we actually saw each other on a regular basis."

"Uh—"

Bobby plunked down two beers and another basket of wings.

"What'd you do to the poor man, sis?" he asked, smirking as Clay rubbed his forehead.

"Family tree discussion."

"Ah. That would do it." He reached across Clay to tug a strand of her hair. "See you around."

And he was gone, disappearing to who knew where. He wouldn't call, wouldn't pop by her office. She knew if she wanted to keep any sort of relationship with Bobby, it was on her to reach out and maintain, and since he didn't return texts, emails, or phone calls, she made bar visits when she was in town.

One out of five in which he'd make an appearance, but that was probably better for everyone.

Because while she loved Bobby, he wasn't the greatest manager or businessman and frankly, the only reason the money her mother had given him for start-up costs hadn't been completely blown was because Heather had personally vetted and hired all the staff at the bar.

Luckily, good food, good location, and good service meant the place pretty much ran itself. It also meant that her loveable but flighty half-brother could disappear for days at a time without disturbing the business.

Of course, *she* got the calls he should be handling, but all in all, Heather would rather have that problem than not knowing where Bobby had flitted off to.

At least the bar kept him close.

Her mother's three other children? Not so much. Last she'd heard, Trix was in Kathmandu, working at a children's health clinic. Kevin was in the Army and the only communication she got from him was the occasional email stating that he was alive. And Will? Well, last she'd heard, he'd gotten into MIT but had instead chosen to go to a community college.

When she'd offered to pay his tuition, thinking that the hefty price tag of MIT might have been prohibitive, he'd cut off all communication.

So, there was that.

Her mother, on the other hand, still sent plenty of *communications*, but they were all either centered on what piece of art she'd recently acquired—she was the curator for a very important museum in New York—or were filled with demands for grandchildren.

No questions about her business, her work, her life. Her mom just wanted her to get married and have babies.

Which was hysterical considering that her mother had five children from five different men and had never bothered to get married.

I'm different from you, pumpkin, she'd said the last time Heather had pointed out the discrepancy. *You're not like me. You need a man in your life for the long haul.*

Not like her.

Well, yup, Heather would take that.

Not like her mother sounded like a damned good thing—

Fingers on her cheek made her blink and realize that she'd been staring at the basket of wings instead of eating them. Or talking to Clay. Or, well, doing anything that a normal person might do.

Her stomach twisted as she forced a smile that quickly transformed into indignation. The basket was empty. "Wing thief!"

"Spoils go to the victor." A grin. "Or maybe, you snooze you lose?" Clay winked and slid the other basket toward her. "All yours."

Since her mouth was burning—*sauce burn, not Clay burn, thank you very much*, she thought with a snort—she fished out a carrot stick and nibbled on one end. "Sorry that I zoned out on you there."

"No sweat." He shrugged before taking a sip of his beer. "Ah. That's good." His eyes met hers. "I'm assuming you helped them pick it out."

Her cheeks felt hot, but she returned his shrug with one of her own. "I might have made a few suggestions."

"Of course, you did."

"What does that mean?"

He grinned, running one hand down the inside of her arm, making her shiver as heat arrowed directly south.

Note to self, the arm is apparently an erogenous zone.

"This place has Heather O'Keith written all over it."

Her brows pulled together, wanting to find an insult in the statement but unable to do so, not when the words were earnest and his eyes kind.

"What does that mean?" she asked softly.

"That the reason it's jam-packed is because this place is well-run with good food and in a great location. It's smart. Successful" —he touched her cheek again—"Like you." He hesitated then said, "I'm sorry your family isn't what you hoped."

Her breath caught.

This man absolutely undid her.

Heather let the sentiment settle deep inside her, holding it tight. Then she made a joke, because . . . shit was getting too real.

"Messy"—she swiped a dot of sauce from the corner of his mouth and licked it off the tip of her finger—"*Yummy*. Like you."

He chuckled, giving her a goofy look that made her like him so much more. "I try." Then he changed topics, and she felt another piece of her heart fall for him. "So, word on the street is that Tony is trying to buy out Sellco. Now that's going to be a—"

"Total disaster," they finished together.

They talked business and Netflix shows and movies they'd seen, then favorite restaurants and places to travel.

She confessed her love of expensive pajamas.

He confided that he hated wearing a suit.

They talked about everything and nothing.

And it was the best night of her life.

EIGHTEEN

Clay

HOURS LATER, he walked Heather to her car. It was just after two and he tried to remember the last time he'd been up this late —escapades with Heather, aside—without a laptop in front of him as he actively crunched data.

College maybe?

But even then he'd been serious, focused on building Steele Technologies into a powerhouse.

His father's company had limped on after the murders, doing fine, the board making safe but boring decisions. Clay wasn't disappointed by that. In fact, he was grateful. Without them he wouldn't have been able to go to college, wouldn't have had money to fall back on when a few of his early business choices didn't pan out.

The board was the reason why he didn't end up in foster care—his father's partner becoming his guardian because Clay didn't have any other living relatives.

Rich had been a single man in his fifties, so Clay had been

shipped off to boarding school, had stayed there in the summers and over the holidays.

But it was better that way.

He'd needed to get away from the sympathy, the pitying looks.

Rich had always told him he was only holding over Steele Technologies until Clay was ready, and that had motivated him like nothing else could. He'd used the time to grow stronger, more confident, and he'd worked his ass off studying business, the marketplace, statistics, everything and anything that might one day be helpful.

That was what having something to prove would do to a person.

And he'd had a hell of a lot to prove.

Rich had retired the day after Clay graduated with his master's degree. He'd been a great listener when Clay needed to hash something out, a neutral third party when the board didn't like one of Clay's suggestions.

He'd been there and was probably the reason that Clay was semi-well-adjusted.

But Rich had died, too.

A year ago, just after the company went public.

And Clay had been alone again.

The lights on Heather's car flashed as she unlocked it, and as he stared down at the sporty little number, the past faded as a grin spread across his face.

So, his girl had a need for speed, too.

"What?" she asked, and he ignored the blip in his mind at the possessive word. Part of him had already decided that this woman was worth whatever risk she might bring.

"Mine's blue."

Her lips curved. "*Oh*. I couldn't decide"—she brushed a hand over the silver surface—"I loved the blue but couldn't justify the extra money for the paint job, not when she was already so expensive, and I hardly ever drive as it is."

"Don't like it?" he asked, moving forward to cage her between the open door and the body of the car.

"No. Hate it. And traffic. And other drivers." She lifted one shoulder. "But I do occasionally give *my* driver a day off."

"What's her name?"

Her brows furrowed. "My driver?"

"No, your car." He took a step closer, loving that Heather's breathing hitched. "You called her a she."

"I don't know," she said. "I've never actually come up with one. She's so pretty that I guess I just always refer to her as a . . . well, a girl."

Clay slipped his arms around *his* girl, shifting her so her back rested against the body of the car, then he leaned closer, his chest brushing hers any time one of them took a breath.

And they were both breathing pretty fast.

"So," he prompted, stepping even nearer, closing every bit of distance between them so she was sandwiched between him and the car.

"So, what?" One of her legs came up to wrap around his hip.

He bit back a groan. "So, what are you going to name her?" His mouth dropped near her ear, and he pressed a kiss just behind it, loving that Heather's hands slid behind his head to hold him there.

"Mmm," she moaned as he kissed her neck. "I'm—" She hissed when he nipped her throat. "Behave, or I won't tell you."

She tugged at his head, drawing him away from her skin and up to her mouth. Their lips nearly touching, her breath warm and hot and with just the hint of mint from the gum she'd chewed earlier.

"I'll behave," he said.

A scoff. "Unlikely," she replied. "Especially when your hands are doing *that*."

Clay hadn't realized he'd moved, gripping her other thigh to coax it around his waist, sliding his palms up and down the softness there. If only those sexy-as-hell jeans weren't in his way.

He smiled. "I like *that*."

Her tongue darted out, swept across his lips. "Me, too. Which is why I'm not stopping you."

"You're also stalling because you can't come up with a good name."

"Nope," she said, a smug grin on her lips. "I came up with one the moment you mentioned it."

"Yeah?" A nod in response that made her lips brush against his, her hips flex just enough to be the most intimate sort of tease. "Well, then tell me already."

Her hips shifted again, and this time he couldn't hold back his groan.

"Kind of liking this *not* telling you thing."

"Heather," he warned, running out of patience that had nothing to do with her car's damn name and everything to do with the fact that he wanted her naked and under him.

"Oh, poor baby," she said, but her words were breathless and a sexy little moan escaped her lips when he slid a hand up under her shirt.

Skin. *Fuck* he loved her skin.

"Name," he demanded, not that he gave a shit about the stupid name any longer. He just wasn't above using any tactic he could to stay where he was, Heather wrapped around him, his cock pressed tightly against her pussy.

She ground against him, and he lost any semblance of control. He bent and—

"Beyoncé."

He froze. "What?"

Her expression was playful. "Yup. She's powerful and strong and full of curves. So, Beyoncé fits."

Somehow it did.

"You're a menace," he said, not wanting to but releasing her legs slowly back down to the ground anyway. If he didn't take advantage of this moment of clarity, he'd be striping her in the back seat and probably getting them both arrested.

Now that would be a news story that would make his board happy.

Cue sarcasm.

"I should let you get home," he said, thinking it was late and that she had to be as exhausted as he was after the week they'd had.

"Follow me back to my house?" she asked, fluttering her eyelashes like the damsel in distress she wasn't. "I think I need an escort."

Her hand drifted toward the waistband of his pants.

"You just want to sleep with me."

A smug smile. "Yeah, so?"

He kissed it off her lips, not releasing her mouth until they were both breathing hard. "Good point," he said with a smirk, coaxing her into the driver's seat, his fingers brushing over that tempting-as-hell column of buttons as he buckled her seat belt. It was just an excuse to touch her. Because she was *his* and he needed to touch her and—

"Give me your address in case we get separated."

NINETEEN

Heather

"OH GOD," she murmured as Clay walked away after promising to bring his car around.

Her heart pounded in her chest, still reeling from his last kiss.

Her fingers came up, brushing against her lips. In the rearview mirror, her eyes were wide, her mouth reddened and slightly puffy, but she couldn't find a fuck to give.

The man *could* kiss.

And he was coming home with her.

Which was a thought that she needed out of her mind if she was going to safely make it back to her house.

"Whew," she said and turned on the car, cranking the air conditioning until the interior felt like the Arctic. "Better," she said as the freezing air blasted her in the face. She might not be able to feel her nose, but at least her brain was clear.

Lights came up behind her, and she saw a bright blue Maserati, the same model as hers, pull to a stop.

Her phone buzzed with a text.

Your escort is here.

Blowing him a kiss in the rearview mirror and hoping he could see it, Heather put the car into drive and pulled out in front of him.

It was about ten miles to her house, but most of it was freeway time, and it wouldn't take long for them to get there. Her body didn't like *any* delay, but her mind thought it was probably better, at least in one way. Ten minutes wasn't long enough for her to reconsider, but it *was* enough time that she could safely tuck away all of those tender feelings that were growing for Clay.

She needed to remind herself that while they were obviously attracted to each other, he hadn't made mention of wanting anything more.

In fact, he'd only discussed wanting that annulment, as quickly as possible.

So, expectations. She needed to temper hers.

A hot fling with a brilliant, sexy man? She could do worse.

Remembering that the fling had a shelf life was going to be the tricky part.

The freeway miles slipped away easily, despite the fact she kept to the speed limit, not wanting to chance a ticket. Clay stayed right on her heels, his lights a constant presence as she took the exit and headed up into the hills.

A few turns—right, left, left, and right—and they were outside her gate. She hit the clicker and pulled forward so he could follow her through.

They parked and turned off their respective, ridiculous sports cars almost in unison, stepping out onto the driveway just as the gate closed.

"Trapped." She smirked and rubbed her hands together, evil-genius style.

Clay stepped close, cupped her cheek. "I think you need an escort *inside*."

"Oh, yes. I definitely need one of those." Heather nodded

eagerly, tugging his hand and pulling him toward the front door then inputting the code to unlock it. "I'm not sure I can find my bedroom."

"Well, with the amount of time you spend traveling"—he swept her up into his arms—"I'm not surprised."

"Wait," she said. "Did we lock that?"

Clay obediently turned to show her that he had in fact locked the door behind them. "Yup."

"And the security system is on function two?" she asked, wanting to reassure him that it was safe, but his expression clouded at the question, and she worried that she might have gone too far.

He nodded, jaw tense. "It is." But then he relaxed, "No assistants will be barging in on us, right?"

Relief made her laughter slightly shrill. He thought this was about Berlin, not his childhood. *Thank God.* She knew she shouldn't have pried into his past, should have let him reveal what he wanted in the timeframe he chose, but she'd been nosy. So, the guilt she was feeling had been well-earned.

"No," she assured him. "I gave her a few days off. She's been working too hard."

Clay brushed his lips across hers. "Have we already had the pot-meet-kettle discussion?"

"Mmm." She nipped at his jaw. "Remind me?"

"How about you tell me where your bedroom is instead?"

Down to business. That worked for her. "Up the stairs, turn right. It's the door at the end of the hall."

He carried her easily, despite the fact she wasn't a small woman. She wasn't fat exactly, but she was taller than average and had curves. She was sturdy. Solid. But apparently not heavy enough to strain Clay's arms.

For which she was extremely happy.

Being held like this—close, secure, gentle—wasn't a bad place to be.

And the man smelled so fucking good.

"Mmm." She rubbed her nose along his throat, inhaled deeply. "I just want to rub myself all over you."

His arms tucked her closer as he finished with the stairs and went right.

"I'd rather you wait for the rubbing until we're both naked."

"I can deal with that," she replied, thrusting both her hands into his hair and kissing him. He tasted faintly of beer laced with the slight burn from the wing sauce and . . . like Clay. All male and spice and heat.

So much heat that she was surprised she didn't actually burst into flames.

Softness pillowed behind her spine as he set her onto the bed, but it was the barest sensation because a heartbeat later Clay was on top of her, the long, lean strength of him pinning her in place.

"Hey," he murmured.

Heather forced her eyes open. Her bedside lamp ran on a timer, so her room wasn't dark. The soft light made him more beautiful than ever, highlighting the sharp lines of his nose, his jaw, making his mouth more kissable. "Hey," she whispered.

"You're beautiful," he said, stroking a finger down her nose.

Her lips curved. "I was just thinking the same thing about you."

"I"—he shook his head—"never mind." He bent to kiss her.

"No." Her hand came up, pressed against his chest, stalling the movement. His heart thundered under her palm "What were you going to say?"

"I—" He wrapped her hand in his, slid it up to his mouth. "I know that we didn't start off in the most conventional way, but I've been thinking."

Her throat went tight, her response squeezed out. "About what?"

"That we could take a little time. See where things went."

Oh fuck. Oh fuck. *Oh fuck.*

She snatched her hand back, shoved hard against his chest, and scrambled out of bed.

"Oof." Heather landed in a heap on the carpet.

He started to slide from the bed. "Shit, sweetheart, are you okay?"

No. *No*, she wasn't fine. She was freaking the fuck out.

"You need to go," she said, pushing to her feet and running into the bathroom. She slammed and locked the door behind her then flicked on the light. Her pale face stared back at her in the mirror while she just focused on breathing.

It didn't work. She *couldn't* breathe.

See where things went.

Take a little time—

For her to grow more attached, for her to get more invested.

For her to end up more broken in the end.

Fuck. Fuck. *Fuck.*

There were footsteps across the carpet, a soft knock on the door.

"Heather?"

She didn't respond, *wouldn't* respond. Eventually, he'd forget she was in there altogether and just leave. Really, he would.

Yes, she understood she was completely delusional.

"D-did I hurt you?"

"No."

The word left her mouth without conscious thought. She couldn't have Clay thinking he'd hurt her. Not when—

Not when he was such a good guy.

"Okay," he said tentatively. "So, this is . . . what exactly?"

A patented Heather O'Keith freak out. Except she didn't freak out. Not ever. Hell, on the rare occasion that she even felt a little panicked, she dealt with it, boxed that shit up tight, and locked it the fuck away.

This—*Clay*—wouldn't stay compartmentalized.

Guys had wanted relationships before.

She'd *been* in relationships before.

So why was she hyperventilating in the bathroom *now?*

"You . . . have . . . to . . . go," she panted, sliding to the floor, her back ending up against the vanity.

"Heath—"

"Go!" she screamed.

Silence from the other side of the door. Then a sigh.

Then footsteps . . . heading away.

Heather plunked her head back onto the cabinet front and clenched her jaw when tears threatened to fall.

This wasn't her. This vulnerable, weak thing that was almost crying.

She was untouchable.

Except that was the biggest fucking lie in history.

She was a fake, just as messed up as everyone else. *Plop.* A tear landed in her lap, leaving a dark mark on her jeans, just on top of her thigh. And suddenly there were more dark drops, and she was huddled on her bathroom floor, crying.

Fuck. She was sobbing like a pathetic heartbroken creature on freezing marble tile when, if she had just played it cool, she could be fucking Clay's brains out right now.

A scraping sound drew her focus back to the door, stoppering up the sobs as she processed that something was being shoved under the gap between the panel and floor. "What?" she whispered, grabbing for the object and seeing it was a bar of gourmet chocolate that Clay must have found in her kitchen. Abby had sent her off with a stash as a thanks for taking Hunter to basketball practice a few weeks before.

Her fingers caught on something on the back, and she turned it over, seeing a Post-It with Clay's handwriting.

It's not cinnamon rolls . . .

Also, I'm sorry.

God, what could he possibly have to be sorry about?

"Oh, Clay," she murmured. "I am so fucked up."

Another scrape, but when her eyes went to the gap there was nothing there. Her gaze averted as such, she missed the handle turning, but not the door opening wide enough for Clay to slip into the bathroom.

"Fancy meeting you here," he said and reached over her to set a bobby pin on the vanity's countertop. For a second, she wondered where he could have found it, then mentally shrugged because God knew she had enough of them lying around.

"So," he said, when she turned her face back to her feet, not wanting him to see how completely wrecked she was. "This is more comfortable than your bed?"

"I—"

Heather wanted to put him off, to tell him to leave again, but that proved to be impossible when she only got the one syllable out before bursting into tears again.

"Oh, baby," he crooned, wrapping her in his arms and tugging her into his lap.

She should have fought the move, pulled back and ended things right then and there. But she didn't have the strength.

For the first time in her life, she didn't have the strength to shove someone away.

"Hey," he murmured, stroking a hand down her back as she buried her face into his chest. "It's okay, sweetheart. I shouldn't have pushed. I—"

Her tears came harder at that. Because she *wanted* him to push.

Desperately.

She just wasn't sure she'd survive it in the end.

"Shh," he said and stood with her in his arms, carrying her back into the bedroom and setting her on the bed.

He stripped off her shoes and pants in a few efficient movements then made quick work of her buttons and bra. She lay there, quiescent and vulnerable and unable to gather her usual armor.

Especially when Clay stripped down to his boxer briefs before tugging his undershirt over her head and smoothing it down over her torso. Not only did the plain white cotton smell amazing, but it also covered her from shoulders to knees and was exactly what she needed, considering how flayed open she was feeling.

He stared into her eyes but didn't say anything as he swiped one thumb under each of her bottom lashes, wiping her tears away.

A kiss to her cheek before he gently coaxed her over and slid into bed next to her. One tug and the blankets were up and over them.

He took her into his arms. "Sleep now."

And miraculously, Heather did.

TWENTY

Clay

CLAY WOKE before Heather and knew it was fortunate he did so.

If she'd been up first, no doubt the bed would be empty and she would've been on the first flight out of the state.

Hell, more than likely, out of the country.

Instead, Clay rose to consciousness with the only woman he'd ever considered his in his arms. And it was fucking fantastic. Unfortunately, *she* didn't think their relationship would last or didn't think she was capable . . . or she knew about his past and didn't think he could protect her.

His spine went ramrod stiff before he stopped himself, forcing his mind to quiet down and consider the evidence clearly.

She'd made a point to reach out to him after he'd panicked in Berlin and hadn't been uncomfortable talking to him after that. Until she'd freaked, she had been her relaxed and typical self with him the night before.

So, it wasn't Berlin.

But had she—? Was it *possible* that she knew what had happened to his family?

He thought about that for approximately two microseconds before he mentally nodded. *Of course,* she had. She hadn't pressed him for answers, but this was Heather O'Keith that he was talking about.

She didn't go into any situation without being fully prepared.

And she'd had him double-check that the locks and doors had been secured when they'd come in hours before.

Of course, she knew. Probably not all the details, because while the media coverage had been pretty heavy twenty-two years before, it was nothing like today.

Thankfully, the worst part of the whole incident—the piece that still tortured him—had never become public knowledge.

Okay. He released a slow, silent breath.

So, she knew.

He turned the information over in his mind. Frankly, not having to rehash the events was almost a relief. She already understood.

But what did that mean for them now? For the future?

He'd been battling the demons of what happened to his family for a long time, demons that Heather knew about and had taken measures to mitigate.

But how could he possibly have a relationship with a woman who wouldn't share her own demons in return?

Hell, just considering entering a relationship *at all* was a first for him.

He didn't do girlfriends. He did one-night stands with the occasional mutually satisfying repeat.

He didn't do connections.

His life was the business.

But Heather made him want more.

Clay watched her sleep in his arms, her face calm, her features so fragile and soft. Words he never would have picked to describe her before.

And yet, she'd broken down only hours earlier when he'd suggested they go for something that wasn't quick and easy and disposable.

He wasn't arrogant enough to think that he was irresistible in any way, shape, or form, but could recognize her reluctance in pursuing a relationship didn't have much to do with him. Or, more accurately, that it probably *was* his fault, but only because this thing between them had the potential to be something really special.

Since he knew a little of what it meant to be frightened of being tied down to someone when the pain of losing them might come back to bite him in the end, Clay could sympathize.

Just thinking about the future made his gut twist.

But he also understood exactly how it felt to lose those closest to him.

And that gave him the courage to press onward.

Heather sighed, shifting in the circle of his arms, burrowing closer even as her breathing changed from long and even to short and staccato.

"I'm awake," he murmured, tugging her closer and rubbing his jaw along her temple. Her hair caught on the day-old stubble there, stirring up the floral and spice scent of her. "And so are you."

She swallowed, kept her head tucked against his chest. "Good morning."

"You okay?"

Her body stiffened. "About that—"

"Hey, before we get into that," he said, running a hand up and down her back, "I wanted to tell you something." He paused. "Or rather, to pose a question first and *then* tell you something."

"Clay—"

"Please?"

The smallest hesitation before, "Okay."

He pulled back, met her eyes. "You know about my family."

She bit her lip as guilt invaded her expression. "That's not a question."

He raised a brow at the obvious non-answer but laid all his cards on the table anyway. "Do you know what happened to my family?"

"Well . . . yes." She winced. "I'm sorry. I shouldn't have researched that far back. It was a total invasion of your privacy—"

"It's okay," he interrupted. "I mean, obviously, it's not easy for me to talk about, but I'm glad you know. I just need you to understand the other part, too."

"Oh no, Clay. You don't have—"

"Sweetheart." He brushed his thumb across her lips, halting the flow of words. "The reason I freaked out in Berlin was because *I* was the one who left the door unlocked all those years ago. *I* was the one who didn't double-check like my mother had asked." He sucked in a breath, forced out the rest. "That wasn't in the papers. Neither was the fact that she'd been dealing with a stalker."

Her eyes glittered with tears. "*Clay.*"

"He killed the security guards my parents had hired, but not before they got out the S.O.S." His eyes closed as the memories swarmed his mind. He'd been playing a video game when the first gunshots sounded and had dismissed them as background noise. But when the sounds had continued indoors, gotten closer, were punctuated with screams, he'd run up from the basement and tried—

He'd been too late.

The stalker had turned the gun on himself. His family was gone.

And he was alone.

Releasing a shuddering breath, he made himself finish telling the story. He'd already gotten this far. "If I had locked the door, we might have had enough time—"

His voice broke.

She pressed her palm to his cheek. "You couldn't have known."

"It haunts me." He covered her hand with his. "To this day, it *still* haunts me. The might-have-been's, the if-only's. But"—he tore off his final layer of armor—"for the first time in my life, I've met someone who makes me want to put the past behind me."

Heather's breath was shaky. "Yeah?"

He pressed his forehead to hers. "Yes."

Another inhale, another wobbling exhale that teased Clay's lips.

She shook her head. "I'm so screwed up, Clay. My parents— my childhood—it . . . there's a very real chance that I will fuck this up. That I won't be any good for you."

"Why don't you let me decide what's good for me?"

"How can I, when you think that *I'm* what's good for you?"

A smile tugged at his lips. "And clearly I'm delusional?"

The stiff set of her shoulders relaxed. "Obviously."

"Well"—he pressed his lips to hers—"then it's clear you need to save me from myself."

He knew he had her when she giggled and said, "So, I'm the knight on the white stallion in this scenario, is it?"

"Exactly"—he waggled his eyebrows—"and I'm the dude-sel in distress."

Her chest was vibrating with laughter as she pushed off him and started to slip from the bed.

He snagged her waist. "Where are you going?"

"To get my trusty steed."

"You—"

One tug and she was back against him, encircled in his arms, her lips curved with a smile as they pressed to his.

Heather was just where she belonged, and all was right in the world.

TWENTY-ONE

Heather

TWO WEEKS later Heather had managed to avoid all relapses of the panic attack she'd experienced that night in her house.

Mostly because of Clay . . . and his keen ability to orgasm her into submission.

But tonight was going to be different. She'd slowly been allowing herself to get used to the idea of a relationship, inching forward out of the safety of her armor, and Clay had been allowing her to move at snail speed.

She'd been content. Everything had been great.

Until he'd left.

He'd been out of town the last four days on a quick business trip to New York and London. It wasn't anything out of the ordinary—these kinds of trips would be part and parcel for their future if they stayed married—

There. She'd said it.

She *wanted* to stay married to Clay Steele.

In fact, she was going to tell him that night.

Work travel sucked, but she wanted it to suck with Clay. She wanted to plan their trips together, to stack their meetings so they could spend as much time with each other as possible.

She wanted to send the collective power of their exceptionally good assistants down upon the business travel world and have them make it their bitch.

Also, this just in, she'd missed Clay, wanted to find a way to make their schedules more compatible.

Bonus—think of all the plane fuel they could save.

Snorting, she put the finishing touches on her makeup and smoothed down her skirt. She'd left work early, wanting to freshen up before slipping into some fancy but very uncomfortable lingerie.

The things it did for her boobs . . . well, Clay wasn't going to be able to take his hands off them.

Another bonus.

With a smirk, she slipped into a fresh shirt, making sure to leave a few of the pearl buttons undone. She loved the way Clay's eyes heated when he saw that little slice of bare skin.

Heather shivered. Maybe he'd tear her blouse open again, buttons popping, his mouth descending onto her flesh and working her body into a slavering frenzy.

"Whew, overactive imagination, much?" she muttered, but undid one more button for good measure.

They'd both been working nonstop, so she figured they deserved a treat.

And, thinking of treats, she couldn't stop her mind from conjuring up their FaceTime conversation. The man had a wicked mind, and Heather could honestly say that she finally understood the appeal of cybersex. Still, it wasn't the same as having him there. Especially since they'd only been able to FaceTime twice in those four days.

But between her business responsibilities and the extra challenge of the various time differences, most of their communication had been via texts.

The man might know his way around a gif—he'd even reduced her to snorting laughter more than once, much to Rachel's amusement—but it couldn't compare to the reality of having him in bed next to her, holding her while they slept.

Her phone pinged, a text from her driver saying he was out front and ready to bring her to the airport where she planned to surprise Clay by picking him up.

A quick jaunt down to Carmel, dinner, a walk on the beach, and a night at a cottage within a stone's throw of the ocean would follow. The overnight trip was also a surprise, and she'd been careful to keep it to only one night, understanding that Clay would probably want to sleep in his own bed at some point, especially considering he'd spent almost every night of the last few weeks at her house.

More than that, she'd wanted to plan something special, something romantic when she told him that she was willing to go all in on their relationship. And, frankly, it was the perfect excuse to keep him for herself, at least for a night.

Heather was feeling greedy since she was flying out early the following week for her own international trip.

Edinburgh, London, Berlin, and Milan this time.

But she definitely wasn't hating the addition of Milan on this trek. Rachel knew her well enough by this point that she'd built in a half day of shopping time in Italy's fashion capital.

That raise had been worth every penny.

But various travel plans aside, she and Clay had three nights together, and she intended to make them count.

After grabbing their bag—she'd snagged him a change of clothes from those he'd left at her house—she stepped into a pair of strappy, heeled sandals then hustled downstairs.

An hour later she was waiting for him on the tarmac.

The stairs unfolded and he hopped down them, his eyes glued to his phone as he typed something.

Her phone pinged with his text a moment later and her

heart, her *fucking heart*, she would swear to God that it grew three sizes, just like the Grinch. She loved the man. Heaven help her, but she was absolutely head over heels in love with Clay Steele.

She was still reeling from the realization when he looked up, eyes widening as a grin spread over his face.

"There's my white knight," he said softly and dropped his bag to cup both her cheeks. The kiss he laid on her was gentle and sweet and almost brought tears to her eyes.

Heather O'Keith, resident watering pot.

"I missed you, beautiful."

"That's my line," she quipped, hugging him tight for a brief moment before tugging him into the car. "Come on, I've got a surprise for you."

"Is it you wearing nothing but a tiny bow?" he asked once they'd strapped in.

A smirk. "Basically," she said, bringing her free hand up to trace the skin exposed by the unbuttoned V of her shirt.

"Heather." His eyes darkened, but then he studied her closer. "That's not it, is it?"

Her teeth found her bottom lip and bit down.

"No. I mean *yes*. I mean *I'm* your surprise, Clay. And not just between the sheets." Her throat went tight, and she was acutely conscious of the driver in the front seat, but she pressed on anyway. "I want the other times, too."

"Yeah?" His fingers laced with hers, tugged so she was sprawled across his chest. "That is the best surprise ever."

"Wait until you see my panties," she stage-whispered.

They didn't even make it to the freeway before her driver had to raise the privacy screen.

"Best. Surprise. Ever," Clay declared awhile later.

And, her head pillowed against his chest, her heart full and buoyant, Heather had to agree.

———

HEATHER GOT the call the next day, just as they were nearing her house.

"Aunt Heather!" Hunter's loud voice made Heather wince and hold the phone away from her ear.

"Hey, buddy," she said. "How's it going?"

A toddler babbled in the background. "Hang on, Carter wants to say hi." Rustling before the voices sounded further away. Having been through this pony show before, Heather knew she was now on speaker. "Hey, Carter."

"He-he!"

"Great," she muttered, "and now my nickname is the same as the chicken from *Moana*."

"You love that movie," Hunter said, still loud, still wince-worthy. "You made me watch it *again* last time you came over because you *love* the music."

She pointed a warning finger at Clay when he snorted and mouthed, "*Moana*." Obviously, her nephews didn't have an issue with volume if he could hear every word they said.

Ignoring him, she told Hunter, "The soundtrack is incredible."

"It's a *girls'* movie." She imagined he was wrinkling his nose.

"Girls," Carter parroted.

And great. "We'll talk gender stereotypes later," she declared. "But all I have to say for the moment is . . . lies in a trash can."

Hunter giggled. "That doesn't make any sense."

"Sure, it does." She smacked Clay when he snorted again. "It means take all of those lies and stick 'em in the trash can."

"Gross," Hunter said.

"G-luss," Carter repeated.

"Boys," came Abby's voice in the background. "Let's give your aunt's ear a break for a second, okay?"

"Okay!"

The noise dimmed dramatically as Abby snagged the phone. "So?" her sister-in-law asked.

"So, *what?*"

"Is he coming over to visit?" Abby whispered.

"Abs," Heather warned. "We talked about this. Meeting everyone is a lot of pressure for him, and things are still so—"

Clay plucked the phone out of her hand. "Is this Abigail?" A pause. "Yes, it's so nice to finally talk to you. I've heard a lot about your work." Heather launched herself across the car, trying to grab the phone back, but he just manacled both of her wrists in one of his hands and held her away from him. Clay's side of the conversation made the hairs stand up on the back of her neck. This couldn't be happening. She wasn't ready. She—

Well, fuck it all.

It was happening whether she was ready or not.

"Yes, I see. No, she didn't." His eyes flicked to hers. "Of course, she's going to come. Oh, no, I wouldn't want to impose." Another beat. "Absolutely. Well then, we'll both see you tomorrow."

He hung up at the same time as he released her wrists.

A pause then, "Birthday party?"

She winced. *Shit.* Hunter's party. They were celebrating early since his actual birthday was so close to Christmas and his friends often couldn't make it to a party when it was held over the winter holidays. "It totally slipped my mind. Damn. Seriously, I'm the worst aunt ever."

"Abby had a few gift suggestions. Should we stop off for a present?"

"Clay," she began. "This isn't—"

His brows pulled together. "I hope you aren't going to finish that sentence with something along the lines of *this isn't something you need to do.*"

"Well, it's just so soon." She stared out the window. *Lame excuse, O'Keith.*

He cupped her cheek, turned her face toward his. "We're married."

"Kind of."

Lush lips pressed flat. "What does that mean? I thought last night—Did you change your mind now that—"

"Stop," she said, placing one finger across his mouth and taking a deep breath. "This is coming out all wrong. Let me try and explain, okay?"

His eyes blazed in frustration, but he nodded.

"I know we're married," she said softly. "And I meant what I said last night. I want *all* the things. I want to try to make this work."

"But?" A murmur against her finger.

"But, it *is* still very new. And a birthday party is a pretty big step, especially when it comes to my nephew."

Clarity across the face she knew almost better than her own. "You're protective."

"Yes." She wrinkled her nose, sighed because . . . "I'm also scared."

He tugged her finger away from his mouth, interwove it with his own. "And look at us discussing it like rational adults."

Sighing, she smacked a hand across his chest. "You don't have any sympathy, do you?"

"Nope." A press of his lips to hers. "Now, I'm going to say something that is guaranteed to freak you out, but I don't want you to say anything in return. Instead, I want you to just accept the words."

"Wh-what?"

He brushed his knuckles across her cheek. "Just promise me you'll keep talking, okay?"

"Clay?" Her heart thudded.

"Don't shut me out, sweetheart." His eyes were calm, his mouth warm against hers.

She gripped his fingers tight when he pulled back. "I could never shut you out, Clay."

His smile lit up her heart. "Excellent," he said in his best evil genius voice before all notes of teasing left his face. "Because I love you, Heather O'Keith."

Oh fuck.

All the butterflies.

All the feels.

But nowhere in there was fear.

Her lips parted to say the words back, but before they could emerge, Clay kissed her, long and deep and hot.

"Not yet, baby," he said when he pulled back, both of their chests heaving. "Just wait until it's right for you."

So, she held tight to the words, tucked them safely against her heart.

And then, just because she could, she kissed him again.

Hunter's present could wait until the morning.

HEATHER COLLAPSED BACK onto her bed, exhaustion in every cell of her body.

Clay, who had flopped down next to her, was first to regain the ability to form words. "I had no idea that kids' birthday parties were so tiring."

She lifted a sneaker-clad foot. "I'm wearing tennis shoes, and my feet *still* hurt."

They had arrived at Hunter's party several hours earlier to find that twenty-something kids between the ages of two and ten had descended upon Jordan and Abby's house to jump in an inflatable house, play video games, gorge on junk food, and just be kids.

It had been loud and chaotic and . . . everything a kid's birthday should be.

Friends, cake, and gaming, little brothers tagging along and disrupting everything. Heather grinned at the memory of Hunter handing Carter his controller in the middle of the game, just because he'd asked and not getting mad when his little brother had spent more time drooling on it than actually pressing any buttons.

Even baby Emma had gotten in on the action, demanding loudly to be fed as the kiddos were being served cake.

Damn straight. She'd needed sustenance, just like the other kids, and Heather approved of the little munchkin going after what she wanted.

Have to start these girls off on the right foot while they're still young, she thought drowsily.

"Your nephews are good kids," Clay murmured.

Heather rolled to face him, a smile lighting her face. "Yes, they are."

"And the baby was cute."

"Emma's a doll."

She had shared—of her own volition, thank her very much, she was rocking this relationship thing—that Hunter had dealt with some serious health issues a few years ago, including a congenital heart condition that had ultimately required a heart transplant. He was healthy and well-adjusted now but obviously had dealt with obstacles no kid his age should have been exposed to. And even aside from his health, his dad had died, his mom had left, and Jordan and Abby had adopted him after his heart transplant. That would have been a lot for anyone, let alone a little kid, but it was great to see that he'd made it through to the other side relatively unscathed.

"I think he liked the Legos," she said, toeing off her sneakers.

"Are you kidding?" Clay said. "I'm not a ten-year-old kid, and *I* wanted that set, just for me."

She snuggled closer. "Are you trying to give me a hint for your birthday present?" A kiss to his throat. "When is it anyway?"

"June fourteenth."

"Noted." Her tongue flicked out, loving the way he tasted. "Mentally ordering *all* the Legos."

"Smart ass."

Her fingers snagged his wrists, drawing his palms down until he cupped her ass.

"Is this my hint?" he teased.

"Literally. Mmm." She moaned when he squeezed then pushed him onto his back, straddling his hips.

A raised brow. "I thought you were exhausted."

"Funny"—she tilted her hips, riding the hard ridge of his cock through the layers of their clothes and making them both groan—"I'm not feeling tired at the moment."

Clay flipped her onto *her* back. "Me neither."

"Hey—"

His mouth slanted across hers, cutting off her words. At the same time, his fingers moved to the waistband of her leggings, tugging them and her underwear off her in one quick movement.

"Clay—"

"Shh." A smirk as he shoved up her shirt. "Lay back and rest that tired body of yours." His tongue traced circles on her stomach, lower. Lower still.

Her eyes slid closed on a moan, and she was thanking all the various deities for gifting the world such a glorious mouth when he used his fingers to spread her wide and gave her a kiss that had her crying out and seeing stars.

"Oh, *oh God*."

Heat spiraled through her, tensing her muscles, a fine sheen of sweat breaking out all over her skin. Too fast, she was at the precipice, trying to control her fall, to slow down and wait for him.

One finger teased the entrance to her body, slid inside.

And there was no hope of waiting, the orgasm had its claws in her, and it yanked her down the other side.

She screamed. Which she would deny outright later because Heather O'Keith didn't do something as uncouth as shriek like a banshee in bed.

But it had definitely been a scream.

Clay rose with a smirk—which she had to face, he'd earned the right to wear—and stripped off his shirt, wiping his chin with it. A stroke of warm hands up the outside of her bare thighs. "I like you like this."

"Bottomless?" she asked, her throat slightly hoarse.

He chuckled, and her insides quivered, banked heat unfurling, spreading out to her limbs.

She didn't know what it was about Clay that made her insatiable, but she loved it anyway.

She *loved* him.

Her pulse was a rapid tattoo against her skin. Not in panic, not this time. The words were right, a piece that fit perfectly into the rest of the puzzle that was her and Clay, completing the image, a perfect fit.

Her lips parted to tell him, to repeat the sentiment he'd given her the night before, not wanting to wait when everything was finally, perfectly awesome.

But Clay didn't give her a chance.

He tugged her shirt and bra up and off and he kissed her, tangling his tongue with hers until she forgot what was so important to tell him, until she forgot her own name, until she forgot anything except sensation and desire.

She gripped his head when he feasted on her breasts, but when he would have slid lower again, she gripped his shoulders.

"No."

Heat in his eyes, but his head shook and he started to extract himself from her hold.

At least, until she reached down to stroke him.

He groaned and dropped his head to her chest, thrusting into her hand.

"Inside, baby," she whispered. "Now."

A nod, his stare filled with emotion as it stayed locked with hers. Then he was sliding home, and she was holding him tight as they both groaned.

"I love you," he said.

And the words came, natural and reflexive. "I love you, too."

His hips froze, his eyes went wide in shock, but it only took him a second to recover, for his smile to brand itself into a special place of her heart.

"I thought you were going to wait," he said.

She leaned up, pressed a fast kiss to his mouth. "I didn't need to." And then she clenched her inner muscles, making him hiss in pleasure. "Now move because I'm about to go gray waiting for my next orgasm."

Mocha eyes lighting with amusement, with affection. With love.

"You are perfect, Heather O'Keith."

She touched his cheek, sensations running over her body, emotions wrapping tightly around her heart, but she had regained enough of herself to say, "I know."

His chuckle morphed into groan halfway through.

But Heather didn't mind at all.

TWENTY-TWO

Clay

CLAY HAD NEVER FELT MORE optimistic or enthusiastic about something that wasn't business-related.

But here he was, smiling like a fool as Heather talked about a book "the girls" had recommended. It had, apparently, made their friend CeCe flush bright red when they'd all video-conferenced to discuss a notorious scene in Chapter Sixteen.

"I didn't realize that someone's cheeks could be that exact shade of crimson, but then Colin snuck onto the screen—they're still on their honeymoon, you know?" She paused, waited for him to nod. "And so, Colin came onto the screen and said, 'I thought we'd already tried that?' And then he laid this kiss on her . . ." She cackled. "It was so fucking hot, and I can't wait to give her shit about it for all eternity!"

"You guys are cruel."

She snorted. "No, I'd fully expect teasing in return, and *I know* they will give me the hardest of all hard times when we eventually cop to a drunken wedding in Vegas." A huff. "And plus"—she lifted one hand—"CeCe knows we love her."

"I hope that's true."

"Oh, hey"—she closed her laptop, the screen now free of her gaggle of friends—"I meant to ask you, how did you like the book I sent you?"

Since he'd learned a lot from that particular volume of literature, most especially, what his woman liked in bed, Clay just grinned, slid his own computer to the side, and tugged Heather into his lap. "I found Chapter Twenty-Two particularly informative."

"Twenty—" Her head tilted, brows coming together in recollection. Then her lips curved. "Oh, you liked *that* part, did you?"

"I did, but I also think that *you* would like it, too."

"Hmm." She nuzzled his throat, sending goose bumps down his arms. God, he loved when she did that. "Maybe I *would* like it."

His fingers drifted down, teasing under the edge of her shirt, button-free today.

Her skin was like silk, and he found himself forgetting about the book, about the scene that he'd imagined Heather would like. Instead, he stroked along her ribs, the undersides of her breasts, inching higher and higher until—

The doorbell rang.

"*Fuuck,*" she muttered and pushed herself up from his lap. "That must be the pizza. You have to answer it"—she pointed at her nipples, hard points that made it obvious she wasn't wearing a bra—"I can't go like this."

Clay snorted and pointed down to where his cock threatened to poke a hole in his jeans. "My problem's worse. I'll scare the delivery boy." But he rose to his feet anyway, pressing a kiss to her forehead, before crossing the room to answer the buzzer when it rang a second time.

After confirming it was, in fact, the pizza they'd ordered, he pressed the button to open the gate and slipped out the front door, hoping that the cool air would take care of his *problem.*

Luckily, it did the trick.

That, along with mentally reciting some data for the business venture he wanted to show Heather that night.

He was still at her house, having spent all of one night at his own apartment in the city over the last few weeks. Knowing it was a total waste, he made a mental note to ask Heather about selling it and moving in here or selling both of their places and buying something together. . . but he made that mental note set about a month from then. No way did he want to push her, to scare her when he'd finally got what he wanted.

Slow and steady had been his motto with Heather.

Aside from the whole drunken marriage thing, he imagined her retorting, which put a smile on his lips that the delivery boy probably thought was for him.

"Thanks, man," the kid said when Clay tipped him an extra twenty for being the creepy, weird, smiling old guy.

"Have a good one," he told the kid with a wave, waiting until the car had driven off and the gate closed behind it before going back inside and locking the front door. He would probably always be extra aware of gates and doors and locks, but Clay's fear had eased. He didn't check them repeatedly as he had in the past. He didn't panic when something wasn't secure.

He was getting there, but he also knew it was something inside him that would never be truly "fixed."

And he'd take being a little overcautious—especially when it came to protecting Heather.

Speaking of which, she'd snagged some plates and napkins along with a bottle of wine and was lounging on the floor of her living room. She'd cleared the coffee table of their laptops and files and squeezed in between to recline against the couch.

"How's your *problem?*" he asked.

"They're great." Her hands came up to cup her breasts through her shirt.

He almost dropped the pizza. "And you're dangerous."

A smirk. "Hell yes, I am. How's *your* little problem?"

After placing the pizza safely on the table, Clay took advantage of her distraction of the meat and cheese to reach down and tweak her nipple.

"Hey!" She jumped back.

He mock-glared. "Little?"

Her eyes danced with mirth. "I'm sorry, I meant gigantic, so big it's an almost painful problem."

"That's more like it," he said and snagged her hand, bringing it against his cock.

"*Ooh.*"

"*Not* little," Clay agreed. "And still very much here any time I'm within six feet of you." He peeled her fingers off when she squeezed hard enough that he wanted to forget about the food and bend her over the couch to— "Now behave. You're hungry."

"Your fault," she accused, but grabbed the plate he held out.

He waited until they both had slices and full wine glasses before reaching behind him for his laptop. "I wanted to show you something. I know that since the Pierce deal fell through, we've both been looking for a similar deal. So"—he clicked open a file— "I came up with a list of companies that we could potentially invest in together."

She'd gone very still as he spoke, her expression unreadable.

"Or not," he said, closing the screen and thinking he'd royally fucked up.

Slow, Steele, he thought disgustedly. *You were supposed to be moving slow.*

Heather turned and grabbed her laptop. "You want me to tell you what I've been working on?" she asked, softly, as she opened a file and showed it to Clay.

It was a list of companies, some of which were the same as Clay's list.

Her expression was gentle. "I'm tired of traveling alone."

"Oh, thank fuck," he said, wrapping her in his arms. "Me,

too, sweetheart. Me, too." His lips found hers, kissing her until all the worried tension about screwing up and moving too quickly and pushing her too hard left in a wave of desire and need and heat. He broke away. "Pizza."

Heather's eyes were knowing, but instead of commenting, she picked up her slice and chowed down. "So," she said after he'd joined her. "Should we compare lists and crunch some numbers?"

"That might have been the sexiest thing you've ever said."

She blew on her nails, buffed them on her shoulder. "I'm just getting started, Steele."

JUST OVER A DAY LATER, Clay watched Heather ascend the steps to RoboTech's private jet and tried not to feel as though she were taking his heart along with her.

He waved when she turned back then leaned against the hood of his car, waiting for the stairs to close and the plane's engines to start up. Only then did he get into his car and drive to his office.

They'd compared company lists the afternoon before, crunched data well into the night and then had moved fast, having their lawyers put in a joint offer that morning. Something extra convenient they'd discovered, and that Clay took as a sign they were doing the right thing, was that their respective businesses were both represented by the same law firm, McAvoy and Associates.

The company they decided on was Helix, a young tech start-up with more orders than they could keep up with.

Helix needed capital to expand and direction with where to place the manufacturing and storage units—Clay's strong suit. Plus, their R&D department wasn't functioning as it should and getting underperforming research to pan out or switch directions was right in Heather's wheelhouse. Helix was their top choice and just about as perfect of a joint investment as they could ever dream to come across.

But since it would be some time before they heard back, Clay focused his brainpower on other projects.

The quarter was ending and there were always reports to go over. Then his head of HR had an issue they needed to discuss, one that had resulted in an emergency meeting after it was discovered that an employee had stolen a very valuable prototype.

It was in that meeting that he finally caught up with his lawyer, Rebecca Darden.

Yes, he'd called in the big guns in order to scare the shit out of Timothy.

And no, he felt no shame.

Bec was a hotshot attorney and had just made partner. She was capable, smart, and a hard-ass.

"Steele," she said, shaking his hand before slanting her eyes to the corner of the room.

Taking her hint, he got up and followed her. "Yeah?"

"I just wanted to confirm that your issue was handled?" she asked. "Sorry again I had to cancel that Sunday as well."

Considering he'd spent the entire weekend in bed with Heather, Clay hadn't minded.

"Not your fault," he said. "Business comes first."

He thought of the marriage license Heather had stolen from his bag. Instead of hiding it, she'd taped it to her bathroom mirror. The action had made him grin and then tug her close so that he could show her exactly how much it meant. "It was a small personal matter," he told Bec, trying to keep the grin from his lips. "But it's all taken care of now."

"Good." She paused before crossing her arms. "So, scuttle-butt says that you and Heather are having naked, sexy time."

He huffed out a laugh. "You're as bad as she is." One female brow rose. "*And* it's none of your business."

"She's my client and my friend." Brown eyes went flinty cold. "So, yes, it *is* my business."

"Scary," he said. "I thought you were *my* friend."

"I've known her longer, so she wins."

"Cold."

"Remember that," she said, lips twitching before all teasing left her expression. She pinned him in place with that patented stare. "Your legal matter didn't have to do with a baby mama, did it?"

Clay didn't consider himself easily intimidated, but Bec was in a whole other league.

"No baby mama," he said. "I love her, Bec."

And that quickly her frosty exterior faded. "You mean it." Her voice held a note of incredulity.

"It's true." He shrugged, mildly annoyed.

"So the infamous bachelor known as Clay Steele has fallen." Despite the teasing she touched his shoulder gently. "I've never seen you look so happy . . ." A pause in her words that had him frowning. "I'm mentally hugging you right now."

"Is there something wrong with hugging in actuality?" he asked.

"Only that I called you over here so that we'd make Timothy more nervous and more likely to give up the goods."

Clay flicked his eyes over his shoulder, saw that his—now former—employee was sweating and looked like he was going to shit himself. "It appears your tactic is working."

"Yup." Bec checked her watch. "But hugging you will ruin that."

"Okay." He closed his eyes.

"What are you doing?"

"Mentally hugging you back."

She snorted and he opened his lids, saw the laughter in her

own eyes.

"Heather does you good."

"That she does," he agreed.

"She'll also give you a hell of a chase."

He nodded. "Maybe. But I think I'm faster."

"I hope so." Bec tilted her head toward Timothy, and they began walking back to the table. "Oh, before I forget, I passed the Helix acquisition to my junior associate while I deal with this. I already sent Heather a text, letting her know. Anything major happens I'll pick it up again, but I'll leave the back and forth to him. Okay?"

"Works for me."

Her eyes narrowed on his former employee as they took their seats, and there was unrestrained glee in her tone when she announced, "Timothy is priority one."

Timothy paled.

It didn't take long for him to give up the goods.

CLAY ARRIVED BACK at his apartment well into the evening and was reheating his takeout that had gotten cold on the drive.

City traffic wasn't something he would miss if he moved into Heather's place.

His phone buzzed the same time the microwave dinged, and he grinned when he saw it was Heather.

Tell me why I love my job again? she texted, punctuating the sentiment with a row of sleepy emojis.

Because you're incredibly good at it? he sent back.

Oh. Well, there's that. Dots on the bottom of his screen. *I don't like sleeping without you.*

He knew what it cost her to send that, how hard it was for her to put herself out there, and the fact that she continued to do it with him? Well, fuck, she absolutely owned him.

I can fly out, he texted, only half-joking.

A rolled eyes emoji. *We can survive five days.*

Orgasms, was his only counter.

She sent him a gif with a curly headed girl giggling. *You're ridiculous.*

He replied with a sad puppy gif. *So that's a no?*

That's an I-miss-you and I-hate-to-go-but-I'm-at-my-first-meeting-no.

Damn, he wrote. *But I love you anyway.*

A gif of hearts in return that had him grinning.

Good luck, sweetheart. Not that you need it.

Night, Clay. Talk to you soon.

Clay ate in front of his TV, catching the final minutes of a Gold Hockey game—they won because Brit Plantain was an absolute beast in the net—before taking his computer with him into his bedroom.

He was just about to fall asleep when his phone beeped with an incoming call.

Thinking it was Heather, he picked it up from the nightstand then frowned at the unfamiliar number. "Hello?"

"Uh. Mr. Steele?"

"Yes," he snapped, wondering who in the fuck had the balls to call him at nearly one in the morning.

"It's Steven, Rebecca Darden's associate. I just . . . she said you were handling negotiations?"

"This couldn't wait until morning?"

"I-uh-this seemed important."

Clay was exhausted, missing Heather, and feeling impatient, but he forced himself to give the poor man a break. His next question was more even-keeled. "What's happening, Steven?"

"Well, we didn't get a counteroffer exactly. It's weird because I thought this was a joint project between Steele and RoboTech, but this looks like—"

"The point, please, Steven."

The other man coughed. "Helix didn't send an explicit counteroffer. Instead, they sent RoboTech's offer over with a note that this was your one opportunity to beat it."

What in the fuck? "They want us to beat our own offer?"

How wrong had he and Heather been about Helix?

"No. This offer isn't the joint one between Steele and RoboTech. It's one that RoboTech submitted on its own."

Clay was clearly delusional because he thought that Steven had said—

The kid had to be mistaken.

"Just email me all of the paperwork, and I'll take a look in the morning, okay?"

"Okay, Mr. Steele. But I think—"

"Goodnight, Steven." He clicked off.

Five minutes later the email came through, and confused and irritated and unable to turn off his brain, Clay opened up the files.

"What the—?"

He struggled to comprehend exactly what he was reading.

Because it looked like Heather had taken the opportunity to undercut their joint bid. To offer more capital for a smaller percentage of the company. To attempt to screw him over while securing a damned good deal for RoboTech.

There was absolutely no way that could be right.

They were in the deal together, and Heather may be a serious businesswoman, but she'd never been underhanded or unethical.

Two things the offer in front of him definitely was.

The first thing he did after reading through the files was call Heather. The phone rang once then went directly to voice mail.

Clay left a message, explaining what had been sent. Then he hung up and went over the files again as he waited for a callback.

And waited.

Another call. A single ring then voice mail again.

The same thing happened several hours later when he called after her last scheduled meeting of the day.

Seriously concerned and knowing that her assistant was holding down the home fort on this trip, Clay called Rachel.

She answered after a couple of rings. "Hey, Clay." Her voice was harried. "Everything good? No—not that one," she said to someone in the background before returning back to him. "Sorry, it's all hands on deck here with the deals in play."

"Heather good?" he asked, wondering what deals she was referring to. "I haven't heard from her."

"She's fine," Rachel replied. "I chatted with her a few minutes ago about the Helix thing. But I need to get her a new— Damn. No! Not that one. Sorry, Clay, I have to go—"

"Bye," he said, but she'd already clicked off.

He tried Heather's cell again, immediately received her voice mail in return.

What the hell was going on? Had he done something? Had—?

His phone pinged with a new email, and when he saw it was from Heather, he breathed a sigh of relief. Maybe cell service was crappy and his calls hadn't been able to get through?

That relief lasted for the barest of moments.

Or only as long as it took for her message to load.

Clay,
It's over

He blinked, trying to understand. There had to be something he was missing.

But when he called her again, it went straight to voice mail.

It's over?

How could it possibly be over?

TWENTY-THREE

Heather

THIS TRIP HAD NOT GONE as Heather had planned.

First, she'd dropped her phone in the toilet while rushing between one meeting and the next—stupid staying hydrated nonsense—then her laptop had up and died in the middle of video conferencing with Rachel and asking her to overnight her a new phone. She'd barely gotten it started back up and had been in the middle of emailing Clay to explain that she didn't have her phone and that her computer was on the fritz before it died again.

Ugh. Technology.

Heather had managed to power through the multiple shut-downs and get a second, and hopefully complete, email out to Clay.

Luckily, Rachel was really good at her job. Even with the middle of the night wakeup punctuated by failed technology, her assistant had been lucid enough to text the driver information to be passed along to Heather—a new phone would be waiting in Berlin.

Clay should be up in the next few hours and would hopefully get the emails she'd sent.

And maybe by the time she made it to Berlin, they could break in the FaceTime feature on her new phone.

Grinning at the thought, Heather shoved the ruined phone—encased in a zip-top bag—deep down in her tote bag. Conveniently, it lay right next to the ruined laptop.

She rolled her eyes. Technology, man.

"I have the rest of your trip's schedule, Ms. O'Keith," Bill, her driver said. "I'll get it printed for you, so you can have it until your new phone arrives."

"Paper," she quipped. "So old-fashioned."

Bill chuckled. "Pretty soon it won't exist at all."

"If only they made waterproof phones."

"That's probably not too far off."

"No," Heather said with a laugh. "Then the cell companies wouldn't sell as many replacement phones."

A tip of Bill's hat. "And that's why you're the businesswoman and I'm just the driver."

"Your job is very important."

"In some ways"—he pulled to the curb, putting the car into park and coming around to open her door—"yes, it's important. In others, not as much. But I like it and that's really the key to a happy life."

She raised a brow. "No happy wife, happy life?"

"That, too." He closed the door behind her. "Try and make sure you're down here at half past three so we can get you to that last meeting on time. Rachel has already emailed me"—he held up his working cell phone, the lucky bastard—"so, I'll have your *old-fashioned* paper itinerary ready by then."

"Thanks, Bill," she said, slipping her tote onto one shoulder and making a mental note to call his boss and report that he'd really gone above and beyond for her. "See you at three-thirty."

"Crazy American. It's *half* past three."

Since they'd had this conversation many times over in the two years since she'd taken over RoboTech, Heather just rolled her eyes, gave a wave goodbye, and headed into her next meeting.

BERLIN WAS a complete and utter shit-show.

She'd had the IT department take a look at her laptop, and it was deader than a doornail. Luckily all her data was backed up to the secure cloud and they'd provided her with a new computer, but the operating system was in German, and while she may be able to speak a word here or there, she was nowhere near fluent enough to operate it.

In the end, she'd given it back and just pinned her hopes on getting her new cell phone when she checked into the hotel.

But when it rained, it poured, because her room hadn't been ready at the hotel. She'd waited in the bar, reading—the only perk of no technology—for several precious hours until one had become available.

Further that, her package with her new phone hadn't shown up, and it wasn't until she called the front desk, the concierge, and then the mailroom itself before she discovered that no, it *had* been delivered, but no one knew quite where it was.

Blowing out a breath, she flopped back onto the bed and closed her eyes.

She'd need to figure out how to set the alarm clock in the room since she didn't trust wake-up calls. The last time she'd scheduled one, it hadn't come and she'd been late.

So alarm.

Then she would try and sort out how to make a long-distance call to the States, because she didn't care how much it cost.

She just really missed hearing Clay's voice.

Sighing and promising that she would only lie there for a couple of minutes, Heather let her body relax into the mattress.

The phone rang what felt like minutes later, but when Heather glanced at the clock, she saw that hours had, in fact, passed.

Another sharp trill set her in motion, and she snatched up the receiver. "Hello?"

A woman's voice spoke in slightly accented English. "Ms. O'Keith?"

"Yes." She cleared her throat, trying to erase the fact that she'd slept the evening away. "Have you managed to locate my package?"

"Ah, yes. It's actually at our other hotel."

She frowned. Weird. "Oh, okay. So, someone will drive it over?"

"Uh—"

"What is it?" Heather asked, knowing by the other woman's hesitation that she definitely wasn't going to like where this conversation was going.

"Well, the package is in the other hotel."

And no more words.

"You said that," she prompted.

"The other hotel isn't in Germany."

Heather rubbed her temples. "Where is it then?" If it was in Italy, she could survive one more day without it.

Thank God, she'd packed her paperbacks.

"It's in Moscow."

Now it was her turn for no more words.

"Ms. O'Keith?" the woman asked after a long moment of silence.

"Yes, I'm still here. Please just have them mail it to this address"—she rattled off the information for her office north of San Francisco, thinking at this point, she would probably beat it there.

And at any rate, with the way this trip was going, it would be easier for her to buy a cheap disposable phone and just use it until her trip ended.

"I will do that, Ms. O'Keith," the woman said. "Sorry for the inconvenience."

Heather thanked her, knowing it wasn't the woman on the phone's fault—but still *argh!*—then hung up.

Two more days and she'd be home.

A quick shower to wash her face, a few minutes to brush and floss, and a pair of cozy pajamas later, and Heather was more relaxed.

It would all be fine.

The shops were already closed, but that wasn't a big deal, she would pick up a phone in the morning. Maybe she'd even send Clay a naughty text or two from the unknown number, just to see what he'd do.

Smirking and settling back onto her bed with her newest book in hand, she let the plot of the contemporary romance lull her into sleepiness. She probably should have been working, going over her notes for tomorrow's meeting, but dammit, she was lonely and without technology—and Clay *and* Netflix.

So, she figured she'd earned a little hooky time.

And bonus, she figured out how to set the alarm clock so that she could make her scheduled flight time to Milan in the morning. She'd even built in time for the phone pit stop.

Go her.

It was just after midnight when she put the book down and flicked off the light.

Probably the earliest she'd gone to bed in ages, especially considering her multi-hour nap that afternoon.

But fuck it all, she was tired and at loose ends, so she'd let sleep take her under.

The hotel phone rang just over five hours later. Scrabbling

with a sleep-muddled brain, Heather managed to grab the receiver and bring it up to her ear. "Yeah?"

Maybe they'd found out that her package wasn't in Moscow after all?

But it wasn't the woman from the night before on the phone.

Instead, the voice belonged to pretty much the last person she expected to call her at zero-dark-thirty, in the middle of a business trip.

"Heather Isabelle O'Keith!"

"Bec?" she asked, still groggy.

"Yes, of course, it's me," her friend snapped.

Aware that she wasn't at her peak level of mindfulness, Heather asked, "What's wrong?"

Which was the absolute *wrong* thing to ask when Bec was in this kind of mood.

"Wrong?" her friend shrieked. *"What's. Wrong?"*

Heather sat up, rubbed a hand across her eyes. "Bec, I love you, but it's barely five and I'm still half asleep, what's going on?"

"What's going on is that I've been trying to get a hold of you for hours." Bec's voice was at an ear-piercing level of shrill now.

"Why? Is there something wrong with the Helix deal?"

Maybe there had been some huge issue and they'd needed both hers and Clay's opinion on it, and since she'd been unreachable—

A sharp, irritated sound punctuated the phone's speaker. "This doesn't have to do with business."

Since she was feeling tired and confused and, yes, by now more than a little frustrated, Heather snapped out, "Then *what*, Bec? What in the fuck is so important that you're calling me now, in full-on New Jersey housewife mode?"

"First, I resent that comment," her friend announced. "Second, I resent that comment."

"Bec," she warned.

"No," Bec said. "You don't get to use that tone, not when *you've* been keeping secrets."

Her gut twisted, and she clenched the receiver tightly. "About what?"

"I think you know."

She did know of *one* thing that would get Bec all riled up like this, but she hadn't expected, hadn't thought . . .

Things had been going so well.

And yet, it made perfect sense.

Of course, it couldn't last.

Of course, it wouldn't work.

"About what?" she asked again, needing Bec to say the words.

"Why in the fuck do I have a marriage license with yours and Clay Steele's names on it?"

Heather's eyes slid closed, and she collapsed back against the headboard, clenching the receiver tightly, waiting for the bomb to drop.

"Why is it sitting on my desk?" Bec went on. "With a note requesting an annulment as quickly as possible?"

That tiny tendril of hope that she'd been holding on to so carefully, protecting so tightly under the armor of her heart shriveled up and died. It turned to ash, right along with Clay's declaration of love, right along with her own tender feelings.

She'd known it was all too good to be true. *She'd known.*

Relationships weren't in her DNA.

But apparently, broken hearts were.

TWENTY-FOUR

Clay

HE STILL HADN'T HEARD from Heather.

Clay had thought she would have *something* to say about the annulment, but apparently, *It's over* was enough of an ending. "Fuck," he muttered, glancing at the clock on his laptop screen and knowing that she'd officially been back for more than twenty-four hours.

And he was sitting in his office well after midnight, trying to figure out how to move on with his life.

The Helix deal was on permanent hold.

His other business dealings were well in hand.

He wasn't needed here, or frankly anywhere at the moment, and yet, he couldn't bring himself to go back to his empty apartment.

Home had become that house north of the city owned by a beautiful blonde.

But Heather didn't want him.

That much had become clear.

He'd called forty-eight times. He'd sent a message to her hotel. He'd emailed. He'd texted copious amounts of gifs.

All with no response.

And so, as much as he wanted to demand answers from Heather, to demand a fucking explanation for torpedoing the deal, for ghosting him, for cutting him more deeply than any other person on the planet ever had, Clay knew he had to set her free.

He loved her, so damned much. He wouldn't force her to stay.

Not when she didn't feel as strongly.

"Fuck," he said again, pushing up from his desk, his hand on the top of his laptop, readying to close the screen.

Ping.

An email.

His heart beat a little faster before he caught himself. Heather wouldn't email at this point. That ship had more than sailed, and it was important he remember that. Still, remembering didn't stop him from clicking over to his inbox, and it certainly didn't stop his pulse from speeding up until it was a rapid tattoo in his chest when he saw that the sender was, in fact, Heather.

Fingers trembling, he opened the message.

Hey Handsome,

Sorry my last message cut off. My laptop has decided to go to that sunny, rainbow-filled place beyond the clouds. Worse than that, and my point of the previous message (which I'm not sure actually went through since the computer went completely black the moment I hit send), is that my life is over! Okay, maybe not, but my phone took a dive in the toilet—insert puking sound here—and so I'm woefully disconnected from the world. Hopefully the replacement will get here soon and the IT department can fix my

computer, but if not, know that I love you so much and that I'm
missing you.
Love,
H
P.S. I feel as though I should insert more puking sounds here
because of the sheer sap level of that last sentence, but because it's
true, I'm leaving it.
P.P.S. Can't wait to see you. Only three days and six hours left
to go.

Clay reread the message three times before he finally understood . . . and realized exactly how much of a fucking idiot he'd
been.

Those weren't the words of a woman who'd just double-
crossed him. They were the warm, teasing words of the woman
he loved, who loved him right back.

Why hadn't he waited for Heather to come back and talked
to her?

Why had he jumped to conclusions?

Why hadn't he trusted in what they were building?

Because he was a fucking moron.

"Goddammit," he said, resisting the urge—barely—to launch
his laptop across the room.

Funny that he worked in technology and it had screwed him
over with the woman he loved. Toilet-dunked phones. Mysteri-
ously dying laptops. Emails arriving way too many days late.

And because of that, he'd had the marriage license delivered
to Bec, along with a request for the annulment. He'd taken their
very private matter and turned it very public.

Heather would never forgive him.

He sank into his chair, head in his hands, fingers threatening
to tear all the hair from his scalp. So, it was just as well that his
cell rang right at that moment.

Sure, fate, throw another thing on his plate.

A swipe across the screen, a jab to turn it on speaker. "What?"

"Uhh . . . Mr. Steele?"

Steven. Bec's junior associate.

Clay sighed. "What is it, Steven?"

"Um, well, I just wanted to get back to you as quickly as possible. I've been doing some research on the contracts from the Helix deal—"

"The deal's dead."

Steven coughed. "Well, I figured as much." A pause. "But I also knew that something wasn't quite right with the counteroffer they'd sent back. So I, um, went through all of the contracts and—" He broke off, papers rustling in the background.

Clay strived for patience. "Get to the bottom line, please."

"The RoboTech offer didn't originate from our office, and it hadn't been approved by anyone in their acquisitions department, either." The more Steven talked, the calmer he got, his words finally flowing in a way that didn't make Clay want to reach through the phone and strangle him.

Finally, some progress.

"But," Steven continued. "I didn't quite understand what was happening until I got a call from one of my former associates. He was wondering why Steele Technologies had put in two offers on Helix."

Clay frowned. "What—?"

"It wasn't a mistake on our end. I checked. We sent the one offer, but when my friend sent me a copy of the second contract, it appeared almost identical."

"Almost?"

"The numbers were different, obviously. But that wasn't all. The logo had been altered slightly and while the signature on the final page matched yours, we didn't have any digital confirmation that you'd actually signed the contract. Because all our contracts are handled electronically, there is *always* a signature confirmation. So, I went back and looked at the one from RoboTech."

Clay leaned back in his chair, already knowing the answer to his next statement. "They didn't have any confirmation of Heather signing either."

"No." Two letters that drove the knife of regret lodged in Clay's heart even deeper. "Apparently, Helix has been trying to play both sides."

"And fucking up while doing it," Clay said, furious.

"I'll take care of it," Steven said. "But I thought you would need to know as soon as possible."

"You did the right thing," Clay told him. "Both times." He sighed, thinking of the mess he needed to untangle because he'd been hurt and impulsive. "Thank you for following this through until the end."

"Who needs sleep?" Steven joked, and Clay thought there might be for hope for him yet.

After saying goodbye, they hung up and Clay stood, shoving his arms into his suit jacket. He knew he should probably wait until morning, but he went straight down to the garage and got into his car anyway.

As he sped through the dark night, he called Heather, but it rang once before sending him straight to voice mail. He was sure she had a functioning cell phone by now, so he was probably blocked. Great.

He hung up and though he knew it was wrong, especially considering the late hour and the fact that she wasn't *his* assistant, he also called Rachel.

It also rang once and went to voice mail.

Shit.

He drove the rest of the way in tense silence, fingers clenched on the steering wheel, his mind running a thousand miles per hour, even as he got no closer to figuring out a way to fix things.

When he turned onto her street, he could see that the gate to Heather's house was wide open. His heart clenched.

It was fine. She had probably ordered a pizza or something.

Except there weren't any lights on in the front of the house and no cars in the driveway.

Throat tight, he screeched through the gate, threw his car in park, and jumped out. A sprint to the front door, his fist rising to knock . . . only to find the door slightly ajar. At that point, Clay's vision went black on the edges, his breaths short and shallow, and sweat broke out on the back of his neck. He frantically searched the dimly-lit hallway for signs of blood or broken glass.

Heather walked out of the kitchen at that moment, a large black bag in one hand, two empty wine bottles in the other.

Seeing him standing there, she screamed and dropped both the bottles and bag.

Glass shattered, garbage exploded all over the floor, but all Clay felt was relief that Heather was alive.

His legs buckled and he landed hard on his knees. She was okay.

She was okay.

"Clay," she said tentatively. "I'm fine."

"Careful of the glass," he rasped out when she made as though to come toward him. "Your feet are bare."

She glanced down, as if surprised to see the shattered bottles mere inches from her unprotected skin. "Let me get the broom."

A shake of his head as he pushed to his feet.

His shoes crunched over the glass as he crossed to her and swept her up into his arms. Then held her for several long minutes.

Until she stiffened and seemed to remember all that had happened over the last few days.

"Please," he said, carrying her over to the counter. "Just let me explain."

There were tears in Heather's eyes, moisture that threatened to break him.

She pointed. "The broom is in that cupboard."

Nodding, though he'd already known that, Clay took the hint and extracted the broom and dustpan. It only took a few minutes for him to sweep up the glass and dump it into the trash bag. Then several moments more to pack up the garbage and take everything out to the cans on the side of Heather's house.

That done, he locked up and returned the broom to the cabinet.

Silence until—

"What are you doing here?"

A soft question, but one that was laced with so much hurt that it sliced Clay right to the quick.

"I made a mistake. It—"

She snorted. "Do you know what I was doing before you showed up? Why the gate was open and the lights were off?" He shook his head. "My friends came over to commiserate, to cheer me up because you'd broken me so thoroughly. *In fact*, your timing was about perfect because they'd just left, and I was finally feeling like myself again. I was finally f-feeling strong, and then you had to show up—" Tears streamed down her face. "I was just trying to take the fucking trash out, and you *had* to make a mess of things. And somehow, I'm the one who's feeling bad? Terrible that I'd scared you because I *knew*, because I understood just how much the unlocked door and dark house must have frightened you—"

He closed the distance between them as her sobs cut off her words, wrapping his arms tightly around her. She pushed him away, but he didn't let go. He *couldn't* let go.

"And . . . you . . . *hurt* me." A sniff. "How could you send Bec the license without talking to me?"

"I'm sorry, baby," he said. "I'm *so* fucking sorry. I—" He began explaining about the contract and the forged offer from

RoboTech, his unreturned phone calls, her partial email, the words pouring out of him. "I thought that it was your way of telling me that you didn't want me." He cupped her face, meeting her tear-filled eyes with his own. "And I couldn't be the thing to force you to stay in a relationship that wasn't making you happy, baby. Not when you're so important to me. I *couldn't* do that to you."

"So, you broke my heart instead."

Words spoken so flatly that ice spread through his gut. "I thought it was what you wanted."

Her cheeks went bright red, and she shoved at his chest. Hard.

Hard enough that he staggered back a step as she slid from the counter and began pacing around the kitchen.

"Dammit, Clay. You *knew* how hard it was for me to try and give us a real shot! You knew how hard it was for me to tell you that I loved you! And I did it!" She turned and ripped open the refrigerator door, grabbing a half-opened roll of cookie dough. She slammed it onto the counter, tore off a chunk, and shoved it into her mouth.

He started to speak, but she pointed the roll at him, its yellow and black wrapper flapping with the motion. "Not a word about salmonella or *so help me God,* I will launch this right at your head."

Absurdly, the threat forced him to bite back a smile. Mad was so much better than hurt. He could deal with fury, but he couldn't look into Heather's pain-filled gaze and have any hope of making things right. Not when he'd hurt her so badly.

"Baby—"

"Don't *baby* me," she snapped, shoving another piece of dough into her mouth. "You fucked up royally, Clay Steele."

He closed the distance between them again, dared to push the roll away. "You'll make yourself sick."

"*You* make me sick!" But then her chin wobbled, and Clay lost his heart all over again.

"I'm sorry, sweetheart. So damned sorry."

She sniffed, buried her head in his chest. "You hurt me."

"I know." He cupped the back of her head. "I'm so sorry."

She inhaled deeply, then let it back out. "I know. That's what makes this harder."

"Yeah."

He allowed himself another minute to just hold her before dropping his arms and stepping back. "I'll leave you to get some sleep." He'd go that night, let her rest because she was hurt and upset and exhausted . . . but he was going to keep coming back every *single* chance he got. Until he proved to Heather that this was just a stupid, albeit horrendous, mistake, until she understood that she was his and his future wasn't worth shit if she wasn't in it.

A smack to his chest. Not hard, but surprising enough that he stared down at her in open-mouthed shock.

"You are a fucking idiot," she said and launched herself back into his arms.

"Wh—"

"Shut up and kiss me."

Blindsided and confused but not stupid enough to deny such a request, Clay slid one hand behind her neck and slammed his lips down onto Heather's. It wasn't a gentle tangling of mouths, but all teeth and tongue, heat and desire.

She broke away, tugging at his neck until her forehead rested against his.

"No matter what"—a gasping breath as her eyes met his with blazing intent—"*no matter what*, you will talk to me, and you *will* trust that I'll give you the same courtesy. Always. No excuses. I will never shut you out." Her expression softened. "Never." Her hand came up, resting on her chest, over her heart. "You're *here*. You're in my heart. Forever."

"I will love you until the day this"—he interlaced their fingers, bringing her hand to his own chest, where his own heart was pounding furiously—"stops beating. I will love you until the moment I leave this earth."

She rose on tiptoe, nuzzled his cheek then whispered, mischievous intent in her words. "Only until your heart stops beating? What about after?"

Muscles relaxing, he brushed his knuckles down Heather's cheek.

"Always so demanding," he teased.

Her smile filled his heart to overflowing. "You know it." A beat, her hands weaving into his hair again. "Now get down here and kiss me again."

In this case, Clay had no issues doing what he was told.

EPILOGUE

Heather

HEATHER WAS FEELING UNACCOUNTABLY nervous as she stared at herself in the mirror three months later.

She wore a white dress—short and sexy, but still white—and blue heels—courtesy of Abby, who held her baby girl on one shoulder while she ran around the house, shouting orders every which way.

"The flowers have to be evenly spaced across the mantel," her sister-in-law declared, and because no one dared argue with a breastfeeding mother who held her newborn in her arms, her decrees were being followed left, right, and center. "No, *evenly* spaced."

Abby popped her head back into the bedroom. "This is awesome! Everyone is listening to me, and I mean *everyone!*" She came up behind Heather, used her free hand to smooth a nonexistent wrinkle. "Can I hire them to come live with me?" she stage-whispered. "No one listens to me there."

Heather smirked, but she also saw right through her sister-in-law. "I know what you're doing."

"What?" Abby asked, all innocent, the faker.

Rachel, who was wearing a killer red dress with matching red lipstick that went perfectly with the olive tone of her skin, smirked. "Abs, everyone knows what you're doing."

Heather turned and hugged Abby tight, careful of baby Emma. "And I love you for it," she said, softly.

"Stop! I still have baby hormones, and you're going to make me cry," Abby wailed, but even as she sniffled, she held on to Heather for dear life. "Now I'll have to redo my mascara."

"What'd I miss?" Bec asked, and Heather flicked her eyes to the mirror, smiling when her friend strolled in all lawyer-like, wearing a perfectly tailored black business suit that showed off her curves, her cell held in one hand, a briefcase in the other. She was all business as she extracted a white envelope . . . well, except for those killer heels.

Those were sexy.

Rachel filled her in. "Abby's still hormonal, and Heather is feeling so sappy that she's declared her undying love."

"Hey!" she and Abby said in unison, turning to glare at her assistant—now in job description only, since she was officially part of their group of friends in real life.

"Because of that," Heather added, pointing an accusing finger at Rachel. "No more pajamas for you."

Bec shuddered. "You fight mean, O'Keith."

"Not O'Keith for much longer," she said, biting her lip.

"Aw," Abby chimed in as Rachel smiled wide and Bec's eyes went suspiciously misty. "Damn, Heather," she said, swiping one finger under her lashes. "You were my only hope."

"No crying without us!" CeCe said, hustling down the hall with Seraphina in tow.

Colin, CeCe's husband and one of Heather's business partners, waved from the doorway. "Looking good, O'Keith," he said in that yummy Scottish accent.

"Steele," Bec called. "Apparently she's going to be a Steele."

Seraphina snorted. "She likes some *Steele*."

"Oh my God," Rachel moaned.

"What?" Seraphina said, plunking her hands onto her hips. The action made her considerable "assets" threaten to burst from her dress. "Why is it funny when you guys make a bad dirty joke, but it's not when I do?"

"Easy there, supermodel. It's because you're too sweet and innocent," Bec teased, tugging up the front of Seraphina's dress as their friend began to protest her innocence. At the same time, Abby moved forward to squeeze Sera's arm, said, "We love you anyway," and then moved to the mirror to fix her mascara.

Newly returned from her ostentatiously long honeymoon, CeCe crossed the room to hug Rachel.

"It's nice to meet you in real life," she said, the women only ever having chatted during their weekly videoconference book club meetings since CeCe had been too busy traveling the world to join them all in person.

Their weekly Horny FaceTime—as they'd termed it—worked out well. Whoever was near enough to meet up, got together in person at someone's house, and the rest conferenced in.

Which is what Clay thought was happening that night at their house and as such, he'd made himself scarce, meeting up with Jordan at Bobby's for wings and a couple of beers.

Meanwhile, Heather had called in the help of her friends.

"Do you have it?" she asked Bec.

Bec nodded, holding up the white envelope.

The gate chimed, and Abby ran to the window, peeking out the curtains. "He's here!"

Heather hotfooted it over to the window, saw Clay's blue Maserati pulling into the drive. He parked behind the line of cars in the driveway and got out, chatting with Jordan as they walked up to the front door.

"Oh God," she said, stepping back and releasing a shuddering breath. "Why am I so nervous?"

"Because this time you won't be drunk during the vows?" Rachel asked.

"You." Heather pointed. "Are both evil *and* right."

CeCe slipped a hand around Rachel's waist. "It's also why she fits right in."

Obviously, Heather had experienced no little amount of teasing about her "drunken wedding." Her friends had been merciless . . . as was only right.

At least they'd waited to tease her until after she and Clay had made up.

And now they were together and happy. Of course, Clay still felt guilty that he couldn't recall their wedding, which was why they were there today.

"Just remember," she told her friends. "Tequila is dangerous."

"And gross," Sera said, probably remembering some drunken night at boarding school, considering Abby and Bec, the other two members of the original trio were shuddering, too.

"No tequila," Bec agreed.

Abby nodded.

"Heath?" Clay called up the stairs. "Is there a reason that a florist shop exploded in the front room?"

"Fuck," Heather said, pacing the room. "I don't think I can do this."

"Just a second," Abby hollered, but Heather was almost too far gone to hear her. She'd gotten it into her mind to give Clay new memories, to show him how stupidly happy and in love with him she was, but what the fuck did she know about grand gestures?

There was no way this was going to be okay—

And just as she was fully entering the panic zone, five pairs of arms wrapped her up tight.

"It's going to be great," Abby murmured.

"Totally," Rachel agreed.

"It's the *perfect* gesture," Seraphina said.

"He's going to love it," CeCe added.

"Men are stupid."

They all froze and looked at Bec, who shrugged and added, "It seemed like the thing to say at the time."

Laughter. The room was filled with pure, unfettered laughter and love and hugs and teasing . . . and because Heather was no longer afraid of getting close to people, no longer terrified of being left behind, or measured and found lacking, she tucked all those lovely emotions close to her heart, shoved her nerves down, and lifted her chin.

"It's go time."

More laughter, and then they heard Clay's footsteps on the stairs. "Baby?" he asked, knocking on the doorframe but not peeking in. "Is it safe to enter?"

"Almost," Abby called then turned to Heather and whispered. "No tears—and I mean it!"

"Anybody want a peanut?" CeCe quipped.

Abby smacked her lightly on the arm. "Shut it, you. I don't see how anyone could possibly like that movie!"

Sera glared. "*The Princess Bride* is an absolute classic—"

"As for you," Abby interrupted, effectively ending the familiar argument before it could really get started. She grabbed Heather by both shoulders and gave her a fierce look. "Raccoon eyes are not sexy, so do *not* ruin your mascara." Then she led the way out, the rest of their friends following suit.

Bec was last. "When are you going to tell her that your mascara is waterproof?"

"Shh," Heather said with a smile. "She's still hormonal." But it was *her* who had to regain control of her emotions when Bec hugged her tight. She was so incredibly grateful for the group of friends, of *family,* that she had in her life.

"Good luck," Bec told Clay, patting him on the shoulder as she pushed by him and into the hall.

"What's happening, sweet—" His words cut off as he stepped fully into the room and saw her in the white dress. "*Wow*, you look amazing. What's the occasion?"

Heather took a deep breath and handed him the envelope. "This."

Clay was grinning as he opened the flap, but the smile faded the moment he began reading what was inside.

"An annulment?" His face went pale, his lips pressed into a tight line. "No, Heather. We're in this together. We'll go to therapy, work out whatever the problem is but—"

Bec was right. Men *were* idiots.

Clay had pulled the obscenely large diamond out of the envelope, the one from that night, the one she hadn't worn since. "This is yours." He crossed his arms. "I'm not taking it back."

"Clay—"

"No, Heather. I'm not giving you up."

And apparently, she'd been right to worry. This grand gesture was going to hell.

"Clay—"

"No negotiation. You promised we'd always talk—"

Since words weren't working, Heather went back to gestures. This time, though, it wasn't a grand one. She threw her arms around his neck and kissed him. His lips were all heat and passion and anger, in equal measure.

Only when her lungs were screaming for air did she pull back.

"Listen, you stubborn man," she panted, sucking in another breath to slow her pulse. "I'm wearing a white dress. There's a flower explosion downstairs. I just handed you a diamond ring. Can you please put the freaking pieces together?"

"What—oh. *Oh*." His eyes lit up. "Really?"

"Yes, really." She cupped his face. "You'll have to pretend that I'm down on one knee, because this dress is way too tight and these heels are way too high, but all of that aside, I wanted to ask, Clay Steele, will you mar—"

"Nope," he said and dropped to his knee. "I love you, sweetheart, but it's *me* who's going to do the asking." He held up the ring. "Heather O'Keith, my love, my heart, my *soul*. I never dreamed that I would feel this way about another person, that the love I feel for you could be this—"

"Yes," she interrupted. "I'll—"

"Shh," he said, standing to cup her cheek with his free hand. "I've had this speech planned for a while."

Tears escaped the confines of her lashes. "Clay . . ."

"I can honestly say that when I tell you I love you, it's because you're the best thing that has ever happened to me. You've given me a family, a home, and I love"—he pressed a kiss to her cheek, capturing the tears there with his lips—"I love"—another kiss on the other cheek—"I *love* you."

She sniffled. "Had to go full Darcy on me, didn't you?"

He touched his lips to hers. "Didn't think I knew it was your favorite movie?"

"Of course, you knew." Her fingers brushed his jaw. "So, can I say yes, now?"

Clay laughed and hugged her tight. "Yes, love, you can."

And so, Heather said yes. Yes to the now. Yes to forever.

And then she fixed her mascara.

Rachel

Rachel watched her boss dance with her second husband—or maybe husband twice over, was a better description?—and gave a little sigh of happiness.

Yes, Heather was technically her boss, but she was also her friend.

She deserved her happily ever after.

The party was just getting started, friends and business associates spilling out onto Heather's back patio that had been decorated with twinkly lights, lots of flowers, and plenty of portable heaters.

Only the Sextant—herself, Abby, Bec, Seraphina, CeCe, and Heather—plus Jordan, Colin, and of course, Clay, knew that the surprise wedding they'd celebrated that night was technically a *second* wedding.

The rest just thought Heather had pulled a fast one on Clay.

Rachel smiled as she remembered the way the couple had come down the stairs, both of their eyes a little damp, but love in every fiber of their bodies.

The vows had been beautiful and—

Ugh. She was getting a little too sappy.

Wiping the tears away before they could escape—and heaven forbid, ruin her mascara—Rachel blew out a breath and set about making sure the food the caterers had delivered was set out properly.

Soon the first dance would be over and then the group of fifty-plus—okay, so she knew that it was actually fifty-*seven* guests, because she was damned good at her job—would descend like locusts on the food tables.

Everything needed to be ready.

So, she went down her mental checklist. Appetizers. Check. Several types of salad. Blegh, but check. Entrees. Pasta, chicken, and vegetarian. Check. Check. Check. And the cake was ready and waiting to be cut.

"This little shindig your doing?"

Rachel froze, all her nerve endings going on red alert.

She knew that voice.

She knew if she turned around she would see *him*.

Him.

Tall, much taller than her, but lean when compared to her

curves. Still, all that lankiness hadn't meant a lack of strength. He'd been all sorts of hard and hot as he'd pinned her against the door and pounded into her.

Rachel cleared her throat but didn't rotate to face him. "Not my doing. I just helped out."

A long pause, probably because normal people usually looked each other in the eyes when they conversed.

"Well, from what I've seen, you've done *a lot* of helping out." He put a hand on the table next to her, and she shifted away, shivering. She remembered what those fingers could do, how they'd traced over her skin, slipped between her legs, slid *inside*.

Shuddering, she smoothed out a wrinkle on the tablecloth.

"For a last-minute surprise wedding, everything is beautiful."

She shrugged before fussing with the placement of the warming dishes.

The man didn't leave.

Why wouldn't he leave?

She dropped her chin to her chest.

"So," he finally said after a lengthy—and silent—moment. "Gay, taken, or not interested?"

"Oh my God," she moaned, one hand coming up to push her bangs off her forehead. "This is *not* happening."

"I—" A beat then his voice was incredulous, "I *know* that moan." Warm fingers grasped her wrist, tugged until she could see him in all his yumminess.

Her moment of weakness. Her hookup because she'd been feeling desperate and lonely and—

"It's you," he said softly.

Yes, it was *her*. Rachel, the good girl who didn't sleep around, who *certainly* didn't hook up with random strangers in a bar.

Rachel, who *had* hooked up with a stranger.

The sex had been damned good. Incredible, actually.

But it had been just that. Sex. And she hadn't been able to let go of the guilt. She'd now slept with a grand total of two men in her life, and one of them had been her husband.

"I—" She tugged at her wrist. "I need to go."

Heather and Clay chose that exact moment to saunter over. *Why universe? Why?*

"Oh, good," Clay said, after a brief thanks to her for all her help with the wedding. "I was going to introduce you two, but I see you've already met my assistant, Sebastian."

Sebastian's expression flickered with shock—no doubt mirroring her own—but luckily, Clay and Heather were too lost in each other to recognize it.

After a few more words, their bosses moved on to talk with a business associate, and Sebastian's blue-green eyes darkened to a deep emerald. His stare was all heat and desire and sex appeal.

But his words made her insides tremble.

"I'm *really* looking forward to working with you."

She tipped over a bowl of salad dressing.

THANK YOU FOR READING! I hope you loved meeting Abby and Jordan, CeCe and Colin, Heather and Clay, and Garret and Kay! The next book in the Billionaire's Club series is BAD HOOKUP. Find out what happens when Rachel's one-night stand shows back up and now she has to work with the insufferably sexy, pushy man...

CLICK HERE TO READ HOOKUP NOW>

NOW TURN THE PAGE FOR THE BILLIONAIRE'S CLUB NOVELLA, BAD DATE...

BAD DATE

A BILLIONAIRE'S CLUB NOVELLA

ONE

Kay

"GO ON A BLIND DATE, they said. It will be fun, they said."

Kay sighed and slumped back into her chair. Nothing like sitting alone for over an hour at the very expensive and chic restaurant her date had insisted upon. She was way outclassed at Ange Bisou and had only agreed to meet there in the first place because she was trying to force herself to step out of her comfort zone.

Routines were her mojo.

In fact, she loved nothing more than following them to a tee.

Which was probably why she was still single.

Ugh.

Kay pull out her phone, as if glancing at it for the hundredth time in the last hour might make a call or text magically appear, as if looking at it might mean she hadn't actually been stood up . . . for a date she hadn't wanted to go on in the first place.

Frankly, she had a hard time thinking that *any* date could possibly be worth her having to change out of her daytime pajamas and into actual adult clothes.

Yes, her normal routine involved daytime pajamas.

She stared at her phone, irritated all over again, because right about now—eight forty-five—she should be finishing up her bath and changing into her sleep pajamas. Maybe with a glass of chardonnay and definitely with a cooking show streaming on Hulu.

Not that she could cook.

Nope. Kay could burn water.

But lack of cooking skills aside, she still enjoyed watching what those chefs could whip up.

Plus, one of her favorite chefs had worked at Ange Bisou. So, despite her having to get out of her pajamas and her routine being completely obliterated, she'd actually been looking forward to eating here tonight.

Until she'd found herself sitting at the table alone.

Kay wished she'd ordered something earlier, but it was too late. She was already an hour in and nursing her second glass of wine, though she *had* given into the urge to get busy with the bread basket ten minutes ago.

She should have ordered the beet salad.

That was Christie's addition to the menu. And, yes, she considered herself on a first name basis with her fave celebrity chef, because watching every episode of a reality cooking competition meant they'd become friends, right?

Well now, *that* was a little slice of pathetic.

Sighing, she caught the waiter's eye.

"Can I get you anything else?" he asked, his gaze deliberately on her face and not the empty chair or unused flatware on the other side of the table.

She shook her head. "Just the bill. Thank you."

"Sure thing."

Kay shoved another bit of bread into her mouth as she waited, watching as the patrons around her ate *coq au vin* and chocolate soufflé.

Oh, good God. They had chocolate soufflé.

Her eyes rolled to the ceiling and she forced herself to breathe. She wished she had the guts to say fuck it all and order dinner, to sit and enjoy it.

But she knew herself.

She'd order the beet salad and the chocolate soufflé, and then she would be miserable and self-conscious eating them by herself.

And this didn't seem like the type of place to pull out a book as a shield.

Nope.

Plus, even if it was, it didn't matter. Because Kay was ready to go home, ready to change into her sleep pajamas and watch repeats of *Great British Bake Off.* They gave her hope that someday she might actually develop some cooking chops . . . instead of cooking *pork*chops into submission.

Because shoe leather had nothing on hers.

Her gaze drifted to the other table, the one with the chocolate soufflé. The woman who'd ordered it had only eaten half and then she nodded to the waiter when he asked if she'd finished.

What kind of monster only finishes half a soufflé?

Kay's nose wrinkled and her inner voice turned all grumbly. She wished *she* had a soufflé. She wouldn't waste it.

And—*ugh*—because *now* the woman reached across the table and her partner or date or husband also stretched his hand out to lace their fingers together, his other palm coming up to cup her cheek. It was sweet and lovely and romantic—

"I want to be home," she whined under her breath. "Right now."

Romance was dead for the romance writer.

How fitting.

Blinking, she dug out her wallet and by the time her waiter returned with her check, she was ready, all but tossing her card onto the little metal tray. He zipped away and back in record time and then she scrawled her name, paying fifty bucks for two glasses of wine and a tip to make the poor guy's night worth it.

Probably not as much as he would have made if she and her nonexistent date had actually eaten, but he'd been nice and not judgy, and hopefully it would take the edge off.

It wasn't his fault that she'd been stood up.

Nope. That particular responsibility lay solely in Garret's lap.

Kay blew out a breath, shrugged into her coat, and picked up her purse. The only good news was that her sleep pajamas were ready and waiting for her, laid out on her mattress.

She strode out of the restaurant, smiling to the hostess as she pushed through the door, and had just turned in the direction of her car when—

Wham!

Her purse dropped to the ground, spilling its contents everywhere, and she stumbled, almost falling, as a man shoved past her, cell phone glued to his ear.

He paused, glanced downing at her as though surprised to see a peon such as her existed. Probably not fair since there was a trace of concern in his gaze, but she certainly felt like a peasant when compared to the god in front of her.

Tall, dark, hot.

Black hair with the barest hint of a wave, tan skin and deep chocolate eyes, a jawline that could have been chiseled out of marble.

Yup. He was easy on the eyes.

"You okay?" he asked, and her heart skipped a beat.

Maybe not *all* men were assholes.

"I'm—" she began.

But once again, optimism was proven wrong.

Tall, dark, and handsome didn't wait for her answer. Whoever was on the phone must have snagged his attention, because his expression hardened and he turned away, saying, "I don't care if I'm late—"

Pieces fell into place.

Garret Williams, her MIA date, was a former rugby player from Australia. He'd recently begun a project with one of Heather's subsidiaries.

Heather O'Keith was an accidental friend—more about that later—and had been pestering Kay about setting up this date for months.

Garret was tall.

Garret was built.

Garret had the most gorgeous chocolate eyes Heather had *ever* seen.

Kay's own eyes flicked back to the man, who was now yanking open the door. Check. Check. Check.

"—You know I didn't even want to do this in the first place."

She'd been expecting an Australian accent, considering he was from Australia, but he sounded American. Well, chalk it up to things she would never know.

The door shut, cutting off anything else he might have said, and leaving Kay alone on the sidewalk, purse's contents strewn in all directions, and temper rapidly rising.

"Stupid"—she grabbed her book, shoved it back into her bag—"men."

Then Kay snatched up her keys, wallet, lipstick, pack of gum, two hair ties, and a few bobby pins and tucked them into her purse, all while muttering under her breath about the irritating creatures of the opposite sex who were hot but didn't appear to give a damn about anyone but themselves.

What the fuck had Heather been thinking?

You know what?

What had *she* been thinking?

Letting that asshole crash into her with nary an apology, allowing him to leave her to crawl across the dirty sidewalk gathering up her personal items. She hadn't even managed to say anything useful, just been blinded by his gorgeous god-likeness and had let him traipse off like a big ole'—

Ugh.

Like a big ole' something that was really insulting and annoying and—

The door opened again, a man holding it wide for his wife. Kay probably would have left at that moment, gone back to her apartment to sulk in peace, *if* the tall, dark, and handsome man she assumed was Garret Williams hadn't still been in the lobby of the restaurant. But nope, he was still there, still on his phone, still talking loudly enough that she could hear every single word through the open door.

And what she heard took her temper from bubbling to boiling.

"What kind of woman writes romance novels anyway?" he said. "She's probably an awkward cow who'll just stare at me through giant glasses the whole time I'm eating."

Kay's jaw dropped open. Her hand snatched at the door handle when it started to close.

He chuckled and said, "*Exactly*," like the snarky little asshole he was.

A vision of a pot boiling over filled her mind, or maybe a tea kettle whistling as steam poured out its spout. Either way, all Kay knew was that she saw literal red as she stormed back into the restaurant.

Just as she approached him, he hung up the phone, tucking it into his pocket and opening his mouth.

"Garret Williams?" she asked.

Furious as she was, she'd managed to hold on to enough reason to make sure the man she was about eviscerate was, in fact, her absentee date.

He rotated to face her. "Yes?"

She reached into her purse, yanked out a paperback of her

latest release. She'd intended to give it to Heather when they met up for coffee tomorrow, but this was more important. Plus, Heather had already read the ebook. The paper version had just been intended as a thank you for being awesome and a good friend and—

Right now that didn't matter.

Kay slapped the book against Garret's chest. The action made a satisfying *smack*, especially when she pretended it was actually her hand making contact with his cheek.

But first, he was so tall she couldn't reach it without a ladder.

And second, she didn't want to be arrested for assault.

Yeah. Minor details.

"What's this—"

She narrowed her eyes and took great joy in cutting him off. "Only your *cow* of a date's latest release. Maybe you should check the *New York Times* the next time you go searching for your decency."

He winced, looked the slightest bit sick. "Katherine?"

Kay lifted her chin, huffed dismissively, and followed up with an insult she would later look upon with pride. For once, she hadn't rolled over and accepted some asshole's judgment. She'd owned him *and* the situation.

"I go by Kay."

A beat.

"But in your case, I go by Fuck-Off-Because-You-Never-Even-Had-A-Chance."

And she walked out of the restaurant.

There should have been trumpets and banners . . . or at the very least, a round of applause as she went.

Instead, the only thing that trailed her was the *click-click* of her heels.

But, for that night, it was enough.

TWO

Kay

"JUST BECAUSE YOU saved my laptop from that Venti Frappuccino doesn't mean you get to torture me," she accused Heather the following day. She flopped down into the chair across from her friend. It was a dramatic move, but Kay held on to enough sense to not spill the steaming cup of tea she'd just purchased.

Her friend winced and took a sip of her coffee. "I'm guessing things didn't go well last night?"

"Well?" Kay snorted. "An unmitigated disaster would be a more accurate description."

"Damn, did he talk about himself too much?" Heather asked. "Sometimes people get nervous and try to impress their dates. Or was he too accommodating? Like he was so worried about you and your feelings that you didn't get to know him at all?"

"Heath," Kay replied. "I'm saying this with the utmost affection but . . . you're losing your touch. Your wonderful hubby has rotted your once sharp and precise brain." She raised a finger when Heather would have argued. "I see it with my characters all the time. They fall in love and they get soft—"

"One," Heather interjected. "Your characters are a product of your brain, so they don't get full human status in this argument and two, RoboTech and its subsidiaries made record profits last year, so my hubby isn't making me soft. Rather"—she waggled her eyebrows—"he's giving me *hard*."

"First," Kay said, mimicking her, "gross. And second . . . gross."

"That's all you got?" Heather lifted a brow. "I thought you were supposed to be some super successful author."

Kay rolled her eyes. "Words are hard."

Heather's mouth curved. "Uh-huh. Okay, so why was your date with Garret a disaster?"

"Before or after he stood me up?"

Kay had to hand it to herself, she'd surprised her friend and *that* didn't happen very often. So, she took great pleasure in the slack-jawed expression currently adorning Heather's face.

"I waited an hour," she said. "Nursed that bread basket like a son of a bitch, downed two glasses of really good wine. But after sitting alone at the table for an hour, I decided I'd had enough punishment and so I paid and left."

Heather winced. "Shit. I'm so sorry. I thought Garret was—"

"I haven't even got to what happened *after* the date ditching."

"Hold on"—Heather took a slug of coffee—I need to prepare myself. Especially since I'm the one who forced you to go out with him." She sucked in a breath, released it. "Okay, go."

"He called me a cow."

The look on Heather's face was scary, Kay had to give her friend that much. *And* it wasn't even directed at her, so really, she hadn't even witnessed the full potential of that glare.

"He. Did. *What?*"

Kay explained leaving the restaurant, the sexy—albeit awful

—man who'd knocked into her, causing her to spill her purse, before overhearing the conversation and—

"Then he basically said only gross cows write romance novels and that he'd purposely come late because he didn't want to be there in the first place." Kay sipped her tea. "And so I walked over to him, slapped him in the chest with one of my books, and walked out."

"You didn't!" Heather gasped.

Kay nodded. "Fuck yes, I did."

"That is amazing," Heather said, and the slight awe in her tone smoothed over the ruffled edges of Kay's temper. "You should have really slapped him though."

Kay sighed and sat back. "As much as I wanted to, you know how I feel about actual violence."

"You and your morals."

"I know"—Kay's lips twitched—"pesky standards."

Heather's phone buzzed, but she kept her eyes on Kay's. "I'm really sorry. Garret mentioned to Clay that he was single and looking to settle down, but that he'd been struggling to find smart, talented woman, I thought, *Who's smarter and more talented than you?*"

Aw.

Another buzz, which Heather ignored. "Obviously, I knew you fit the bill, but I didn't know he'd be such a douche. Next time—"

"There will be no *next time*, Heather O'Keith." Kay narrowed her eyes.

Heather's phone buzzed for a third time, and she sighed. "I need to go."

"Not until you promise no more blind dates."

Avoiding Kay's eyes, she stood up, tossed her purse over one shoulder and turned to leave. "It was good to meet up. I can't wait for your next book!"

"No more new books unless you agree to no more blind dates."

Heather winced. "You're mean."

"I'm practical. That was torture, and I'm old enough to only want to do things that *I* want to do." All well and good in words, but Kay had serious pushover tendencies, which Heather certainly knew . . . and would probably exploit if the chips were on the table.

"It's for your own good," Heather began.

See?

"I'm happy with my life," she told her. "Would I turn the right man away if he dropped into my lap? Hell no. But I'm not actively looking for a relationship, and I'm totally fine with that."

"But you're a romance writer," Heather said. "You create stories that make people happy, and you deserve to have some of that happy for yourself."

Kay smiled and pushed to her feet. "Thank you for caring." She hugged Heather. "But I *am* happy and if you read some of my reviews, you'd see that I make plenty of people miserable." Her smile widened to a grin. "Plus, consider this whole horrible event fodder for my new book. I'll name someone Garret, kill him off, and then move on with my life in blissful abandon."

Heather considered that for a few seconds. "Okay, fine." She finally glanced down at her cell and made at face at what she saw on the screen. "I just don't understand how he transformed from Mr. Nice Guy into Sir Asshole."

"Either way," Kay said. "He's not Mr. Right. So"—and she wanted to make this crystal clear because Heather was a master negotiator and had a penchant for finding workarounds and loopholes—"repeat after me: No more blind dates."

Her friend nodded. "No more setting you up on blind dates. Got it."

And with a quick squeeze and a promise of dinner soon, Heather left.

Kay stared after her, trying to figure out why that interaction had come off as weird. Heather's agreement had been almost too easy, but then again, she *had* felt bad about the disaster of a date, so maybe that was it.

Huh. Kay shrugged mentally as she pulled out her laptop.

Weirdness aside, Heather was a woman of her word. If she promised no more blind dates, she would follow through with that.

It was only later that Kay would realize that while Heather had promised no more blind dates, what she *hadn't* promised was to forgo dates altogether.

Words, man. Sometimes they came back and bit a girl on the—

THREE

Garret

HE'D KNOWN he'd fucked up from the moment he'd watched the beautiful blonde come his way, pretty chocolate eyes molten and all but shooting sparks.

Garret knew he'd pissed her off, but hadn't comprehended why.

Had he broken something when he accidentally bumped into her?

He knew he probably should have stopped to help her pick up her things, to make sure she was fine, but he'd already been late and wanting to get the evening over with.

Not to mention the rant. He'd been spouting off to his best friend and former teammate, Kevin, like he'd earned a gold medal in ranting.

But then the woman had approached with fury written across her face, and so Garret had quickly hung up his call, pocketed his cell, and opened his mouth to apologize. But he hadn't managed to get more than a syllable out before she was assaulting him with a paperback and then telling him to check out the *New York Times* listings.

And *that* was the precise moment he realized the degree to which he'd fucked up.

Because the beautiful blonde wasn't just a stranger he'd bumped into on the street.

Nope. She was his date.

A date he hadn't wanted, but one that had been his investor's idea. Heather O'Keith was a legend in the business world, and when she'd found out he was single and potentially looking for that status to change, she'd all but forced one Katherine Hart on him.

What was he going to say? No?

Of course not.

He wanted RoboTech's investment, and he was counting on Heather's business acumen.

So he'd agreed to the date.

But inwardly, he'd groaned and moaned and bitched as if his coach had dressed him down in front of the guys. And this inner whine-fest had only grown louder when Heather told him how she'd met Katherine and that her friend was a romance novelist.

First, Garret was a realist. He didn't have room in his life for someone who spent time fantasizing over fictional eight-packs and happy endings that rarely came to fruition.

Second, he'd pictured a woman who looked like those from the backs of his mother's books. Bodice rippers still cluttered her nightstand and, well, this was going to make him sound like a Class-A asshole again, but the women whose pictures were on the back of those hadn't exactly been his type. They appeared a little frumpy, slightly awkward, and old enough to be his . . . *well*, his mother.

Of course, what he *hadn't* expected was tall, lean, and gorgeous with angelic features and lush lips that any man would dream of kissing. Even her glasses had added to her allure.

Katherine—or Kay as she'd told him she went by—definitely had the sexy librarian vibe happening.

And if there was one thing that Garret dug, it was the sexy librarian look.

Contrary to his size as an adult, he'd been little growing up. But now he was six-feet-four, two hundred and fifty pounds, and while he didn't have that fictional eight-pack, he was in damned good shape considering his professional rugby career had ended five years earlier. Still, he'd been the shortest in his class for years and as skinny as a beanpole. The library had been his happy place, somewhere he could pretend to be strong and tall or a superhero or a Greek god.

And he'd had a crush on Mrs. Phillips, the librarian.

That had all ended, the summer before his junior year which had brought him eight inches and forty pounds. Not his love for literature, but his pathetic crush.

He'd done little over those months except eat, sleep, and groan during the miserable growth spurt. Every bone in his body had hurt, including his toes.

But he'd come out the other side and had picked up rugby.

Which wasn't typical in the States—except Garret had been born in California to an American mother and an Australian father, so he had love for both countries. His parents had divorced when he was in high school, his dad moving back to Australia and Garret's summers permanently spent in a foreign country.

Not that Australia wasn't great. There were parts that were amazing, and he loved the beaches, the people, and rugby. That he'd loved even before his growth spurt. After, he'd gotten good at the sport—so good that he'd managed to play professionally.

The only bad thing about spending summers in Australia had been being away from his friends and missing out on all the high school parties.

His lips curved when he remembered how upset he'd been

about missing Beverly Hawkins' swim party. The girls had skinny dipped, and he hadn't been there to witness it.

God, he'd been such a perv.

Was still a perv.

He was also fucked, he realized the moment that Heather walked into her office. He'd been waiting for the better part of forty-five minutes, her assistant plying him with coffee and snacks, and him assuming that another meeting had run long.

What he *hadn't* expected was for Heather to come in, guns blazing, having already spoken with Katherine—Kay.

How did he know that she'd spoken to Kay?

Probably because she strode across the room, lifted her hand as though to slap him—though she didn't—and glared. "I should slap you," she muttered. "God knows you deserve it. But Kay has this pesky policy against physical violence, and so I'm going to abide by it, as much as it pains me to say."

"I do deserve it," he said.

She indicated he should sit before she crossed behind her desk and sat down herself. "Yes." Her eyes went flinty, steel entering her expression in a way that made this woman way more terrifying than any of his coaches had ever been. "Next time you lie to me, our deal is off the table. I don't fuck around, I don't play games, and I don't force people I work with to date my friends."

"I—"

"Frankly, it was hard fucking enough to get Kay to agree to the date in the first place. She hates meeting new people, and going out in general is like a worst-case scenario for her."

She seemed to be waiting for a response from him, so he told the truth. "Me, too."

Heather threw up her hands, as if she knew he'd say that. "Yes. *Exactly.* Which is why I thought you two would hit it off. She's beautiful and brilliant *and* a homebody." Blue eyes narrowed further. "Like you."

Garret winced. "I—"

"Fucked up."

He nodded. "I was an ass."

"A total ass. A slap-deserving ass." She stood up and started pacing the room. "How dare you call her a cow! Do you know how insulting that is? How fucking dismissive and disgusting?"

"Look"—he pushed to his feet—"Yes, I was an asshole, but I don't need a dressing down from you. I was a prick, case closed, and I already apologized . . . or well, I sent an apology to Kay's apartment this morning."

Heather stared at him long enough that he struggled not to squirm.

"You apologized?" she eventually said.

A nod. "Yes." He sighed. "I shouldn't have said that. It wasn't fair to her or even, women in general. I was showing off for a friend and being a dick. And, not that this matters at all, but I read the book she gave me"—*cough*, hit him with—"last night. It was damned good."

Another long moment of staring and subsequent resisting of squirming.

Why would a grown man feel the urge to squirm in front of a woman half his size?

Because Heather was Heather fucking O'Keith.

And there was just something about her that made people fall in line.

"What happened in chapter twenty-eight?"

"You mean where the hero realized he was an ass and then went to grovel for forgiveness?"

Her lips curved slightly. And it *was* slight, but that barely-there smile was enough to allow Garret to relax.

Marginally.

"I hope you took notes," she said.

"I did. I sent her a gift card to the local bookstore along with a ridiculously expensive notebook and stationery set I picked out myself."

"Hmm."

"And flowers and chocolates and a handwritten note."

Heather crossed to her chair, plunked down into it. "Good. And you're going to ask her out again?"

Garret blinked. "Well, I think I fucked that particular option up, don't you?"

"Hmm." Heather opened a folder on her desk. "Well, it just so happens that I need another man to round out my table at RoboTech's fundraiser this Saturday."

His brows rose, hope bubbled up in his blood. "And will your table include one Kay Hart?"

"Of course, it will." A sage smile. "Now, about your proposal . . ."

FOUR

Kay

FOR THE SECOND time in only a week she was out late, not in bed, and *not* in her sleep pajamas.

Her heels made a little *click click* as she walked into the venue that was housing Heather's fundraising event, and she had to resist the urge to tug at the straps of her bodice. She didn't often wear dresses, and certainly not ones that were so limited in the fabric department.

But after the disastrous date with Garret, she'd wanted to feel sexy.

So, she'd ditched her glasses, put in contacts, and squeezed into her best pushup bra.

Paired with the long navy chiffon gown and she'd pulled her own teen movie makeup montage. The point was that Kay could be glam when she had to—or in this very rare case, when she *wanted* to.

Garret Williams could just stick that up his incredibly yummy ass. Which was so not the point, but still a nice thought.

Who was the cow now?

Hmph. He'd even had the nerve to send her flowers and expect her to accept his apology for being a jerk.

And chocolates, her brain reminded her. *And a gorgeous journal and pen. And—*

"Enough," she growled.

"Are you all right?"

The college-aged boy running the coat check gave her a concerned look, and Kay realized she'd paused in the middle of taking off her jacket and was talking to herself.

Aloud. In public.

Yup. That was absolutely perfect.

Sighing, she forced the frown lines between her brows to relax and curved her lips up into a smile.

"I'm fine." She shoved the coat at him, mentally promised that she'd give him a big tip for being weird later then hurried off with a cheery, "Thank you!"

"Get it together, Hart," she muttered under breath once she was out of earshot. "You'll go in there, say hello, have a bite to eat, a drink, stick around the requisite amount of time, then GTFO."

Feeling better after reminding herself of her plan, Kay lifted her chin and walked through the double doors. Inside, the ballroom had been filled with round tables. They were adorned with gleaming white tablecloths, glittering candles, and gorgeous floral displays.

Each table had a different theme, and the accessories—flowers, vases, and other decorations—had been carefully selected to fit in with that theme.

How did Kay know all of that, just by striding through the door?

Well, the proceeds from tonight's benefit were going to a local literacy charity and because of Kay's experience in publishing, Heather had sicced her assistant Rachel on her. Together they'd selected a different genre of book for each table before going crazy with theming the items.

Kay hadn't minded, however.

The one thing she'd never been able to get enough of was books, and getting to arrange an entire party around the love of her life?

She couldn't lie. It had been the most fun she'd had in ages.

Besides the silent and live auctions, all the centerpieces would be sold. And she had her eye on table ten, which held the historical romance wares. Kay wanted that early edition of Pride and Prejudice, dammit, and she didn't care who she had to take down in the process of getting it.

Heather walked by her then did a double take, jaw falling open.

"Kay?" She stopped, backed up a few feet. "Holy shit. You look amazing! That dress is incredible."

"Thanks—"

Clay, Heather's husband, walked up. "I'm sorry to interrupt, but—Kay?" he exclaimed. "Wow. That's a beautiful color on you."

Kay blushed. That was the reaction she'd wanted from getting dressed up, of course, but she wasn't used to people noticing the way she looked. Still, she was going to take the confidence booster and leave it at that.

Look at her, all mature and shit.

"Go do what you need to do," she told Heather. "I'm going to grab a drink. Are we still sitting together? Or did you bump me for someone more important?"

Heather grinned. "Would I do that to my favorite author?"

"For more donations?" Kay asked. "I would hope so."

"And that"—Heather squeezed her arm—"is why you're a good friend. I'll see you later. Table ten."

Kay waved before heading to the bar.

Once there, she ordered her normal Cosmo before leaning back against the bar top to look around the room. Rachel had worked her magic, turning what could have been a bland ballroom into a really beautiful event. And, though she'd only played a small part in it with the tables, Kay had to admit she was proud of her contribution.

"Here you are," the bartender said.

She turned around, tipped him, and then returned to leaning against the bar, only this time with her Cosmo in hand.

Yeah, she thought as she took a sip, *that was so much better.*

"This must be up your alley."

Kay froze, martini glass at her lips, eyes darting to her left.

She knew that voice.

And the last time she'd heard it, he'd been calling her a cow.

Okay, not exactly the *last time*, but taking a little creative license now and then was kind of her thing.

Garret mirrored her position, leaning against the bar as his eyes trailed down and back up. "You look *incredible*," he said, lifting a bottle of beer to his lips.

Kay sucked in a breath and nearly choked on her drink. But, hot damn, there was something about a man who drank straight out of a bottle. No fancy glass or prissy cocktail, but a man's man who drank and fucked and—

Apparently, she'd gone too long without writing a true alpha.

Because Garret screamed alpha, especially in that form-fitting suit that showed off his broad shoulders and lean hips and, fuck, but his thighs. There weren't any chicken legs in sight because Garret had *great* thighs.

Kay's mind drifted for a minute, imagined those thighs shoving hers apart as he thrust home. Or maybe her straddling him, riding them both to completion. Or maybe—

She coughed again and then almost choked for a second time when hot, calloused fingers brushed the bare skin of her back.

Had she mentioned that her dress was backless?

A fact that Kay was simultaneously thrilled and dismayed about in that moment.

"Are you okay?" Garret asked, the brush turning into a gentle pat as she coughed. He snagged her glass from her hand, set it on top of the bar.

She nodded, slowing her breathing as she attempted to not cough up a lung.

"Fine," she eventually managed to rasp. "Thank you."

"Sorry if I startled you." Chocolate eyes met hers. "And I'm sorry for the other night. I was an asshole."

Her lips parted as a surprised breath slipped out.

An apology? No qualifications, no excuses? Just sorry?

Fingertips brushed her spine again. "I didn't want to be there, and I shouldn't have taken it out on you. Further that, what I said was—"

Except, Kay had stopped listening after I *didn't want to be there*.

She'd waited an hour for the man, missed out on her beet salad *and* chocolate soufflé for a jerk who hadn't even wanted to come in the first place.

She'd gotten out of her daytime pajamas for the man.

What. The. Fuck?

The callous fingers on her bare skin lost their appeal, the intimate fantasies speeding through her brain faded away.

"—completely inappropriate and wrong and—"

"I'll have you know—" she started to say before stopping and shaking her head. This man would never get it. "You know what? Never mind. Thanks for the apology. Have a nice life."

She grabbed her glass, started to turn away.

"Wait." He snagged her wrist, causing her cocktail to slosh over the rim of the cup, splashing all along her arm. "Shit." Still holding on to her, he turned for the bar, snagged some napkins from the pile and held them out to her. "Sorry."

"Lot of that going around," she muttered, slipping free of his grip and wiping her arm. She'd need to go to the bathroom to wash it, otherwise she'd be walking around with a sticky hand all night.

Snorting inwardly at that thought—sticky hand, *te-he-he*—Kay dropped the wad of napkins back onto the bar and lifted her chin. "Goodbye, Garret."

"Wait," he said again, though this time he didn't grab her.

"No, I don't think I will." She whipped around.

He darted around her, stepping right in front of her and forcing her to skid to a stop on her heels. And fuck, because she really didn't want him to, but he smelled amazing.

"I'm fucking this up."

"Ding. Ding. Ding." She took a step to the side and he mimicked the movement. "For God's sake, why won't you leave me alone?"

Garret winced. "Because I'm not normally an asshole."

"Well," she grumbled. "Reiterating the fact you didn't want to go on a date with me at all certainly isn't the way to prove that."

"I—" He sighed. "That's not what I meant."

Kay rolled her eyes. "I mean, I got that loud and clear simply by the fact that you didn't show up."

"I—"

"Then there's the small factor of the bovine reference to my appearance and making fun of my career."

"I—"

"So, yeah, you're not batting that high of an average with the whole *not asshole* thing."

"I read your book."

Kay froze, pulse speeding up.

"I liked it. A lot."

She bit her lip, felt his gaze lock onto the spot, and though she'd written about it in many of her books, imagined it in her author brain plenty of times, Kay had never actually experienced the sensation of a simple look creating such a tangible feeling.

It. Was. Incredible.

She could feel his eyes, could actually *feel* her blood shift, moving toward her lips, plumping them, making them tingle.

Her tongue darted out and his chocolate stare heated, going molten until she could almost sense that melted sweetness dripping down her spine.

He leaned down. Her breath caught.

"I really am sorry."

Just like that, the spell was broken . . . or if not broken exactly, then at least she'd regained a few of her senses.

Kay stepped back and glared at him. Why was he pushing this? Because she didn't believe for one second that he was truly sorry. Sorry he got caught, maybe. Sorry his asshole move might jeopardize—

"Don't worry," she said, clarity finally hitting her brain. "I know that Heather is your investor. I won't do anything to change that."

He waved a hand. "That's not why I'm apologizing. Yes, I'm in business with Heather. Yes, it would be a blow to lose her investment, but this isn't my first rodeo. I'd figure it out."

"Great. Well, kudos to you." She blew out an exasperated breath when she tried to step around him, only to be blocked by him again. "What?" she snapped and poked a finger into his chest. "What's so special about me that you're pushing this?"

He caught her hand, and Kay bit back a gasp at the spark of desire that shot through her at the simple contact. "I—" He shook his head. "I don't know."

And then he was close again. Too close.

Not close enough.

She swallowed hard, heart pounding in the back of her throat, breaths coming in rapid inhalations.

He was going to kiss her.

Oh God. Did she want him to? He was such an ass—

He'd apologized. Seemed to genuinely mean it . . . or at the least was very determined that she believe it.

Garret brushed back a strand of her hair. "I'm not going to say anything," he told her. "Every time I do, I stick my foot in my mouth."

"You're saying something right now."

His lips curved. Her thighs clenched.

Shit. *Shit*. She . . . wanted his mouth to slant across hers.

"You're beautiful." One hand gently cupped her cheek. "And I'm so, *so* sorry."

More words, but she wasn't hearing them because he was coming closer, warm breath on her cheek . . . on her forehead.

He pressed a gentle kiss there before straightening, meeting her no doubt surprised eyes with warm chocolate ones. "I hope someday you'll give me a chance to prove that I'm not usually an ass."

Then he reached behind her, making her breath catch all over again and picked up a glass.

Somehow during all of the apologizing, he'd managed to order her another Cosmo. Her anger eased, not gone completely, but tempered, along with her hurt feelings.

Maybe he wasn't so bad after all.

Carefully, he handed over the drink.

"You didn't drug this, did you?" she blurted.

A raised brow. "Will it get you to accept my apology?"

She shook her head. "Not a chance."

"Damn." Garret smirked. "Not my speed, sweetheart."

She eyed the drink then him.

"I'm happy to pay for a fresh one if you want to watch the bartender mix it up."

Kay bit her lip, watched his eyes heat and drift to that spot again. "No," she said, trying to pretend she wasn't breathless. "That's okay."

One more brush of his fingers, this time along the outside of her arm and making her shiver. "I'll see you later."

And then he was gone, taking the rest of her anger along with him.

Maybe she was a pushover who forgave too easily.

But . . . maybe she wasn't.

FIVE

Garret

HE SAW the moment Kay clued into the fact that they would be sitting next to each other at dinner.

Consternation rolled across her expression, followed by softness and then maybe irritation. She was almost an open book with those feelings written on her face, and he had the feeling that if he got to know her better, he'd be able to read them as easily as one of her books.

And he *wanted* to know her better.

Whether or not she believed it, since that night he'd thought of little else aside finding a way to win her over, to prove that he wasn't always a jerk, and to convince her to give him a second chance for a first date.

Garret pulled Kay's chair out for her and waited for her to sit, feeling as though he were playing an intense game of chicken.

Would she cave and sit?

Or would he be relegated to the reject table?

Heather was on Kay's other side. "Sit, please, everyone." Kay, next to him, released a barely audible sigh, but did sit.

Heather glanced back at him and winked.

Garret plunked down into his chair, lest Kay change her mind about relegating him to the rejects.

"Did you like the journal?" he asked, not wanting to remind her of their disastrous first date any more than necessary, but also more than a little desperate to see if he'd picked correctly.

Her expression gentled, and he sent up a prayer that he might have actually chosen something right to say for a change.

"Yes, I did," she said. "It was absolutely lovely."

He shrugged. "The least I could do."

She dropped her chin to her chest, sighed, and Garret's stomach clenched. *Shit*. What had he done now?

And, *fuck it all*, but why did he care so much?

"Can we just start over?" she asked.

If he'd been hit over the head with a two-by-four, Garret wouldn't have been more shocked. "Do you . . . do you *want* to?"

She glanced up at him from beneath her lashes, smiled shyly. "Yes."

His heart skipped a beat, and he realized he was in the best type of trouble. The kind that led to monogamy and picket fences and, yes, it was way too fucking soon to even be considering that in the slightest . . . but—

There was something different about this woman.

Something he knew he wanted to explore further.

"Okay."

Her smile widened. "Okay."

The servers were coming around with salads and so Garret waited for their plates to be delivered. "Why writing?" he asked once the waiter had retreated.

Kay bit her lip again and that little flash of white against pink, the glistening of soft skin from the moisture left behind, the desire for it to be *his* teeth all contributed to making his cock twitch.

He hadn't touched her, and he was at risk of embarrassing himself.

"I was super shy as a kid," she said and shrugged. "Stories gave me a way to get all my words out and onto a page without worrying if I was going to stutter or screw up or miss something." She reached into her purse and pulled out a tiny notebook, along with a pencil and an eraser shaped like a fox. "My weapons!" she joked. "The best part was that this one"—she made the little fox run across the tablecloth—"has magical erasing powers."

"A marvelous feat of engineering."

She smiled up at him. "Exactly." Then shyness seemed to take over because her gaze drifted down. She seemed to realize her plate was still full and took a bite of salad.

He did the same.

"So," she said a few moments later, "why rugby?"

Garret shrugged. "I loved watching it growing up. My dad's Australian, and it's obviously much more popular there. When my parents split up, I'd go there and visit my dad, and I sort of fell into it."

One half of her mouth turned up. "Fell into it so well you were good enough to play professionally."

"I got lucky, and I definitely was never the best guy on the team." He speared some lettuce with his fork. "Do you know anything about rugby?"

Amusement played across her gorgeous face. "I know I like rugby romance."

He tilted his head to the side. "That's a thing?"

"Oh yeah, it's a thing."

"Well, damn."

She grinned, pointed at his plate "Eat your salad before your jaw falls off."

He snorted but shoved the bite hanging off his fork into his mouth, chewed and swallowed. "Where'd you grow up?"

They exchanged first date pleasantries, finding out that

they'd both grown up in California, though Kay was born and raised in the Bay Area, while Garret had been in L.A. until his rugby career had taken off. He'd moved back to the States and up to Northern California just a few months before.

"Did you learn to surf?" she asked, after they'd both discovered they were only children.

Garret shuddered. "No. The guys tried, but I'm hopeless."

Kay smiled. "I learned. The water was freezing, and I was freaked out the whole time that a Great White was going to attack me, but I managed to get up on a couple of waves at least."

"Nice." He raised his fist for her to bump, and their eyes met when even that tiny bit of contact made his nerves spark.

"Why does that keep happening?" she breathed.

"I don't know." A beat. "But I don't hate it."

Her laughter made his heart skip a beat—something that was starting to become a regular occurrence with this woman.

They talked about her books during the main course, laughed over a few of Garret's rugby stories during dessert—an American rookie had led to no small amount of good-natured teasing and pranks. She had him in absolute stitches as she relayed a tale about how she'd been so mad at a former boyfriend that she'd made him the impotent villain in an early book as the live auction was going on.

He clamped a hand over his mouth, nudged her with his shoulder. "You almost made me buy that trip to Maui," he said with a mock-glare.

"I'd make you take me," she teased.

He bent close. "Should I be worried you're going to make *me* impotent in a future book?"

She leaned in conspiratorially. "I *was* going to kill you off."

"What about now?" He turned, and suddenly their lips very close together.

"I'm considering my options."

"I—"

Applause broke out around them and Garret blinked, trying to sort out the reason until he realized the first portion of the live auction was over.

Kay stood. "I'm going to hit the ladies room before they start bidding on these babies." Her fingers traced over the centerpiece of books in the middle of the table. "I've had my eye on this one since I first gave Rachel the idea for them."

He rose as well. "Do you want me to get you another drink? I promise I won't spill this one on you."

Her smile lit up her face, and Garret knew in that moment that he'd do anything for this woman. "That would be great. Thank you." And with a quick word to Heather—asking her to watch her purse—and a soft touch to the spine of one book in particular, a whispered, "I'll be back for you," she hurried across the room.

Heather glanced up at him, raised her brows.

"I'm an idiot, and you know all."

Clay's mouth quirked. "Words my wife loves to hear."

"She's amazing."

"Of course, she is," Heather said. "She's *my* friend."

SIX

Kay

SHE WAS TRAPPED in the bathroom.

Kay was literally trapped in the bathroom, and her Jane Austen book was in danger.

Why had she decided to pee?

Or more importantly, why had she decided to leave her purse and, inside of it her cell phone, with Heather?

Oh yeah, because she hadn't wanted to wrestle with her full-length dress and heels *and* a purse all while trying to hover so her butt didn't touch a gross public toilet seat.

"Hello?" she said again, trying the door handle for the umpteenth time.

It still didn't budge, and she'd lost count of how many times she'd knocked on the door, trying to get someone's attention. All she knew was that she'd been locked in the room for what seemed to be an inordinate amount of time.

"*Hello?*"

Why did the stalls have to be floor to ceiling with actual doors?

What she wouldn't give in that moment to be able to crawl out beneath that shin-high gap most public bathrooms sported, dirty, germ-filled floor aside.

Who cared? Her Austen was *in danger*.

"It's going to be fine," she murmured. They were auctioning the tables from one upward. Her Austen was number ten.

She had plenty of time.

Except . . . how long had she been trapped?

"Shit!" she muttered then raised her voice. "Help!" she called. "*Help!*"

Finally, she heard footsteps. "Hello?"

"Hello?" she said. "I'm stuck in the stall."

"Oh no," came a female voice. "This one?" The handle jiggled from the outside.

"Yes."

"Okay, let me try." It wiggled some more. "Can you turn it at all?"

Kay and her mystery female help worked for a few minutes more, trying to get the handle to move or the lock to disengage, all to no avail.

"Shoot," the woman eventually said. "I can't get it to budge. I'm going to see if I can find an employee. Maybe they have a key or a screwdriver or something."

"Thank you so much," Kay said, even though her heart was sinking as the minutes passed. There was no way the auctioneer wasn't getting close to her table, and the likelihood of that early edition of *Pride and Prejudice* being added to her collection was dropping with each passing moment.

A few minutes passed, and the woman reappeared . . . or at least her voice did. "I found an employee, and they called maintenance, but are you by any chance Kay?"

"Yes," she said. "Why?"

"Because there's a guy out here named Garret. I guess he got worried and came looking."

"Oh."

That was sweet.

"He says he can try to fix the handle if you're comfortable."

"I'm comfortable with anything that gets me out of this stall."

"I had a feeling," the woman said. "Let me grab him."

A few moments later, Kay heard quick footsteps across the tile floor. "Sweetheart? Which stall are you in?"

Her pulse jumped at the endearment—too soon and yet she liked the way it made her feel. As though she were special to him. "I'm here," she said, knocking on the door.

"Okay, I'm going to try . . ." And he spent a few minutes repeating the process Kay had tried by herself and also with her female helper, without success. "Damn," he muttered. "You're really stuck. Let me see if there's any progress on the maintenance guy. You okay in there for a few more minutes?"

It wasn't like she had a choice, but Kay bit back an annoyed reply. Garret was trying to help, and getting snappy wouldn't help.

The Austen would be there when she got out, or it wouldn't.

That was just the way it was going to be.

Garret came back into the bathroom, relaying he'd been told it would only be a few more minutes before they came, but when a solid fifteen minutes passed, he ordered her to stand back.

And with a grunt and hard shove of his shoulder, he broke the lock, slamming the door into the stall. It crashed against the wall with surprising force, and the half of her that was impressed with his strength was really glad she'd been standing well out of the way.

The other half of her launched herself over the splinters of wood and into his arms.

"Thank you!" she exclaimed, squeezing him tightly. "Thank you so much." She stepped out of his arms, turned to the petite blonde standing in the doorway. "And thank *you* for not leaving me. I was really worried there for a minute."

"I'm Claire," the woman said. "And I glad you were rescued."

"Kay." She laughed. "But I guess you knew that already. Thank you again."

Claire left as Kay spun back to face Garret. "I've got to see if I can get back for the table auction. My Austen—"

Her gut clenched.

Because his expression said it all.

"It's gone?"

He nodded. "I'm sorry. I heard the bids close on it when I went to find the maintenance guy."

"Oh." She sucked in a breath and pushed down her disappointment. It was only a book. There would be others. "Did it go for a lot?"

"Over two thousand."

Kay's eyes widened. "Really? Well, at least they got their money's worth."

"Yeah." He took her hand. "Do you want to go back to the party?"

"Not really."

"Okay." Garret tucked her palm into the crook of his arm. "I'll walk you to your car."

"I took an Uber."

His lips twitched. "I'm grasping at straws here. So, should I call you an Uber or do you want a ride home?"

Kay shook off her disappointment. "Sorry," she said. "I'm just a mixture of bummed about the book and shook up from being trapped in a bathroom stall for . . ." She paused. "How long exactly?"

"Close to an hour."

"Shit."

He snorted. "Literally."

"Garret!" But then she was laughing, too, and by the time they both stopped, she felt better. "Thanks," she said. Her hand still rested on his forearm, and she gave the hard muscle a squeeze.

"You're welcome."

"Did you bring a coat?"

"Yes," she said. "I just need to get the ticket out of my—" She smacked her forehead. "My purse! I'm an idiot. I forgot I left it with—"

Garret held it up.

"She got pulled away from the table. I promised to keep it safe." He pretended to model it for a few seconds and had her in hysterics. "I think it goes with my outfit, don't you?"

She patted his arm. "Only a truly secure man would say that."

"You know it." He handed her the purse then steered them toward coat check. "Let's grab your jacket, and I'll drive you home."

"That sounds great."

HER COAT FELT a little heavy when she put it on, but she attributed it to exhaustion from her crazy evening. First Garret, then the bathroom, and now the multitude of sparks flying as he drove her home.

He held her hand, stroking little circles on the back of her wrist as they drove. Bolts of pleasure shot up her arm and then down. Straight down between her thighs.

Yup, she was getting hot from a simple caress.

Thus was the power of Garret Williams.

He regaled her with a few more tales but didn't take over the conversation. For as much as he spoke, he seemed to make sure she talked twice as much, and his questions were interesting and fun, ranging from thoughtful to simple small talk.

She'd answered everything from "Where do you come up

with your character names?" to "What's your favorite thing to binge right now?" to "What did your parents do growing up?"

Her answers had been: she had a master list of character names she added to every time she heard a good name, *Killing Eve*, and school teachers, respectively.

"Star Wars or Star Trek?"

She slanted her eyes at him, felt her lips twitch and then they both said, "Star Wars" at the same time.

He laughed, brushed his fingers along her wrist again, and her breath caught.

Garret was . . . well, he was being the perfect date.

Of course, he was also spinning a web around her, drawing her in, tugging her close—

Or maybe that just what her body wanted.

Or her brain.

Shh, her mind said. *Don't ruin this for us.*

Apparently, all of her wanted Garret and she couldn't just chalk it up to hormones. Nope. He was smart and funny and kind, and the hug after he'd rescued her from the bathroom hadn't been nearly enough contact.

Damn Heather for her matchmaking skills. If she liked Garret and went out with him then she'd never hear the end of it—

And now Kay was grasping at straws to distance herself.

Because she was scared.

Because she really liked him.

Ugh.

"Take a right at the signal," she said softly.

As though sensing she was going around in circles in her mind, Garret just nodded and then silently followed the rest of her directions until he was pulling into her driveway. She owned a house south of the City and though it was ridiculously small—she mentally shook her fist at the price of Bay Area real estate—Kay was very proud of it. The little Craftsman had a wide front porch that was dotted with pots of hardy flowers she'd somehow managed to keep alive.

And considering her black thumb, *that* was saying something.

"Thanks," she said softly and then bit her lip, unsure what to say and suddenly nervous.

"This place is great," he said, staring at her house. "Is it blue or gray? It's hard to tell in this light."

Her lips curved, and she relaxed. "It's blue-gray. Do you"— she sucked in a breath—"do you want to come in?"

There.

That might have been the bravest thing she'd ever done with a man. Inviting him into her house and not even under the guise of a nightcap. She wasn't necessarily the type of girl to sleep with someone after a date or two, however good or bad they were. But with Garret, she thought she *could* be.

Quiet filled the car, and Kay felt her cheeks heat.

Chocolate eyes locked onto hers, desire in their depths, and yet he didn't move to get out of the car.

His expression went rueful. "I *want* to come in, but I'm not going to. I consider myself on probation after our first date."

"Probation?" she asked, head tilting to study him. A mix of relief and disappointment coursed through her, which told her he was probably right in his decision to not come in. Yes, she wanted him, but yes, there was also a part of her waiting for the asshole to reappear.

It was just too soon.

He cupped her cheek. "You need time to get to know me." One half of his mouth curved. "The not jerky version."

"How long do you propose this probationary period to last?"

"Hmm. Three months should do it?"

Her heart jumped. *Three months?* He was considering—

Fingers on her wrist again. "Will you go out with me some-time next week?"

"I'd like that." She reached into her purse and handed him her card. "Here's my email."

"No phone number?"

She shook her head, reached for the handle. "We'll work up to it."

A grin that made her thighs clench. "I'm good with working up to things. But"—his eyes scorched her—"I'd like to kiss you goodnight."

Her mouth went dry, longing pulsed through her.

But then his expression transformed, going all innocent as he shrugged. "I mean, if you want to. No big deal."

Amusement filled her. "Nope. No can do, bucko," she told him. "You're on probation, remember?" Disappointment crossed his gorgeous face, and Kay bit back a smile. "But . . . I can kiss you because *I'm* not the one aboard the paddy wagon."

One brow rose. "Paddy wagon?"

She leaned across the console. "Shut up."

She kissed him.

From the moment her lips touched his, all was right in the world. His mouth had been slack with surprise, but he quickly recovered, sliding his hands into her hair, tugging her close, angling her head so they fit perfectly together. Kay might have been the one to initiate the kiss, but Garret was the one to own it.

To own *her*.

His tongue slipped inside, tangling with hers. Heat and moisture and . . . *fuck* but he could kiss good.

Not proper English in the slightest, and her editor would be appalled at her grammar. But as his hands trailed down her spine and his tongue slid in and out of her mouth in a rhythm that had her seeing stars, all she could think was—

Good.

More.

Naked.

Now.

And that was the moment Garret pulled back. He pushed out his door, walked around the front of his car, and opened hers.

He extended a hand, and her desire-addled brain had Kay trailing him mutely to the house. "Keys?" he asked once they'd stopped on the porch.

She blinked, pulled them out of her purse.

Garret snagged them from her, unlocked the door. Then he kissed her one more time, slipping a hand underneath her coat, wrapping it around her waist, and pulling her flush against him. His chest hard and his cock . . . well, *that* was hard, too. She arched, aching to be closer, for the thin layers of her dress and his clothes to disappear.

His hand slid a little lower, fingertips teasing the top of her ass, before he pulled back with a curse. "You'll be the death of me, sweetheart." And though he was breathing hard, his eyes danced. "Dangerous kisses. Assaulting me with paperbacks—"

Kay felt her cheeks go red. "I'll have you know, I'm not normally prone to violence."

A kiss to her forehead as he opened the door.

"I certainly deserved more than the potential risk of a paper cut."

He nudged her inside.

"It's ok—"

"Three months," he said softly and nudged her inside before closing the door, leaving them separated by the planks of wood. "Lock up." His voice was muffled.

She reached for the handle. "Garret—"

"*Lock up.*"

Kay sighed loud enough for him to hear, but her lips were curved.

She locked the door, pulled out her phone, scrolled down to Heather's number, and shot off a quick text.

"Garret?" she called as she waited.

"Yes?"

Buzz. Buzz.

Her fingers moved furiously across the keyboard . . . and *send*.

"Kay?"

"There's my number," she said.

"What—" He broke off, no doubt felt the buzz of the text she sent him "*Oh.*"

"Consider it supervised release."

He laughed, a loud guffaw that resounded through the door and warmed her heart.

"Goodnight, Garret."

"Goodnight, sweetheart."

She heard his footsteps as he crossed the porch and made his way down the steps. Then listened to the slam of the car door and the rev of the engine as it started up. Kay was just starting to shrug out of her coat when her cell buzzed.

Look in your right coat pocket.

"What?"

Her hand darted down, felt something hard and rectangular and—

She pulled out a book.

The book.

She opened it, surprised when a note fell out. Scooping it up from the floor, she unfolded it and read:

Sorry I was late rescuing you. I had something really important I needed to bid on. Heather promised the other books would be delivered next week sometime. I figured you would want to keep this one safe.
-G

When had he found time to write her a note?

But then she smiled, remembered Garret talking to the kid at the coat check stand. He'd been there awhile, longer than it should have taken to just pick up her jacket.

Sneaky man.

Wonderful man.

She held the book to her chest as she typed out a text.

Thank you. So, so much. Then before he could reply, she added, *I think you should be up to unsupervised release now.*

His response made her laugh aloud.

Two months and twenty-nine days.

SEVEN

Garret, Two months and twenty-eight days later

HE WHISTLED as he hopped up the stairs leading to Kay's house then softly knocked on the front door.

They'd fallen into a pleasant routine over the last few months. During the week, he'd pop over after work and they'd eat dinner together. On the weekends, they would hang out, walk around the city, go to the beach or see a movie. It was funny —in a crazy-because-it-felt-so-right-way rather than a funny-but-weird way—but since the night of the fundraiser they hadn't gone a day without seeing each other.

Garret liked that. A lot.

In fact, he loved it.

He loved *her*.

When his quiet knock wasn't answered—Garret used his key to let himself in. They'd learned a lot about each other over the last months, and one of the first things he'd needed to grasp—or risk the wrath of his woman—was that if Kay was writing she didn't like to be interrupted.

Typically, she'd be waiting for him when he got there, snuggled up in cute pajamas and a glass of wine in her hand as she answered the door.

But if she didn't answer the knock, that meant the muse was still talking and it was better for everyone—and most especially *him*—if he didn't interrupt Kay while she was working.

His first—and only—interruption hadn't been intentional. In fact, he'd been worried when she hadn't answered her door or her phone. Finally, after multiple rings of the bell, she'd pounded down the stairs, whipped open the door, and he'd learned the hard way to not interrupt the Beast—his teasing nickname for her author persona—at work. No way did he want to endure another round of glaring and grumbling.

She'd apologized later for being grumpy, and he'd teased her by threatening to put *her* on probation. But Garret got it. A jarring intrusion while working on something important was bound to make anyone cranky.

Smiling, he silently let himself into the house, closing and locking the door behind him.

He'd wait thirty minutes then order a pizza.

It hadn't taken him long to understand that the smell of pepperoni tended to lure Kay out of her writing cave.

Plan in mind, he was mentally patting himself on his back as he turned for the living room.

Only to stop halfway, his jaw falling open.

Kay stood on the bottom step, wearing only a pair of underwear and bra.

Lacy underwear.

A see-through bra.

His cock hardened, his pulse jumped, and he didn't think, just strode over, wrapped his arms around her waist, and lifted her up. Her mouth found his, tongues meeting, twining together, dancing in a pattern they'd perfected over the last months.

But this? Kay nearly naked in his arms?

They hadn't perfected *this*.

Probation wasn't up for another day.

Yes, he'd been counting.

Kay broke away, gasping for air as he kissed his way down her neck, trailed his mouth across her collarbone, nipped the top of one breast. She gasped, wound her hands into his hair to hold him in place and so he repeated the action, soothing it with a flick of his tongue before moving to her other breast.

Then somehow her bra disappeared—or rather, his mind hazed over the specific details of the undressing because suddenly, he had a gorgeous pair of breasts in front of him that he *needed* to get his mouth on.

"Yes," Kay said, tugging him toward one nipple. "Please, Garret. Oh *God. Yes*."

He switched sides as her hands reached for the button on his slacks, fumbling with the little circle until it slipped free and she was able to reach inside his boxer briefs to grip him.

Stars flashed behind his lids, his hips thrust forward, and he groaned.

He'd been imagining this for three long months, planning all the things he was going to do to make the night incredible and perfect and unforgettable for his woman. Yes, they'd touched each other, engaged in some seriously heavy petting, but it had all been through clothes. Garret had insisted on it, despite her pleas, despite his near perpetual blue balls, because he'd promised himself that he wouldn't sleep with Kay until she trusted him completely, whether that took three months or three years.

They'd spent many nights together, but he hadn't slept over.

They'd touched, but not skin to skin.

They'd kissed, but only from the throat up.

But last week, he'd finally seen it.

Kay's last wall had fallen, the final bit of distance she'd kept between them had disappeared, and Garret knew his patience— and hers—had all been worth it.

He trusted her like he'd never trusted another person. She knew everything about him, good and bad and in between, and . . . he loved her, more than he'd thought possible to love another person.

She was his heart. It was as simple as that.

And, as usual, this beautiful, wonderful, kind woman had surprised him.

This time it wasn't assault by novel or confronting him in a restaurant or getting locked in a bathroom stall.

Instead, she'd decided she'd had enough and was going after what she wanted.

"Garret?" she asked, stroking him and making every single one of his carefully laid out plans poof right out of his head.

"Yeah?" he gritted out, clambering for control and not finding it.

"Can we"—another stroke that had him groaning—"skip the foreplay. Just this once?"

His eyes shot to hers.

She shrugged. "We've kinda had three months of foreplay already."

Good point. *Excellent* point.

Garret nodded. "You're right." He swept her up into his arms, pounded up the stairs. He was inside her bedroom seconds later, tossing Kay onto the mattress, tearing off his clothes.

She slipped out of her panties, tossed them aside. Breathtakingly naked, Kay reached for a packet from her nightstand. "Catch." She lobbed it at him.

Gotta love a woman with a plan.

Garret caught the condom, tore it open, and rolled it on. He was on top of her by the next second, spreading her thighs, kneeling in between, and then . . . his heart had him pausing.

"You sure?" he asked.

Her eyes softened and she reached up to cup his jaw. "I'm sure."

"Good," he said and thrust inside. "Because I'm keeping you." Her eyes had flitted closed as he'd pushed home, lips parting on a moan, but at his words she peeled back her lids.

Warmth. This woman just imparted so much fucking warmth.

He looked at her and felt . . . everything.

Possessiveness, desire, heat . . . *love*.

She made him want to write sonnets and horrible love songs, to shout her name from rooftops.

"I love you," he said.

Her hand came up to rest on his chest, just over his heart. "I love you, too," she said, tears making the pretty brown of her irises glitter.

They stared at each other for a long moment. Then Kay shifted beneath him, hips undulating and sucking every rational thought from his mind. "I know I'm supposed to be the romance writer here, and I should be appreciating you and the loveliness of this moment, but can we appreciate it later?" She shifted again. "Because I *really* need you to move."

"Yeah?" He pulled out, slid back in.

She nodded. "Fuck now. Romance later."

Another thrust. Another shared moan.

"Words to live by?" he managed to ask.

"I'd rather live with you," she said.

"Me too, sweetheart, me too."

Then they weren't talking, or at least they didn't have any more room in their brains for talking. The moment became about sensation—for nerves to fire, for caresses and soft touches to leave goosebumps in their wake, for pleasure to build, orgasms to pull them each over into the abyss, and . . . for hearts to feel.

After, as they lay together, bodies intertwined, Garret knew *his* heart wouldn't ever belong to another.

Kay owned it.

And that was perfectly fine with him.

Thank you for reading! I hope you loved meeting the Billionaire's Club crew! The next book in the Billionaire's Club series is BAD HOOKUP. Find out what happens when Rachel's one-night stand shows back up and now she has to work with the insufferably sexy, pushy man...

CLICK HERE TO READ HOOKUP NOW>

And if you enjoyed BAD BILLIONAIRES, you'll love the sexy, sweet, and close-knit Breakers Hockey crew. The first book in the series, BROKEN, is now live!

"It is sexy, hot, adorable and such a fun read. You will not be able to put this down!" —Amazon Reviewer

Her life was a disaster...Don't miss the hilarious Life Sucks series, starting with TRAIN WRECK. Derek Cashette was determined to salvage the train wreck of her life...and she was just as determined *not* to let him be the hero.

DOWNLOAD TRAIN WRECK FOR FREE >

I so appreciate your help in spreading the word about my books, including sharing with friends! Please leave a review on your favorite book site!
You can also join my Facebook group, the Fabinators, for exclusive giveaways and sneak peeks of future books.

SIGN UP FOR ELISE FABER'S NEWSLETTER HERE:
https://www.elisefaber.com/newsletter

BAD DIVORCE

BILLIONAIRE'S CLUB BOOK 5

Get your copy at

https://www.elisefaber.com/bad-divorce

Bec

Bec closed the file she'd been working on and stretched her arms above her head. Her shoulders ached, her eyes burned—she gone way over the thirty minutes of continuous computer screen time her optometrist recommended—and she was the absolute last person left in the building.

Seriously.

Security had come by her office an hour before, telling her they'd locked up and the high-rise was empty.

Except for her.

She probably should have been lonely, being the singular human presence around, but Bec loved this time of night. It was after one, and she'd been in the office since six the previous morning working on a case that was preparing for trial.

But fuck, did she love finding a legal loophole in a contract and being the one to decisively close it.

Nothing was better than that.

Not being made partner several months before. Not the money or the power. Not having a slew of paralegals whose job it was to go line by line through all the paperwork pertinent to her cases and find loopholes like the one she'd just spent hours scouring for.

Those were all intoxicating in many ways.

But still, nothing topped the law itself.

The different interpretations, the way it morphed based on a court's or judge's decision, how it changed from year to year to year, even finding this particular loophole after all others before her had failed.

One lawyer to rule them all.

Snorting at her inner SciFi nerd—not that she'd had much spare time to indulge in any form of hobby as of late . . . okay, as of the last five years, if she was being honest—Bec knew it was all worth it. Law was her first love and it was a constantly shifting spider's web, a fragile and intricate and complex lover.

But it also made sense to her when so many other things in her world did not.

"And now I've killed my own buzz," she muttered before logging off of her computer, grabbing a stack of files from her desk, shoving them into her briefcase, and then slipping on her suit jacket and black pumps.

Down the elevator, through the locked door to the garage, and into her car.

Quiet.

So quiet.

She'd grown up in New York—or at least spent enough of her formative years in the Big Apple for her accent to reflect her time there—and felt more comfortable in big cities. San Francisco was a nice metropolis, but it had a definite sleepy time . . . or at least the district where her office was located did.

Normally, she liked that, preferred it over the way New York had always buzzed with activity.

But Bec had been . . . feeling weird as of late.

She was used to city life—the expensive rents, the exhaust fumes that hung in the air at all hours of the day, the horns and sirens and screeching brakes.

But this quiet? Fuck, did it hit her straight in the gut.

Or maybe it wasn't *quiet* so much as disquiet?

Bec was a simple woman. She didn't censor herself, didn't trouble over hurt feelings or someone's toes being stepped on. She took care of business in the quickest, most efficient way possible.

That was Rebecca Darden. What she was famous for—at least in the legal world.

No prisoners. Decisive. Smart as hell and not a fucking pushover.

She'd spent a lifetime studying and working and losing sleep and clawing and fighting and struggling against the pressures of being in a male-dominated field to become that woman.

And yet . . .

"Fuck," she muttered and turned on her car, making her way through the quieted city to her apartment. "I'm losing it."

Because she couldn't help but feel that now she'd finally met her goal of being partner, of being revered and feared and even sometimes reviled—all fine qualities in her opinion—that she was missing out on something.

There.

She'd said it.

Rebecca *fucking* Darden felt that somehow along the way of all her success that she'd missed out on *something*.

Unfortunately, she couldn't figure out what the fuck that *something* was.

A bigger challenge?

Nope. A month before, she'd taken on a case with impossible odds and had just that evening figured out how to win it.

Longer hours?

Hell no. At this point, she was paying for an apartment she was hardly ever in.

More money? No. She already had an obscene amount.

Better relationship with her parents? Nope. Things were fine at this point. Probably the most settled she'd ever been with them.

Different friends?

No fucking way. Her group of women—and now a few men —were the shit. They kept her sane and laughed at her jokes and were really incredible people.

She loved them and *that* was saying something, especially coming from her and her limited tolerance of bullshit. She didn't like easy, let alone *love* easily.

And she loved every one of them.

So what?

That was the fucking problem. She *didn't* know. Normally, she'd just turn that particular puzzle over in her mind until she figured it out, as she'd done with the contract that evening.

But she'd been turning this freaking enigma over in her mind for months and Bec was no closer to discovering the exact source of her unease.

"Boo fucking hoo," she murmured, pulling into her parking spot and making it up to her floor via her private elevator.

The lift went directly to her penthouse—yes, the apartment she hardly spent any time in was a ridiculously expensive penthouse—and required a code to access it.

So Bec really didn't expect to see another person waiting for her when the doors opened with a soft *ding* and she stepped off.

But there *was* another person waiting just outside her front door.

A person she never expected to see again.

Luke Pearson.

Her ex-husband.

It was one-fucking-thirty in the morning, and her ex-husband was sitting on the floor outside her apartment.

Asleep.

Fuming, she marched over to him and kicked his shoe. Hard.

"Luke," she snapped. "Why in the ever loving fuck are you here?"

His lids peeled back, sleepy green eyes met hers. "Becky," he murmured. "You're gorgeous as always." The drowsiness began to fade from his expression. "Did you just come from work?" He glanced down at his phone. "Do you know what time it is?"

"Of course, I know what time it is—" Bec bit back the words. Fuck, but wasn't this conversation an exact replica of the broken record one they'd had *way* too many times over the course of their relationship?

She crossed her arms. "Never mind that." A glare that had withered balls much bigger than Luke's "Why did you break into my apartment?"

He stood, towering over her. Once, Bec would have said that his size made her feel petite, feminine, soft, which was atypical for a giant Amazon such as herself. Today, it just pissed her off. She was tall for a women, almost six feet in heels, and was used to using that fact to her advantage.

No longer hunching her shoulders to appear shorter. Hell, no. She wore heels if she wanted and as high as she wanted—

And she had this man to thank for that fact.

"Stand tall, sugar pie," he used to say.

Yes, Luke had called her—world-famous, tough as shit lawyer—*sugar pie.*

But that had been long ago, when she'd been broken and . . .

Her heart, the one she liked to pretend didn't actually exist, throbbed pulsed with old hurt.

Because she'd merely been an entertaining side project for

him, a broken toy to fix, a puzzle to figure out and one to discard when he couldn't find a satisfactory answer.

Memories.

Aw.

Motherfucking memories.

"First, I didn't break into your apartment. This is the hall. Second," he hurried to add when she opened her mouth to argue semantics, "I didn't break in. You used our anniversary as the code."

Oh, for fuck's sake.

Well, she was changing that tomorrow . . . today . . . fuck, *yesterday*, now that—

"Go away, Luke," she said, pushing past him and unlocking her door while blocking his view of the keypad that was identical to that of the elevator. Her front door's code was *not* the date of her anniversary with her ex.

But Luke probably already knew that, given that he had been sitting on the floor of her hallway rather than on her couch, beer in hand, feet making prints on her glass coffee table.

Men.

Fucking men.

She slammed the door closed behind her and threw the dead bolt. The knock approximately one second later did not surprise her. Bec dropped her briefcase to the floor then opened it just enough to shoot angry eyes at him through the narrow gap the dead bolt allowed.

Serious green eyes fixed onto hers. "We need to talk."

"Luke," she snapped. "I'm exhausted. It's the middle of the night. I wouldn't have any patience to talk to my best friends right now, let alone my ex-husband."

"Funny story about that," he said, his lips curving. "Turns out that I'm not actually your *ex*-husband."

BAD FIANCÉ

Get your copy at

https://www.elisefaber.com/bad-fiance

Seraphina

SERA WAS GOING to lose her mind.

Or throw a fucking tantrum.

And see? There it was. A curse word.

Seraphina Delgado did *not* curse. It wasn't seemly or lady-like, and . . . she was a thirty-something-year-old woman who still saw her mother's disapproving face in her mind any time she dared utter a curse word.

Well, know what?

Fuck. Fuck. Fuckity-fuck.

There. *Ha.*

Mental diatribe somewhat satisfied, Sera turned to the source of her wannabe tantrum.

Tate Conner.

Tech genius. Real estate client—

Or, rather, *former* real estate client because he was a giant pain in her as—*tush*.

Congrats, Mom. I sound like a four-year-old.

But Tate Conner had become a *former* client because he *was* such a pain. He didn't like any of the houses she'd selected, and he never showed up for appointments. In fact, she'd lost count of how many times he had *forgotten* about a scheduled showing after number twelve.

So yeah, she'd kissed away any hope of a giant commission and told Tate they would no longer be working together.

That had been four months ago.

And now he was here in her office, looking all . . . Tate-like.

Super helpful description, she knew, but it just wasn't fair. Weren't these tech guys supposed to be nerdy and unattractive? Because Tate Conner *definitely* didn't fit that description.

He was tall and lean but strong. Months ago while en route to one of the appointments he'd actually made, Sera had gotten a flat tire. She'd managed to get her car to the showing then had called AAA, and Tate had shown up while the man was struggling with her lug nut—poor phrasing, but so not the point. *Anyway*, he'd approached the tow truck driver, tweaked the angle of the wrench, and the nut had popped right off.

Again, more poor phrasing, but—

Sera mentally shook herself.

He'd claimed it was all about leverage, but she'd seen the way his muscles had rippled under his T-shirt. He was strong, and she could tell it was more of a natural strength rather than a result of spending loads of time in the gym.

Want to know the worst part?

Besides the whole strong and as tall as her—hard to do considering she was over six feet—Tate was also pretty.

Really pretty.

A chiseled jawline, a straight nose, lips that were totally kissable, and a pair of dimples that only made the rare appearance.

He also had the prettiest blue eyes she had ever seen and sandy blond hair that was more appropriate on a surfer than an executive.

That hair had been her undoing. Well, that *and* his brain. He was the head of a huge tech company, brilliant, and—insert a long mental sigh here—he was also funny. Tate had a quiet wit that never failed to make her smile.

So, as she always did, Sera had fallen in love.

Fallen fast. Fallen hard.

For a man who had absolutely zero interest in her.

Her friends—none of whom had ever dreamed about finding their happy endings and several of whom had been decidedly against them, she felt required to point out—were all married or paired off. Abby had babies. CeCe was due any day, and—

Sera was alone, pining after a man who'd created the latest social media craze.

Yup. Her life was *ah-maz-ing*.

Tate cleared his throat, and Sera realized she'd been staring at him dumbfounded for a good couple of minutes.

"I'm sorry, Mr. Conner." She stood, forcing herself to shake his hand. "I was woolgathering."

Sparks. The moment their skin touched, she felt *actual* sparks.

Just like every time before.

And just like every time before, she was the only one affected.

He smiled—eliciting more sparks, because her body was a stupid jerk—and said, "I've been known to do that from time to time."

Sera indicated for him to sit in the chair in front of her desk as she sank into her own chair. He continued to stand, but she started talking anyway, desperate to get this conversation over with. "How can I help you today?" she asked. "I do hope"—*Do hope? What was she, British? Ugh.*—"I-uh . . . I hope you were able to find a house. The agents I passed along are very good at finding unique properties, and I even gave them a few locations to start with . . . " She bit her lip, attempting to stop the ramble.

"No."

Just no.

Um. Okay.

He lifted a hand, rubbed the back of his neck. The movement made his shirt lift, exposing several inches of flat stomach and tan skin and, oh God, a trail of blond hair leading south. Her mouth watered, desperate to trace that path with her tongue—

Sera sucked in a breath, popped to her feet.

"Ah. I'm sorry." She picked up a random file, pretending to know what was in it. "I'm actually really busy, so this will have to continue another time."

Like never.

She rounded her desk, forced a smile. "Mr. Conner," she said when he didn't move. "I'll have my assistant schedule something soon."

"Seraphina."

She shivered at the sound of her name on his lips—soft, a little raspy, and deep enough to conjure all sorts of unhelpful fantasies in her mind.

Shaking herself, she moved to open the door.

Suddenly, Tate was there, hand on hers, body inches away, spicy scent inundating her senses.

Sera's breath caught. "What are you—?"

He seemed to be arguing with himself then finally, those piercing blue eyes locked onto hers. "I need you to marry me."

BAD BOYFRIEND

Get your copy at

https://www.elisefaber.com/bad-boyfriend

Kelsey

"WHO IS IT THEN?" she asked through stiff lips.

Because it couldn't be. Her brother didn't know about them. She'd made sure of it. They'd kept things on the down-low and . . . then she'd nursed her broken heart two thousand miles away in college.

"Tanner."

Her gut twisted.

Double fuck.

And a shit for good measure.

"That's fine, right?" Bas asked. "You guys seemed to get along great." Concern rippled across his face. "Is there something wrong. Did—"

"No," she said quickly. "That's great. I'm sorry. I'm just preoccupied with my new project."

He grinned. "Always work with you."

She blew him a kiss. "You know it."

"Great. So you'll be paired up with him. And I know it's been a while, but he's coming into town next week to catch up." He tapped the roof of her car, took a step back. "You want to grab dinner with us?"

"I'd love too," she lied before getting into her car and with a wave that hopefully didn't show her dismay, Kelsey drove away.

Paired up with Tanner.

Been there, done that.

Got the souvenir broken heart.

Triple fuck.

BAD BLIND DATE

Trix

BUT JET HAD BROKEN HER.

He was the *one* man she'd let in, with whom she'd shared her past and hopes, her pain and desires. So maybe he wouldn't understand how important what she'd shared was because she'd spent so long being closed down with everyone around her. Maybe he couldn't have realized how hard it had been for her to give what she'd given. But part of her felt like . . . he *should* have known. Especially since he'd shown about as much care with her exposed and vulnerable heart as a physician tossing a soiled bandage onto the floor.

For a nurse to pick up.

Because that was all she'd ever been to him.

A convenient place to stash his dick before he'd tossed her aside, dirty and used, and she had to cobble herself together enough to throw away those pathetic hopes she'd been hanging on to.

"Trixie," he murmured.

She smiled brightly and picked up the menu. "I've heard the prickly pear margaritas are delicious," she announced to the table at large.

As she knew it would, that turned the conversation to Kelsey, who had proclaimed her love of the cocktail far and wide as they'd all chatted a few minutes before. This jumpstarted the bantering with the table at large, and pretty soon, the waiter came over to take their orders.

All through dinner, she managed to keep the conversation light, to keep her physical and verbal distance from Jet while still pretending to get to know him enough to satisfy the others at the table.

Her fatal flaw began when she slipped away to use the bathroom.

Because when she came out, Jet was standing in the hall.

Sniffing, she started to move past him.

His hand on her arm stilled her.

"What, Jet?" she snapped. "What could you possibly have to say to me?"

A growl. "Nothing."

"Good."

"*Everything.*"

He kissed her, and the world went topsy-turvy.

BAD WEDDING

Get your copy at
https://www.elisefaber.com/bad-wedding

Molly

BAKING WAS HER FAVORITE.

The people weren't bad either. She loved getting to know them, to see them change, their lives grow full and happy, their kids get older. She loved *feeding* people, even if they weren't regulars.

There was absolutely nothing better than seeing someone's happy smile when they bit into something tasty.

Speaking of, the bell above the door tinkled as her first customer of the day strode into the bakery.

"I'll be with you in a second," she called, continuing to fill the case with lemon muffins.

"I did always love to see you like this."

Molly jumped, eyes shooting up.

It had been so long since she'd heard that voice.

I love taking bites out of you.

It had rumbled back then, too, rasping along her skin, skating down her spine, and making her shiver.

The first man she'd baked for.

The man who'd given her the money to open this place.

The one who'd *named* it.

And the one who'd left her at the altar. In the white dress. With the venue booked. With the caterer and the DJ set up. With the guests packing the pews on both sides of the isle.

Jackson Davis.

Jackson *Fucking* Davis.

"Jackson," she murmured and slid the back of the case closed.

"I'm back, honey."

She'd regret her actions later, but in that moment, with the memories of the full church and the people and their pitying expressions and *this man*. Not. Fucking. Showing. Up.

Molly snapped.

She threw the baking sheet at his head.

BAD ENGAGEMENT

Get your copy at
https://www.elisefaber.com/bad-engagement

Kate

IT WAS JUST . . . Christmas.

All of her family in one place. The huge party with the whole neighborhood. Everyone paired off and happy and gathering under the mistletoe her mother hung in each and every doorway.

And her.

Alone.

The pitying gazes plentiful.

Or worse . . . the copious conversations where all the happy people constantly threw every single male with half a brain cell in Kate's direction.

My cousin is in town and fresh out of a relationship . . .

I have a coworker who's new to the area. He's looking for someone . . .

My ex-husband would be perfect for you—no really, he's actually a great guy . . .

And more.

Kate just couldn't take it, couldn't stand the idea of another Christmas party at her parents' house matched with someone who didn't fit her, or worse, spending the entire extravaganza alone and in the corner, playing wallflower.

She wanted excitement.

She wanted someone who could be unequivocally hers.

She wanted someone who saw inside her and didn't run off in a panic.

". . . and Katie, love, he's going to be at dinner this Friday so that you two can get to know each other better—"

Fucking hell.

Family dinner *and* the Christmas Extravaganza?

Please. God. *No.*

"Um, Mom—"

"Remember he's got all his hair—"

"Actually, Mom. I'm kind of seeing—"

"And his stomach doesn't hang over his belt—"

"That's not—I don't really care about that—"

"*And* he's got the loveliest blue—"

"I'm engaged!" she screamed, cutting off her mother's soliloquy of all things doctor, and successfully drawing the attention of random strangers on the sidewalk. Which was a hard thing to do in San Francisco—because it was San Francisco, and these streets had seen a lot of shit—but also could only further confirm that she'd screamed it like a complete and total lunatic.

Shrieking *I'm engaged* on street corners.

What every man wanted.

It was a wonder she was single.

"Katie?" her mom asked. "Did you say you're engaged?"

No. No, she wasn't. Not even close. She was on a break from anyone with a Y chromosome, mostly to save them from herself.

But also . . . there was joy in her mom's tone.

Absolute joy that she had never heard directed at her. She'd heard it leveled toward her siblings. To her brother, when he'd announced he was proposing to Steph, who was really fucking cool and way too good for her brother—something he'd be the first to admit . . . because he was really fucking cool. She'd heard it expounded lavishly again at his wedding this last summer (during which Kate had spent her time fending off the worst setup of all setups, The Can't Take No For An Answer Setup). And obviously, it had rung with crystal clarity in her ears when her sister had announced she was pregnant, and again after her adorable niece had been born.

But her mom had *never* given it to Kate.

Which was probably the reason she let the crazy keep rolling along instead of stopping the joy in its tracks with truth.

Why instead of saying, "No, Mom. You heard wrong," she said, "Yes, I am, and you'll get to meet him Friday at dinner."

Horror flowed through her as intensely as her mother's excitement poured through the airwaves, expressing her *joy* at meeting him, her *joy* at Kate having finally found a slice of her own happy.

"What's his name, honey?"

Oh fuck.

"What's that?" Kate asked, panic swarming to overtake horror. "You're breaking up."

Oh shit. *Oh shit.* She hadn't thought this through. She needed—

"I asked his name—"

"Hello?" More panic. More horror. More pretending the call was cutting out because she had to end this conversation now. Hell, she should have never picked up the call in the first place. "Mom? *Hello?*"

"Katie!"

Shit. Shit. *Shit.* "I can't hear you," she said. "If you can hear me, I'll call you later." She hung up.

Call her later.

Ha.

More like never.

As in, she'd *never* call her family again. As in, she was moving to a deserted island and changing her name and living off the grid in a tent with the most technically advanced thing being one of those compostable toilets.

Fuck.

She hated camping.

Which meant . . . she'd be there at the family dinner.

Because despite all of the setups and the pity and the fact that they'd found their happy, she loved her family. So. Damned. Much. And she also loved that stupid fucking Christmas party, even when she was lonely.

"*Ugh.*" Kate groaned, feet sliding to a stop on that dirty San Franciscan sidewalk.

She had a choice here.

She also knew she wasn't going to make the right one.

Because, instead of calling her mother back and telling her that she wasn't engaged, Kate opened Instagram, tapped on the profile of a man she'd been following for a while now, who'd followed her back and commented on a few of her posts, and . . . sent a message.

Later, she'd want to pretend she'd been drinking.

But in *that* moment, the only thing she was consumed with was desperation.

And lust. She couldn't deny lust was also her downfall.

Because surprisingly, shockingly, *insanely* the man from social media, the one whose abs had made her fall just a little in love with him, who had an actual man bun, but not one of those gross, greasy ones that looked like octopus tentacles—a nice one, sleek and shiny and way better than any bun she could wrestle her own locks into. But anyway, that handsome stranger . . .

He said yes.

And suddenly, Kate had a fiancé.

BAD BRIDESMAID

Heidi

SHE WAS WEARING a violet bridesmaid's dress and holding a leash.

Not the strangest sentence ever uttered.

Unless, perhaps she included what was on the other end of the leash.

Because she'd been escorted down the aisle by a rooster name Sir Fuzzy McFeatherston, or Fuzz for short.

He was cute. He was cocky—*ha*—and he was not happy to be on a leash.

Heidi sniffed and dashed away a tear as the officiant declared the newlyweds officially married before they strode down the aisle hand-in-hand.

And she strode—hand-in-leash?—with a rooster.

Well, if that wasn't an apt description of her dating life . . . she didn't know what was. She could find a man who wanted to sleep with her—*cough*, cock—but couldn't find one with staying power.

"Not the point," she muttered under her breath, somehow getting herself and Sir Fuzzy McFeatherston safely down the aisle, the rest of the bridal party pairing off and following her.

They snapped some pictures, but eventually the Fuzz got tired of the paparazzi and Heidi wrestled him into her arms and took him to the crate Kate had ready for him.

She was just bending to stick him inside, trying to slip off the harness without letting him escape when she felt someone come up behind her. Assuming it was Kate, she said, "I'm fine, Katie girl. Go enjoyed your husband. I've got your"—she giggled, a twelve-year-old at heart—"cock well in hand."

Silence instead of her friend's cackling.

Shit.

Heat stained her cheeks, and Heidi yanked the leash and harness out before slamming and locking the cage. Then she shored her spine and spun around.

Tall. Dark. A smirk on a gorgeous mouth.

One that grew as his gaze traced her down then up. "Sure you can handle that cock, baby?"

She *had* handled that cock.

Six months ago, Jaime's brother Brad had stopped in the Bay Area for a quick visit, and she'd had a few too many glasses of wine. He'd offered her a ride home . . . and then he'd given her a fucking *ride*.

So yeah, she'd had that cock, and, she couldn't lie, it had been *incredible*.

But . . . he'd been gone before she'd woken the next morning.

And she might be tough on the outside, she might be a strong, independent woman who hadn't been expecting a ring and a relationship, but she'd thought she at least warranted a note or a text or a fucking goodbye.

Heidi sniffed. "I've handled plenty of cocks in my life," she said, chin lifting, eyes narrowing. "And none are more than I can handle."

She pushed past him.

He snagged her arm.

She yanked it free, stepped back when he went to grab her again. "Don't," she snapped. "Just because I made a mistake once doesn't mean I'm easy prey now."

A cocky—no pun intended—smile. "Mistake? I happened to think we were—"

"*That* was your mistake," she said, glaring. "*Thinking*."

Pretty hazel eyes flared. "Baby—"

"Not your baby."

A sigh. "Heidi."

"Yes, Brad, groomsman, who should be paying attention to his brother's wedding instead of bothering a woman who *isn't interested*?" It wasn't a sweet question, for as sickly saccharine as her tone was.

"I think—"

She rolled her eyes. "Not *that* again."

Heidi didn't mean to, but it all happened so fast.

Brad grabbed her arm.

She shoved him back at the same time the crate door burst open and Sir Fuzzy McFeatherston shot out of the pen.

The rooster took off running.

Brad lost his footing, crashed into a waiter, who was carrying a large tray of appetizers.

The food went flying.

Brad went flying . . . into the cake table.

Sir Fuzzy McFeatherston went flying, feathers scattering in all directions.

The tray came down.

And Heidi didn't think she'd ever forget the sound of it colliding with Brad's head.

Nor how much joy it gave her.

At least until she turned back for the bridal party, promptly tripped over the fucking rooster . . . and ended up sprawled across Brad's chest.

Fuck, she loved that chest.

BAD SWIPE

Get your copy at
https://www.elisefaber.com/bad-swipe

Stef

"MARRY ME, FRED," she murmured, tugging her man close and wrapping her arms around him.

He nuzzled into her throat, his warm breath on her skin—

And then started licking her face.

Full stop.

With completely unattractive, smelly breath.

"Ick," she grumbled, burying her face in her pillow to get away from her eighty-five-pound golden retriever.

The only man in her life.

He was hairy, had the aforementioned smelly, doggy breath, but he was loyal and didn't cheat. So, although he would go home with anyone who offered him the smallest morsel of food, his tail always went propellor when he saw her, and he always nuzzled close, especially when she was feeling down.

Yeah, she picked up his shit and waited on him hand and foot.

But how was that different from anyone she'd ever dated?

Spoiler alert . . . it wasn't.

Fred continued licking, thinking her burying herself into her pillows was now the best game ever and attacking her in earnest.

"Okay," she said, pushing him off and sitting up. "Do you want breakfast?"

Breakfast being the magic word, since it sent Fred sprinting from the bed and skidding toward the kitchen, his claws clicking on the tile loudly enough that she could mentally track his path the entire way.

Sighing, she tossed the covers back. She needed to get up anyway, to take Fred on his walk, and then get him off to doggy day care before she headed into work.

Carefully, she shifted out of bed, wincing a bit when she put weight on her ankle.

She'd broken her ankle a few months before—well, Fred and his obsession with a squirrel had been the cause of her injury—and it was still a bit weak and tender. Because of that, she was still going to physical therapy, even though the cast had been off for a while now, and her doc said that she might have to undergo another surgery at some point to remove her "jewelry."

That jewelry being the six screws and two plates currently freeloading their way around town in her body.

And causing her pain when she walked too far or stood too long or, really, just turned in the wrong direction. So truly, it hurt most of the time unless her ass was parked on her plush gray couch or propped up in bed on the special pillow that her friend Heidi had bought for her right after her surgery.

Ah, to be a woman in her thirties.

Sadly single.

Hobbling like a motherfucker.

Pretty soon she'd be bent in half like an old crone, sporting a bedazzled cane. Which—she paused, considered that—might be cool. She could see herself rocking some rainbow sparkles.

They'd go perfectly with her numerous T-shirts and skinny jeans (*and* side part, so take *that*, Gen Z!).

Before she could go too far down her obsession with TikTok, Fred whipped back against the corner, bull in a china shop style.

"Sit!" she ordered, and since he was a good boy, he did just that. Unfortunately because he was eighty-five pounds and had been moving at approximately the speed of light, his sitting didn't mean he actually stopped moving forward.

His ass hit the floor.

His body kept sliding . . . right into the wall.

"Oh, Fred," she murmured as he righted himself just as quickly, sliding some more, his nails clicking on the tile like he was a tapdancing crab until he was finally sitting in front of her.

His tail thumping on the floor.

She stepped by him, careful to not mention the b-word (breakfast), in case he did some more slip and sliding and took her out.

And she did not need *that* on a Monday morning.

"Come on," she said, once she was out of the line of fire, because—like the good boy he was—Fred had waited where she'd told him to sit. And aside from his squirrel obsession, he really *was* a good boy. He was just big and clumsy and all legs and no sense of balance.

Like her.

Ha.

He danced around her legs as she scooped his food, added his vitamins, and then a scoop of supplements that kept his teeth clean and was supposed to battle that doggy breath of his.

Stef wasn't convinced that it helped.

Or it could be a million times worse without it.

Either way, it wasn't something she was going to find out.

Then she sprinkled some shredded chicken because Fred was her boy and yes, he was spoiled as hell.

Once his bowl was in front of him and he was scarfing it down, she got the coffee going, and the moment the bitter, smokey fumes hit her nose, she started feeling less like a Monday Monster and more like an actual human being.

Bagel in the toaster.

Cinnamon cream cheese on the counter.

Plate from the cupboard beside it.

To-go mug open and ready to be filled.

Other mug put in place of the pot and filled with the steaming brew. She took a large sip as her bagel toasted, enough to further chase the Mondays away, and then when it was done, she set about slathering on the cream cheese and doing her level best to replace her blood with the spicy, tangy spread.

It was her absolute favorite.

She bought it by the tub at the local bakery—now bakery chain—Molly's.

And by *the tub*, she meant by the *double* tub, because she always (always!) had a spare container in her fridge.

A girl never knew when she might need a spoonful to chase away the reality of being thirty-five and her longest relationship being with a furry, non-human male who liked to pee on fire hydrants.

Sufficiently caffeinated, she went to pull on a pair of sweats and her tennis shoes then tugged her hair back into a ponytail.

The moment she pulled out the leash, Fred stopped licking his bowl. A walk was the only thing that would convince him to get up because he lived his life alternating between thinking he hadn't gotten every last drop from his dish and worrying that he would never ever eat again.

"Come on, buddy," she said as he trotted over, clipping on his leash and reaching for her oversized hoodie.

They'd do a quick turn around the block and then she'd

come back and shower, bundle him into the car for doggy day care, take herself to work, and it would be another glorious Monday.

"Joy of joys," she muttered.

But truthfully, she didn't mind the walk, didn't mind the cool morning air on her face, the quiet of the neighborhood. There weren't many cars on the road at this hour, not with the sun still mostly below the horizon, and it was a peaceful way to start her morning.

Just her and her man.

Smiling when Fred did a little butt wiggle as they moved down the front steps of her condo, she set them on a quick pace as they turned right, looped down through the dew-covered grass in the small park at the end of the street, then back up a block over, before turning onto her street and completing their loop.

His tongue hanging out, Fred sprinted back over to his bowl the moment she opened the door and took off the leash, returning to the business of licking up every last crumb.

Stef flicked the lock and headed into the bathroom to shower.

Was *mid*-shower with shampoo suds dripping down her spine when the doorbell rang.

She ignored it.

Continued washing her hair.

It rang again.

Sighing, since she'd just slathered conditioner on, she kept the water running—yeah, yeah, she knew about the drought, but also, she knew it would take even more water to warm up her shower since her water heater sucked ass—snagged a towel, wrapped it around her head, grabbed her robe, and made her way to the front door . . . just as the bell rang for a third time.

A glance through the peephole made her want to spin around and head right back into the shower.

But she also knew that the knocking wouldn't stop.

Not with Jeremy.

Girding her loins, she unlocked and opened the door. "Yes?" she asked, purposefully blocking the opening so he couldn't just stroll his way into her place. He'd lost that privilege when he'd unceremoniously dumped her months before.

"Where is it?" he snapped, shoving at the door so roughly that she stumbled back a step.

Fred spun around the corner, nails clicking, excitement at seeing a new person—any new person, and especially one who'd occasionally fed him in the past—fueling his barreling. "Wait," she ordered before he could burst out the front door and take her on a sprint through the neighborhood.

He waited, skidding to a stop.

She grabbed the door, pushed the panel back, returning it to its previous position of only being open a crack. "What are you talking about, Jeremy?"

"I'm asking where it is," he growled. "And I'm asking where it is *right now*."

Water was dripping down her spine. The cool air that had felt good on her face earlier now felt like shit because she was wet from the shower and fucking freezing. "What the hell are you talking about?"

A sharp sigh. "You know."

Why had she been forced onto this particular merry-go-round so fucking early on a Monday morning?

Did the universe hate her?

Was the god of evil ex-boyfriends determined to make her life miserable?

"No, Jeremy," she said, grasping at the straws of her calm. "I *don't* know. However, if you'd clue me into what you're looking for, I'm happy to tell you."

Silence.

Narrowed eyes and a clenched jaw. God, once she'd thought he was the handsomest man she'd ever laid eyes on. But now as she was looking at him, she could only see an angry, sad man and wonder how in the hell had she wasted so much time being upset about the breakup.

"Vase. Blue with white flowers."

She frowned, searching her brain, before remembering that she did, in fact, have the vase. It was sitting on top of her bookcase and was actually quite pretty. One of the few things that Jeremy had bought her that she'd actually liked. But, "You gave me that for our anniversary."

His lips pressed flat. "My mom gave it to me. She's flying in today."

Stef read between the lines. He needed it back or his mom would freak the fuck out, and . . . here her petty streak came out because it was so tempting to refuse, knowing that Jeremy would get an earful from his uber-controlling, feelings-hurt-at-the-drop-of-a-hat mother.

It would be glorious.

But . . . *here* her rational streak came out. If she fought Jeremy over this, he would stay, and he wouldn't give up. He'd browbeat her into giving it back, or at the very least, he would annoy the shit out of her until she was so fed up that she chucked it at him.

And then she'd have glass in her entryway, and she'd be further contributing to the drought because she would have another delay returning to her shower.

Namely having to clean up the glass.

Still, it was tempting . . .

Fred whined.

Reminding her that her pupper would eventually lose all self-control and really burst out the front door, equaling more shower delays.

Lastly, now that she remembered the vase and knew that it hadn't been a gift from Jeremy but rather a regift from his mother, the pretty blue container had lost most of its appeal.

"Wait here," she said.

He narrowed his eyes.

She repeated, more firmly this time, "*Wait* here."

Then she closed the door, threw the lock, and moved to the bookcase. It wasn't far, thus, it didn't take her very long to retrieve it, but Jeremy was already knocking again by the time she made it back to the entryway.

God, why did she have such horrible taste in men?

Sigh.

She flicked open the lock, turned the handle, and thrust the vase at Jeremy. "Anything else?"

He scrambled to hold on to it. "Um . . . no."

"Good." She narrowed her eyes. "If you show up on my porch again, banging on my door, I *will* call the police."

Jeremy's lips parted, anger flooding his blue eyes.

"You remember I have another vase or something else, you text, and I'll get it to you when it's convenient for me." Her voice was harder than it had ever been, and she saw the surprise trailing over his expression. Good. The only positive from this morning's call was that Stef was now certain there wasn't a speck of longing inside her for this man. "Now, go home."

"Stef," he began, and she would have to have been an idiot to not miss the sudden interest in his face.

Nor the way his eyes went to her breasts.

As though the first sign of her temper—which she could truthfully admit wasn't something she'd ever shown him, even in their two years together—was a turn-on.

But seriously, yeah. No.

Maybe she'd been so invested in making the relationship work that she'd hidden parts of herself. Okay, no *maybe* about it. That was the truth. She'd definitely hidden whole facets of herself in order to keep things smooth sailing with Jeremy.

Pathetic. It really was.

Well, no more.

She slammed the door, not caring that it was close to his face, not caring if it *hit* his face.

Then she threw the lock and went back to her shower.

Shutting the door on Jeremy, on the person she'd been with him. Forever.

And good riddance.

For the record, her shower was absolutely divine.

BAD GIRLFRIEND

Tammy

Are you really breaking up with me via text?

Tammy winced as she read the text message and started to set down her cell.

But it vibrated again.

While I'm in your bathroom?

She winced. Okay, so her timing wasn't ideal.

Sighing, she tugged the covers back and pulled on her robe. Her frumpy, holey, old flannel robe that absolutely dwarfed her and was so unappealing that it had run off more than her fair share of men.

Which was why she only pulled it out for very special occasions.

Her period when she felt horrible and crampy and exhausted and just wanted to veg on the couch and pretend that her uterus wasn't shredding itself to pieces.

The other very special occasion?

This.

The inevitable breakup.

The bathroom door cracked open as she was belting her robe, and a very pretty—probably too pretty for her—man walked out. Naked. She picked up his clothes, turned them right side out, and handed them to him.

"This is me breaking up with you," Tammy said. "Not in the bathroom," she added when he opened his mouth to say something she didn't want him to say, didn't want to *hear* him say. "Not that we were together in the first place."

"We've been sleeping together for three months."

She lifted a brow. "We've been *fucking* together. That's it. That's what I made clear from the moment I brought you home from Bobby's."

"That's not—" His face crumpled and she allowed herself to feel like shit for a moment.

Just a moment.

Because she'd been clear with him.

But also like shit because clearly she'd fucked up, and he was hurting and that was on her. She wasn't a monster. She didn't like people feeling crappy, especially because of something she did.

Liking it or not, she still had to end this.

The longer it went on, the more he would expect her to give, and the more she would feel like she was kicking a puppy.

Good times.

Which was why she pulled her shroud of bitch around her.

"It's not?" she asked archly, yanking it tight, buttoning it up for good measure. They'd discussed this that first night, and again after, when it had been so good neither of them wanted just one time together. They'd talked about it many times over the last twelve weeks—that this was for mutual pleasure and not building a connection—never building a connection—and they'd usually done it when her instincts had prickled and told her that he might be feeling more than her.

She should have listened to her gut.

But he'd said all the right things, given her all the right reassurances.

And he was seriously talented at giving her orgasms.

But tonight had been different.

He'd made it clear they weren't just fuck buddies—or he didn't see *her* as a fuck buddy, while nothing about him had changed for her.

She wanted pleasure.

She wanted fun.

She didn't want a possessive, growly male who thought it was his right to claim her time and body—even if he was pretty.

"We've been together for three months—"

"Not together."

"We've..." He trailed off, probably realizing where he'd gone wrong.

"What?" she asked baldly, though not cruelly. She knew she needed to be firm in order for this to be a clean break. Clear boundaries. Not bending or giving in because that just made everything worse when it inevitably came down to this. "What?" she repeated when he didn't speak. "You thought you'd change my mind, even though I've made it clear I'm not interested in a relationship?" Catching herself fussing with the tie on her robe, she forced herself to stop, to not reveal this was uncomfortable, that she didn't like doing this. No cracks in her armor for him to slip back in. "We have fun together. I like your cock. I like *you*, but I don't want a boyfriend, and that's what you're trying to be. So, it's gotta be done, Adam."

"I—" He broke off again, and she pointed to the clothes. His shoulders straightened, and his expression went from hurt to mulish and—sigh, he was going to make this even harder. "You like me. We could be good together. I love—"

Panic washed over her, and quickly she shook her head, throwing her hand up, cutting him off with a sharp order. "Get dressed." Then she moved to the bedroom door, cloaking herself in sharp words before he got the rest of that statement out. "I'll clue you in," she said, zipping up the shroud of bitch jacket, pulling up her bitch pants, slipping her feet into bitch socks and shoes for good measure. "You're just upset because you're the one who usually ends things, add in that you're used to women fawning all over you because you're pretty." A beat. "And you are. You're gorgeous."

His face had changed from mulish to pained to gentle during her speech. When she called him gorgeous, that expression became determined.

Uh-oh.

"Just a little more time," he murmured, coming close and stroking his knuckles down her throat in the way that always made her shiver. He bent, trailed his lips along her jaw, and Tammy remembered why she'd brought him home in the first place.

And she almost gave in...

Almost.

Because the man had a cock that was...

"Please, love," he murmured. "I need—"

That snapped her out of it. He needed what she couldn't give him. What she wouldn't ever be able to give him. She couldn't be open in a way that would make him happy, and eventually, he would choose someone else.

It would be much less messy to end things now.

She gripped his shoulders, and though it was tempting to draw him near, to have one more time, she knew she couldn't.

Tammy shoved him back. "I'm done."

He reached for her again. "But—"

She shoved him away. Again. "*Done*," she repeated, having done this too many times to do anything but end it here and now. Adam was a nice guy, and she'd kept him around for so long because he'd seemed on board to be a fuck buddy, but tonight... tonight he'd been different.

Tonight he'd made love to her.

Tonight hadn't been about mutual attraction.

He had feelings for her, and she couldn't let that stand. Better to cut ties now before he grew even more attached, before things got messier.

"Get dressed," she said again, exiting the bedroom and walking down the hall, moving to the front door.

It was better to be by an exit.

That made things less complicated...and easier to slam and lock the door.

A minute later, Adam emerged from the bedroom, shoving his cell and wallet into his pocket, his eyes blazing, but his expression gentle again. His lips parted as he lifted his arms, prepared to take her in his arms.

Fuck.

She sidestepped, gripped the doorknob, and opened the door.

"Bye, Adam," she murmured.

"Baby, come on," he pleaded, taking a step toward her. "We'd be good together."

"No," she said, stifling a sigh. This was seriously getting old fast. "We wouldn't."

"You like me."

She clenched her jaw. "Look, you're a nice guy, but—"

He came close, lowered his head, mouth closing in.

She put up her hand, pushed him back. "No."

"Tammy—"

"It's not you. It's me."

That finally seemed to penetrate, probably since it was such a shitty line, such a crappy thing to say. But at least it had the result of Adam backing away, his eyes furious. "Seriously?"

Tammy just lifted her brows.

He made a disgusted sound, but she was far too well-versed in this to feel guilty.

"Goodbye, Adam," she said.

A shake of his head, but he didn't say anything further, just walked down the steps.

She watched him get into his car, screech out of her driveway.

Sigh. Now she'd need to find a new source of orgasms. Rolling her shoulders, she started to turn to go back inside.

"It's not you, it's me?"

That voice was silk brushing along her thighs, dipping up to test the moisture between them. It was heat in her abdomen, fingers grazing her nipples. It was...instant sexual attraction, the same heady feeling she'd experienced the moment she'd laid eyes on Fletcher King. Eyes catching his as she'd strode to her office, desire pooling as she took in those blazing blue irises, his dark brown hair, so dark that it was nearly black. She'd clocked sexy stubble, a built body, and a great smile.

But he wanted *it*.

It being a real relationship, a girlfriend, a wife, and the picket fence. *It* being everything she couldn't give, because she wasn't a relationship, girlfriend, or wife and picket fence kind of woman. She'd heard him talk about *it* at work, heard the sadness in his words when he and his ex had broken things off.

She, on the other hand, wanted freedom.

More than she wanted the gorgeous man standing in front of her now.

"What are you doing here, Fletcher?"

"I need a favor."

The refusal was already on her lips. A favor that brought her sexy co-worker to her house on a weekend certainly didn't bode well for her.

But then he smiled, and she actually had to force her knees to lock so she didn't melt into a puddle, and...*that* right there illustrated just how much she didn't want to be in a relationship.

Because she'd been resisting this attraction with Fletch for an entire year.

Locking her knees, ignoring the melting, denying the temptation of him.

But that sexy smile, highlighted by the setting sun, the warm lights of her porch...undid her.

That sexy smile had her refusal staying lodged in her throat.

That smile had her saying...*yes*.

Eventually.

BAD BEST FRIEND

Get your copy at
https://www.elisefaber.com/bad-best-friend

Cora

CHEETOS WERE REALLY the best thing on the planet.

Okay, maybe not the *best* thing.

Because she *could* list a few things that were better than the faux cheese crunchy deliciousness—those being her mom's chocolate pecan pie, the croissants from Molly's in her new hometown (San Francisco had a lot of perks compared to the small suburban city that she had grown up in, not the least of which were the delicious treats from her favorite bakery), and sitting at home in her fuzziest socks while watching the Hallmark channel on repeat.

Those were all better than Cheetos.

But truly, they were all a close second. At that moment anyway.

Which was mostly because she had her bag of chips propped on the couch next to her, her orange powder-covered fingers—on her left hand, always, since the right hand was reserved for the remote so she could pause for a heartfelt sigh at all the perfect parts. And to rewind and watch them again.

And to sigh again.

She also had a box with baked goods on her coffee table—minus one croissant because she couldn't wait until the morning —and hell, why should she? It was Friday night. She was single since her brothers had decided to chase off the last man she'd dated.

Truthfully, she couldn't complain too much.

Six brothers equaled a lot of testosterone, and when they got it in their heads that she needed protecting, it was nearly impossible to get them to stop.

They were dogs to a bone.

Mostly because they had been protecting her almost her whole life.

Five. She'd been five years old when her dad died. The youngest. The baby. The long-awaited girl after *all* those boys. She needed to be protected. Coddled. Looked out for. It was sweet but stifling. Loving but overbearing. Coming from a genuine place but sometimes so absolutely infuriating that she wanted to tear her hair out.

Her older brothers had made it their full-time jobs—complete with benefits, plenty of PTO, and 401k plans—to watch over her.

Her dad had ingrained it in them.

Her dad, whom she loved...but—she sighed—she just wished she had the memories her brothers did, her mom did.

Everything she had was blurry on the edges, more feelings and smells than crystal clear memories.

Being tossed up in the air, flying so high that she felt like she could grab the stars twinkling overhead.

The smell of his skin, his hair.

The feel of his strong arms hugging her tight.

It was enough...and it wasn't *nearly* enough. She wanted what her brothers, her mom had, but knew she would never get it. So, she contented herself with the stories, the fractured memories, and pushed the longing she felt for all that she'd missed out on deep, deep down.

So many people had it worse.

She could suck up her daddy issues, be grateful for her family—even for the big lugs that seemed determined to mess up her love life—and enjoy her Cheetos and Hallmark.

"Exactly, Cor," she whispered to herself. "Cheetos. Croissants. Forests in Vermont where small-town girls find their happy endings with lumberjacks who have thick, bushy beards and plaid shirts that threaten to burst from the sheer size of their biceps."

Pleased with herself—go, new positive Cora!—she hit play on the remote and allowed herself to get wrapped back up in the story.

And God, seriously, those colorful leaves were *gorgeous*.

She was thinking that she really needed to plan a trip to Vermont when there was a knock at her door.

"Ugh," she groaned, wishing she could ignore it. But if it was one of her brothers, they would just let themselves in anyway, and if she wanted to protect her Cheetos from their Hoovering abilities, then she needed to be proactive.

Which meant answering the door.

After stashing the bag of Cheetos behind the pillow.

Sighing, she paused her movie, did her stashing, wiped her Cheeto fingers on the napkin she had draped over her leg for just that purpose, then stood.

A glance through the peephole had her sighing again, this time paired with shaking her head. It was so much worse than her brothers.

It was *him*.

She tugged open the door.

"Rafe," she grumbled, plunking her hands on her hips, "which of them sent you?"

Yeah, she had six brothers, but she might as well have a seventh because Rafe had hung around Jeremy, Wyatt, and Asher—her eldest three brothers who had all come within three years of each other (her poor mother)—all the way through elementary, middle, and high school and well into adulthood.

Case in point, he just shrugged, barged into her house, and said, like it was absolutely no surprise (and she supposed it wasn't), "All of them."

She muttered an epithet, closed the door he'd just left wide open, and hurried past him, lest he try to steal her croissants.

With six brothers, she'd learned to protect what was really important.

Which was why she grabbed the bag of Cheetos right after she'd safely secured the box of pastries.

He dropped a bag on the floor—right in the middle of her living room—and sank onto the couch, picking up the remote and changing the channel, like he'd visited a hundred times before.

And she supposed he had.

He always seemed to tag along.

To *protect* her.

And yes, she was mentally doing air quotes to go along with that thought, even as she shoved his feet off the coffee table. "What are you doing here?" she growled, snatching the remote back and returning the television to its rightful place—the Hallmark channel.

But she didn't get to rewind the movie back to where she'd left off.

Because Rafe shrugged his bulky shoulders, nodded at the bag, and said—

"I'm moving in."

BAD REBOUND

Get your copy at
https://www.elisefaber.com/bad-rebound

Jeremy

"FUCK, YES, I WIN!"

God, she was frustrating.

Gorgeous. Smart. Funny.

And frustrating.

Teresa tossed her head back and laughed loud and deep, showing off the innate confidence she had. She was a woman who liked what she liked, who lived big and unafraid.

And she was fucking intense when it came to any form of competition.

Brutal.

As in, she took an opponent down with precise strategy and absolutely no sympathy.

Case in point...

His utter destruction at her hands in Spoons.

"I'm out," he muttered, tossing his cards—and let it be noted, he couldn't toss his spoon on the table because he'd lost...again.

Teresa had shown up about the time the board games got really serious and had jumped right in, just like she always did.

During the three years she'd worked for Rafe, his best friend and brother, for all intents and purposes, she'd become an honorary Hutchins.

At Sunday dinners.

At game nights.

At family events and holidays and birthdays and—

She was there.

Always.

And...she was hot and sexy and gorgeous. And he wanted her.

But she was seeing someone.

So, he stayed away, kept his distance, rolled his eyes when she crowed, snarked back when she led with sarcasm, huffed out laughter when she threatened him...and generally acted the part of the annoying older brother.

Inside?

Inside, he'd cataloged enough fantasies to write a dozen romance novels.

"We can play something else," Kate offered.

He shook his head, smiled at his sister's friend. "Nah. I'm good. My eyes need a break." A nod to the fridge. "I'm gonna grab a beer."

There were offers to join him, but he waved them off, and in the end, he went out onto Cora's back deck alone, plunking into one of the chairs, holding his bottle of beer by the neck, and staring up at the sky.

He'd finished nearly all of it by the time the slider opened.

Footsteps on the deck.

He glanced up, expecting to see his twin, but it wasn't Wyatt clomping out on the wooden slats. It was...Teresa.

She looked beautiful that night.

Jeans, sneakers, a simple T-shirt. Her hair pulled back into a ponytail. No makeup.

No pretense.

Just...Teresa.

And she was the most beautiful woman he'd ever seen.

But she didn't seem to see him sitting in the corner of the deck, and in fairness, he'd purposely taken the area that was mostly in shadows because he'd just needed some time alone.

In the Hutchins family, there wasn't much to be said for alone time.

Normally, he would have said something to announce himself, would have made some snarky comment just to have her snapping back at him. In fact, he'd opened his mouth to do so, but before he could, he saw it.

It.

She wiped her eye.

Then the other.

And fuck...was she crying?

He'd hopped to his feet before he even processed he was moving. "Teresa?"

She jumped, spinning toward him and clamping a hand to her chest. "What the fuck, Jeremy?"

He was hauling ass toward her, fingers coming to her jaw, turning it toward the lights, and yeah, *there.* Her eyes were damp, tears glistening on the ends of her lashes. "What's the matter, T? Who hurt you? I'll—"

She huffed out a laugh, shook her head. "You can't help but be a protective older brother, can you?"

What he felt for Teresa was the furthest thing from brotherly there was.

"This isn't about me, baby." He slid his hand to her nape, holding her in place. "This is about why you're crying."

She rolled her eyes. "I have plenty of annoying older brothers, Jer. I don't need you to join their ranks."

His fingers flexed. "What. Happened?"

A sigh. "Seriously?"

He just held her stare.

She sighed again, but probably because she had experience with annoying older brothers, she gave in—saved them both the trouble by not drawing out the locking of horns. But she didn't do that giving in softly, it was laced with plenty of fire and spice, plenty of *Teresa*. "For fuck's sake," she snapped. "It's nothing, okay? Sam broke up with me. That's all. My ex-boyfriend is an asshole and—"

"Did he hurt you?"

Was that question too intense considering he had no claim over this woman?

Yes.

Did he care?

Nope.

Teresa glanced over his shoulder, but he didn't miss her rolling her eyes again. Nor did he miss the way that roll of her eyes felt in his heart, how it amused him, tempered the edge of his anger, let that haze of fury ease, especially when she explained, "He dumped me. So, it's not like that feels good, but no, he didn't physically touch me in any way that I didn't like." She glanced back at him. "Or yell, or threaten, or get in my face," she added, stymieing his next questions. "Sam just...stepped on my heart, okay? And that sucks." She wrinkled her nose. "Not that *you'd* know that, considering you're so fucking hot girls are throwing themselves at you."

Jer shook his head. "They don't throw—"

Her brows went up. "That bartender in the restaurant?"

"It wasn't like that," he said quickly. "She just wanted some advice on her—"

Now her lips joined the party, tipping up at the edges. "I

know you're not going to tell me she wanted advice on her golf game now, are you?"

"She just—"

"Needed help with her backswing?" Laughter bubbled up, dancing across her lips, drawing his focus there. Fuck, but she had the most kissable mouth. "Or was it back *seat* that she called it?" A smirk. "Probably because she was desperate to get there with you—"

"T," he warned.

"Or how about the waitress who slipped you her number?"

"She just—"

"Or I know!" She was laughing outright now, barely able to get the words out, and even though it was at his expense, her amusement settled deep inside him. He liked her. A lot. So freaking much that he didn't care she was laughing at him, so long as she was *laughing*. Of course, through that laughter she gave another so-called example. "Remember the jogger who pretended to twist her ankle? Oh! And the—"

"T."

"And—"

"Teresa."

She blinked, stopped laughing, stopped talking about women he couldn't give one fuck about. And how could he? He *loved* Teresa. Had been pathetically in love with her for too fucking long. Everyone knew it.

Except her.

She looked up at him. "What?"

He shifted his hand on her nape, sliding it so that he was cupping her cheek. "You ever wonder why I never took any of them up on their offers?"

Silence.

Long. Long enough for him to hear the crickets, the crinkling of the leaves as the wind blew through the trees.

"What?" she asked again, though this time it was a whisper.

"You," he said instead of repeating *his* question. "You're the reason I never accepted any of them."

Wide, wide eyes. Another whisper. "What?"

"I like you, Teresa," he said, and since he was already *in* this, already laying it out, he just gave her the rest of it, gave her *all* of it—or well, *almost* all of it because he wasn't about declaring his undying love, not when she was looking at him with that much shock in her pretty eyes. "I like you a lot."

She sputtered. "I-I...but *you*—"

"You've been dating someone, baby," he murmured. "And I don't—I'm not the kind of guy who'd get in between or jeopardize your relationship or who—"

Her lips pressed flat, released, plumping up, tempting him. "Who what?"

"I'm not the kind of man who fucks around with someone else's woman," he said baldly.

She sucked in a breath, released it slowly. "But I'm not someone else's woman."

"No."

Not anymore.

Wide hazel eyes on his.

"You're mine."

Her lips parted. Tempting him.

And...he might have ignored it, ignored it like he had for years.

But then her body drifted closer, thighs rubbing against his, breasts brushing his chest, hands coming to his arms.

And...he just had to taste her.

So, he did.

BAD ROMANCE

Melody

SHE WATCHED Jeremy slip the ring on Teresa's finger and couldn't have been happier for either of them.

They deserved it.

They deserved each other.

They deserved a life that would lead them to happiness.

But she couldn't lie and deny that it hurt, seeing them in their blissfulness.

Mel couldn't begrudge them, *wouldn't*.

It was just that she...

Well, she had spent the last months putting on a damned good front.

She was in therapy. Look at her go, trying to get better!

She went to Game Nights and Girls' Nights and Reality TV Binge Day and work events that needed a twinly escort and

Sunday Dinners and days like this—celebrating big milestones that people deserved to be celebrated.

It was easy to stay unobserved—though less so than the previous years because everyone had seemed to take it upon themselves to look out for her after she'd been raped.

She'd. Been. Raped.

Drugged. Beaten. Violated.

Raped.

And...

She was still here, still in therapy, still in the support groups.

And she still felt dirty, used.

Violated.

It had only been three months, the therapist had told her. Give it time.

But how long was she supposed to feel like this?

He got a few moments of pleasure...

And she'd gotten this.

Aching, throbbing, open wound in her belly that never fucking closed, never got clean, never—

"Mel."

She blinked.

Realized that Teresa and Jeremy were now kissing like the newly engaged couple they were, realized she was staring but not really seeing.

Realized that it was Asher who was standing behind her and talking to her in that careful tone that did nothing to help and everything to piss her off.

So careful.

So tentative.

Everyone had tried really hard to treat her like normal.

Everyone except for Asher.

Who looked at her with guilt in his eyes and regret in his bearing and pity on his face.

It made her feel sick.

"Are you sleeping?" he asked, still gentle.

Fuck no, she wasn't sleeping.

She hadn't slept without nightmares, not since that night.

But she wasn't going there. "Of course," she said, turning from the kissing couple, but not turning enough to have to fully face him—to face the man who'd seen her broken and bloody and *raped*, to face the man who'd held her through her nightmares for weeks on fucking end.

Until she'd finally gotten a clear look at *his* face and realized what she'd been doing to him.

Destroying him slowly from the inside out.

His guilt eating at his veins, his regret gnawing at his bones, his pity straining his muscles until they'd reached their breaking point.

"I'm fine," she said, still not meeting his eyes but glancing at his bottom lashes.

Close enough.

Close enough that no one saw the difference.

Because most people didn't actually look each other in the eye, they just connected for quick glances before looking away.

The bottom lashes were close enough, she'd realized.

Especially, when paired with her normal, pre-rape quiet demeanor.

People didn't look too close.

But Asher did.

He looked uncomfortably close.

His rough fingers drew along the edge of her jaw, tilting her head up, and after the assault, she didn't allow herself to shy away—it would be too easy to never allow touch again. But with Asher it was different.

She had to hold herself away, lest she allow her body to crave his touch.

To crave *him*.

He didn't want her.

He'd made that crystal clear before she'd been raped, and after, well, she didn't want someone who only saw her as a victim, as a belonging to protect, a broken object to try to piece back together.

Who only wanted her because something had happened to her.

Not because of who she truly was inside.

But because she didn't pull away that night, he held her close, capturing her eyes, holding her gaze, studying her like he could see every thought inside her head.

And then his hand was sliding over her cheek, along her throat, down her arm.

His fingers were wrapping around her wrist, and then weaving through her own.

Warm.

He was warm and strong and...

The bolt of feeling through her belly was a sick mix of pleasure and poison.

Enough jarring juxtaposition that she didn't fight him when he led her onto the front porch, when he closed the door behind them, when he drew her down to sit on the top step beside him.

"You're not sleeping," he murmured, his free hand lifting, his thumb brushing lightly beneath each eye.

More touch.

More pleasure and poison.

"Don't," she whispered, drawing back.

He didn't fight her, just immediately let her go, let her retreat.

But he didn't step away, didn't leave her alone and go into the house.

And they sat there, in silence, in pain.

"What can I do?" he whispered, after long moments.

Nothing.

There was absolutely nothing he could do.

This was her burden to carry, to shoulder, to dispose of...maybe.

Or maybe it would always be with her.

"I wish I'd never called you."

He went stiff, as though there was an electrical current running through his veins. "Why?" he asked, agony in every word. "Why would you say that?"

"You saw me like that," she murmured. "You saw me, and now we're connected and..."

"What?"

"And you didn't want me before, didn't want me then, and you're only hanging around now because I called you that night, and you think it-it's some fucking moral obligation to help me." Her voice grew stronger the longer she spoke. "But you don't really want me. Not *me*, not this broken fucking woman that I've become. I'm not some used-up puzzle you have to help piece back together. I'm fine on my own."

Charged silence greeted her words.

"I don't see you that way."

"Liar," she hissed, spinning toward him, the anger, oh God, the rage, it boiled beneath her skin, desperate to be released.

He stilled again and for a long moment, just stared at her.

Then his hand cupped her jaw, the warm fingers making her gasp in surprise.

She'd slipped back into cold, into that frigid apartment and the memories that froze every cell in her body.

But Ash was hot, warm embers coating her skin, threatening to alight.

"Good," he said approvingly. "It's good to see you with some fight."

His hand fell away and then he stood, moved toward the house.

She tore her gaze away, forced her breaths to even out.

"But Mel?"

She jerked, refused to look back at him.

"The only thing I ever *did* lie to you about?"

Phrased as a question.

But one he didn't wait for her to an

Want a free bonus story? Hate missing Elise's new releases? Love contests, exclusive excerpts and giveaways?
Then signup for Elise's newsletter here!
https://www.elisefaber.com/newsletter

And join Elise's fan group, the Fabinators https://www.facebook.com/groups/fabinators for insider information, sneak peaks at new releases, and fun freebies! Hope to see you there!

ALSO BY ELISE FABER

Benched

Breakaway

Breakout

Checked

Coasting

Centered

Charging

Caged

Crashed

A Gold Christmas

Cycled

Caught

Breakers Hockey (all stand alone)

Broken

Boldly

Breathless

Ballsy (April 26,2022)

Love, Action, Camera (all stand alone)

Dotted Line

Action Shot

Close-Up

End Scene

Meet Cute

***Love After Midnight* (all stand alone)**

Rum And Notes

Virgin Daiquiri

On The Rocks

Sex On The Seats

Life Sucks Series (**all stand alone**)

Train Wreck

Hot Mess

Dumpster Fire

Clusterf*@k

FUBAR (March 29,2022)

Roosevelt Ranch Series (**all stand alone, series complete**)

Disaster at Roosevelt Ranch

Heartbreak at Roosevelt Ranch

Collision at Roosevelt Ranch

Regret at Roosevelt Ranch

Desire at Roosevelt Ranch

Phoenix Series (**read in order**)

Phoenix Rising

Dark Phoenix

Phoenix Freed

Phoenix: LexTal Chronicles (**rereleasing soon, stand alone, Phoenix world**)

From Ashes

In Flames

To Smoke

ABOUT THE AUTHOR

USA Today bestselling author, Elise Faber, loves chocolate, Star Wars, Harry Potter, and hockey (the order depending on the day and how well her team -- the Sharks! -- are playing). She and her husband also play as much hockey as they can squeeze into their schedules, so much so that their typical date night is spent on the ice. Elise changes her hair color more often than some people change their socks, loves sparkly things, and is the mom to two exuberant boys. She lives in Northern California. Connect with her in her Facebook group, the Fabinators or find more information about her books at www.elisefaber.com.

facebook.com/elisefaberauthor

amazon.com/author/elisefaber

bookbub.com/profile/elise-faber

instagram.com/elisefaber

goodreads.com/elisefaber

pinterest.com/elisefaberwrite

ACKNOWLEDGMENTS

This is the point in every book that I'm reminded of exactly how many people it takes to turn my books into something that you as readers can enjoy! I quite literally could not do it without you! My editors and friends who I bug constantly with ideas (and too many curse words ;)) and YOU, my readers. Thank you for supporting this series!

If you'd like to catch up on all my other releases, please check out my website: www.elisefaber.com. There you can sign up for my newsletter (with monthly bookish giveaways, woohoo!), check out my other books (everything from paranormal romance to hockey romance to contemporary stand alones), and get to know more about my dorky self (hockey, chocolate, Star Wars . . . okay, I'm pretty boring).

You can also find me on Facebook (@elisefaberauthor), via my FB fan group (facebook.com/group/fabinators), or Instagram (@elisefaber). I look forward to talking with you soon!

—XOXO,
    E